His Uncle's Favorite

LORY LILIAN

Meryton Press

Oysterville, WA

HIS UNCLE'S FAVORITE

ISBN: 978-1-9360-0925-1

Graphic design by Ellen Pickels

Special thanks to Margaret Fransen and Ellen Pickels
for their support and assistance in publishing this book.

Chapter 1

The journey to London was a challenge; it was exceedingly cold, and the horses plodded cautiously on the frozen road.

Inside the carriage, however, Elizabeth was cheerful as she entertained her little cousins. Opposite her, Jane remained in complete silence, her attention drawn outside, while Mrs. Gardiner observed her children with loving looks.

Elizabeth quickly glanced at her dear aunt. It was Christmas time, the most heart-wrenching month for Mrs. Gardiner two years after her husband's tragic death.

There was little Elizabeth could do to comfort her beloved aunt. All of them missed Edward Gardiner exceedingly, and they would never forget him. He had been an excellent husband and father—and a dear uncle and brother for the Bennets. Mrs. Gardiner was desperately trying to overcome her pain for the benefit of her two children. Eleanor was six and Edward, seven. They were so young when the tragedy occurred that they never understood why their mother cried every time their father was mentioned.

A lady in her late thirties, Mrs. Gardiner was as amiable and intelligent as she was beautiful and elegant, despite her deep mourning. She looked at her favourite nieces with an affectionate and understanding smile, pleased that she enticed them to accompany her to London. Both girls needed a diversion: an escape from the fresh memory of Mr. Bingley for Jane and from Mr. Wickham's presence for Elizabeth.

During a short stay at Longbourn, Mrs. Gardiner had seen Mr. Wickham a few times and enjoyed sharing pleasant conversations with him. They had a subject of mutual interest: Derbyshire and, more precisely, Pemberley. There Mr. Wickham had grown up, and it was only five miles from the little town where Mrs. Gardiner had spent the first years of her life.

Mrs. Gardiner became reticent when Mr. Wickham explained to her—in great detail—the present Mr. Darcy's mistreatment of him. Mrs. Gardiner did not feel comfortable with Mr. Wickham's ease in discussing such an intimate story with a new acquaintance; that was not expected of a proper gentleman.

Even less easy was Mrs. Gardiner with Elizabeth's high opinion of Mr. Wickham.

That fact determined her narrowly to observe them both. Without supposing them, from what she saw, to have a serious inclination, their preference for each other was plain enough to make her a little uneasy; at the first opportunity, she spoke to Elizabeth on the subject and represented to her the imprudence of encouraging such an attachment. Mrs. Gardiner was pleased to receive a light, teasing reply from Elizabeth and her assurance that she was not—at present—in love with Mr. Wickham.

However, Elizabeth did admit that Mr. Wickham was, beyond all comparison, the most agreeable man she had ever met. If not for the abominable Mr. Darcy leaving him in poverty, she might have become attached to him.

When Elizabeth accepted the invitation to spend the next month in London with Jane, Mrs. Gardiner was relieved. Surely, Elizabeth's heart was not seriously touched by Mr. Wickham; she felt no disappointment in being separated from him for a time.

As for Mr. Bingley's departure, Mrs. Gardiner knew these things often happened, and she told Elizabeth as much when the two of them had discussed the matter privately.

"My dear, a young man, such as you described Mr. Bingley, so easily falls in love with a pretty girl for a few weeks, and when accident separates them, so easily forgets her that these sorts of inconstancies are very common."

However, Elizabeth did not blame Mr. Bingley as much as she blamed his sisters and his friend Mr. Darcy. "It was not an accident, Aunt," Elizabeth had replied. "It was a premeditated and malicious scheme of his sisters and his friend to separate him from Jane!"

"Poor Jane! I am sorry for her because, with her disposition, she may not get over it immediately. It had better have happened to you, Lizzy; you would have laughed yourself out of it sooner. But do you think Mr. Bingley to be truly so blameless? How is it possible that he trusted his heart and his wishes so little? That is not a good sign to me. Surely, he would be able to stand up for himself against his sisters and against his friend."

Elizabeth could not contradict her aunt. In her opinion, Mr. Bingley was indeed lacking the determination and self-confidence of a true gentleman. Nevertheless, she was inclined to blame Mr. Darcy for the turn of events. A gentleman who had so grossly mistreated his long-time friend Mr. Wickham surely would have a harmful influence upon the young and inexperienced Mr. Bingley.

Jane declared that Mr. Bingley was no longer in her thoughts. She hoped that, by Caroline Bingley's not living in the same house with her brother, she might occasionally spend a morning with her friend without any danger of seeing him.

Elizabeth's thoughts, however, were different. On closer examination, she did not consider the situation entirely hopeless. It was possible, even probable, that they would meet Mr. Bingley in London, either during a call to his sisters or on some other occasion.

The Gardiners were accustomed to being out in society frequently before Mr.

Gardiner's tragic death. They had many influential acquaintances among the *ton*, as Mr. Gardiner had been very successful in business during his last years. His skills, knowledge, and intelligence had increased his fortune while Mrs. Gardiner's perfect manners, elegant taste, and amiable disposition secured his position among his acquaintances—some of them illustrious members of society.

Consequently, the number of invitations grew from one year to the next, and parties in the Gardiners' house—an impressive building purchased three years before his death—were always well attended and much appreciated by their guests.

Of course, Mrs. Gardiner knew that most of their 'high class' friends never overlooked that the Gardiners' fortune was from trade. However, Mrs. Gardiner cared little about such talk and bore any unpleasant remarks or looks with humour and wisdom. She felt content with her situation, her two beautiful children, and the company of a loving, caring husband. She would not change her position for an entire earldom and considered herself the most fortunate woman—until fate decreed otherwise.

Mr. Gardiner's wisdom in business assured his family a comfortable situation. In fact, his legacy, besides the wonderful memories, was a considerable fortune, so neither his wife nor his children had any reason to worry for their future security.

That year, in an attempt to offer her nieces some diversion and to return to a sense of normalcy, Mrs. Gardiner promised her nieces that she would accept invitations to a few parties or small balls from those she still considered family friends. *That would be a very good thing, both for my aunt and for Jane,* Elizabeth thought, hoping all of them would manage to traverse the Christmas season with a modicum of good humour.

With these considerations in mind, Elizabeth's confidence in a chance meeting between Jane and Mr. Bingley was strong. And if it were to happen, Elizabeth was certain his affection might be reanimated and the influence of his friends successfully combated by the more natural influence of Jane's attractions. If only Mr. Bingley were allowed to do anything without the custody of Mr. Darcy!

"Dear girls, I am happy to tell you that we have a dinner invitation to honour three days from now on Christmas evening and at least a ball to attend in a fortnight."

"I am not in need of balls and entertainments. Your company is enough for me, Aunt."

"Jane dearest, we already discussed that we will attend a few events. Will you do this for me? I confess I want to surprise everybody by introducing them to my beautiful nieces."

Jane tried to smile for her aunt's sake, and Elizabeth decided to support Mrs. Gardiner.

"I promise I will do my best to look beautiful, but I must warn you, I may not be as successful as you hope; it is well known that I am not anywhere near as pretty as Jane, nor do I have as happy a disposition as Lydia. Mama can testify to that."

"Oh, I have no fear that you will do just fine, Lizzy. If only you would not scare young gentlemen with your sharp teasing. Few gentlemen are fond of a bright lady."

"Thank you, dear Aunt, though I wonder whether that was a compliment." Elizabeth laughed.

"You are most welcome! Now, about that dinner invitation on Christmas evening: Lizzy, you will adore the earl; I am sure of it. He possesses your father's love of books but is more inclined to enjoy the amusements of the world outside his library. However, I have to warn you: the earl takes great delight in teasing and vexing those around him, and he has a peculiar sense of humour. As his daughter, Lady Selina, frequently says, 'I am afraid he enjoys himself a little too much at times.'"

Jane looked at her with alarm while Elizabeth laughed.

"Do not worry, Jane. I am sure your beauty will charm the earl, and he will find no reason to tease you at all! You have no faults about which to laugh! As for me, I will be more than pleased to be the recipient of his interest in that regard."

"Is his wife like him in disposition?" inquired Jane.

"Unfortunately, the earl's wife passed away a decade ago. But he has two sons —both unmarried—besides his daughter. Lady Selina has been happily married for four years now."

"Oh, so the earl must be older than my uncle," continued Jane, puzzled, and a moment later she frowned and turned pale. "I am sorry, Aunt; I should realise that—"

"Jane dearest, do not reproach yourself. It is time to speak about Edward openly no matter how painful it is. You are correct; the earl is your father's age, so he was ten years older than Edward. Despite his superior situation in life and the difference in age, he was a kind and reliable friend to Edward—and our entire family."

"I am sorry I have not had the chance to meet him until now," said Elizabeth. "I am curious about him and his daughter. I can hardly believe such titled people can be pleasant company. Mr. Darcy was not titled at all, and he barely spoke to or looked at anyone in Hertfordshire. How fortunate not all members of the *ton* are as disagreeable as he is."

"Lizzy, let us try to forgive Mr. Darcy's faults for at least a few days, shall we? So, it is settled then; we shall have dinner at Lord Marlock's."

"Certainly, whatever you wish, Aunt. You say the earl is very much like Papa in disposition and his love of books. Too bad he is not younger as he seems like my ideal sort of gentleman; I am sure I would easily fall in love with him." Elizabeth laughed while her aunt smiled.

Jane looked at them with reproach. "Lizzy, you cannot speak like that about an earl who is our father's age! Falling in love is not a subject for jest." She averted her eyes towards the carriage's window.

Mrs. Gardiner affectionately patted Jane's arm and then turned to her other niece. "You know, dearest, the earl has two sons, and I can easily say the younger is the most charming gentleman I have seen in quite a while. He is a colonel in His Majesty's army."

"An earl's son—and a colonel! It is fortunate you did not mention him at

8

Longbourn, or I am certain other members of our family would have insisted on joining us in London." Elizabeth laughed, feeling somehow guilty for her cheerful disposition.

"Oh, it is so beautiful," Jane cried rapturously, suddenly animated, and all looked out to observe the sight that aroused her attention.

The winter night was cold, and a light snowfall was adorning the trees, houses, and roads in a white gown that sparkled under the moonlight.

"It is like a fairy tale," Jane whispered, and Elizabeth smiled.

Yes, it was like a fairy tale, and she had a very good feeling about it!

It was the second day of their arrival in Town, and Jane's spirits fell even lower. That morning, she had accompanied Mrs. Gardiner in her quest to purchase accessories for their new dresses. The opportunity took her to that part of Town where Caroline Bingley resided in her sister's house; so Jane called on them, confident they had received the letter she sent before they left Hertfordshire.

Later that day, Mrs. Gardiner told Elizabeth how poorly Mr. Bingley's sisters had treated them.

"I hate to speak ill, but they were so ridiculously pleased with themselves that they appeared foolish to me! I could not care less about their pretence to greatness, but Jane—"

"Oh, dear Aunt! Was it truly so bad? Poor Jane!"

"Well, judge for yourself. First, they were reluctant to invite us in, and seemed amazed that we were there. Then they spoke and looked at us with obvious disdain; they even had the nerve to reproach Jane for not sending them notice of her coming to London, though I am certain they got her letter. And even more, Jane inquired of Mr. Bingley, and they answered that he was well but so much engaged with Mr. Darcy and his sister that they scarcely saw him! Poor Jane turned pale, and I was afraid she would faint."

"How horrible," Elizabeth cried. "Poor, sweet Jane!" She hurried from the room so quickly that Mrs. Gardiner was forced to call her three times before she heard and returned.

"Lizzy, wait a moment, child. Let us sit and talk because I, too, am concerned about Jane."

"What is it, Aunt? I have to go to Jane and speak to her; she needs me. Unfortunately, no matter how worried we might be, there is nothing we can do—"

"Oh, but there is. No *lady* who dares humiliate my niece will be unrewarded for such *manners*," Mrs. Gardiner said sharply, and Elizabeth looked at her in complete puzzlement. "If only... Elizabeth, are you certain you were correct in your judgment of Mr. Bingley's feelings about Jane?"

"What can I say, Aunt? Apparently, I have been utterly incorrect, considering Mr. Bingley is now so engaged with Miss Darcy! I am sure she is equally as unpleasant and annoying as Mr. Darcy. She must be since Miss Bingley is so fond of her!"

"Wait a moment; let us not be hasty in disapproving the entire Darcy family so easily. Miss Bingley said many things, and none of them seemed true to me. She was obviously attempting to deceive Jane and make her abandon any hope of Mr. Bingley. So I would not be surprised if the story about Miss Darcy was a pure fabrication."

"I told Jane the same thing when she got the first letter from Miss Bingley in Hertfordshire. But I do not know what to believe now. Should we encourage Jane's hopes? What if Miss Bingley is correct? How will Jane bear even more disappointment?"

"Dearest, there are only two ways to settle the matter. Mr. Bingley either is the worthy gentleman you believed him to be and was deeply enamoured of Jane —in which case he could not possibly be interested in another young lady after only three weeks of separation—or his infatuation was without substance, and he showed no consideration for the hopes he had fostered in Jane. In the latter case, he is unworthy of her affection, and we both will help Jane to see that and to understand she has lost nothing of value."

Elizabeth stared at her aunt. Animated, her eyes brightened by anger, her lips pursed together, Mrs. Gardiner looked even more beautiful than usual, much younger—and a little frightening. Elizabeth laughed, trying to control her emotions.

"Dear Aunt, your self-confidence is contagious! I agree with you, utterly and completely, and I will do everything to help Jane see reason. But I am at a loss as to how you plan to discover the truth about Mr. Bingley's worthiness and his true feelings for Jane."

"Niece, I am certain, absolutely certain, that we will have a chance to meet Mr. Bingley. And if an opportunity does not arise by itself, we must use our intuition and skills to create one. After all, Mr. Gardiner did not choose a smart woman as a wife for nothing!" Mrs. Gardiner gave Elizabeth a playful wink. "Now, go and comfort Jane, and I will supervise dinner preparations."

A COUPLE OF HOURS LATER, Elizabeth's efforts seemed rewarded as Jane looked more tranquil, and her face had regained some colour. She was still affected, and she barely gathered herself enough to speak, but at least she agreed to dress herself for dinner instead of retiring to the seclusion of her own room as she intended earlier.

They both expected a pleasant, informal family supper and entered the dining room together; but the sound of voices stopped them in the doorway, and they needed a moment before Elizabeth finally stepped forward, pulling her sister by the hand.

In the middle of the room were two guests: an older gentleman and a beautiful lady, younger than Mrs. Gardiner. The gentleman's figure was impressive and intimidating; he was speaking animatedly with their aunt, his tone so insistent that it seemed to admit no contradiction. The lady only smiled at the others in a friendly way.

Their conversation stopped, and Mrs. Gardiner smiled at the girls, inviting them to enter. They obeyed hesitantly, Jane's eyes seeking those of her aunt as if begging for support; Elizabeth gazed at the guests with curiosity. With each step, she was more certain she had never seen the gentleman before in her life, yet his features appeared curiously familiar to her.

She felt him watching her with equal interest, and when their eyes finally met, she attempted a polite smile, awaiting the introductions.

The gentleman came near, and his voice thundered unceremoniously: "You must be Miss Elizabeth Bennet! And you, beautiful as a goddess and shy as a little lamb, must be Miss Jane Bennet."

Elizabeth's eyebrows instantly rose in wonder at such a statement, and she turned to her aunt, awaiting her guidance, while the young lady burst out laughing.

"Papa, you have a peculiar notion of what constitutes *proper* introductions."

"Indeed, your lordship, these are my dear nieces." Mrs. Gardiner attempted to hide her amusement. "Please allow me to present to you Miss Jane and Miss Elizabeth Bennet. Jane, Elizabeth, I am honoured to introduce you to our very special guests, Lord Matlock and Lady Selina Brightmore."

All three ladies curtseyed properly while the earl apologised to Mrs. Gardiner for interrupting her and then, with no further consideration, interrupted his own daughter who had started to talk to Elizabeth. Elizabeth could not restrain a peal of laughter and hurried to cover her mouth with her hand. Jane barely kept her countenance.

"Miss Bennet, there is no cause for uneasiness. I am not as frightening as I might appear on first acquaintance. And you, Miss Elizabeth—you should never hide your laugh; there is nothing more charming than a beautiful woman's laugh!"

"And you, dearest Papa, should not speak so frankly to young ladies you have just met. It is not acceptable behaviour," Lady Selina said. Lord Matlock only waved his hand without much consideration for his daughter's concern.

"Thank you for the compliment, your lordship," Elizabeth answered, moving to the couch, followed closely by Jane, and whispering: "At least I think it was a compliment..."

"It certainly was a compliment. Did it sound otherwise?" Lord Matlock inquired, and Elizabeth was afraid she might have upset him.

Mrs. Gardiner seemed amused as did Lady Selina. Jane was positively lost, unable to say anything to the earl.

"No indeed, Lord Matlock," Elizabeth replied neutrally and politely. "Thank you."

"Heavens, I certainly hope you do not intend to thank me the entire evening, Miss Elizabeth. That is not what I expect from you."

Jane's eyes widened in shock. The earl had the strangest manners she had ever seen!

"And may I dare ask what exactly your lordship does expect from me?" Rather than being intimidated, Elizabeth's spirit rose; and her boldness, encouraged by her aunt's clear approval, defeated any shyness. If the earl was as Mrs. Gardiner described him and showed so little consideration for decorum and the rules of politeness, then why would she feel embarrassed? After all, she had done nothing wrong; even his daughter openly disapproved his directness.

"Ahhh, very good, you have spirit! Well, let us see: from what Mrs. Gardiner told me about you, I expect interesting subjects, witty conversation, amusing stories about your home—and maybe some music after dinner. I understand you are very talented."

"I am afraid your lordship might be disappointed because, unfortunately, my aunt grossly exaggerated my merits and my talent in music."

"Really? What a shame... Then I shall have to be content with your charming presence. Of course, I would say the same thing about Miss Bennet, whose appearance is as bright as a summer day, but she seems determined to ignore me completely. I am quite positive she has come to detest me in only a few minutes—"

"Oh no, no, please do not believe that... I beg your forgiveness. I would never dare to... Please forgive me," said Jane, pale, her eyes moving from her aunt to her sister and then back to the earl.

Lord Matlock's expression changed instantly, and to everyone's surprise, he came closer and bowed to Jane, his voice gentle and perfectly polite.

"Miss Bennet, it is I who should beg your forgiveness for placing you in a distressful situation with my poor attempt at a joke. I hope you will accept my apologies and not harbour any hard feelings towards an old man."

"Indeed, Miss Bennet," Lady Selina intervened kindly. "We intruded upon you unexpectedly, and it appears we did not choose the best of moments. You have nothing about which to be sorry. As for our familiarity, which perhaps trespassed the limits of decorum, it is only due to our close friendship with Mrs. Gardiner. Perhaps we should leave now. We only wanted to inform you that we decided to have dinner at my father's house tomorrow evening."

Jane smiled nervously as she swallowed some more water. "Oh, please do not consider leaving. I am very happy to meet you, Lady Selina...and Lord Matlock. It is just that I have not felt well today. Please do not presume it is your fault."

Elizabeth's eyes searched the earl's face, and she could see he was regretful. Again, a strange sensation of familiarity crossed her mind; he reminded her of somebody, a person well known to her, yet she could not identify the puzzling resemblance.

"I think we should let this distressing moment pass, your lordship...Lady Selina," Mrs. Gardiner kindly intervened. "It is nobody's fault that it occurred. Jane is not feeling well, as she said. As for harbouring any hard feelings, certainly, neither she nor any of us would take offence at a mere joke. Let us resume our places. Dinner is ready."

As Mrs. Gardiner hoped, the incident passed, and by the second dish, Jane dared to join Elizabeth and Lady Selina's conversation and even to answer a couple of the earl's questions. However, the earl proved to be consistent in his regret and considerate towards her; his tone and the nature of his questions as he spoke to Jane remained gentle, and he put aside any attempt at mockery.

Yet, another uncomfortable moment occurred when the earl asked Jane whether she enjoyed the morning ride with Mrs. Gardiner; for no apparent reason, Jane turned pale and remained silent again. From that moment, the earl did not insist further in drawing Miss Bennet into conversation. Lady Selina, however, continued to speak to Jane warmly.

"So," Lady Selina told both Jane and Elizabeth, "I have two elder brothers. I am the only lady in the family as I have two boys of my own. Can you imagine how spoiled I am?"

"I have four sisters, and poor Papa is the only man in the family, so I really cannot imagine how it would be to be surrounded only by gentlemen." Elizabeth laughed.

"Well, you will be able to experience that in our house as we will have many male cousins attending the dinner, and my husband, who is out of town now on some urgent matters, will also be there," replied Lady Selina.

"Indeed, I have lots of nephews," Lord Matlock approved. "Among them there are a couple of nieces but I tell you: there is far too little beauty in our family," Lord Matlock concluded, resigned, sipping some wine.

"You have a lovely family, your lordship, and having had the pleasure of meeting your sons, I dare say they are as handsome as they are worthy and admirable," Mrs. Gardiner said.

"Well, well, they are, I agree, and I thank God for that. However, as I said, there is far too little beauty in our family," he repeated, to the ladies' utter amusement.

"Well, then your lordship can only hope all your sons and nephews will marry beautiful ladies and solve your problem," Elizabeth replied.

"You are correct, Miss Elizabeth. However, appearance is not the only thing a woman needs to bring beauty into a man's life." Once more his expression, the small smile hidden on his lips, and the furrow between his eyebrows looked annoyingly familiar to Elizabeth.

When dinner finished, Jane dared to announce she would retire to her room as she was still not feeling well. The earl wished her a restful night and insisted she should take care of herself. Lady Selina took her hands and even kissed her cheeks; her gesture pleased Elizabeth exceedingly as it erased any offence that Bingley's sisters gave her earlier. Jane took her leave with grace and perfect politeness, accompanied by Elizabeth who helped her to her chamber.

"Oh, Lizzy, I made a fool of myself. What will the earl think of me? And Lady Selina —I could not believe how kind she was. Both were kind, in fact, though the earl is so frighteningly outspoken at times; I hope he was not upset with my lack of spirit.

"Jane, do not be silly! You did nothing wrong; it was the earl who behaved strangely. He is indeed a little frightening, though his daughter is adorable. If I did not know better, I would never guess he is a peer; his manners are more than…questionable. But at least he was amiable enough to understand when he crossed the line, and he sincerely apologised. That is also strange for an earl, I presume." Elizabeth laughed.

"He is strange indeed, but he was considerate with me. Lizzy, are you sure he does not persist in believing I detest him? How could he imagine that?"

"You worry too much! You must sleep until late tomorrow morning; do not forget that in two days' time we are invited to Lord Matlock's for dinner. You surely need all your strength to bear an entire evening in his company. In the meantime, I will try to draw his attention upon me. If I could bear Mr. Collins for an entire set and manage to escape his marriage proposal, I surely can bear Lord Matlock's mockery."

They separated in the hall with a warm embrace, and Elizabeth watched her sister until she disappeared upstairs. Jane was indeed not well, not well at all. Fortunately, she would regain her spirits soon, and no doctor would be needed. Yet, Elizabeth had to admit that Lord Matlock had been very kind in offering his assistance. And what were those meaningful glances between her aunt and Lady Selina?

LESS THAN A QUARTER HOUR later, Elizabeth re-joined the others. The conversation was easily carried—light, open and friendly. Gradually, Lord Matlock's attention was directed entirely towards Elizabeth.

"So, Miss Elizabeth, your father's estate is entailed from what I heard. That must be very uncomfortable."

"It might be, but for the moment we have no reason to worry. My father, thank the Lord, is in perfect health, and we hope to have him with us for many, many years."

"And in the meantime, I am sure you will all marry and quite well. If all your sisters are as beautiful as you and Miss Bennet, you truly have no reason to worry," said Lady Selina.

"Your ladyship is very kind; Jane is indeed beautiful, and all my sisters are pleasant girls. However, as they are young yet, I surely hope they will not marry any time soon."

"So, do you like London, Miss Elizabeth? Have you been in town often?" asked the earl.

"Not often. My father hates London."

"Ah, a country gentleman who hates London; I surely can sympathise with him. I would hate London too but, unfortunately, I cannot indulge that."

"How is that, your lordship?" Elizabeth asked with amusement.

"Well, until a few years ago my daughter used to drag me to London every season. Now my eldest son appears to have little skill in the management of our investments, so I need to come to Town more often that I would wish."

"I am sorry to hear that."

"You must not believe all of my father's statements, Miss Elizabeth. I never dragged him to London; he insisted on coming to watch over me. He was afraid I would not marry to his liking. If you had chosen my husband, dearest Papa, I would still be single as no man was to your liking." Lady Selina laughed affectionately.

"You are correct in that," he admitted then turned his attention to Elizabeth once more. "So, Miss Elizabeth, your aunt told me you are a great reader. What books do you favour?"

"Lord Matlock, my aunt is very partial to me, and I am afraid she tends to praise me too much. I would not dare to call myself a great reader, but indeed I

14

enjoy reading very much."

"Do you play and sing, too? Mrs. Gardiner said you do. May I ask for some music?"

His request was friendly and unpretentious, and his daughter insisted too. Elizabeth, after mentioning once more that they must not expect too much, indulged them.

"You play very well, Miss Elizabeth, but indeed not exceptionally. I imagine you do not spend much time practicing. However, it was a delight to hear you."

"Thank you, your lordship. You are correct; I do not practice as much as I should. I play only when it gives me pleasure. I am relieved you were not disappointed."

"Not at all; quite the contrary. Your performance is like yourself: pleasant, merry and natural. I appreciate that."

"You are very kind! I imagine you are accustomed to superior performances."

"It depends what you understand by superior. I notice all mothers insist their daughters waste their time learning all manner of silly things in order to become *accomplished*—whatever that might mean. And I cringe when I hear a young girl play with no passion or feeling, only good technique. That is not superior if you ask me."

"I must say I agree; but then again, your theory is advantageous for me, so I might be partial," Elizabeth replied, laughing.

"Music depends on talent. My daughter learned to play for years and had the most prodigious masters. Yet, her performance is not nearly as good as yours."

His statement surprised Elizabeth by its directness, but Lady Selina did not seem at all bothered; she only nodded in agreement with the same open smile.

"On the other hand," he continued, "my favourite niece, who is only sixteen, performs like an angel. I could listen to her forever. She is as shy as your sister, by the way…"

"My sister is not especially shy," Elizabeth replied tentatively. "She is not feeling well at the moment, but she is very easy in company…most of the time."

"I see… I confess I am convinced she is either shy or ill. If not that, then she has experienced some disappointment in love." He gave a satisfied laugh until he saw Elizabeth's countenance change. Lady Selina and Mrs. Gardiner exchanged another quick glance.

"I…I would rather not speak of my sister. She will be well soon; that is all that matters."

"Of course we should not talk about Miss Bennet's private affairs. Forgive me; I tend to speak with you as I speak to my family, and that is unacceptable. I apologise if I offended you."

"No indeed; there was no offence at all. We may speak of *my* private affairs if your lordship wishes." Elizabeth was enjoying the conversation; she liked Lady Selina, and even came to be at ease with the earl. Instead of feeling offended, she appreciated that he was speaking to her, a tradesman's niece, as if he were speaking to his own children.

"Are you suffering from a disappointment in love too, Miss Elizabeth?"

"Unfortunately for the development of our conversation—not at all, sir."

"I would have guessed that. But are you by any chance engaged or soon to be engaged?"

"This is not a proper question either, Lord Matlock. And, before considering whether I should answer, may I ask why you are interested in knowing?"

"Because, Miss Elizabeth, I confess you have charmed me utterly and completely. And, since I am too old to pursue you myself, I am seriously considering marrying you to one of my sons."

"Papa!" cried Lady Selina. "You will embarrass Miss Elizabeth completely!"

"Lord Matlock," intervened Mrs. Gardiner, who had attended them in silence until that moment, "would you like another glass of brandy? And may I suggest postponing the marriage arrangements for a while? After all, you only met Lizzy this very evening. You might discover she is not always as nice as she seems."

"I surely hope that is true. A woman who is pleasant all the time would be very boring. Very well, I will have another drink and be silent for a minute or two. That would be my fourth, I think. I am already feeling a little too well humoured. Now, you know my sons very well, Mrs. Gardiner. Do you think Miss Bennet would be suited for either of them?"

"Or, better said, Aunt, do you think I could be prevailed upon to marry one of them?" Elizabeth smiled, and both the earl and his daughter turned to her with surprise.

"Miss Elizabeth, that is a very interesting statement. You mean to imply that you would refuse an offer of marriage from an earl's son?"

"I would certainly refuse an offer from any man I could not respect and care deeply for, sir. I believe there is nothing worse than a marriage without affection."

"Respect and affection might come later in marriage; you should know that. But then again, perhaps you are too young and impulsive to consider all aspects." The earl watched Elizabeth with equal interest and disbelief.

"They might come later, but I would not risk presuming so. I would rather wait to be certain of my feelings before accepting a proposal."

"Miss Elizabeth, I wholeheartedly agree with you!" said Lady Selina enthusiastically.

The earl stared at Elizabeth with a smirk on his lips. "You express your opinion very decidedly for someone so young, Miss Elizabeth. I appreciate that very much —very much indeed."

"Thank you, my lord," Elizabeth replied with a friendly smile. She knew the earl had no intention of marrying her to either of his sons, yet she could also sense the honesty in his praise. She was pleased to be complimented in such a manner by an illustrious—though very strange—gentleman.

"So, while we try to decide your future in marriage, Miss Elizabeth, let us speak of literature. Who is your favourite author?"

Elizabeth breathed deeply, relieved at the change of topic from delicate to completely safe. Yes, discussing literature would do.

Chapter 2

The next day, late in the afternoon, Lord Matlock was sitting in his library, deep in the study of his ledgers. He took another glass of brandy—one too many, his daughter would say.

"Good day, Father. May we keep you company?" Colonel Fitzwilliam sauntered into the room with Mr. Darcy in his wake.

"Of course, of course. What a pleasant surprise! My favourite nephew finally comes to see me. Where did you find this stranger, Son?"

"Good evening, Uncle. Forgive me, I did not mean to neglect you. As you know, I just returned to Town a couple of weeks ago, and before that I was at Pemberley, so—"

"Yes, yes, I know you are quite busy and dutiful. Now you had better tell me how you have been. Will you surprise me with any interesting news? Any interesting lady?"

"I am sorry to disappoint you, Uncle. I have no interesting news to share and most certainly not about interesting ladies. Unfortunately, I cannot surprise you."

"Well, I am indeed disappointed, but there is little I can do about the situation. It is quite fortunate that my son here always has interesting news to share, usually involving a lovely smile and beautiful eyes. However, I might surprise both of you tomorrow night as I plan to introduce to you the most interesting young lady I have met in many years. I have to say I was quite taken with her, and I am curious to know your opinion."

His son laughed. "May I presume I am soon to meet my future stepmother?"

"Don't be an idiot, Son; she is much younger than Selina. However, you should prepare as it is likely you will meet a woman whose eyes will charm your senses and whose wit will bewitch your mind. I cannot wait to see you lost like a schoolboy."

His son laughed again, heartily. "I accept the wager, Father. That will never happen unless… Does she have an interesting dowry, too?"

The earl gulped his brandy and shook his head. "We shall see if you ask about her dowry tomorrow night."

"Uncle, perhaps we should find another subject? I am not comfortable with this conversation. Suppose someone were to speak in the same manner about my sister? Or about Selina?"

"Oh, don't be so boring, Nephew. I speak with the deepest respect. The young lady I describe is the niece of my late business partner, Edward Gardiner."

"I see…" both younger gentlemen whispered, and there was silence for a few moments.

"So, I understand you had a pleasant call on Mrs. Gardiner yesterday," said his son.

"Indeed I had—very pleasant. Her nieces are visiting, and it was a delight to meet them both. Very beautiful girls, though so utterly different…"

"Well, you have me curious and anxious about tomorrow night, I grant you that."

"Good. What about you, Nephew? Are you curious, too?"

"Not really, Uncle. I am curious to meet Mrs. Gardiner as I know of the high opinion you and Selina have of her; and I never heard you praise a man as much as you did Mr. Gardiner. However, more than anything, I was hoping for a quiet, pleasant, Christmas evening with our family. I really need that after all the turmoil…" His last words were no more than a whisper, and his uncle looked at him with unconcealed curiosity.

"Are you well, Nephew? Is anything wrong?"

"I think he is just worried, Father. As we arrived, he was telling me how he managed to save a friend from a disadvantageous union with a young lady who did not share his affection."

"Really? Well, well—that is an interesting story indeed. Will you not indulge me, or it is too private for your old uncle?"

"There is not much to say, Uncle. As you may know, my friend Bingley's heart is…quite easy to impress. He became attached to a young lady whose beauty was indeed remarkable, but it was not enough to outweigh other important aspects—"

"Important aspects? May I inquire of what aspects you are speaking? Am I to understand the lady was beautiful but lacking in behaviour or disposition or good sense?"

"Not really. I could not say she lacked in any of these but—"

"You said she did not share his affection. If that is the case, it is good he has to bear the disappointment now rather than later."

"Yes, I agree with you. Hopefully, his spirit will rise again soon. He could not possibly bind himself to a young lady whose family was so much beneath him and whose affection for him was questionable."

The earl gulped some wine while examining his nephew's face with extra care.

"So her affection was questionable? That would mean you are not certain about it. What is your friend's opinion? And what is the situation of the young lady's family that is so beneath him?"

"Uncle, why are we speaking of this? It can be of little interest to you."

"The matter is of little interest to me, but you are of *great* interest to me, and you seemed preoccupied with the situation."

"I confess I am preoccupied because I really want to find the best resolution for my friend. His well-being is my main concern, and his sisters agreed with me that—"

"His sisters agreed with you? And you are concerned about his well-being? Come, Nephew; that is quite ridiculous. As far as I know, he is a worthy gentleman, well capable of taking care of his own interests. May I ask what precisely you did for his well-being?"

"I advised him it would be best for everyone that he stay in London for the winter. I am sure you would agree with me if you saw the shocking behaviour of the entire Bennet family—their lack of manners and education. I will admit that the two elder Miss Bennets were beyond reproach in every regard, but the rest of the family—"

"The Bennet family?" The earl moved to the wine decanter.

"Yes, that was the name of the young lady—Miss Jane Bennet."

The earl stopped in the middle of the room, forcing his nephew to cease his pacing. A few moments of silence followed until the earl poured himself another glass of wine.

"I see...and Miss Bennet's father... What does he do for a living?"

"He has an estate in Hertfordshire, but the estate is entailed to a cousin."

"So Mr. Bennet is a gentleman, and he owns an estate. However, I suspect Miss Bennet does not possess an impressive dowry."

"I imagine she does not, but that was not the reason—"

"Yes, yes, the main reason was her family's behaviour. You were appalled by their lack of manners, and in this, you had the agreement of his sisters, whose behaviour and manners are always beyond reproach."

"Uncle..."

"And your friend? How does he bear the situation?"

"Worse than I anticipated, I am afraid. I was hoping his attachment was a superficial one, but it appears his heart was touched more deeply than I thought."

"Well, neither he nor his attachment means much to me at the moment if he changed his mind so easily. Perhaps you did the lady a favour after all. And as long as you are preoccupied with his well-being and the lady's feelings did not equal his, everything is for the best."

"I hope so. But, sir, you must not blame my friend. You know he is an honourable man."

"He is honourable; there is no doubt about that. But I do wonder how much of a man he is." His son laughed.

"What about Miss Bennet's sisters? You mentioned earlier that the two eldest 'were beyond reproach.' Did I understand you correctly? Does she have a sister who is not the object of your complaints?"

Darcy averted his eyes, and his answer was delayed a moment too long. "You understood correctly, Uncle. Miss Bennet's younger sister—Miss Elizabeth—is one of the most accomplished ladies I have met in a long time."

"This is quite astonishing; there seems to be something you approve in Miss Bennet's family! And most accomplished, above all... Well, well..."

"I... There is... I confess I had the chance of being in Miss Elizabeth's company a few times, and I will not deny that I noticed many qualities that are rarely seen together in a young lady."

"I see... Well, at least I am relieved to know you and Bingley do not admire the same Bennet daughter. For a moment I suspected you had an interest of your own in keeping your friend separated from the lady."

"Uncle, you must not—'

"Do not worry; I no longer suspect such a thing. I understand perfectly well that your only concern was your friend's well-being. Despite Miss Bennet's many accomplishments, we must not forget their family's lack of manners—and most likely fortune as well."

"True! But, Uncle, I have the strange feeling that you are mocking me, and I cannot understand why. You know I dislike it when you take my words lightly"

"Have no fear, Nephew; this time I take your words seriously indeed. Well, well —that was an entertaining conversation. Let us return to our plans for tomorrow evening. I can hardly wait to see my dear niece again. That sweet girl is like an angel who always succeeds in lightening my old heart."

"We are looking forward to tomorrow night, too, Uncle. I hope we will have a lovely, peaceful family dinner."

"You may rest assured, Nephew—it will be a lovely dinner, indeed!"

After his guest left, the earl remained near the window, staring at the white streets.

The mischievous smile on his face caused a frown on his son's, and he demanded an explanation that never came. The younger gentleman continued to insist, with little success, until the earl became weary of his inquiries and dismissed him for the rest of the afternoon.

LORD MATLOCK'S HOUSE WAS EVERYTHING Elizabeth expected: grand, impressive, lit by hundreds of candles, and crowded with servants preoccupied with accomplishing their duties perfectly. Lady Selina, on the arm of her husband, Lord Brightmore, hurried forward to greet them.

Immediately behind her were two young gentlemen, one of them maintaining a serious—even stern—countenance, the other smiling openly as his eyes instantly met those of Elizabeth. She smiled back at him. Lady Selina performed the introductions to her husband and brothers, the viscount Lord Fitzwilliam and Colonel Fitzwilliam, and for the first time in his life, the colonel was speechless. He vividly remembered his father's mischievous smile from the previous day and felt deeply sorry for his cousin. Indeed, there would be little peace for him that evening.

The gentlemen's dispositions allowed the Bennet sisters to recognise which son was which. However, with no little surprise, Elizabeth saw the colonel's smile vanish from his face when the introductions were made. She had no time to wonder about it as a moment later both gentlemen greeted them in a friendly manner.

"My Lord, Colonel Fitzwilliam, I am so delighted to see you again," said Mrs. Gardiner.

"The pleasure is all ours, I assure you," shouted the earl from the doorway.

He offered his arm to Mrs. Gardiner while the colonel accompanied the younger ladies, already bewitched by both of them. The expected shock and distress his cousin would likely suffer in a short time suddenly became of very little importance to the colonel.

ELIZABETH WAS PLEASED WITH THE visit so far. The colonel was delightful company, his easy manners and conversational skills putting even Jane at ease. From the first moment, he declared both the Miss Bennets were more beautiful than his father reported. Since he could not choose between them, he decided to court both, at least for the time being. Elizabeth laughed; Jane smiled and blushed.

Half an hour passed in pleasant conversation. Then the opening of a door and the sound of a well-known voice startled Elizabeth. She turned to her sister and saw her face pale; she feared Jane might faint. The earl left their little group to greet the newly arrived guests, and a moment later from the doorway, he declared with unconcealed amusement:

"Dear ladies, please allow me to introduce to you my favourite nephew and niece."

Elizabeth silently considered that, if Jane should faint, at least she would not faint alone; the gentleman whom the earl introduced was considerably paler. He remained motionless in the doorway, staring at their party, and his gaze turned to Elizabeth. She breathed deeply, instantly recognising the disapproving glare that always made her uncomfortable, and allowed a satisfied smile to twist her lips.

Holding his gaze, she stepped forward until she was close enough to see his eyes, even darker than usual. Only then did she greet him with perfect politeness.

"Mr. Darcy, such a wonderful surprise to meet again. I never would have imagined how small London is, after all."

LADY SELINA EMBRACED HER COUSINS with great affection. Both Mr. and Miss Darcy expressed their pleasure in meeting Mrs. Gardiner, and the lady replied with genuine warmth.

With the Miss Bennets, however, the Darcy siblings showed considerably more restraint, which credited the memories Elizabeth had of Mr. Darcy's behaviour. Surely, his sister was no different!

Jane appeared unable to look at either of the Darcys, and Elizabeth sensed her distress. How horrible for Jane to be introduced to the girl who was her rival for Mr. Bingley's affections!

With a small voice and a furtive glance, Miss Darcy finally managed to express

21

her delight in making their acquaintance.

"Miss Bennet...Miss Elizabeth?"

Both ladies turned to face Mr. Darcy; startled by his voice. Jane's eyes lowered while Elizabeth's eyebrow arched in expectation.

Darcy stared at them in complete silence for a moment. Lady Selina laughed, but he eventually found his voice. "I wanted to ask whether you have been in London long. It is a lovely surprise to meet you both again."

"We just arrived three days ago, sir," whispered Jane.

"I see... Well, this is indeed a lovely surprise," he repeated, but neither his voice nor his countenance showed any pleasure.

"My sister Jane sent a letter to Miss Bingley, informing her of our arrival. And the day before yesterday, Jane called on Miss Bingley with my aunt. Did they not mention it to you?"

"No... No... In fact, I have rarely seen Miss Bingley or Mrs. Hurst. I visited my estate after we returned from Hertfordshire; I had some urgent business..."

"Oh, I see. It is fortunate you left Hertfordshire in time to attend to your urgent business," Elizabeth concluded with a smile while Darcy remained silent, his eyes searching the fire with great interest.

Once they entered the drawing room, most separated into two groups: the silent and the talkative. Jane remained a little apart on a settee, her eyes travelling shyly from Mr. Darcy to his sister and then to Elizabeth.

Though heavyhearted from Jane's distress, Elizabeth remained equally intrigued and amused by the situation, wondering about the strange coincidence and Mrs. Gardiner's duplicity. Surely, her aunt was aware that Lord Matlock was a close relative of the Darcys. How could she not say a word, even when Elizabeth complained about Mr. Darcy's character and faults? Such a mischievous scheme was unlike Mrs. Gardiner. And certainly, Lady Selina was not oblivious to the situation. What was the purpose of those arrangements? Was it only a plan to allow Jane to meet Mr. Bingley again as Mrs. Gardiner suggested the day before? And why would the daughter of an earl agree to engage in such matchmaking?

"So, Miss Elizabeth, what is your opinion of my sons? Which of them is more to your liking?" the earl loudly whispered to be heard by the entire room.

"Papa!" cried Lady Selina.

Elizabeth blushed as she tried to answer discretely. "Surely, your lordship cannot expect me to answer such a question. Besides, even if I were tempted to answer —which I am not—I would not dare express an opinion about someone I have barely met."

"Fair enough" The earl laughed. "We shall postpone this conversation until after dinner."

Elizabeth easily noticed that neither Mr. Darcy nor the viscount appreciated the unseemly exchange. Once again, she felt Mr. Darcy's disapproving stare. He might be upset by the situation, but she cared little for his opinion. She daringly smiled at him and then turned towards her other companions, ignoring the gentleman's insistent gaze.

Miss Darcy spoke not a single word once she took the seat near her brother, but she watched Elizabeth and Jane with obvious curiosity. This was proof to Elizabeth that her suspicions were correct: Miss Darcy was as proud and disagreeable as her brother—just as Mr. Wickham declared her to be—and she clearly had an interest in Mr. Bingley. Otherwise, why look at Jane with such interest?

Deciding the Darcy siblings would not ruin her disposition, Elizabeth entered into a pleasant conversation with Colonel Fitzwilliam, whose company she enjoyed exceedingly. The colonel, attentive and polite, insisted that Jane move closer to them and take a seat near her sister. Blushing, Miss Bennet joined the animated group, and it was not long before a smile finally came to Jane's face, and her loveliness overcame her distress. Elizabeth could not be more grateful to the colonel.

Shortly thereafter, Lord Matlock invited the gentlemen to accompany him to the library before dinner.

Lady Selina approached her cousin and whispered something to her. Miss Darcy seemed to hesitate a few moments, looked with alarm at her brother, and then finally joined her cousin near the settee where the other ladies were sitting. A tentative conversation thus began.

"Miss Elizabeth, I am pleased finally to make your acquaintance." Elizabeth heard Miss Darcy's low voice.

"Finally, Miss Darcy?" She smiled and tried not to sound impertinent. "Have you heard of me before this evening? How is that possible?"

The girl sketched a tentative smile. "Yes, my brother used to write me from Hertfordshire quite often—"

"Mr. Darcy mentioned me in his letters to you? Oh dear, I dare not imagine the terrible things he must have said." She laughed, looked at her aunt meaningfully, and then turned back to Miss Darcy. The girl was pale.

"Miss Elizabeth, have I offended you in some way? I am so sorry... I do not... I mean... Why do you presume that my brother—"

Miss Darcy's shy, trembling voice and wide, blue eyes left Elizabeth with no words. Hesitantly, Elizabeth touched the girl's hand and forced a smile.

Lady Selina spoke gently. "Georgiana dearest, do not distress yourself. I am sure Miss Elizabeth is speaking in jest. If Darcy mentioned Miss Elizabeth in his letters to you, I am sure he spoke well of her."

Elizabeth barely repressed a laugh. "Indeed there is no need for distress, Miss Darcy. You did not offend me at all. I am only surprised that Mr. Darcy took the time to write about me, considering he and I are not friends. He has always been my severest critic, and I can safely declare that his opinion of me cannot be high, so you must understand my concern about what he might have told you."

She continued laughing, hoping they would join in her amusement. However, Miss Darcy interrupted her again, quite determined.

"That cannot be true… My brother mentioned to me that he missed my playing the piano but was fortunate to enjoy your performance a few times…and he expressed his approval of your interest in books. I fear I do not read as much as I should, and he…"

Elizabeth stared at Miss Darcy, unable to trust this revelation. *Mr. Darcy expressed his approval of me? There must be some sort of mistake!* She was tempted to declare her doubts once more, but Miss Darcy seemed so honest and trusting in her own words that Elizabeth dared not upset her again. She smiled and whispered a polite, "Thank you."

"Well, this is a surprise," said Lady Selina. "Not only does Darcy seem to be an acquaintance of the Miss Bennets, but you appear to know Miss Elizabeth very well."

"Oh, not very well, unfortunately," Miss Darcy replied, suddenly more inclined to talk. "But my brother wrote me almost every day from Hertfordshire…and I also heard accounts from Mr. Bingley…"

Jane instantly grew pale, and Elizabeth was intent on knowing more.

"Mr. Bingley is a friend of yours, I understand. Miss Bingley told me as much."

Miss Darcy hesitated a moment, and Elizabeth was certain she understood the reason.

"Mr. Bingley is a close friend of my brother. He is a very amiable gentleman; it is such a pleasure to listen to his stories."

"Do you see Mr. Bingley often?" Elizabeth continued, and Mrs. Gardiner was ready to intervene; however, Miss Darcy's answer came easily, along with a slight smile.

"No…I only saw him twice after he arrived in town. The first time was almost a month ago, and he seemed very eager to return to Hertfordshire. For the entire dinner, he shared recollections of his friends from there. He seemed very fond indeed of Netherfield Park," she concluded, and Elizabeth was once more at a loss for words.

She turned to her sister, only to see Jane's eyes moist with tears. Miss Bennet suddenly rose from her seat and hurried to pour herself a cup of tea. Her hands trembled so that she could not hold the cup properly, and Elizabeth went to help her.

"That was kind of Mr. Bingley," Lady Selina declared. "I hope he returns soon to his estate."

"I am not certain of his future plans," the girl continued, oblivious to Jane's distress. "The second time I met him, he seemed quite preoccupied, and we spoke very little. I imagine he had some business that interfered with his plans."

"Well, we can only hope his business will be resolved soon in the best possible way," Lady Selina concluded, and with that, Mrs. Gardiner changed the topic.

A short glance from her aunt confirmed to Elizabeth that the subject of Mr. Bingley was closed for the evening, and she did not dare disobey. Besides, she needed no further details; their short conversation held shocking revelations.

Miss Darcy had no romantic interest in Mr. Bingley—anyone could see that

—and she even tried, shyly and not very skilfully, to become friendly with both of them. Even more, her words gave rise to hope and proved once more the lack of honesty in Miss Bingley and Mrs. Hurst. As for those ladies' much declared intimate friendship with Miss Darcy, Elizabeth was certain it could not be further from the truth.

I wonder how Mr. Wickham could have been so wrong in his estimation of Miss Darcy's character... She surely does not seem anything like her brother—quite the contrary.

"Miss Darcy, I am glad we had the chance to talk," Elizabeth said, and a smile spread over the girl's face.

"As am I, Miss Elizabeth."

"You know, my dear Georgiana, Mrs. Gardiner grew up in Lambton." Lady Selina brought a new subject into the conversation, which changed Miss Darcy's spirit in a moment.

"Truly? In Lambton? I was not aware of that! Have we met before, perhaps? And have you been in Derbyshire lately?" she asked, allowing little time for answers between questions.

"That is indeed surprising, Mrs. Gardiner." Mr. Darcy's voice interrupted their exuberant conversation. "Did your father possess an estate in the neighbourhood?"

Elizabeth looked at him for a moment, wondering how long he had been there. A smile twisted her lips as she tried to imagine his expression at hearing Mrs. Gardiner's revelation about her family. She feared his usual behaviour might distress her aunt, but would he dare be disrespectful to a guest in his uncle's home?

Mrs. Gardiner answered with perfect composure and a warm smile.

"No, sir. My father had a small shop in Lambton."

"Oh, I see..."

As Elizabeth anticipated, Mr. Darcy was surprised, and he remained disconcerted for a moment. She expected him to return to his usual aloofness and leave their company, but he looked at the ladies and finally replied:

"Lambton is a charming little town."

"Yes, it is. And Derbyshire is the most wonderful place in the world."

"I shall not argue with you, Mrs. Gardiner; I should be pleased to speak with you more about Derbyshire at any time," Mr. Darcy concluded. Then with a proper bow to the ladies and a warm smile to his sister, he joined the other gentlemen.

Elizabeth stared at her aunt with a puzzled expression, trying to remember whether she had ever heard Mr Darcy speak with such warm politeness. Her aunt smiled.

DARCY REMAINED IN THE HALL, close enough to hear the ladies' voices chatting amiably. He had yet to recover from the shock of seeing Elizabeth in his uncle's house, and he was yet unable to breathe, talk, or behave properly.

This could not be; he had left Netherfield a month before, trying to put her out of his memory and ease his conscience for his participation in Bingley's departure.

Yes, he had been certain that his judgement of Miss Bennet's feelings for Bingley had been correct. Yes, he was certain that it was better for Bingley to escape from marriage to a beautiful lady who did not share his affection. Besides, he was not sure that Bingley's feelings for Miss Bennet were real or would last more than a month; he had seen him in love many times before.

But he could not deny his own interest in removing from Netherfield, and that was the reason for his lack of sleep during the last month. He was also in danger of being trapped. Her smiles, sparkling eyes, teasing and witty replies, dark hair playing along her nape—all made his days and nights at Netherfield a torture, and there was little improvement once he left. But he had been certain that, with time and distance, his strength and self-control would conquer the feelings he battled.

And now she was there, and she likely would be around for some time as his uncle made it clear that he found the Bennet ladies pleasant company.

Darcy felt the urge for a glass of brandy as he remembered the conversation with his uncle the previous day. The earl allowed him to make a fool of himself when he related his disapproval of the Bennet family. He had not felt so dreadful in a long time. He was tempted to take Georgiana and return home that instant. But did he have the right to ruin everyone's evening by behaving in such a savage manner? And what explanation could he find for an impromptu leaving? Besides, Georgiana seemed to be enjoying herself. She seemed to feel at ease with the Miss Bennets, which was surprising—or was it? Was it surprising that anyone, even a person as shy as his sister, felt at ease with Elizabeth and Jane Bennet? His uncle had met them the day before and liked them instantly, and the earl generally liked few people on such a short acquaintance. On the other hand, it was not a surprise that the colonel was charmed by both of them as he himself declared. But he was not to be taken seriously; he was even worse than Bingley when it came to beautiful, young ladies. Darcy was more cautious in judging people; he did not approve of either sister at first meeting. *Miss Bennet used to smile too much. And Miss Elizabeth was not handsome enough to tempt me to dance with her.*

Suddenly, his thoughts sounded ridiculous. Surely, those were not the reasons he disapproved of them in the beginning! There must have been other things to form his poor opinion of them, and the most important was their family's behaviour and situation, which could not be forgotten or dismissed. But Miss Bennet does not seem to smile any longer—not at all! And Miss Elizabeth... He could not think of any lady more handsome—or more tempting.

"Darcy, what on earth are you doing here? Let us return to the ladies; dinner is ready." The earl's voice startled him, and he could not reply before his gleeful uncle continued.

"And I absolutely need your opinion: Which of my sons should marry Miss Elizabeth Bennet, do you think? We could not reach an agreement, and you seem to be an expert on difficult problems of the heart. I shall put her near you during dinner so you can observe her behaviour towards both of them and inform me

26

whether you sense any partiality to one or the other. Oh—and do not worry about her family's faults; I dare say her charms are adequate compensation."

His uncle and cousins passed nearby, and he heard their laughter from the dining room; Darcy remained motionless in the hall, staring after them and forgetting to breathe.

All hope for a peaceful evening had vanished. He could only pray that his uncle continued to mock him and that none of his words was taken seriously—except for the fact that he would put Elizabeth near him at the table. Could it be true? Would he spend the entire evening only a few inches from Elizabeth? *Miss Elizabeth, of course,* he corrected himself and hurried to the dining room. He did not need the earl's assistance to make a fool of himself; he had been a fool since the first moment he met her, and neither time nor distance had changed that.

Chapter 3

Taking her place at the dinner table, Elizabeth paid little attention to her surroundings. Her thoughts were preoccupied with the revelations of the last hour. Aside from the unique behaviour of Lord Matlock's entire family—which included the earl's amusing but tiresome insistence on her marrying one of his sons—she was puzzled by Mr. Darcy and, more importantly, his intentions.

Elizabeth had not the slightest doubt that Mr. Darcy convinced Mr. Bingley to remain in London just to keep him from Jane. Mr. Bingley's sisters must have played an important part in the scheme, but surely, Mr. Darcy had a more powerful influence over his friend. What his reasons were, Elizabeth could not guess.

Elizabeth's initial suspicion—and Miss Bingley's own declaration—about a future connection between the Darcys and Bingley was obviously far from the truth. Miss Darcy's sincere description of her conversations with Mr. Bingley confirmed that she had no romantic interest in him and that Mr. Bingley's affections remained in Hertfordshire.

It was understandable that Miss Bingley—whose main interest in life seemed to be Mr. Darcy and everything related to him—and her sister would not want Mr. Bingley to enter into a marriage that could bring him neither wealth, position, nor any other benefits aside from the love and honour of a wonderful woman like Jane.

What Mr. Darcy's interest was in such a dishonourable scheme, Elizabeth could not understand. Was he so selfish and proud that he planned to force a union between his sister and Bingley despite their wishes? Or did he simply despise the entire Bennet family, wanting to be as far from them as possible?

If she were tempted to accept the worst about that gentleman before their brief interaction, the evening revealed some unexpected details.

He had appeared quite surprised—even shocked—to see her and Jane in his uncle's house, but he showed nothing but politeness towards them, much more politeness than he had shown in all the time he spent in Hertfordshire. To Mrs. Gardiner, his behaviour was not merely proper but almost friendly. Surprisingly, he expressed his intention to talk more about Derbyshire with Mrs. Gardiner, the daughter of a small shop owner from Lambton. Though he was obviously influenced by the earl's friendship with the Gardiners, it was a pleasant change from his past aloofness and disturbingly proud behaviour.

But the most shocking revelation—one that Elizabeth still could not believe —was the notion that Mr. Darcy had mentioned her—Elizabeth Bennet—in his letters to his sister. She remembered an evening during her stay at Netherfield when poor Miss Bingley insistently begged him to include a few words of admiration from her in his letter to Miss Darcy, and he refused her. Was it possible that he found time and space to put in his letters such things as her playing the pianoforte or her 'extensive' reading?

Were these the actions of a man who only looked at her to find fault and whose long, insistent, reproachful stares only made Elizabeth uncomfortable? If he had such a poor opinion of her entire family, why waste time writing his sister about her in an apparently positive manner as Miss Darcy declared? His affection for his sister was beyond any doubt, and his attitude towards her was protective and warm. He would surely be careful regarding news he shared with her and people he introduced to her—even through letters.

And another intriguing thing: He left the gentlemen in the library and came into the drawing room to join their conversation for a few minutes. That was uncommon behaviour, and she certainly would not expect it from Mr. Darcy. Or perhaps he just wanted to see whether his young and painfully shy sister was comfortable amid so many new acquaintances. Yes, that was a logical explanation —and one that gave him much credit as a brother.

Such puzzling information about that gentleman; it almost made her dizzy.

She remembered their conversation from the ball when he asked her not to sketch his character. That night she had said she might not have another opportunity. Well, she seemed to have been wrong about that as there obviously would be many other opportunities after that evening unless he took his sister—as he took his friend—and left London immediately to avoid further encounters. Perhaps that would not be so bad, after all, because she had little interest in discovering his character. No, that was not entirely true; she was interested in knowing him better, so she could understand his reasons for ruining Jane's chances of happiness and challenge them. Yes, that was what she would do!

Her eyes met Mrs. Gardiner's worried gaze, and she smiled at her aunt. She did not miss the reproach and silent scolding on her aunt's face, and once more, she wondered how Mrs. Gardiner seemed to read her mind.

Suddenly, her own thoughts seemed unreasonable as she remembered a previous talk with Mrs. Gardiner. How was it that her anger and reproach for Jane's situation turned on Mr. Darcy alone? Where was Bingley, after all, and why could he find no other way of securing his happiness than amusing Miss Darcy with pleasant stories of Hertfordshire? Surely, a man should do a great deal more to protect his desires and future happiness. *Unless I misjudged his true wishes and desires as Mr.*

Wickham misjudged Miss Darcy's character. Or perhaps Jane misjudged his worthiness and gave him more credit than he deserved.

A moment later, the earl's voice startled her from her musings. She tried to answer but could not remember the question, so she took her seat and tried to smile as she drank some cold water; she was suddenly very warm. She was about to refill her glass when she noticed on her left the presence of the very person whose character she was so desirous to sketch.

"Mr. Darcy…"

"Miss Elizabeth… Please allow me to pour you a glass of water."

"I… Thank you, sir," she said, taking the glass hesitantly and avoiding his eyes.

Situated next to Elizabeth at his uncle's right, it was not difficult for Darcy to notice the earl's friendly care for Mrs. Gardiner and consequently for her nieces if for no other reason than the gratitude and respect he had for the late Mr. Gardiner.

He also knew that the earl disapproved of his intervention in Bingley's situation. He could remember every moment of his conversation with the earl from the previous day, and now he understood why the earl's tone and expression changed the instant he mentioned the name *Bennet*. Yes, his uncle was displeased, and he would continue to show his displeasure for a while, one way or another.

Still, Darcy was certain that his judgement of the Bennet family's lack of proper behaviour was correct, and surely, the earl would agree with him if he met them. And he was certain that, despite the earl's mocking declaration, he would not allow either of his sons to join a family whose situation was so beneath them.

He stared at Elizabeth's face, and he could see that she was deep in thought. Her eyebrow was arched, and she was biting her lower lip—two sure signs of her preoccupation. He had spent uncounted minutes in Hertfordshire watching her and silently studying every small gesture as she read, played, talked to others or danced. He always watched from afar, and now, suddenly, he was inches away and felt suddenly warm. He needed a glass of cold water, too, he thought, glancing at her again. Her lips were still wet and red and apparently very soft, and he could not look away.

"So, Miss Elizabeth, what have you done these last couple of days? Have you enjoyed London?" asked the colonel, and Darcy suddenly turned his attention to him.

"We have done little, sir. I spend most of the time at home or walking in the park with my little cousins; Lord Matlock and Lady Selina's visit a few days ago was the only special event since we arrived in London. Oh, and yes—my aunt and sister called on Miss Bingley a couple of days ago, but I did not join them."

"Do you have some specific plans for your stay in London, Miss Elizabeth? And Miss Bennet?" The viscount's direct question took both sisters by surprise, and for a moment, they looked at each other, uncertain who should answer.

"No, nothing of the sort," Jane finally replied. "We intend to spend as much time as possible with our aunt and cousins. We have few acquaintances in London."

"Oh, you must not worry about that, Miss Bennet," Lady Selina spoke up. "After the ball next week, a lack of acquaintances in London will be your last worry."

"A ball? I do not think that… We did not…"

"We were not aware there is a ball next week to which we are invited," Elizabeth said, her pleased voice covering Jane's small whisper. "May I ask who will host this ball? Not Mr. Darcy, certainly, as I know he is not fond of dancing."

She knew it was impolite to address such a comment to Mr. Darcy, but Jane's sad countenance compelled her to punish a *certain person* for her sister's distress.

"Miss Elizabeth, I am curious to know how you can be so sure of what my nephew is fond! May I dare ask how well you came to know each other during his stay in Hertfordshire?"

The viscount coughed, Lady Selina and her husband chuckled, and the colonel laughed and added, "I would like to ask the same question if I may be so bold."

"Uncle, we all know you well enough to appreciate your humour, but I do not believe it is fair to expose Miss Bennet and Miss Elizabeth to such a conversation. Besides, the answer is quite simple. I had the pleasure of first meeting them during an assembly, and I am sure there was no doubt in anyone's mind that it was not my favourite pastime. More so, if I remember correctly, Miss Elizabeth heard me declare openly to Bingley that I do not enjoy dancing."

Mr. Darcy's intervention and his veiled scolding of his uncle took the others by surprise. Even Elizabeth, who bore the earl's behaviour and questions easily, was startled by Darcy's long speech, clearly meant to protect her sensibility. Before he ended, her attention and her eyes were fixed on his face, and she could see he was, indeed, solemn. At his last words, he turned his eyes to her, and his gaze locked on hers.

"And to Sir William, if *I* remember correctly," Elizabeth added, and to her shock, she saw him puzzle a moment before a tentative smile lit his face.

"You do remember correctly," he answered.

"I thank you for clarifying my dilemma, Nephew. I am also grateful that you brought the impropriety of my question to my attention. It is providential to have such a detached mind among us, always attentive to propriety and decorum. I have often wondered whether it is not tiresome to be a man without fault."

The earl's reply sounded offensive, and Miss Darcy, together with Jane, stared at him in shock. Elizabeth did not know what to expect next; she looked worriedly at her aunt, but a moment later, the earl and the colonel began to laugh loudly.

With no little wonder, Elizabeth noticed Mr. Darcy himself shaking his head in disapproval before smiling and turning to his uncle. He laughed, too, and then replied with a small voice, his eyes turned to his uncle but his words clearly directed to her.

"I have enough faults myself, as you well know, Uncle, and I am occasionally inattentive to propriety and decorum; Miss Elizabeth must remember that, too."

His voice—words with hidden meaning—and smiles she had rarely seen before all suggested to Elizabeth that there could be only one reason for Mr. Darcy's strange behaviour: he indulged himself with one glass of brandy too many before dinner! Moreover, the earl and the colonel apparently kept him company!

The first course was served, and that briefly put an end to their conversation.

"So, Miss Elizabeth, you met Darcy first at an assembly. That sounds like an interesting story."

"Yes we did, Lady Selina, but I am sorry to disappoint you. There was nothing interesting, only a common introduction," Elizabeth said lightly.

She was not certain whether it was only an impression or whether Mr. Darcy suddenly had become tense next to her. Was he worried, perhaps, that she would reveal more of his behaviour during the assembly ball and expose him to additional teasing from his uncle? She smiled to herself and tried to keep her eyes on her plate.

"Well, I hope you are fond of dancing, Miss Elizabeth…both you and Miss Bennet, I mean," the viscount intervened once more.

"Of that, you may have no doubt, sir," said Mrs. Gardiner. "I am proud to tell you my nieces are both proficient dancers."

"Excellent," added the colonel. "I must ask for at least one dance from each of you ladies, and I intend to secure my dances this very evening."

Jane gave him a disconcerted look while Elizabeth began to laugh again.

"Colonel, may I inquire once more of what ball we are talking and who will host it?"

"My sister, Selina. It has been a family tradition for the past five years to have a ball at her house on the first evening of the New Year."

"Oh, I see…" Elizabeth knew very well that neither she nor Jane had the proper gowns for such an event, and it was not possible to order new dresses in such a short time. Fond of dancing or not, they would certainly not attend the ball.

"We thank you for your kind invitation, Lady Selina, and we happily accept it," said Mrs. Gardiner with perfect composure, and Elizabeth's puzzlement increased.

Even her dear aunt seemed to behave strangely that night, and everything distressed Elizabeth's state of mind. However, she quickly decided to put aside what she could not solve immediately and pay attention to the aspects that might have a favourable resolution that evening—like discovering more about Mr. Bingley and his plans from Mr. Darcy himself. After all, she could not ignore the opportunity of having the gentleman a few inches from her all evening.

As the second course was served, Elizabeth turned to her companion, keeping her voice as low as possible in order not to draw the attention of the others.

"Mr. Darcy, I hope Mr. Bingley is well."

He hesitated a moment. "Yes, he was, the last time I saw him. Unfortunately, I have not met with him as much as I would wish to since we returned to London."

"I am surprised to hear that; Miss Bingley told my sister and my aunt that Mr. Bingley was very busy and closely engaged with you and Miss Darcy."

She did not dare meet his eyes as she spoke, but she could feel his gaze on her face. *I should not have said that!*

"Miss Bingley's estimations about certain things are not always...accurate."

She lifted her eyes to meet his. "That must be true as I am sure you know her very well. She declared she has been an intimate friend of your family for many years."

"As I said, Miss Bingley is not always accurate in her estimation of people...or situations."

She thought she could detect a smile and a trace of sarcasm in his voice, and she was amused, but only for a moment.

"Miss Bingley said that Mr. Bingley does not plan on returning to Netherfield. Is this accurate, do you think?"

"Well, I am not certain. It is very likely he will spend little time there in the future."

"I see...so in this, at least, Miss Bingley's *estimation* seems to be accurate. Then perhaps it would be better for the neighbours that he left Netherfield."

"Yes, that could be one of his plans. I would not be surprised if he were to do that."

Elizabeth suddenly abandoned the subject and asked Lady Selina something about the theatre. The next moment, both the viscount and the colonel joined them, and the conversation became animated. She could feel Darcy's stare and could not say whether her cheeks turned red because of him or because of the anger caused by this new revelation. So it was true that Mr. Bingley did not plan a return to Netherfield! She wondered whether Lady Selina knew the Bingleys well enough to invite them to a private ball.

Until the end of the dinner, she did not speak directly to Mr. Darcy again. She thought of nothing but the arrogance in his voice when he informed her that Bingley had left Netherfield forever. He must rejoice in his success!

She was angry with him and furious with herself as she was aware that she actually enjoyed speaking to him. What a mistake! Yes, he was fond of and careful with his sister. Yes, she admitted he was a clever man, well read, and well educated. Yes, he could be pleasant when he wished to be. Yes, he had been polite, even friendly, with all of them—no doubt, because the earl demanded it. But his pride and disdain for those beneath him, his selfishness in imposing his will regardless of the way his actions might affect others—these never would change!

AFTER DINNER, THE GENTLEMEN DID not retire as expected. Instead, they enjoyed their drinks in the pleasant company of the ladies.

Elizabeth took a cup of tea and retired to a corner, trying to maintain a pleasing countenance. With no little surprise, she noticed the approach of Mr. Darcy; he asked permission to speak to her. She hesitated and looked around but could find no reason to refuse him.

"Miss Elizabeth, may I ask whether I offended you in any way? Forgive my boldness, but I cannot ignore that I had the pleasure of a conversation with you, and then suddenly you seemed to avoid my presence. Please allow me to apologise if—"

"You have not offended me, sir. I thank you for your concern, but it is unnecessary."

"Then...are you unwell?"

"I am very well, thank you. I just do not feel inclined to speak."

"I understand that but—"

"If you will excuse me, sir, I would like a few words with my sister. Again, thank you for your concern." She left before he could reply. She felt his gaze on her and was content. Surely, his pride could not bear the notion that she would amuse him no longer with trivial conversation about nonsense. It was such a pity that Miss Bingley was not there to mend his pen and comfort his wounded ego.

"So, Miss Elizabeth, I hope you will not refuse to play for us! We are all eager to hear you," said the viscount. The others pleaded with her, but she was still angry and tired. She could not play and sing for Mr. Darcy!

"Oh, I could not... I am in no disposition to... I am sure we would all be much happier to hear Miss Darcy play. I have heard so many wonderful things about her talent that I could not possibly miss the opportunity to hear her. I am certainly not as accomplished as she is, and I would not want to ruin your evening with my performance."

While speaking, she took a seat near Miss Darcy and sketched a smile to her, but the girl had turned pale and was struggling to speak. As occurred earlier, the effect of her words upon Miss Darcy took Elizabeth by surprise, and she did not know what to do. She saw Miss Darcy searching the room for her brother, and once their eyes met, Mr. Darcy moved towards them.

The earl took his niece by her shoulder. "My dearest Georgiana, nobody will force you to play, but I would be delighted to hear you. We are all family and friends here, after all, so you have nothing to fear. Unless you do not want to play for your old uncle..."

He was coercing her with his warm words. Elizabeth could easily see that and was about to intervene, ashamed that her attempt to avoid a tiresome request had put the girl in an unpleasant situation. But her brother was there in a moment, assisting his sister as she expected.

"I would love to hear you play if you wish to, my dear," Darcy said gently. "And I would also love to listen to Miss Elizabeth play if she cares to indulge us."

His tone of his voice was different, and if a few moments earlier Elizabeth would have refused him without hesitation, she now remained silent, staring at him.

She finally averted her eyes and looked at Miss Darcy. Their eyes met, and almost the same moment, they smiled at each other.

"Miss Darcy, it seems useless to try to change their minds. I would suggest finding a way to sing and play together, perhaps holding hands tightly for courage." Elizabeth laughed.

Miss Darcy turned her wide eyes to Elizabeth and then to her brother and suddenly replied, "It might be a good idea to sing together, Miss Elizabeth; however, holding hands would make our playing at the pianoforte a bit more difficult."

The others stared at her in disbelief at such a playful answer, and both burst out laughing. The earl kissed her hair and then politely kissed Elizabeth's hand.

The colonel offered each of them an arm and took them to the pianoforte, but he soon returned to the settee as his help turning pages was not needed.

From the corner to which he retreated after speaking with his sister, Mr. Darcy followed their performance. From time to time, Elizabeth could feel his eyes on them, and she acknowledged again his care and protection of Miss Darcy.

They played and sang together twice, and then each of them performed one song while the other turned the pages. More than half an hour later, with many thanks from their companions, they returned to the others. Darcy remained in the corner.

With a glass of brandy in his hand, the earl approached and took a seat near his nephew.

"Are you enjoying the evening so far, Nephew? I certainly hope so, and I hope you have some useful observations to share with me regarding the small assignment I gave you."

Darcy gulped some brandy then cast a glance at the animated group.

"I would not have suspected you to trap me this way, Uncle. I have been completely honest with you, and you hold my honesty against me and force me into this awkward situation—"

"Of what situation are you speaking, Nephew?"

"Come, sir, let us play games no longer. It was not fair to throw me into an unexpected meeting with Miss Bennet and Miss Elizabeth without warning, nor was it fair for them. I feared Miss Bennet would faint when she saw us. She surely deserved no such treatment."

"Again, of what treatment are you speaking? Are you suddenly preoccupied with Miss Bennet's feelings? You thought little of them a month ago."

"That statement is unfair, Uncle—"

"Is it? Come, Darcy, you know I value you as much as I care for you; however, you were in error in this case. Admit it! Have you seen Miss Bennet tonight? Does she not seem like a lady who suffers from love?"

"I was not in error. I see Miss Bennet is more shy than usual, but I also notice she is as polite and friendly as usual. Besides, all the other difficulties remain; you do not know Mrs. Bennet and her younger daughter, and—"

"I do not know Mrs. Bennet, but I do know your Aunt Catherine and Bingley's sister; I am also aware of my own improper behaviour at times! So spare me your understanding of other people's manners. As long as you have nothing against the lady's character and Bingley is not displeased with her lack of dowry, this conversation is ridiculous."

"You would not be happy were your sons to marry someone so far beneath them, despite all your jokes and insinuations."

"Perhaps not; but then again, Bingley is not the son of an earl. Let us be honest; if we are to speak of family situations, Miss Bennet is the daughter of a gentleman while Bingley's fortune is from trade. She is superior to him, is she not?"

"If you put it that way—"

"I do put it that way! And even more, I would not disapprove of my sons marrying either of the Miss Bennets if they developed an attachment. They could surely do worse than Jane and Elizabeth Bennet."

"Surely, you are joking," Darcy interrupted him abruptly.

"Surely, I am being serious, unless you have some strong arguments against the idea. From what I have seen, you have quite a history with Miss Elizabeth. What on earth did you do to that girl that she dislikes you so intensely?"

"Excuse me?" Darcy asked so loudly that the others turned to them. "What do you mean she dislikes me intensely? From where did that idea spring?"

"Where? For heaven's sake, Nephew, are you blind? First you insist Jane Bennet has no feelings for Bingley when anyone can see she still suffers for him, and now you misread Miss Elizabeth's feelings for you that are equally strong but of a completely different kind."

"You think Miss Elizabeth dislikes me? I have always believed we were on friendly terms. We always had lively conversations and—"

The earl rolled his eyes and patted his shoulder, laughing.

"Darcy, may I inquire as to how many women you have known—*really known* —before now? Damn, you seem oblivious about whether a woman likes or dislikes anything. I hope you are not equally oblivious to other things a woman might like or dislike!"

Darcy choked and spilled wine on his coat then started to cough.

DARCY'S FACE WAS STILL RED from coughing, and he desperately tried not to draw the attention of the group. His uncle's words whirled in his head, but he could not accept that the earl was correct with regard to either lady.

Yes, Miss Bennet seemed out of spirits, but on the other hand, he had never seen her especially lively, even when Bingley was present. A simple indisposition of the lady did not prove he was in error.

Memories of his conversation with Elizabeth during dinner flooded back to him. Moment by moment, word by word, he managed to recollect the precise instant Elizabeth's demeanour changed and she seemed disinclined to speak to him again. It occurred when he informed her that Bingley had no intention of returning to Netherfield.

He sat alone, the glass of brandy in his hand, staring at Elizabeth as she talked and laughed with the colonel, Selina, and his own sister. He looked at Georgiana, in a joyful mood after she played with Elizabeth, and then he looked at Miss Bennet, who smiled politely, although her eyes betrayed a distracted lack of interest in the conversation.

He had been honest in his beliefs when he decided that Miss Bennet did not share Bingley's feelings; he could not have been so partial and unfair in his judgment! Or could he? No, that was not the proper question. Was it his right or his duty as a friend to judge Bingley's feelings for a young lady or that lady's feelings for him? That was the question he must answer.

And the earl said he would be pleased for his sons to marry either lady. Was he serious? Surely, that would never happen. But what if it did?

What of Elizabeth's feelings towards him? He had been certain that she had an inclination towards him. He had even been careful not to encourage this tendency as he could not possibly consider binding himself to her.

And now the earl declared that she deeply disliked him and suggested he would agree for his son to court her. That could not be! Robert, as a second son, could not afford to marry a woman with no dowry; besides, Elizabeth could not possibly form a positive opinion of the colonel in so short a time! Or could she? After all, she apparently liked Wickham from their first acquaintance. Why could she not like Robert, who was an honourable gentleman with a happy demeanour and the son of an earl?

ELIZABETH CONTINUED TO TALK TO the colonel, but from time to time, her eyes returned to Mr. Darcy. He remained in the corner, and she began to feel uncomfortable whenever she felt his stare. What was he thinking? And why did he keep looking at her in such a way? Something obviously upset him, and she did not much care what it was except that his behaviour made her uneasy.

She went to pour herself another cup of tea, and she noticed the earl close to her. They smiled at one another, and he thanked her once again for her lovely performance.

"I hope you are having a pleasant evening, Miss Elizabeth."

"Indeed we are, your lordship. We are truly grateful for your invitation. This party was a pleasant diversion for my aunt and my sister...and for me, of course."

"I hope we shall meet again soon. I hope you have not been disappointed with my sons."

"Not at all, sir. I enjoy their company, and I especially appreciate a gentleman who secures a dance for a ball a week early." She smiled, and the earl laughed.

"Well, a man never should be timid about securing a beautiful lady's company and a place on her dance card."

She looked at the earl with surprise and curiosity, not daring to inquire further.

"Are you unwell, Miss Elizabeth? Did I say something wrong?"

"No, no...it is just that...a friend of mine told me the same thing some time ago, just before the ball at Netherfield. He asked me for a dance a week before the ball and—"

"Truly? That is quite unusual. I used to tell my boys that when they were younger, but I doubt my words of wisdom are as well known among strangers. "

Elizabeth forced a smile. "Well, they might be, after all. Or perhaps he heard you speak of it. Mr. Wickham told me he grew up at Mr. Darcy's estate and—"

"Wickham? George Wickham, you mean? Do you know him?"

"Yes indeed. We met in Hertfordshire. He was in the militia and—" She looked at the earl carefully, trying to guess his opinion of that gentleman. With no little surprise, she felt the earl move her a few steps away as he spoke in a quiet voice.

"If he asked you to secure him a dance, I imagine you were on friendly terms."

"Yes we were; in truth, I can say we were very good friends."

"I am glad to hear that. I hope he is doing well, but let us speak about this on another occasion. That little rascal George Wickham was always a favourite of mine, but these boys seem not to like him much, so we had better not mention his name here for the moment."

She wondered whether she should take him seriously, but a moment later when the colonel approached them and the earl suddenly changed the subject, she had her answer.

The rest of the evening passed in pleasant conversation on a variety of subjects. The only one who remained silently apart was Mr. Darcy, who seemed determined to watch from afar.

It was quite late when the guests finally took their leave.

The earl offered his arm to Mrs. Gardiner, and the colonel was ready to do the same for Elizabeth. It was an unexpected surprise, then, that Mr. Darcy stepped away from his sister and invited Elizabeth out, leaving the colonel to care for Miss Darcy.

Careful not to slip on the frozen path, Elizabeth held his arm tightly, her eyes lowered, reflecting that it was the first time—except for the requirement of dancing—that he had offered her his arm since they met.

"Miss Elizabeth, I am pleased I had the chance to see all of you tonight—such a pleasant surprise! And I am certain Bingley will be equally pleased when I tell him of this dinner party. I should meet with him in a few days."

He released her hand, helped her enter the carriage, then bowed to them—and smiled.

Uncertain whether she had heard him correctly or rightly understood his words, Elizabeth had no time to return his farewell before the horses began to move.

It was snowing again.

Chapter 4

Elizabeth was not certain whether she had slept an hour the entire night. She could remember falling asleep a few times, but she would waken after only a few minutes. After she recollected, more than once, every minute of the previous evening, the image of Mr. Darcy's expression right before their departure would not leave her mind.

Did he mean what she believed he did? Would he tell Mr. Bingley about their presence in Town? Could she expect Mr. Bingley to visit them soon? If so, should she tell Jane? But what if Mr. Darcy did not keep his word? Was this possible? Would he mention such an important thing if he did not wish to do it? And what if he told Mr. Bingley, but that gentleman still did not come to visit Jane? What if they all misinterpreted Mr. Bingley's affection for Jane? Would Jane be able to bear another disappointment? No, indeed. There was nothing to be shared with Jane for the moment.

And Mr. Darcy…was it possible that he changed his mind about Mr. Bingley and Jane? Why would he do that? What if she had misjudged him from the very beginning? What if he was not responsible for Mr. Bingley's decision to leave Netherfield?"

"No, this will not do," she said loudly, furious with her own thoughts. She rose from the bed and went to open the window. The cold winter wind assaulted the room instantly while flakes of snow fell on her face. She shivered but remained in the window frame, looking along the empty, white, frozen street. The snow had covered everything in white, and she closed her eyes, allowing herself to be wrapped in happy memories. She had loved winter and snow since she was an infant and used to spend her days skating, playing, or simply walking in the snow, or riding in her father's small sleigh.

None of her sisters—not even Jane—shared her love for the cold and for snow, and Mrs. Bennet spent every winter complaining that Elizabeth would catch a very bad cold and die from it, and her nerves would never recover after losing a beloved—though wild and disobedient—child.

With a smile frozen on her lips and missing her family, whom she had only left three days ago, she wondered how they spent their Christmas and whether it were snowing at Longbourn; Elizabeth then shut the window and, shivering, hurried to the warmth of her bed.

It was dawn and a deep sleep finally wrapped her.

WHY HE HAD PROMISED HE would talk to Bingley, Darcy could not explain to himself.

Did it take so little for him to change his mind? He believed himself to have been fair and correct in his opinions; he rightly insisted that Bingley should remain in town for the winter. However, he was forced to admit privately that his insistence was increased by his wish of keeping himself away from Hertfordshire —away from Elizabeth Bennet, the same Elizabeth who had been brought by fate into his uncle's house on Christmas evening.

When they departed and he promised he would speak to Bingley the next day, Elizabeth had been surprised by his words—pleasantly surprised and incredulous, looking at him with her eyes , her lips half parted. And that moment he understood the reason he made the promise: precisely to see her looking at him with wonder. Had he completely lost his reason? What purpose could it serve?

On the subject of lost reason, surely that was the case with his uncle. Darcy could easily understand why and how the earl had been charmed by Elizabeth Bennet as soon as he met her. But to express his admiration for her so publicly and to insist that both his sons should court the Bennet sisters—that was unacceptable. Suppose one of them took his words seriously? He might raise expectations and hopes impossible to fulfil? Surely, he could not be serious about wanting both ladies in his family? The earl had taken his information about the Bennet family and dismissed it instantly. Yet, only one evening in the Bennets' company—as at the Netherfield ball—would surely change the earl's intentions immediately.

In any case, such a union was not possible. If Miss Bennet *was* attached to Bingley, she could not possibly accept the courtship of another man—even a viscount —so easily. If she did, that would mean that he—Darcy—had been correct in his judgement all along, and he would have every reason to congratulate himself on saving his friend from such a disastrous relation.

As for Miss Elizabeth, she appeared to enjoy the colonel's company, and it was obvious that he was smitten with her. Robert was easily taken with any beautiful woman, but he also made no secret of his intention to pursue an advantageous marriage as he had long declared his disbelief in lasting love.

Oh, for heaven's sake, I am being ridiculous! This is not about my uncle or my cousins! What should I do tomorrow?

Yet, he knew there was only one thing to do.

Just before sleep took hold, he remembered Georgiana's lively chat on their way home: how pleased she had been to meet the Bennet sisters and how she and

Selina planned to call on them the next day. He knew he should be alarmed by the recollection, but he was too tired to think about it.

"You must admit that you owe us an explanation, dear Aunt. What happened last evening could not have been a mere coincidence."

Elizabeth had purposely wakened early to spend time alone with Mrs. Gardiner. The latter smiled.

"What sort of explanation do you wish? On what subject?"

"Hmm… Let me consider… Perhaps on Mr. Darcy's connection with the earl's family? Or Mr. and Miss Darcy's unexpected presence at the dinner where we were also invited? And a few words about why you allowed my severe criticism of Mr. Darcy without even mentioning that you are well connected with his relatives?"

"Not so hasty, my dear. The only blame I take upon myself is that I kept Mr. Darcy's presence at dinner a secret. I could easily see that both you and Jane were surprised to see him so suddenly. I should not have trifled with your feelings."

"No, you should not. I imagine you planned this little charade together with Lady Selina. Was the earl part of the scheme, too?"

"No, indeed. And it was not a charade; as Lady Selena informed me, it is a family custom to have dinner together on Christmas evening."

"I imagine so, but that was no excuse for your secrecy. Indeed, you are culpable —not on my account but for poor Jane."

"You are right. However, I trust Jane's time was not entirely unpleasant. She seemed to have formed a friendly acquaintance with everybody, including Miss Darcy. And even Mr. Darcy was more amiable than I would have expected considering your stories about his many faults and his evil character."

Mrs. Gardiner's irony did not escape Elizabeth.

"I never believed that Mr. Darcy had an evil character, Aunt! And I never declared he had many faults…only pride, haughtiness, an uncivil attitude, and disdain for everybody around him—oh, yes, and his unfortunate influence over his friend Mr Bingley."

Mrs. Gardiner laughed. "Not many faults, indeed…"

"However, I truly liked Miss Darcy," Elizabeth declared seriously. "Making her acquaintance was one of the good things to come from the evening. And speaking of Miss Darcy, I cannot be more certain that there is no attachment of any kind between her and Mr. Bingley. She has a good opinion of him but nothing more. I am convinced that Caroline Bingley tried to deceive Jane—and us—regarding Miss Darcy's attachment to Mr. Bingley. Hateful woman!"

"In this, I completely agree with you, my dear. And what other good things?"

"What do you mean 'other good things'?"

Mrs. Gardiner smiled again. "You said Miss Darcy's presence was *one* of the good things to come from our gathering. What are the other good things?"

"There were many good things, but the most important…Mr. Darcy mentioned

41

to me that he will inform Mr. Bingley of our presence in Town. What do you think of that?"

"Of Mr. Darcy?"

"Aunt, please do not tease me! Do you think he will keep his word? Should we expect Mr. Bingley to call soon?"

"Lizzy, please take a seat and let us talk calmly, child. Neither good nor bad anticipation are desirable regarding Mr. Bingley or Mr. Darcy. I am inclined to believe Mr. Darcy will keep his word, but I am not confident that, in doing so, all the problems suddenly will be solved. Besides, from my knowledge, Mr. Bingley has been out of town for the last few days. That is why Lady Selina and I did not call at his house yesterday," concluded Mrs. Gardiner to an incredulous and silent Elizabeth.

It was almost midday when the first visitors to Gracechurch Street were announced. The joyful appearance of Lady Selina, together with a shy, blushing Miss Darcy brought equal pleasure and disappointment to Elizabeth. Yet, she admitted, it would have been strange for Mr. Bingley to appear at the door so quickly, so she decidedly welcomed the guests and called for tea and refreshments.

"Such cold weather," exclaimed Lady Selina, taking off her gloves.

"I am not fond of cold weather, either," admitted Jane with a smile.

"It is cold indeed, but the snow is wonderful," replied Elizabeth. "I confess I rather love winter. I was tempted to play with my cousins in the snow this morning."

"Really? Well, Georgiana actually did play with my boys in the snow earlier, and I thought that was singular," laughed Lady Selina while Miss Darcy averted her eyes in embarrassment, incredulous that her cousin had revealed her secret.

"Not singular at all, Miss Darcy. Please let me know next time you intend to have an outing, and I will join you," Elizabeth offered, and her laughter stole a smile from her guest.

"May I dare ask where you have been so early in this weather?" inquired Mrs. Gardiner.

"I went to my modiste to assess the progress of my ball gown, and it suddenly crossed my mind that neither Miss Bennet nor Miss Elizabeth likely has a proper dress for such an event. So I made an appointment for you later today, and she promised she will have your dresses ready in time for the ball."

Elizabeth and Jane looked at each other while Mrs. Gardiner only replied, "Thank you, Selina, you are very considerate as always."

"Good! By the way, Georgiana paid a visit to Mr. Bingley earlier; did I mention that?"

"No, you did not," their hostess said while her nieces remained speechless. "You found Mr. Bingley in good health, I hope?"

"My brother and I took our daily walk, and he asked me to join him in calling on Mr. Bingley. My brother loves snow, too. At Pemberley, we used to play in the snow all the time when I was a child. Even now, he is so kind as to keep me company as much as his time allows. I always enjoy walking with him," Miss Darcy said, a smile warming her expression.

For a moment, Elizabeth struggled to imagine the proper Mr. Darcy playing in the snow and then abandoned the daunting task and asked whether Mr. Bingley was well.

"I could not say. Unfortunately, he has been out of town for the last few days. My brother asked Mrs. Stewart, the housekeeper, of his whereabouts."

"Do you know whether Mr. Bingley will soon return?" Jane's question took everybody by surprise, even herself, as she proved by the redness that spread over her cheeks and neck.

Miss Darcy seemed to understand her uneasiness and comforted her with another smile.

"Mrs. Stewart seemed unaware of Mr. Bingley's location. However, my brother had some business to discuss with him, and I trust he will find his direction soon enough."

Lady Selina agreed. "Darcy always finds things that are of interest; since we were young, I cannot remember an instance when he wanted something and did not succeed in achieving it."

"As I once said, Mr. Darcy seems a gentleman with numerous merits and few faults." Elizabeth smiled meaningfully to her aunt.

Miss Darcy watched her carefully and spoke with a low voice and more seriousness than the moment required. "I am pleased to see you have such a high opinion of my brother, Miss Elizabeth. Indeed, he is the best of men."

Again, Elizabeth struggled to respond. Though she had spoken in jest, Miss Darcy took her words in earnest. She glanced to her sister, who appeared lost in her thoughts, and then to her aunt, who was watching her with interest.

"However, if Darcy discovers our missing Mr. Bingley in time, I will face a difficult dilemma: can I invite Mr. Bingley to the ball without his sisters? Upon my word, I have never in my life been in the difficult position of liking a gentleman so much while disliking his sisters so completely."

Miss Bennet and Miss Darcy blushed in embarrassment while Elizabeth laughed. "I am pleased to see we are similar in our dislikes, Lady Selina."

"Miss Bingley and Mrs. Hurst might be difficult sometimes, but they are nice persons," offered Jane, and Miss Darcy kindly approved her.

Lady Selina interrupted them with a harsh gesture. "I am confident you are taking their side only because you are both kind and generous, else I would be upset over your poor judgement of character. They are arrogant, impolite, too pleased with themselves, too inconsiderate for others' feelings—and they share a horrid taste in gowns," she concluded as Elizabeth hid her mirth behind a teacup.

"I fear you must invite the entire family to the ball to enjoy Mr. Bingley's presence," Mrs. Gardiner replied, and Lady Selina rolled her eyes in displeasure while

Jane paled at the prospect of Mr. Bingley's attendance.

"Yes, I know. My only comfort is that my brothers, my husband, and Darcy will be even more displeased as I will force them all to dance with Miss Bingley."

Her remark made the other ladies chuckle, and the time passed in pleasant conversation. Miss Darcy showed little interest in the ball as she had no plan to participate, but she was delighted to make arrangements for a night at the opera in three days' time. Also, the visit to the modiste for the next day was arranged, including an unexpected invitation to her house afterward from Miss Darcy, an invitation gladly accepted.

Half an hour later, an interruption brought their conversation to an end. Strong voices, the fresh air of winter, and three gentlemen entered, stealing smiles from the ladies.

Mrs. Gardiner greeted the new visitors with proper courtesy and obvious pleasure. "Lord Matlock, Lord Fitzwilliam, Colonel Fitzwilliam—so delighted to see you all!"

"Mrs. Gardiner..." The earl bowed to her then cast a quick glance around the room. "Well, soon enough you will be invaded by the entire Fitzwilliam family."

"Be assured I am always happy to see you, your lordship."

Lady Selina placed a kiss on her father's cheek. "I will allow you gentlemen the privilege of entertaining these beautiful ladies as I have to leave. My husband must be home by now, and I will not have him waiting for me. Georgiana, should I take you home?"

"Dearest, do not leave; Darcy will fetch you shortly," the colonel intervened, and all the ladies turned to him. "I met Darcy an hour ago. He had some business, but he will join us soon to take you home."

After a moment of hesitation, Miss Darcy resumed her place on the settee while Elizabeth wondered what extraordinary event might entice Mr. Darcy to Cheapside. Did Mr. Darcy even know where Cheapside was?

"Miss Elizabeth, I hope I am not interrupting your thoughts," said the earl.

"No, your lordship," Elizabeth replied warmly. He remained silent a few moments before a smile spread over his face as he asked Elizabeth for coffee. She obliged and offered him a cup.

"So, Miss Elizabeth, you had the pleasure of meeting Wickham recently?"

"Mr. Wickham? Yes...yes, I did."

"Was he in good health? When did you last see him?"

"Yes, he was in excellent health. I saw him a few days ago."

"Really? What on earth was that rascal doing in Hertfordshire? I hope he is not in any trouble." Unlike his words, the earl's voice sounded caring; his concern was obvious.

"No indeed; why would your lordship believe him in trouble? Mr. Wickham is an officer in a militia regiment encamped in Meryton for the winter."

"Oh, I see... He is an officer now? Well, I imagine he looks very handsome in uniform."

"He does." Elizabeth laughed. "All the ladies in Meryton share my opinion."

"So, did you fall under the charms of Wickham, too?" The earl's question would have offended Elizabeth had his voice and open smile not shown utter amusement.

She laughed. "I am not certain what you mean, sir. Mr. Wickham and I are good friends."

"I am happy to hear that. Well, I am content to know he is well for now. He would have approached me if he were otherwise, I suppose."

He remained silent, and Elizabeth was not certain how to continue. She looked around the room and noticed Miss Darcy looking at them intensely.

"Lord Matlock, may I dare ask… Are you well acquainted with Mr. Wickham?"

"Quite well, indeed. His father had the management of Pemberley for many years. Oh, forgive me; Pemberley is Darcy's estate. My late brother Darcy was Wickham's godfather. I have known Wickham since he was an infant."

He seemed lost in his thoughts, and again, Elizabeth could not find the proper words to inquire further. Fortunately, the earl continued his confession.

"Yes, since he was an infant…that little rascal… Miss Elizabeth, do you think you could find something stronger than this coffee? Some brandy, perhaps?"

"Sorry? Oh, yes, certainly. I will take care of it immediately." Elizabeth hurried and asked the servant for some brandy then returned to the earl.

"I am pleased to know Mr. Wickham had you to support him in times of need, Lord Matlock. It is a relief to know he is a favourite of yours. I know he had little support from Mr. Darcy. They do not appear to be on the best of terms."

"You are correct, Miss Elizabeth. Now they are grown, neither Darcy nor my sons are very fond of Wickham."

"I imagine they are reluctant to share a friendship with someone beneath them…"

"In this I am not certain you are correct. If they changed their behaviour towards him, they had good reasons. Some of the reasons I am aware of, some not, but I cannot blame any of them, nor can I intervene between them. And I cannot demand they be as forgiving as I am of Wickham's faults."

"I am sure Mr. Wickham has his faults, but do not we all? And I think the punishment should be no more severe than the fault."

"You must not worry, dear Miss Elizabeth; no matter what Wickham might have told you, you must not take it seriously. No one is punishing Wickham, though he has changed in the last few years, and not for the better. I can understand why my nephew and my sons are not easy with his misbehaviour."

Elizabeth tried to control her temper, though it was difficult. She could not understand how the earl could declare his affection for Mr. Wickham and accept so easily his rejection by the younger men in the family.

"It might be correct—or not. Miss Elizabeth, you have a quick mind and hasty judgement. I enjoy speaking to you, but if you were my daughter, I would warn you to be cautious when you form your opinions. It might be dangerous…"

He was speaking in jest, so she replied in like manner. "Sir, had I the honour of being your daughter, I would happily accept your warnings."

He kissed her hand, and they moved together to the settee where the others were gathered. A few steps away, Miss Darcy poured herself a cup of tea. Elizabeth offered to help her whilst the earl asked for the favour of a second glass of brandy. He then turned to Georgiana and whispered so only she and Elizabeth could hear.

"Georgie sweetie, can you keep a secret? I was just speaking to Miss Elizabeth about Wickham. She met him in Hertfordshire; he has joined the militia. What do think of that? And Miss Elizabeth testified he looked handsome in uniform."

Miss Darcy turned white, her hands trembling, and she dropped her cup of hot tea on her dress. Elizabeth hurried to see whether she had harmed herself. Mrs. Gardiner and Jane joined them and, with great distress, discovered that Miss Darcy's hand was injured. Tense moments followed, and the ladies retired to the music room where Miss Darcy was given proper care; the gentlemen remained silent and confused.

Miss Darcy's hand was only slightly burned; it was red and a trifle painful, but her embarrassment was greater. She continued to assure her hostess that she was well and apologised for her clumsiness, asking them to return to the gentlemen.

After a quarter hour, Mrs. Gardiner declared everything was fine and they could all return to the drawing room. Unexpectedly, this time Miss Darcy hesitated.

"Mrs. Gardiner, please be so kind and tell my uncle and my cousins that I am perfectly fine and I will return shortly. I do not want to give anyone reason to worry."

Mrs. Gardiner understood that the girl wished to avoid being the centre of the gentlemen's attention and would rather return after Mrs. Gardiner gave them the details and explanations. She could easily sympathise with her.

"I will remain with Miss Darcy a little longer," said Elizabeth, and Mrs. Gardiner seemed pleased with her offer. She and Jane left the room while Elizabeth turned to Miss Darcy.

For a few moments there was silence; they both searched the room with curious gazes, stared at the fire, and then the piano.

"It is a fine instrument," Miss Darcy said.

"It was a gift from my uncle for my aunt's birthday three years ago. He loved music..."

"Oh, I did not mean to... I am sorry; I know it might be difficult to—"

"Do not worry, Miss Darcy. I miss my uncle very much, and though it makes me sad, I enjoy speaking of him."

"I understand you perfectly well, Miss Elizabeth. Since my parents—" She suddenly stopped, uncertain whether she should continue her confession. "Oh, look, it is snowing again!" After a brief moment of confusion, they hurried to the window, staring outside at the white beauty before them. A short glance was enough approval for Elizabeth to open the window, and like children, they leaned outside to allow the snow to fall over their faces and hands.

The door opened abruptly, but neither of them heard it as the wind blew their hair; a strong voice calling Georgiana diverted their attention, and both girls were shocked to see Mr. Darcy in the doorway, staring at them.

All the way to Cheapside, Darcy struggled to escape the feeling that he was making a mistake. He had no reason to be there, and his mind and common sense insisted that he should return and allow his cousins to take Georgiana home. Was it acceptable for Georgiana to stay at Mrs. Gardiner's so long? He would fetch her and leave shortly; that was his decision. He had no reason to remain a moment longer than necessary. His sister had stayed too long already.

When the driver stopped and invited him to step out, Darcy's first thought was to admire the house. The second was to take off his gloves; his hands felt unusually warm, though the air was freezing.

He entered and allowed the servant to introduce him, wondering whether the others would be pleased to see him. Did they know he would come? *The colonel probably informed them—that is if he remembered my request and is not preoccupied with his other companions,* Darcy thought as the door opened widely.

He glanced around the room, and the first thing he noticed was that *she* was not there. A moment later, while he was greeting his hostess, he noticed his own sister was not there either. Surely, it was expected of him to inquire about Georgiana. He was informed about the little accident and about Georgiana's being in the music room with Miss Elizabeth and instantly replied, "I wish to see her—thank you." As his steps took him closer to the music room, he felt worry and concern taking control; a cold shiver travelled along his spine, and his skin burned under his neck cloth.

The servant was dismissed, and Darcy stood a few moments before the closed door, breathed deeply, and finally entered—only to stand still again. Near the open window, leaning outside with hands and hair fully exposed to the falling snow and the cold wind chilling their brightened cheeks, were his sister and Elizabeth!

The surprise was so great that he did not know what to do. In fact, he did know, but he did not want to interrupt them—yet. His eyes locked on Elizabeth's nape where the snow had turned into drops of water and slid down to her shoulder. He saw her shiver under the cold snow and heard her lively laughter. His sister was laughing too, and for a moment, he wondered how it was possible that he only heard Elizabeth's voice, despite the fact that he should have been worried for his sister.

"Georgiana!"

They both startled, and Elizabeth's embarrassment was apparent. She properly greeted him, and he bowed to her then turned to his sister and asked whether she was well. Georgiana declared she was very well indeed. Only then did he observe her bandaged hand and become concerned, inquiring about her injury.

"Oh, nothing important; there is no need to worry. I dropped the teacup and burned my hand a little. Trust me, Mrs. Gardiner's care was completely unneeded; do not be misled by the bandages. But, Brother, you know what I have discovered?

Miss Elizabeth likes winter as much as we do! It is snowing so beautifully! We shall go for a ride in the sleigh tomorrow. I must make the arrangements!"

Georgiana's cheerful answer and her excitement as she revealed that small piece of information made him smile in relief; she seemed very well, indeed.

"Dearest, I am pleased you are not hurt," he said gently. "But I will only be able to join you for the ride after noon as I have some business in the morning."

"I was speaking of Miss Elizabeth and me," Georgiana replied. She saw her brother's confusion and hurried to add, "But you are welcome to join us if you wish."

That was astonishing, and Elizabeth was equally amazed, so he did not know what to answer except to say, "Thank you, we shall see tomorrow," and to politely inform his sister that it was time to leave.

The insistence of the others convinced Darcy to stay a quarter hour—but no longer. He felt uncomfortable in the room full of people as his eyes kept turning to Elizabeth and her red cheeks and neck. He had to leave quickly as he intended.

When the carriage began to move, he suddenly felt safer— at least for the moment—but he would have to meet her again soon. Riding in a sleigh? Surely, he could not possibly consider joining them. The earl had invited all three ladies to the opera; yes, there he may go—he must go, for sure.

"William?" He startled and returned his attention to his sister while she spoke hesitantly. "My uncle was speaking with Miss Elizabeth about Mr. Wickham… That was why I foolishly dropped the cup of tea."

They looked at each other for a moment then turned to the window. The wind was blowing, and the carriage suddenly became more chilled than the road.

Chapter 5

Fitzwilliam Darcy was a young boy when he first understood that he and his cousins must follow rules that were not imposed upon their friend. In truth, it seemed as though George Wickham had no rules at all.

Young master Darcy had the best tutors and a fixed schedule for study. George Wickham kept him company in class but only until he became bored, which happened frequently. It was understood that young Darcy must improve continuously to be worthy of his name and able to bear the responsibilities of his inheritance. George had no responsibilities, only the benevolence of his godfather and Lord Matlock.

Master Darcy was taught to enjoy success and strive to be the first in any challenge. If he failed at something, it was an opportunity to try harder. If George Wickham could not finish an assignment, however, he was excused and never forced to repeat it. Mr. Darcy and Lord Matlock were severe with their children occasionally but always indulgent with Wickham.

George Wickham came to understand that he could expect and demand to be treated leniently. It was a fact universally acknowledged that he was a charming and likeable boy—and young man. It was simply his nature, and he skilfully enhanced that quality over the years as he improved his ability to take advantage of his charm.

Though he was aware of Wickham's true character, it took Darcy more than ten years of struggle to deny his requests for support. He might have continued to allow himself to be deceived by Wickham's false promises had the scoundrel not tried to wound Georgiana's innocent heart. He remembered the moment he discovered the appalling scheme Wickham and Mrs. Younge had planned. Darcy was so angry that his first thought was to punish Wickham in such a painful way that he would never deceive anyone again. Then he stood face to face with Wickham and listened as he claimed his only interest was to make Georgiana happy; he wanted nothing except the living he was promised so he could support himself. Darcy's most powerful feeling was disgust for the person Wickham had become, and he blamed himself for not taking measures to prevent it when the signs were there for all to see.

Darcy was not surprised that Elizabeth was on friendly terms with Wickham; he knew that other women, more experienced than she, had surrendered to Wickham's charms. He could not expect Elizabeth to understand Wickham's faults after so short an acquaintance. Yet, he believed and trusted her to be wise and show prudence in everything that involved George Wickham.

On the other hand, Darcy knew Elizabeth did not dislike him. The earl was completely wrong about that! She smiled at him, teased him, and followed him with her eyes when they were together. She was not indifferent to him, and he struggled to keep a proper distance from her and conceal any preference for her. He could not allow himself to raise expectations that could never be fulfilled.

Fitzwilliam Darcy was certain of two things: he never had been as enchanted by any other woman, and he never would be able to propose marriage to Elizabeth Bennet. He thanked God for the disastrous situation of her family, or he would have been in real danger.

He remembered the first time he had seen Elizabeth—and yes, he refused to dance with her. Then she refused him—twice. When she finally accepted, he could still remember the feeling of her hand in his and the pleasure of speaking with her. Even then, she mentioned Wickham with obvious insistence and interest, clearly trying to imply something. Was it possible that Wickham shared some of their history with Elizabeth? Was there nothing Wickham would do or say to give him an advantage?

He looked at his sister again and called her name, smiling at her.

"So, dearest, did you have a pleasant time today?"

THE HOUSE WAS SILENT AGAIN, especially silent after the departure of their guests. Suddenly, the ball—and the lack of proper gowns for the event—became the most important topic for all three ladies. While Mrs. Gardiner sent a quick note to the modiste asking for an urgent appointment the next morning, Jane paced the room in obvious preoccupation.

"Lizzy, do you think Mr. Bingley will return in time for the ball? It would be such a nice surprise to meet him again…"

"We cannot be certain, but I have no doubt that, had he known there would be a ball you would attend, he would return in an instant. But, dearest, if you expect to see him, it will not be a surprise anymore." Elizabeth laughed.

"May I say you seem to be enjoying your time here, girls?" Mrs. Gardiner smiled. "And dare I presume you are not so opposed to the idea of a ball now, Jane?"

"I am glad to see *you* are not completely displeased with the ball, either, dear Aunt," Elizabeth said. Mrs. Gardiner turned pale.

"You think I should not go, Lizzy? Would you agree to attend without me? Perhaps I should stay home. I am not very inclined to… I do not think I am yet prepared to…"

"Oh no, by no means! You must go even if you do not feel inclined to dance. We certainly will not go without you—and you surely cannot disappoint Lady Selina by your absence."

Mrs. Gardiner tried to argue with them, but at that moment, the children entered the parlour, and the discussion ended. Only later at dinner did Jane and Elizabeth insist upon the subject again and force the promise that, without any doubt, they all would attend the ball.

THEY HAD BEEN IN TOWN less than a week, and each day had brought revelations for Elizabeth, some proving her previous opinions, others changing them completely.

First, there was the conversation she had with Lord Matlock about Mr. Wickham and, partially, about Mr. Darcy. She recalled the expression on the earl's face when he spoke of Mr. Wickham; it left no doubt that the earl was genuinely fond of the younger gentleman. Then how was it that he seemed not to worry about Wickham's situation in life and the misfortune he suffered at the hands of Mr. Darcy?

Perhaps it was true that Mr. Wickham had made mistakes, but those had been severely and unfairly punished by Mr. Darcy as well as the earl's sons—no doubt out of some obligation to support their cousin—by withdrawing their good opinion and their friendship. Also, Elizabeth remembered the earl's statement that Mr. Wickham knew how to turn things in his favour. What could he possibly mean by that?

And last, but by no means least, she was surprised that Mr. Wickham had been incorrect in his description of Miss Darcy's nature; the young lady had dropped the cup and burned her hand precisely when the earl spoke of Mr. Wickham. The entire story must by more complicated than she knew.

Lady Selina was a daily visitor, sometimes accompanied by her husband, her father or her brothers. In addition, she invited them to dine at her house, and it was apparent that Mrs. Gardiner was a familiar presence in her ladyship's home.

Even more, Lady Selina's mother-in-law, Lady Brightmore, had invited them all to dinner that evening. As Lady Selina said with delight—a gathering of almost thirty people "with great prospects of dancing and a lovely preparation for the ball I will host in two days' time."

Elizabeth was intrigued by the fact that, for some strange reason, Miss Darcy —by her own choice— had joined Lady Selina at Gracechurch Street every day. Even more shocking, her brother seemed aware of these visits, and instead of forbidding them as Elizabeth expected, he called once himself.

To both Elizabeth and Georgiana's disappointment, the planned sleigh ride had to be postponed as the clouds dissipated unexpectedly that morning, and the weather warmed just enough for the snow to melt. But as Miss Darcy said, it was only delayed until the perfect moment came. Mr. Darcy himself had suggested that, if they really wished to enjoy such a ride, they should take a tour outside town, an idea the ladies appreciated.

"Oh dear, it is snowing again," said Lady Selina, leaving the carriage in a great hurry, as they all returned from the modiste and were invited for tea at Gracechurch Street. Jane and Mrs. Gardiner followed her, while Georgiana and Elizabeth, in a customary gesture, lifted their faces to allow snow to caress their cheeks; Miss Darcy's foot slid, and she almost fell, but fortunately, Elizabeth took hold of her arm. They laughed at each other under the reproachful gazes of the other ladies.

"I know all this white landscape is wonderful, but I confess I dislike what the snow is doing to my shoes, my gowns, and my hair," Lady Selina continued, shivering.

"I enjoy walking in the snow!" Elizabeth replied, enthusiastically.

"Lizzy, you enjoy walking in any weather," added Jane, and Mrs. Gardiner agreed.

"My brother told me you walked almost three miles to visit Miss Bennet when she was ill," said Miss Darcy and both Elizabeth and Jane stared at her in utter surprise. That Mr. Darcy shared such a thing with his sister was difficult to believe, and Elizabeth attempted a joke.

"Miss Darcy, I am afraid to ask what else Mr. Darcy told you about me. I am amazed that, after hearing so many preposterous stories, you can still speak to me."

Miss Darcy seemed disconcerted for a moment, looked at her cousin, then turned her attention to Elizabeth again, and a huge smile of relief spread over her face.

"Miss Elizabeth, I confess at first I was puzzled by your remarks regarding my brother, but now that I have come to know you better, I understand you are only speaking in jest. It is amusing that, for some reason, you always joke when referring to William while he is always serious when he speaks about you."

Elizabeth was at a loss for words at such a statement, and as happened on their first meetings, she could not be certain whether Miss Darcy was serious or not. She noticed some looks exchanged between her aunt and Lady Selina, but this was neither the moment nor the place to inquire further.

THE PARTY HAD BEGUN HALF an hour before, and Caroline Bingley was still uncertain whether it had been wise for her to attend Lady Brightmore's dinner with Louisa and her husband. She knew Lady Brightmore to be a difficult widow with extravagant tastes and weird notions and habits. Once her ladyship came to dislike someone, that person would never be on her guest list again, so Caroline wisely chose to remain silent and watch the others, hoping to see a friendly face. There were a few young gentlemen with whom she would like to become better acquainted—if only someone might introduce her into their animated conversations. On such occasions, Charles had always been helpful. However, she would rather not talk to anyone the entire evening than risk having Charles in London and meeting some…undesirable persons.

She was slightly impatient, and she knew she did not look her best since she did not feel her best. The worst thing was that she was in town, Georgiana Darcy was in town, Mr. Darcy himself was in town, and instead of enjoying time in their company, she must find a way to avoid them! What in God's name came over Mr. Darcy that he would inquire so insistently about Charles's location? Could he not see the danger? And Georgiana—she could not forget Georgiana's unusual chitchat about the time she had spent with Mrs. Gardiner and the Miss Bennets. Had they all lost their reason? How had the Bennets become the most popular family in Town?

As if all her prayers had been heard, with unconcealed pleasure Caroline Bingley saw Mr. Darcy and his sister enter the room. Only a few moments passed before Lady Brightmore hurried to them. Caroline had always wondered why the Darcys treated Lady Brightmore with such apparent warmth when they were not even real family.

Finally, the Darcys approached her. "Miss Bingley...such a nice surprise to meet you here."

"Likewise, sir... I have—"

"Miss Bingley! What a pleasure to see you. I did not know you were on my mother's guest list of. Are you alone?"

"Lady Selina...Lord Brightmore..." By that point, Caroline Bingley turned from frustration to anger. She was certain Lady Selina was purposely trying to interrupt the lovely conversation she started with the Darcys. "I came with my sister and my brother Mr. Hurst."

"Oh, I see... I know Lady Brightmore is closely acquainted with Mr. Hurst's mother. I hope Mrs. Hurst is in good health—the elder Mrs. Hurst, I mean."

Caroline was vexed and at a loss for words. How on earth would she know if Mr. Hurst's mother was in good health? She had barely seen the old lady in the last five years.

"I hope Charles will be here tonight. He has been missed at the club. Where is he?" Lord Brightmore intervened, and a glance at Mr. Darcy told Caroline that he was about to ask the same question. She breathed deeply and was about to reply when she was stopped by Louisa's desperate gaze and improper waving.

When she turned towards the main door, the entire room became dark and began to spin. It was Caroline's worst nightmare: in the middle, closely attached to the arms of Colonel Fitzwilliam and the viscount, were Jane and Eliza Bennet! She hoped and prayed her eyes were deceiving her, and she staggered a few steps to the nearest chair. She sat, shocked to see her companions abandon her for the newly arrived guests. She was too distracted to notice Louisa's approach.

"I do not really know, sir. My brother left town a month ago, and all I know is that he is visiting friends; he will likely remain at their estate for the next few months," she answered, but Lord Brightmore was too far away to hear.

"What on earth are the Bennets doing here? And with Lord Matlock and his sons? How could the earl allow country nobodies to enter on the arms of his sons? Does he not know what rumours will arise? And why is their aunt from Cheapside on the earl's arm?"

"Caroline, mind your temper! This is not the time to make a scene! And stop looking at Eliza Bennet that way," Mrs. Hurst scolded her furious sister.

Caroline Bingley did heard no more than a couple of words; her complete attention was engaged in following the Bennet sisters around the room. She saw Eliza Bennet sitting with Lady Brightmore on one side and Georgiana Darcy on the other. She hesitated a few minutes and then began to move, closely followed by her sister, and did not stop until she was a few steps from the object of her despair.

"My dearest Jane, how happy I am to see you here! And Mrs. Gardiner! Miss Eliza! I could not hope for a lovelier surprise."

"Miss Bingley, Mrs. Hurst..." Mrs. Gardiner replied with polite composure. Jane was slightly embarrassed by the friendly approach but greeted the ladies with her usual kindness.

Elizabeth forced a smile. "Miss Caroline Bingley... I confess I had lost any hope of meeting you again after we waited in vain for you to return my sister's call. It seems fate wished for us to renew our acquaintance. And Mrs. Hurst...so nice to see you."

Caroline was lost for words in the face of such impertinence, and she failed to notice Lady Selina's chuckle. How could she respond to Eliza's preposterous suggestion that she should have called on them in Cheapside?

"Well, I confess I was surprised myself to see Miss Bingley here tonight," Lady Brightmore intervened. "I would not have guessed that you know each other, my dear Mrs. Gardiner."

"We had the pleasure of meeting Miss Bingley and Mrs. Hurst in Hertford-shire; Mr. Bingley leased an estate near our father's property," explained Elizabeth, smiling at her ladyship while Caroline Bingley struggled to appear indifferent in the face of Lady Brightmore's veiled offence. The old lady seemed to find great enjoyment in suggesting—again—that she had not invited Caroline personally. What a horrible person!

"Oh, by the way, where is that dear boy Charles, Miss Bingley?"

"My brother is not in town, Lady Brightmore. He left with a party of friends, and it is likely that he will spend some time with them." She could not help but look with satisfaction at her sister when she noticed Jane Bennet's sudden pallor. This was a battle Caroline surely would not lose!

"Such a pity. I have rarely liked anyone from the first moment as I liked Charles. Although, he might have some companions in that competition, as I just met Miss Bennet and Miss Elizabeth, and I liked them instantly. Now, if you will excuse us, Miss Bingley, Mrs. Hurst, I want to introduce my new guests to the others."

They had little choice but to return to their previous place near Mr. Hurst, who had already enjoyed a few glasses of brandy, while on each arm, Lady Brightmore bore a Bennet sister to their introductions.

"I AM SORRY IF I was rude, dear girls, but Caroline and Louisa always bring me to the edge of my patience. It is a shame; their father was a worthy man, and so is Charles."

"You must not apologise, your ladyship. I can well understand your feelings." Elizabeth laughed. "You met Mr. Bingley's late father?"

"Yes, I did. He took care of some of my business for a few years. He was a great help to me and my son. After he passed away, I was a little lost until I had the good fortune to meet Mr. Gardiner. Such an extraordinary gentleman… What a loss for us all. I am so happy to see Madeleine here tonight after such a long time. But who could blame her? Losing such a husband as Edward so early in her life… My dear husband, God rest his soul, could have learned a thing or two from Edward Gardiner if they had ever met. Oh well, we should not allow the Bingley sisters to ruin our appetite. I trust you will enjoy my dinner. Oh, and girls—do any of you play or sing? I would love some music. I have three musicians to play in case anyone might want to dance. My dearest Selina is so fond of dancing, but still, I would love to hear you."

Half an hour later, Elizabeth and Jane had been introduced to the other guests —all of them relatives of her ladyship or Lord Matlock—and a few old family friends. There were many illustrious names, and Elizabeth could remember only a few.

What remained vivid in her mind, though, were the reactions to their introduction as most of the guests were not as friendly or as pleased to meet them as Lady Brightmore was. The ladies in attendance especially received them with restraint and prudence, barely addressing a few words to them.

"I absolutely need to rest a little," said Lady Brightmore, and Elizabeth and Jane took her to the settee where Mrs. Gardiner was waiting.

"Mother, you should not make so much effort, you know that," said Lord Brightmore reproachfully while Lady Selina offered her mother-in-law a cup of tea.

"Oh, nonsense… Selina dearest, please give me a glass of wine. I am tired of tea."

"Mother! Selina, no wine for her!"

"Matthew, mind your own business, son. You may have tea if you want! Selina sweetie, please indulge your mother…or must I ask a servant?"

With obvious disapproval and a meaningful shake of her head, Selina obeyed. Lady Brightmore enjoyed her wine and looked around with a contented smile.

"Such a joy to have so many young people around! So much youth, so much liveliness… You have the liveliest eyes I have seen in a long time, Miss Elizabeth?"

"That is a fair statement," approved Lord Matlock, approaching with his sons and Mr. Darcy. "Lively and bright, much like Miss Elizabeth herself." Elizabeth felt her cheeks warming and averted her eyes for a moment. From behind the colonel, she saw Mr. Darcy staring at her, and for a moment their eyes met; to her greater surprise and embarrassment, Mr. Darcy smiled at her, approving the earl's words.

"Your lordship is purposely trying to make me feel uncomfortable, I can see that," Elizabeth said, attempting a joke. "Or, you are trying to flatter me in order to ask something of me."

"I declare myself defeated, Miss Elizabeth. Indeed, I plan to ask you something; I would appreciate it if you play and sing something for us tonight. I dare not ask Georgiana, but I hope you might be easier to persuade."

Elizabeth looked at Miss Darcy for a moment, looked around the enormous ballroom, and then turned to the earl. She tried to keep a smile while replying seriously.

"Lord Matlock, I would gladly respond to any request you may have in the future, but I have no desire to perform tonight; there is no way I could be persuaded."

"But Miss Elizabeth, we—"

Darcy intervened. "We would be happy to listen to you play and sing on another occasion in the future, Miss Elizabeth, but by no means will we insist upon a situation that might make you uncomfortable."

Elizabeth stared at him, surprised at his unexpected rescue. What *could* she answer?

"Darcy is right, Father," said the viscount.

"Of course he is right," accepted the earl after a moment of hesitation. "Though not surprising—Darcy is always right." The earl laughed.

Mr. Darcy shook his head in mocking reproach at his uncle's teasing; then he turned his eyes for another moment to Elizabeth. With surprise, she saw another smile on his face—so she smiled back.

The uncomfortable moment passed. At Lady Brightmore's request, four young ladies offered to play and sing, eager and proud to display a small measure of their accomplishments acquired during years of diligent study.

During the entertainment, most of the guests moved about the room, trying to approach—as much as propriety allowed—those of the opposite sex who were the recipient of their interest and hoping that, during the coming dinner, they would be seated as close as possible to the favoured lady or gentleman.

Elizabeth spent most of the time talking with Lady Brightmore and Miss Darcy. Jane—due to the kindness of her heart—accepted small talk from Caroline and Louisa, closely watched by Mrs. Gardiner who was speaking with Lady Selina and her husband.

In another corner of the room, the viscount, the colonel, Mr. Darcy, and a few other gentlemen, seemed overwhelmed by a group of beautiful young ladies who were skilfully trying to gain the gentlemen's attentions.

Elizabeth's eyes were diverted in their direction, amused by the difference between Mr. Darcy and the other gentlemen. He appeared as aloof and silent as he was in Hertfordshire, despite the fact that his companions were superior to those in Meryton. From time to time, her eyes met his, and each time, she was certain she could see a forced, uncomfortable smile on his face.

"He is handsome, is he not? He looks much like his father," Lady Brightmore whispered to Elizabeth. She startled, then smiled and whispered back, noting that her ladyship was enjoying a second glass of wine.

"Of whom are we talking? I have to confess I see many handsome gentlemen here."

"Yes—many handsome gentlemen indeed! When I was young, it was customary for a gentleman who liked a young lady to attract her attention, but these days things have changed. All these girls, so willing to catch a man with wealth and connection…a little strange to me. By the way, do you like anyone in particular, Miss Elizabeth? Please feel free to spend your time with them; you need not stay with me."

"I assure you, it is a pleasure to talk with you, Lady Brightmore." She was amused by the conversation. "But I am still curious—about whom were you talking?"

"Well, well—what kind of question is that? You were looking closely at their group, so you can tell for yourself. Which of them is the most handsome, do you think?"

Elizabeth felt herself blushing, but it was too late to stop the discussion; she looked at the group once more, aware that Lady Brightmore was watching her.

"All of them could be called handsome if you ask for my opinion."

"True, true, they are all handsome, but—"

She was interrupted by Lady Selina, who sat near them. "Of what are you and Miss Elizabeth talking so seriously, Mother?"

"We were talking about the most handsome gentleman in that group, my dear."

"Oh, you are talking about Darcy again. What did he do this time? I notice he barely speaks a word while Mary, Sophia and Florence are all over him. Poor man—just wait until the music begins. I will ask to dance with him, and he will be forced to dance with other ladies, too." She started to laugh while Elizabeth silently stared at the gentlemen. *Mr. Darcy?*

How did Lady Selina know that the ladies were *'all over him'*? And why did she not hesitate a moment to identify the *'most handsome'* gentleman as being Mr. Darcy. Of course, he was handsome—nobody could deny that—but the others were good looking and also pleasant and amiable. He only appeared silent, distant, and haughty.

Her eyes met his again, and he smiled at her; his entire face seemed lit, and his lips parted as though he were trying to say something. She hurriedly averted her eyes and returned her attention to her companions.

"Mr. Darcy is his usual self," she said.

"Yes, he is mostly the same when he is in a large company. I think his aloofness is what appeals to all these young ladies, besides his wealth—that and his figure, of course. And the way he wears his clothes." Lady Selina laughed, and Lady Brightmore joined her.

"You are so right, my dear! One can easily estimate a man's qualities and assets by looking at how his clothes fit his body."

"I can testify to that, based on my own experience with my dear husband. Our marriage proved that my early judgement of his qualities were all correct."

Elizabeth blushed violently at Lady Brightmore's statement and Lady Selina's reply, shocked by the highly improper exchange and not knowing how to reply. Lady

Selina patted her arm. "My dearest Miss Elizabeth, I am afraid we have offended you with our language. Please forgive us; my mother and I have a particular way of speaking that is far from what decorum would require. Will you forgive us?"

"Lady Selina, please call me by my given name. After such a conversation, it feels strange to be addressed in such a formal manner."

Lady Selina and her mother-in-law began to laugh openly while Elizabeth could not decide whether she should be shocked or laugh with them. She struggled not to notice how their clothes fit on some of the gentlemen in attendance—but with little success.

Immediately after dinner, the music began, and though tentatively, a few couples took their places on the dance floor. Lady Selina and her husband were the first, followed closely by three other pairs. The colonel asked Elizabeth while the viscount invited Jane.

For the next two dances, both Bennet sisters were asked by other gentlemen; Mr. Darcy showed no interest in dancing until Lady Selina almost forced him to dance the third with her. After an hour and a half, Elizabeth finally took a seat near Miss Darcy. Only after she was seated did she notice Mr. Darcy a few steps behind them. Her cheeks were red from the exercise, and she arranged a lock of hair she could feel on her nape.

"Miss Elizabeth, would you like something to drink?" Mr. Darcy's amiable tone took her by surprise. She accepted, he offered her the drink, and had nothing more to say.

"So, here you are, Miss Elizabeth," said the colonel, approaching. "I would be honoured if you would dance another with me."

"I thank you, colonel, but I am afraid I have to refuse you this time. I would like to rest a little; I hope you do not mind?"

"Not at all! But, in order to compensate for this refusal, you must save me the first two sets at the ball the day after tomorrow! I hope I am not too late with my request."

"Gladly, sir, and no, you are not too late. Nobody has asked me to save a dance and only two days until the ball." Elizabeth laughed.

"Well, a man cannot be too careful about these things," he said and departed after asking Darcy whether he was injured after being forced to dance with Selina.

Though she could see he was offended by the colonel's remark, Elizabeth could not help laughing, as did Miss Darcy. Mr. Darcy remained serious for a few moments; then he smiled.

"You may laugh at me, Miss Elizabeth, but this is how I am. I do not feel comfortable dancing unless I know my partner really well. I do not appreciate that my cousins are amused at my expense, but there is little I can do about it."

"You could exercise a little more, perhaps? I am certain there is more than one young lady in this room whom you know well enough and who would be happy to dance."

58

"Perhaps… I shall try to follow your advice…in the future."

"A very polite answer—as polite as your intervention earlier when you kindly saved me from the torture of playing before all these people. I have to thank you for that."

"You are most welcome, Miss Elizabeth. I know how it feels when someone insists on something you do not wish to do."

She blushed at the hidden reproach then smiled at him.

"I understand your meaning, sir, but it is not the same. I did not feel comfortable to perform because I do not play the piano as well as I would wish to, and that is precisely because I do not take the trouble to practice. But you are a skilful dancer —as I have the pleasure of knowing myself—so you have no excuse."

"Perhaps you do not take the trouble to practice the piano, but certainly you have employed your time much better. No one admitted to the privilege of hearing you could think anything wanting. It seems neither of us performs to strangers," he said, holding her gaze.

No word came from Elizabeth for some time. Finally, she replied. "Yes, so it seems…"

"Brother, do you think we could go for a sleigh ride tomorrow? It has snowed all day long." Georgiana turned the conversation in a most welcome way. "It is quite a shame that I promised Miss Elizabeth and I could not keep my word."

"It is very likely you will have a beautiful day for a cold journey around London tomorrow. I will ask Oliver to have the horses prepared in the morning."

"Will we have your company, Mr. Darcy?" asked Elizabeth, and a moment later she blushed in embarrassment. *What came over me to ask such a preposterous question? What will he think of me? What will Georgiana think of me?*

"Unfortunately, I have fixed plans for tomorrow morning, but I thank you for your question, Miss Elizabeth. I can only hope that another opportunity will arise soon."

He was smiling at her with perfect amiability, and she could do nothing but smile back. The last quarter of an hour spent in his company, their conversation, his change in manners, and his words with hidden meanings were completely new and difficult to accept. She still anticipated any minute to see him behave as he did in Hertfordshire. And her silly reaction, including her improper question about his joining them on the sleigh ride, made her even less comfortable. She smiled with unconcealed pleasure and relief when the earl moved near her.

"So, dear Miss Elizabeth, are you pleased with your evening so far? What do you think of Lady Brightmore? I noticed you spending a lot of time in her company."

"I am grateful to her ladyship and to you, sir, for this lovely evening. I am having a wonderful time, and so is Jane. As for Lady Brightmore, I cannot imagine a more pleasing or agreeable lady. I loved spending time with her."

"Yes, I imagined you would. She was equally pleased with you, as I expected. Well, you will have more opportunities to spend your time in Town in an entertaining way. And speaking of entertainment, I noticed that Bingley's sisters spoke with Miss Bennet. You know, they are amusing only if one does not give much credit to what they say."

"I know that; thank you, sir." She laughed.

A moment later, the earl moved a step closer to her and leaned slightly to whisper playfully. "And also speaking of entertainment…would you like a short walk in the park with an old man? The day after tomorrow, maybe?"

At her puzzled look, he confessed with a trace of guilt, "A mutual friend of ours is passing through town for a few days, and I plan to see him, but I would like to keep it secret from my sons—and from Darcy, of course. I thought *you* might like to meet him briefly."

"Mr. Wickham is in town?"

The earl barely had time to nod in agreement before he exclaimed cheerfully, "Darcy, you are here. May we help you with something, Nephew?"

Elizabeth hesitated a moment before she felt composed enough to turn and face Mr. Darcy. He seemed somehow disconcerted, as it was obvious he had interrupted their conversation, but he stepped forward and bowed politely to Elizabeth.

"You cannot help me with anything, Uncle, but I was wondering whether Miss Elizabeth would be kind enough to help me correct one of my major faults." Both Elizabeth and the earl stared at him, eyes wide, so he continued, clearly amused.

"Miss Elizabeth, would you do me the pleasure of dancing the next set with me? In order to improve my skills by practicing more, as you wisely advised me earlier."

Elizabeth was certain the earl's laughter was heard by the entire room, so, without further thought, she put her hand into Darcy's and followed him to the dance floor.

The music finally began.

Chapter 6

Mrs. Gardiner and her nieces were among the last guests to leave Lady Brightmore's party. The late hour, the freezing wind that struck them the moment they left the house, the excitement of the evening, and the stressful anticipation of the days to come were reason enough to fall asleep as soon as they entered their rooms in Gracechurch Street. In Elizabeth's case, however, *soon* meant rather late.

The extraordinary event of Mr. Darcy asking her to dance—only a few minutes after he took the trouble to explain his opposition to the pastime—needed an extraordinary explanation, but Elizabeth had none.

He had asked her to dance in Hertfordshire, and even there his gesture puzzled Elizabeth exceedingly. During the entirety of that ball, she could see how appalled Mr. Darcy was by the behaviour of the attendees—and principally her own family. Yet, he asked her—Elizabeth Bennet—to dance with him! And, if any doubt remained, their harsh conversation during the dance only proved to him once more that his invitation was unwise, which made it unlikely that he would repeat such a mistake again. Had he forgotten those things? He must have; there was no other explanation for his renewed request.

Mr. Darcy of London seemed a wholly different person from Mr. Darcy of Hertfordshire. If Elizabeth had any remaining doubts about this, they vanished with their conversation during the set. Though Elizabeth could not recall every subject of their discussion, his amiability was vivid in her mind.

On further reflection, however, she admitted that, as Lady Selina pointed out, with the others around him, he was his usual self. Even in the matter of dancing —except for a compulsory dance with his cousin Selina and the one with herself —he did not dance at all. The satisfying feeling that she was the only lady in the room on whom he had bestowed such attention was difficult to deny—as it was also difficult to deny the fact that she had enjoyed the company of *this* Mr. Darcy quite a lot.

Just before sleep defeated her, three things still spun in her mind. First—Mr.

Bingley's presence at the forthcoming ball seemed more possible than ever. Second —she must wake up early and prepare for the sleigh ride, as she would meet Miss Darcy at ten o'clock. Third—among all the gentlemen at the party, Mr. Darcy was indeed the one whose clothes were most flattering to his figure. It was fortunate that Lady Brightmore and Lady Selina had pointed out that feature to her; she had never paid close attention to it before with any gentleman.

"LIZZY, YOU LOOK PRETTY AND rested, my dear. May I presume you slept well?"

Not at all, Elizabeth was tempted to reply, but instead she smiled approvingly at her aunt. She felt rested, though, and anxious for a long ride in the freezing, December air.

"Lizzy dearest, are you sure it is wise to ride in this weather?" Jane asked with a trace of worry. "It has been snowing since yesterday."

"My sweet Jane, the problem with a sleigh ride is that its success depends precisely on snow." Elizabeth laughed while pouring herself a cup of tea. "Do not worry; I am sure we will be perfectly safe in Mr. Darcy's sleigh. And, of course, any of you are more than welcome to join us. I am sure Miss Darcy would like that."

"Thank you for your kind invitation, my dear," smiled Mrs. Gardiner. "We will save our strength for tomorrow's ball."

"I fail to understand how a sleigh ride would drain your strength, Aunt. However, I shall not insist further, but I am sure you will come to regret your refusal."

"I would rather take that risk, dear," Mrs. Gardiner concluded.

Half an hour after they finished breakfast, Miss Darcy arrived. Elizabeth prepared herself in a few minutes while Eleanor and Edward ran from their mother to Elizabeth, begging to ride with them. Elizabeth kissed her cousins and renewed her promise that she would take them to the park the next day; even Miss Darcy promised to join them. The children were not happy about the result but had no other choice than to accept the offer.

Elizabeth and Miss Darcy left the house and bravely confronted the snow and wind while holding each other's arms. The servants—Mrs. Gardiner's doorman and the groom—helped them into the sleigh. They sat near each other and wrapped themselves in warm blankets. With a tinkle of bells, the horses started to move, and soon there was no sight of them. Mrs. Gardiner and Jane reluctantly retired from the window.

"This is a beautiful sleigh, Miss Darcy! And such wonderful snow!"

"My brother said he cannot believe I have found someone to agree to do this with me." Miss Darcy smiled. "I thank you; the sleigh is beautiful indeed. My brother gave it to me five years ago. And the horses are splendid, would you not agree? We brought them from Pemberley when we came to town."

"They are splendid, indeed, but I confess I am not fond of horses. I have always been a little…scared of them since I was a child."

"You do not like horses?" Miss Darcy asked, disconcerted. "How can that be?"

"I am sorry to disappoint you; unfortunately, there is little I can to do remedy this fault." Elizabeth laughed at this, but Miss Darcy changed her countenance immediately.

"Oh, forgive me, I did not mean to… It is just that… I am sorry if—"

"Miss Darcy, if we are to spend time together in this sleigh, we should make an agreement: we must not use the words 'I am sorry' or 'forgive me' unless it is absolutely necessary and no more than once per hour."

Miss Darcy smiled shyly. "That sounds a convenient agreement, Miss Elizabeth."

"Also, if it is not inappropriate for me to suggest it, please be so kind as to call me by my given name."

Again, Miss Darcy seemed surprised by the request. "That would be lovely —Elizabeth."

"Thank you, Miss…Georgiana." This time the girl laughed.

"Elizabeth, this is our house," she said suddenly, and Elizabeth turned to look at the place in front of them. Through the dense snow, she could see little, but the building seemed impressive as she would expect for Mr. Darcy. For a moment, she wondered whether the gentleman was at home and looked with much attention at the house.

"Oliver, please stop a moment," Georgiana said, and Elizabeth looked at her, puzzled. "I would like to see whether William is home. He mentioned his affairs would not take long. Would you come inside for a moment, please?"

Elizabeth had little time to answer as Georgiana had already left the sleigh; she followed her, and the next moment a servant came from the house and retrieved the blankets.

"My child, it is so good to see you home. I am glad you finally took my advice." A lady in her late fifties came to greet them and remained silent when she saw Elizabeth.

"Mrs. Spencer, this is my friend Miss Elizabeth Bennet. We will only stay a moment; the sleigh is waiting for us."

"I am so pleased to meet you, Miss Bennet! Please come in! Would you like some tea? Are you not hungry? I will order some refreshments immediately and—"

"An admirable, though unsuccessful, attempt, Mrs. Spencer, but I doubt you will keep them inside by offering tea and food."

"William, I am so happy you are home. We just stopped for a moment to check on you."

"Miss Bennet…"

"Mr. Darcy… I hope we did not interrupt you with our impromptu visit. We will leave in a moment." She felt her cheeks burning, but she was certain it was due to the heat from the fireplace.

"No interruption at all… I am pleased to see you. Yes, I understand you are in a hurry. Georgiana, you will need some dry, warm blankets. Where do you plan to go? I would suggest the direction of ------."

"That would be a lovely idea. But how are you, Brother? Did you finish your appointments? Would you not like to join us? It is snowing beautifully. That is —if you have time…"

The request obviously took him by surprise; Elizabeth could see that clearly. Their eyes met for a moment, and she had a strange feeling that he was awaiting her approval, which was a ridiculous notion. Why would he need her approval in his house—and in his sleigh? She smiled at her own folly, and to her surprise, he smiled back.

"I would not want to impose on you with my presence. Are you certain I will not ruin your plans? Perhaps you and Miss Bennet have private things to talk about."

"Oh, forgive me, Elizabeth; I should have asked your opinion first. Would you mind?"

"My dear Georgiana, you have been so kind to invite me on a lovely ride in a beautiful sleigh. Do you think I could possibly mind that the master of the sleigh joins us?" Elizabeth smiled, slightly flustered.

"Well, Miss Bennet, the master of the sleigh is actually Georgiana. And being a guest, you are entitled to refuse any presence that might disturb you."

Though Mr. Darcy's intervention was surprising, his light, teasing tone and the mirth in his eyes left Elizabeth speechless. She swallowed the lump in her throat. "Thank you, sir. I would surely refuse any presence that might *disturb* me, but I would be glad for you to join us as I understand you are familiar with the places we might visit."

He did not answer as he seemed preoccupied in staring at her; Georgiana chuckled and asked her brother to prepare himself as quickly as possible while she and Elizabeth took their seats in the sleigh. A few minutes later, Mr. Darcy appeared and, after giving the driver brief instructions, took a seat in front of them.

The snowflakes were falling gently, and everything around was white and frozen. They passed near Hyde Park when Georgiana suddenly addressed her brother.

"Elizabeth seems to be similar in passions to me except that she does not like horses, which I can hardly understand. Do you remember when father gave me Duke?" She turned to Elizabeth to offer more explanation. "I was about three years old, I think, and Duke was of the same age. He is sixteen now, you see. I loved him so much from the first moment I saw him! I shall introduce you to him when you come to Pemberley. I am sure you will love him. How can you not like horses?"

Mr. Darcy looked at her with increased attention, and Elizabeth felt as though she had been caught doing something wrong by not liking horses. She would have been amused if she were not growing increasingly uncomfortable with Georgiana's genuine excitement. She could sense that Mr. Darcy did not entirely approve of the familiarity between them. She clearly discerned a frown when Georgiana suggested as a certainty that sometime soon she, Elizabeth Bennet, would visit Pemberley.

She hoped her voice was light enough when she answered, forcing a smile. "Well, perhaps if I had a horse of my own, my opinion on the matter would be different now. We only had two horses that, when they were not in the fields, were usually ridden by my father or Jane; and to be perfectly honest, I have to say the horses did not seem to like me any more than I liked them."

Georgiana laughed, and her brother smiled. Elizabeth breathed deeply, allowing the cold air to assault her. She felt Mr. Darcy's gaze upon her still, but this time she was not certain whether he was looking at her to find fault.

THEY HAD BEEN IN THE sleigh for more than an hour, and Fitzwilliam Darcy still could not believe he was there—nor understand why.

When Georgiana informed him of their plan, he approved it without hesitation, but he never considered he might join them. And yet, there he was! Perhaps he was still tired after the previous night's party and could not think properly. It was true that he had barely slept; as soon as he arrived home, he enjoyed a couple of glasses of brandy to put his thoughts in order. The only result had been an increased disorder of his mind and a restless night.

He had enjoyed the party exceedingly—more so than he could remember in a long time. But he knew—and was afraid—that he enjoyed the party because of *her* presence. And, even more dangerous—she had enjoyed his company, too; he was certain of that.

He had left Netherfield after the disastrous ball and after a most enchanting dance with her. He had left—first of all—in Bingley's best interest, but he had been content and relieved to do so. He had wisely put many miles between himself and those sparkling eyes.

And there she was—right in his face—cuddled under blankets, laughing and chatting with Georgiana, her cheeks red from cold, her hair partially escaped from her bonnet, wet and frozen from the snow, her eyes sparkling and laughing—at him.

When he first heard her voice in his house, he thought he imagined it. He exited his office to find her in the middle of the room, and then he barely remembered what happened. Georgiana invited him to join them, and Miss Elizabeth had asked him at the party whether he would accompany them. What more clear indication could he expect? How could he refuse them both? He accepted because he had to.

She had been in town for only a week, and Georgiana was charmed by her. They were already calling each by their given names. And, without much consideration, Georgiana had invited Miss Elizabeth Bennet to Pemberley! What should he do?

He must have the strength to make a decision; he knew he would be in real danger if he continued to see her so often. But could it be avoided? Her aunt was a close friend of his uncle's family, and his sister seemed eager to gain her friendship. What should he do?

"Oliver, stop, please," Georgiana said suddenly, and he startled, looking around. "Oh, this is beautiful!"

They were near a small forest on a hill. Everything around them was completely white; it was no longer snowing, and no breeze disturbed the trees. Everything seemed frozen. The horses stopped, and both girls freed themselves from the blankets and stepped out into the snow, which was higher than their ankles. Darcy knew he should demand they return, but their joy was so infectious that it enticed him, too.

Eventually, he stepped out of the sleigh and instantly felt the snow invading his boots. He could imagine how frozen their feet must be in their thin shoes. There was still a long ride home, so he asked them to re-enter the sleigh.

Georgiana and Elizabeth returned and resumed their seats in the sleigh, but their appearance was distressing. Their shoes were heavy with snow, and their dresses looked positively frozen. They tried to shake the snow from their shoes and gowns but with little success, as their hands were chilled. This failure made Darcy cast them a disapproving look, and they fought to hide their laughter under obedient glances.

At Darcy's request, the sleigh resumed its ride. "If you remain like that until we arrive home, you will both catch a dangerous cold, ladies."

"Oh, let us hope not, sir. I would be deeply saddened if Georgiana should suffer because of her generosity. It was my fault; I unwisely suggested that—"

"Miss Bennet, I have seen Georgiana many times in similar situations, and I doubt it was your fault. But neither of you can remain like this."

To Elizabeth's shock, he bent to his knees and, with his gloved hands, brushed the snow from Georgiana's bonnet, her gown and shoes; then, without hesitation, he did the same for Elizabeth. She forgot to breathe for some moments. *This cannot be happening!*

He finally resumed his seat, removed his gloves and reached towards them, demanding, "Now your gloves, please, ladies!" Elizabeth did not move, incredulous at the meaning of his words. Georgiana, however, stretched her hands to him, and he pulled her gloves then rubbed her hands to warm them and covered her with the blankets.

"William, I cannot believe you still treat me like a child." Georgiana laughed, but he raised his eyebrow in reproach.

"My dear, apparently not much has changed since you were a child, and I still wish you to avoid catching a cold. So the treatment must be similar."

Then he turned to Elizabeth, waiting. She stared at him, her eyes and mouth wide open. *Surely, he would not presume to—*

Without warning, he took her hands, removed her gloves, then covered them in his warm palms. Her hands were still, not daring to move; he looked at her, and their gazes held for a moment. He continued to hold her hands then clasped and pressed them together—her cold hands wrapped in his, taking warmth from them. She could not say how much time passed, but she was certain it was improperly long. Eventually he released her hands, and as he did with Georgiana, he covered her in a blanket.

"Brother, we are fortunate that you came with us. Would you not agree, Elizabeth?" asked Georgiana.

Elizabeth hesitated a moment. "Indeed we are…"

A few minutes later, light conversation resumed. Halfway home, Elizabeth's hands were still warm, but her feet were becoming colder. She briefly thought she should have removed her shoes the same way as the gloves, but instantly she felt her cheeks warming as she remembered the way her gloves had been removed.

It was already one o'clock, and it began to snow again.

"Elizabeth, would you like to come in and have a cup of hot tea with us?" Georgiana asked. "You could warm yourself by the fire and return home later in our carriage."

"I thank you for your invitation, but unfortunately I must refuse. Jane and Aunt Gardiner are waiting for me; you know we must prepare for tomorrow's ball."

"Oh, but is still very early and—"

"Georgiana, we must not abuse Miss Bennet's time," her brother intervened. His voice was kind but determined, clearly expecting no opposition.

"You are correct, of course. I am sorry Elizabeth, it is just that—"

"Georgiana, I must say I am disappointed with how easily you broke our agreement," Elizabeth replied, and both the Darcys looked inquiringly at her. Miss Darcy finally understood her meaning and laughed under the puzzled gaze of her brother.

"Please forgive me," Miss Darcy said, and both started to laugh openly.

"Would you ladies be so kind as to inform me of your agreement and the reason for your sudden amusement?" Mr. Darcy asked, obviously disconcerted.

"I cannot speak for Miss Darcy, but from my point of view, I would rather not share the agreement with any gentleman," Elizabeth said. Georgiana nodded approvingly, and though she was afraid Mr. Darcy might be offended, Elizabeth saw him smiling at her.

"As you wish, Miss Bennet. I would by no means suspend any pleasure of yours." She recognised his words from the Netherfield ball, but his voice and his expression were so utterly different that she could not believe it was the same Mr. Darcy.

"I thank you for your understanding, sir." She smiled tentatively.

When the sleigh stopped in Gracechurch Street, Mr. Darcy stepped down and handed Elizabeth out. She collected her wet, dirty gloves, put them in her pocket, then took Mr. Darcy's offered hand. Unlike the freezing air, his hand was strangely warm; he continued to hold her hand tightly, to protect her from slipping on the icy stairs. He released her hand only when they reached the main entrance, and with a proper bow, he departed. Elizabeth remained in the doorway until the Darcy sleigh disappeared from sight.

When she finally entered, the housekeeper, Mrs. Burton, informed her that Mrs. Gardiner, her children, and Jane were visiting Lady Selina; they were not expected for an hour or two. Surprisingly, Elizabeth found herself relieved by the news as she wanted nothing more than to change her gown, enjoy a cup of hot tea—and think of that day's events.

Her plan, however, had only partial success when the servant announced that a Miss Bingley and a Mrs. Hurst were there to see Mrs. Gardiner and Miss Bennet.

For a moment, Elizabeth considered there must be some great misunderstanding, because it was difficult to believe that these ladies would take the trouble of such a long ride to Cheapside, let alone in such terrible weather. Then she thought something tragic must have happened to cause them to make such an effort, but Miss Bingley's well-known voice, complaining about the snow and the stairs, proved she had no reason to worry. Still, she had to face them—alone—and that was tragedy enough.

Just before the visitors entered, Elizabeth considered how pleasant it would have been to accept Miss Darcy's invitation for tea.

"Miss Bingley, Mrs. Hurst, what an extraordinary surprise!"

"Miss Eliza… We happened to be in the neighbourhood, visiting a friend, and we took the opportunity to call on dear Jane. Is she home, I hope?"

"Unfortunately not; she and my aunt are visiting a friend. Oh, but you must know her—Lady Selina?"

"Lady Selina?" Mrs. Hurst seemed shocked. "Jane is visiting Lady Selina?"

"Well, to be more accurate—my aunt took her children to play with Lady Selina's boys. I understand they are all good friends."

Miss Bingley seemed suddenly to need air, so she sat on the nearest chair, joined by her sister. Elizabeth offered them some tea while she watched them with a sense of power, which—she knew—did not give her much credit. She felt she was being malicious, but remembering Jane's suffering, her guilt dissipated. She was ungenerous but not more than both visitors deserved.

"Jane should return soon. She cannot afford to delay much as we are busy preparing for the ball tomorrow night. Will you be there? At Lady Selina's ball, I mean?"

Mrs. Hurst and Miss Bingley turned white while the latter tried to formulate an answer.

"My sister and I have other fixed engagements for tomorrow night, so we will not be able to attend. But I can understand your excitement; it is certainly different from the balls to which you are accustomed."

"I am sure it is, and I truly look forward to it," Elizabeth replied sweetly.

"Perhaps now you will understand more clearly why we were all so eager to return to Town," Mrs. Hurst intervened. "One who has had the pleasure of enjoying parties in Town cannot be content with small country gatherings."

"True, true…" Elizabeth replied, the same smile on her face. "And speaking of returning to Town—do you have any news of Mr. Bingley? He is well, I hope."

"Oh, he is very well indeed. He sent me word that he is enjoying his time exceedingly and most likely will return to town no sooner than two months from now. He is in a large party of ladies and gentlemen and…I dare say he has special reasons to prolong his stay."

"Special reasons, Miss Bingley? I cannot imagine what you mean."

"Oh, but it is not difficult to imagine what special reasons might keep a young gentleman away from his family."

"Surely you cannot mean Mr. Bingley has romantic interests in that group. Not after you were so kind to inform Jane about his close attachment to Miss Darcy and your hopes regarding a certain union in that direction?"

Both visitors stared at her, and she could not help smiling and enjoying her tea.

"I... Well... I love my brother very much, but he has always been open to romantic interests. One would be unwise to take him too seriously," Mrs. Hurst intervened, and Elizabeth took the offence with humour.

"You must be correct, Mrs. Hurst. So it is fair to presume that, if he has some romantic interests in that group, they will pass soon enough. Besides, we are eager to see him again soon, so please send him our kind regards when you next write to him. Or, perhaps I should ask Mr. Darcy to do so, as I will meet him tomorrow night, and it is likely we will have plenty of time to talk."

Miss Bingley choked on her tea and almost dropped the cup. Her face turned white and then red while her sister tried to help her regain some composure but with little success.

They took their leave a few moments later. Elizabeth expressed her wish that they would all meet again soon and remained in the doorway until their carriage departed.

Still in the doorway, peering through the dense snow, Elizabeth had the impression she recognised a familiar gentleman's silhouette across the street. She even waved slightly, but the gentleman walked away. She closed the door, preoccupied with all that happened that day. She was hopeful for what would come on the morrow—rather the next evening as the morning would be occupied with ball preparations. She smiled to herself, wondering what had made her be so well humoured and eager for the event.

She stopped in the middle of the room, suddenly recollecting a fact that had completely escaped her mind: the next morning she was supposed to meet Mr. Wickham.

She remained still for a few moments, considering the situation, and as she climbed the stairs to her room, she wondered whether it was proper for the earl to extend her such an invitation without informing Mrs. Gardiner.

Chapter 7

"I cannot understand what these women hope to accomplish," said Aunt Gardiner in a tête-à-tête with Elizabeth after dinner. "What was the purpose of their visit? And why suggest Mr. Bingley's interest in another lady? Are they not aware that their schemes will be discovered as soon as their brother returns?"

"I cannot imagine their purpose, nor do I give them much consideration, Aunt. I believe they are desperately trying to keep Mr. Bingley away from Jane by any means. Oh, but where can he be? This will not do; he cannot simply disappear! I will certainly speak to Mr. Darcy about him at the first opportunity!"

"But was not Mr. Darcy to blame for his departure in the first place? Would it be wise to raise such a delicate subject with Mr. Darcy? After all, you are not the best of friends, and he might be displeased with such familiarity."

Elizabeth could read the inquiring irony in her aunt's voice despite Mrs. Gardiner's genuine smile. Indeed, with everything Elizabeth said about Mr. Darcy in the recent past, it would be unthinkable to approach him about his friend's whereabouts and return—just as it was unthinkable that Mr. Darcy had knelt before her to clear snow from her dress and shoes and to warm her hands...

"I... Mr. Darcy has expressed his intention of finding Mr. Bingley and informing him of...recent events, so I believe such an inquiry would not upset him."

"I am sure you are right, my dear. By the way, how was your sleigh ride? Did you and Miss Darcy have a pleasant day?"

"It was wonderful, Aunt! Miss Darcy is the most pleasant company. She is so amiable that she actually invited me to visit Pemberley." Elizabeth laughed with a trace of uneasiness that did not escape her aunt's notice.

"That is quite astonishing, considering your brief acquaintance. Then again, I would expect Miss Darcy to be a remarkable young lady, just as remarkable as her parents. And I dare say, any qualities Miss Darcy possesses at her young age must be the result of her brother's influence. Would you not agree?"

"I do agree. Miss Darcy was but an infant when her mother passed away and still a child when her father died. How painful it must have been for Mr. Darcy to lose his parents and be alone with such a young sister! He was almost a boy himself at the time."

"True, my dear. I am glad you have found something positive in Mr. Darcy, after all."

"I never denied Mr. Darcy's qualities as I could not ignore his faults. But I was surprised to observe his warm behaviour towards his sister. You should have seen him in the sleigh cleaning the snow from her clothes. I never would imagine his being so kind and tender."

"Am I to understand that Mr. Darcy kept you company today?"

"Yes he did, but it was not a previous arrangement. Georgiana decided to stop at her house for a few moments, and Mr. Darcy had finished his businesses earlier and decided to join us. He said he wanted to be certain we did not put ourselves in danger."

"That was thoughtful of him," Mrs. Gardiner concluded just before Jane returned. The conversation moved to the subject of the ball until they retired for the night.

THE EARL'S UNANNOUNCED VISIT WAS a surprise for Mrs. Gardiner; she invited him to sit, but the earl declined the invitation. Mrs. Gardiner was even more perplexed.

"I will be happy to stay for tea later today, Mrs. Gardiner. I come now to fetch Miss Elizabeth for our secret stroll in the park," he said well humoured.

Mrs. Gardiner turned to her niece for an explanation. Elizabeth blushed, hesitated a moment, and tried to form an answer for her aunt; then suddenly, she declared she would be ready in a moment and ran to her room. Mrs. Gardiner followed her.

"Elizabeth?" Her aunt's voice was gentle but determined as was the lady's inquiring gaze. Elizabeth twisted the bonnet in her hands, forcing a smile.

"Lord Matlock invited me for a short walk when we were at Lady Brightmore's party."

"That is lovely…but also quite unexpected. Just you and the earl? I know he enjoys your company, but you barely know each other. And why is this stroll so 'secret'?"

Elizabeth sat on the bed, breathed deeply, and held her aunt's gaze.

"Lord Matlock will meet Mr. Wickham. He thought I might enjoy seeing him, too, but he did not want his family to know about it. None of them is fond of Mr. Wickham, and they disapprove the earl's affection for him. They are clearly partial to Mr. Darcy, so they share his opinion…and his feelings." Her animation increased with every word while her aunt's countenance darkened.

"Let me see if I understand: you secretly planned with a gentleman of your father's age to deceive his family and yours in order to meet another gentleman with a questionable reputation and behaviour. Is that correct, Lizzy?"

"No, I did not mean to… I am aware it is not a proper situation, but…it was somehow difficult to refuse the earl. And I do not think Mr. Wickham's reputation or behaviour is 'questionable.' He has done nothing to us to deserve that."

"Lizzy, you were always a smart girl, and I trust you grew up a wise lady, so I shall not forbid your meeting Mr. Wickham if you wish. But please allow me to question the behaviour of a man who does not hesitate to share with you intimate and painful information about his life at your very first meeting and prefers to meet the earl during the early morning in the park because he has not enough courage to stand up for himself and confront the earl's family."

For several moments after her aunt left the room, Elizabeth still could not decide what to do. She heard the earl's voice, and she wondered whether Lord Matlock would be the recipient of Mrs. Gardiner's displeasure. Elizabeth finally returned to the living room and, to her surprise, found the others quite relaxed.

"I must beg your forgiveness, your lordship, but I cannot join you. I am sorry I made you come all the way here... Please forgive me."

The earl looked at her closely, obviously surprised by the sudden change of events. He glanced at Mrs. Gardiner, who returned a proper smile, then back at Elizabeth.

"I understand. Well, I am sorry to miss your pleasant company this morning, and I am sure our friend will be disappointed, too. But certainly there will be other opportunities."

"I would be delighted to keep you company on another occasion. And please send my regards to Mr. Wickham. I hope he is well and enjoying his time in Town."

"Oh, I am sure he is well enough. He has the ability to enjoy himself most of the time—maybe too much on occasion." Lord Matlock laughed, taking a proper farewell of the ladies. "I shall share the news with you later tonight, Miss Elizabeth," he promised, and all three ladies answered with only a polite smile.

The two sisters spent the next hours preparing for the ball, but Elizabeth remained unsatisfied with her own behaviour regarding Mr. Wickham and the meeting with him.

Two days before, she was excited at the possibility of seeing the gentleman again. She had only pleasant memories of him and no reason to doubt his character. Yet, after the previous day—and the ride with Miss Darcy—her interest subsided to the point where she could see the impropriety of such a meeting. She had felt almost relieved when her aunt discovered and disapproved the plan.

Nevertheless, she could not accept her aunt's reproaches. Mr. Wickham surely could not be blamed for his trust in her when he shared his misfortunes. If such behaviour was wrong, what could be said about another gentleman who spent his time offending those around him— a gentleman who did not have the least courtesy of dancing at a ball even if the lady was *'barely tolerable'*? Mrs. Gardiner did not witness either behaviour, or she would surely not be so inclined against Mr. Wickham to the benefit of Mr. Darcy.

It could not be denied, however, that Mr. Darcy was the sort of man who improved on further acquaintance. Among his friends and family, he showed amiability, kindness, and a tender care that seemed unlike him. Even the friendly way he addressed his housekeeper was uncommon. Elizabeth never would have believed he was a kind master—fair, maybe, if someone did not *'lose his good opinion*' forever, but kind—never. Yet, he appeared to be so. It was also true that he refused—quite rudely—to dance with her at the Meryton assembly but knelt beside her and brushed the snow from her clothes.

Elizabeth felt her cheeks grow warm and returned her attention to arranging Jane's hair quickly. The ball was approaching, and Lady Selina surely would not admit any delay.

Inside the carriage, three ladies shared the same anxiety, though for different reasons. Elizabeth knew her aunt was not completely at ease with attending the ball; it was her first in two years, and her heart must still be burdened with sadness. It was unlikely that Mrs. Gardiner could enjoy herself with music and dancing.

Jane's nervousness was equally apparent; she was staring out the window with great interest, as though trying to find someone special.

On Elizabeth's part, it was childish to feel anxiety of any kind. She had always found pleasure in making new acquaintances, especially during a ball, and there was nothing new or special for her at this particular ball. Lady Selina was the hostess, and her entire family would be there. In addition, the colonel had already invited her for the first set, so she would have at least two dances secured. For the rest—if she were fortunate, she might dance another set or two.

Any anxiety the ladies might have experienced vanished the moment they entered the house and saw the friendly faces of the earl, his sons, Lord Brightmore, and especially, Lady Selina.

In the entrance of the elegant ballroom, Elizabeth and Jane glanced around. What was assumed to be a small, family affair had become an event with at least 50 people in attendance.

"Are you looking for someone in particular, ladies?" whispered the colonel.

"No, not really, I was just surprised to see so many people," Jane whispered.

"Oh, I am so happy to see you, Madeleine," Lady Brightmore cried out the moment she saw them. "You look lovely, my darling. And these sweet girls—oh, look at you, you are both so beautiful! Stunning! Come and sit near me. These are my nephews—oh, Robert darling, please be sweet and make the introductions."

The interest showed by the other guests was difficult to ignore. It appeared that many of them were acquainted with Mrs. Gardiner, so all hidden glances were directed towards the Bennet sisters. With patience and good humour, the colonel introduced them to the others, and Elizabeth managed to count about fifteen "cousins" before she abandoned the task. She did not remember more than three names—Mr. Bertram, Lord Rowley, and the young Lord Montgomery, all Lady Brightmore's nephews.

DARCY COULD NOT BE CERTAIN when the ball started; he did not feel comfortable speaking to either of the Miss Bennets; he only greeted them and Mrs. Gardiner briefly, as politeness demanded, then stepped away and was content to look around, silent and preoccupied.

He looked at Elizabeth as she danced with his cousin, gracefully smiling at her partner. Robert always had been easy in the company of ladies, and he was never careful about concealing his partiality. Everyone could see that Robert Fitzwilliam was charmed by Miss Elizabeth Bennet—not to mention that he had requested her for the first set of the ball. That sort of attention could affect Miss Elizabeth's reputation. She seemed to enjoy the colonel's company as well, but she was her usual self: inclined to favour voluble, amiable men such as Bingley and Robert —and Wickham.

The room was exceedingly warm; he could use some fresh air—or perhaps a ride in the sleigh. That would be refreshing, indeed. Darcy hid his smile behind a glass of brandy while his mind was gripped by vivid memories of Elizabeth walking through the snow, her hair wet and frozen, her cheeks red, her eyes sparkling with excitement, and her small hands resting shyly in his palms...

She danced with the colonel, her hand in his. *Robert should not smile so obviously at her; it is not difficult to guess that he is courting her.*

Darcy looked at the pair dancing happily, and wondered whether the colonel would make her a marriage offer. What would she say? Surely, no woman would refuse to marry Robert Fitzwilliam and certainly not a woman of such poor connections and lack of fortune as Miss Elizabeth Bennet. If Robert proposed, she would certainly accept, more so given that the earl openly declared his wish for such a union.

Darcy took a gulp of brandy then another; the room grew warmer, and he could barely breathe as his eyes remained fixed on the couple. Suddenly, his eyes were caught by hers. He felt embarrassed, as though doing something improper, but his gaze remained steady, holding hers. She appeared surprised, but while she continued to dance, she did not avert her eyes. Even more, she smiled at him, a small, barely perceptible smile, charming nevertheless and meant only for him.

For the rest of the set, their glances as well as their smiles met more than once. He counted the steps, anticipating each turn in the dance when she would face him again—and smile at him.

"So, Nephew, are you enjoying yourself? You know, admiring a beautiful woman is a pleasant occupation, but holding her in your arms is more rewarding."

"What do you mean, sir," he said in a low voice.

"I mean go and dance, young man! That is the only way you can hold a woman in your arms...in a ballroom...in public, I mean." The earl laughed.

"I am not fond of dancing," Darcy replied. The next instant he felt his arms trapped.

"Oh, we all know you are not fond of dancing, Mr. Darcy. But I cannot believe you will refuse to dance with me, especially if I insist upon it." Both gentlemen turned to face a young lady whose daring smiles and determined expression allowed no opposition.

"Lady Sinclair." Darcy bowed politely.

"Eve darling, you look beautiful as always," the earl declared.

74

"Thank you, Lord Matlock. And you are as flattering as always, while this gentleman here"—she turned to Darcy, a mischievous smile on her face—"is as handsome and haughty as ever. I cannot believe you still do not dance the first set, Mr. Darcy. I presume you have yet to find a young lady worthy of that honour."

"You are too kind, Lady Sinclair, and give me too much credit. I do not dance the first set, but I also do not dance the second or the third if I can avoid it," Darcy replied, forcing a smile. Lady Sinclair put the other hand on his arm, holding it tightly.

"Well, I am afraid you will not be able to avoid it any longer. I demand a dance, sir. I will only allow you to choose which one."

"Oh, I doubt you will convince him, Eve." The earl laughed again.

"You should not doubt my ability to get what I desire. So, Mr. Darcy, which will it be? You dare not refuse me or you will not be allowed to dance with any other lady this evening."

"Such a punishment for him! Please be gentle." The earl laughed.

Darcy glanced towards the dance floor where Elizabeth was moving through the last steps of the first set. She appeared to listen to the colonel as her gaze returned to the place Darcy stood. He smiled at her, but she seemed not to notice it.

Darcy returned his attention to his companion, who was still holding his arm. He abandoned the fight. "Lady Sinclair, will you do me the honour of dancing the next set with me?"

That would do. He would dance with her as soon as possible and be done with it.

Elizabeth promised herself that she would enjoy the evening as much as possible, but she could not avoid worrying for her aunt as well as for her sister; both appeared sad and out of spirits.

Her heart ached to see her sister scrutinise each gentleman in the room, look towards the door frequently, and startle at each manly voice. Jane Bennet still hoped Mr. Bingley would come to the ball, but her hopes were in vain.

Where could Mr. Bingley be that Mr. Darcy did not locate him as he promised? What if Mr. Bingley knew of Jane's presence in town but chose not to return as he had lost interest in renewing their acquaintance? Was it possible that Mr. Darcy did not keep his word and only pretended to search for his friend? Could Mr. Darcy be so unworthy of trust? She turned her attention to the gentleman, who was now talking quite amiably with his uncle...and with a young lady. Who could be the lady attaching herself tightly to Mr. Darcy's arm? Perhaps one of his many cousins? The earl laughed quite loudly at something the lady said, and Mr. Darcy seemed to approve of her.

Mr. Darcy can do as he pleases, Elizabeth thought. It was obvious that he was not pleased to speak to her since he had avoided her from the beginning of the ball. He said no more than three words to them when they arrived and then put a significant distance between them. That was understandable. He could not allow himself—Heaven forbid!—to be seen in the close company of someone so beneath him. The earl and Lady Selina had no restraint in declaring their friendship with Mrs. Gardiner and to present them—Elizabeth and Jane Bennet—as their friends. But not Mr. Darcy—no indeed! No doubt, he knew enough to behave in a friendly manner—even caringly when they were in private—but not in large gatherings! Surely, he could not compromise his name by displaying a connection with someone from Cheapside! She had even wondered whether he would ask her to dance—what a joke! Surely, that was as far as possible from his intentions.

Such a strange man! The entire time she danced with the colonel, she had the clear impression that Mr. Darcy was searching for her gaze and that he smiled at her; she was certain that he showed some sort of interest in her. She had no doubt that he would ask for the next set. Such a silly presumption! The dance came to an end, and the colonel walked with her towards her family, but at the same time, Mr. Darcy offered his arm to the lady next to him and accompanied her to the dance floor. Elizabeth tried to show a calm and proper countenance the moment they stepped near each other. She could swear he was smiling at her—a barely visible smile but a smile nevertheless. Hateful man!

"MISS ELIZABETH, YOU ARE A skilful dancer," the earl said as she sat near Lady Brightmore.

"Indeed, my dear. You are just beautiful, and so is Miss Bennet. I doubt you will have a moment to rest this evening. All the men in the room are eager to dance with you," Lady Brightmore declared, and Elizabeth laughed.

"You are too kind, and your praise is most undeserved in my case, your ladyship. As for Jane—one cannot find a more beautiful, sweet and generous person. She is truly wonderful."

"Your love for your sister makes you even more praiseworthy, dear," said the lady, enjoying a gulp of wine. "Oh, but what miracle is this? Is Darcy dancing? With whom?"

"With Eve Sinclair." The earl laughed. "And there is no miracle; she practically demanded a dance. I am sure he accepted only to escape the punishment of her insisting further."

The colonel laughed. "Darcy is the only man who would want to escape Eve Sinclair."

"She is insistent in an obvious, unladylike manner," Lady Brightmore admitted. "She is a married woman after all; she could be more…discreet."

"She is beautiful," said Elizabeth, unaware that she spoke aloud.

"She is indeed," the earl admitted. "I have rarely seen a woman with such a perfect complexion. Her beauty helped her make an advantageous marriage."

"With a man twice her age and twice her wealth," Lady Brightmore added.

"Of whom are you speaking?" asked Lady Selina, appearing on the arm of her husband.

"Eve Sinclair."

"Oh, Eve." The lady smiled, exchanging a glance with her husband. "She is pretentious and demanding, but she can be agreeable when she wants."

"And she never hid her interest in Darcy; why would she do so this evening?" Lord Brightmore intervened, and his wife silenced him with a sharp glance. He looked puzzled.

"What did I say? You know she was always after Darcy—before and after she married."

"Nonsense, husband. Do not speak so about Eve—or about Darcy."

"Well, he did not say anything bad about Darcy," the colonel intervened. "It is only that he and I and half the men in the room have wondered whether she managed to convince Darcy to satisfy her…interest."

Lord Brightmore, Lord Matlock, and the colonel laughed openly, joined by Lady Brightmore. Lady Selina struggled to hide a smile while Elizabeth felt her cheeks burning. Unconsciously, she looked towards the dance floor and met Darcy's gaze. He was clearly staring at them, and she wondered whether it was possible that he heard them.

"I would appreciate it if we could change the subject," said Mrs. Gardiner. "I do not find it amusing to joke at the expense of a friend who is not here to defend himself. Perhaps you could express your wonder in the presence of Mr. Darcy himself."

Lady Selina instantly stopped laughing while the colonel bowed to Mrs. Gardiner.

"Please accept our apologies, Mrs. Gardiner," the earl intervened. "You are perfectly right as always. We should not speak of others when our own behaviour is far from faultless."

Elizabeth remained silent, uncertain what to believe about their conversation. What everyone implied about Mr. Darcy and Lady Sinclair whirled in her mind. Elizabeth understood her to be a married woman. Where was her husband? And was it possible that Mr. Darcy—? She looked towards the dance floor again. They were dancing together, and the gentleman did not seem exactly displeased that he had been '*forced*' to dance. And he was looking at Elizabeth again with the same smile on his face. What could he mean by it?

"Miss Elizabeth, I have warm regards for you from an old acquaintance," the earl suddenly whispered. "I hope you do not mind."

"Not at all, sir." She smiled. "How is Mr. Wickham? I trust he is in good health. Will he be in town long?"

"He is in excellent health; he will stay a few days more as he has some unfinished business. He seemed eager to meet with you."

"I would like to see him, too. If you have the chance to meet him again, please let him know that I would be more than happy to receive him in Gracechurch Street."

"I will inform him; I might accompany him."

"That would be a perfect arrangement, sir," she replied politely, though she felt she was not quite as anxious to see Mr. Wickham as she pretended to be. She noticed that the set had ended and briefly wondered where a certain gentleman might be.

"Miss Elizabeth, if you are not otherwise engaged, would you do me the honour of dancing the next with me?" Mr. Darcy's request, which Elizabeth had ceased to expect, was as shocking as his appearance and his friendly voice. He was smiling tentatively, awaiting her answer. He was only a few steps away, and Elizabeth felt uncomfortable again. *He always makes people feel uneasy around him. Well, not all people; apparently Lady Sinclair felt quite well.* She felt her face warming from her outrageous thoughts and averted her eyes.

"I…thank you, yes…"

Lord Matlock said something, but Elizabeth did not comprehend his words; Mr. Darcy took her hand, and they stepped together to the dance floor. A cold sensation prickled her spine as she felt the pressure of his fingers upon hers. Yes, it was beyond any doubt: he always made her uncomfortable in a way that no other man did.

"Miss Elizabeth, my sister asked me to convey to you her regards. She is eager for your visit tomorrow."

"Thank you, sir. I look forward to seeing her, too. I expected she would not be here tonight, but I confess I secretly hoped for her presence."

"Usually she attends small gatherings at Lady Selina's, but when she discovered the number of guests for tonight's ball, she preferred to remain at home. She is not fond of large gatherings. Nor am I, but I could not afford the luxury of refusing my cousin." He smiled again as if he were expecting her to understand him.

"So you were forced to be here tonight, sir? That is not a kind thing to say; it might offend some people." She tried to mirror his smile.

"I hope it did not offend *you*, Miss Elizabeth; that was not my intention."

"I am not so easily offended, sir." She laughed, and he looked slightly uncomfortable.

"But you seem to enjoy your time very well. I feel fortunate to have secured a dance with you as I imagine your card is full. I took a chance, and I was rewarded."

"Had you asked earlier, you would have known that my card is not full." She stopped and averted her eyes again. What came over her to say such a thing?

"I would have asked earlier, but I did not dare disturb you. You appeared always to be surrounded by old and new acquaintances."

"As were you, sir."

For the next minutes, they continued to dance in silence, looking at each other. Their gazes held; their hands met briefly when the dance demanded it.

"I noticed you met all our and Lord Brightmore's cousins," Darcy said.

"Indeed. Most of them seem to be pleasant and friendly, at least on a first impression."

"Most of them are. Though sometimes first impressions can be misleading, that is not necessarily the case with our cousins." His voice was light, and he was smiling at her, but she was certain she could guess the hidden, tacit censure directed at her.

"One does not always need a long time to make a friend of a new acquaintance

—or to decide that an acquaintance will never be a friend, no matter how much time passes."

"True. However, previous experiences have shown me that one should be guarded before deciding which acquaintance deserves to become a friend if one does not want to be disappointed."

"I am not sure that I agree with you, sir. I would rather be disappointed from time to time than avoid making new friends. People deserve a chance to prove themselves worthy before their characters are judged, even those who are below one's situation in life."

"I have always admired your wisdom. Let us make an agreement: both of us shall allow new or old acquaintances a chance to prove their worthiness before judging their characters. Shall we?" He sounded more serious than a ball conversation would require.

"It is strange that you are interested in an agreement with me under any circumstances, Mr. Darcy. However, such an agreement cannot but be accepted."

"I am glad you approve. I have been interested in reaching an agreement with you many times, but somehow it seems we are meant to argue whenever we meet. More than once I have wondered whether one or perhaps both of us purposely search for subjects upon which to disagree."

"Of one thing you may be certain, sir: any argument we might have had was never purposely begun on my part."

"That is a great relief."

"However, I am not as sure of your motives," she continued.

The music stopped, and he offered her his arm, good humour obvious on his face.

"It appears we shall have to continue our conversation later—and most likely our argument, too," he said, slightly inclining his head towards hers. Holding Mr. Darcy's arm and stepping towards her family and friends, Elizabeth fought the same feeling of uneasiness.

"Oh, Darcy, what a lovely idea to ask Miss Elizabeth to dance! I was wondering whether you would do it, considering how rarely you dance, and I really cannot understand why, my boy," said Lady Brightmore. "You are such a handsome young man, and you dance so well. You should smile more often; smiling is quite becoming on you. Oh, look at those pretty dimples; you look so much like your father! I had a crush on the late Mr. Darcy, you know?" her ladyship whispered to Elizabeth, her cheeks red and her eyes sparkling. Elizabeth tried to hide a smile: her ladyship clearly had enjoyed one glass of wine too many.

She turned to Mr. Darcy, hardly restraining her laughter; he looked embarrassed, a trace of redness colouring his cheeks, and she noticed that she was still holding his arm.

The invitation to dinner came as a relief. They walked together, Elizabeth still on Mr. Darcy's arm while the viscount accompanied Jane. However, once they reached the table, Mr. Darcy had to leave them as his seat was separate from theirs.

As he walked away, Elizabeth found herself wondering whether he felt regret or relief that he could not stay with them. She briefly asked herself the same question but rejected it instantly as the colonel took a chair next to her.

Dinner was mostly a pleasant affair, though Elizabeth was not quite herself —nor was Jane. From time to time, Elizabeth could not resist searching the room; Mr. Darcy was not too far away, but he was content to speak to Lady Selina and Lord Brightmore. Lady Sinclair—seated at least four places away from Darcy —was the heart of the conversation with everyone around, and more than once she asked specifically for Mr. Darcy's opinion. Each time he replied politely but briefly, and Elizabeth could not hide her smile, remembering a similar situation with Mr. Darcy and Caroline Bingley.

Elizabeth's thoughts were occupied primarily by Mr. Darcy's puzzling behaviour and their conversation. In truth, there were times she was certain he was purposely arguing with her only to reveal her flaws, and other times she was certain he enjoyed her company. No, not certain—with Mr. Darcy, one could never be certain of anything. And there was also Lady Sinclair and... *Why did I think of Lady Sinclair? She should not be a subject of interest for me.*

After supper, the gentlemen retired to the library and their brandy.

The room was warm, and there was such a din of voices that Elizabeth rose from her seat and left the ballroom, convinced that no one would notice her brief absence. She walked along the hall until she reached the music room. She entered the room, closed the door, then touched the piano briefly, remembering the evening she and Miss Darcy played together. Poor Georgiana was so frightened to sing in front of her relatives. How could she possibly be Mr. Darcy's sister? Was he ever frightened—of anything?

Elizabeth could not say how long she stayed in the music room. She knew she should return before her aunt and Jane looked for her. She opened the door carefully as she could hear voices from the hall; two ladies were talking. The music room was dark, but a few candles tentatively lightened the hall. With no little surprise, Elizabeth recognised one of the women as Lady Sinclair. Elizabeth was about to open the door and greet them when the subject of their conversation stopped her.

"What other reason could Darcy have to dance with her? He never dances; he barely danced with me, which I would find offensive from any man except Darcy."

"Other men would have danced with you, Eve."

"True, my dear." Lady Sinclair laughed. "Oh well, it will be interesting to follow. He could not have any serious designs on her; she is a country nobody. Perhaps that is precisely what is attractive about her—nobody will expect him to have a serious attachment."

"They all seem to be under Lord Matlock's protection. I seriously doubt Mr. Darcy would have any improper thoughts regarding his uncle's protégée. He is well known as a gentleman of honour. Am I wrong?"

"You are not wrong. But nobody can control one's thoughts. As for Darcy, he has few choices, regardless. I imagine he will shortly marry Anne de Bourgh. I am tired of hearing about their never-ending engagement, and I have hopes that marriage will change his perspective." Lady Sinclair laughed.

"Heaven forbid someone could control your thoughts, Eve. And speaking of marriage—yours surely changed your perspective. How is your husband, by the way?"

"He is on a hunting party; I expect him to return to London in a week."

"But he will not remain in town long, I imagine, as I do not expect you will be tempted to leave London in this weather."

"To both your questions the answer is no." Lady Sinclair laughed again. "Come—let us return to the ballroom. This wine makes me particularly tempted to dance again."

The ladies left, and for some time Elizabeth could not move. Her chest felt crushed by an enormous burden, and she could not breathe. She leaned against the wall, gathering her strength and struggling for air and then hurried along the hall to the entrance. Under a servant's surprised glance, she opened the main door and stepped outside.

The chill wind whipped across her face, and the snow on her cheeks mixed with warm tears of anger and helpless disappointment. She could only hope she misunderstood the words spinning in her mind. Were they truly speaking about her—and in such preposterous terms? Why would they do that? Mr. Darcy was engaged to Anne de Bourgh? Was she not his cousin? And if he were engaged, why should she care? He never spoke or behaved improperly, nor did he ever mention he was engaged. But why would he? After all, it was his private business. She could not care less if he were engaged!

She gathered herself and returned to the ballroom. Her aunt and Jane were in the midst of Lord Matlock's family. Mrs. Gardiner inquired about her and Elizabeth forced a smile as she confessed she was not feeling well. She admitted to a piercing headache and pretended her eyes could not bear the light because of the pain. Lady Selina invited her to retire to one of the guest rooms, but Mrs. Gardiner declared she would take Elizabeth home to rest. Immediately, Miss Bennet supported her idea, and shortly all three ladies were ready to depart despite Lady Selina and Lady Brightmore's insistence. They declined any attempt to call for one of the gentlemen to keep them company. Mrs. Gardiner had her coachman waiting and decidedly said they would be perfectly safe. They did not wish to raise unnecessary concerns nor ruin the pleasure of the ball for the other guests.

So, with little recourse, Lady Selina accepted her friends' decision, taking a warm farewell of them and asking to see them all the next day. Mrs. Gardiner promised they would come for tea, and Lady Selina was content with the prospect.

Hours passed, and Elizabeth could find no rest. Although she threw herself in bed as soon as they were home and assured her aunt and sister that she was feeling better, it only became worse. She recalled every word, every gesture, every face, and every glance from the ball. Were other people also thinking so ill of her?

Morning came, but it brought little peace for Elizabeth. She did not leave her bed nor join the family for breakfast. Mrs. Gardiner encouraged her to sleep as much as she wanted, but she declared she would send for a doctor, as she was worried about Elizabeth's indisposition.

To avoid such a drastic measure, Elizabeth finally dressed, declaring she wanted to eat a little and rest later. Content, Mrs. Gardiner postponed the idea of fetching the doctor.

During the noon hour, Mrs. Gardiner remembered they promised to have tea with Lady Selina. Jane seemed pleased with the idea, and Mrs. Gardiner declared she would take the children, too, so they could play with Lady Selina's boys.

Elizabeth asked to be forgiven but expressed her trust that she would be much better the next day. With some arguments and no little worry, the ladies finally left.

For Elizabeth, the empty house and the silence surrounding her were a blessing. She hurried to her room and lay on the bed, closing her eyes and remembering once more all the details of the previous night. She became angrier at each passing moment, not so much against a certain lady but against herself for allowing the events to bother her so. The lady had danced with Mr. Darcy too; how dare she make such insinuations after a dance? And Mr. Darcy himself—how could he be friends with such a disrespectful woman? And what kind of friends were they, after all?

She was surprised by the sound of the doorbell and hurried to the parlour. A servant announced the visitor, and to her utter amazement, Mr. Darcy walked into the room.

He bowed to her politely, but she could scarcely greet him properly, so preoccupied was she to discover the reason for his presence.

He took a seat and inquired after her health, confessing he was at Lady Selina's with his sister when Mrs. Gardiner and Miss Bennet arrived. He had been surprised not to see her and was worried to hear she was not feeling well, especially after their sudden departure from the ball.

She assured him she was well and thanked him for his concern. Then she asked about Georgiana and was told that she remained at Lady Selina's. He had come alone, and Elizabeth's consternation grew. As she watched him attempt to start a conversation, it was obvious to Elizabeth that he had slept ill as well. His countenance was pale, his eyes showed dark circles, and no smile lit his face.

After a silence of several minutes, he came towards her in an agitated manner, still standing, and finally spoke.

"In vain have I struggled. It will not do. My feelings will not be repressed. You must allow me to tell you how ardently I admire and love you."

Chapter 8

Elizabeth stared at Mr. Darcy, her cheeks burning, and for a moment, she wondered whether he was making fun of her. Her head felt painfully heavy, and the daylight was intolerable. His words sounded loud and clear, but their meaning was uncertain. He seemed slightly uneasy, and the trace of fatigue on his face became more visible with each moment. He looked at her as though waiting for a sign to continue, and she knew she should stop him.

"Miss Bennet, please forgive my intrusion and the manner of my declaration. I can understand your surprise, your shock; to be honest, my presence here is a surprise even to me. I have thought of little else since last night, and I confess I did not sleep a single moment as I considered my decision to speak with you. But surely you cannot be surprised by my words as you must have noticed my inclination for you since we were in Hertfordshire."

She continued to stare at him in silent astonishment. Of what was he speaking? His inclination for her? *'She is tolerable, I suppose, but not handsome enough to tempt me.'*

"Almost from the beginning of our acquaintance, I came to admire you. Yet, I must admit that, for a long time, I struggled with my feelings because of the obstacles presented by the differences between our families. I never would consider attaching myself to someone whose situation in life was so far below mine. I have always known my duty, and I am aware that I must fulfil my expectations and those of my family. And then, when I met you again in London among my uncle's friends, seeing how pleased my sister was to be in your company and how happy I was myself, I became more and more certain that I might come to a decision, even one against my judgement, because what has judgement to do with matters of the heart? It finally became clear to me that there was no other way to manage this painful situation, so I came here to plead for your acceptance. And I trust it might be to the advantage of us both to…"

He continued to speak, more hastily with each word as if he were trying to convince not just her but also himself. While speaking, he paced the room, and she found it increasingly difficult to comprehend his statements. *He has admired me from the beginning of our acquaintance? He is aware he should not even consider marriage with someone in my situation? And now he has come to propose some sort of arrangement?* She felt her eyes stinging.

"Mr. Darcy, I am afraid I cannot allow you to continue upon this subject. As you mentioned, I am shocked by your presence here and even more so by your words. I never noticed any inclination you might have for me; the only thing that does not surprise me is your disapproval of my family; that I have long noticed."

She looked around for a chair. A lump in her throat forbade her from speaking louder, and she struggled against the tears that threatened to overcome her.

"You cannot seriously consider that I would accept such a proposal, so my answer will not be a surprise to you. And if you are truly disappointed, I hope it will be of short duration. I trust that your judgement eventually will overcome your regard and you will find other ways to solve any painful situation that might arise in the future."

She finished her reply and took a deep breath. As she spoke, his complexion paled, and the disturbance of his mind was impossible to ignore. He obviously struggled to maintain his composure as he stared at her, unable to reply. Elizabeth, her eyes riveted by his, felt the urge to sit. At that moment, he should have understood the ridiculous situation in which he had put himself and leave. After some time, in a voice of forced calmness, he spoke.

"And this is all the reply which I am to have the honour of expecting! I might wish to be informed why, with so little endeavour at civility, I am thus rejected before I had the opportunity to finish my plea. But it is of small importance."

"You wish to know why you have been rejected? I would also wish to know why, with so evident a design of offending me, you chose to tell me that you liked me against your will and that you cannot attach yourself to me through marriage? How dare you come here and speak to me in such a way? What would your family say had they known of your proposal?"

"My family? It is not for them to have an opinion in this matter. I have done what I felt I should, and I was certain you would expect and welcome such a proposal. Since we met in London, I could not miss your properly displayed but nevertheless obvious inclination towards me, but it seems my judgement was wrong. Or perhaps, after being so unanimously admired last evening by so many eligible gentlemen, your inclination towards me is less than it was, and you suddenly search for reasons to think ill of me."

His eyes turned darker, and she could see he intentionally offended her. Her anger overcame any other feelings, and suddenly her heart began to beat wildly.

"Any inclination you pretended to see on my part is as presumptuous as the reason for your visit today. I did try to behave more civilly than in the past, I shall not deny that, and I did so against my better judgement. But even if there were an inclination on my part, that would not change my answer in the slightest. I have

84

every reason in the world to think ill of you; I do not need to search for more. No motive can excuse the unjust and ungenerous part you acted in separating Mr. Bingley from my sister. You dare not, you cannot deny that you have been the principal, if not the only means of dividing them from each other!"

Elizabeth finished her tirade with a sense of emptiness and a fatigue that defeated her strength. She held his gaze while demanding an answer.

With assumed tranquillity and stern countenance, he replied, "I have no wish of denying that I did everything in my power to separate my friend from your sister while they were in Hertfordshire. At that time, I was certain it was the best decision for him."

Elizabeth could hardly breathe from anger. "And may I ask who you are to decide for and to impose upon everybody around you? The best decision indeed! And what about Mr. Wickham? Was it the best decision to deny him what was his right and to reduce him to his present misery? On this subject, what can you have to say?"

"You take an eager interest in that gentleman's concerns," said Darcy in a less tranquil tone, his face slightly coloured.

"Who that knows what his misfortunes have been can help feeling an interest in him?"

"Yes, his misfortunes have been great indeed. It is such a relief that there are always those who have feelings for him and an inclination to comfort him."

"And *that* you cannot understand. Since the very beginning of our acquaintance, your manners impressed me with the fullest belief of your arrogance, your conceit, and your selfish disdain of the feelings of others. After we met again in London, influenced by the amiability and gentleness of your family, I was tempted to judge you more favourably, but now you prove me wrong. I have no doubt that sympathy and kindness are feelings with which you are unaccustomed, and for that, I am sorry for you, sir. That is precisely why I will not mention this visit to either my aunt or your uncle. I do not wish to create an unpleasant situation for the others, nor do I want to hurt them with the disclosure of your dishonourable behaviour."

"And this," cried Darcy, as he walked across the room, "is your opinion of me! This is the estimation in which you hold me! I thank you for explaining it so fully. My faults, according to this calculation, are heavy indeed and your refusal easy to understand, though I still cannot comprehend why my proposal is so appalling and dishonourable to you."

Elizabeth grew angrier every moment, yet she struggled to speak with composure.

"Your insolence matches your arrogance, sir. You came here professing your ardent admiration and love for me and assumed—unreasonably—that I share such feelings. Then you made it perfectly clear that you would never bind yourself in marriage to someone with an inferior situation such as mine. You then offend my family, admit your unfair role in the present unhappiness of my sister, and propose to me a 'way of solving your painful situation, by an arrangement which could be to the advantage of both.' And all this while you know very well that you are engaged to marry Miss Anne de Bourgh. What would you call such behaviour, Mr. Darcy?"

Her neck was burning, her hands began to shiver and her lips were dry. She could speak no longer, as she felt all her strength abandon her. She prayed that he would have an atom of consideration and finally leave, or she was in danger of crying in his presence, for which she would never forgive herself.

He looked at her with an expression of mingled incredulity and mortification. He remained silent, staring at her. He had no apparent intention of leaving; he took a few steps forward, and she moved away from him. His countenance changed again; his gaze was dark, and his face seemed as white as new fallen snow.

"Miss Bennet, if I say that your words offended me in a way that no one has ever done before, it would not do justice to my present feelings. I came here today and spoke to you with equal sincerity and admiration. I admitted feelings to you that I have tried to conceal, and I am not ashamed of doing that. Disguise of every sort is my abhorrence, and I was certain that you, with your wisdom and brightness of mind, would appreciate my honesty. I still consider that all my struggles were natural and just. Could you expect me to rejoice in the inferiority of your connections? To congratulate myself on the hope of relations, whose condition in life is so decidedly beneath my own?"

She felt her own anger matching his and tried to interrupt his speech, but she could not; he continued to walk back and forth, his voice growing in volume and bitterness.

"Those, Madam, are the reasons I have tried to hide my preference for you—and God knows I should not have changed my mind. But I did, though with every passing moment, I wonder why. And this, Madam, is the motive of my visit today: to explain my past behaviour and to offer you my hand in marriage. I cannot understand why my words hurt you so deeply or by what mysterious means you came to the conclusion that I came to make you a dishonourable proposal. God knows I am shocked that you could even have such a preposterous notion. I am deeply pained by your complete distrust of my character, but I am even more pained by your distrust of your own worthiness. No man who had the pleasure of knowing you would ever dare to make you such a proposal. Yet, your misjudgement must be the result of your feelings, which I now perfectly comprehend, and I have only to be ashamed of what my own have been. Forgive me for having taken up so much of your time, and accept my best wishes for your health and happiness."

And with these words, he hastily left the room, and Elizabeth heard him the next moment open the front door and quit the house.

THE TUMULT OF HER MIND threw her into a hole of dark coldness; she could see nothing around her, and she lay on the settee, closed her eyes, and ceased fighting her tears. She did not want to let her mind reflect on what had passed, as she was certain she would not be able to bear the pain, but her thoughts returned unbidden to each moment of his extraordinary visit. What had happened, and how was such an event possible? That he should have been in love with her for so many months, so much in love as to wish to marry her in spite of all the objections he was anxious to declare, was incredible. That she could utterly misinterpret his proposal was even more difficult to fathom.

He had insulted her and her family; that was beyond any doubt. But she had offended herself much worse. What was she thinking? What evil force drove her to think the worst from the moment he began to speak? She vividly remembered his countenance when he said, *'God knows I am shocked that you could even have such a preposterous notion.'*

She was a complete fool! Everything she had believed about herself proved to be wrong. Elizabeth Bennet was nothing but a simpleton who allowed gossip to defeat her judgement. She must surely possess paltry judgement, after all.

As she reflected on each word she said, unbearable shame overwhelmed her. How dared she even mention to a gentleman the possibility of a dishonourable proposal? She was a young, unmarried lady; propriety demanded that she not even know of such things!

The extraordinary fact that she received an offer of marriage from Mr. Darcy repeatedly burst upon her mind, but she fought against those thoughts. All she could think of was how she ever would be able to speak to him again or even meet his eyes. Yet, it might be easier than she feared; surely, he would not want to see her or speak to her— nor meet her eyes ever again.

She ceased fighting her tears, closed her eyes and covered them with her hands. The light of the sun, warming the frozen day, was too much for her eyes and her heart.

She cried until the sound of voices in the main hall brought her back from the darkness. She tried to escape to her room but had no time as the main door opened and a whole party burst into the room, starting with her little cousins and Lady Selina's children. She forced a smile, looking from one to another, until the shock of a familiar face left her breathless.

THE COLD BREEZE BLEW FURIOUSLY against his face, but he barely felt it, as his entire body seemed trapped in a hole of ice. He had to fight to move his feet, to demand that they take him as far as possible, as soon as possible. He must run from her—far, far away—farther than a month before when he had run from Hertfordshire to London in an effort to escape. His carriage was waiting for him in front of the house, but he hurried along the street instead; to enter the small space of the carriage was unthinkable. The entire town—the entire world—was not large enough to bear the torment of his mind.

This must be some nightmare; he must have fallen asleep since he had not slept for many nights before. He had just proposed marriage to Miss Elizabeth Bennet, and she refused him in the worst way a man could be refused.

Every glance, every word, every gesture had been signs of her inclination to-wards him—he was certain of that. He was not at all inexperienced in the matter of ladies' feelings; he had no doubt that he was correct in his judgement. But she pretended the opposite with such determination that all his certainties vanished.

He suddenly crossed the street, so unexpectedly that his carriage, which was following closely, almost hit him. He did not even notice, only entered a small park and sat on the bench. It was full of fresh snow, but he did not bother to clean it. He stroked his forehead with his hands to erase the pain and then looked towards the house he had just left.

One month before he never would consider calling on someone who lived in Cheapside. He remembered Miss Bingley and Mrs. Hurst laughing about Eliza-beth's relatives in London, and he never thought to contradict them. How could he imagine that her infamous relatives were such close friends of his uncle and cousin? How could he have predicted that all the reasons for leaving Hertfordshire —and taking Bingley with him—all her family's faults that persuaded him she was completely unsuitable and determined him to put aside any intention regarding Miss Elizabeth Bennet would disappear only days after their reunion?

He had proposed, and she had refused him.

A day earlier, he would not dream that such a thing could happen. He admitted that she possessed all the qualities he desired in a wife, and he did not deny that his house seemed warmer since her visit; his sister Georgiana was happier since they became friends, and he himself was different since they spent more time together... and since he knelt in front of her to clean the snow from her shoes.

That day in the sleigh, he did not miss the emotion in her eyes or her reaction when he warmed her hands. He still could feel the gentle movement of her frozen fingers in his palms and the regret he felt when he was forced to release her. No, he did not misjudge all these things...

Despite all her accomplishments, despite the fact that her image never left his mind nor allowed him to sleep for weeks, despite the feelings she aroused in him, he never considered proposing to her—until that morning.

The previous night at the ball had been torturous. The moment she appeared, he could look at and think of little else. She had danced almost every dance, and jealousy, a feeling he never thought to experience, took control of him. Each smile she directed at other men—and each time Robert took her hand—were too much to bear. He was aware of his own foolishness, but it overwhelmed him. Their eyes met, and he was certain she smiled at him and held his gaze. Every time it happened, it was as if they silently spoke to each other. Then they danced; he held her hand, and they spoke—and she teased him again. For the second time in his life since the Netherfield ball, he wondered how a set could end so quickly.

With surprise and worry, he discovered she had left the ball with her aunt and sister, and he departed soon after, but home was even worse. He had no hope of sleeping and spent the rest of the night in front of the fire with successive glasses of brandy, waiting for daybreak. With each passing moment, his mind desperately searched for a way to end its torment.

He almost dragged Georgiana with him to visit Selina, hoping he might receive some news of Elizabeth, but he saw only her aunt and sister; Elizabeth remained at home as she was not feeling well. Could she be as miserable as he was? Georgiana was worried and declared that she missed Elizabeth, and then everybody spoke only of her, again and again.

Finally, Fitzwilliam Darcy, a man who always prided himself on his wise restraint, made a decision that was meant to change his life—and hers!

He excused himself, and shortly found himself in Gracechurch Street. He planned first to ask after her and be sure she was not seriously ill. If so, he would not disturb her rest. But the servant directed him to the living room where Elizabeth was reading. He could see that she was surprised and somewhat embarrassed; she tried to smile, though unconvincingly, but she was not displeased to see him; he was certain of that. He also was certain that his proposal would astonish her, so he thought to explain his decision and his previous struggles and hesitation in great detail. His tumult and weariness did not allow him to think very clearly, and his words seemed to tumble out with their own will.

'In vain I have struggled...' he had proposed, and she refused him.

Even worse, for some unfathomable reason, she presumed that he was proposing that she... Dear God, how could she think such a thing? Which of his words drove her to such a conclusion? What had he said? And her strange comment about his being engaged to Anne... How was it possible that she imagined he would come in her house and...

'...your manners impressed me with the fullest belief of your arrogance, your conceit, and your selfish disdain of the feelings of others... Your insolence equals your arrogance... I have all the reason in the world to think ill of you...' It was possible. He, Fitzwilliam Darcy, had been completely, deeply, painfully wrong about Elizabeth Bennet's feelings.

He could not find the strength to move from the icy bench. With a sideward glance, he saw his carriage waiting. He should leave, but go where? He could not return home, not for a while. He needed time to decide what to do next. He must depart immediately to avoid seeing her again. He would never be able to speak to her or meet her eyes—never again. He looked up and cold drops fell on his face. It was snowing again.

He gradually became aware of the cold, and tried to wrap his coat more tightly. Only then did he notice he was not wearing it. He looked around, stroked his hair with his bare hands, and found it wet and half frozen. He likely had left his coat in the house. A sharp sense of panic made him rise to his feet; he must recover his coat immediately. If Mrs. Gardiner discovered his coat there and demanded answers, how would Elizabeth explain its presence? He decided to send his coachman but abandoned the idea. He would return himself to fetch the coat and then depart instantly. The doorman would not dare to ask any questions, and surely, *nobody* would notice his return.

He crossed the street again, and a moment later ,he was at the door. His coachman had already turned the carriage and was slowly following him. He knocked. The doorman appeared, and his surprise was impossible to conceal. Darcy briefly wondered what the servant must think of his appearance, but one word was enough, and the man returned in a moment, handing him the coat.

His carriage was only steps away, and he was prepared to enter when two other carriages stopped impetuously in front of the house.

"Darcy, what on earth are you doing here? And what happened to you? You look horrible!"

"Brother, what a lovely coincidence to meet you here! I left you a note to come and fetch me later, but this is even better. How did you know we would come to see Elizabeth? Oh, but what happened to you? You look so wet and cold. Are you well? You do not look well at all!"

"Darcy, why in hell do you walk in this horrible weather? Have you lost your mind, Nephew? You are all wet and dirty like a lunatic! Surely, you do not intend to call on Miss Elizabeth in such a state! She is ill enough; she does not need to be frightened to death."

"Mr. Darcy, such a pleasure so see you, sir!" Mrs. Gardiner's gentle voice and her hand clasping his arm startled Darcy, as he was completely lost in his thoughts. "A dry, warm towel and a glass of brandy will do miracles. I am glad you finished your business so soon."

He froze next to his carriage as his mind desperately searched for a way to escape. "I am afraid I cannot stay. I must leave immediately; some urgent business is waiting and…" he insisted in a lost voice but the earl and the colonel pushed him towards the house with little chivalry.

"Come, Darcy, shall we not enter immediately? I am freezing. And surely you jest if you plan to attend to business in such a state!"

He felt helplessly ridiculous; he should protest, but he refused to make the situation worse by arguing in the street. He would enter and then leave immediately. Under no circumstances would he see her again—not for a single moment.

The main hall was too small for such a gathering. Darcy freed himself from Mrs. Gardiner and his sister and instantly stepped back to hide his presence behind the door.

She was there in the middle of the drawing room. Some of her hair had escaped its pins, and it fell on her neck and around her temples. All the sparkle had vanished from her eyes, now dark and lifeless. Her face was pale and her lips dry; she tried to form a proper greeting, but he could not hear her voice. He stepped back further.

Her eyes finally met his, and he feared she would faint. She supported herself on a chair but did not avert her eyes from him. He felt the melted snow falling along his neck and instinctively brushed his fingers through his hair. He surely looked horrible—everybody said so—but he was not concerned about that; her opinion of him was already so ill that his appearance could not make it worse. Everything was already as bad as it could possibly be.

IF NOT FOR THE DIN of voices that invaded the entire house, Elizabeth would have been certain she was dreaming. This could not be happening. *He* could not be there. But he was, and though he refused to enter, he was staring at her. His eyes were unknown to her, and his pale, stern countenance expressed nothing. She saw him step back gradually; without a doubt, he wished to depart from her, and she wondered by what coincidence he met the others and was forced to enter. But why was he still nearby? He had left more than an hour before, and his hair and his face were so wet… Where had he been all that time?

'You must allow me to tell you how ardently I admire and love you…'

One more step and he would be at the door, but as he did so, the door opened.

Together with the chilly air and the fresh smell of winter, an amiable and joyful presence burst into the house, his voice covering all the others.

"Darcy, why on earth are you standing in the doorway? And where have you been that you look so wet? Miss Elizabeth, such a great pleasure to see you again! I was so sad earlier when I noticed your absence from Lady Selina's! I was just telling Miss Bennet"—Jane blushed violently—"that I was looking forward to seeing you again. How are you? Not very well, I understand, but it is still delightful to see you!"

All her strength left her, and Elizabeth dropped unceremoniously onto the settee. She looked at the visitor with wide eyes and gaping mouth, and tried to gather her wits for a reply.

"I am well, thank you. I am happy to see you again, Mr. Bingley…"

Chapter 9

Though Mr. Darcy had left some time before, Elizabeth still could not avert her eyes from the door. Between the extraordinary events of Mr. Darcy's proposal and the shocking appearance of Mr. Bingley, Elizabeth's mind whirled with a tumult of questions while her heart remained imprisoned in a cold void from which it could not escape.

A sharp pain tortured her forehead, and she barely managed to keep her eyes open. Miss Darcy's concern, repeated inquiries for her health, and wishes to go skating soon made Elizabeth acknowledge a shameful distress. It was unlikely that she and Miss Darcy would meet again on such friendly terms. She had no concern that Mr. Darcy would betray the secret of their encounter, but she also was sure he would not allow his sister to continue their friendship. Besides, how could she bear Miss Darcy's gentleness after she had abused her brother so abominably? That he had been neither polite nor considerate in his address was also true. However, that did not diminish her own error in the slightest. She was certain she would die of shame if Miss Darcy—or anyone—ever learned of the appalling discussion between her and Mr Darcy.

Mr. Bingley's voice interrupted her thoughts. "Georgiana, if you and Miss Elizabeth plan to go skating, I would be happy to keep you company. And perhaps Miss Bennet might be tempted to join us? I dare say it is a lovely idea. Would you not agree, Miss Bennet?"

Elizabeth glanced at Jane, wondering whether her sister would admit that she did not enjoy skating. Quite the contrary, she replied that she would be delighted, though she was not a proficient skater. Naturally, Mr. Bingley immediately offered his assistance, and Jane blushed even more as Miss Darcy expressed her joy at these new additions to their group. Elizabeth's heart grew heavy; there would be no skating.

She was in danger of losing the struggle against her tears, so she gently excused herself to Miss Darcy, quickly embraced her, and then said goodbye to Mr. Bingley and the other visitors. She declared she was not well enough to remain in their company but assured them there was no reason for concern. Surely, she would feel better after a long rest, she said, but nobody gave much credit to her whispered, unconvincing assurance. As soon as she left the room, Mrs. Gardiner sent a servant to fetch the doctor.

The visit in Gracechurch Street was far too brief in Mr. Bingley's opinion. In the carriage with Lord Matlock and the colonel, he talked incessantly about how happy he was to return to London and how grateful he was that they were kind enough to accompany him home, and how delightful it had been to meet Mrs. Gardiner and to see Miss Bennet and Miss Elizabeth again, and—

"Bingley, I venture to say you are quite excited to be here." The colonel laughed, but the earl rolled his eyes in exasperation.

"Where the hell have you been all this time, young man?" the earl demanded, and Mr. Bingley's smile paled.

"I was at my friend Matthew Morton's estate, your lordship, as I previously had the honour of informing you. I—"

"Yes, yes, I know all that, but why on earth did you disappear without a word? Darcy searched after you all around the country."

"I… Please forgive me, your lordship. I was not aware that anyone was looking for me. I was not feeling at all well in London, and I wished to be alone for a time. Had I known that—"

"Then how the hell are you feeling so damn well in London now?" the earl continued, and the colonel could not contain his laughter. Poor Bingley looked like a schoolboy scolded by his headmaster. He did not dare either to lie or tell the entire truth.

"Oh, I… It is just that—"

"Besides, did your sisters not inform you of Miss Bennet's presence in town and Darcy's search party? And speaking of your sisters, you should do something to improve their social skills. You are aware, I hope, that they are rude and frequently misbehave. From what I hear, they have treated Miss Bennet and Mrs. Gardiner abominably. You might want to insist they apologise for their lack of civility. So, you previously met Miss Bennet and Miss Elizabeth in Hertfordshire, am I correct?"

Bingley was powerless to understand everything the earl was disclosing. He blinked a few times and tried to find an answer that—he hoped—would satisfy Lord Matlock.

"I beg your forgiveness for my sisters, your lordship. Without a doubt, I will speak to them. Indeed you are correct, sir. I had the honour of meeting both Bennet ladies in Hertfordshire. I feel very fortunate to call them my friends, and I was so happy to see them again today. I truly miss Netherfield. Those months spent in Hertfordshire were the happiest in my life."

"Truly? I never would have guessed that, considering you left after only two months. No master leaves his property, and no man leaves his supposed friends after such a short time unless he is determined to abandon them forever. You should not have taken the trouble of leasing the place or making new friends if you were not capable of keeping them. So, you are a friend of the Miss Bennets?"

Mr. Bingley had long lost all his joy and—apparently—his ability to speak coherently.

"Yes, I dare say I am and—"

"Then it is a shame that you did not make an appearance last night. You would have been very proud to see how admired they were. Every man in the room was impressed with their beauty," the earl continued, enjoying a cigar and smiling at a pallid Bingley.

The colonel intervened, barely keeping his countenance. "Well, I for one am happy you missed the ball, Bingley, as it allowed me more time to dance with Miss Bennet and Miss Elizabeth. Can you imagine that Miss Bennet was engaged for every dance? I was tempted to ask her for a second set, but her card was already full. Thomas himself seemed very enchanted by her. I would not be surprised if she were to become family some day."

"Well, I surely would not be opposed to such an arrangement, son. So, Bingley, why did you say you left Netherfield? And why did you not inform your sisters of your whereabouts? And who is taking care of the estate at present?"

Bingley's pallor and long silence were almost too much to bear, and the colonel wondered whether they had been too cruel towards him.

The earl recalled his first encounter with Miss Bennet, and he felt that Bingley needed the torment and punishment just to compensate for her distress. Darcy deserved similar punishment though he had earned a measure of forgiveness for admitting his error and bringing Bingley back to town.

"By the way, where is Darcy? He looked like a wet puppy, lost in the middle of Cheapside. What was he thinking to appear like a lunatic at Mrs. Gardiner's door? I surely hope he did not plan to call on Miss Elizabeth in such a state. Did he not know that she was home alone?" The earl seemed seriously displeased, and Bingley vacillated between worry for his friend and relief that Lord Matlock had transferred his censure to Darcy.

"I am worried about Darcy, to tell the truth," the colonel replied. "I cannot remember seeing him other than properly attired since we were infants. I should go and speak to him after dinner. It is fortunate that Miss Elizabeth did not see him in such a state while she was home alone; she seemed quite ill. She looked feverish with her face and eyes so flushed. To be honest, I am quite concerned about her. If I did not know her disposition, I would imagine she had been crying. I think we should send a note later and ask Mrs. Gardiner about her state."

"I would be happy to return to Gracechurch Street later, ask about Miss Elizabeth, and return to you with the news," offered Bingley, and the earl rolled his eyes again.

"Your generous offer is impressive but unnecessary," said the earl. "I dare say we have disturbed Mrs. Gardiner more than enough for one day. A note will do perfectly well."

Mr. Bingley dared not say more on that subject or any other until the carriage stopped in front of his house. He entered after inviting his companions to join him for a glass of brandy. Both refused him, and he did not insist.

"Thank you, Miles, that will be all for now. I shall ring if I need you."

From his bathtub, Darcy could hear the servant closing the door behind him. He still did not open his eyes but leaned back in the hot water and swallowed another gulp of brandy. It was the third since he got home, and he knew he should stop, but he did not intend to do so or even to contemplate it. In truth, he did not intend to think or do anything at all. He would set his mind on sleep and not allow any thought or memory to intrude. He was determined to maintain the same darkness in his mind that existed in his heart.

Darcy looked around, his head spinning with a sharp pain, wondering how long he had slept. He was still in the bathtub, shivering in cold water, the empty brandy snifter in his hand.

He hurried out of the tub and, wrapped in his robe, walked towards the window. The street, though frozen and white, was quite animated, and he wondered what the time was. He continued to stare out at people, carriages, and sleighs with unseeing eyes. He remembered that the previous night he was preparing himself for a ball. Those twenty-four hours seemed as distant as a year. A cold claw gripped his stomach; he needed something to drink. The room was dark, but his mind was unbearably light and clear.

He had proposed marriage to Miss Elizabeth Bennet, the daughter of a small country gentleman, and she had the nerve to refuse him most offensively. It was unthinkable and unacceptable. How could he have exposed himself to such a situation? Surely, it must be the result of too little sleep and too much brandy —otherwise such an outrageous event never would have taken place. She accused him of absurd things that were not worth the trouble of denying! She was invariably hasty in judging his character—and others! It was such a disappointment to hear of her sympathy towards Wickham. God knows what that miscreant might have told her, but still…she should know better than to believe such a man.

And he should have known better than to propose during a moment of insanity. *'Your manners impressed me with the fullest belief of your arrogance, your conceit, and your selfish disdain of the feelings of others.'*

How dare she judge him so unfairly? And on what grounds? He had never behaved other than considerately and politely towards her! In fact, he was more amiable with her than with any other woman. He certainly did not deserve such an offensive reply, and she likely did not deserve his trust and admiration. What a disappointment!

She believed Wickham to be an honest, honourable man—what a joke!—while she was convinced that he, Darcy, had come to propose that she be his—! Where on earth did she learn of such things? How was a young country girl of twenty familiar with such…arrangements? And how could she make such an blunder? Surely, there was nothing in his words to suggest such a disgusting idea. He could remember their conversation word for word, and he was certain he was not to blame. He had been honest, open and fair, presenting his feelings, his hopes, his hesitations… And she pretended he had offended her? Surely not! He was the one who had been deeply and unfairly offended without cause. He might have upset her by taking Bingley from Netherfield, but he had done it for his friend's benefit and felt no regret about it. To Bingley, he had been more considerate than to himself. And he was still not convinced of his fault. And even if he was, how could she possibly be certain of his involvement?

Well, at least she had seen Bingley, and she would understand that he tried to make amends for his past misjudgement. He hoped she would recognise his effort and regret her harsh words. In truth, she looked unwell from what he could see from the hall. Surely, she could feel no worse than he did. She even accused him of being engaged to Cousin Anne. How could she imagine that he would break his word to another lady by proposing to her?

'You proposed to me a "way of solving your painful situation, by an arrangement which could be to the advantage of both," while you know very well that you are engaged to marry Miss Anne de Bourgh.' Why would she say such a thing? And how does she know Anne?

In truth, the words as she put them were confounding, but surely she twisted his meaning. He could not—

Miles entered, and Darcy startled, casting a sharp, reproachful glance at him. The servant remained immobile in the doorway.

"What is it? I do not remember ringing for you!"

"Forgive me, sir, I thought… Miss Darcy was concerned and asked whether she could speak to you. I knocked, but I received no answer, so I— It is dinnertime."

"Tell her I am well, but I will be dealing with some urgent matters. I shall not join her for dinner tonight; please send her my apologies."

"Yes sir, as you wish. May I be of any help?"

"No, you cannot! How many times do I have to repeat myself? Please leave!"

He knew he was being unfair, but he could not find the strength to behave politely. And he surely could not speak to Georgiana and bear her stories about the time she spent in Gracechurch Street. For a moment, he wondered how Elizabeth reacted after his departure. Did she remain to entertain guests? Did anyone else notice her altered spirits? Or were they really altered? Did her unfair judgement even slightly embarrass her?

He toyed with the idea of joining Georgiana for dinner and proposing that they leave for Pemberley. They could be gone by the end of the next day and not return to Town until spring. There was nothing in London for them. Yes, that was what he should do!

He started to dress while enjoying another glass of brandy. He knew Georgiana would not oppose his plan; she never did. They both would be happy at Pemberley. Surely, the estate was buried in snow, and Georgiana would love long rides in the sleigh.

Memories of their ride in the sleigh two days before produced a sharp pang in his chest. *Her* eyes were full of joy and sparkle, her cheeks crimson as she laughed at him and— That would never happen again. Earlier that day, Elizabeth's eyes were tearful, empty and lifeless. That would be the image he carried with him when he left.

He gulped another glass of brandy and leaned back in the chair, staring out the window. How could he even consider going to dinner?

It was finally silent in the house. Elizabeth had prayed to fall asleep since she closed herself in her room, but in vain. *'In vain I have struggled…'*

Every word and thought that crossed her mind unbidden carried the memories of what occurred earlier, and each time she closed her eyes, his image sharply returned to trouble her—his image from the hall when he was forced to return to the house after their horrible fight—wet, dirty, frozen, offended, hurt, and obviously searching for an escape!

A sharp pain seized her chest, and breathing became difficult. What would happen in the next days? How could she bear to face him again? Or would she ever face him again? He likely would avoid her as his worst enemy and surely would forbid his sister any further visits. What should she do? His close relatives were intimate friends of her family; how could she avoid wondering glances, insinuating questions, and awkward situations? How would she manage to keep such a secret?

Hours passed, and Elizabeth's memories only returned more vividly. She easily could remember every word, every gesture, and every glance, but still she was unable to judge properly what had happened. *'…both of us shall allow new or old acquaintances a chance to prove their worthiness before judging their characters…'*

She had long judged his character, and she could not say whether she had been wrong. His insufferable pride and his inconsiderate and ungenerous involvement in Mr. Bingley's departure were not things to be forgiven or forgotten. It was true that Mr. Bingley had returned, but that did not diminish Mr. Darcy's fault in the slightest. And there was still his obvious disgust when he spoke of Mr Wickham. He seemed unmoved about his unfair treatment of his boyhood friend—the son of his father's steward. She could not imagine herself attached to such a man, especially through marriage, and certainly not after such an insulting proposal.

Nevertheless, his behaviour was not an excuse for hers. She was not even clever enough to understand his intentions—not that morning and not before.

'I have been interested in reaching an agreement with you many times, but somehow it seems we are meant to argue whenever we meet. More than once I have wondered whether one or perhaps both of us purposely search for subjects upon which to disagree.'

So many words from the past, so many small gestures, so many smiles and glances should have been a sign of his interest in her, but she missed them all. Yet, she did not miss hearing Lady Sinclair speak of him…and his own family making fun of his pretended relationship with that lady…and Mr. Wickham confessing their past relationship…

The room was too warm, and she could barely breathe, so she threw open the window.

Mr. Darcy asked her to marry him, and she refused him—the worst possible refusal.

FOR ALMOST A WEEK, MRS. Gardiner's parlour was a daily host to pleasant, entertaining guests. Since his return, Mr. Bingley had called each day, and his visits were highly improper: he came too early, stayed too long and, not rarely, just left and returned again an hour later.

Yet, Mrs. Gardiner had no cause to establish new rules since Mr. Bingley seemed to be the most proper gentleman, and his mere presence brought complete and instant happiness to Jane's eyes. Besides, his gesture of bringing his sisters with him one day, in which they behaved in a faultless manner during the entire visit, was greatly in his favour.

Miss Darcy also visited them three times, and Lady Selina and Lord Matlock, sometimes together with Colonel Fitzwilliam, were regular presences in Gracechurch Street.

That morning, just before breakfast, Mrs. Gardiner heard the main door and could barely hide a smile. Mr. Bingley was much too early; he would have to wait some time before Jane would be ready to receive him.

To her surprise, however, Lord Matlock barged in without an introduction, apologised briefly and asked for a glass of brandy before he spoke with obvious distress. "Mrs. Gardiner, please forgive my impromptu visit but things cannot continue in this manner. We must take proper measures before more harm is done. Is Miss Elizabeth better today?"

Mrs. Gardiner raised her eyebrow in surprise. "I think so, sir; as I had the pleasure to inform you yesterday, she is somewhat recovered. She had a very bad cold, and she is still tired and somewhat indisposed, but other than that—"

"Yes, yes…but do you remember the precise day of her indisposition? It was the day after the ball; am I correct?"

"You must be, sir—"

"So—you all left the ball early because she was unwell. Then, the second day, she refused to visit Selina and stayed home, and when we came here, we found Darcy in front of the house. Do you remember?"

"I do, but—"

"Then, the very next morning, Darcy returned to Pemberley without informing anyone—except for a brief letter to Georgiana—and since then, Miss Elizabeth has barely left her room. Do you not see the extent of these coincidences, Mrs.

Gardiner?"

His hostess looked at the earl in silent disbelief. She needed several moments before she could speak, and the earl sat near her, gently touching her hand.

"Mrs. Gardiner, I cannot say how sorry I am that—"

"Lord Matlock, what exactly do you suppose happened? It is difficult to imagine a situation involving Lizzy and Mr. Darcy. I was quite surprised that Lizzy danced with Mr. Darcy at the ball, and they seemed to be on amicable terms. I never suspected anything except a headache forced her to leave the ball early, and the next day... Oh dear—what do you suspect?"

"I am not sure...not sure at all...but something must have forced them both to behave so strangely. It is hard for me to imagine anything improper regarding my favourite nephew. I always have trusted him as the most honourable of men. I could trust him with my life. His behaviour has always been beyond reproach. I confess I was surprised that he asked Miss Elizabeth to dance, and a couple of days before, he joined Miss Elizabeth and Georgiana in a sleigh ride. I have seen young men lose their minds over a beautiful young woman... Did he harm her in some way, do you think?"

"No, that cannot be. It is not possible. Lizzy would have said something. But what if—? What should we do? What is to be done? I—" Mrs Gardiner started pacing the room, her anxiety increasing. The earl poured himself another brandy.

"I shall send for Darcy. I shall speak to him and force him to tell me the truth. He will do his duty to resolve this situation; you must have no doubt, Mrs. Gardiner. I—"

"Lord Matlock, perhaps we are too hasty... We are worrying about a situation that is a complete mystery to us. Did your lordship speak with anyone else about these suspicions?"

"No, I have not. I came here directly."

"Please be so kind as to allow me to speak with Lizzy before attempting any action regarding Mr. Darcy. Would you agree to return later in the afternoon and continue this conversation?"

"As you wish, madam. I trust your judgement more than my own for the time being. If you need my assistance, I should perhaps wait here and—"

"That will not be necessary, sir. I would be grateful if we could discuss this further in a couple of hours." A moment after the earl left, Mrs. Gardiner ran up the stairs; she stopped in front of Elizabeth's door to regain a composed appearance and then knocked.

Elizabeth was sitting near the window, reading. She looked at her aunt with surprise and forced a smile. Mrs. Gardiner briefly pondered the best approach in such a delicate situation, but she had little time for consideration.

"How are you, Lizzy? Are you feeling better, I hope?"

"Yes, thank you. I felt like reading."

"I see... Can we hope you will join us for dinner later? Mr. Bingley is expected...

And Miss Darcy might call later in the afternoon."

"Mr. Bingley is here so often that he is hardly a guest any longer. It is likely he intends to make up for all the dinners he missed."

"True, but Jane is happy with his company, so I am happy too. It is fortunate that Mr. Darcy brought him back to town."

Elizabeth tensed instantly, and Mrs. Gardiner did not miss it.

"Miss Darcy is worried by your indisposition, Lizzy. Is there any reason you are not as anxious to spend time with her as you were before?"

"No, not at all... Miss Darcy's company is always a joy. It is just that... To be honest, I was amazed that Mr. Darcy did not take his sister with him when he left town. I am not sure he would approve of Miss Darcy's visits to us."

"Why would he not approve? He never seemed displeased with your friendship with Miss Darcy before. And why would you presume he would take his sister with him when he left?"

"I was just thinking that..." She appeared unable to justify her statement and suddenly turned crimson. Mrs. Gardiner took a few steps then turned and stopped in front of her niece.

"Lizzy, we must talk. You must tell me at once what happened between you and Mr. Darcy before the earl and I are forced to take extreme measures."

Elizabeth frowned, staring at her aunt with anxious eyes.

"Aunt, of what measures are you speaking? The earl? What does he have to do with this? And what do you expect me to tell you? There is nothing to tell!"

"Dearest, surely, you cannot say it was a mere coincidence that you became unwell shortly after you danced with Mr. Darcy and then asked to leave the ball early! And can you convince me that, the next day at the same time you stayed at home alone, Mr. Darcy happened to be in the neighbourhood? Then he left town impromptu, and you did not abandon your room for almost a week. You must understand that both the earl and I are concerned for you! If Mr. Darcy did something to you, it must be revealed at once and—"

"Aunt, please, please stop this... Please..." She could no longer fight her tears and threw herself on the bed, sobbing, her face buried in the pillow. Mrs. Gardiner, pained and breathless, could do little but caress her hair as her panic increased. Her niece had been gravely hurt while under her protection!

After some time, Elizabeth rose and wiped her eyes; Mrs. Gardiner offered her a glass of water mixed with wine, and she took it with trembling hands. "My love, I am so sorry for your pain. I would do anything to—"

"Dearest Aunt, please do not be kind to me. If you only knew how horrible my behaviour has been, you would be ashamed of me. And Miss Darcy never would speak to me again if she knew how abominably I abused her brother. Oh, and the earl... I never would be able to face him again. I beg you; you must promise me you will not tell the earl anything. I—"

"*Your* behaviour? You abused Mr. Darcy? Lizzy, of what are you talking, child?"

Mrs. Gardiner took a few steps back as if to see her niece better. The tumult of emotion was too much for Mrs. Gardiner, and for a moment she considered that Lord Matlock's request for early morning brandy might not be unreasonable.

Mrs. Gardiner resumed her place on the bed and took Elizabeth's hands. "Dearest, let us start from the beginning, and I promise everything we discuss will remain in complete secrecy on my part. You did admit something happened between you and Mr. Darcy, did you not? Surely it cannot be as abominable as you say, so please tell me all the details, and we will see what is best to be done." She attempted to smile, but Elizabeth averted her eyes and remained silent.

"I... We... Mr. Darcy and I had a horrible argument that day...quite horrible..."

"An argument with Mr. Darcy? On what possible subject, my dear?" With every word, Mrs. Gardiner felt more relieved; the situation seemed far from what she feared.

"The subject is of little importance, Aunt. We spoke, he said some things that upset me, and...I replied in the most offensive manner. It is no wonder he left; I was tempted to do the same as I will not be able to face him ever again!"

"I see..." Mrs. Gardiner gently embraced her niece, puzzled and deeply curious but wisely fighting the temptation to force a more detailed confession. Elizabeth began to sob again, her body tense and trembling.

"Lizzy, did Mr. Darcy hurt you in some way?"

"Yes he did... He did hurt me very much. He had the arrogance to admit his involvement in separating Jane from Mr. Bingley, and he pointed out the faults of our family, and he seemed so insensitive about everything he did to Mr. Wickham..."

"Well, well," Mrs. Gardiner whispered in surprise. "Then it is no wonder you replied in the same manner, dearest—"

"Not in the same manner, Aunt, but much, much worse: I accused him of being dishonourable and of having malicious intentions, and I spoke of some horrible things—which should not even be mentioned—and he told me he expected me to distrust his character, but he was surprised by my distrust of my own worthiness, and he was correct that—"

"My love, you are surely too harsh on yourself. I understand you regret everything you said to him, but it is not so horrid; I am sure he has regrets too. He is a most honourable gentleman, after all. I am sure there will be many opportunities for you to make amends and overcome this delicate situation."

"The manner of his address was dreadful—but I still feel deeply sorry for my words, and I would like to apologise, but I am sure he will never speak to me again."

In the agitation of her turmoil, Elizabeth was not aware how much of her secret she revealed. Every word brought Mrs. Gardiner closer to the truth though Elizabeth refused to disclose the *subject of her argument with Mr. Darcy.* The revelation shocked Mrs. Gardiner exceedingly; she never would have suspected such a circumstance, considering the history between the two. She knew she would have to think calmly and patiently about the situation, but for the moment, she needed to calm her niece's troubled heart.

"Lizzy… What should I do with you, my love?" Mrs. Gardiner smiled and embraced her again. "I am glad we finally talked, and I confess I am relieved that things are not as bad as I feared. I am sure we will find a way to settle the entire situation better than you hope at the moment. You must trust me in this, will you?"

"I am glad we talked, too, Aunt, and yes, I do trust you. But I beg you, do not ask me for other details of my discussion with Mr. Darcy because I cannot say more. And I trust you will keep my secret in the strictest confidence."

"Have no fear, dearest; I promise I will not ask anything more. Now, this is what I suggest: you should prepare yourself and come down for a good breakfast. Then, you will go with Jane and your cousins for a walk in the park. Miss Darcy no doubt will come with Mr. Bingley later, and they can join you." Elizabeth tried to disagree with no success.

"Lizzy, Miss Darcy is your friend, and despite any arguments you might have with her brother, you cannot punish her. For the moment, you must continue to behave as you did before and wait to see whether the future requires any change in your relationship."

Elizabeth could see the reason in her aunt's words, so she listened carefully as Mrs. Gardiner told her what she should do that day. After being so wrong in her own decisions, what else could she do except listen to someone wiser!

The joy in her cousins and sister's eyes was precisely what Elizabeth's spirit needed to rise again; an hour later when Mr. Bingley and Miss Darcy arrived, together with Lady Selina and her children, the happy reunion made her almost forget the past week's torment. She had little time to answer all the questions about her health before the entire group left the house and walked to the park in a din of happy voices and horse bells ringing along the frozen street.

Mrs. Gardiner poured herself a glass of wine and sat to enjoy it, closely observed by a concerned housekeeper who had never seen her mistress imbibe before dinnertime.

An hour later, the earl returned. Mrs. Gardiner smiled with her usual calmness and asked for some refreshments.

"Your lordship will be relieved to find that your favourite nephew did not betray your confidence. Except for some unfortunate words at an unsuitable moment, which upset Elizabeth exceedingly, he did nothing wrong. And before you rush to blame him, my niece confessed she did not remain in his debt with offences and harsh replies, so I would say they are quite even." At the earl's incredulous expression, Mrs. Gardiner continued to mingle seriousness with jests in order to convince the earl without disclosing too much.

"Indeed, sir, there was nothing more than a heated argument, generated by some disagreements. The only thing you can do is teach Mr. Darcy better manners. Lizzy had just managed to forget his refusal to dance with her at their first meeting—calling her *tolerable but not enough to tempt him*—and now he finds a new way to offend her. I wonder who he resembles with this unappealing attitude!"

The earl seemed unable to comprehend her words; he remained silent for some time and then hurried to pour himself a brimming glass of brandy.

"So Darcy came here, argued with Miss Elizabeth, offended her, and she offended him back—good for her!—then he left town without a word?"

"That would be a correct summary." Mrs. Gardiner laughed.

"Damn! Darcy is smitten with her! I should have known it from the first day they met in my house! And he had no idea that she completely disliked him—poor oblivious idiot! I told him as much, but he refused to listen! God knows what he might have said to her that made her angry! Well, good to know he did not make himself completely ridiculous by asking for her hand. That would make him the laughingstock of the town!"

"Lord Matlock, please! This is not something to joke about, sir! And we cannot presume to know who is smitten with whom, nor should we speculate about it! Whatever the reason for their argument, clearly it affected both my niece and your nephew, and we should not laugh at their trouble!"

"Please forgive me, Mrs. Gardiner. I did not mean to sound disrespectful, but—"

"No need to apologise, your lordship. I am deeply grateful for your concern and for your attentive care for my niece. If you had not discovered the connection between all that happened, we still would be worried about Elizabeth, and I never would have considered searching for the truth. But you must promise me, sir, that you will not do anything nor will you speak to anyone about this, not even Mr. Darcy himself. Our conversation must remain between us. You must promise me, Lord Matlock!" When she finished her speech, her hand was holding his arm quite tightly, and her insistent gaze demanded obedience.

The earl smiled politely and took her hand, placing a polite kiss over it.

"I promise I will do or say nothing regarding the delicate subject of our conversation. So, do you have any news from your family in Hertfordshire?"

The conversation continued for some time until, suddenly, the earl started to laugh.

"Damn, I cannot help myself! How on earth can Darcy be brilliant in so many ways and then idiotic in others? I wonder why so many women are interested in him, and I have to say I can only think of two reasons: either his wealth or other qualities of which we are not aware. I am really praying it is the latter." The earl laughed with all his heart while Mrs. Gardiner blushed and hid her face behind her cup of tea.

ANOTHER WEEK PASSED WITH THE same routine for Elizabeth. Not a night passed without remembering each moment of her past encounters with Mr. Darcy. She still did not regret refusing his proposal—his marriage proposal—but she felt flattered at touching the heart of such a man. During those nights, the reproaches against herself grew and were more difficult to bear. Eventually, she concluded that she had not been at all fair in judging Mr. Darcy's character; she was always inclined to weigh his faults heavier than his admirable qualities. She admitted to herself that she never forgave his unpardonable fault of calling her '*not tolerable enough.*' If not for his rude remark on that first evening, her dislike probably would have been less intense. In fairness, his behaviour towards her had always been beyond reproach—excepting that first evening, of course. Though his offensive words regarding her family were difficult to hear, they were not unjustified. The way her family—her mother, Mary, Kitty, Lydia, even her father—behaved each time Mr. Darcy was present was justification for his poor opinion of them.

Her judgement of Mr. Darcy was based on his behaviour towards others: poor Mr. Wickham, Mr. Bingley and Jane, even the way Lady Sinclair spoke of him. Elizabeth was furious that she believed the words of a stranger whose behaviour was not beyond reproach. The information that he was engaged to his cousin Miss De Bourgh seemed easy to reject, though he did not specifically deny it. His wounded countenance and his surprise on hearing her accusations were proof that he had proposed to no one else. But how could she have known that? Even Mr. Wickham had mentioned the union of their two estates.

If she should ever have the chance to speak with Mr. Darcy again, she would only apologise for not keeping the promise she made to him during Lady Selina's ball: that she would allow new or old acquaintances a chance to prove their worthiness before judging their characters.

Elizabeth's nights were weighty and restless, indeed.

Nevertheless, her days continued to improve until the moment she was able to smile at Miss Darcy again, make plans for skating together, and even to receive reasonably well the news of Mr. Darcy's being delayed by important business at Pemberley. Miss Darcy would mention her brother from time to time but not so often as to make the others uncomfortable.

It was near the end of January, and the Bennet sisters were missed at Longbourn. In every letter, either Mr. or Mrs. Bennet inquired about their returning, and though it was not easy to leave their aunt, their time in London would not be long.

However, Mr. Bingley declared he had already requested his servants to prepare Netherfield for his return, and he invited everyone to be his guests.

Elizabeth had mixed feelings about returning home, and she could not be certain whether she more wanted or feared leaving Town and never speaking to Mr. Darcy again. Yet, 'never' seemed unlikely with the predictable development of Mr. Bingley's attachment to Jane. As that certain event became clearer, she expected that she would have to face Mr. Darcy at least once more. Whether he would want to speak to her was another matter entirely.

One afternoon, Elizabeth—together with Jane and Mr. Bingley—was shopping for some lace and trinkets for her sisters. It was planned they would meet Lady Selina and Miss Darcy at the modiste, but they arrived a little early and were admiring the shop windows.

From across the street, Elizabeth felt a familiar presence, and her curious gaze encountered Mr. Wickham. Surprised, he greeted her from afar and walked towards her. Elizabeth was pleased and eagerly anticipated their conversation.

They were a few steps away and Mr. Wickham had already called her name and declared his delight in seeing her when a carriage stopped, and Lady Selina and Miss Darcy stepped out. When the new companions appeared, Mr. Wickham froze in the middle of the street, and to Elizabeth's surprise, Miss Darcy took a step back, her face pale and frightened. Lady Selina, however, looked angry, and her cheeks became red. Elizabeth had little time to react because Mr. Wickham greeted them briefly then excused himself and departed in some haste.

"Miss Darcy, are you well?" asked Jane, and Mr. Bingley hurried to take Georgiana's arm as she leaned against a post.

Miss Darcy declared she was well; Lady Selina hurried them into the shop and asked the modiste for some tea. Elizabeth remained puzzled, but it was not the time or place to inquire further. They spent the next hour in reasonably pleasant preoccupations with lace, bonnets, and the most fashionable colours for each of them, but Elizabeth could think of little except Miss Darcy's pallor and the sight of her blue eyes gaping in shock.

Why would Mr. Wickham's presence elicit such strong reactions in both Darcys and Lady Selina? Mr. Wickham had secret liaisons with Lord Matlock but avoided even greeting his daughter and niece. What was behind these strange encounters?

If she could talk to Mr. Wickham, perhaps he would explain to her what was happening; he trusted her and had offered his friendship from the moment they met.

The next day after breakfast, the ladies at the Gardiner home were surprised by a visitor—Mr. Wickham. He entered—alone—as charming and handsome as ever. They received him with perfect politeness and amiability, and he expressed his pleasure in seeing his friends again.

"I cannot believe we have been in town for so long together and we have not had the chance to visit," the gentleman said.

"True, Mr. Wickham," said their aunt, "but I imagine a young gentleman has so many obligations in Town that he can hardly accommodate them all. I imagine there were other priorities that kept you away from us until now."

"You are too kind, Mrs. Gardiner, but I cannot help blaming myself. Nothing should be more important than seeing you," he replied, looking pointedly at Elizabeth.

She smiled, but her heart beat as regularly as ever. Inexplicably, the image of both Darcy siblings—pale and rigid the moment they saw Mr. Wickham—vividly invaded her mind.

"Well, we did have the pleasure of seeing you yesterday, Mr. Wickham, though for a brief moment. You must have had something important to attend to, I imagine..."

Mr. Wickham looked at Elizabeth, uncertain of the meaning of her words. "I... well, I noticed you were in larger company, and I did not want to intrude."

"Very thoughtful of you, but I imagine you are well enough acquainted with

Lady Selina and Miss Darcy to feel at ease in their presence. Old friends are always a joy to see as soon as possible, and you would have been pleased to see that Miss Darcy has changed since you last saw her; she is not at all proud but affectionate, pleasant and kind—as you said she used to be as a child."

"Well, I…"

Mrs. Gardiner excused herself for a moment as she was needed by the children; Jane took the opportunity to ask for refreshments, so for a few moments, Elizabeth remained alone with their guest. He took the opportunity to sit close to her.

"Miss Elizabeth, I have to say I was looking forward to meeting you again. I was disappointed you could not join Lord Matlock a couple of weeks ago; I have been anxious for some time to speak to you undisturbed."

"I am sorry for the disappointment you had to bear, but I hope your suffering was not too intense," she teased him, and he smiled back. "However, if you were anxious to see me, you must have known that you were always welcome in my aunt's house."

"Yes, perhaps but… I came to the neighbourhood a few times, but I was shocked to discover Mr. Darcy visiting you too, and I could not take the risk of meeting him. I wanted to avoid an unpleasant situation for you or Mrs. Gardiner."

"So thoughtful of you, sir! Will you be in London long? You are having a pleasant time, I imagine. Please have some refreshments; I hope you are not in a hurry. We expect Lord Matlock and Colonel Fitzwilliam to visit; I am sure they would be delighted to see you."

Mr. Wickham unfortunately had urgent business, and he was in quite a hurry, so he departed less than half an hour later, long before the earl, the colonel and the viscount arrived.

Without any special agreement among them, none of the ladies though it necessary to mention Mr. Wickham's morning call to their newly arrived guests.

That night, Elizabeth had one more reason to lose sleep and pose questions without answers. She dare not speculate about the events between Mr. Wickham and the Darcys or about the contradiction between the earl's favourable inclination towards Mr. Wickham and the strong dislike of the rest of his family.

She remembered her past conversations with Mr. Wickham and began to wonder about the veracity of his words.

Mr. Wickham had said many things, but on closer scrutiny, many of them proved to be untrue. He declared Miss Darcy to be a proud, disagreeable young lady, and that was untrue. He said he would come to the Netherfield ball, but he did not appear. He declared he would never say any unfavourable words about Mr. Darcy, but as soon as the gentleman left Hertfordshire, Mr. Wickham's secret dealings with him became public knowledge.

Yet, until the day she witnessed the strong reaction of Lady Selina and Miss Darcy, Elizabeth never questioned his motives or his character, and she could not understand why. Could it be that he was handsome and charming and always showed a preference for her? *He* never called her 'tolerable.'

Was it possible that, for the same shallow reason, she misjudged Mr. Darcy and Mr. Wickham equally wrongly, but in different ways?

THREE MORE DAYS PASSED, AND their return to Hertfordshire was three days closer.

Elizabeth took long walks in the park across the street as often as she could, including just after dusk and just before dawn. Her aunt and the housekeeper worried and completely disapproved of her habits. A young lady ought not to spend time alone outside in the dark—regardless of whether the dark was late at night or early in the morning—so a servant was summoned each time to watch her from afar. Elizabeth could not but be amused, considering the streetlight was lit until late in the evening, and even in the morning, she usually saw one or two others walking silently along the frozen lane.

That night she managed to sleep for more than two hours, and she knew she had no reason to stay in bed longer. She roused and dressed herself, put on her bonnet without even catching her hair in pins—who would see her at that hour?—and silently left the house. She stopped, overwhelmed by the fresh breeze and the new snow falling.

She took a few careful steps—it would not do to fall in the middle of the street—and, walking slowly, she reached the park. There were only a few silhouettes at that hour—no doubt as sleepless as she—and she remained in the lane from where she could see her aunt's house.

After some time, cold and wet, she decided to return home; the snow was falling heavier, and the visibility was poor.

She felt another person's presence near her long before she noticed it was a man; she stopped and allowed him to approach and step by her, hoping it was not an acquaintance as her appearance was quite improper.

However, he seemed unwilling to pass by, pausing a few steps away, so she lifted her eyes.

Her body was cold, but it suddenly froze completely; even if she had wished to depart, her feet seemed trapped in stone. He took one more step forward and bowed to her.

"Miss Bennet, forgive me if I frightened you."

"Mr. Darcy! I… I did not expect to see you, sir. I was told you were out of town and—"

"I returned two days ago, but I asked my sister to keep it private for the time being as I am not certain for how long I will remain. I am sorry to disturb you. I have been walking for some time with the hope of seeing you alone for a moment. Would you do me the honour of reading this letter?" His voice was as uncertain and gentle as his gaze.

He handed her a letter, and the snow covered it instantly, so without thinking, she tucked the letter under her cloak. She raised her eyes briefly, he thanked her and apologised once more, and then she watched him depart through a curtain of snow.

Chapter 10

D arcy had appeared a day earlier as unexpectedly as he left, and his sister was not certain whether she was happy to see him or frightened by his strange behaviour.

If someone asked, he would not have been able to explain why he returned, nor would he dare tell anyone that he returned because Pemberley was cold and lonely in the winter.

He had been angry for many days and nights—so angry and hurt that he could do nothing, not even sleep. He spent considerable time on horseback, and some days he exercised three mounts and was still not satisfied or tired from riding across the snowy grounds.

Then he received the first letter from Georgiana, and she spoke of her concern regarding Miss Elizabeth, who had not left her room for almost a week. He could not help worrying and wondering about her illness. He felt deeply for her—the sharp pang in his chest was clear proof—and he was furious with himself for caring about a woman who cared so little for him.

During the next few days, worry surpassed his anger. In fact, he was still infuriated with her, but he would rather know she was well and healthy. He replied to Georgiana, asking for more details, and she finally informed him that Miss Elizabeth was better. It appeared she was more tired and exhausted than truly ill, but she improved satisfactorily.

So, she had been unwell for a week. Could it be that their argument had affected her so? Certainly, she could not remain untouched after such a quarrel; nobody could.

When he received another letter from the colonel, inquiring about his plans and mentioning that the Bennet sisters would soon return to Hertfordshire, Darcy became restless. He knew he should have been happy that she was leaving town. Briefly, it crossed his mind that it would not be long before Bingley likely proposed to Miss Bennet, so future events and situations would probably throw them into each other's company. For the time being, he should be happy that she was leaving Town.

But he was not.

His anger towards her was equally as strong as the anger towards his own weakness, so in order to discover new reasons to feed this anger, he spent an entire day and night reviewing every moment he spent in her company since they first met.

In the end, he was spent, deeply ashamed, and appalled at his own behaviour, shocked by the revelation that, indeed, she had every reason in the world to think ill of him and to accuse him of arrogance, conceit, and selfish disdain for the feelings of others.

He had offended her on the first evening of their acquaintance, refusing to dance with her and describing her as only tolerable. And she heard him; he had proof of that. In a short time, his opinion of her changed, and he found her to be considerably more than tolerable—but she never knew that. How could she? She had only the evidence of his rude behaviour in Hertfordshire.

He was aware that, since they met again in London, things had changed slightly between him and Miss Elizabeth Bennet. It might have been the positive influence of his family—perhaps the earl, perhaps Georgiana's sweet manners—but he sensed that Elizabeth was more favourable towards him. The day of the sleigh ride, he felt her strong reaction as he brushed the snow from her clothes.

At the ball, he was certain she was not displeased to be in his company and to dance with him. She had smiled at him, and when they danced, she flirted with him. That was precisely what drove him to the conclusion that she would welcome his proposal.

Consequently, he had presented himself before her with a proposal expressed in the worst possible manner; Darcy could acknowledge it once he regained control of himself. With disbelief and severe reproach, he recollected the entire discussion and understood that her criticisms were less than he deserved. He had been insensitive to her feelings, and he severely offended her family. His choice of words could easily mislead any woman into believing his proposal was not an honourable one, especially if she was induced to believe he was already engaged. From what quarter that information had reached her was not even worth considering—perhaps from Wickham, perhaps from others. He was aware of the rumour and did nothing to contradict it—until the damage was impossible to repair.

She had been unfair in her accusations, certainly, but he was no gentleman in his manners—not at all! He had no hope that she would ever speak to him again, nor could he hope she would ever forgive him.

The revelation that Elizabeth still held Wickham in high esteem was especially disturbing, and while he admitted to himself that he was jealous, he also worried that she might discover Wickham's true character when it was too late. He decided then that, if there were no possible way for him to make amends and win her forgiveness, there was one thing he could do. It was his duty to share his side of the story of his past dealings with Wickham.

It was highly unlikely that she would agree to speak to him privately and listen to his arguments; in fact, it was unlikely that she would agree to speak with him at all, ever again. Finally, he understood there was only one solution, so he spent the entire evening and night putting together the most detailed and difficult letter he had written in his entire life. When morning came, he began the lengthy journey back to London.

When he arrived in Grosvenor Square, the expression on Georgiana's face melted his heart. He had abandoned her without any explanation. She had every reason to feel the same degree of anger as he felt of guilt, but she smiled and cuddled to his chest, happy and relieved.

At dawn the next day, he decided to call on Mrs. Gardiner and ask her permission to give Elizabeth a letter. He could have asked Georgiana to deliver the letter privately, of course, but he could not expose either his sister or Elizabeth to such a delicate situation.

Once he made the decision, he could not bear to wait for a proper visiting hour, so he fetched the carriage and drove to the park where he walked around to clear his thoughts. Fortunately, the park was empty, barren and frozen. No reasonable person would venture outside at that hour and in such weather—almost no reasonable person.

A few steps ahead of him, stepping carefully along the frozen path, lost in her thoughts, her hair down and covered with snow, was Elizabeth. The moment he had desired for so many days was upon him. She was alone, and he meant to use that chance to speak to her, to apologise for his outrageous behaviour, to explain to her that—

Her eyes met his, and he could see she was frightened, shocked, frozen, disturbed and…she had no desire to speak to him at all.

"Would you do me the honour of reading this letter?" She was still silent, staring at the letter, and then she took it—and he left. It was done.

UNABLE TO UNDERSTAND THE HAPPENSTANCE of such an unexpected meeting and struggling to comprehend what compelled Mr. Darcy to write her a letter, Elizabeth stared at the two pieces of paper—written quite through in a very close hand—now lying open on her bed, drying.

She changed her clothes, and for a moment, she looked in the mirror and wondered what he might think after seeing her in such a dishevelled state. Yet, that was the least reason for concern; his opinion of her must be so low that her appearance mattered little.

So he returned to Town—why did Georgiana not say a word?—and he spent time writing her and came to hand the letter to her in person. How long had he been walking around the cold park?

With the strongest curiosity and equal worry, she began reading.

Be not alarmed, Miss Bennet, on receiving this letter, by the apprehension of its containing any repetition of those sentiments, or renewal of those offers, which were
110

earlier so disgusting to you...

You will, I hope, pardon the freedom with which I demand your attention in reading this, but I felt it was necessary. Two offences of a very different nature, and by no means of equal magnitude, you laid to my charge, and both need to be clarified. The first mentioned was, that, regardless of the sentiments of either, I had detached Mr. Bingley from your sister...

Her eyes eagerly ran along the page, anxious to discover his explanation regarding the role he had played in separating Mr. Bingley from Jane. At first, Darcy's admission of his interference and his poor attempt at excusing himself by explaining his reasons made her angry and resentful. The fact that he admitted his error and made efforts to reunite the couple did not diminish his mistake. If fate had not made them meet again, or Mrs. Gardiner had not been a friend of the Matlocks, it was likely that Jane and Mr. Bingley would have been separated forever and their chance of happiness ruined. For that, he could not be forgiven so easily. However, since her sister's present state of joy was a source of comfort, these revelations did not affect Elizabeth as much as they would have two weeks earlier.

Then, when she reached the part where he referred to Mr. Wickham, she continued to read word after word, her eyes burning, her head spinning, her breathing heavy.

... My father and Lord Matlock were not only fond of this young man's society, whose manners were always engaging, they also had the highest opinion of him, and hoping the church would be his profession, my father intended to provide a living for him. As for my cousins and me, it is many years since we first began to think of Wickham as unworthy of such benefaction. The vicious propensities and the want of principle, which he was careful to guard from the knowledge of his best friends, could not escape the observation of young men of nearly the same age as himself who had opportunities to observe him in unguarded moments, which my father and uncle could not have.

As for my cousin Lady Selina, she had her own share of hurtful experiences with Wickham, who tried more than once to insinuate himself with her with—probably —the hope of using his charms to accomplish a most advantageous marriage. With little hesitation, Selina rejected him, and he had no other choice than keeping his distance ..."

Lady Selina? Mr. Wickham tried to insinuate himself with her? That cannot be! Was Lord Matlock aware of the dishonourable scheme against his beloved daughter?

... All connection between us seemed now dissolved, though I knew he had maintained a sort of friendship with my Uncle Matlock, who considered him an amiable rascal. You might wonder why, if we were aware of Wickham's

*true character, we did not try harder to convince the earl to put an end to their
friendship. I shall only mention that we tried, but Wickham's influence seemed
quite strong, and for reasons that are not to be shared, we had a strong belief
that any further insistence would pain the earl exceedingly. Yet, the colonel
lost no opportunity to inform his father about one or another of Wickham's
'accomplishments,' and though the earl used to take everything in jest and find
excuses for Wickham's wantonness, we at least were content that he seemed to be
aware that Wickham was more charming than trustworthy.*

Elizabeth vividly remembered her first conversation with the Earl about Wickham, and that passage from the letter confirmed her own observation. She hastily whipped the tears from the corners of her eyes as she read further.

*… last summer, he was again most painfully obtruded on my notice. I must
now mention a circumstance which I would wish to forget myself and which no
obligation less than the present should induce me to unfold to any human being.
Having said this much, I feel no doubt of your secrecy, but I will kindly point out
that, except for my cousin the colonel, no one is aware of this, not even Selina or the
earl. My sister Georgiana was left to the guardianship of the colonel and myself, as
you might know. About a year ago, she was taken from school and an establishment
formed for her in London, and last summer she went with the lady who presided
over it to Ramsgate; thither also went Mr. Wickham, undoubtedly by design, for
there proved to have been a prior acquaintance between him and Mrs. Younge, in
whose character we were most unhappily deceived …*

By the time she finished the part of the letter that painfully related Georgiana's attempted elopement, the shame and anger towards herself felt like a sharp claw that took her breath away and defeated Elizabeth's strength as tears clouded her eyes.

She immediately remembered Georgiana's pallor and Lady Selina's anger at seeing Wickham on the street. She remembered that Miss Darcy had burned her hand at the mere mention of Wickham's name. Poor, dearest, sweet Georgiana!

Elizabeth struggled to read the last few lines while tears dropped on the paper.

*At my sister's heartfelt pleading, I agreed not to share this story with the earl—whose
reaction against Wickham surely would have been violent, despite their previous
friendship, as my uncle's affection is divided equally between Selina and Georgiana.
Also, my sister begged me not to tell Selina as she would be too ashamed to bear a
dear cousin's compassion. Not wanting to pain my sister further, I obeyed her wishes,
but I still hope that she might feel strong enough in the future to tell my uncle and
Selina about Wickham's schemes. Colonel Fitzwilliam, as my best friend and one
of the executors of my father's will, has been unavoidably acquainted with every
particular of these transactions, but he kept the secret.*

You will, I hope, acquit me henceforth of cruelty towards Mr. Wickham. I know not in what manner, under what form of falsehood, he has imposed on you, but his success is not, perhaps, to be wondered at. Ignorant as you previously were of everything concerning either, detection could not be in your power and suspicion certainly not in your inclination.

There is just one thing further that must be addressed: my supposed engagement to my cousin Anne de Bourgh. I do not know how you received such information, but you will believe me, I hope, when I say that I am not and never have been bound by either affection or honour to any other woman. On this, I have no other explanation to offer.

You may wonder why these things were not explained to you two weeks ago. I was not then master enough of myself to know what could or ought to be revealed. Even now, after so many days, I am not certain that what I have related in this letter is written well, but I am at peace with myself that I did everything in my power to present you a faithful and honest narrative of all events.

I will only add, God bless you.
Fitzwilliam Darcy.

Elizabeth put the letter down on the bed, unable to move.

Any shame, disappointment or horror she felt while reading the letter were against herself. Yes, Wickham proved to be unworthy of her approval, but she also was unworthy of everyone's admiration. She was not wise, witty, or smart: nothing her family and friends—or Mr. Darcy—thought her to be.

All the outrageous things she discovered about Wickham disgusted her, but they did not surprise her as much as they should, not after the last days' events. If she had been told all this two weeks earlier when her opinion of Mr. Wickham was unsullied, her reactions probably would have been disbelief and denial. However, after time to think properly of all she had witnessed, she had already admitted her errors in judgement.

She recollected meeting Mr. Wickham in Hertfordshire. She accepted his malicious words against Mr. Darcy and Georgiana without questioning his reasons for sharing such intimate information with a complete stranger. She—Elizabeth Bennet—was a careless simpleton who succumbed to Mr. Wickham's questionable charms, and he used her as an instrument against Mr. Darcy. It was clear now that his motives could not have been honourable; he was either deceived regarding her fortune, or he was gratifying his vanity by the preference she showed unwisely and openly. She was horrified and humiliated, admitting she felt flattered and enchanted by Mr. Wickham's attentions in the same empty-headed way that Lydia was flattered by any officer's attention.

Sometime later, she cleaned herself and changed her clothes, whipping her tears furiously. She would not allow herself to cry; her behaviour did not deserve such relief.

Mrs. Gardiner, Jane, and her cousins were already at breakfast; Elizabeth joined them and tried to conceal her preoccupation, but she could not drive away her thoughts. Yes, she was silly and careless, but what about Lord Matlock? How was it possible that an admirable man allowed himself to be deceived by someone whose character was questioned by his own children? Was he blind? Old Mr. Darcy himself seemed to have been unfairly partial to Mr. Wickham, but since then, many things had happened—things that should have demonstrated proof of Wickham's unworthiness.

After breakfast, Elizabeth returned to her room and read Darcy's letter again. With every word, she could feel his worry and suffering for his sister and Georgiana's shame and love of her brother, who was like a father to her.

A young man and little girl—almost a child—lost their parents and took care of each other alone, Mr. Darcy buying his sister a sleigh and teaching her to skate, Mr. Darcy being forced to deal with Mr. Wickham…

From the first moment of their acquaintance, Mr. Darcy's repulsive manners were the only thing that impressed her, and though she had occasions to witness proof of his admirable character, she ignored them. She never saw anything that betrayed him of being unprincipled or unjust; Wickham himself recognised his qualities as a brother, and all his acquaintance esteemed and valued him, but she had simply ignored any contrary information. Only when she met him again in London did she begin to recognise more than she admitted regarding his worthiness. Even then, she was hasty to believe the worst of him, to accuse him of the most immoral intentions and to reject him in the most despicable manner.

Two hours later, they had visitors. She hurried downstairs, only to meet the happy faces of Lord Matlock, Mr. Bingley, Lady Selina, and Georgiana.

She greeted them and, without a second thought, suddenly embraced Miss Darcy tightly. She felt the girl hesitate for a moment and then respond to her caring gesture.

"Well, what a nice idea! Should we all embrace each other, do you think?" The earl laughed, and Miss Bennet blushed instantly while Mr. Bingley could not control a huge smile.

"I am afraid only those who enjoy sleigh riding are allowed to embrace each other," Elizabeth attempted to joke, hiding her emotion, but a moment later she coloured, praying nobody would mention that Mr. Darcy also was in the sleigh.

Nobody did, so they seated themselves, and a servant entered with refreshments.

"Oh, speaking of the sleigh, Elizabeth, I have news," said Georgiana. "Miss Bennet, Mr. Bingley and I decided we will have a long sleigh ride before you leave town! Miss Bennet was very curious after everything I told her, so she will come with us, and Mr. Bingley was so amiable that he agreed to join us! What do you say?"

"Well, it sounds quite charming if you are willing to freeze," said Lord Matlock, "but you must plan it carefully not to interfere with my own plans; in two days'

time, I am expecting you all to dinner. No exceptions and no excuses are allowed."
The earl paused a moment, looked at his daughter, and then turned to Bingley.
"You should bring your sisters, too, Bingley."

"I thank you, your lordship. I am sure they will be grateful and delighted to
be there."

"So shall I be." The earl poured himself another glass of brandy. "Oh, did I
mention Darcy is back in town? He called earlier, but I could not convince him
to come with us. He had some urgent business to attend. Damn, that boy always
is caught up in some sort of business. Unlike my sons..."

"Mr. Darcy has visited us many times in the past, and I am sure he will do so
again soon. We should not bother him with our insistence," Mrs. Gardiner said.

"I am sure my brother would be delighted to visit you, but he was reluctant to
intrude on you unexpectedly," Miss Darcy intervened. "He said it was not proper
to make an appearance when nobody expected him. He said he did not want to
bother you..."

"Oh, nonsense! He is troubling himself too much...unlike my sons..." the earl
replied, and everybody smiled.

"Mr. Darcy is as considerate and thoughtful as ever," Elizabeth said. "We understand his reason and appreciate his restraint. If...when he considers the time
acceptable, we hope to meet him again...sometime soon. We would not wish to
intrude on his plans, however..."

For a moment, it was silent in the room, and Miss Darcy looked at Elizabeth
with curiosity. Mrs. Gardiner and Lord Matlock exchanged a glance.

"I look forward to having dinner together," Lady Selina said to Elizabeth. "You
know, my mother-in-law asks about you constantly. She will be very pleased to
see you again, too."

"Oh, Lady Brightmore will be there, too? I truly miss her," said Elizabeth.

"The entire family will be there," the earl replied. "We are happy to have you as
our guests before you leave."

"Though I am sure we will all meet again very soon," Lady Selina added.

"I would be happy to have you all at Netherfield," Mr. Bingley hurried to assure
them, and everybody laughed while Lord Matlock rolled his eyes in exasperation
once more.

A few minutes later, Elizabeth took another cup of tea and noticed the earl
alone in a corner, watching the others. She approached him hesitantly, and he
greeted her with a smile.

"I am glad to see you better, Miss Elizabeth. You will be missed when you return
to Longbourn, you know. Your presence here was most beneficial to your aunt
and a pleasant addition for the rest of us."

"Your lordship is too kind. We shall miss you all dearly. We cannot say how
grateful we are for the generous friendship you and your family have shown us
during our time here."

"My niece Georgiana is uncommonly close to you. She rarely attaches herself to a stranger."

"It was a joy and a privilege for me to spend time with Lady Selina and Miss Darcy. And I have to say I was surprised to see how many things Miss Darcy and I have in common—including our preference for music and for winter." Elizabeth tried to smile.

"Well, I hope your acquaintance with Selina and Georgiana will not end when you leave town. We hope to receive news of you from time to time."

"And so you shall, your lordship." She paused for a moment, watching the earl closely, and she suddenly changed the subject to the one that was most interesting to her.

"Have you seen Mr. Wickham lately? Did I mention he paid us a visit a few days ago?"

"No, you did not. So…I hope his visit was a pleasant one?"

"Mr. Wickham is always a pleasant conversationalist. But I have to say, there is something that intrigued me. A day before Mr. Wickham's call, we met in town —and I was quite pleased to see him—but he departed immediately when he saw Lady Selina and Miss Darcy. They seemed displeased to see him, and he seemed uncomfortable to meet them."

"Yes, I can understand your puzzlement. If you remember, I mentioned to you that my sons and even my daughter are not on friendly terms with Wickham —and Darcy even less so."

"I can understand that, but considering their old acquaintance, I would expect that Mr. Wickham would at least greet Lady Selina and Miss Darcy briefly but civilly. Considering how well behaved and polite both ladies are, I am sure they would have responded to him with the same politeness despite their like or dislike of him. But he left quite hastily."

"You are right, of course. Wickham was rude, I might say. Perhaps he did not want to put you in an uncomfortable situation…"

"Please forgive my impertinence, but do you not find it strange that Mr. Darcy —who you confessed to be your favourite nephew and whose character I have heard you praise many times—and your sons and your daughter and even your favourite niece are all so completely against Mr. Wickham? And he avoided meeting any of them? Can a mere dislike explain this? At the same time, Mr. Wickham has the benefit of your friendship, and you even favour him with secret meetings while you mentioned to me long ago that I should not trust everything he told me? I confess I do not know what to think of all these—"

The earl's countenance changed as Elizabeth spoke. He stared silently for a few moments, and though Elizabeth tried to smile, his expression remained stern.

"It does sound strange, Miss Elizabeth, now that you put it that way. I have been accustomed to our family's history for years, but the situation might appear difficult to explain for someone outside the family. There is not much I can explain, though..."

"I do not expect an explanation; I was merely wondering. Someone told me once that I have a quick mind and hasty judgement—so I am trying to correct this fault."

The earl smiled. "I surely enjoy your quick mind, Miss Elizabeth."

Less than an hour later, the servant announced a new visitor, and a most surprising and welcome appearance broke their conversation, entering with a breeze of fresh, cold air.

"I shall never again struggle against my common sense and venture myself on the road in such horrible weather. Well, well, I hope I am not interrupting you!"

Mrs. Gardiner cried in surprise while Elizabeth and Jane ran to embrace him.

"Papa, what a lovely surprise! What are you doing here? You are so cold; come in! Oh, I am so happy to see you!"

"Well, girls, step away and let me enter," Mr. Bennet demanded with a brief kiss on their cheeks while Mrs. Gardiner hurried to invite him in and performed the introductions.

AFTER A BRIEF INTRODUCTION, MR. Bennet retired to the guest room to change after his long ride. Mrs. Gardiner, along with Elizabeth and Jane could not contain their joy at his arrival as they speculated about the reason for such an unexpected trip. He was well known for rarely leaving his home and never in the midst of such unfriendly weather.

Lady Selina had to return home, and her brother offered to accompany her as he had another engagement. Miss Darcy, Lord Matlock and Mr. Bingley continued their conversation until, half an hour later, the newly arrived guest joined them.

Mr. Bennet declared he was hungry, so plates with food were brought for everyone.

"Brother, I am so happy to see you! We did not expect you to come—not for the world!"

"Well, you know I like to make my appearance when I am least expected! Lizzy dearest, may I have a glass of brandy, please?"

"Of course, Papa. I am happy to see you; I truly missed you! But what enticed you to come so unexpectedly? Did you come to take us home? So good of you!"

"I missed you and Jane, too, my child. You have been cruel to leave me alone for so long, you know! I have barely had a rational conversation since the two of you left. And yes, you may say I have come to take you home; it pleased your mother very much. She demanded I bring you home immediately."

"Will you leave tomorrow?" Bingley asked, worry mixed with panic.

"No, we will not, Mr. Bingley, but soon. Did you have some plans that I ruined?" Mr. Bennet asked while Mr. Bingley and Jane turned equally crimson. The earl laughed.

"No sir... I mean...I shall return to Netherfield too, and I thought... I..."

"I am not quite certain about the exact day of our return as there are things I must take care of. Tomorrow I have some urgent business with my solicitor.

Unfortunately, he could not leave town, so I had to come here. Such bad timing; it is so cold, and the roads are so bad…"

"Urgent businesses can be annoying," the earl said. "I hope you have a good solicitor. It is so difficult to find someone trustworthy and knowledgeable in business affairs."

"I could not agree more, Lord Matlock. Since my brother Gardiner left us, my business has become a nightmare. My solicitor is Mr. Gordon; my brother used to work with him…"

"I know Mr. Gordon. He is trustworthy, but he is nothing compared to Mr. Gardiner; I can testify to that. In fact, I do not believe there are many people in town to compare to Mr. Gardiner. He is impossible to replace—as an adviser and as a friend."

Elizabeth saw her aunt turning pale, but Mrs. Gardiner's gentle smile assured her she was fine. As always, any remarks about Mr. Gardiner brought painful memories, but she seemed to bear them better than before.

"I am glad we share the same opinion, Lord Matlock. I have to say—I am quite honoured I have made your acquaintance."

"The pleasure is mine, I assure you, Mr. Bennet. And the moment could not be more perfect. I am hosting a dinner party, and I would be delighted to have you as my guest."

"I thank you. Let us hope tomorrow will be a good day. I hope Mr. Gordon's advice will be helpful… I truly need good advice…"

"Papa, did something bad happen? Are there any troubles at home?"

"Oh, do not worry, Lizzy—usual estate business, nothing for you to trouble about. You have known for years that your father is not the best landlord. I have always admitted that Longbourn could have been more successful with another master, but…well, what can we do? Maybe after I pass away and my cousin Mr. Collins inherits, things will improve." Mr. Bennet laughed, taking another gulp of brandy.

"Papa!" Elizabeth cried, obviously reproachful and upset. "Please never say that again; it is not something to joke about!"

"Come, Lizzy, do not take be so serious! I have great hopes I will own Longbourn and manage it very ill for many years. So, how did you lovely ladies spend time in London? Miss Darcy, such a pleasant surprise to make your acquaintance! So, Lord Matlock, you are related to Mr. Darcy? Well, well, this is a small world indeed. By the way, how is Mr. Darcy? He is in good health, I hope. Is he in town?"

"Yes, my brother is in town, thank you, sir. I am very happy I made your acquaintance, Mr. Bennet. Elizabeth has told me so many things about you," Miss Darcy said with a smile.

The earl stroked his chin. "You know, Mr. Bennet, speaking about Darcy—he is the one who could surely help you with business advice. That boy has managed Pemberley flawlessly since he was a pup. He has people who take care of the estate, but all decisions belong to him, and none of them have proved to be wrong."

"Oh, I am sure Mr. Darcy does everything perfectly, but I doubt he would take the trouble to advise me—that is, if I ever dared bother him with my insignificant problems." Mr. Bennet replied with such obvious irony that Elizabeth felt equally ashamed at her father's tone and embarrassed at the possibility of his talking to Mr. Darcy.

"I know my nephew does not possess the most charming manners, and he might appear unapproachable, but I assure you: there is no one more trustworthy or reliable. I shall send him a note. Perhaps we can all meet tomorrow at my house?"

"I would not want Mr. Darcy to alter his plans for my business. Is your lordship certain that Mr. Darcy could meet us?" Mr. Bennet glanced at Elizabeth, amused by the hilarious prospect of Mr. Darcy offering advice about how to manage Longbourn.

"I am sure my brother will be happy to speak to you on any subject you wish, Mr. Bennet," said a confident Miss Darcy.

"Well then—be it as you say. I am grateful for any help."

Elizabeth was unable to say a word, her head spinning painfully. Mr. Darcy was to be asked to advise her father and be part of the problems at Longbourn? After everything that had happened—after the letter he wrote her when she was not even convinced that he would want to see her again? A worse situation could not be imagined!

DINNER AT GROSVENOR SQUARE WAS pleasant, and Georgiana Darcy could not hide her enjoyment at having her brother's company again. They were relishing the dishes in relative silence until he asked about her day.

"Oh, I had a wonderful time visiting Mrs. Gardiner! They asked about you, quite insistently, you know."

"I somehow doubt that." He laughed. "I dare say I am little missed on such visits as I am the least reliable at entertaining people."

"I speak the truth! Mrs. Gardiner asked about you, and I told them what you said...to excuse you..."

He suddenly became serious. "May I ask exactly how you excused me?"

"I said you did not wish to intrude when nobody expected you..." Miss Darcy replied then returned her attention to her plate. After another moment of silence, he continued.

"And? What did they say?"

"Uncle said you are troubling about business too much. Mrs. Gardiner said you would be welcome anytime, and Elizabeth said...let me remember her exact words... she said, 'We understand his reason and appreciate his restraint. If...when he considers the time acceptable, we hope to meet him again...sometime soon. We would not wish to intrude on his plans, however...'"

"Those were Miss Elizabeth's words? Are you certain?" he inquired impatiently.

"I am certain. Elizabeth seemed quite serious when she said it."

"Truly?" He said nothing for some time, and his sister continued to watch him closely.

"Was Miss Bennet well, I hope? And Miss Elizabeth…"

"Yes, they were. When do you believe it will be 'soon'?"

"I beg your pardon?"

"When do you believe it will be soon enough to call on Mrs. Gardiner? It is obvious you would not intrude. They leave town soon, you know."

"I am aware they will leave soon, but I cannot answer you this instant."

"The day after tomorrow, Uncle will host a dinner. We will attend the dinner, I hope?"

"Yes…yes… I do not believe we have any reason to decline."

"No indeed! I look forward to that dinner. Oh and I have another extraordinary piece of news: Mr. Bennet just arrived in town!"

"Mr. Bennet? That is indeed a surprise."

"Yes…apparently he has some business."

"Business? Nothing urgent, I hope?"

"Some estate problems, I guess…and quite urgent, I understand. Brother, may I ask… Are you and Mr. Bennet well acquainted?"

"No, not really… I mean, we did speak a few times but nothing more than brief pleasantries… We have few interests in common. Why do you ask?"

"I am afraid Mr. Bennet does not know you well enough. Uncle said you might be helpful and advise Mr. Bennet in his estate management, but Mr. Bennet declared he never would dare bother you, and he seemed incredulous that you would be willing to help him. I felt so unhappy that he said that, and I think Elizabeth felt the same way."

To her surprise, Miss Darcy noticed a trace of redness on her brother's face.

"You must not feel bad, dearest. I am sure Mr. Bennet has a low opinion of me and rightfully so. My behaviour towards him was not without fault. In fact, I am ashamed to admit that my behaviour in Hertfordshire was not without fault."

He returned his attention to his plate, and Georgiana was silent for a time.

"But, Brother, will you?"

"Will I what, dearest? "

"Will you help Mr. Bennet?"

He looked closely at his preoccupied sister, and for the first time in many days, he offered her a large, open smile that brightened his face.

"Mr. Bennet might not know me very well, as you said. But you do…"

"I most certainly do, Brother. Uncle invited Mr. Bennet to his house tomorrow at eleven o'clock. Perhaps you could join them for coffee…if you have no fixed plans, I mean…"

"I have no other plans. And I must say you have become very wise lately, dearest. Yes, coffee would be just fine, indeed…"

Chapter 11

Elizabeth's anxiety became insupportable. Her father had left Gracechurch Street immediately after breakfast and had not yet returned, though it was quite late in the afternoon.

Earlier, Lady Selina and Georgiana Darcy called briefly on their way to the modiste, asking Elizabeth and Jane to keep them company and perhaps order new gowns.

To Mrs. Gardiner's surprise, Jane accepted the invitation while Elizabeth politely refused. Elizabeth recognised her aunt's puzzled expression, but she chose to feign ignorance. She was not disposed to have a conversation with Mrs. Gardiner.

Where could her father be? Was the present financial state of Longbourn so seriously damaged? Or perhaps he had finished his business long ago, and Lord Matlock had invited him to his club? Did her father still need Mr. Darcy's advice? Did the earl inform Mr. Darcy that her father might need help?

She had come to know him—such a painful process of discovering his worthiness!—well enough to know that he would not refuse to offer help to her father. But in what way would this new situation influence his opinion of her family? She could not imagine how she would bear to see him again—or whether she would ever see him again. After all, even if he were to help her father, that was no reason to see her.

She was still deeply upset by his cruel words regarding her family and his lack of consideration in hurting her feelings! His improper way of professing affection and his indelicate proposal deserved no less than a rejection—but not such a rejection!

She wondered whether Georgiana had related to him any of their conversation. He was thoughtful enough to avoid putting her in a stressful position by appearing at her door unexpectedly, but she was daring enough to send word that she was not opposed to seeing him again—that is, if Georgiana thought to pass it on.

Elizabeth knew she could expect nothing but polite, cold behaviour when —and if—they should meet again. She hoped at least for the opportunity to thank him for the trouble of writing the letter, to apologise for the cruel accusations she bestowed upon him, and to assure him she would keep the secret he chose to share with her. She wanted him to know he could trust her.

She had little patience for staying in her room, so she returned downstairs and moved to the small library, searching for a favourite book.

It was not long before her solitude was broken by Mr. Bennet's appearance. He was alone, so Elizabeth allowed him only an instant before she started questioning him.

"Have a little patience and a little pity for your old father, child. How do expect me to answer all these questions?"

"Forgive me, Papa; but I was worried about you. You left early this morning and… Did you finish your business? How are you feeling? Are you tired? Do you want a glass of wine?"

"I am very well indeed. I have great hopes that things will settle quite satisfactorily —and no, no wine for now. I had the pleasure of enjoying the earl's brandy for some time, and I dare say it was enough for the time being…at least until after dinner."

"A very wise decision, Papa." She sat near her father, searching for a way to continue.

"What about you, Lizzy? Why are you home? I understood Miss Darcy and Lady Selina had plans involving dresses and lace. Surely, you could not resist such temptation."

She laughed. "I did resist, Papa—quite shocking, I admit."

"Well, well—so fortunate your mother is not here. Your behaviour would truly vex her! She is still upset with you, you know!"

"I imagine… I am afraid she will never forgive me." Elizabeth smiled.

"No, indeed. Unless you marry someone much better than Mr. Collins—a task that should not be difficult to accomplish—someone with at least 5000 a year: a viscount or a handsome colonel, perhaps."

"Oh, you met the earl's sons." She laughed.

"I have indeed. Had I not known better, I would say Lord Matlock has decided to marry you into his family. Your mother would worship the earl if she heard him speaking. Perhaps I should write her—"

"Papa, please do not mock me with this! You must promise you will tell Mama nothing about the earl's jokes. I dare not imagine her agitation at such news!"

"Oh, you are too serious, Lizzy! You should allow me enough credit to know your mother's nerves intimately, and I never mock them. But I have to say, I felt quite proud to discover the earl's favourable opinion of you, my child."

"Lord Matlock is too kind. You know me well enough to realise he is exaggerating."

"He is exaggerating a little, I admit; yet it does not make me less proud of you. I am quite pleased to see that such illustrious people as Lord Matlock, Lady Selina and Miss Darcy are fond of you, Lizzy. Not to mention Mr. Darcy himself, who, I dare say, seems to have improved his opinion since that evening he refused to dance with you."

Mr. Bennet smiled tenderly at his daughter while a mischievous smile appeared on his face.

A cold shiver struck Elizabeth; she stared at her father, her mind unable to accept the meaning of his words. "What do you mean, Papa? Have you spoken with Mr. Darcy?"

"I most certainly have! Oh, I forgot to tell you—the strangest coincidence occurred: precisely a few minutes after I arrived at the earl's house, Mr. Darcy called! To be sure, I believed he would excuse himself and leave, but instead he declared himself pleased to see me and inquired about my arrival in town. Mr. Darcy himself, can you believe that?"

"Strange coincidence, indeed…" she whispered.

"But a fortunate one—very, very fortunate. You will not believe, Lizzy, how knowledgeable Mr. Darcy is in everything that involves estate business. I was overwhelmed; I must say I did not give much importance to Lord Matlock's suggestion yesterday—about asking for Mr. Darcy's support. But that young man is quite impressive, you know. He said he was confident things can improve at Longbourn in the future, and he was exceedingly amiable—unexpectedly amiable. Well, not quite like Mr. Bingley, but I have to confess, Mr Bingley can be quite annoying at times with his perpetually smiling expression. By the way, Lizzy, can you remind me why we disliked Mr. Darcy so much—in the past, I mean—because I have come to like him quite a lot in the last hours. I have to say I felt quite ashamed of myself for my poor opinion of him, not to mention that I had already expressed my scepticism to Lord Matlock yesterday. I hope he will not betray me to Mr. Darcy."

Elizabeth stared at her father—who had obviously enjoyed Lord Matlock's brandy a bit too much—and struggled to understand his words. There was no doubt that her father had spent no little time with Mr. Darcy, and despite his present euphoric state, Mr. Bennet's favourable report about the meeting could not be doubted.

Was it a coincidence that Mr. Darcy visited his uncle precisely when her father was there? Or not? Did she dare imagine too much?

"I would truly appreciate it if you could help me to my room now; I need to rest a little. I am not accustomed to leaving the house during the winter and—"

"And you are not accustomed to such fine, strong brandy, either." Elizabeth laughed, holding her father's arm.

"That, too," Mr. Bennet admitted. "Oh, I forgot to mention—Mr. Darcy might stop by later with some papers. He kindly offered to bring them to me himself. You know—another strange thing—he was somehow under the impression that you would be bothered by his appearance. How amusing! I know you are not too fond of the man, but why would you be bothered by his visit? Anyway, I assured him you would be more than pleased with his visit, so be so kind as to inform me when he arrives—and try to be a charming companion in the mean time. I know he once called you only tolerable, but it is excusable for someone who spends time burdened with business affairs to have poor taste in ladies' beauty. And do not be upset that he refused to dance with you. Believe me, dearest, if I were he, I would not dance with anyone at a country ball. Upon my word, I am not he, and I never liked to dance at country balls, not even when I was young!"

ELIZABETH CLOSED THE DOOR TO her father's chamber and leaned against the wall. He would stop by to bring her father some papers. What papers? Could he not send a courier? Of course, he could. Will he come in person? Surely, he knows that she will be at home. Was he willing to talk to her? If not, why come? What would he tell her? What should she tell him? She must thank him for taking the trouble to write the letter, and she must apologise for everything she said to him, but he should apologise, too. Was he aware that his behaviour was wrong? He must be, or else he would not bother to explain himself in such a long letter... and he would not be so kind to her father...and he would not come to visit her... Would he truly come?

An hour passed in turmoil and unanswered questions. Her aunt was taking care of the children, and Jane had not yet returned; she likely was having an enjoyable time with Georgiana, Lady Selina and Mr. Bingley. Dearest Jane—she deserved as much enjoyment as possible after the pain she bore for so long.

Elizabeth took up her needlework, but she was unable to attend to it; she then took a book and began to read without comprehending a single word.

When she heard the doorbell, her heart beat wildly as she sensed the visitor's name long before the servant announced him and invited him in.

"Miss Bennet." He bowed with perfect politeness, his uneasiness obvious.

"Mr. Darcy," she whispered, wondering whether he heard her.

"Please forgive my intrusion. I did not mean to interrupt you—"

"No intrusion, not at all. My father mentioned you might visit us."

"Mr. Bennet is at home?"

"Yes, he is. He is resting, but I will inform him you have arrived."

"He is well, I hope?"

"Yes, very well...just a little tired..."

"Then perhaps you should allow him to rest a little longer?"

She stopped in the middle of the room, puzzled, her cheeks burning again.

"And you? Are you well, Miss Bennet?"

"I...yes, thank you."

He was still standing, looking around uncomfortably. She suddenly remembered her duty.

"Please do sit down, sir. I mean...that is, if you are not in a hurry."

"No... Yes, thank you. I am in no hurry... Are you certain I am not disturbing you?"

"Very certain."

A moment of silence followed. They looked around, and their gazes met for a moment, then both averted their eyes.

124

"They are very important, I imagine…" she said.

"I beg your pardon?"

"The documents you brought for my father… They must be very important, or else you could have sent them."

"Would you have preferred I sent them rather than coming myself? Would that have been more comfortable for you?" Her face was warm, but she held his gaze a moment longer.

"No…not at all."

He paused a moment, and their eyes met again.

"The papers are not so important… I could have sent a courier, but I wished to come myself."

Her heart skipped a beat, and she felt the blood drain from her face. What did he mean?

"Thank you…" she whispered. "Thank you for helping my father; he told me that—"

"Miss Bennet!" he interrupted her abruptly. "I have been dishonest. I used these papers as an excuse to come here today without appearing ridiculous. But my real reason was the hope of finding a few moments to apologise, though no excuses would—"

"Mr. Darcy, it is I who should apologise… Everything I said… You must allow me to thank you for your trust…and for explaining to me… Your letter…"

"I cannot allow you to apologise because I cannot allow you to carry the blame. If not for my outrageous behaviour and my offensive attempt at…proposing, nothing would have happened… I should not have—"

"Sir, you cannot take all the blame upon yourself… I cannot deny that—"

They were only steps apart, and each seemed more preoccupied with speaking than listening. So caught were they in their argument, that they did not observe Mrs. Gardiner's entrance.

"Mr. Darcy! I thought I heard voices! Welcome! I am quite pleased to see you back in London. Are you well, I hope?"

He stared at his hostess, surprised by her appearance, and struggled to find words for the proper answer. Mrs. Gardiner smiled warmly, awaiting his reply.

"I am well, thank you. Please forgive my intrusion—"

"Oh, say nothing of that! We have been inquiring after you lately; your presence was deeply missed. We were hoping to see you soon—were we not, Lizzy?"

Elizabeth was caught by surprise, and she could not answer immediately.

"Yes, we were. I was just telling Mr. Darcy the same thing, and I was thanking him for his help and support regarding my father's business."

"Please sit down, sir," Mrs Gardiner invited him. "I sent a servant to fetch my brother Bennet. Lizzy, has Jane not yet returned? It is already dark, and it is snowing again…"

"I just met Miss Bennet earlier… I happened upon them… She was shopping with my sister and Selina. Bingley was keeping them company, so I am sure they are safe."

"Oh, I have no doubt they are safe. Mr. Bingley is very trustworthy." Mrs. Gardiner smiled.

"Yes he is… I… If I am not disturbing you, I shall wait for my sister and take her home when they arrive."

"That sounds like a lovely arrangement except that I cannot allow Miss Darcy to leave immediately; she must join us for a cup of tea, at least."

"And you, sir, must join me for a glass of wine," Mr. Bennet interrupted from the doorway. "Mr. Darcy, how kind of you to come! I am quite delighted to see you again! Are the papers ready so soon? I am afraid I have ruined your day entirely, sir…"

"Not at all… A glass of wine would be fine, Mr. Bennet. And in the meantime we can continue our earlier discussion." He glanced at Elizabeth then followed Mr. Bennet to the library. Elizabeth looked after them in disbelief.

EARLIER, ELIZABETH WAS TORN BETWEEN wishing and fearing that Mr. Darcy would visit, wondering how she could better apologise and afraid of how he might behave and what he might say to her. Now that he had come, everything she expected proved to be wrong.

She was certain he would be polite but cold, avoiding her as much as possible and speaking only as propriety required. Instead, he admitted he had come of his own will; he apologised, and appeared to be on amiable terms with her father. What was the meaning of it? Any man would be appalled to be in the company of the woman who had hurt him so deeply. He was embarrassed, that was true, but he did not seem appalled in the slightest.

Or was she misjudging his thoughts and his behaviour again as she had done so often in the past? But how could she misjudge the 'coincidence' of his appearing at his uncle's house precisely as her father was there? And what about all the help he willingly offered?

Half an hour later, her sister returned together with Miss Darcy and Mr. Bingley. All seemed in excellent spirits, and Elizabeth noticed that she had never seen the shy Jane and Georgiana so animated. Poor Mr. Bingley was completely lost to Jane.

After admiring the gifts Jane purchased for their sisters and their mother, Elizabeth offered to inform Mr. Darcy about their presence. Unable to conceal her impatience, she hurried to the library and timidly knocked on the door.

"Come in, Lizzy dear," Mr. Bennet invited her. "Mr. Darcy, now I think that perhaps we should have invited Lizzy to our discussion. You will not believe it, but my Lizzy is very proficient in business matters. If she were a son, all my problems would cease to exist, no doubt. Such a pity—though I confess I would not trade my Lizzy for five men."

There was no answer for a moment, so Elizabeth turned towards Darcy; their eyes met, and—to her utter shock—a smile lit his countenance.

"I... Mr. Bingley and Miss Darcy are here. I just wanted to inform you, sir."

"Thank you, Miss Bennet. I think it is time for us to depart."

"So soon? I confess I do not remember when I last had such a pleasant day, Mr. Darcy. Your company has been a rare luxury," said Mr. Bennet with genuine regret. "And your help is invaluable. I will not—"

"Mr. Bennet, the pleasure was mine, I assure you," Darcy interrupted the words of gratitude. "I hope we shall meet again tomorrow as we planned."

"Tomorrow we are invited to dinner...by Lord Matlock," Elizabeth said.

"So we are," Darcy replied. "But Mr. Bennet and I shall meet again tomorrow at noon."

"I would gladly take you, Lizzy, but Mr. Darcy invited me to his club, and I doubt you would be welcome there." Mr. Bennet laughed. "Besides, I am sure you have better things to do than discuss estate business—buying some lace, perhaps? Well, well, let us go then. I am sure my sister Gardiner has prepared dinner."

Sooner than later, the guests prepared to leave. With perfect politeness, Darcy thanked Mrs. Gardiner for her hospitality and apologised for staying so late. Mrs. Gardiner assured him his presence was most pleasant, and she thanked him for his help with Mr. Bennet's problems.

"Mr. Darcy, surely it is we who must thank you for spending your day with us," Mr. Bennet concluded. "Your help was as valuable as it was unexpected."

"I say, Darcy, yesterday Mr. Bennet was reluctant to approach you. Surely, he believed you to be some sort of ogre who would rather eat people alive than help them, which is not completely untrue." Mr. Bingley laughed.

Elizabeth was silent with mortification, staring at Mr. Bingley who seemed nothing but amused. Miss Darcy blushed slightly, casting an embarrassed glance at Elizabeth.

"Mr. Bingley, you seem to be in a joyful disposition, sir. Not that this is a surprise," Mr. Bennet replied. "However, Mr. Darcy, I shall not deny that Mr. Bingley is correct: considering our previous, brief acquaintance, I never would have dared bother you with my problems. I confess my previous opinion of you was...different."

"Do not trouble yourself, Mr. Bennet. Any opinion you might have had of me was surely correct, based on my behaviour in Hertfordshire. I am deeply sorry that I missed many opportunities to have a pleasant time—in Hertfordshire, I mean..."

"Well, do not be too upset, sir. In fact, perhaps it was for the best. Everybody was impressed with your ten thousand a year and your handsome appearance. If your behaviour had been half as pleasant as it was today, there would have been no escape for you. Every lady in the neighbourhood would have fallen for your charms—my wife included."

The most extraordinary thing happened: Mr. Darcy's face turned crimson as he dared to look at Elizabeth with a lost expression. Elizabeth laughed—an open, amused laugh, directed at him—which she tried unsuccessfully to stifle with her hand on her lips.

PREPARATION FOR THEIR RETURN TO Longbourn grew intense the next day. Mr. Bingley declared he would open Netherfield and the staff was informed to prepare for his arrival. He was not yet certain whether his sisters would join him, but even sweet Jane gave little consequence to that possibility.

After countless sleepless nights, Elizabeth woke with a feeling of intense relief and high spirits. She found herself smiling as she remembered Mr. Darcy's expression in the face of her father's teasing. He surely was unaccustomed to anyone making sport of him, but he did not seem upset.

She wondered more than once about her father's meeting with Mr. Darcy at his club. She knew that Mr. Darcy's attentions to her father were a compliment to her, and she felt equally flattered and ashamed; he was more generous than she deserved. The purpose of his politeness or his intention to continue their acquaintance she did not dare consider.

The day passed with easiness and eager anticipation for the upcoming dinner with Lord Matlock. In the afternoon, Mr. Bennet returned; Elizabeth hoped he might have company, but he entered alone. In a jovial disposition, he declared he had a lovely time with Mr. Darcy, the earl, and the colonel and declared he would rest before dinner.

It was already dark and had started to snow gently when the Gracechurch Street party arrived at Lord Matlock's house.

Their reception was as amiable as they expected; Lady Selina and her husband were present as well as Lady Brightmore, who was entertained by the colonel and Miss Darcy. The viscount was absent, as urgent business required his presence out of town for two days. From a corner, Mr. Darcy greeted them warmly but did not approach. Mr. Bennet was introduced to those who had not yet met him, and the conversation began easily.

"I hope Bingley is not late; I am already hungry," said Lady Brightmore.

"I am sure he will be here shortly. He is not late; we were early," Lady Selina replied.

"I know he will be late if he brings his sisters!"

"Mama! That was unkind!"

"Oh hush, Selina; you know I am right. I have known the Bingley siblings from infancy, and the girls grew up with pretensions of greatness, exactly like their mother. Old Bingley was a pleasant, hardworking man. It is fortunate that Charles has only the looks of his mother; in character, he is all his father. By the way, Jane dear, are you pleased that Bingley has returned? You positively look happier than I last saw you."

"Mama!" cried Lady Selina while Jane turned crimson.

"Selina, you are annoying today! Nothing is to your liking. What did I say?"

"Darcy also looks remarkably happier than the last time I saw him," said Lord Matlock, and Darcy almost choked on his wine. He stole a glance at Elizabeth, whose cheeks now matched her sister's, and after a short pause, he spoke to the earl.

"You are as perceptive as always, Uncle."

"Well, well—such a short, meaningful answer, Nephew. So, Miss Bennet, Miss Elizabeth, what about you. Are you happy or sad to return home?"

"That is not an easy question, your lordship," Elizabeth replied. "We are happy to see our mother and sisters and sad to leave our friends."

"Yes, yes—happiness is never easy," the earl concluded as the colonel began to laugh.

"I told you Bingley would be late because of his sisters," Lady Brightmore repeated, and Elizabeth brushed her fingers over her lips to cover a laugh. She lifted her eyes and saw Darcy's smiling eyes staring at her. She felt herself blushing, but she returned the smile, and for a moment, their gazes held.

"Well, well, you are finally here," Lord Matlock exclaimed as the newly arrived entered.

Elizabeth returned her attention to the room and saw Miss Bingley and Mrs. Hurst entering. Their appearance was faultless, as were their manners. They greeted everyone with perfect politeness and displayed their surprise at the new addition to the group.

"Mr. Bennet! Are you alone, or is your entire family in town?"

Mr. Bennet responded with a slight move of his head and an amused grin while Elizabeth replied sharply, forcing a smile.

"We thank you for your inquiry, Miss Bingley. My mother and younger sisters are still at Longbourn. But you will be pleased to see them on another occasion since Mr. Bingley is returning to Netherfield."

Miss Bingley reddened, but Mr. Bingley, oblivious to Elizabeth's irony, rhapsodised about living in Hertfordshire again. With every word, Jane shone while his sisters blanched. Elizabeth was content.

The dinner table was large enough to accommodate a great number of people. No formal arrangements were made, so Lady Brightmore demanded that Elizabeth sit by her. Miss Darcy took the remaining place beside Elizabeth while Jane sat near her aunt. Mr. Bingley needed only a moment to claim the free chair next to Jane.

Miss Bingley was thrilled to find herself at Mr. Darcy's left; however, that gentleman appeared more interested in Mr. Bennet, who was on his right. Nobody was as pleased as Mr. Bennet, who had the good fortune to sit between Mr. Darcy and the earl, and across the table from his favourite daughter.

"Miss Eliza, you are eager to return home, I understand? I imagine you are not accustomed to being in town for so long."

"I am eager to return home, indeed, Miss Bingley." She returned her attention to her plate.

"I hope you and Jane had a lovely time, but Meryton is not London, and it must be more daunting than pleasant to move from a Meryton assembly to a ball in London."

Georgiana turned pale while Darcy looked at Elizabeth, attempting to reply. Elizabeth smiled at him with calmness and amusement.

"You have no reason to worry, Miss Bingley. I had the benefit of illustrious company, which helped me overcome any difficulties."

"Oh, such nonsense!" Lady Brightmore intervened, enjoying a glass of wine. "Elizabeth was perfectly at ease at the ball; her only daunting task was to choose whom to dance with."

Miss Bingley stared at her for a moment then redirected her attention.

"My dear Georgiana, I dearly missed you lately. Have you been away?"

"No, I have been in town for the last month," Miss Darcy replied gently.

"Oh, such a shame! You did not come to see me at all. And I called a couple of times, but you were not at home! Where could you possibly go in such horrible weather?"

"I was out most of the time…" Miss Darcy replied uncomfortably.

"With the Miss Bennets," said Lady Selina. "In truth, since they arrived in town, I do not think there were two days in a row when we did not visit."

Lady Selina smiled while Miss Bingley's gaping mouth needed a long moment to close.

Dinner then passed pleasantly; afterwards, the earl invited the gentlemen to join him in the library while the ladies remained to amuse themselves.

More than once, Miss Bingley's rudeness irritated everyone but Elizabeth, to whom it was chiefly directed. Elizabeth struggled to remain calm since, no matter how undeserving both ladies proved to be, they were Mr. Bingley's sisters and —with God's will—would soon be family. Furthermore, Elizabeth now understood that Miss Bingley's insolence to her was due to jealousy. It was quite pitiful the way Miss Bingley struggled unsuccessfully for Mr. Darcy's attention.

"Caroline dear, you are a handsome woman but so annoying! Why do you keep fretting Elizabeth? For heaven's sake, no man will marry you if you continue to be bitter and mean." Lady Brightmore took a last gulp from her wine glass.

The ladies frowned, and Jane and Georgiana stared at each other in shock while Caroline Bingley pressed her chest, gasping for air, until her sister helped her sit.

"Miss Bingley, a little water will help," Mrs. Gardiner said gently, handing her a glass, and Lady Selina declared it was time for the gentlemen to return—and hurried to fetch them.

As the next day was the last before their departure, the long-planned sleigh ride was anticipated. Elizabeth wanted to ask Miss Darcy whether her brother would join them. It was a daring presumption, considering the circumstances. Besides, the thought of spending time in relative privacy with Mr. Darcy was not at all comfortable for her, so perhaps it would be for the best if he did not come. However, if he were willing to come, it would not be fair of her to reject the idea —that is, if he were informed about the sleigh ride at all.

"I say, Mr. Bennet, you must admit I was right in suggesting you ask for Darcy's help," said the earl, enjoying his brandy. "Upon my word, this young man is the best landlord I know—I dare say even better than his father!"

"Uncle, you are too kind, and your praise is generous but undeserved. Let us change the subject." Mr. Darcy seemed completely uncomfortable as he briefly glanced at Elizabeth. She looked at him, intrigued, wondering at the disappearance of the proud, aloof man whose cold look of superior contempt would intimidate anyone who might happen near him.

"If I may be so bold as to give *you* advice, you should learn to bear praise better, Mr. Darcy, especially when you deserve it," said Mr. Bennet.

"Darcy, are you coming with us tomorrow? In the sleigh? I mean—it is your sleigh, after all," Mr. Bingley inquired, and for a moment, Mr. Darcy seemed pleased with the change of subject. Yet, the new one made him equally uneasy as Mr. Darcy looked at his friend and then at Elizabeth. When he met her inquiring gaze, he averted his eyes for a moment.

"Oh, Brother, you cannot miss such an opportunity. The weather is lovely, and we will all be together. You must come!" Miss Darcy said, animatedly.

"I would be happy to join you, but I have another engagement..."

Elizabeth's struggle to keep her countenance was unsuccessful; she acutely felt the regret, and only that moment did she admit her wishes: she wanted and hoped that he would come. She was furious with herself for allowing him to see her disappointment, as she was certain he did not miss it. He had other engagements... Of course...

"I invited Mr. Bennet to visit. It seems that we share a passion for books, and he was eager to see my library. I... He will be my guest tomorrow. Otherwise, I would be pleased to keep you company. I hope you have a lovely ride."

Elizabeth raised her eyes, hardly believing her ears. That was his 'engagement'?

"And, as I can imagine how frozen you will be after the ride," he said as Elizabeth blushed violently, remembering his hands warming hers, "I shall await you all with hot tea and refreshments."

"Very well, I guess that is as perfect as it can be," Mr. Bingley concluded. "I have just one request: may I have a glass of your fine brandy instead of that hot tea?"

Miss Bingley declined the invitation at the revelation that Mr. Darcy would not participate in a silly sleigh ride—what nonsense; it surely must be Eliza's idea! The others would never consider spending half the day in freezing weather, so Mr. Bingley remained the only gentleman to keep company with the Bennet sisters and Miss Darcy.

Half an hour later, the earl reminded both Elizabeth and Georgiana of their promise to play and sing together. He was surprised that his shy, restrained niece accepted without hesitation. She took Elizabeth's hand, and they stepped together to the piano, followed by Darcy's insistent gaze.

The earl looked closely at his nephew; he was surprised to see Darcy wear an expression of warm delight on his face when he looked at Miss Elizabeth. His restrained nephew never bestowed such a tender gaze upon any young lady except Georgiana. Despite any quarrel Darcy might have had with Miss Elizabeth a couple of weeks earlier and any disagreements they might have had in the past, they seemed perfectly capable of reconciling them.

The earl was exceedingly pleased with himself; he had been correct when he asked his sons to abandon any attempt to court either of the Miss Bennets. It was simply not meant to be. From their first acquaintance, he was aware that neither of his sons was appropriate for his favourite Bennet sister.

DARCY PACED THE LIBRARY, CAREFUL not to disturb his guest.

He briefly looked at Mr. Bennet and could not restrain a smile; the elder gentleman seemed under a spell from the moment he entered the library. He had spent long moments in front of each shelf, perusing every book and tentatively touching rare editions as if he were afraid he might damage them. Darcy had encouraged him to borrow any book in which he might be interested. Mr. Bennet thanked him heartily, but Darcy felt ashamed, as he knew he had another motive for encouraging Mr. Bennet to borrow books: a justifiable reason to visit the Bennets...and soon.

Mr. Bennet's presence and company made Darcy feel ashamed for other reasons, too. He had lived in Hertfordshire for quite some time and never bothered to begin even a superficial conversation with Mr. Bennet. He judged him an indifferent father and husband, unable to control his wife and younger daughters, and occasionally displaying improper behaviour—a simple, country gentleman who did not deserve Darcy's interest.

When they first met in London, Darcy had no genuine interest in Mr. Bennet. He was Elizabeth's father and needed help; his problems were also Elizabeth's problems. He made the effort to spend time with the gentleman only for her—to prove to her that he could be a different man than she accused him of being.

However, he soon discovered the real Mr. Bennet: a well-read gentleman, full of wit and humour, sensible and perceptive, and capable of amusement at his own expense as much as at others'. He enjoyed spending time with Mr. Bennet, whom he was earlier incapable of recognising due to his selfish pride—exactly as Elizabeth had described him.

Then she seemed somehow to forgive him. She behaved quite friendly— though a little embarrassed—during the first moments they met. She tried to apologise and to thank him for his help, and she even smiled at him a few times. The day before when they spoke of the sleigh ride: was she disappointed he did not attend? She seemed so, but again—he could not depend on his judgement about anything regarding Elizabeth Bennet.

She would leave the next day, but he felt somewhat relieved; more than two weeks had passed since his dreadful proposal, and they seemed able to forgive each other and to maintain a polite acquaintance, though that was not enough for him. Since the moment he saw her again and she smiled at him, he knew it was not enough. His feelings had not changed in the slightest, but the future would depend on her feelings and wishes alone.

Perhaps it was for the best that she returned home. She needed time: time to forgive him and perhaps to forget his worst behaviour. Someday she might allow him to speak to her again...about his wishes and desires...

In a short time, she would be in his house again. He could picture her appearance: her eyes sparkling with exercise, her cheeks red and chilled, her hair shining from the snow, and her hands cold and trembling...

Mr. Bennet's voice brought him back to reality, inquiring about the provenance of a book. They began to discuss it, and Darcy asked his guest whether any of his daughters shared his passion for books. For the next half hour, Mr. Bennet delighted his host with anecdotes about his favourite daughter—Lizzy—and her love for books. Mr. Darcy declared with complete honesty that he had not had such a pleasant time in a while.

Mr. Bennet returned to his book, and Darcy left the library to speak with Mrs. Spencer. The doorbell and the din of voices were clear signs of his guests' arrival. Darcy greeted them at the door and smiled. They looked exactly as he expected.

Miss Bennet was slightly flustered and obviously very cold, but her appearance was as impeccable as ever.

His sister and Miss Elizabeth were another story; he could easily guess that they had spent time out of the sleigh as the hems of their gowns were frozen and their shoulders were heavy with iced snow.

Mrs. Spencer hurried to Georgiana while Mr. Bingley helped Jane to remove her coat.

"Oh dear child, look at you! Your bonnet and your coat are completely frozen; I cannot even unbutton it! You will not be pleased unless you catch a cold, upon my word!"

Miss Darcy laughed while she bore the reproaches.

"Oh, I am fine; Elizabeth is much worse—just look at her! She lost her mittens in the snow, and she cannot even move her fingers! And I fell when we got down from the sleigh, and she tried to help me, but we fell together!"

"It is not nice to throw me in the middle, Miss Darcy," Elizabeth laughed.

"It is not nice, indeed," Mr. Darcy replied, moving closer until he was only a step away. Elizabeth lifted her eyes and met his; suddenly, she felt exceedingly warm.

"Please allow me, Miss Bennet," he said, and before she had time to answer, he began to unbutton her coat. She frowned. He gently removed her coat and his palms lingered on her shoulders a moment longer, then his fingers began to untie her bonnet. She scarcely breathed. The ribbon was wet and frozen, and he needed real skill to unloosen it. Each movement of his fingers brushed and warmed the skin of her neck. She never felt the touch of a man's hand before, and she never imagined it might arouse such feelings inside her. Her heart beat so wildly that she was certain he could hear it. He continued to struggle with the ribbon until he finally defeated it. She closed her eyes and felt him remove the bonnet, then he gently brushed the snowflakes from her hair. She grimaced when his hands took hers and gently squeezed them. She needed to sit, as she was not the master of her strength any longer.

"You are chilled through, Miss Elizabeth. Come, we must remove your shoes, too," he said, and his voice made her tremble. Surely, he cannot mean that—

"Mrs. Spencer, please take my sister and Miss Elizabeth to Georgiana's room. I trust you will do everything that is needed to make them dry and warm."

"Do not worry, sir. If you allow me full responsibility and insist they both listen to me…"

"You are fully responsible, and we all will follow your advice on this matter," Mr. Darcy replied with perfect seriousness while Mrs. Spencer quickly directed them both upstairs.

Only then did Elizabeth realise that Mr. Darcy was still holding her hands.

The guests reunited in the living room as soon as Elizabeth's gown was dry, and hours flew in pleasant conversation. Mr. Bingley and Jane sat close to each other on the settee, while Elizabeth and Miss Darcy each took a chair near the fire. Mr. Darcy took another chair a short distance away.

The warmth of the fire and the hot tea turned Elizabeth's cheeks crimson, and they kept their colour for some time.

THE MORNING OF THEIR DEPARTURE for Hertfordshire proved to be more difficult than expected. The earl's family, together with Miss Darcy, came for a last, short visit, and their regrets were all genuine and heartfelt as was their acceptance of Mr. Bingley's invitation to visit Netherfield. Miss Darcy asked Elizabeth to write her as soon as she arrived home, and it was decided that their correspondence would be regular and detailed.

Elizabeth dared not ask about Mr. Darcy, though his absence was equally surprising and disappointing. The earl informed her that Darcy was already out when he stopped to fetch Georgiana, so it was likely he had some urgent business. Of course he had, she admitted. After all, he could not be expected to neglect his business just to say good-bye after he had spent the entire previous day with them.

The guests departed, and the three Bennets awaited Mr. Bingley. The gentleman was kind enough to take them in his carriage, as it was large enough to accommodate at least six persons, and his sisters decided to extend their stay in town. He finally appeared—well spirited, ready for the trip and closely followed into the house by Mr. Wickham. Elizabeth frowned while Mr. Bingley spoke animatedly.

"Are you ready? You are, as I can see! Well, allow my men to take the luggage. Oh, did you see Mr. Wickham? Can you imagine the coincidence? I happened to meet him on my way here; he was about to return to Meryton today by post! I invited him to join us. I was sure Miss Elizabeth would be pleased."

"Mr. Bennet, Miss Bennet, Miss Elizabeth, I would by no means disturb you. Please tell me if my presence is an inconvenience; I can very well travel by post."

"Oh, nonsense, we can use another man— if only for helping us if we get stuck on the way. Strange coincidence indeed—have you been in town all this time?" inquired Mr. Bennet.

Elizabeth's head was spinning, and she was tempted to ask her father to reject Mr. Wickham's presence. What was he doing there? She was certain it was no coincidence; only Mr. Bingley's kind heart could believe such a poor excuse. How did Wickham discover they were about to return home? And what was his purpose in joining them? She was about to enter the carriage when her father's voice stopped her.

"Mr. Darcy! So good to see you, sir! Another minute and you would have missed us!"

Elizabeth stared at Darcy, and she could not conceal her joy at seeing him—nor did she wish to. She smiled at him, and he greeted her with a polite bow and warm smile. A moment later, his countenance paled and his eyes turned dark and cold.

"Darcy...what a surprise to see you," said Mr. Wickham, but Darcy turned to Mr. Bennet, completely ignoring Wickham.

"I am glad I arrived in time, Mr. Bennet. I wish you good bye and a safe trip home."

"Thank you. I hope we shall see you soon in Hertfordshire."

"I… I am not certain yet, but I shall inform you...Bingley, I mean…"

"Darcy, you know you are always welcome—no need to inform anyone. You may come when you please!" said Mr. Bingley.

"Arrange to come when you are least expected, Mr. Darcy." Mr. Bennet laughed. "I know I am doing so, and it is much more amusing."

"I shall try to follow your advice," Mr. Darcy attempted to joke with little success.

Elizabeth was still not able to move. She looked at Darcy, searching for a way to dissipate the sadness from his face. What might he think to see Wickham there? And she would not have the chance to speak to him and explain...

"Miss Elizabeth, have a safe trip home," he whispered and turned to leave.

"Mr. Darcy!" She did not allow her mind to consider properly what she intended to do. "Sir, if you have a moment, there is a matter of some urgency that I would discuss with you. I forgot to tell Georgiana earlier, and—"

He moved a step back, surprised and puzzled. She looked around; Wickham and her father were only a few steps away, but she needed to speak to him.

"Miss Elizabeth, it is quite late and cold, and it has started to snow again. You should not stay outside …" Wickham intervened.

"It is cold indeed," said Mr. Bennet as he entered the carriage. "Lizzy, you should go inside and speak to Mr. Darcy if you wish. But no more than a moment; we must leave!"

"A moment will be enough," she said, and with a quick glance at Darcy, she returned to the house. Darcy followed her. In the main hall, they stared at each other: he, wondering what urgent matter must be said, and she, struggling to begin.

"Mr. Darcy, I just wish to assure you that I carefully read your letter," she tentatively began, and his puzzlement only increased. *The letter?*

"I would like to thank you—again—for your trust and to assure you that there is no need for the colonel to testify on your behalf. I do not doubt a single word of that letter, and everything you had the kindness to tell me was taken to heart. I have been wrong in my first impression of certain people, but that is all corrected now."

He finally understood. He looked at her in silence, and then he tried to force a smile.

"What is Wickham doing here? Forgive me, I know I have no right to inquire, but believe me, my reason is only your safety—and your family's, of course."

"He just arrived… He pretended he planned to return to Meryton and met Mr. Bingley by chance. Of course, Mr. Bingley had no other choice than to invite him to join us."

"It was no coincidence; nothing is a coincidence with Wickham."

"I am well aware of that and"—she put her hand on his arm— "I thank you for your concern, sir. It is much appreciated but I dare say unnecessary. My father and Mr. Bingley will be there. What could happen?"

"You are correct, of course… Would you… Georgiana would be happy to receive a letter from you as soon as you arrive home."

"And I shall be happy to write it. I must leave now. Would you assist me to the carriage?"

"Certainly." Her hand was still on his arm, and he gently covered it with his own. They carefully stepped down the main stairs and approached the carriage.

Inside, Jane and her father were on one seat with Mr. Bingley and Wickham opposite them. The latter opened the carriage door.

"Miss Elizabeth, take my hand," he said, making room for her to sit near him.

"I thank you, but I already have Mr. Darcy's hand," she said as she sat by her sister.

When she was in, Mr. Darcy's hand was still holding hers. She glanced at him and saw his face lit by an attempt to smile. "Thank you, Mr. Darcy."

"You are most welcome. Have a safe trip, and please convey my greetings to your family." He then closed the carriage door and remained in front of Mrs. Gardiner's house, following the carriage with a worried gaze until it disappeared from sight.

Inside the carriage, Elizabeth closed her eyes, and for the first hour, she spoke very little, pretending to sleep. She could hear Mr. Bingley and Jane talking, and her father intervening from time to time. More than once, she recognised Mr. Wickham's animated, amused voice, mentioning Mr. Darcy's name—once, twice, three times…then again.

Elizabeth could not be certain how much time had passed before Mr. Bennet decided to interrupt Wickham's discourse.

"Mr. Wickham, I greatly appreciate your talent at entertaining us with little, amusing stories of your misfortunes. However, if you say another word against Mr. Darcy, I shall ask Mr. Bingley to drop you at the next inn. Travelling by post is not so bad, after all…"

Chapter 12

There was no doubt that Mrs. Bennet missed her daughters dearly and was content to see them back home, but nothing could compare with her happiness at the sight of Mr. Bingley. It was without doubt Mrs. Bennet's best day in many years.

Elizabeth felt relieved that Mr. Bingley was an amiable and tolerant gentleman, or else he would have hastily departed for Netherfield. Instead, he expressed his delight in seeing Mrs. Bennet again and eagerly accepted her impromptu invitation for dinner, as he could appreciate the advantage of a meal in the midst of pleasant company versus dining alone.

As soon as she retired to the comfort of her room, Elizabeth remembered her promise to write Miss Darcy—not that she would have forgotten for a moment. Nor could she forget Mr. Darcy's insistent gaze when he gently suggested she inform them as soon as she arrived safely. He was worried for her—that was obvious! He was worried, caring and understanding, and he seemed elated that she had read his letter and trusted it. Surely, she could do as much as to write his sister a short letter immediately.

A sharp knock on her door interrupted her, and she was surprised to see her father requesting entrance.

"Certainly, Papa! What is it?"

"It is about Wickham. I know he was your favourite, but he really irritated me. I sense a sort of duplicity in his behaviour, and I truly dislike his continuous references to how badly Darcy persecuted him. It has become quite tedious. I could tolerate him reasonably well in the past when I had the liberty of retiring to my library, but I found it impossible to bear him in a small carriage. I hope I was not offensive; I would not wish to spoil your pleasure of dancing with him in the future."

She felt her cheeks warm with embarrassment, and she forced a laugh. "I thank you for your concern, Father. I am sure I will manage at the next ball even if I have no partner. I think your words to Mr. Wickham were well deserved. I used to consider Mr. Wickham a friend, but that changed some time ago. I am ashamed to admit that I was wrong in my first impression of his character."

"Good—for a while, I was worried that you resembled your mother and youngest sisters more than I would like. My mind is at ease. I think I shall go and rest a little. Oh, I forgot—please do me a favour and send a letter to Mr. Darcy."

"Excuse me? I cannot write a letter to Mr. Darcy! Papa, are you teasing me?"

"Oh come, Lizzy, do not be missish. Just drop him a few words in my name to inform him we arrived safely and apologise that I cannot write him myself. My eyes hurt, and I am in no mood to write, but I think I owe him as much. He was considerate to come and say good-bye, and I appreciate his concern; he seemed genuinely worried about our trip. I tell you, that young man is a continual surprise to me. He is uncommonly kind and friendly, considering our brief acquaintance."

"Very well, Papa. In truth, I was about to write Georgiana, so I suppose I could send a short note for Mr. Darcy, too."

"Thank you, my child." He took a few steps and then suddenly returned. "By the way, Lizzy, I am quite curious—what was the urgent thing you wanted to tell Mr. Darcy? If it is not too great a secret…"

She froze and for a moment was lost for words. She stared at her father, both waiting. She bit her lower lip, desperately seeking a convenient answer.

"I… It was not such a great secret but…I did not want Mr. Wickham to hear us."

"Oh?" Mr. Bennet's puzzlement mixed with apparent interest.

"I…I have to confess that Mr. Darcy and I spoke quite a lot while I was in London…and we talked a little about Mr. Wickham. Mr. Darcy kindly offered me a bit of information that helped me to understand that Mr. Wickham's easy cordiality is not always genuine. And…when Mr. Darcy saw Mr. Wickham in our carriage, I was certain he would be displeased…and I thought he deserved to know that I did not take his words lightly and it was not I—we—who invited Mr. Wickham to join our group."

"I see…well, well—such a surprise. Not Wickham—I could have told you the same without knowing the details—but Mr. Darcy talking to you about Wickham. I would not expect that, considering he seems to be a very private man. I think you did well in speaking to him before our departure if only because your secret conversation made Wickham angry! So amusing, truly! I shall go to sleep now. Please remember to write Mr. Darcy, though I somehow doubt there will be any danger of your forgetting."

He left with a last glance at his daughter; by that time, Elizabeth was sitting in the chair, silent again and positively flustered. Mr. Bennet felt too tired to think properly of everything he just discovered, but there would be time in the next few days. He felt more pleased and lively than he had been in many years.

Elizabeth finished her letter to Georgiana and folded it carefully. Then she took another sheet and breathed deeply before she started.

Mr. Darcy,

Allow me to convey my father's apologies for being unable to write this letter himself and to inform you that we have arrived home safely after an uneventful trip. Everything was perfectly fine on the road as well as at Longbourn, and we kindly thank you for your concern.

She read the short note and found it cold and impersonal, but she did not dare write anything more private. Yet, if she were to receive such a letter, she would be disappointed. She thought for a bit, put the paper aside, then took it again and added:

You must not worry that my father did not write this letter personally. He is quite well; his eyes are just a little tired from the delightful effort of enjoying, during the entire trip, one of the books you kindly loaned him. I am afraid he is a little too eager to finish each book as soon as possible in order to move on to the next, an eagerness quite easy to understand.

I thank you for offering my father this opportunity as well as for all of your help.

Sincerely,
Elizabeth Bennet

She read it once more and folded it immediately, afraid that she might change her mind. A moment later, she handed both letters to John to be sent as soon as possible.

Darcy had dined alone with his sister countless times, but that night the silence seemed heavier. Neither of them appeared interested in conversation, and as soon as the meal was finished, he retired to his study while Georgiana returned to her rooms.

Darcy was pacing his office impatiently. Many things required his attention, but he could concentrate on none of them. His mind was completely occupied remembering his last conversation with Elizabeth—her last smiles, her hand resting in his, her sharp replies to Wickham, her daring invitation to speak to him privately in the presence of her own father…

She had courage and determination, and her gesture had more meaning than he first understood. She had willingly broken with propriety for his benefit only; she had nothing to gain from their brief conversation, but she insisted upon it for his sake. She guessed his distress when he saw Wickham, and she was concerned enough to seek a way to dissipate it. She also discovered a means to express her opinion about the letter and to assure him of her confidence in his words. She did all those things for him—because she cared for him! There could be no other reason!

He dared not consider the nature of her caring for him nor ask himself whether she would ever offer him the opportunity to propose again. Those were questions whose answer was yet to be found. Nevertheless, he was certain that her poor opinion of him had improved. She no longer hated him, nor was she indifferent to his feelings and concerns. Whether that happened because of the letter, because of her father's partiality for him, or because of her attachment to his sister, he could not be certain nor even speculate. He was content that, at least, he was given another chance to prove he was worthy of her good opinion. He knew it was more than he hoped in the last weeks and more than he deserved.

Until the last moment, he unwisely considered returning to Netherfield with Bingley, and if only his wishes were considered, he would have done it. However, there were two persons more important than himself whose well-being was his main concern: Georgiana and Elizabeth. He knew his sister would be happy at Netherfield, if only to be close to Elizabeth, but Wickham's proximity required supplementary measures in order to protect Georgiana. As for Elizabeth—he knew he was too insistent in forcing the acquaintance with Mr. Bennet and frequently imposing himself in the Gardiners' house during the past three days. Moreover, by helping Mr. Bennet with business advice, he was aware that he had obliged Elizabeth to behave politely towards him, even had she wanted to distance herself. Making an appearance at Netherfield—when surely Bingley spent most of his time at Longbourn—would put him in Elizabeth's path again, and she would have little choice but to accept his presence whether she liked him or not. It was fortunate that her feelings for him seemed to be changing; there was no reason to force her trust. Therefore, he decided it was impossible to join Bingley at Netherfield for the time being.

However, when he saw Wickham's impertinent face and discovered his mischievous scheme to impose himself in Bingley's carriage, his previous resolution dissipated; for a moment, he was decided to go to Netherfield with them. Happily, he needed little time to realise how ridiculous such a gesture would be—and even happier, Elizabeth guessed his struggle and put an end to it with a few wise words and a smile.

Yet, he had no rest as he lay on his bed; countless thoughts spun in his head as he wondered what Wickham's plans might be.

The next day, after a silent breakfast and a brief chat about their plans for the day, Georgiana inquired how long it would take for a letter to arrive from Longbourn.

"I am sure the letter will arrive as soon as possible. I think it would be helpful if you visit Selina while you wait for news."

"Perhaps I will. And I plan to stop at Mrs. Gardiner's for a tea. She invited me."

"Excellent. I am sure you will have an agreeable time, dearest."

Darcy returned to his library while Georgiana prepared for the day. Half an hour later, Colonel Fitzwilliam made a welcome appearance.

"Darcy, I came to take you to the club. Father and Thomas are already there."

"I am not certain I can interrupt what I am working on—"

"Nonsense. Get your coat; there is not the slightest chance I will leave without you."

"You seem in an excellent disposition, Cousin."

"No more than usual. How are you, Darcy? And Georgiana?"

"She is visiting Selina—and Mrs. Gardiner, I think. So, I understand you were assigned to fetch me. Are you being punished for something?"

"So amusing—I am glad to see you so well humoured." The colonel looked at Darcy briefly. "You did not sleep well. Any thoughts keeping you awake?"

"Quite a lot."

"Will you share them?"

"Not likely."

The colonel laughed as Darcy took his coat, and they left the house together. Only when they were inside the carriage did Darcy speak.

"Yesterday I went to say goodbye to the Bennets. I had some business in the morning, so I arrived only a few minutes before they left."

The colonel smiled to himself, tempted to ask his cousin why he did not leave with them. However, Darcy's countenance was too serious for mockery.

"And? Did anything happen? You seem worried."

"Wickham was there. Apparently, he just happened upon Bingley that morning, and he was also on his way to Meryton. So Bingley asked him to join them."

"Wickham? Did you not say he was in Meryton? How long was he here?"

"Wickham was in town for almost a month. He resided at Mrs. Younge's as usual."

"How do you know that? Do you have people watching him?"

"Once he had the impudence to cross paths with me in Meryton. I wanted no more surprises from him, so I took appropriate measures."

"I see… But what the hell is the scoundrel doing around the Bennets? And what is wrong with Bingley? He should know better than to befriend Wickham!"

"Bingley knows too little about Wickham to avoid him; you cannot blame him. And you know how insistent Wickham can be when he has something to gain."

"Do you believe Wickham just wished to benefit from a ride at no charge? He is well capable of that. So it has nothing to do with the Bennets?"

"You cannot believe me so naïve; surely it was no coincidence. Unfortunately, I can only speculate what his interest might be." Darcy remained silent as the colonel waited.

"Well? What speculations? What do you suspect?"

The answer did not come easily, and the colonel needed to repeat his impatient question.

"Wickham has a… From the beginning, he showed an interest in Miss Elizabeth."

"Oh come, you cannot be serious! I am quite charmed by Miss Elizabeth, but we must honestly admit that her situation does not recommend her as one of Wickham's usual targets. She must have a small dowry, if any."

"You are not wrong in that; I am not certain about Wickham's interest, but surely he does not intend to trap her into marriage."

"I am not in the slightest worried about other kinds of interests he might have. Miss Elizabeth Bennet would eat him alive if he dared exercise his charms with her! Even an idiot like him must see she is not a woman to trifle with."

Darcy hesitated a moment. "Miss Elizabeth is a very young and...genuine lady. It would not be impossible for her to be deceived and... Nevertheless, that is not the issue here. I have not the smallest doubt that she never would do anything improper. Besides..." He hesitated again then cast a quick glance at his cousin. "I had an opportunity to speak with her about a number of things and...I told her of my past dealings with Wickham."

The colonel stared in shock. "You mean—about Georgiana and Ramsgate? Why would you do such a thing? Do you think that was wise?"

"It was necessary. Do not worry; I trust Miss Elizabeth's secrecy completely."

"You trust her more than your own relatives?"

"I do not... I would not say that. The situation was a special one. I struggled over the decision for some time, and I believe I was not wrong. Please let it be. And about Wickham: let us hope his only interest was to pinch a free ride to Meryton."

"But how the hell did he know that Bingley planned to return to Hertfordshire?"

Darcy's countenance became even sterner, and his uneasiness increased.

"Robert, there is no one I trust more than you, and I see no other way to tell you that... I am sorry to upset you but...I am afraid the earl might have informed Wickham."

"My father? Surely, you are joking! My father is not even aware Wickham was in town."

"Uncle is well aware of Wickham's presence in town. He even met Wickham a few times." They looked at each other, both embarrassed by the subject.

"I am truly sorry, Darcy. I do not know what to say. You know my father means well but... his attachment to Wickham seems... I am stunned. I am certain he kept silent in order not to bother us; you know he never would favour Wickham over you. His affection for you...

"I do not doubt the earl's affection for me or my family, and I will not hold against him his inclination towards Wickham. After all, my own father favoured him more than he deserved. I would just wish that uncle saw more in Wickham's behaviour..."

"Darcy, I do not mean to sound rude, but perhaps you should trust my father as much as you trusted Miss Elizabeth. You should tell him everything about Ramsgate."

"I shall consider the entire situation carefully. Let us speak no more about it for now."

They finally arrived at the club where Lord Matlock and Lord Brightmore were expecting them. The rest of the day passed in pleasant conversation until two gentlemen of middle age approached their table.

"Lord Sinclair, it is good to see you!" said the earl. "How long have you been in town? We were told you were with a hunting party."

"The pleasure is mine, Lord Matlock. Darcy, Colonel, Brightmore... Yes, I was in the country, and I would have preferred to stay there, but my wife insisted we return. She complained of feeling lonely and bored, so I had little choice. I wish she would find something to amuse her. I am not in the mood to attend balls and parties. Women are quite tiresome sometimes, but that is the price one must pay for having a young wife." He laughed loudly.

"True... Will you stay longer? I hope you will join me for a glass of brandy one day."

"I would be delighted. By the way, I did not forget about your invitation to hunt at your estate. As soon as spring arrives, I shall remind you."

"No hunting party would be complete without you, Sinclair."

Lord Sinclair departed with a last greeting, and Lord Matlock laughed to his companions.

"Well, boys, you heard the man: he must find a way to keep Lady Sinclair amused."

"Do not count on me; I care only for my wife's entertainment." Lord Brightmore laughed. "Other young women should be the responsibility of unmarried men."

"I might attempt to help, but I do not trust I will accomplish much," the colonel replied. "On the other hand, no one can doubt Darcy's success, had he ever bothered to try."

Their amusement was a contrast to Darcy's severe countenance.

"Robert, your comment is quite rude and I would be grateful if that is the last time you bring up such an improper subject. You know that kind of joke appals me—now more than ever."

"Nephew, do not be upset; you know we are only joking. But you are right, as usual. Even Mrs. Gardiner scolded us; we should have listened to her."

"What do you mean, Uncle? When did Mrs. Gardiner scold you?" Darcy inquired.

"Oh, during the ball." Lord Brightmore laughed. "We made some improper comments about you and Lady Sinclair. Mrs. Gardiner censured us most deservedly."

"You discussed this matter in the presence of Mrs. Gardiner? Were...were either of the Miss Bennets there?" Lord Matlock thought he had never seen his nephew so pale.

"Miss Elizabeth was," Lord Brightmore replied. "But she has an excellent sense of humour. I am certain she was not upset—slightly embarrassed, perhaps, but not upset."

"You cannot presume to know how Miss Elizabeth felt," Darcy said harshly. "And you surely cannot presume to know how I feel—or any others you make sport of."

"Darcy, there is no reason to be angry with us. We were only—"

"Uncle, perhaps it would be better if you considered your words and your actions before they hurt people instead of trying to justify your misbehaviour afterwards. Forgive me; I have no disposition to continue this conversation. I shall see you all soon. Good evening."

He withdrew hastily, leaving his companions in complete bewilderment. Outside, facing the wind and snow, he breathed deeply, trying to gather his thoughts. He needed to walk, and his carriage followed along. It was dark and cold, but he felt only his own turmoil.

The ball—yes, that happened before his disastrous proposal. She had heard his relatives teasing about him and a certain lady—a married one—the one with whom he was dancing. He could now remember clearly her stern expression as he danced with Eve Sinclair. And the next day he proposed to Elizabeth, and she believed he intended to... No wonder she rejected him in such a way!

The next morning during breakfast, a footman arrived with two letters. Georgiana eagerly opened hers, declared it was from Elizabeth then ran to her room.

Darcy glanced at his sister's letter, envying her the opportunity of receiving news from Elizabeth. Then he returned his attention to his own envelope, which he hoped was from Mr. Bennet, and his heart skipped a beat; the writing on his letter was similar to that on Georgiana's. Surely, it was not possible that—

He took his letter to the library and closed door behind him. With tentative fingers, he opened it, and his eager eyes travelled along the paper. He read it repeatedly, each time discovering different meanings in the words, which he did not dare trust.

The last part of the letter seemed to have been written from her rather than Mr. Bennet; it was not necessary for the news she intended to share, but she wrote it nevertheless. And she thanked him—with perfectly proper words—but there was a warmth that came through the cold paper, and he did not miss it.

He held the letter to his chest, closed his eyes and leaned against the armchair. Alone in his library, in the darkness lit only by the fire, Darcy smiled.

ELIZABETH WAITED FOR MISS DARCY's letter with a good deal of eagerness, though she knew she should not expect special news. However, the first letter she received was from Charlotte, who found many things to relate about her peaceful happiness in Kent and all the satisfactory arrangements, including Lady Catherine's kindness. Elizabeth read it in a hurry and put it down; she loved Charlotte dearly, but she could not bear the details about a pretended happy marriage with Mr. Collins. It was simply too much.

Charlotte continued to insist that she should visit them in Kent, but Elizabeth was sceptical about accepting such an invitation. She felt a sort of curiosity, which she admitted to be highly improper, regarding Miss Anne de Bourgh, but it was not enough for her to make such a long visit to Rosings.

Two days later, the letter from Georgiana arrived with another letter for Mr. Bennet from Mr. Darcy himself. After she read Georgiana's letter several times, a servant asked her to the library. To her surprise, her father invited her to enter and handed her a piece of paper.

"This is for you, Lizzy. It is a short note from Mr. Darcy. He put it inside my letter, opened, so I could see its contents. Very considerate of him, do you not think?"

She felt her cheeks flaming, and her lips suddenly became dry; she could not think properly of all the implications of such a gesture. He wrote to her and asked her father's permission to do so? Did he realise what that could mean?

"Thank you, Papa, I shall go to my room," she said hastily, and her father smiled as he turned the page of his book.

Once inside her chamber, Elizabeth lay on the bed as she ran her eyes over the letter. She laughed nervously, remembering Miss Bingley's comment about the evenness of his writing.

Miss Bennet,

Thank you for your considerate message. I am pleased to know your journey went as well as I hoped.

I am also pleased that Mr. Bennet enjoys the books, but as I informed him personally, there is no reason to hurry—he may keep the books as long as he wishes. I trust he will take as good care of them as I would. I shall look forward to sharing opinions with Mr. Bennet regarding this subject some time very soon.

I shall give to my sister the pleasure of filling her letter with all the details of our last days in London. I am sure she will tell you that it snowed again and that she deeply regrets she missed the opportunity to skate with you, as I am sure she will tell you that your presence is already missed—as she has told me more than once.

I shall only add my best regards, and please allow me to repeat that there is no reason to thank me for doing something I did most willingly.

Fitzwilliam Darcy

She read the letter repeatedly, her heart beating more wildly each time. There could be no misunderstanding: he told her he would come to Hertfordshire soon, and he let her know he still remembered they did not go skating together as had been planned right after the ball and just before their argument. And he told her she was missed! Yes, he did! He dared to do so with the risk of being noticed by her father. And he declared once more that everything he did for her father was most willingly done.

She threw herself on the bed, the letter to her chest, and closed her eyes. No, there was no misunderstanding!

The next weeks passed slowly with lots of snow, visits from Mr. Bingley, and hopes of a marriage proposal from him.

Mr. Wickham rarely visited. She saw him only three times in more than five weeks. He was as polite and friendly as ever but more restrained. The news was spread in the neighbourhood of his interest in Miss Mary King, a pleasant young lady with a dowry of ten thousand pounds. Elizabeth felt equally relieved for her tranquillity and worried for Miss King, hoping her family would protect her from any imprudent alliance.

Mr. Bingley's sisters did not return to Netherfield by the end of February, nor did his friend. Despite Elizabeth's hopes, Mr. Darcy remained in London with his sister.

Elizabeth knew he maintained a regular correspondence with her father; also, she and Georgiana wrote to each other at least once a week, and each letter received from Miss Darcy contained some reference to her brother, which Elizabeth was pleased to read. He did not write another letter to her personally, but more than once Mr. Bennet told her that Mr. Darcy commented about something concerning her.

Overwhelmed by Charlotte's insistence and disappointed in herself for her fruitless waiting amid daily hopes and speculations, Elizabeth decided to visit Kent for two weeks. Surely, it would be a pleasant change from her own thoughts, and she could not forego the chance finally to meet Lady Catherine and admire the windows of Rosings.

She told Georgiana of her intention to accept Charlotte's invitation, and she was highly amused by Georgiana's reluctance to express an opinion. She began the journey the last week of March, together with Sir William and Maria Lucas, with her spirits in a high state that was difficult to understand. When they arrived at the parsonage, Elizabeth realised how much she missed her dear friend and how little marriage had changed the parson's manners.

Mr. Collins welcomed them with the liveliest pleasure and ostentatious formality to his 'humble abode,' and punctually repeated all his wife's offers of refreshment.

The first evening was spent chiefly in talking about Hertfordshire and making plans for their stay in Kent. More than once, Mr. Collins expressed his hope that they would be invited to dine at Rosings at least once and that they would be overwhelmed by Lady Catherine's kindness and generosity. In the solitude of her room that evening, Elizabeth meditated upon Charlotte's degree of contentment and the meaning of happiness in marriage.

Just before sleep took her, she briefly wondered when Mr. Darcy last visited Rosings.

As Mr. Collins anticipated and prayed for, an invitation for dinner at Rosings arrived the next day, and his triumph could not be quelled.

He repeatedly assured Elizabeth that she had no reason to feel unease for her modest gowns, and then he pointed out that Lady Catherine was very strict regarding punctuality; finally, he made sure that everybody was aware of the import of such an invitation and that it was all due to Lady Catherine's favourable opinion of him.

The moment they entered, both Sir William and Maria were awed by the grandeur surrounding them. They both turned silent by the time they were introduced in the enormous room where Lady Catherine, her daughter, and Mrs. Jenkinson, the companion, awaited them.

Lady Catherine was a tall, large woman with strongly marked features, which might once have been handsome. Her air was not conciliatory, nor was her manner of receiving them such as to make her visitors forget their inferior rank. Whatever she said was spoken in so authoritative a tone as marked her self-importance.

Miss Anne de Bourgh was quite the opposite: thin, sickly, and pale, obviously intimidated, and glancing around as if frightened. She spoke little except in a low voice to Mrs. Jenkinson. There was neither in figure nor face any likeness between Lady Catherine and her daughter.

The dinner was exceedingly handsome, and it mirrored precisely everything that Mr. Collins promised in terms of servants, plates, and dishes.

During and after the dinner, there was little to do but listen to Lady Catherine. She addressed a variety of questions to Maria and Elizabeth but especially to the latter.

Once her curiosity was satisfied on the subject of the Bennet family, Lady Catherine seemed unwilling to speak much with Elizabeth. She demanded everybody play cards, and the rest of the time passed in such a way. From time to time, Elizabeth could feel her ladyship's insistent stare upon her, but she bore it reasonably well. With great amusement, Elizabeth could not help imagining what would have happened had she accepted Mr. Darcy's marriage proposal two months earlier and been presented to Lady Catherine as her future niece. Now that would have been a memorable moment, indeed!

At the end of the evening, Mr. Collins spared no effort to thank and praise Lady Catherine until the moment they left the house.

The next morning, Elizabeth woke early and, as the house was still silent, took the chance to escape for a quick walk in her surroundings. She allowed herself to be distracted by the beauty of the estate in the early spring until the parsonage remained far behind.

The sound of galloping hooves made her turn; she watched as a dark horse approached across the field, and before her eyes could trust their recognition of the horseman, her quickly drumming heartbeat disclosed his identity. She stopped, her hand seeking support against a tree. Mr. Darcy dismounted and bowed politely, his eyes capturing her amazed expression.

"Miss Bennet! What a wonderful surprise to find you here at this early hour."

Elizabeth stared at him, unable to credit his unexpected appearance. He was there, standing in front of her, smiling tentatively, his expression more delighted than surprised. How did it happen that he was there? Could a more surprising coincidence exist?

"I hope I did not frighten you?"

"No, not really, it is just that...I did not expect to see you in Kent, sir. We arrived only yesterday and—"

"Yes, I know." He hesitated a moment, then the smile spread over his face as he confessed.

"Georgiana informed me of your trip to Kent. Robert and I usually visit Aunt Catherine every year before Easter; I thought the timing could not be better. We shall stay for a fortnight."

Her face was crimson, and her heart nearly stopped for a moment. *What did he just say? He purposely set his visit to find me here and confessed it with such easiness? What should I answer to such a statement?*

"It is ideal timing, indeed," she heard herself saying, and his smile opened even more. She said it; there was nothing to be done now. He was being honest, and so was she.

"How is Georgiana?" she whispered.

"Very well, thank you. She missed your company very much, as you must already know."

"I…I missed her company, too. Is she here by any chance?"

"No…only the colonel, and he is anxious to meet you again. We planned to call at the parsonage later. It is such a wonderful surprise to meet you here so early," he repeated, and she laughed against the sudden lump in her throat.

"We shall be happy to receive you at the parsonage. I am sure Charlotte will be pleased to see you…and Mr. Collins, too. But I should return now; it will soon be time for breakfast."

"May I keep you company on your way back?"

"Certainly…thank you. How is Lord Matlock? And all your London family?"

"They are all well. I see the earl and Lord Brightmore quite often, but Selina and Lady Brightmore not so much. I understand they keep a close acquaintance with Mrs. Gardiner. Unfortunately, I did not have much time to visit Mrs. Gardiner after…after you left town. I called on her with Lord Matlock twice but…"

"I am sure my aunt understands the demanding responsibilities to which you must attend. Rare visits might be more valuable if they are sincere."

As they walked together, Elizabeth struggled to keep her eyes from him, not an easy task as she could feel his insistent gaze on her face. The horse stepped obediently behind them, following his master. Darcy offered her his arm. She took it reluctantly.

"My father is well," she said suddenly, and her voice sounded silly to herself.

"I know…but thank you for telling me, nevertheless. I have the pleasure of a regular correspondence with Mr. Bennet. A couple of days ago, he told me he has finished the books I loaned him, and I understand you showed interest in some of them as well."

She blushed again and raised her eyes to meet his. "I did. But do not worry; I shall be extremely careful with them."

"I am not worried in the slightest. I am only trying to find a proper occasion to bring Mr. Bennet additional books…" He spoke lightly and warmly; her mind remained trapped by the hidden meaning of his words, and she could not meet his eyes.

The way back to the parsonage seemed shorter than she remembered. They took their farewell with the expectation of seeing each other again soon. Elizabeth entered the house and ran to her chamber, still incredulous about what had happened. Mr. Darcy was in Kent!

Elizabeth kept the secret of her morning meeting, but after breakfast, as soon as Mr. Collins returned from his daily visit at Rosings, his manic gestures and breathless voice brought the extraordinary news of Mr. Darcy and Colonel Fitzwilliam's arrival at Rosings and their declared intention of calling on them.

"I may thank you, Eliza, for this piece of civility. Mr. Darcy never would have come so soon to wait upon me," Charlotte said.

Despite their previous conversations upon that subject, Elizabeth said nothing to contradict her, and Mrs. Collins's surprise was apparent.

The gentlemen—Mr. Darcy and Colonel Fitzwilliam—arrived at the parsonage within half an hour of Mr. Collins's announcement.

Colonel Fitzwilliam greeted his hosts properly then expressed his delight in seeing Elizabeth again. Mr. Darcy paid his compliments with his usual politeness and congratulated Mr. Collins for his house and garden. With Elizabeth, he had every appearance of composure, and only his gazes resting on her face and a small smile in the corner of his lips betrayed his feelings. After a brief moment of silence, he found a chair a little apart from the others.

"Miss Bennet," said the colonel, "you must return to London as soon as possible. I cannot possibly tell you how much you are missed. Georgiana and Selina speak of you all the time, and to be perfectly honest, so do my father and I—and even Darcy here."

"You are as kind as you are charming, Colonel; it is good that I am already accustomed to your manners, and I know too well you are not completely serious." Elizabeth laughed.

"Dear Cousin, I am sure you did not mean any affront to the colonel, but you must be aware that an officer in His Majesty's army is not to be trifled with nor his words doubted," Mr. Collins intervened, alarmed by any offence she might give to Lady Catherine's nephew.

"So true, Mr. Collins! A lady never should doubt my words." The colonel laughed and politely kissed her hand. "Such a pity that Miss Elizabeth knows me too well indeed."

For some time, Elizabeth, the colonel, and Mrs. Collins continued to speak of London, Kent and Hertfordshire, with frequent and insistent intervention from Mr. Collins. Only Mr. Darcy remained silent, watching them from his corner chair. Several times Elizabeth looked towards him, and each time she met his eyes. She could not be certain whether he enjoyed his time or not. She felt disappointed, though she was not sure what precisely she expected from him.

"Miss Bennet, I look forward to meeting you again at Rosings soon. Your presence will surely make Rosings more beautiful," the colonel said as the gentlemen prepared to leave.

"My dear Colonel Fitzwilliam, I would not wish by any means to contradict you, but I have to say that, though I believe my fair cousin Elizabeth is worthy of admiration, it would not be possible for anyone to make Rosings more beautiful as perfection cannot be improved."

Elizabeth laughed while Charlotte blushed slightly in embarrassment at her husband's outrageous comment. The colonel hurried to reply, but it was Mr. Darcy who spoke first with perfect composure.

"I must agree with Mr. Collins. Miss Elizabeth's presence may not make Rosings more beautiful, but surely she will make it more radiant and spirited," he said while bowing politely to his hosts.

Later, though Mr. Darcy and Colonel Fitzwilliam had left long before, Elizabeth still was unable to attend to any of her cousin's remarks.

Chapter 13

Despite their desires and expectations, no invitation for dinner arrived that evening from Rosings—nor did one arrive in the next several days. Furthermore, it rained two days in a row—a cold, sharp, spring rain that kept them all inside. Between her cousin's poor library and his endless stories regarding Lady Catherine, together with his delight at having been visited by Mr. Darcy and Colonel Fitzwilliam, Elizabeth found little to keep her mind from further struggles, questions and restrained hopes.

The morning of the third day, Mr. Collins's loudly expressed joy was a clear indication that the long-awaited invitation had arrived.

For the first time since she arrived in Kent, Elizabeth wondered whether she had a proper gown for such an auspicious dinner and whether Charlotte's maid would know how to fix her hair. Annoyed by her own childish behaviour, she found a better way to calm her nerves: she left for a walk before anyone could offer to keep her company.

As she enjoyed the beauty of the grounds, her steps took her towards Rosings. She stopped for a moment, admiring the splendid gardens; Mr. Collins might have exaggerated in many ways, but his praise of Rosings's gardens was well merited.

She heard her name called and turned to see Colonel Fitzwilliam hurrying to her. His expression was nothing but happy, and she could do little else than smile at him.

"Miss Bennet, such a pleasure to see you! This weather was killing me. If I had to stay one more day inside, I would become ill, mark my words."

"Colonel Fitzwilliam. You become ill from indoor air; I understand." She laughed. "I have to say I sympathise with you completely, sir.

"Upon my word, I have not slept so much in years, yet I do not remember the last time I felt so tired. Are you going somewhere, Miss Bennet?"

"No sir, I was just walking and enjoying the gardens of Rosings." She smiled.

"May I keep you company, then?"

"Certainly," she said as she took his offered arm and they walked together along the garden path. She wished to inquire after Darcy, but she did not dare.

"So, Miss Bennet, we shall have dinner together, I hear—such a delightful diversion."

"Lady Catherine was kind enough to invite us."

"Lady Catherine is all kindness," the colonel replied, and Elizabeth laughed.

"Her kindness does not go unnoticed or unappreciated. There are few people who would be as grateful as my cousin for all her ladyship's attention."

"I have no doubt of that. Mr. Collins has already visited us today to express his gratitude."

She blushed slightly, embarrassed by her cousin's behaviour. The colonel seemed oblivious to her uneasiness and continued. "Mr. Collins was very fortunate in choosing his wife—strangely and unexpectedly fortunate. Mrs. Collins appears to be a very sensible lady."

"She is, indeed. However, it is possible to say that she was fortunate, too."

"I have many doubts about that," the colonel replied, and Elizabeth tried to hide her laughter.

"Charlotte seems perfectly happy, and in a prudential light, it is certainly a good match for her. As long as she is content, I cannot but be content for her."

"I am certain that your opinion about marriage is different. I somehow doubt that you would judge the prospect of a match only in a prudential light."

"My own opinion is of little importance in this, Colonel. May I ask—how are Lady Catherine and Miss de Bourgh?" she tried to change the subject, slightly uncomfortable.

"My aunt is busy with something—not sure what—and I confess I am not curious to find out. Anne was taking a walk with Darcy; I think they are still somewhere in the garden. Oh, here they are!" the colonel exclaimed, pointing to a spot in a corner of the garden.

Not far away, somewhat protected by some rose bushes, were Mr. Darcy and Miss de Bourgh, walking arm in arm at a slow pace. Elizabeth had the impression that they had spotted them, too. Before Elizabeth could say a word, the colonel called his cousin, waving to him. A few moments later, they had moved closer, greeting each other.

"I found Miss Bennet hiding in the back garden, and I was just telling her how pleased I was to see her. These last days have been so boring; I could not bear any longer the silence of Rosings. Nobody sings, nobody plays, nobody laughs. I so look forward to dinner tonight!"

Elizabeth startled, embarrassed by the colonel's inconsiderate remark. Did he not see that Miss de Bourgh was present? How could he declare he was bored spending time in her house and in her company? She briefly met Darcy's eyes and noticed his own uneasiness. At his side, Miss de Bourgh became paler, and her hand clenched her cousin's arm.

"Rosings is beautiful, inside and out," said Mr. Darcy. "I am certain you could have found something with which to amuse yourself if you were willing to do it."

"I have rarely seen a house and surroundings as beautiful as Rosings," Elizabeth approved. "And from what I saw, there is a beautiful library and a beautiful music room…"

"Yes, but nobody uses them." The colonel laughed again.

"I am sorry…" Miss de Bourgh whispered self consciously, her eyes to the ground.

"No need to be sorry, Anne. I am sure Miss Bennet will play for us tonight," the colonel said.

Elizabeth glanced to Darcy, and his discomfort was obvious. She smiled at Miss de Bourgh, but she avoided Elizabeth's gaze. "I feel a little tired. I shall return home," she whispered.

"As you wish," Darcy replied. "Let us return. Good day, Miss Bennet…Robert…"

They departed together while the colonel offered his arm to Elizabeth again.

"Poor Anne, she is not accustomed to staying outside long. It is better for her to rest as much as she can. Well, Miss Bennet, where to? Do you have a special place you would like to see?"

"No, not particularly. In fact…if you do not mind, Colonel, I think I shall go and rest a little too. Then I need to prepare for dinner. Shall I see you later?"

"You most certainly shall, Miss Bennet. And I do mind a little, as you force me to retire to lifeless Rosings too soon; that is not very kind of you. For this, you must play at least twice tonight. And I shall turn the pages for you; it is settled."

"We shall see." She smiled. He kept her company until they approached the parsonage. Not partial to the prospect of returning to Rosings alone, the colonel stood for another half an hour, allowing himself to be amused by Mr. Collins's meaningless conversation and by Maria's anxiety.

As soon as the colonel left, Elizabeth excused herself and went to her chamber. Her heart felt heavy and restless from the moment she saw Darcy with Miss de Bourgh. Though she reasoned that it was unlikely Mr. Darcy was bound in any way to his cousin, there was no doubt that Mr. Darcy had tender feelings for Miss de Bourgh, which was perfectly reasonable.

Two months earlier, he made her an offer of marriage, but how could she be certain of his present feelings? She had rejected him; it would be reasonable that he turn to someone who cared for him and welcomed his attentions. He admitted that he had come to Kent with the special purpose of meeting her, but that very day, he behaved coldly again—he barely looked at her and did not speak more than two words to her. How could she understand his intentions? And she would meet him again that evening. How should she behave?

After an hour, she lost patience. She tried to read, but her mind seemed drawn away, and time passed painfully slowly. She took her pelisse and her bonnet and left again, this time away from Rosings. She was not in the mood for company; she only needed exercise so she could rest before dinner. A long walk would do perfectly well.

So lost was she in her thoughts that she did not hear the voice calling her name. She looked around, a little nervous, only to see Darcy appear from behind the trees.

He dismounted and greeted her with gentle politeness. Elizabeth's only hope was that he would not notice her embarrassment.

"Mr. Darcy...this is the second time we have met so unexpectedly, sir." She forced a smile. "Such a coincidence that your riding paths always cross my walks."

"It is no coincidence; I was looking for you. I just called at the parsonage, and Mrs. Collins was surprised not to find you in your room."

"I imagine so; I was careless to leave without telling her. She was not too worried, I hope?"

"No, not too worried." He smiled. "I assured her that I would look for you and bring you back home safely. But I am surprised to find you so far from the house. Did you walk here?"

She laughed and blushed, looking at her shoes, dirty with mud. "I obviously did. I have to say I am similarly surprised to find myself so far. I am afraid I will not return in time for dinner."

"Of course you will; take my horse, and you will be at the parsonage in no time. As soon as you get there, just release him; he will return to me on his own."

She stared at him—eyes wide. "Surely you mock me."

"No, I do not. Do not worry about the horse; we have been together since his birth. He will come back to me."

"I...I can barely dare to look at your horse; nothing on earth would entice me to ride him."

"Very well, than we must find another way. I could go home and return with a carriage. Or, we can return through the wood; I still remember a few shortcuts."

She hesitated a moment, unable to take her eyes from his smiling ones. He was positively amused, his face bright, a mischievous twist on his lips.

"What if we return together?"

"It will take us at least an hour to walk back."

"Very well, I shall take the offer with the shortcuts. And please do not think your help is unappreciated, sir, as well as your sacrifice to walk rather than ride."

"As I said on a previous occasion, please do not thank me for what I do willingly."

She dared a quick glance at him then began to walk at a fast pace. "Miss Bennet? On the left, please," his voice stopped her, and she obeyed instantly.

"We will climb a small hill then go down and trespass the grove behind the parsonage, and we are there," he said, offering his arm, which she took instantly.

"It sounds very easy and fast...like a short stroll around the house." She laughed.

"Yes, almost. You must be careful; the grass is wet and slippery."

After a few moments, Elizabeth looked back and continued to do so from time to time.

"Is something wrong, Miss Bennet?"

"No, not really, but...the horse is actually following us. And he is free, is he not?

You are not holding the reins… He is like an enormous, black, restless shadow."

"Black, restless shadow… I think Thunder would like your description. Why are you surprised? I told you he would follow me. Did you believe I deceived you?"

"His name is Thunder? Well, that certainly puts my mind at ease. I am most eager to ride him at the first opportunity… Thunder…" Darcy laughed out loud.

"Have you ever ridden, Miss Bennet? Have you always disliked horses?"

"I have ridden a few times, but each time I felt more anxiety than enjoyment. Papa said I fell from a horse when I was five. I have no memory of it, but the fear has remained. However, I like horses very much; they are beautiful animals, and I love watching them—from afar. I think the last time I rode I was fifteen."

They walked in silence for a short while. "Look, you can see the parsonage already."

"Excellent. I am glad we will arrive in time; my cousin would never forgive me if we were late for dinner."

"Nor would Lady Catherine, you know…" He appeared serious, but the mirth in his eyes betrayed him. "Nor the colonel… He seemed anxious to hear you play and sing."

"Yes, the colonel… May I ask where he is? He seemed desperate to return to Rosings earlier today. Why is he not riding with you?"

"I…did not inform him of my plan to ride," he replied with some hesitation; she turned to him and their eyes met for a moment.

"And Miss de Bourgh? She seemed unwell when I met her. Perhaps she was just tired? I hope she was better after she rested."

"I am sure she is better; I have not spoken to her since we returned home. I believe she was tired indeed."

"You seem close to Miss de Bourgh. She was… It is obvious she trusts you very much. She looked like she felt safe in your company."

"I am close to Anne, indeed. She is the reason I come to Rosings every year around Easter," he admitted. A strange silence followed, only the wind blowing through the trees and the heavy steps of Thunder behind them could be heard.

"I am as close to Anne as I am to Selina. They both are as dear as sisters to me. But Selina has a large family who adore her, and Anne is alone most of the time… with my aunt, I mean, but…she rarely receives other guests except us."

She said nothing; as from its own will, her hand tightened the hold of his arm, and he continued.

"Robert is fond of Anne, too. He would never do anything to hurt her on purpose." He did not say more, but his meaning was impossible to miss.

"I am sure he is. But he is not always careful with his words." Elizabeth smiled.

"You seem close to Robert," Darcy said, his voice lower.

"The colonel is one of the most pleasant gentlemen I have ever met. He is amiable and smart and possesses such friendly manners that make everyone easy around him. I enjoy his presence exceedingly," Elizabeth said, glancing at him. His countenance was stern, and his gaze was searching somewhere ahead. She felt his arm tensing.

"Robert has been praised for his manners and for his friendly behaviour. I am glad you enjoy his company; he is an excellent man, and I know he admires you very much."

He continued to walk carefully, his eyes fixed ahead. Elizabeth tried to keep pace, still holding his arm, her head turned to him, puzzled by his cold attitude. For a moment, she felt offended and was tempted to tell him that he could learn some manners from his cousin.

"Robert and I are very different," he said, his voice even lower. Revelation turned her cheeks crimson as she tried to hide the welcoming warmth that touched her heart. *Is he jealous?*

"I do enjoy his company very much," she admitted, her voice as low as his. "In truth, I always feel at ease with him. I am never nervous in his presence, I never wonder what he might think of me, and I never struggle to guess the meaning behind his words. I know he admires me, but his admiration does not trouble me at all. I admire him too in the same way I believe I would admire a brother... if I had one."

From the corner of her eye, she noticed he had turned his head and was staring at her, but she dared not meet his gaze. Her eyes searched the grass and the trees around them, fighting to hide a smile that threatened to escape her lips. *Yes, jealous, indeed!*

The walk followed peacefully and silently. Neither spoke, nor did they look at each other until the parsonage was in view. They walked down the hill and crossed a small, wild garden. After a few more steps, they stopped; in front of them was a brook, which ran along the main path, separating the parsonage gardens from the rest of the estate. Due to the rain in the last days, the small stream was larger and deeper than usual; the water barely reached Darcy's ankles, but Elizabeth had to stop.

She cast a quiet glance around and then turned to Darcy.

"Well, here we are, only minutes from the house. What should we do now, sir?"

He held her gaze, uncertain how to reply and unable to conceal his amusement.

"As far as I see, we only have two options: Thunder can take you to the other side, or..."

She laughed nervously. "I already like the second option better..."

"Or *I* can take you to the other side."

She stared at him, her eyes and mouth wide. "Excuse me?"

"I could easily carry you to the other side. It would take but a moment."

"Or I could pass through the water myself and be home in a few minutes."

"True. But it might be difficult to explain why you were missing for so long and returned wet and dirty." He smiled, strangely well humoured, and she took a deep breath, half-upset and half-amused by the situation and by his attempt at mockery. Yet, he had a point. She looked towards the house once more; she was certain she spied Mr. Collins in the garden. She took one more step and watched the horse carefully.

"Will you hold the reins? That is, if I am ever able to reach the saddle."

"Of course," Darcy replied.

He took her gloved hand and put it slowly on the horse's strong neck, then covered her hand with his and moved her fingers against the horse's shining skin. She stood still, looking at the splendid animal; she could feel Darcy's protective presence behind her. She turned and faced him from mere inches away.

"Let me help you," he said, and a moment later, she felt herself held and lifted; she barely had time to take a breath before she was settled in the saddle. She clasped her hands, afraid that she would fall any minute.

"Are you comfortable, Miss Bennet?"

"No, I am not. But the situation will not improve any time soon."

He laughed, and his hand briefly caressed her arm. "It will take only a minute."

He took the reins and walked slowly; the horse followed him instantly, stepping in the water. Elizabeth sighed, and her heart skipped a beat. Darcy turned to her, walking backward so he could watch her carefully. She smiled at him. "I am fine."

"Good." They were shortly on the other side, and Darcy stopped—as did the horse. Elizabeth dared to look around; only then did she realise how tall the stallion was.

Darcy stretched his hands to her; she hesitated only an instant before allowing herself to slide down. She felt his arms surrounding her, and she was imprisoned for a moment. He released her immediately and stepped back.

Elizabeth tried to breathe regularly before she dared to look at Darcy; then she turned shyly and reluctantly to the stallion and gently petted his neck and caressed his mane. The horse neighed, and she startled and stepped back then laughed at herself and returned to caress him.

"Thank you, Thunder." She smiled.

She started to walk at a quick pace, eager finally to be home. Just before she was about to open the gate to the parsonage, Mr. Collins appeared in the yard.

"My dear Cousin Elizabeth, where have you been? We have been worried sick! Sir William believed you were lost or kidnapped!"

"I thank you for your concern, sir; I am perfectly well. I shall hurry to prepare myself for dinner if you will excuse me."

"Oh, please make haste, make haste! Lady Catherine will be very displeased to hear about your little escapade; I dare not imagine how upset she will be if we are late."

He was a living image of desperation, so Darcy needed to call his name three times before Mr. Collins heard him. "Yes, Mr. Darcy?"

"Sir, I understand your concern, but I would think that you of all people could appreciate Miss Bennet's imprudent walk. Only imagine—she is here for the first time. How could she resist the beauties of Rosings, even the beauties of the parsonage? It is understandable that she was spellbound and lost track of time."

"Indeed you are right, sir! How could I overlook that? Surely, you are correct. I remember myself walking around for days, admiring the gardens of Rosings and—"

"And Mr. Collins, perhaps it would be wise if you do not tell Lady Catherine. You know her ladyship is easily impressed; we would not want to upset her for no reason. I am sure Miss Bennet will be ready in time. I look forward to seeing you all soon."

"I could not imagine myself doing other than you suggest, sir—such wise advice, indeed."

"Very well then, it is settled. I shall leave you now. Good day, Miss Bennet, Mr. Collins."

"Mr. Darcy, can you wait a moment, please?" asked Elizabeth, and to the gentlemen's surprise, she approached and petted the horse once more.

"Thank you, Thunder." Then she stepped closer to Darcy and curtseyed politely to him as she whispered, "I would thank you too, sir, but I have learned that I should not thank you for things you do most willingly."

IMMEDIATELY AFTER HE ARRIVED AT Rosings, Darcy retired to his room. He pretended not to hear the colonel and his aunt calling his name; he wished for a little solitude and tranquillity. His heart was light, but his mind was tormented with restless thoughts. That day turned out to be more than he could have hoped —and it had not ended yet. He would see her again soon.

As hard as he had fought it, sharp jealousy defeated his reason each time he saw his cousin with Elizabeth Bennet. That morning in the garden, he had spotted them long before his cousin called his name, but seeing them walking arm in arm, looking at each other and laughing, he did not trust himself enough to disturb them.

When they approached and he could see Elizabeth holding the colonel's arm, the icy hole in his stomach grew. And then Robert started his insensitive, thoughtless conversation, and he could see Elizabeth's disapproving expression. He felt obliged to return home with Anne, though he wished nothing more than to stay. And then she left with Robert.

Not for a moment did he imagine that Elizabeth might share the same feelings seeing him with Anne—yet she did, as she betrayed herself during their walk. She was jealous, too. And she was relieved to find that he was caring for Anne as for a sister, but not half as relieved as he was to discover the nature of her attachment to Robert.

She was extraordinarily smart, and she always found the perfect means to allow him to guess her feelings after his disastrous proposal. And then today he had spent an hour alone with her, an hour that brought him the joy he needed. She was pleased in his company, too; he could not doubt that.

He had been tempted to bring up the subject of his proposal again, to offer more apologies, and to explain to her what remained unexplained, but somehow he felt it was not needed; things seemed quite clear between them for the moment. Sometime in the future, if their newly born friendship grew as he hoped, there would be need for more words, for more explanations, and for more confessions.

For the time being, he allowed himself to enjoy the warmth of their new friendship. He allowed himself to enjoy her company, her smiles, her jokes, her fears, her teasing, her touches… He could still feel her body touching his when he lifted her onto the horse and then when he took her down. For a moment, she had been in his arms—touching his, brushing against his—and her breath had warmed his face for an instant. He knew he would not be able to find rest or sleep for a long time, just recollecting that sensation.

Elizabeth had stolen his peace since the first day he was enchanted by her beautiful eyes.

Elizabeth took a final look at her image in the mirror and was reasonably pleased.

Since she entered the house, she had spent time preparing for dinner, fighting the temptation to lie on her bed and recollect each moment of the last hours.

She could not think of what happened and what was said without feeling her entire body tingle. She was not certain whether it was embarrassment, shame, or some other strange sensation she had never experienced before, equally pleasant and frightening.

She loved to be alone with him; she was forced to admit that to herself. She loved to see him so different than in the past—smiling, laughing at her, teasing her at times, protecting her when necessary, touching her, holding her… Her hand still felt his touch—their entwined fingers, caressing Thunder's strong, soft neck—then he held her in his arms. That was what he did. She remembered the moment he took her off the horse; she slid into his embrace and her body touched his. Cold shivers travelled along her spine at the recollection. If he had tightened his grip only a little, she would have been breathless. In truth, she was breathless anyway.

As she tried to ignore the memories, she forced herself not to anticipate what would happen during dinner. She expected him to be as restrained and behave as propriety demanded. She could not hope for more. But there would be another day —and she had one more week at Rosings. Then she would return to Longbourn and he— No, she could not think of that yet.

With much excitement from Mr. Collins and his continuous praise in anticipation of the evening, they arrived at Rosings where they were directed to the dining room.

The colonel seemed glad to see them, and he did not hesitate to mention that their presence was a welcome and pleasant addition. Lady Catherine asked why they were five minutes late; Miss de Bourgh and her companion greeted them briefly and silently.

Mr. Darcy moved to them and bowed politely; his manners were not as open as his cousin's, but he was friendlier than usual. He did not say more than a few words, but his eyes fixed upon Elizabeth and captured her own. She smiled and felt herself blushing, but she did not avert her eyes until the colonel asked her a direct question. He invited her to sit, and she sat by him; she cast a quick glance at Darcy, but he had already resumed his place by his aunt.

Lady Catherine began to talk with Mr. and Mrs. Collins and Sir William about various issues that demanded her ladyship's wise opinion. The colonel engaged Elizabeth and Maria in a most agreeable conversation of Kent and Hertfordshire, of travelling and staying at home, and of new books and music. Elizabeth was as pleased as ever to speak with the colonel, and the uneasiness of noticing Darcy's eyes turned repeatedly towards them made her more talkative than usual. They conversed with so much spirit and flow as to draw the attention not only of Mr. Darcy but of Lady Catherine herself, who did not scruple to call out,

"What is it that you are saying, Fitzwilliam? What is it you are talking of? What are you telling Miss Bennet? Let me hear what it is."

"We are speaking of music, madam," said he when no longer able to avoid a reply.

"Of music! I must have my share in the conversation if you are speaking of music. There are few people in England, I suppose, who have more true enjoyment of music than myself, or a better natural taste. If I had ever learnt, I should have been a great proficient. And so would Anne if her health had allowed her to apply. I am confident that she would have performed delightfully. How does Georgiana get on, Darcy?"

"Georgiana gets on wonderfully, ma'am. She is extremely gifted, and I enjoy seeing her daily progress. I am truly proud of her."

"I am very glad to hear such a good account of her," said Lady Catherine, "and pray tell her from me that she cannot expect to excel if she does not practise a great deal."

"I assure you, madam, that she does not need such advice. She practises constantly."

"So much the better. It cannot be done too much, and when I next write to her, I shall charge her not to neglect it on any account. I often tell young ladies that no excellence in music is to be acquired without constant practice. I have told Miss Bennet several times that she will never play really well unless she practises more, and though Mrs. Collins has no instrument, she is welcome to come to Rosings and play on the pianoforte in Mrs. Jenkinson's room. She would be in nobody's way in that part of the house."

Elizabeth was more amused than offended, but she could see that Mr. Darcy was ashamed of his aunt's ill breeding. She smiled at him as she thanked her ladyship politely.

When dinner was over, Colonel Fitzwilliam reminded Elizabeth of having promised to play for him, and she sat down directly to the instrument. He drew a chair near her. Lady Catherine listened to half a song and then talked to her other guests.

Mr. Darcy moved slowly to the pianoforte and stationed himself so as to command a full view of the fair performer's countenance. Elizabeth was certain that her increased emotions and trembling fingers made her perform poorly, so she took the first convenient pause.

"Darcy, you interrupted Miss Bennet! Why on earth are you staring at us so seriously? You are quite scary, you know. I wonder if Miss Bennet will be able to play again. Take a seat; it will be more comfortable for all of us."

"Do not worry, Colonel, I am not scared of Mr. Darcy." She laughed, her eyes daringly holding Darcy's gaze. "It is true that Mr. Darcy's presence is intimidating, and it makes me nervous and sometimes uncomfortable. I always wonder what he thinks of me and whether he looks at me to find fault; I am never easy in his company, but I am not scared either."

She spoke while their eyes remained fixed on each other, and a smile twisted his lips. The colonel was only inches away, but they seemed oblivious to his presence.

"I shall not say that you are mistaken," Darcy replied, "because you could not really believe me to look at you to find fault. If I make you nervous, I heartily apologise; I shall do anything I can to make you more comfortable in my presence. Would taking a seat, as the colonel suggested, help?"

Elizabeth laughed heartily. "Taking a chair would be a good start—thank you."

"Now, as my cousin is neither frightening nor intimidating, and he does not make you nervous, he might as well stand. Cousin, be so good as to allow me to sit by Miss Bennet; I shall turn the pages for her."

Colonel Fitzwilliam stared at his cousin in disbelief. He had little time to react before Darcy gently but disarmingly grabbed his arm, removed him from the chair, and then seated himself. Elizabeth was as shocked as the colonel, blushing and barely concealing her laughter.

"So, Miss Bennet, what shall we play?" asked Darcy while the colonel, shaking his head in disapproval, moved to the other guests and was immediately claimed by Lady Catherine.

"Please forgive my aunt's rudeness. Your performance is lovely as I have told you many times," Darcy said, his voice a whisper.

"You are too kind as I have told you many times." She smiled. "Lady Catherine is right; I should practice more if only I had a real interest to do it."

"Perhaps you should do it. Perhaps you should come and practice every day as my aunt suggested. I would be delighted to follow your daily performance."

She glanced at him, and her cheeks reddened while he continued.

"Or perhaps you could employ your time better. Walking is very beneficial, and this season is perfect for such activity. Practicing indoors can wait until the rainy, cold days."

She suddenly stopped her song and tried to find another. Darcy offered her the music sheets, and she took them, her hand trembling slightly. Their fingers touched for a moment, and neither hurried to withdraw them; when he finally did, his fingers brushed against her in a gentle, tentative caress. Turning the pages became impossible for her.

"I have to tell you, sir, that you are not successful in making me less nervous." He released a low rumble of laughter, though she could see he was also ill at ease.

Here they were interrupted by Lady Catherine, who called out to know what they were talking of. Elizabeth immediately began playing again. Lady Catherine approached and, after listening for a few minutes, said to Darcy:

"Miss Bennet would not play at all amiss, if she practised more and could have the advantage of a London master. She has a very good notion of fingering though her taste is not equal to Anne's. Anne would have been a delightful performer had her health allowed her to learn."

"I heartily agree with you, Aunt, with regard to both matters. I have no doubt about Anne's exquisite taste, and yes, Miss Bennet has a very good notion of fingering. She only has to practice more under the close guidance of a master."

While Lady Catherine demanded that her nephew take her back to the couch, Elizabeth stopped her playing and watched after them in disbelief. What had Mr. Darcy just said?

THE REST OF THEIR STAY in Kent passed with little event. Three more days it had rained; the three dry days, as in mutual understanding, Elizabeth and Darcy spent the entire morning on long walks, discussing such varied subjects as music, books, weather, Georgiana, Bingley, Longbourn, and Pemberley. Nothing more personal was attempted between them, but each day made them more familiar with each other. Elizabeth did not dare to ask about his plans after leaving Kent; it was only decided that she would remain a few days in London with her aunt Gardiner while Sir William and Maria returned home.

Lady Catherine was very displeased that her nephews decided to leave so soon; she insisted that at least Elizabeth should stay longer and was highly displeased to receive a rejection. Her ladyship insisted on knowing all their travel details. She showed surprise that her nephews would leave the same day as the other guests; she insisted several times that their carriage was too small and uncomfortable and it was fortunate that the gentlemen would ride back to London. As they took their farewells, her ladyship did not forget to mention that Darcy's attachment to Rosings seemed to increase every year.

Elizabeth spent most of the journey watching through the window, admiring the beauty of the fields and the splendid posture of Thunder, who was riding proudly near the carriage under the gentle guidance of his master. In a few hours, they would be in London, and there would be no opportunities for long walks and private conversation. Suddenly, Elizabeth realised she did not like London quite as much as she did before.

Chapter 14

Elizabeth's reception in Gracechurch Street was as warm as she expected. Her little cousins missed her exceedingly and did not hesitate to prove it. Their genuine love and demands for attention were most welcome distractions from her thoughts.

Sir William and Maria stayed long enough to enjoy tea and some refreshment then resumed their travel home.

"Dearest, do tell me all. How was your visit in Kent? How is Charlotte? What a lovely coincidence for Mr. Darcy and the colonel to visit Rosings at the same time..."

"Yes, lovely coincidence indeed. Charlotte is fine; she made herself a very comfortable home. She seems to be pleased with her present situation. I am happy for her."

"I am glad to hear it; you will have to indulge me with a detailed report during dinner. In the meantime, I have some news, too. Next week we are all invited to Lord Matlock's estate for a hunting party. The earl and Selina insisted so fervently that they left me little choice. I had to accept, though hunting is not my favourite amusement."

"A hunting party? That is quite intriguing, I must say, but I am afraid I will not be able to join you. I should return home in a few days. I miss Longbourn, and I know they miss me, too."

"Surely, you cannot hope to escape so easily, Missy. The earl also sent an invitation to Mr. Bingley and your father. As you might imagine, my brother Bennet refused to travel so long for a week of hunting, but he generously offered to send you and Jane. Jane will arrive the day after tomorrow in the afternoon. So you see—all is settled."

Elizabeth was uncertain how she felt about the prospect of such a party, so she did not answer immediately. One question was particularly troubling, but she dared not ask it.

"The colonel did not seem aware of such a party," she said.

"It was a hasty arrangement made by the earl, but the colonel will surely be there. I understand there will be quite a large party besides the family. Selina is very excited about it—and so is Miss Darcy."

"Georgiana? I would never imagine her hunting."

"She will most likely not hunt but enjoy her time at Matlock Manor. Miss Darcy said her brother is a skilful hunter. But again, if we were to take Miss Darcy's word, Mr. Darcy is skilful at everything." Mrs. Gardiner laughed and Elizabeth forced a smile.

"I hope you remember I do not ride. I would feel awkward to walk while others ride."

Mrs. Gardiner laughed loudly. "Yes you would. I am afraid you will have to spend your time taking care of your cousins, dearest. I have every intention of taking advantage of this week; it has been so long since I last rode. And you cannot count on Jane to keep you company, either.

"So, unless you learn to ride quite well in the next few days, you will have to find a way to entertain yourself. Or perhaps one of the gentlemen will sacrifice himself and abandon the hunt in your favour."

She blushed and laughed. "If my aunt and sister are prepared to abandon me without mercy, I dare not hope that a gentleman would prefer me to a hunt. It would be uncommonly strange."

With such jokes, the rest of the day passed, and dinnertime arrived with the promised detailed report from Elizabeth. Every parcel of Mr. Collins's garden was described, as well as the windows and rooms of Rosings. Lady Catherine was quoted at least five times, including the matter of proficiency through excessive practice. When they retired to their chambers, Mrs. Gardiner was exhausted from laughter and amusement. She had not been so entertained in many years, nor could she fail to notice the frequency of Mr. Darcy's name being mentioned during her niece's narrative.

BREAKFAST HAD JUST FINISHED WHEN a servant announced Miss Darcy. She hurried to embrace her friend, who received her with the warmest feelings.

"I am so happy to see you, Elizabeth! I wished to come yesterday, but William said I should let you rest after your trip. He was right, of course. He had some meetings fixed for this morning, and as soon he was gone, I came to see you. How are you? You look very well!"

"I missed you too, Georgiana. You should have come yesterday; no rest is as important as seeing you. How are you? Mr. Darcy and I spoke about you recently. I really missed you."

"Oh, I am fine. Before I forget—Selina asked me to tell you that tonight we will go to the theatre. All is settled. Selina will come to see you soon; she had to prepare the children first."

Elizabeth was equally amused and touched to see Miss Darcy so happy at their meeting and to watch the young girl becoming so lively. Her previous shyness seemed to be gone. She embraced the girl again, and then they both moved to the settee together, holding hands.

"Thank you for your invitation; I would love to watch a play."

"Oh, Mrs. Gardiner, did you tell Elizabeth about the hunting party? We all will be there; I am so happy. Matlock estate is beautiful. Only Pemberley is more beautiful," she exclaimed with genuine enthusiasm. She blushed, slightly embarrassed. "Please do not think I am being rude or vain, but Pemberley is truly the most beautiful place. You will see for yourself."

Miss Darcy seemed so proud of her home and so certain that her friend would have the opportunity to see it for herself soon that Elizabeth felt unable to make a proper reply.

"I can testify as to your statement, Miss Darcy," Mrs. Gardiner happily intervened. "Pemberley is indeed a magnificent place, though I only have had the pleasure of being inside a couple of times. Is Mr. Darcy well after his trip?" Mrs. Gardiner masterfully changed the subject from what appeared to be a momentary indiscretion.

"Yes—yes he is. I think he will come to call on you later... I heard him saying so..."

"Georgiana, I was talking to my aunt yesterday. Do you really hunt?" Elizabeth finally managed to intervene in the conversation after spending the last minutes wondering about the probable opportunity of seeing Pemberley sometime soon.

"Hunt? No, not really—I could never hunt a living animal..."

"I imagined as much." Elizabeth laughed.

As expected, Lady Selina called shortly with her two children and Lord Matlock.

"My, my, you truly look beautiful, my dear Miss Elizabeth. Where have you been all these months? I am pleased to see you are unharmed after spending a fortnight with my sister Catherine. How is your cousin? Still busy kissing Catherine's footsteps?"

"Papa, please!" Lady Selina scolded him. "I am sure Miss Elizabeth had a most pleasant time at Rosings. Aunt Catherine is a very attentive host."

"Robert said it rained most of the time; he said he had a most boring time," the earl added.

"It did rain, but there were a few beautiful days, which fully compensated for the rainy ones," Elizabeth answered, hoping nobody would notice her blush.

"My brother told me he enjoyed his stay at Rosings very much." Miss Darcy tried to support her friend, oblivious to the reason for Elizabeth's crimson cheeks.

"Perhaps Miss Elizabeth and Darcy found a way to employ their time much better than Robert," the earl concluded.

"Well, Robert is not very fond of spending time in the country unless there is a hunting party or some other activity that requires a challenge. Do you notice how eager men are to challenge each other?" said Lady Selina.

"My dear, all male creatures are eager to challenge each other; it is a manly way of living. I confess I like a good challenge anytime," the earl said.

"I know you do, Papa. Sometimes I would prefer that your young spirit was tempered more frequently by the voice of wisdom."

"My love, man and wisdom are two words that rarely go together." The earl laughed and—not surprisingly—none of the ladies tried to contradict him.

"My brother is a very wise man," Miss Darcy said a few moments later.

"Yes dear, we all know Darcy is very wise and perfect in everything," replied the earl.

"I thank you for your trust, Uncle. I shall prove my wisdom by struggling to avoid the challenge raised by your mocking tone," Mr. Darcy answered from the door. He was staring at them, a large smile twisting his lips as he looked at his uncle challengingly.

"Here you are, my boy. Come—let me see you. And do not pretend to be offended. You know very well that you are not much wiser than the other men of our family."

Darcy moved to Mrs. Gardiner and greeted her politely, kissed his cousin and then shook his uncle's hand. Finally, he turned to the place where his sister and Elizabeth were and smiled.

"Well, I am glad we are all here to clarify a few things. I have fixed our leaving for next Wednesday, and I do not wish to hear about any urgent business delaying our departure." The earl cast a meaningful glance at Darcy.

"Do not worry, Uncle; we shall be ready for Wednesday."

Mrs. Gardiner called for some refreshment, and the discussion continued animatedly. Darcy took a glass of wine, and after a brief hesitation, he sat on a chair near Elizabeth.

"I hope you rested after your trip," Darcy said a few moments later.

"I did, thank you… I was not really tired but more anxious to see my friends," Elizabeth answered. "How is Thunder?" she asked and he glanced at her with surprise.

"He is fine. I think he misses the long walks in Kent," Darcy said, and Elizabeth felt a wave of redness spreading over her neck. She daringly held his gaze.

"Thunder is wonderful," said Miss Darcy. "And my horse, Duke, is wonderful, too," she added, and Elizabeth smiled. She could feel Darcy's eyes on her.

"Mrs. Reynolds—our housekeeper at Pemberley—says that Thunder is strong and intimidating but gentle and trustworthy—just like William," Miss Darcy whispered.

Elizabeth turned her head for an instant, enough to see Darcy's face redden with embarrassment. She returned her attention to her friend. "I am sure Mrs. Reynolds is right."

At that point, they were interrupted by Lady Selina asking for details regarding their presence at the theatre that evening.

"If it is convenient for you, Georgiana and I will take Mrs. Gardiner and Miss Bennet," said Darcy, waiting for Mrs. Gardiner's approval.

"That would be a perfect, thank you sir," Mrs. Gardiner answered.

The guests left with the promise of seeing each other again soon.

In the solitude of her room, while choosing her gown for the theatre, Elizabeth was not easy with everything she had learned that day. The hunting party
166

sounded strange, and the more she thought about it, the more uncomfortable she felt, though the reason for her low spirits was hard to determine. Most disturbing was Georgiana's comment about seeing Pemberley soon. Could she dare hope for a summer invitation to Pemberley? She knew the Bingleys had spent summers at Pemberley before, so the prospect was not impossible, yet she could not allow herself to speculate much upon that subject.

At the perfect time, Darcy's carriage arrived. They spoke little during the ride, but Elizabeth's eyes turned insistently to Darcy, and each time his gaze was upon her, ready to catch her eye. She tried to keep her attention outside the window; the streets were crowded, and the gentle, spring breeze touched them with the fresh smells of tree flowers.

The theatre entrance was more crowded than Elizabeth anticipated. The earl was already there, together with his sons, his daughter, and his son-in-law.

Lord Matlock approached them and politely engaged Mrs. Gardiner to walk with him. The colonel took a few steps towards them, but Darcy had already offered his arms to both Elizabeth and Georgiana.

As soon as the small group reunited, they entered the main hall. There was another moment of greetings and exchanged politeness with a large number of their acquaintances. Elizabeth's attention was drawn to a group that approached them, calling Lord Matlock's name. She startled to see, in the middle of the group, Lady Sinclair on the arm of a handsome gentleman who seemed in his late fifties.

"Lord Sinclair, I did not expect to see you here." Lord Matlock laughed.

"I did not expect to see myself here, but I could not escape my wife's stubborn insistence. You know Eve and her notions of entertainment."

"Lord Sinclair, you should not make a fool of yourself; everyone knows you are more than willing to keep me company," Lady Sinclair replied with a mischievous smile. She looked beautiful; Elizabeth was forced to admit the truth.

"I was a fool when I decided to marry a woman less than half my age," he said with an adoring glance at his wife, which contradicted his harsh words.

"Good evening," Lady Sinclair said with a charming smile to them. Elizabeth did not miss Lady Sinclair's displeasure the moment she saw her.

"We should go to our places," said Lady Selina. "We will be in Darcy's box. If I remember correctly, your box is on the opposite side, Lord Sinclair."

"You have an excellent memory, Selina. It was a great pleasure to see you all. If I had known you would be here, I would not have asked my husband to keep me company. I am certain there would be an extra place for me in your box," Lady Sinclair said to Darcy. "In any case, I shall see you again in a few days. Lord Matlock, I know you are hosting a hunting party, but I rely on you to entertain us with some dances, too."

Elizabeth was unable to take her attention from her, trying to comprehend her words.

"We should go," Darcy said, and with a short greeting to the other group, he walked away, followed by his relatives.

They reached the box, and Elizabeth briefly noticed that it was perfectly situated for the most advantageous view of the stage. Georgiana asked her to take the last seat on the left side of the box, then she seated herself at Elizabeth's right. At the other side of Georgiana were Mrs. Gardiner and then Lady Selina. The gentlemen sat in a second row of chairs behind the ladies. Mr. Darcy took the seat behind Elizabeth; near him were the colonel, then the earl and lastly Lord Brightmore.

Some lights were extinguished and the play was about to start.

With Darcy only a short distance behind her, Elizabeth's mind was not clear enough to understand what she had just seen. She could not understand how it was possible that Lady Sinclair dared to flirt openly with Darcy while she was on the arm of her husband. And how was it possible that she was invited to the hunting party? Who else would attend? She vividly recollected Lady Sinclair's offensive words about her at the ball; she could only speculate what she would say after seeing her on Darcy's arm. Lady Sinclair was determined to claim Mr. Darcy's interest. She was even more insistent and impertinent than Caroline Bingley, but at least Caroline's desire of marrying a gentleman like Mr. Darcy was easy to understand. But Lady Sinclair? What did she propose to accomplish with her insistence? The answer instantly came to her mind, and Elizabeth felt her ears and neck burning. It was not difficult to guess what Lady Sinclair wished to accomplish; even Darcy's relatives were well aware of that. They said as much at the ball in January.

At Elizabeth's right, Georgiana spoke with the colonel in whispers; their subject seemed to be highly amusing, as they barely contained their chuckles. Elizabeth turned her head to them briefly and then frowned; from behind, she could feel Darcy leaning gently towards her until he could whisper in her ear.

"Lord Sinclair has been my uncle's friend for many years, and Lady Sinclair is distantly related to Lord Matlock. We have known her since we were children."

She did not dare breathe; how did it happen that he knew what was troubling her? And what was he thinking to remain so close to her that she could feel his warm breath on her neck? She struggled to form an indifferent reply, to show him she was not preoccupied by Lady Sinclair. Then she remembered his confession from his first day at Rosings. He admitted he had come for her. They had discussed Anne and the colonel, and each of them was relieved to know the nature of their feelings. Now she wished to give him the same honesty.

She whispered back, "Thank you for letting me know, sir. I was wondering about…the nature of your relationship with Lord and Lady Sinclair. Your family relationship, I mean…" She blushed with embarrassment.

He replied, each of his words warming the skin of her neck. "There is no relationship between me and Lady Sinclair, nor has there ever been since we played together as children, fifteen years ago."

She heard the answer, and for a moment she sighed in relief; a moment later, however, her mind was invaded by a single thought: if she had leaned back a little or if he had moved his head an inch closer, his lips would have touched her skin.

The play finally began, and fortunately, nobody observed the trembling of her hands.

Never in his life had Darcy been less interested in a play.

He barely managed to calm himself after the meeting with the Sinclairs. In truth, Eve Sinclair had become more irritating with each passing day. He was not interested in judging her behaviour; he knew very well that most marriages arranged for social reasons soon ended with at least one if not both partners finding entertainment outside of marriage. Even if that fact was customary and easily accepted among the men, it was well known but silently ignored that quite a few ladies of the *ton* also developed particular preferences for one or more gentlemen.

Though he considered such a situation appalling and completely unacceptable, he did not give the fact much consideration. So Eve Sinclair was free to do as she wished—as long as she refrained from bothering him. Could she really imagine that she would be successful in her attempts? He would have to lose his mind entirely to consider accepting Eve's attentions.

And Elizabeth was troubled by Eve; even more, she was jealous.

He felt her hand tighten over his arm the moment Eve appeared, and then, while she spoke to him, he could sense Elizabeth's body tensing beside him. She was still upset when they took their seats; that was obvious. He considered what he should do: ignore the situation or try to clarify it—as much as was possible in a crowded theatre box. Then he saw his sister whispering with the colonel, the earl whispering with Mrs. Gardiner, and Brightmore whispering with Selina. He hoped his gesture would not draw undue attention from the gossips, so he leaned towards her and whispered in her ear; her scent made him dizzy and he felt overwhelmed by the desire to place his lips on her skin. His struggle was almost lost when she gently turned her head and whispered back to him. That very moment, he could see her lips moving slowly a couple of inches from his. If he moved his head a little forward, his lips would actually touch hers...

The sound of the play starting brought him back from his mind-numbing thoughts, and he recollected himself while leaning back against his chair. However, that posture offered him a most torturing, enchanting view of her neck, her bare shoulders, the silky locks of hair gently touching her nape... If he moved a little forward, his eyes could easily travel down along the cleavage of her dress, which was moving with the rhythm of her breath. If he could only brush his fingers against her shoulder...

How could he allow his common sense to be defeated by such thoughts in the presence of his family? What was happening to him? He had never been in such a state, not even when he was a lad experiencing the first quivers of desire.

He was startled when the first act ended. During the interlude, their group left the box for a short walk in the hall. That time the colonel was quicker, and he immediately secured Elizabeth and Georgiana, offering each an arm. Elizabeth accepted the colonel's company while glancing at Darcy; her smiling eyes and the mischievous twist of her lips were enough compensation for him, so he silently followed them. After all, it was perhaps better that people not see him and Elizabeth arm in arm again. Surely, anyone could see his preference for her, and most of them probably noticed his improper, intimate behaviour towards her; he should not fuel more gossip.

At the colonel's arm, Elizabeth tried to amuse herself with his comments about the people they met during their stroll. It seemed like nobody in Town was unknown to him; many young ladies gazed and smiled at him while looking at her with curiosity. She met a few gentlemen who pretended they had known her from the January ball and danced with her; unfortunately, her memories about that ball were sparse and not entirely happy, so she tried to compensate for her oblivion with her most charming smile.

The second act of the play began shortly, and Elizabeth was pleased to resume her place.

She spoke only a few words to Darcy during the interlude, yet she felt at ease and almost comfortable in his presence. Even the nervousness caused by his closeness turned out to be pleasant in a most tormenting way.

A few minutes after the play resumed, Elizabeth felt herself shivering and wondered whether it had turned suddenly cold in the room or it was just her impression. She looked around and saw Georgiana and Lady Selina putting on their cloaks. Mrs. Gardiner was already wearing a thick but elegant shawl so Elizabeth decided to put on hers.

She slowly turned to the back of her chair, looking for her shawl, but she could not find it—surely, it had fallen down. Trying not to draw attention towards herself, she blindly searched around the chair on her left. She remembered seeing it there during the interlude, and she proved correct as she felt it immediately. The next moment she frowned—the shawl was picked up and handed to her by Darcy, so the moment she took it, her fingers touched his and remained still.

They were both seated on their chairs, apparently attentive to the scene; only their left hands were joined lower, on the shawl, waiting. His fingers moved slowly, searching for hers through the soft fabric; she did not dare move her hand—she did not dare even breathe. But her fingers, of their own will, slid along and met his and then entwined, but only for the length of a heartbeat. He withdrew his hand, together with the shawl, stretched the fabric and gently tried to place it on her bare shoulders. She leaned forward a little to allow him enough space; while arranging the shawl, his fingers briefly caressed her neck, and his touch felt softer than the fabric that finally covered her. His hands lingered on her shoulders a moment longer than needed and finally withdrew, reluctantly. She was no longer cold as every spot on her skin burned.

Elizabeth needed some time before she was able to breathe steadily again. She slowly looked around, but everyone seemed enchanted by the play; she wished to see what he was doing, but did not dare turn her head to him. Her head was whirling with reproaches to herself while her heart seemed overwhelmed with joy.

She allowed herself to be rapt by the music and hoped it would calm her turmoil. When the play came to an end, she was no calmer, but at least she was able to present an appearance of composure. Yet, she did not dare meet Darcy's eyes.

However, the moment they left, without a single word, Darcy gently took Elizabeth's hand and placed it on his arm. He briefly looked at her to search for a sign of disapproval, but she could not hold his gaze. Instead, her hand tightened the hold of his arm and a shy smile twisted her lips.

The carriages were waiting patiently; Lady Selina and her husband were the first to depart. Lord Matlock and the colonel helped Georgiana and Mrs. Gardiner into the carriage, while Darcy handed in Elizabeth., the bright sky filled with stars and a shining moon. The streets were silent; only a few carriages could be heard.

"What a wonderful night," Elizabeth suddenly exclaimed.

"I was prepared to say the same thing," said Miss Darcy. "Just look at the stars! It would be a perfect time for a long, night ride, would you not agree?"

"I cannot say; it never crossed my mind to ride at night." Elizabeth laughed. "However, I trust your word completely."

"It would also be the perfect time for a walk," Mr. Darcy intervened, a small smile on his face. "For those who are not fond of riding, I mean…"

Though she felt her face colouring, Elizabeth daringly held his eyes for a moment and did not attempt to conceal her laughter.

"Thank you, sir. You are very considerate to those of us who are not fond of riding."

"But, Elizabeth, what will you do next week?" Georgiana asked in concern. Elizabeth laughed again.

"At the hunting party, you mean? I do not hunt and I do not ride; so I have only two choices—to stay in London or to go and take care of the children as my aunt suggested."

"Or you may learn to ride," Miss Darcy said, and Mrs. Gardiner approved her immediately while Elizabeth laughed, a little nervous.

"Of course I may; in five days I can easily become proficient in riding."

"William could easily teach you to ride. He taught me when I was three years old."

"I am sure Mr. Darcy could easily teach anyone anything," Elizabeth concluded, trying to laugh, and Georgiana chuckled.

"Matlock is a beautiful estate, and perhaps the best way of enjoying its beauties is by walking," Darcy said in earnest. "Its surroundings are exquisite in the spring."

"This is an excellent suggestion, thank you."

"Besides, no matter how fond we are of riding and hunting, I doubt very much that we will spend the entire ten days in such a way. I am certain you will find someone to keep you company on your walks."

"I shall keep you company, Elizabeth. Hunting is not my favourite way of spending time, after all," Miss Darcy said, and though the conversation was mostly in jest, Elizabeth could not be insensible to Miss Darcy's generous offer nor to Mr. Darcy's subtle one.

JANE'S ARRIVAL IN LONDON THE next day was a moment of joy. Miss Bennet looked more beautiful than ever, and Elizabeth could easily see that Mr. Bingley's presence had been beneficial for her. In addition, Mr. Bingley seemed more bewitched than ever. His adoring gazes and smiles directed at Jane, his hurry to guess her small wishes and comply with them—everything was undoubted proof that Jane could expect a happy future.

The journey began early in the morning and lasted until late afternoon.

As Georgiana had told her, the Matlock estate was one of the most beautiful places Elizabeth had ever seen. It had all the grandeur of Rosings and the same wonderful gardens, but it possessed what Rosings lacked completely: warmth, joy, and liveliness.

The moment they arrived, Lady Selina's children climbed from the carriage and started to scamper along a path, followed closely by Mrs. Gardiner's children. The governesses attempted to scold them, but Lord Matlock stopped them.

"Let them play—there is nothing more lovely than children's laughter. Just keep your eyes on them; the grounds are extensive, and you could easily lose them," he said, entering the house and giving specific orders to the servants.

"And please keep them out of our way," Lady Sinclair said harshly. "I do not remember joining my parents at hunting parties when I was an infant."

"Indeed, I have to agree with you, Lady Sinclair," said Miss Bingley, casting a reproachful glance at the children who were rolling on the grass, in the small, front garden. "Children are nice as long as they can be seen but not heard."

"Seen, but not too much," Mrs. Hurst intervened with a meaningful look to her sister.

Elizabeth looked at her aunt who was only a few steps away from their exchange and was positively pale—then to Lady Selina, who turned red. Lady Selina stepped towards the other ladies. When she spoke, her voice admitted no contradiction.

"Eve, please remember that this estate is my children's home. They may do whatever they please, together with their friends and with their parents' permission. My family will do everything to ensure that you all have an excellent time, but we shall not keep our children locked away to gratify your inane sensibilities. If there is anything that bothers you—or you," she said, turning to Bingley's sisters, "this would be the perfect time to alter your plans for attending our party. The carriages await your pleasure."

Elizabeth could see Lady Sinclair colour with anger, while Miss Bingley and Mrs. Hurst seemed unable to breathe. Mrs. Gardiner tried to maintain her usual, elegant temper, while Jane and Georgiana became pale with embarrassment.

"So, ladies, shall we enter?" The colonel was the first of the horsemen to approach, a happy expression on his face. A moment later, he noticed the tension on their faces.

"Are you well? You seem preoccupied and too serious for my taste."

"We are perfectly well, Brother. We were just discussing the children."

The gentlemen turned to watch the noisy, laughing children, who were playing carelessly, closely watched by their governesses.

"I just love my boys," Lord Brightmore declared, with a loving smile at his wife. "In fact, I love all children, but then again, it is easy for me to say that as long as my wife is the one who takes care of them. And I love my wife, too," he whispered, while he placed a soft kiss on his wife's hand, and was rewarded with a loving glance.

The servants arrived and invited them to their chambers, so the discussion ceased, but Elizabeth continued to think of it even after she entered her splendid room.

She admired the furniture for some time, then opened the balcony and stepped out to enjoy the view. Yes, Mr. Darcy had been right once more: Matlock was a wonderful property, and the gardens, the groves, the hills deserved—nay demanded —to be known on foot, step by step.

She unpacked and lay on the bed a moment; it was established that they would all meet downstairs for dinner, so she had time to rest, but she did not feel tired at all.

She wondered what her aunt was doing and was tempted to search for her then changed her mind. Most likely she was resting. She went to the balcony again and looked along the outside wall. There were a few windows open, but she could not spot where the others' rooms were. The Manor seemed to have countless rooms all around.

Her attention was drawn by a mix of voices in front of the house. She looked down and stood still, her sight held by the image in front of her. There was her aunt, walking around the yard with Lord Matlock, Lady Selina and Georgiana; in a near garden, all four children were laughing and clapping. Near them, two ponies waited, and a few steps away stood Lord Brightmore and Mr. Darcy. Each of the gentlemen took two children and put them together on a pony, then held the reins and walked them around. Thomas Brightmore, the eldest, who was riding with Edward Gardner, demanded that his father release the reins, as they were grown enough to ride alone. His father refused to listen, and the boy insisted until his mother stepped away and whispered a few words to him and the boy became silent immediately, enjoying the peaceful and safe ride.

From the balcony, Elizabeth covered her lips with her hand to stem her laughter. Mr. Darcy lifted his eyes and saw her. He waved to her with a small gesture, and she waved back. It was all that was needed for Georgiana and Lord Matlock to spot her. After a brief hesitation, Elizabeth took her spencer and left the room.

The joyful party in the yard welcomed her. Edward and Eleanor, her little cousins, barely had time to breathe while they told her everything they saw since they arrived.

"How is your room, dear Miss Bennet? Are you comfortable?" asked Lord Matlock.

"Surely your lordship is mocking me. I do not think the mere word 'comfortable' could be fairly used in regard to your estate. My room is magnificent, thank you."

"I am glad you like it," the earl replied, pleased by the compliment. "I confess I love my home, and I am glad my children seem to maintain a strong affection for it."

"I have rarely seen a place so beautiful. I saw Rosings, too, and it is impressive, but Matlock is much more…alive. I do not know if you understand my meaning."

"I do understand your meaning, Miss Bennet. I thank you; your words bring me joy."

"It is beautiful," she repeated while turning around.

"You must see Pemberley; you will absolutely love it," Lady Selina intervened. "I love my home, but I have to admit, Pemberley is the most perfectly situated place I have ever seen. Besides all the care my uncle and my cousin have put in it, nature has given it everything one could hope…perfectly situated, indeed."

"I cannot deny that," the earl admitted, and Elizabeth had little to reply. She saw Mr. Darcy watching them with interest, but she was not certain whether he heard their words.

"Will the children not disturb the other guests?" Mrs. Gardiner inquired. "I know they are resting before dinner; perhaps we should take the children inside until—"

"The other guests have rooms in the opposite wing; their windows are to the back gardens. This wing is for family only," the earl explained.

Elizabeth and Mrs. Gardiner quickly looked at each other, their surprise obvious while trying to properly comprehend the earl's words, neither of them finding anything to say.

Lord Brightmore approached together with Mr. Darcy. The children had been taken off the ponies to resume their play in the grass.

"Darcy, when do you plan to go to Pemberley? We were just talking with Miss Elizabeth Bennet about it," asked the earl.

He hesitated a moment, then answered as his eyes turned instantly to Elizabeth.

"I am not certain yet. I promised Bingley I would stay at Netherfield for a while. I have some business to discuss with Mr. Bennet, and I think this would be a perfect time. It is likely that we will go to Pemberley for the summer."

"Seems a well thought plan, indeed. Bingley will be thrilled that someone finally accepted his invitation. That is—if he does not decide to take the step in the mean time."

The conversation stopped abruptly as the children became tired and restless. Mrs. Gardiner and Lady Selina, together with the governess, retired to their rooms. Lord Matlock had some business to attend to, while Lord Brightmore followed his wife.

As there were only the three of them, the moment turned slightly awkward. Elizabeth needed to gather herself after the revelation that he planned to return to Netherfield. He had business with her father?

"Ladies, would you care to join me for a short walk? If you are not very tired, I mean."

"I am not tired, but it depends on Georgiana. If she wishes to…" Elizabeth said.

The girl hesitated a little then looked from Elizabeth to her brother.

"I am a little tired, I confess. I would rather rest before dinner. But you should not abandon the walk because of me."

There was another moment of silence; Darcy looked at her, but Elizabeth was unable to decide. She wished to have a few moments with him, but the house was full of people. If they were seen, the gossip and speculations would never end —especially from Miss Bingley and Lady Sinclair.

"Perhaps I should go and rest, too. Maybe another time would be better," she said.

The expression of disappointment on his face was unmistakable, and she immediately regretted her decision, though she knew it was the only acceptable one. Before realising her own words, she continued.

"I am sorry; it would have been lovely to…but I think another time would be better."

"Then I shall come," said Miss Darcy.

"Pardon me?"

"I know you wished to go for a walk, but you cannot because of my absence. I shall go."

Stunned, Elizabeth looked at the girl who barely dared to express her opinion only a few months ago. The determination in her voice was equally touching and amusing.

"Georgiana, you may go and rest, dearest. Miss Bennet and I will go for a walk. We will return shortly," Darcy said with a voice that admitted no contradiction, and before any of them had time to reply, he put Elizabeth's hand on his arm and started walking.

After a short glance at them, Miss Darcy returned to the house at a slow pace with a contented smile that lit her eyes. She was not tired at all.

BOTH OF THEM LOOKED STRAIGHT ahead while the path took them towards a small grove at the end of the side garden.

"Are you upset?" he asked. "That I forced you to come?"

She smiled. "You did not force me, sir. And no, I am not upset."

"I will come to Netherfield after we return to town." His tone was hesitant. "I hope it is not an inconvenience for you?"

"No, no…I am just a little surprised. My father did not mention—"

"We discussed this possibility, but it was not settled until recently. And…there is another thing I would like to ask you. I have wanted to ask you for some time now. I shall write to Mr. Bennet, too, but I need to be certain of your answer first."

He stopped, and she had to do the same; they faced each other for a moment, and she felt all her strength abandon her. Her knees were unable to support her, and she briefly looked around for a support. Did he intend to propose to her again? Was it possible? So hastily? It never crossed her mind that he might do that. How did it happen? She looked at him, searching for the proper words.

"I would be honoured if you accept my invitation to spend the summer at Pemberley...in July and August. Georgiana and I would be happy for you to be our guest. Not just you alone— I shall send an invitation to Mr. Bennet...for the entire family. It will be his decision... I hope Mrs. Gardiner will be there too. I wished to be certain that this idea would be agreeable to you before asking Mr. Bennet."

She had already stopped breathing, so when he finished his question, she continued to look at him in disbelief. He invited her to spend the summer at Pemberley. And she thought— She was such a simpleton! If he only knew how ridiculous she had been...

She needed some time to regain her composure before she was able to reply.

"I thank you. I would be very happy to accept your invitation if my father agrees to it."

"Excellent." All the time they spoke, his gaze never abandoned her face; she could feel his eyes searching for her feelings, and the fear that he understood her foolish thoughts embarrassed her deeply.

He resumed their walk at a slow pace; she still held his arm, but her hand barely touched it.

As they walked, she noticed they were tracing a circle. They had departed a little, but now the path was taking them back. She startled again when he spoke.

"We shall be back in a few minutes. I thought it would be best if we do not go too far...today. It is quite late, and we should prepare for dinner."

"It is for the best, indeed."

He pointed out another path that left the grove and seemed to go towards a hill.

"That road would make a wonderful walk. This path travels up to the hill in front of us—there—see? It goes along up to the peak; you cannot see it very well from here because the hill is covered in woods. But the view from the top of the hill is spectacular. I could not describe it to you. You must see for yourself someday."

Elizabeth leaned her head and tried to follow the path with her eyes. Mr. Darcy tried to show her where to look, and in doing so, their heads almost touched. He gently put his arm around her shoulders for a moment.

"I would like very much to see it...someday..." she whispered.

He said nothing, only took her hand and placed it properly back on his arm, continuing to walk to the house. When they almost reached the main gate, he said sternly.

"At these kinds of parties, people are used to staying up very late in the evening and sleeping late in the mornings. If one woke around seven, there would be plenty of time for a walk before breakfast."

Silence fell again, as she did not know how to answer.

"I rarely sleep after seven," she eventually replied just before they entered the house, and she hurried to her room to prepare for dinner.

Chapter 15

"You are beautiful, Lizzy," Mrs. Gardiner said from the doorway.

Elizabeth abandoned her image in the mirror and glanced at her aunt. "*You* look beautiful, Aunt. I really believe this trip suits you very well indeed."

"Thank you, dear. I am just enjoying the pleasant company, and I am glad to see my children so happy."

"I am grateful to know you have good friends like Lord Matlock and Lady Selina. I am well aware that your situation is perfectly safe and there is no need to worry for your and my cousins' well-being, but the comfort of a close friend is more valuable than anything."

"True, dearest; Lady Selina and her family have been of great help. I could never thank them enough," Mrs. Gardiner replied, and Elizabeth saw that her aunt was slightly embarrassed.

"And I have to say, aunt, I felt honoured and a little overwhelmed that Lord Matlock offered us rooms in the family wing. It is quite astonishing."

"I was surprised, too. I never thought that... It is an honour, indeed. Lord Matlock is very kind, and he is truly fond of you, dearest. I wonder whether he still tries to marry you to his sons," Mrs. Gardiner tried to joke. "Did you speak with Jane? How is she?"

"Yes, I did. I visited a little earlier. She has a splendid apartment on the corner, just at the end of this wing. I thought we easily could have stayed together; there was no need to have separate rooms. I miss talking to Jane. I think she has a lot to share, and I have not spent enough time with her these last few days."

"Well, you will have plenty of time to spend together when you return to Hertfordshire. And, with God's will, perhaps she will have even more things to share then. I wonder when Mr. Bingley will take the plunge."

"Mr. Bingley seems completely bewitched, poor man. I think he cannot even breathe without her. He must do something sometime soon; I am certain of that."

"And what about you, Lizzy, do you not have anything to share?"

"No…nothing to share at the moment. I think we are expected at dinner; it is quite late."

Elizabeth's estimation about being late proved correct. By the time they arrived, the entire party was gathered in the drawing room.

Their hosts greeted them and then seated them near Jane and Georgiana. Elizabeth cast a quick glance to Darcy; he was seated in a corner next to the colonel and the viscount.

"Lady Selina was so kind as to offer me one of her horses," Jane whispered to Elizabeth.

"I have one for Mrs. Gardiner, too." Lady Selina smiled. "Tomorrow we shall go for a long ride to become accustomed to the horses. We do not want surprises during the hunt."

"What about you, Miss Elizabeth? Did you bring your own mount?" Lady Sinclair asked.

"Oh, Eliza does not ride. She is much fonder of walking," Miss Bingley replied.

"Walking? What do you mean walking? Surely you cannot pretend to walk on country roads—any farther than the back garden!"

"Eliza is quite fond of walking on country roads. I remember one time she walked more than three miles to Netherfield, and it was just a day after rain," Miss Bingley continued.

"You cannot be serious," Lady Sinclair replied, looking straight at Elizabeth, her tone as contemptuous as her gaze.

"I am perfectly serious, I assure you," Miss Bingley insisted. "Eliza is here; she can tell you all the details."

Both women looked at her, but Elizabeth remained silent, holding their stares. From the corner of her eye, she could see Darcy and the young Matlocks obviously on edge. She turned to Darcy for a moment, and their eyes met enough to share a smile. He took a gulp from his wine. She did not need his help; her smile told him as much.

"Well, Miss Elizabeth?" asked Lady Sinclair impatiently. "What have you to say? Is it true you do not ride? And did you really walk three miles?"

"I could say quite a lot, but I will restrain myself from doing so. I have learned that it is a lady's virtue not to say everything that crosses her mind," Elizabeth said with sharp mockery. "As for whether I prefer riding or walking, Miss Bingley seems excessively familiar with my likes and dislikes; it must be a proof of her affection and friendship—for which I am grateful."

"But if you do not ride, I am certain you do not hunt either. Why did you come to a hunting party?" Lady Sinclair asked impatiently. The rudeness of her question made Georgiana and Jane turn pale and took Elizabeth by surprise.

"That is not—" Darcy began firmly, but Elizabeth interrupted him as she replied.

"I do not ride and certainly do not hunt, but I can still enjoy the beauties of Matlock, and I dare say that is sufficient reason to accept Lord Matlock's generous invitation. I am certain I will find other pleasant ways to employ my time. Besides, though your ladyship enjoys riding and hunting, I am certain those are not the only reasons you decided to join the party, Lady Sinclair," Elizabeth said, her expression light and amused.

Lady Sinclair needed a long moment to reply.

"I am an excellent rider and an excellent hunter," she stated impetuously.

"Nobody doubts your hunting skills, Eve," said Lord Matlock, approaching and patting her shoulder. "You need not share it so openly. I would suggest more discretion, dear."

The colonel's laughter burst out like a gust of wind while all the others seemed dumbfounded. Darcy properly hid his laugh behind his glass while Bingley looked completely lost, uncertain whether he should laugh or not. Jane's apparent discomfort forbade his being amused.

Lady Sinclair's anger changed her countenance; she looked pointedly at Elizabeth and demanded a glass of wine as she struggled to regain her composure.

"Why are you laughing, Robert? More discretion would do you no harm either from time to time, boy," Lord Matlock continued, oblivious to the tension around him. It was difficult to ignore that he had already enjoyed a few more brandies than he should have.

The colonel laughed louder; this time, Mr. Bingley considered it safe to join him.

"Eve was questioning Miss Elizabeth about why she came to the party," explained Lady Selina. "It seems Eve is equally displeased with the children attending the party and with Miss Elizabeth, but unfortunately we can do little to improve her comfort."

"Well, I can easily understand Eve being displeased with Miss Elizabeth's presence. Come, let us go the dining room; dinner is waiting. I am starving; brandy always makes me hungry. Eve darling, do not be upset; hunting skills are not always successful," the earl concluded, attempting to take Lady Sinclair's arm.

But she turned her back to the others, walked alone to the dining room, and then seated herself towards the middle of the table without asking whether there were fixed arrangements.

Elizabeth remained a few steps behind while the pairs followed Lord Matlock: Jane and Bingley, Lady Selina and her husband, the colonel and his brother.

The Darcy siblings stayed with Elizabeth. Mr. Darcy was silent and seemed preoccupied while Miss Darcy was positively worried.

"Eve is very impolite; she always has been," whispered Georgiana.

"Miss Bennet." They turned and looked at Mr. Darcy, surprised by his intervention. His eyes were locked on Elizabeth's face.

"I understand your wish of my not interfering, but if this kind of conversation continues, I shall not remain silent." He seemed severe and preoccupied, and Elizabeth smiled at him.

Dinner passed uneventfully as their attention was deservedly directed towards their plates and the skilfully prepared dishes meant to satisfy the most pretentious and severe tastes.

Afterwards, the entire party returned to the drawing room, where coffee and drinks were served together as Lord Matlock declared he was not inclined to separate from the ladies; shortly, he kindly asked the ladies to play and sing for them.

Georgiana instantly paled, looking at her brother with obvious worry. However, she had no reason for concern. Miss Bingley, Mrs. Hurst, and Lady Sinclair instantly responded to the request, eager to entertain the gentlemen.

Elizabeth could not help wondering why such a beautiful woman as Lady Sinclair was trying so hard to raise Mr. Darcy's interest—and with apparently so little success. She slowly turned to watch his expression closely. He was speaking with his uncle and his cousins without a trace of interest in the performer at the pianoforte. He caught her glance and their eyes locked an instant; a small, barely visible smile appeared at the corner of his lips. She smiled back, slowly averting her eyes from him.

After the ladies performed, the guests took their places around the card tables. Mrs. Gardiner declined playing as did Elizabeth.

"Miss Eliza, you still despise playing cards?" asked Miss Bingley.

"I do not despise playing cards, Miss Bingley, as I previously had the pleasure of informing you last year at Netherfield. I am simply not inclined to play at the moment."

"Miss Elizabeth Bennet always prefers reading to cards." Miss Bingley smiled with irony.

"I am not surprised," Lady Sinclair replied. "Reading is exceedingly boring. Mr. Darcy, why are you still standing, sir? Will you not come and play with us?"

"No…no thank you. I am not inclined to play cards at the moment, either. In fact, I would rather read if I could only find a book to raise my interest." He then turned to Elizabeth and said with perfect composure:

"I am considering searching for a book in the library. Miss Elizabeth, Georgiana, would you care to join me? I am sure you will find something to interest you."

Lady Sinclair and Miss Bingley stared at him, anger and offence mingled in their expressions. Elizabeth bore the surprise as well as she could, but she did not answer immediately. Finally, as he waited patiently, she simply rose and followed him together with Georgiana. She heard the disapproving voice behind her but did not turn to listen.

If she believed Mr. Darcy was somehow joking, he proved her wrong. He directed them to the library and opened the massive door to invite them inside.

"So, Miss Bennet, what kind of book would you prefer? You may choose whatever you like; here are…" He spoke calmly, presenting her each section of the library with an inviting gesture. Georgiana remained a little behind, taking a seat near the window.

Elizabeth followed his gestures, curiosity mixed with disbelief that he actually
180

left the other guests to escort her from the room. Slowly, her passion for books overcame the discomfort she felt. She became more and more fascinated by the shelves, and she approached so she could examine each book as she gently brushed her fingers over them.

Darcy took a few steps back, watching Elizabeth with vivid interest.

At some point, as she stretched to reach a book, Elizabeth's eyes were caught by three small pictures near each other on a high shelf; she could not see too well, but she discerned a beautiful woman near a young boy, pictured at different ages,. With surprise and wonder, Elizabeth recognised a younger Mr. Wickham, smiling charmingly at her.

"So, you really are looking at books? I thought you planned to compromise Miss Bennet and force her to marry you. Really, Darcy, I am quite disappointed" The earl, entering impromptu, was followed by the colonel, who started to laugh; Georgiana turned pale while Elizabeth's cheeks and neck coloured instantly.

"Uncle, for heavens' sake—that was a poor and offensive joke!" Darcy said severely.

"Dearest Miss Elizabeth, you must not be offended," the earl said with amusement. "I have the greatest affection for you. I was just thinking that I easily could understand a man trying to make you marry him by any means.

"I am not offended, sir. I know you are very of jests though they are not always entirely proper."

"That was very harsh but well deserved." The earl laughed. "Please forgive my rudeness… So, what are you doing here? I am sorry to interrupt you, but I would suggest returning to the other guests before more gossip arises. If you want to take a closer look at the books, I would suggest you do it tomorrow, Miss Bennet. Please consider Matlock your home, and do not hesitate to do anything you like."

"Thank you, your lordship, your kind generosity is much appreciated. I will be happy to keep the company of the children and of your library in the next days." She laughed.

They eventually returned to the other guests, who were still engaged in playing cards.

Not long after that, Mrs. Gardiner and Lady Selina declared they were tired and wished to retire; Miss Darcy joined them, and after a short hesitation, the Bennet sisters said good night and followed the other ladies.

Just before she left the room, Elizabeth dared a glance at Mr. Darcy; he was looking after her insistently with no attempt to conceal his interest. It was almost midnight.

Elizabeth spent nearly an hour talking to Jane until her sister gently suggested that she could keep her eyes open no longer, and then she returned to her room.

Jane was happy—that was beyond any doubt—even if Mr. Bingley seemed undecided or not courageous enough to propose. She did not allow Miss Bingley and Mrs. Hurst to deceive her with their pretensions of friendship any longer, but she managed to keep an amiable relation with them, and she seemed content with that state.

Elizabeth fell asleep when it was almost dawn; the sunshine gently caressed her face through the window, and she almost jumped from her bed. It was past seven, and though she knew her behaviour was childish and slightly ridiculous, she panicked—first, because she was afraid he might presume she would not come and second, because she had not time enough to prepare herself as she would like.

While hurrying to put on her gown and fix her hair, she briefly considered that he might not even be there. He surely had stayed later the previous night, and it was likely that he did not wake up earlier.

The house was still and silent; not even a servant could be heard. She needed only a few minutes to trespass the front garden and reach the small grove where they had met a day earlier. Even before she was close enough, she sensed that her worries about his not being there were groundless. Her doubts had been unjustified once again.

Darcy turned to face her as she approached. He took a few steps to meet her, and his welcome smile spoke eloquently of his delight in seeing her. She laughed nervously.

"I am sorry for being late. I slept longer than usual."

"You are not late—in fact, I do not remember having a fixed hour to meet."

"That is the most perfect answer." She laughed again as she slowly regained her spirits.

"Shall we?" he asked while offering her his arm, which she took and held instantly. Thunder followed them at a few steps distance.

"It is a beautiful morning," she said.

"Indeed—it will be a warm day. Did you sleep well, I hope?"

"To be honest, neither very well nor very long. I spent quite some time speaking with Jane."

"Is Miss Bennet well? She seemed quite well, if I might say."

"Yes, she is, thank you. And I think Mr. Bingley is quite well, too," she replied meaningfully.

"Yes, I noticed. I do not remember seeing him as happy before."

"It was fortunate that some of his friends advised him to return to London and then to Netherfield…back in January, I mean…" she said, choosing her words carefully.

He did not respond immediately. "It would have been even more fortunate if his friends had not advised him to leave Netherfield in the first place. Some advice should not be given even if it is required."

"But then again, there are times when one can be wrong though one means well. It is important to recognise one's own error and to correct it if possible."

"You are too kind. I cannot help wondering what would have happened had we not met in London and had you not given me sufficient information to correct my error."

"And I also wonder what might have happened had we not met in London and had *you* not given me sufficient information to correct *my* error…"

A long pause followed as they began to climb the hill; neither dared to say more.

He gently covered her hand, which was resting on his arm, with his palm.

"I hope you will have a lovely time with the hunting party," she finally broke the silence.

"Yes… To be honest, I am not quite so fond of hunting… I…" he turned his head and looked at her; she could feel his gaze and turned her eyes to meet his. He looked as though he was not certain whether he should continue.

"I would not have come had I not known you would be here," he said.

She held his gaze, speechless, her heart beating wildly and her cheeks burning.

"I do not ride, and I surely do not hunt. The only reason I came was for the company…and for long walks," she whispered, flustered, then laughed to hide her embarrassment. "Lady Sinclair was correct in asking me why I came."

"Lady Sinclair was not correct in anything she said," he replied severely. "I apologise for her; she is rude and spoilt, and she believes everybody outside her circle is beneath her and not worthy of civility. She is accustomed to having her own way in everything. She needs to be put in her place; I shall not allow her to offend you again."

He seemed troubled by the difficult situation in which she was put; Elizabeth was equally amused and pleased with his reaction. He suddenly stopped again and turned to her.

"I was the same, was I not? When I first came to Hertfordshire, I mean."

The question took her by surprise, and she searched a long moment for the proper answer.

"Yes, I was. Your silence answers my question."

"You were haughty and aloof, and yes, I imagine you believed everyone to be beneath you," she eventually admitted. "You were not the most pleasant company, but you have never been rude in such a way."

"Yes, I imagine I was not the most pleasant company…"

"But it is important that you recognised what was wrong and tried to make amends. As for Lady Sinclair, please do not feel you need to intervene. I am quite amused; she reminds me of Miss Bingley, and I dare say I am quite capable of handling them both."

Another long moment of silence followed. She looked around; sunbeams were playing through the leaves, and the silence was broken only by the gentle breeze.

"I need to intervene because Lady Sinclair and Miss Bingley's rudeness is mostly caused by me. It is my fault and I cannot—"

"Oh, that is quite a vain statement, sir. You mean to imply that I have no personal qualities that might make Lady Sinclair and Miss Bingley hate me? That is unkind!"

"I did not mean to imply that… I…" He looked so embarrassed that she started to laugh.

"Sir, I was joking. I know you are the main reason for their rudeness," she laughed, blushing. "But there must be other reasons, too. Miss Bingley has been rude to me almost from the beginning of our acquaintance, long before you had any particular interest…"

She looked at him and expected him to smile, but he looked even more uneasy.

"That is…not entirely correct," he replied, hesitantly

"What do you mean?" He stopped and made her do the same; he gently turned her, so they faced each other before he continued.

"Do you remember one evening at Sir William's when he suggested I should dance with you? When I asked you to dance and you refused me?"

Her eyes laughed and sparkled as she replied. "I remember. I know I had offended and upset you, but I was truly not inclined to dance."

"You did not offend me and surely did not upset me—not in the way you believe. But that evening, Miss Bingley noticed our interaction, and she asked where my thoughts tended. I said I was thinking of your beautiful, sparkling eyes," he concluded as she stared at him in disbelief, certain there must be some mistake.

"But… That happened so long ago…even before I attended Jane at Netherfield."

"Yes… I imagine that was one of the reasons for her continued rudeness."

"But…how is it possible? I never imagined that… I would never believe that… I noticed you often looked at me, but I was certain it was only to uncover my faults."

He found nothing to say, as she looked very troubled. He knew he should find a way to calm her, but he could think of nothing proper. She was as surprised as he had been when he discovered his own error in his estimation of her feelings.

It was Elizabeth who continued to speak.

"It appears Miss Bingley is much more perceptive than I," she confessed. "As was Charlotte—she told me many times that you might have a special interest in me."

"Mrs. Collins is a very wise woman." Darcy smiled. "Miss Bingley—much less so."

"Well, I cannot possibly speak of others' wisdom since I am humbled by my own…"

"You must not judge yourself so harshly. I am ashamed to admit that, for a long time, I tried valiantly to conceal my interest in you. It appears that I was quite successful."

They reached the top of the hill, and he stopped. He gently put his hands on her shoulders and turned her to look down at the view. She gasped then sighed deeply at the beauty spread at their feet. Her heart was filled with joy while her mind was in turmoil.

His palms continued to rest on her shoulders, and he was only a few inches behind her. She barely dared to breathe when he leaned and whispered to her, "I have always admired this view, but it has never seemed as beautiful as today."

"Thank you," she said a few moments later. "Thank you for bringing me here and showing me this beauty. I know you did it most willingly, but I still want to thank you."

"You are most welcome." He smiled. "I must thank you for joining me here. I did not dare hope you would really come. Do you want to sit for a few minutes?"

Elizabeth agreed, instantly feeling the loss of his touch and closeness. He moved to Thunder, took a small blanket from the saddlebag, and spread it on the grass. She was pleasantly surprised and smiled, blushing: he just said he dared not hope she would come, but he was prepared anyway—prepared for her.

She sat on a corner, allowing him space near her; he hesitated until she specifically asked him to join her. Then each of them turned to look straight ahead at the valley, both embarrassed by the solitude and intimacy.

"You have been successful, indeed," she resumed their previous conversation. "I did not at all suspect that you might have a particular interest in me…"

He was surprised but seemed relieved that she decided to continue their delicate discussion. He stared at her another moment, then he averted his eyes towards the view in front of them, and she did the same as suddenly it was too hard to bear the other's eyes.

"Not even when we met in London in January? Not even at the ball?"

"There were some indications that made me wonder, but I could not possibly be certain, and I did not dare presume… But may I ask—why did you try to conceal your interest? I mean—you did not hide it from Miss Bingley, after all…"

"I did not want to raise expectations. I was certain you were aware of my feelings and shared them…and at that time, I never considered I could marry someone outside my own circle… So I thought it would be only fair to keep a reasonable distance from you. What do you think of my vanity now? I was equally stupid and conceited."

His voice became lower and more hesitant as though he were ashamed of his faults.

"Perhaps it was my fault, too. I must have done something to make you believe I sought your attentions."

"No, it was not your fault at all," he hurried to assure her. "It was my pride and my selfishness that made me believe what was most convenient for me. You are not to blame."

"And…what made you change your mind?" she dared to inquire. "About marriage, I mean… Less than two months later you proposed…"

"I cannot say what changed my mind—what gesture or word or smile defeated my resistance. I just awoke one morning and realised my life would not be complete without you…and that it was my choice how my life would be. By that time, I was even more certain that you expected and would welcome my addresses, but I was wrong again—not about my wishes but about yours," he said sadly.

"No…you were not wrong…not completely wrong. I cannot deny that my feelings changed after we met in London. It is true that I did not expect a proposal—and not of that kind… And I was still upset and angry with you because I suspected that you convinced Mr. Bingley to leave my sister, but you were not completely wrong…perhaps just a little hasty."

"Are you still angry…or upset with me?" he whispered, casting a quick glance at her.

"No…no, I am not…" She felt his gaze but could not bear to meet it yet.

"And I shall not be hasty any more…but I must know… and you are too generous to trifle with me… Would you please tell me—are your feelings as they were in Hertfordshire…or as they were in London? My feelings and wishes never changed, but yours…?" he asked tentatively, his voice slightly trembling.

She was certain her heart would stop, and she wondered whether it ever would beat again as her chest clenched. How could she even speak?

"My feelings…my feelings are…different than they were in Hertfordshire and… different than they were in London," she whispered breathlessly.

She slowly turned her head to him, and his eyes were there, waiting for her. The expression of heartfelt delight on his face lit his eyes. She smiled—shy and nervous—and he smiled back—joyful and relieved—as they finally faced each other and remained still, stealing happiness from each other's eyes.

Then he edged even closer and removed his gloves then took her hands and removed hers. He placed a gentle, warm kiss in each palm then held her hands in his, never releasing her gaze. She licked her lips, and his eyes lowered to her mouth. She struggled to swallow as he slowly released her hand, untied her bonnet and put it down then daringly placed a soft kiss on her cheek, brushing the corner of her mouth. His lips rested there, close to hers, burning her skin and making her wish for more. She even turned her head a little, but he slowly pulled back; she kept her eyes closed as he put back her bonnet.

"We should leave; it is quite late," he said unexpectedly, and she sighed with disappointment. She could not hear his words perfectly well, so she did not move. He took her hand and made her rise while he placed another soft kiss on the back of her hand.

As he arranged the saddle and she tried to find support for her weak knees, he took her hands again. "We shall be home in no time if we ride rather than walk. Do you trust me?"

She nodded in acceptance, unable to think what he truly meant, but she did trust him. He lifted her in his arms and put her on the saddle; then he climbed up behind her.

The saddle was too small for two people, so she felt herself crushed against him as he tried to arrange her as comfortably as possible. She was seated in his lap, her legs hanging over his left side. His arms embraced her while his hands took the reins, his left hand against her thigh and his right hand against her hip.

He leaned near her ear and whispered, his lips touching her skin. "Are you comfortable?"

"No, I am not. But I do trust you," she replied, her hands clinging to his arms while Thunder stepped proudly down the path.

The view before them was splendid, but the ride down the hill was frightening;

her heart was filled with overwhelming happiness while her body was tormented by a storm of fire and ice at his touch: every move that brushed them against each other and every whisper that caressed her ear. Seated between his inner thighs, she could feel his warmth and his strength. He was a skilful rider as he was accustomed to order and control. She did not feel comfortable, but she felt safe and protected. Their hands found each other and their fingers entwined. She was so close to him that she could hardly breathe, but she barely needed breath.

Matlock Manor suddenly came in sight, and he stopped the horse; she turned to him, surprised, and he watched from mere inches away. Their faces were so close that they could feel each other. He leaned even closer.

"You shall decide when and what you want me to say, as well as when and what you want me to do. I shall not rush you, but please remember—I am impatient." He smiled.

His eyes seemed on fire as she had never seen them before. His voice, however, was tender and caring, and his countenance serene.

"I will remember," she said.

Her lips were dry again, and she could hardly speak; her eyes closed, and she leaned forward until his lips finally dared to meet hers, touching, caressing and tasting them in a soft, gentle kiss that ended too soon, leaving her breathless and him regretful for his promise not to be hasty. He had strong doubts that he would be able to keep it.

In the small grove just beside Matlock's front garden, Mr. Darcy dismounted and helped Elizabeth down. By the time they entered the house, the servants were about, a clear sign that the other guests had awakened. Even more, Lady Selina and Mrs. Gardiner appeared from the living room and called Elizabeth, asking where she had been.

She did not dare turn her head again, but she could feel Darcy's eyes on her back while her body still held the warmth of his embrace and her lips still carried his taste.

Chapter 16

Darcy closed the door behind him and lay back in the large armchair by the window. Alone in his apartment, he found it difficult to credit that the morning walk was real.

Had all the nights of struggle, disappointment, anger and self-reproach finally come to an end—and so easily? Had he only to be honest and openly display his feelings for her to make a choice in his favour? And did she truly choose so readily?

For some time she had led him to understand that her feelings for him had changed and she was not opposed to accepting his attentions. However, her expressions, her reception of his confession, her acceptance of his kiss—all so exceeded his hopes that he still feared their reality.

He closed his eyes and allowed himself to be overcome by the feelings he tried so long to deny. When he could gather himself enough to think rationally, he realised they had not actually come to an understanding, but how could there be a more complete understanding than the way they spoke to each other? They confessed their past faults and mistakes, their present feelings and desires, and their future hopes.

'I trust you,' she had said, and that statement was all he needed and desired. He did not actually propose to her again, but he allowed her the complete freedom of her wishes.

He had kissed her on her cheek cautiously, careful not to upset her; he knew he should not take that liberty so soon, but he was not strong enough to fight the temptation. She was not upset, however—surprised, nervous, and shy but surely not upset. He smiled to himself as he remembered that his lips stopped near hers —almost touching them—and she had timidly moved her head towards him. If he had turned that kiss into a real one, she would not have rejected him, of that he was certain. They had been alone with their newly discovered and shared feelings, and the temptation to allow his love and passion to conquer her was overwhelming and difficult to control.

However, it was not quite as difficult as it was to bear the sweet torture of their shared journey home. She did not hesitate a moment when he asked her to ride with him; she said she trusted him, and she proved it. He could feel her tension and perhaps even fear—especially when Thunder clambered down the hill—but he knew she had entwined her fingers with his from more than mere fright. She enjoyed the caress of their hands as much as he did; he was certain of that, but he was also certain that their nearness affected her less than it did him. He whispered to her a few times, and her scent as well as the silky warmth of her skin made him dizzy. Each of the stallion's steps brought her closer and brushed her against him such that every fibre of his body was painfully aware. As he felt her relax in his firm embrace, with every passing moment, he became tense, nervous—and angry with himself for behaving like a schoolboy.

And the kiss—the real kiss—was her desire as much as his. He had allowed her the liberty to decide—and she did. He smiled with tenderness at her obvious lack of experience while his heart paced wildly at the remembered soft taste of her lips.

He startled violently when a servant insistently called his name, bringing him back from his thoughts. He was expected downstairs for breakfast. Yes, it was breakfast time; he should have known that.

As he apologised for the delay and took his seat at the table, he glanced at Elizabeth; she was speaking with her aunt, but his eyes made her turn towards him, flustered.

He was suddenly aware of a dilemma: should he wait until they returned to Hertfordshire to speak to Mr. Bennet or should he write him immediately? In any case, it was imperiously necessary that he clarify with Elizabeth the nature of their understanding just to be certain there were no misunderstandings remaining. Moreover, he absolutely must call her *Elizabeth*—at least when they were not in company.

"So—are you ready?" Lord Matlock inquired impatiently. "The horses are waiting."

The party was prepared for the ride, planned the previous day. While the others were eager to spend time outdoors, Georgiana seemed worried as she approached Elizabeth.

"You know, I think I should stay with you. After all, I am riding Duke, and I surely do not need to become accustomed to him.

Elizabeth gently took her hands and laughed. "I shall be forever grateful for your care, my dear friend, but you must not worry for me, truly. I have already rejected Jane's offer, and I would feel guilty if you cannot enjoy your ride because of me."

"But it is such a lovely day! Perhaps I should ask uncle to prepare a carriage."

"I know it is a beautiful day; I had a wonderfully long walk earlier. In fact, I am a bit fatigued; I think I will rest a little while you are out."

"My dear, we should go," Mr. Darcy said, smiling at them. "I would suggest that Miss Bennet rest a little while we are gone," he added, and both ladies laughed.

189

"Elizabeth just told me she wished to rest a little." Georgiana explained their amusement.

"I see… Well, it pleases me to see that Miss Bennet and I share the same thoughts," he replied, looking pointedly at Elizabeth.

"I thank you both for your care." Elizabeth smiled. "Please enjoy your time; I shall see you again soon," she added as the Darcys reluctantly left the house.

Elizabeth followed them with her eyes then hurried to her room. She opened the window and hid herself by the curtain as she looked with great interest at the departing group, attempting to recognise each person. Even from a distance, it was not difficult to recognise Mr. Darcy and Thunder, just as it was not difficult to recognise Lady Sinclair, riding impetuously near him.

Elizabeth had to admit to herself that jealousy—even when unjustified and unreasonable—was a disturbing feeling.

She stood at the window, gazing after them for a while until they became small, restless points moving across the fields; she was soon nestled in her bed under the covers. She knew she should be happy, relieved, trustful and grateful for everything that unexpectedly happened that morning, but she was still not convinced it was real.

Her fears, wonderings, questions and doubts were at an end. He opened his heart to her—again—and offered her hope, answers, and certainties. He admitted his errors and took all the blame upon himself; he was generous in vanquishing her guilt, and she enjoyed receiving his generosity though she knew she did not deserve it.

Her heart melted as she remembered how easily her words brought joy to his handsome face. She was no longer afraid to admit to herself what she began to understand but feared to hope for so long: he was exactly the man who, in disposition and talents, would most suit her. His understanding and temper, though unlike her own, would answer all her wishes, and from his judgement, information, and knowledge of the world, she would receive a benefit of great importance. It would be a union that—she hoped—would be to the advantage of both. She knew he needed little to complete his character, and she had little to offer him except her feelings, but perhaps—yes, perhaps—her ease and liveliness would soften his mind and improve his manners.

In the solitude of her bed, she smiled, recollecting the way his manners towards her had improved since they first met—well, perhaps not improved but certainly softened.

Slowly, her mind returned to their early meeting: every word, every glance, and every touch. She recalled his fingers entwining with hers, his arms holding her tightly, his warmth, his strength, the intoxicating feeling of his lips on hers, his voice and his gaze—the feeling of having a bond between them…and the chill as he left.

She briefly considered that she was exhausted and needed to sleep a little before she spent time with the children. It took only an instant for her to fall into a deep asleep.

Elizabeth did not wake until a din of voices from the yard invaded her room through the open window. The party had returned from riding, and she was still in bed!

As if she were late for an important meeting, she hurriedly changed her clothes and put up her hair as well as she could. It was quite late in the afternoon—or so she thought.

She expected the others to be in the drawing room, but there it was all silence. She met a young maid who smiled, greeted her politely, and then informed her that the guests had retired to their rooms and she expected them down in an hour's time for tea and refreshments. The children, the maid said, were in their apartments, sleeping.

An hour—of course, what was she thinking? Surely, everyone needed to rest and change from their riding clothes! She felt slightly embarrassed by her childish eagerness as she thanked the maid. She had an hour to wait and needed to find a way to employ her time.

She briefly considered returning to her room but abandoned the idea and walked towards the library instead. She would find something to read.

Even before she opened the heavy door, curiosity began to war with her better judgement. The temptation to take another look—closer and more attentive—at the pictures of Mr. Wickham was compelling.

She entered the large room and walked slowly along the walls, glancing at the impressive shelves, then stopped in front of the small paintings, studying them with great interest.

"Miss Bennet?"

She startled so violently that she needed a moment before she finally turned and lifted her eyes to meet Darcy's inquiring ones. He smiled, obviously pleased to see her.

"Forgive me—did I frighten you? I just came from the drawing room—a maid told me you might be here—and to be honest I hoped I could speak to you privately a moment."

"I was in the drawing room a few minutes ago, and I was told everybody was upstairs resting. You did not frighten me; I was just surprised. Did you have a pleasant ride?"

She tried to smile while she felt her heart beating wildly. He took her hand and invited her to sit on the couch.

"Not particularly pleasant... I mean, it was an ordinary ride. I confess I prefer riding in much smaller company."

She laughed. "You are not fond of large parties, I have noticed."

"No, not fond, indeed..."

"I hope Georgiana had a pleasant time."

"She did." He hesitated and averted his eyes from her for a moment then looked at her again. "I hope you do not mind; I took the liberty of telling her...about our discussion..."

She blushed but held his gaze. He appeared uncomfortable and worried.

"I do not mind, but pray tell me—what did you tell her?"

"I told her that we talked and that I have your permission to court you..."

"I see...and what did she say?"

He hesitated again, and she noticed he fought to cover a smile.

"She said, 'Surely you are joking!'"

Elizabeth looked at him in complete puzzlement. She did not expect such a reaction.

"Why would she say that? Why did she believe you were joking?"

"Well, I asked her the same, and she replied, 'You just began to court her? But I believed you were courting Elizabeth in London! I hope you are telling me that you finally came to an arrangement!' I confess I never saw my sister so disappointed."

Elizabeth laughed, her face burning. He still held her hands.

"I am sorry to be the reason for Georgiana's disappointment."

"No indeed—she was disappointed with *me*—and rightfully so. It made me think..."

His countenance changed again, and he tightened the hold on her hand.

"All these hours I thought of what I said earlier today, and I wondered... As the recent past has proved, there are times when I express myself rather ambiguously," he said, mocking himself. "So...I shall keep my word not to rush you, but I must ask...was it beyond any doubt that I intend to ask for your hand in marriage? You may take all the time you need to be certain, but..."

He was completely distressed again, his fingers unconsciously caressing hers while his voice, grave and deep, was overwhelmed with emotion. She felt grateful that she was sitting, or else her knees certainly would have betrayed her.

"I confess I had some suspicions about your intention, but as the recent past has proved to us, I am not very perceptive, and I dare not make any assumptions... so—no, your intention was not beyond any doubt..." She hoped he noticed that she was joking.

"I see... Then please let me try to rectify my fault, Miss Bennet." His serious, preoccupied gaze captured her eyes, and she could see his expression softening with her every word. He rose from the couch, and she mirrored his move. Slowly, he lifted their joined hands to his heart and spoke, his emotions hardly bearable.

"In vain have I struggled. It will not do. My feelings will not be repressed. You must allow me to tell you how ardently I admire and love you."

She instantly recognised the words, but his voice, his expression, his eyes caressing her face, his hands tenderly holding hers, his lips forcing a smile—everything was so new that the meaning of his declaration became utterly, frightfully different.

She said nothing, so he continued.

"I know I have said these words before, but I need to repeat them because only now do I understand them in depth. I did love and admire you in January, but my love was defeated by my selfish desire—the desire to have you—because I was aware that I could have no peace or tranquillity or joy without you. I thought of little else than how I could have you for myself, and it never occurred to me that I might not have my own way. I believed you to be wishing, expecting my addresses. I came to you without a doubt of my reception, and you taught me the hardest and most useful lesson of my life. You showed me how insufficient were all my pretensions to please a woman worthy of being pleased."

Her strength had long betrayed her, and she was certain she would not be able to contain her tears any longer. She wished him to speak more, to wipe away all the painful memories of that day, to confess to him her own fears and self-reproach, but for the moment she could bear no more. She freed her hand from his tight grip and pressed her fingers against his lips to silence him. His lips, half opened, brushed warmly against her trembling fingers. He paused.

"Mr. Darcy… There are so many things that need to be said between us that a whole day would not suffice. We might be interrupted any moment, so I shall not quarrel with you for the greater share of blame annexed to that day. The conduct of neither, if strictly examined, would be irreproachable; even more, there were other reasons that contributed to our misunderstanding. Perhaps we should delay this discussion for another time. I confess I am still not completely certain of your intention…whether you proposed to me or not…"

The emotion made it difficult for her to speak, and her attempt to dissipate her anxiety with a light tone met with little success. He struggled to continue, but she still held her fingers to his lips, so Elizabeth was the one who spoke further.

"However, there is something that needs to be said this instant. I do feel that the words you just repeated to me were the same yet so different, as I do feel that your…affection for me has changed. I can see it in every glance, every gesture, every word. I could see it long ago when you kindly offered me your trust, though I had so abominably abused you. I could see it in your generous support for my father and—"

He gently captured her hand again to release his lips, which daringly hurried to silence her. She gasped in surprise, but a moment later, she forgot everything she wished to say. His hands abandoned hers and wrapped her in a breathtaking embrace; her own hands tentatively slid around his waist in search of his warmth and his tender support. Her lips shyly tried to learn how to respond to his kiss as her heart beat wildly.

As unexpectedly as it began, Darcy withdrew from her but kept her in his embrace. He gently walked her back to the settee, took her hands again then slowly knelt by her, his face only a few inches from hers, and spoke clearly and simply.

"Miss Elizabeth Bennet, would you do me the honour of marrying me? There is no need to answer me now; you may take all the time you wish—"

"Mr. Darcy?" Her voice interrupted him, serious and determined.

"Yes?"

"As Georgiana said earlier—'surely you are joking, sir'! I thought I already gave you my answer, but it seems you are not very perceptive, either."

He looked at her in disbelief, wondering whether he understood her correctly, and she laughed nervously and tearfully. She then moved slowly and, as he was still kneeling, allowed a shy kiss of her own to give him the answer he needed.

It was no wonder that, when the library door opened and Miss Darcy appeared, searching for Elizabeth, neither of them noticed her presence.

Embarrassed at her intrusion, Miss Darcy slowly retreated, closed the door behind her and propped herself against the wall, catching her breath. Then she joyfully ran through the halls as she did as a little girl. For the first time in her life, she had dared to mock and scold her brother—and with so much success! It seemed that Fitzwilliam Darcy had already made the proper amends to rectify his error. He had always been a man of action—no doubt about that.

LATER THAT DAY THE ENTIRE party was gathered in the drawing room, waiting for dinner to be announced. Still overwhelmed by the events that had changed her life in a heartbeat, Elizabeth had little to say to the others. Her eyes frequently encountered Darcy's own, and more than once she saw Mrs. Gardiner watching her with great interest. She knew she would have to speak to her aunt soon, but she needed a little more time to become accustomed to her unexpected happiness.

Besides, she and Darcy decided not to make their arrangement public until they returned to Hertfordshire and spoke to Mr. Bennet. It would be only a few days delay, but Mrs. Gardiner, who was exceedingly attentive, surely would notice even the smallest change in their behaviour, so it would be difficult to keep the secret.

Earlier, Jane expressed her wish to speak privately, and Elizabeth wondered —briefly—what her sister had to say. It could not be anything grave, as Jane seemed very happy.

Elizabeth noticed Darcy exchanging a few words with Georgiana, and the girl's happy glance allowed little doubt about their discussion. Elizabeth smiled at them both then turned to Jane, who was just whispering something, ashamed that she neglected her sister.

"Jane dearest, I was wondering... After dinner perhaps we can find a few moments to talk—just the two of us? You must tell me about your ride."

"Oh, I would love that, Lizzy. I have so much to tell you—"

"About riding?" Elizabeth laughed, and Jane blushed violently while she whispered.

"No, not really. I mean—the ride was very pleasant..."

"You know, I did not expect Miss Bennet to be such a skilful rider," Lord Matlock intervened. "I was quite impressed. Beautiful and brave and with the sweetest disposition—I say, Miss Bennet, there must be many young men vying for your affection, and very few of them deserve it. You must be stern and particular in your choice," the earl added, and Jane became crimson while Mr. Bingley blanched.

"Bingley, be so kind as to give me a glass of brandy, would you, son? And perhaps you should consider one for yourself; you look quite distressed," Lord Matlock concluded while the colonel quickly moved near Darcy, both struggling to keep their countenance.

Elizabeth did not miss their amusement, but she was not willing to make fun at her sister's expense, so she cast a sharp glance at them. The next moment, the earl's attention found another object.

"What about you, Miss Elizabeth? How did you employ your time? Were you not bored? When do you plan to commence riding lessons?"

"Excellent attempt, your lordship." Elizabeth laughed. "Not very successful, though. It is true that I have significantly changed my opinion about riding during the last few days, but I still prefer walking—"

"I am sorry to hear that, Miss Elizabeth. I had great hope that you would be persuaded to change some of your earlier preferences, but it appears my confidence was undeservedly bestowed. Persuasion is a rare virtue, apparently, and needs much effort, but success is even more worthy," he said with sharp mockery, hidden beneath apparent seriousness.

"Persuasion is indeed a rare virtue, as are patience—and wisdom," Darcy intervened as he moved a few steps nearer. "Besides, I consider it a great merit for a young lady not to change her preferences and opinions easily. Success in convincing a young lady of exceptional wit and self-confidence is worth any effort."

As he spoke, Darcy glanced at Elizabeth and their eyes met and held. Every word brought her equal joy and embarrassment, and she wondered briefly whether the other guests understood to whom they were referring.

"True, true..." the earl added. "Patience and wisdom are great virtues but only if they do not crush and defeat passion and daring."

"You are right, of course, Uncle, but passion and daring require a strong character and superior mind to keep them under good regulation."

During the entire exchange, Darcy barely took his eyes from Elizabeth and looked at his uncle only briefly. She felt increasingly flustered, and breathing became more difficult with every passing moment. She wished to speak, but her lips became so dry that she struggled to open them. Suddenly, she heard herself whispering.

"I would love to learn how to ride if it is possible..."

The others stared at her in utter bewilderment, as her words seemed to have no relevance to the conversation. Mr. Bingley was uncertain about the subject of the discussion, so he gulped some brandy to hide his puzzlement. Then the earl started to laugh, took Elizabeth's hand and kissed it gently.

"I am very happy to hear that, my dear—very happy indeed."

"Not happier than I am, I assure you," Darcy concluded in a lower voice, a mischievous smile lighting his face as he continued to look at Elizabeth.

The earl laughed again.

"I am very happy that you are all happy, gentlemen," Elizabeth finally replied, attempting to sound perfectly light and easy. "Had I known that my riding lessons would bring you so much happiness, I surely would have broached the subject earlier." She forced a laugh.

"The timing was perfect, I assure you, Miss Elizabeth," Darcy replied. "Neither sooner nor later would have been as adequate."

"I cannot argue with you in that, sir," Elizabeth admitted, her eyes still locked with his.

Miss Bingley and Mrs. Hurst were certain that their eyes and their common sense betrayed them when they saw Lord Matlock kissing Eliza Bennet's hand. It was worse than anything they imagined before.

The butler finally invited them all to the dining room. Darcy offered Elizabeth his hand; she took it and began to rise from the settee, but flustered from the earlier conversation and Darcy's meaningful gaze, Elizabeth forgot about the coffee cup in her left hand. The coffee spilled into her lap, a large, dark stain spreading over her gown. She let out a small cry, which caused Darcy to ask if she were hurt.

"No, no, *I* am not hurt—only my pride," she said, crimson and self-conscious, attempting to make light of her carelessness. "Please forgive me; I shall change in an instant. I beg you, proceed with dinner; do not wait for me," she addressed Lady Selina then left the room in a great hurry, while Jane followed her immediately.

"Please forgive me; we will be back shortly." Mrs. Gardiner politely excused herself and left to follow her nieces.

Darcy looked around for a moment, uncertain what he should do and hoping their indiscreet and improper conversation did not upset Elizabeth. He should not have said so much without her permission.

"You seemed preoccupied, Cousin. And very lost in her eyes if I may say so..." the colonel teased him as they walked to the dining room. "Miss Elizabeth is well, I hope?"

"Yes...I believe she is. And feel free to make fun of me, Robert, but please do it privately. I do not want to embarrass Elizabeth more than I already have."

"So—she is 'Elizabeth' now?"

Darcy hesitated a moment. "Yes, she is."

"I see... Is there anything else I should know—anything else you might be tempted to share with me? You know you can trust me when needed."

"I know that. I do not doubt your secrecy. But I beg your patience a little longer."

"I can be patient if you wish me to. I can be the soul of absolute discretion, but I am no fool, so I cannot pretend I do not understand what this means. I shall, but not with you."

"Thank you—your discretion is appreciated." Darcy smiled.

They took their seats at the dinner table, joining the conversation. It took only a couple of minutes for Miss Bingley's comment to arrive.

"I find it strange that anyone could spill coffee on themselves. A lady should be careful how she behaves, especially in company. But of course, we cannot expect someone who rarely leaves her small country estate and the nearby *four and twenty families* to behave properly in illustrious company."

"May we cease speaking about this incident? It is quite irritating. I need more pleasant and witty subjects to enjoy my dinner," said Lady Sinclair sharply.

"Yes, I agree, your ladyship," said Miss Bingley.

"Then, by all means, do introduce some witty subjects, ladies," said Darcy severely. "I have long desired such an unusual event to occur." His voice was as rude as his words, and his sister stared at him in disbelief.

"Mr. Darcy, you seem in low spirits," Lady Sinclair replied. "Is there anything we can do to improve your disposition? Your mood has spoiled my appetite."

"Forgive me, your ladyship. From now on, I shall take your appetite into consideration before allowing my disposition to be openly displayed," Darcy answered coldly.

"Oh, am I wrong, or has Mr. Darcy's disposition changed for the worse since Miss Eliza retired to her room? I have to say, sir, that this revelation is quite astonishing to me. I remember a time when you were not at all partial to Miss Eliza's charms; in fact I remember your avoiding her as much as possible—not to mention her mother. Do you remember when they all invaded us at Netherfield? You even had an argument with Mrs. Bennet; it was *so* amusing. But then Miss Eliza managed somehow to improve your opinion, and at some point you even called her pretty..."

Darcy lifted his eyes from his plate and put down his tableware.

"Yes, I did find Miss Elizabeth pretty, but that was only in the beginning when I did not know her well enough. It has been many months since I have come to admire Miss Elizabeth Bennet and to consider myself privileged to be her friend."

The astonishment of Mr. Bingley's sisters, as well as Lady Sinclair's incredulous disdain, brought an awkward silence to the dinner table. Lord Matlock, interrupted in his animated conversation with Lord Sinclair, turned to Miss Bingley with a sharp smile.

"Miss Bingley, I have long wanted to tell you something. You are a handsome, intelligent young woman and fortunate enough to have a nice dowry. Young men should be clamouring for your attention. Sadly, you are bitter, mischievous, and spiteful. I have yet to hear a single kind or generous word from you about anyone unless you have an interest in flattering that person. Why is that? These are appalling traits to a man, you know. I have to say that, if you continue this way, you will end a spinster; I hope you are aware of that. Lady Sinclair and Mrs. Hurst are not kind either, but they can afford it; they have already secured their husbands while you have not been so fortunate."

Miss Bingley turned white as the blood drained from her face; for a moment, Darcy wondered whether she was able to breathe and briefly considered that she might need help, but he did nothing, barely able to contain his mirth.

Lord Sinclair, who normally should have been offended by the severe criticism of his wife, laughed heartily and emptied his glass of brandy.

Angrily red, Mrs. Hurst and Lady Sinclair looked furiously at Lord Matlock, but their anger turned wild when they noticed Eliza Bennet, smiling from the doorway.

In the midst of that dreadful moment, Mr. Darcy and Mr. Bingley rose and invited the ladies to their seats. Jane took her place near Mr. Bingley, and at the other side of her, Mrs. Gardiner sat to the left of Lady Selina. At the opposite side of the table, Elizabeth was almost forced by Miss Darcy to take the seat between her and her brother.

The footmen brought the next course, and the food was the object of everyone's attention for some time. The gentlemen, warmed by brandy and wine, opened multiple and various conversations, and soon the din of voices made it difficult to understand to each other.

"You seem very quiet," Darcy said to Elizabeth in a low voice. "Are you well?"

"Yes, thank you. I was just thinking… It seemed you had an entertaining debate while we were gone," she whispered, a smile on her lips.

"'Very entertaining' is a description that does not do it justice." He smiled. "May I dare presume that you heard a part of it?"

"I did. I have to say, sir, that for someone as reserved as yourself, who is always in perfect control, you are doing a poor job of concealing your feelings. If you continue in this way, our secret will last until tomorrow at the latest." She cast a quick glance at him, her eyes sparkling with amusement.

"Please forgive me. I have no excuse for not keeping my word but—"

"Excuses are not needed." She smiled teasingly. "I was just wondering—perhaps you should write my father after all. In some circumstances, a week can be a very long time."

He stared at her, and she turned her head to meet his eyes; for a heartbeat, they looked only at each other, oblivious to their surroundings. His expression spoke to her more eloquently than words, and the gleam in her eyes was all the reply she need offer.

"Miss Bennet seems exceptionally happy tonight," Darcy said a few moments later.

"Yes, she is; she just shared some extraordinary news with us. But I presume you already know, do you not, Mr. Darcy?"

He hesitated a moment. "Yes, I do; Bingley and I spoke earlier, and I expected he would do something when he returned from riding."

"I see… Did you… Did he propose because you told him to do so?" Her voice was suddenly hesitant and expressionless. He stared at her intently.

"I hope you are still mocking me. You cannot imagine that Bingley proposed to Miss Bennet for reasons other than genuine affection; he has waited long enough."

"Forgive me; I did not mean to imply otherwise… It is just that…"

"There is no need to apologise. You have every reason to fear my interference, whether for good or ill. It is also true that I spoke to him and encouraged him a little."

"Does Mr. Bingley do anything without your approval?"

"Dear God, I surely hope he does," he replied seriously, and she covered her mouth with her napkin to cover her laughter. "He just… As my uncle said earlier, patience is a virtue only when it does not crush passion and daring," he whispered. "Bingley has had much patience and wisdom recently, but too little daring. In that, I confess I encouraged him."

"Yes, but you said…" She paused a moment and looked around to see whether others might hear her then leaned to whisper back. "You said that passion and daring need a strong character and a superior mind to keep them under good regulation. Is that the difference between crushing the passion and keeping it under good regulation? If it is, pray explain it to me because I confess I do not see one, sir."

"It is an extraordinary difference, Miss Bennet. But I cannot explain it to you, as I am afraid it would be difficult to put into words. However, I dare to promise that you will understand it for yourself quite soon."

His words were difficult to understand indeed, as she could barely hear him, and his low, whispered voice increased her anxiety, unsuccessfully hidden behind a tentative smile. She was not certain of his meaning, but what her mind did not comprehend, her heart and her body sensed and yearned for.

Her sister Jane was happy now; Mr. Bingley had finally proposed to her, and Elizabeth anticipated that they would be the most wonderful, kind, and generous couple.

It was now time to allow herself to feel her own happiness.

She startled when he leaned and whispered to her again. "As for your riding lessons, Miss Bennet—I would suggest we start them either at Longbourn or at Pemberley."

She fought to keep a calm voice when she replied. "I shall take your suggestions to heart, sir. What would you consider to be the perfect time?"

"Pemberley," he said gently but decidedly, and she could not contradict him.

Chapter 17

The hunting party set out at dawn.

From the window of her room, Elizabeth watched them depart, heavy-hearted and regretful. The sun was just rising, and it was impossible to decide whether the sky or the fields looked more beautiful. She should have learned to ride earlier.

She could see Jane near Mr. Bingley, and she smiled, imagining how happy her sister must feel.

Though their engagement had yet to be approved by Mr. Bennet, Mr. Bingley proved to be incapable of withholding such a secret—so much so that the happiness of it seemed to illuminate his face. Generously, Mrs. Gardiner took on the task of writing Mr. Bennet herself, and she did not hesitate to assure Mr. Bingley and Jane that they would surely have Mr. Bennet's consent and blessing. Hence, the engagement lost its secrecy almost immediately.

Miss Bingley and Mrs. Hurst were shocked and angered by the news, and their rudeness increased accordingly. Though they made an effort to display civil behaviour, their displeasure and disapproval could hardly be concealed.

Lady Sinclair wasted little time and even less interest on the event, but she could not be remiss in congratulating Jane for the good fortune of "securing a husband whom you surely could not hope to find in your own neighbourhood." Kindly, Jane thanked her for the good thoughts while Elizabeth wondered how Lady Sinclair managed to be even more disagreeable than Miss Bingley.

Still attempting to bring order to the storm of thoughts that invaded her mind and heart, Elizabeth returned to her bed as soon as the house quieted.

When she woke again, the sun was up, and a beautiful, warm, sunny day invited her outdoors. She hurried downstairs and found the children and their governesses having breakfast together. Three little boys and a girl instantly claimed her notice with restless determination, and their joy soon captured Elizabeth's complete attention.

Immediately after breakfast, the children went out and played together on the front lawn under the close supervision of their governesses.

Alone in the house, Elizabeth tentatively returned to the library and, more precisely, to the subject of her deep curiosity.

As she had spied a few days before, on the shelves were miniatures in which she could easily recognise Lady Selina, the colonel, the viscount, Mr. Darcy and Georgiana—some alone and others with their parents. For a moment, Elizabeth took up and looked closer at a portrait of the entire Darcy family: a beautiful, blonde lady and a handsome and impressive father together with their young son and baby girl.

At length, Elizabeth reached the miniatures that had intrigued her earlier. Undoubtedly, in all three of them, Mr. Wickham was pictured—at various ages—with a lady who should have been his mother. Her handsome features were inherited by her son, and their eyes seemed as similar as the pictures were able to reveal. Elizabeth looked at each with growing interest and no little puzzlement, trying to uncover the mystery that induced Lord Matlock to keep those miniatures close to his family's. After all, Mr. Wickham was merely the godson of his brother-in-law.

The only answers she could find gave her little satisfaction, so she abandoned the struggle, and for some time she allowed herself the delight of reading a favourite book. Then, a couple of hours later, she returned to the miniatures—to those of the Darcy family—lost in her thoughts and troubled by other worries: What would Lady Anne and Mr. Darcy say about their son's choice? Would they accept for their heir a woman from a situation so below their own? Would they ever have accepted her?

She was abruptly interrupted by a din of voices, and she barely had time to raise her eyes before she saw Lady Selina and her husband, Mrs. Gardiner, Jane, Mr. Bingley, Georgiana and Mr. Darcy filling the large room. All were dressed in their hunting attire, obviously tired but in high spirits, followed by the children, coming in search of Elizabeth. As Lady Selina and Mrs. Gardiner were instantly claimed by their brood, Lord Brightmore and Mr. Bingley hurried to find drinks for everyone. Mr. Darcy moved towards Elizabeth, and their smiles met halfway.

His hand asked for hers, and only then did she notice she was still holding the miniature of the Darcy family. She blushed in embarrassment and struggled for an excuse.

"I was looking at the pictures..." she said, showing him the miniature.

He appeared surprised and glanced at the picture then at Elizabeth.

"I remember when that one was drawn. Georgiana was so small... My mother held her but she was not feeling well...so my father took her from time to time, but she was not accustomed to his arms so she cried all the time. Poor father was so distressed." He laughed nervously as he explained, his countenance changed by evident emotion.

"Your mother was very beautiful," she whispered.

"My sister was one of the most beautiful women I have ever seen." Lord Matlock's interruption startled them both; they were still holding the miniature with their joined hands and had no time to separate. The earl seemed not to notice their improper posture.

"I think Georgiana will be just like her one day. She is still very young, but she looks very much like Anne."

"Forgive me, your lordship, I did not mean to intrude; I just found the miniatures and—"

"Oh, do not trouble yourself, my dear; there is no intrusion at all. You will find many other pictures in the house. There is even a larger gallery upstairs. You may look as much as you want. George Darcy was very lucky to marry my sister; I think every bachelor in London hoped to court her, but he was the fortunate one. He was a good man; he almost deserved her." The earl laughed as he fought a tear. "Mathew, be so kind as to pour me a full glass of brandy, son; it is the least you can do since you took away my daughter." His son-in-law obeyed instantly, laughing in good humour, oblivious to their conversation.

The earl enjoyed a generous gulp of brandy. "Miss Elizabeth?"

"Yes, your lordship?" she whispered, her hand finally separating from Darcy's.

"Anne always hoped and prayed that her children would have a happy life; she wished nothing less and nothing more for them. As for George Darcy—he was not a man easy to please, but he would approve of you very much."

Elizabeth stared at him in disbelief; with a large smile on his face and with sadness impossible to conceal in his eyes, Lord Matlock watched her with tender care. She struggled against her own emotions, considering what she should say and briefly wondering whether the earl knew about their arrangement or was only perceptive enough to guess the truth. Finally, still uncertain how to proceed, she allowed her heart to guide her, so she gently embraced the earl and only whispered, "Thank you."

"There is nothing to thank me for, my dear." He took another gulp from his glass then returned to the other guests, followed by Elizabeth's smiling eyes.

Darcy and Elizabeth were alone again, face to face, a short distance from the others; their intense gazes needed no words to convey their feelings.

"I wrote your father last night, and I asked Miles to send the letter early this morning. I suspect your father might receive it tomorrow," he eventually broke the silence.

"Oh," she said. So he had already written her father; he had little patience for waiting. She felt content—and happy.

"I also asked him to keep the news private for now. I think we should wait a little longer before making an announcement. I do not wish to suspend Bingley's joy. He deserves to be the centre of attention for a time. I hope you approve my plan."

"I do—most heartily." She smiled. "I can wait as long as you think necessary."

"Not too long. Though I care about Bingley's joy, I care more about my own. I have been a selfish man all my life, and I surely shall not start being generous now."

THE ENTIRE PARTY RETIRED TO change and prepare for an early dinner. Elizabeth spent some time with her sister, who seemed not fatigued at all. Jane was more talkative than ever before. Elizabeth never would have imagined Jane displaying her happiness so openly, and though she did not entirely agree with Jane's praise of Mr. Bingley, her heart melted seeing that Jane had finally found the happiness she long desired.

Though they did not have Mr. Bennet's response yet, Jane hoped their father would approve a wedding date at the beginning of October. Elizabeth smiled in tender understanding; surely, there was no reason to worry about Mr. Bennet's consent.

Dinner began earlier and lasted longer than usual. The conversation was mostly dominated by discussions of the hunting party and the performance of each rider. Lady Sinclair had the pleasure of being much admired and praised for her skills; more than once, she commented that she raced against Mr. Darcy, and only the superiority of his horse allowed him to win the competition. After the third mention of her defeat by Darcy, the gentleman finally intervened.

"Lady Sinclair, I must beg your pardon; I was not aware that we were racing. I thought we were merely riding with the others. Had I known it was a competition, I gladly would have allowed you to win it."

"You are most generous, sir, but I do not like easy victories. There would be no need for you to allow me to win. I always find a way to win competitions that truly interest me."

"I dare not contradict you further," he said briefly, and Elizabeth wondered whether it was possible that Lady Sinclair did not recognise his sharp irony. He was not being generous but slightly rude.

Not long after this exchange, dinner ended, and Lord Matlock invited the gentlemen to join him in the library. At that moment, Mrs. Gardiner excused herself from the other ladies, explaining that she was tired and needed to retire to her room. Soon after, Lady Selina followed Mrs. Gardiner's example, so in the drawing room there were only Elizabeth, Jane and Georgiana to face Lady Sinclair, Mrs. Hurst and Miss Bingley. Neither of them spoke much to each other, so the situation became a bit awkward. A few minutes later, Lady Sinclair rose unceremoniously, said a cold "good night," and suddenly left the room.

A brief moment of disconcertion followed; then Mrs. Hurst and Miss Bingley declared it had been a lovely but tiring day. Consequently, they expressed their regret for not being able to stay longer. In a short while, Elizabeth, Jane and Georgiana found themselves happily alone in the large drawing room.

"I think Lady Sinclair is fatigued from chasing William too much," Georgiana suddenly said sharply, and Elizabeth and Jane stared at her in disbelief.

"Please forgive me; I know I am being rude, but she was such a nuisance the entire day! I almost fell from Duke because of her! William was very upset."

"Mr. Bingley and I were afraid you were hurt," Jane said with kind understanding.

"You were hurt? What happened?" Elizabeth asked with equal worry and distress.

"Oh, nothing really; do not worry. But she is such a— Ahhhhh, I cannot stand her!"

"Come, dearest, do not let her bother you overmuch." Elizabeth laughed. "She will leave in a few days, and fortunately, you will not see her much in the future."

"I certainly hope not! But Miss Bingley just told her she was invited to Pemberley for the summer, and Lady Sinclair asked William why she did not receive an invitation! Can you imagine the nerve of the woman?"

"Will she be at Pemberley?" Elizabeth tried to appear less distressed than she was.

"No indeed! She will never receive such an invitation—of that I am certain."

"Mr. Bingley was upset about Miss Bingley's indiscretion," Jane whispered.

"Mr. Bingley is so amiable; it is always a pleasure to have him around. William is fond of Mr. Bingley, and he speaks very highly of him."

It was easy for Jane and Elizabeth to understand Miss Darcy's statement: Mr. Bingley was the only reason his sisters were tolerated.

"What would you suggest we do now? Shall we wait for the gentlemen? It might be a while, though, considering their animated conversation." Elizabeth laughed.

"I…I enjoy talking to you but…if you do not mind, I would like to retire, too. I did not sleep well the last few nights, and I am a little tired," Jane said tentatively.

"Do not worry, dearest; you may go and sleep. I shall stay a little longer with Georgiana until she abandons me as well. I am certain she is also tired."

"I am not tired at all," Miss Darcy declared. "Last night I slept better than I have in a long time," she said, meaningfully, and Elizabeth smiled at her. "So, what shall we do now?"

"What would you suggest—maybe play something?"

"That would be a lovely idea, but if the gentlemen return, I do not wish to… Elizabeth, would you like to go to my room? I have a small instrument there; my uncle bought it for me a couple of years ago. And we can speak without interruption."

"Really? That would be a perfect arrangement," Elizabeth approved, and Georgiana needed no other encouragement. She asked a maid to bring them a tray of refreshments upstairs then took Elizabeth's arm and left the room. Inside Georgiana's apartment, which was a little larger than hers, the small entrance room was dominated by a piano. Georgiana opened the windows and lit additional candles. The night was dark and cooled by a gentle breeze; heavy clouds covered the moon and the stars.

"It will rain," Georgiana said. "Quite a storm, I'm afraid."

"Well, it is fortunate that it did not rain last night; imagine how it would have been to ride through muddy fields."

"Yes, fortunate indeed." Georgiana laughed. "I am very pleased we can talk a little, Elizabeth. I have long wanted to tell you how happy I am that you and William…"

"Thank you, my dear. I cannot tell you how happy I am that you approve."

"I most certainly do! I cannot wait. Did you fix a date yet? Oh, forgive me for asking; I know you have not informed Mr. Bennet yet."

"Do not worry; you may ask anything you like. And no, we have not fixed a date. In fact, I still cannot believe this is truly happening. We have informed no one yet except you."

Their conversation continued in the same manner for some time; they played the piano a little then returned to their discussion. Georgiana asked more about Elizabeth's home and told Elizabeth about Pemberley. She seemed equally happy and self-confident with no trace in her countenance of the shy, insecure girl from previous months.

She asked Elizabeth to play a duet with her again. This time, their performance was more animated and less accomplished than it should have been, as their skills were adversely affected by their merriment. Elizabeth finally asked whether their playing at such an hour would not disturb the other guests who might be sleeping; they wisely stopped playing and continued to speak, finding amusement in every subject.

"We should play cards," Elizabeth suggested.

"Playing cards? Only the two of us?"

"Well, we can ask Miss Bingley and Mrs. Hurst to join us if you wish. They seem fond of card playing. Besides, they are known to be your intimate friends."

"You are very considerate, Miss Bennet. Thank you."

"Forgive me; that was a mean remark. I think I still cannot forgive Miss Bingley for her ungenerous interference between Jane and Mr. Bingley."

"I understand...but all is well now. Your family will be happy at the news of Miss Bennet's engagement, I imagine."

"Yes, very happy." Elizabeth laughed.

"What about you? I mean, about your engagement. Will they approve of William?"

Elizabeth hesitated a moment and felt her cheeks blush in embarrassment.

"My mother's approval will be difficult to temper, I am afraid. As for my father, I am happy to say that he and Mr. Darcy—William—built a strong relationship during our stay in London. My father came to know and greatly admire Mr. Darcy. I think he will be very happy with our engagement."

"It must be nice to have a large family. Your house must be so lively. Silence can be difficult to bear sometimes..." Georgiana's voice wore a trace of sadness, and Elizabeth felt the girl's emotion.

She squeezed her hand gently and forced a laugh. "Dearest, if we all come to Pemberley, you will beg for silence, I warn you."

"Oh, I cannot wait! Pemberley has been silent for too long, I am afraid—"

A thunderclap broke the stillness of the night and startled them; the wind gusted fiercely against the windows, and Georgiana hurried to close them.

The next moment, the sky seemed to erupt, and rain fell violently.

"I think the windows are open in my room, too. Excuse me for a moment; I must run to close them," Elizabeth said and left the room immediately.

As she expected, the wind had extinguished all the candles, and she barely found her way in the darkness. She stepped carefully towards the windows; the rain had wet the carpet and the curtain. She closed the windows and looked around for something to light the candles then decided she would get a lighted one from Georgiana.

She was in her doorway when she noticed steps and movement in the hall.

She remained still, hidden in the darkness, and the next moment she frowned. A woman's figure—dressed in a nightgown and carrying a small candle, her hair falling about her shoulders—stopped at Mr. Darcy's door, looked about, then blew out the candle and entered cautiously.

A cold shiver ran through Elizabeth; even in the dim candlelight, she easily recognised Lady Sinclair. What was she doing in Mr. Darcy's room at that hour? She stood there, stunned, unable to decide what she should do. She expected to hear raised voices and witness Mr. Darcy's forcible removal of Lady Sinclair from his room. Why would a woman put herself in such a situation? Suppose others should hear of it! How would Lord Sinclair react to this scandal? She looked along the hall, but no movement could be heard—only darkness, and the rain falling heavily, striking the windows. Why was she in his room so long?

Elizabeth startled violently when Georgiana called her name. The girl seemed worried and asked whether she was all right or needed help with the windows. Elizabeth needed time to reply; suddenly, she realised how embarrassing it would be for Georgiana to witness her brother arguing with a woman in the middle of the night.

"I am fine; I just need a lighted candle. Let us return to your room."

They entered and closed the door behind them; Elizabeth poured herself a glass of water while her mind tried to comprehend and find appropriate answers.

Georgiana, preoccupied by her friend's obvious change of spirit, attempted a few more questions but received only short answers. A few more minutes passed; Elizabeth said she felt tired and wished to retire to her room. Georgiana did not try to contradict her, but a tentative yet decided knock on the door interrupted them. They looked at each other with wonder; then Georgiana opened the door only to meet Mr. Darcy's smiling appearance. Elizabeth turned pale and sat on the nearest chair.

"Forgive me for interrupting you, I was just... May I come in?" he asked, and Georgiana gladly invited him in.

"Miss Bennet..." he greeted her with a smile. She stared at him, speechless.

"I hope I am not intruding. I was walking around the grounds just before the rain began, and I heard the piano. I imagined it was Georgiana... So, what do you think of this storm? Were you doing anything special?"

He was smiling in obvious good humour, and Elizabeth could not take her eyes from him.

"We played the piano a little earlier...before the storm interrupted us...but Elizabeth is tired; she was just retiring to her room."

"Really? I am sorry to hear that," he said, and Elizabeth finally managed to answer.

"I was a little tired, but I can stay a little longer. I... We did not expect to see you here."

"I did not expect to see you here, either." He laughed. "May I keep you company for a few minutes? Perhaps card playing for three?"

"That would be lovely, Brother. Elizabeth just proposed we invite Miss Bingley and Mrs. Hurst, but I dare say we would enjoy your presence much better."

"Really? I must say, your sharp irony frightens me a little, dearest. I notice in you a dangerous resemblance to our uncle in the last few days!"

"I dare say she also resembles her brother." Elizabeth laughed, more spirited as her distress began to subside.

"That would not be possible. Georgiana was always the kind, sweet, generous part of our family," Darcy declared.

"As I said, very much like her brother," Elizabeth repeated, her eyes fixed on his face; he seemed a little disconcerted by her compliment.

"You are very generous with your praise, though I know it is not entirely deserved."

"Yes, it is," Georgiana intervened, smiling at her brother. "We were talking about Elizabeth's family. I cannot wait to be all together at Pemberley."

Darcy glanced quickly at Elizabeth then to his sister again, and he did not reply for a moment. Elizabeth laughed. "Mr. Darcy seems more worried than anxious. I know he does not enjoy large parties, and he is already accustomed to my family's…particularities."

"I do look forward to having you at Pemberley, Elizabeth—and your family, too. I have great hopes that each of them will find something to employ their time as they please."

"Thank you, sir. You are very generous," Elizabeth said, becoming crimson.

Georgiana giggled. "So, what should we do? Oh dear, what a storm," she said as thunder crashed and lightning again lit the sky.

"Could you play a little for me, dearest? Anything you wish," Mr. Darcy pleaded.

"I will, but…will you play something for me and for Elizabeth?" Georgiana asked, and Elizabeth startled in surprise, staring at him. He turned red.

"So, you have betrayed me, dearest. I shall not forget that." He smiled at Elizabeth while he tried to devise an explanation. "My mother loved music, and she was an exquisite performer. We used to spend quite some time together in the music room…"

"And William used to play to me when I was little…when I could not sleep or I was sad or frightened. He used to play for me, and I sat on the carpet at his feet, looking at him. I think I first learned to play only to be able to stay with him more."

Elizabeth could hear Georgiana's voice, but her eyes never left Darcy's face; his countenance was a mix of embarrassment and anxiety, and he attempted a smile. Deep emotion overwhelmed the room, so Darcy spoke with forced lightness.

"Very well then… Make room, dearest," he said and suddenly sat at the piano. He then turned to his sister. "I shall play one song, and then you will play for us. Elizabeth is excused for the moment, but her turn will come soon," he added, glancing at Elizabeth. She made no reply as his gaze spread cold shivers through her.

Georgiana agreed, and he started to play while Elizabeth watched, mesmerised. Georgiana slowly sat on the carpet, her beautiful gown spreading across the floor unheeded. A smile lit Darcy's countenance, and his eyes abandoned the music sheet to glance briefly at Elizabeth. As the music filled the chamber, Elizabeth followed Georgiana's example and joined her on the carpet. The smile on Darcy's face brightened.

By the time he ended the song, neither Elizabeth nor Georgiana could speak. He indicated to Georgiana that it was her turn, and she obeyed while he took her place on the floor near Elizabeth. Their backs leaned against the settee, and after briefly gazing at each other, he took her hand while Georgiana started to play.

For a time, there was only the rain pouring wildly outside, and their hands and hearts joined, wrapped within the music.

When Georgiana finished her performance, it was quite late, and they were reluctant to rise from their reverie. Eventually, Darcy rose from the floor and stretched his hand to help Elizabeth. She supported herself on his arm and rose quickly, but the next moment, with a small cry, she fell down. Darcy and Georgiana rushed to help her, but she set them at ease and attempted to laugh at her own folly.

"I am such a fool; my leg felt numb as I stood on it. I think I twisted my ankle; how fortuitous—now I can neither ride nor walk."

"Let me see," Darcy said, serious and worried. He helped her to the settee and put her legs up. She smiled, red-faced and embarrassed.

Darcy hesitated a moment, then slowly removed her shoe; he glanced at her for an instant then returned his attention to her leg. His fingers gently touched her ankle, pressing carefully against it.

"Does it hurt?"

She would have been unable to feel the pain even if there were any; his fingers warmed her skin through the stocking, and each touch seemed to run along her leg and spread over her entire body. She felt ashamed of her sensations, so inappropriate compared to his genuine care, and especially in the presence of Georgiana.

"No...it does not hurt. I am certain it will be fine by tomorrow..."

"I am not so certain; if you feel any pain in the morning, we shall fetch a doctor."

"Oh, please do not do that; it is not necessary, trust me. I shall rest tonight; a good night's sleep is all it needs."

"You are probably right; besides, I think we should all go to sleep. It is very late."

Equally worried for her friend, Georgiana did not attempt to contradict her brother. Darcy helped Elizabeth to rise and offered her his arm; she took it and held it tightly.

"I will need a lighted candle; the wind blew mine out," Elizabeth said, and Darcy took one from the table.

"I shall help Elizabeth to her room," he briefly explained to Georgiana.

"You must promise you will not worry for my leg," Elizabeth told the girl. "It is just a silly accident; my mother will tell you it has happened to me many times before."

"I promise I will try not to worry. Good night; I will see you first thing in the morning."

Elizabeth hobbled slowly along the hall, holding Darcy's arm, wearing only one shoe and struggling to decide whether she was more amused or embarrassed by the situation. They entered her room, and he helped her to the bed then hurried to light a few candles. She climbed on the bed, her back against the pillows. A slight pain was trying her foot.

"Should I send you a maid to help you prepare for the night?"

"No, please do no such thing. I do not want to disturb anyone at this hour."

"I could help you," he said, and she frowned, staring at him. "I could bring you your nightgown and put it on the bed. I did not mean to…"

She averted her eyes, her cheeks burning at her silliness. What was she thinking?

"I should leave now," he said a moment later, but his hands did not move from her legs.

"Yes," she replied then suddenly startled.

"But let me see the leg once more." He sat near her and took off her other shoe; for a few moments, his hands caressed both ankles, examining them.

"It seems to be fine; it is not swollen at all."

"Thank you for your care, but I told you it would be fine; it only hurts a little."

He did not cease pressing her ankle gently, searching for any sign of discomfort. She knew his caresses meant nothing but worry for her safety, but she could not temper the shivers inside her. His palms cupped her heels as his fingers brushed along her ankles. A moan escaped her lips, and his movements stopped.

"Does it hurt?"

"No…no," she whispered, averting her eyes.

"I am glad," he said; she felt his gaze searching her face. "I should leave now; it is very late, and you must be tired." His hands still rested on her ankles, burning her through the stockings.

"I am not tired. I had such a wonderful time with Georgiana—and with you," she confessed, daring to meet his eyes. "I hope we spend many evenings like this after we—" She stopped, uncertain whether it would be proper to continue. To her surprise, he tried to subdue a smile that was twisting his lips. She looked at him, her inquiring eyes awaiting an explanation.

"There is no doubt that we will spend many wonderful moments together with Georgiana after we marry, but those moments will never happen at such late hours. I am afraid you will have to bear my company…alone…at times like that."

As he spoke, he leaned slowly towards her until their faces were only inches apart; his voice became lower and his stare more difficult to bear; she closed her eyes. The gentle press of his lips started as tender and sweet as she expected, and her own lips parted to welcome his growing passion. She was breathless, so she leaned back against the pillows; his eager lips refused to abandon hers as his weight soon pressed against her; her hands encircled his neck, and her mind completely abandoned the struggle against her senses.

"I absolutely must leave now," he said, caressing her face with tenderness.

"Yes…" she admitted, as she attempted to regain her breath. However, neither of them seemed willing to separate. He placed light kisses along her jaw.

"I never dreamed that I could feel so much happiness, Elizabeth. I simply cannot bear to leave you; your presence brings me such joy!" he said as his arm tightened around her.

Her head rested on his shoulder, and she whispered, her lips touching his ear. "I am still afraid it is just a dream. When we came here a week ago, I had some hopes...but I never imagined my life would change so completely in only a few days. I used to tell Jane that I would only marry for the deepest love...but I never imagined love could feel this way..."

"Elizabeth, will you—? I know I promised to be patient, but we both know I cannot. I beg you to consider... I would be grateful if you would consider a date... for our wedding."

"I will consider... We shall speak about this tomorrow."

"Yes, tomorrow... I really should leave now," he said, placing a quick kiss on her hair.

He attempted to withdraw from her, and she followed him with her eyes then suddenly realised that he would return to his room.

"Please wait... I..."

He looked at her in puzzlement, and she was barely able to breathe from embarrassment. She knew she should tell him the truth, but how could anything so absurd be explained?

"Is something wrong?"

"No... Yes... I..." She fought the intense mortification as she tried to speak. "Earlier, when the rain began, I came to my room to close the windows, and...it was very dark in the hall and... I saw Lady Sinclair enter your apartment..."

Darcy looked at her with complete miscomprehension, his eyes and mouth agape.

"Excuse me? Lady Sinclair? Surely you must be mistaken."

"No, I am not mistaken. Forgive me, I did not mean to intrude. I saw her enter and—"

"Are you certain? Forgive me for questioning you, but I am surprised. I did not expect—"

"I am certain. I was surprised, too. I could not believe that..." She was highly embarrassed, as though she had done something inappropriate.

He suddenly smiled and took her hand then placed a soft kiss on the back of her palm.

"I am truly sorry for the trouble this situation caused you."

"It is not your fault."

"No, it is not, but I am sorry nevertheless. I shall talk to Miles tomorrow; he must know what this is all about."

He was holding her hand, sitting only a few inches from her as they gazed at each other. They were both uneasy, finding their words with difficulty.

"May I ask you... When I entered Georgiana's room, you seemed quite unwell...

preoccupied with something. Was this the reason?"

"Yes. I was surprised to see you at the door. I believed—"

"Did you believe that I invited Lady Sinclair?" His voice changed, betraying his discomfort, and she answered with obvious uneasiness.

"No, I did not suspect you invited her—quite the opposite. I was certain you would demand she leave the room immediately, and I waited to see her leave. But the minutes passed, and I wondered what happened…so, when I saw you at Georgiana's door, I was surprised. Then I understood that you had not been in your room at all, and I assumed she must have left. I am glad everything ended quietly. I confess I was afraid that a scandal would arise and you would be blamed for it."

She seemed distressed by the entire situation, and he kissed her hand to comfort her then suddenly laughed.

"Forgive me, I do not mean to seem ungrateful for your worry; I was just thinking that, even if a scandal should arise, when a woman is found in a man's room in the middle of the night, the man can hardly be blamed."

"I suppose you are correct. I cannot help wondering why she would do such a thing. What did she hope to accomplish by entering your room in the middle of the night?"

She could see her question only increased his amusement, and his eyes were equally puzzled and mischievous as he tried to maintain a serious countenance. Her cheeks and neck felt warm from embarrassment, but she daringly held his gaze as she became angry.

"I am not a complete simpleton, sir, nor am I so naïve! I do know why she came to your room!" His amusement seemed to increase, and his eyebrow rose in surprise at such a statement while her embarrassment grew. "I am just surprised that you cannot see the gravity of the situation! You may laugh at me, but if anyone should discover…"

He became serious in an instant. "Please forgive me; I do not laugh at you. Forgive me if I upset you more, but I shall not deny that I find this situation amusing because…" He hesitated a moment then continued, trying to search for the proper words. "I still hope that it is somehow a mistake. I have never done or said anything that might encourage Lady Sinclair to visit my room, so I am not worried about this situation. And I must be completely honest with you; I can see you are jealous, and selfishly I find this pleasing. I know it upsets you more, but it is the truth. What will you think of me now?"

She stared at him in disbelief, still trying to comprehend his words. Did he just admit that he was pleased to witness her distress? What should she say to such a disclosure?

"Forgive me," he repeated. "I would do anything in my power to protect you from distressing situations. As for this particular incident, I am certain Miles attended the situation properly if needed."

"It is fortunate that you have such a reliable valet," she said bluntly.

"It is indeed; Miles and I grew up together. He is only three years my senior. His father served my father with great loyalty. I trust Miles's intelligence and his common sense as much as his discretion. He is skilful at solving such awkward problems."

His voice sounded light and gentle, and she understood he wanted to put her mind at ease, but his words had the opposite effect.

"I see…and does he… Have there been many similarly awkward problems for Miles to solve?" She averted her eyes as she spoke, and when she dared to meet his eyes again, she encountered his incredulous stare.

"Miss Bennet, surely you have not asked what I believe you are asking."

"I apologise. I know it is not my right to speak of such things. I believe we have taken this conversation on a forbidden path. We should sleep; it is very late." Her voice trembled as she became aware and ashamed of the scandalous situation in which she placed herself. He surely must be appalled by the lack of decorum in her manners.

She expected him to leave, but he did not. Instead, he gently caressed her chin and made her raise her eyes to him while his right hand took hers.

"Elizabeth, please… I agree this is a most awkward and distressing conversation; I would never imagine discussing such a subject with you—especially so soon after our betrothal—but since we have come to this point, it would be better to clarify what troubles you. So please ask me what you wish to know. Forgive me for my previous amusement; this is not a trifling situation."

His voice was gentle but serious and comforting; there was no trace of amusement or flirtation in his eyes. She forced a smile.

"There is nothing I wish you to answer; it was only a silly remark, and I am ashamed of my folly. I do not know what is happening to me; I never believed I could behave so unwisely. You are right: I do feel jealous, and you have every reason to laugh at my foolishness." She felt tears of anger stinging her eyes, and she swiped at them with a childish gesture. She was making a fool of herself, and she could hardly bear the thought.

"Elizabeth…" His gentle voice only made her more furious with herself, and she refused to meet his eyes. "Almost from the beginning of our acquaintance, I have felt jealous of every man who was the recipient of your attention; each smile you offered to someone else was a sharp cut inside me. I spent sleepless nights wondering who the man would be to conquer your heart and have the right to kiss your lips and sparkling eyes. I had nightmares that Wickham might deceive you, and…I was overcome by my own foolishness for so many months that I could think of no way to escape."

With each word, her tears turned into bright twinkles, and joy returned to her eyes. Her fingers entwined with his in their joined hands.

"It seems impossible to decide which of us is the greater fool, Mr. Darcy. We are hopeless."

"So it seems…" he admitted, while slowly leaning towards her as his lips captured
212

hers with gentle determination. Unexpectedly, she broke the kiss a few moments later.

"William, I hope you know you have no reason to be jealous of Mr. Wickham or anyone else. My feelings have never been of such a nature with any other man. I have never—"

"I know." He silenced her with a brief kiss, looking at her with a mischievous glint in his eyes. "I noticed your…lack of experience when I first kissed you."

She stared, surprised by his words, then paled. He continued, his fingers caressing a lock of her hair.

"That made me exceedingly happy, my dearest, loveliest Elizabeth, and it made me even happier to be gifted with your tender passion…and to witness firsthand your extraordinary improvement." He laughed, and his lips joined hers again.

She quickly broke the kiss. "I am quite surprised by your words, Mr. Darcy. I did not expect that my lack of experience would be so easy to recognise. I imagine you need extensive practice for such performances," she said sharply. He laughed again, placing a soft kiss on her forehead.

"I am also quite surprised by your earlier statement, Miss Bennet. I would not expect that a lady with so little experience could possess extensive knowledge of the reasons a woman might enter a man's bedchamber in the middle of the night."

Her face coloured instantly, and she stared at him, open-mouthed, unable to form a reply, attempting to understand whether he wished a serious answer or was only speaking in jest. She was lying against the pillows, and his face was inches from hers.

"I would presume that your knowledge is due to your extensive reading," he concluded, his voice low and insinuating, keeping a serious countenance, his lips almost touching her skin as he spoke. "After all, it is well known that you are a great reader and prefer reading to cards; that must be an advantage in this peculiar situation."

His amused countenance defeated her embarrassment, and though she was still flustered and self-conscious, she began to laugh, too. "It is fortunate that you admire women who improve their minds through extensive reading, Mr. Darcy."

Her teasing laughter was instantly subdued by an unexpected kiss. His lips were neither patient nor gentle, and his released passion left her breathless; the shock of his tongue testing her lips shattered her body, and she let out a moan that seemed to increase his overwhelming eagerness. Then he stopped again.

"We must go to sleep this instant. I shall not delay a moment longer," he declared and rose abruptly, then returned and sat near her again. He kissed her hands and stared deeply into her eyes with perfect seriousness.

"Good night, my dearest Elizabeth. And thank you for spending this night with me."

"Good night…my love," she whispered, blushing from the strength of words she had never said before, averting her eyes from his burning stare.

He rose and slowly moved from the bed. When he had almost reached the door, she called his name again. He stopped and turned to her; her eyes captured his, and the power of her feelings defeated her shyness.

"Good night, my love," she repeated.

A FEW HOURS OF SLEEP were enough for Darcy to wake up rested and in excellent spirits. The hours spent with Elizabeth filled his heart with joy, and he found himself smiling continuously. The recollection of their improper discussion still made him laugh. How was it possible that he spoke of such things with her? And how was it possible that he dared to take so many liberties with her—to kiss her as he did—when their engagement was not even publicly acknowledged, and how was it possible that she accepted his improper liberties so willingly? He congratulated himself on the wisdom of returning to his room while he was still able to control his desires; however, it was clear that a long engagement was not acceptable.

He briefly looked at Miles, who was preparing his clothes. The valet seemed preoccupied and less talkative than usual, but Darcy found that beneficial. He was not in the mood for easy conversation at that time of the morning, though he usually enjoyed Miles's company.

He did not inquire about the previous night and Lady Sinclair's supposed visit; it was too ridiculous. Besides, he knew Miles would inform him if anything unusual had happened.

When Darcy was finally prepared for breakfast, Miles asked for the privilege of a few moments of his time. The request worried Darcy, and for the first time that morning, he looked at his valet with interest.

"Miles, is everything well? You do not seem your usual self."

"No, sir, nothing is well—quite the contrary. I know it is not the way to compensate for all the trouble my betrayal will cause, but please believe that I would gladly give you my life to protect your reputation if my life is worth anything at all."

Darcy looked at him with intense curiosity and complete miscomprehension. Miles was a tall, handsome man, with an impressive figure, who was now behaving like a schoolboy awaiting punishment.

"Miles, what on earth are you talking about? Have you taken leave of your senses? Why are you being so dramatic?"

"Mr. Darcy, please allow me to take advantage of your generosity for the last time. I only need you to listen to me for a few moments, and you shall decide what you wish to do with me. Though I know too well no punishment—"

"For heaven's sake—explain yourself, man! I apologise for speaking so bluntly, but you seem drunk. If so, I would recommend you sleep a couple of hours; we can speak later."

"I am not drunk, sir, though guilt has affected my reason. Sir, I... Mr. Darcy, last night I was waiting for you to retire for the night as usual. It was past midnight, and you had not returned; I dared not go to my room without your approval."

"I am sorry, Miles; I forgot to inform you I would be late."

"Sir, please do not apologise. I do not deserve such consideration. As I said, I was waiting for you, and I employed my time reading from your book. I was sitting in the armchair near your desk, and I must have fallen asleep because I do not quite remember what happened. I woke up, but the room was completely dark.

214

My guess is the wind blew out the candles. I remember hearing the rain and..."

The servant paused and looked at Darcy, his countenance pale, betraying the deepest distress and shame. Darcy looked at him, puzzled, waiting for the story to continue, still convinced that his man had enjoyed too much of his brandy.

"I was awakened by... In the darkness I felt... I was assaulted by a woman and...I could not see who she was, but her insistence... I mean...please forgive me, sir. I cannot say what... I swear on my father's memory that at first I tried to stop her, but she did not allow me to speak at all, and then her seduction was... I had too little strength to stop her, and my weakness overcame my reason, and I could not help myself. I ceased saying anything and allowed myself to take advantage of the situation, though I knew it was a mistake. The lady did not know who I was. She believed me to be you, and I cannot pretend to have any excuse. I behaved in a most dishonourable manner and... At the end, I took advantage of the darkness and left the room silently. I did not know what I should do...and then I heard the door, and I imagined she had left and... All I could think was what you would say if you returned, and I hurried to change the sheets and. Sir, I know my words are worth nothing; I only wish you to know that—"

"Miles, stop, STOP!" The valet frowned in silence. "My God, Miles, my head is spinning. For heaven's sake, speak to the point and clearly. Did I hear you properly? You allowed yourself to be seduced by a woman in my room?"

"Yes!" Miles did not dare to breathe.

Darcy paced the room in distress, reluctant to inquire further. "Miles, do you know who the woman was? Did you recognise her?"

"I did, sir. It was Lady Sinclair." The valet only voiced what Darcy had guessed.

"Damn it, Miles!" Darcy was unable to control his fury. "Have you lost all sense? Should Lord Sinclair ever discover this, I cannot guarantee your life!"

"Sir, my life does not worry me, as it is not worth much. My concern is for your honour and safety, sir. I would gladly give my life to protect yours. If Lord Sinclair discovers this, you could be in danger, sir. That is what worries me!"

"Miles, be quiet! Not a word, do you understand me? Not a single word to any breathing creature! And you shall forget we ever had this conversation! Go now!"

Pale, his shoulders stooped and his eyes on the ground, Miles silently left the room while Darcy stared as the door closed behind him, his mind in turmoil at the madness he had discovered; he quickly poured himself a glass of brandy. As he paced the room, he started to laugh, thinking of his conversation with Elizabeth and admitting she was right to be worried.

Half an hour later, Darcy appeared for breakfast. The meal progressed with a discussion of the previous night's storm and plans for the last few days of their stay at Matlock Manor. Elizabeth was seated between Georgiana and Jane, across the table from Darcy. They exchanged a few glances and smiles, but each of them was content to speak with their table neighbours.

After breakfast, Lady Selina and Mrs. Gardiner joined their children on the back lawn, and the gentlemen retired to make plans in the library while the ladies discussed the opportunities to employ their time for the day.

Elizabeth, Georgiana, and Jane decided to spend some time in the music room. As they departed, Darcy followed them and asked to speak to Elizabeth. Georgiana and Jane walked ahead, allowing them a bit of privacy as they moved through the large hall.

Darcy had succeeded only in inquiring whether she slept well when they were interrupted by Lady Sinclair's voice, calling his name. They stopped and turned to her. Lady Sinclair approached, a charming smile lighting her face, addressing Darcy while completely ignoring Elizabeth.

"Mr. Darcy, I would like a moment with you, sir."

"May I help you in any way, Lady Sinclair?"

"Not exactly, sir. I wished to speak to you alone. Miss Elizabeth, please excuse us," she demanded without even favouring Elizabeth with a glance.

"Miss Elizabeth and I were on our way to the music room. You may join us if you wish."

"I really do not wish; as I said, I would like to speak to you alone. I believe you owe me at least such a courtesy."

Elizabeth glanced at Darcy briefly and decided to put an end to the awkward situation.

"I think Georgiana and Jane expect me. I hope I shall see you both later." She left them, though she felt her heart uneasy, wondering what Lady Sinclair wished to tell him.

Darcy turned to his companion. "How may I help you, Lady Sinclair?"

"I do not need your help, Mr. Darcy," she said, moving closer and placing her hand on his arm. He only looked at her, waiting. "I was wondering...did you sleep well last night?"

"Quite well, thank you."

"Really? I did not sleep well at all..."

"I am sorry to hear that. You had better rest then."

"I do not need rest, thank you. You are very considerate, but that is not a surprise. However, it was an enormous surprise to discover how passionate you are," she said, her gaze as insinuating as her voice. "Passionate and generous and tender; it was worth my effort after all."

"I am afraid I do not understand what you mean, Lady Sinclair."

"Of course you know...and I am disappointed to discover that you attempt to deny it—as I was disappointed at your sudden disappearance from your room last night. Why did you run from your own room? Did I scare you, Mr. Darcy?"

He took a step back and removed her hand from his arm then replied sternly.

"Lady Sinclair, if you are joking, and I shall try to be amused, but I cannot possibly imagine what you mean when you say you frightened me and I ran from my own room. Surely, you cannot mean that you were in my room last night."

"I see… So you prefer to deny the truth and play at ignorance. Be it as you wish, sir, but you cannot expect me to join you in this disappointing game. I expected more from you, Mr. Darcy. You are less a man than I believed you to be."

"Lady Sinclair!" he interrupted her unceremoniously, and she looked at him impatiently.

"Lady Sinclair, listen to me carefully as it is the only time I shall tell you this; after that, I shall forget this conversation and all the facts behind it. Last night I did not return to my room until nearly dawn. Miles, my valet, was there—alone —waiting for me. Miles was there," he repeated, looking at her pointedly.

At first, she held his gaze incredulously, showing nothing but daring and disdain for his presumed weakness; then the truth became clear and anger utterly changed her handsome features. She began to tremble with helpless fury, her eyes betraying only hate and rage. She turned without a word, and her steps retreated at a quick pace until she disappeared around the corner.

Darcy looked after her, telling himself that he should feel sorry for her. The situation was deeply disturbing; to know that she ended by seducing his servant must be something she could not easily bear, and he briefly wondered how she would be able to face him again—or to bear the shame. But everything that happened was of her own fault and recklessness. She selfishly and carelessly played the game of seduction with him on a whim with no consideration for the distress she might cause to others, and now she had to face the result of her own behaviour. He should feel sorry for her—but he could not.

He considered whether he should go to the music room but decided that fresh air would be more beneficial to his present state. He went to the stables and was pleased to find Bingley and both his cousins ready for a ride.

When they returned to the house an hour and a half later, they received the surprising news that Lady Sinclair and her husband had to return to London immediately. Lord Sinclair's sudden departure was regretted by all the gentlemen, as the earl was known as the soul of any successful hunting party. But, after all, as Lord Matlock wisely concluded, the hunt was over.

AFTER THREE MORE DAYS SPENT in pleasant and less agitated company at Matlock Manor, the entire party returned to Town.

Elizabeth and Jane were expected to remain with Mrs. Gardiner for only a couple of days before returning to Longbourn together with Mr. Bingley, his sisters, and Mr. Hurst. Mr. Darcy settled his plans to return to Netherfield with Miss Darcy, which brought much joy and happy anticipation to all those involved.

The evening of their arrival in town was spent by each family at their own house with a peaceful dinner and pleasant recollections, so it happened that neither Jane nor Elizabeth succeeded in sleeping until well after midnight as they found countless things to share. With complete trust in her sister, Elizabeth did not hesitate to reveal the extraordinarily news of her own engagement.

After the first moments of surprise and disbelief, Jane's happiness was all the reward Elizabeth needed. Jane declared she had always admired Mr. Darcy, and she was certain he would be an ideal match for Elizabeth; the animated, happy conversation continued until late into the night, keeping the sisters awake until dawn.

On the other side of town, the Darcys did not sleep either but for different reasons.

After the many days and nights spent in Elizabeth's company, Darcy bore the silence and solitude of his large dining room with great difficulty. He was alone with Georgiana, attempting to have a pleasant conversation during dinner, but that easy task suddenly seemed difficult unless the subject of the conversation included Elizabeth.

As the second course was served, the housekeeper rushed in unceremoniously.

"Mr. Darcy, excuse me for interrupting you, sir. Miss Anne de Bourgh has just arrived," she managed to explain before Anne entered the room.

Anne's appearance surprised them exceedingly, and Darcy, after a moment of disbelief, hurried to offer her a chair and a glass of water. She looked exhausted; her face was pale, her eyes surrounded by dark rings and her gown in disorder.

While Darcy looked for Lady Catherine and wondered why she remained behind, Anne spoke weakly, pleading with her voice as well as her eyes.

"Forgive me for coming here at this hour, Cousin; I did not know where to go… I had a violent argument with Mama and left Rosings. May I stay here for a while?"

Darcy was certain he did not hear her rightly. Did she say she had left Rosings?

"Of course you may stay here; there is no need to apologise! This is your home for as long as you want, but who brought you here? Where is your luggage? Does Aunt Catherine know you are here?"

"I came alone in my phaeton," she declared, and Darcy exchanged a shocked look with his sister. "I have no luggage," she added while Darcy and Georgiana were still unable to reply. "And no, Mama does not know I left; I think she believes I only went for a ride."

She paused a long moment, then continued to speak in a low, trembling voice, her face coloured with embarrassment.

"Mama received a letter last night by express. It said that you are involved in a relationship with Miss Elizabeth Bennet. You cannot possibly imagine how angry she was and what she said. I argued with her because I could not bear her tirade any longer. I never argued with her before, and it affected me so! You cannot possibly imagine…"

Darcy smiled warmly at his cousin, attempting to calm her distress while struggling to conceal his own anger; then he gently squeezed her hand in comfort and support.

"I can easily imagine, my dear. Please do not worry about this unpleasantness. You must rest now, and tomorrow I shall take care of everything."

Chapter 18

The next morning found Elizabeth speaking animatedly with her aunt while the others slept. She was aware that her aunt had long suspected the truth about her and Darcy, but she still owed Mrs. Gardiner the entire truth.

As Elizabeth expected, her aunt responded with a tender embrace and trembling voice, declaring she had not felt so much happiness in years.

"My dearest girl, I cannot say how much joy your words bring me and how proud I am of you. I feel so grateful that you found your proper match! You could not possibly bestow your affection on anyone more deserving, and I am certain you will prove yourself worthy of the great honour of being Mrs. Darcy. Oh, your uncle would be so proud of you! You deserve nothing less, Lizzy!"

Elizabeth's tears were impossible to stem. She embraced her aunt, and for a few moments, they sobbed in each other's arms, laughing at each other's folly.

Shortly, Mrs. Gardiner regained her composure, and she immediately recollected how intensely Elizabeth disliked Mr. Darcy when she came to London in December and held him responsible for every misfortune in the kingdom. Tearfully, Elizabeth laughed, admitted how wrong she had been, and promised never to contradict her aunt again.

"I imagine my brother Bennet will be pleased with this news, dearest. And your mother—the day she received the news that her two eldest daughters became engaged to such remarkable gentlemen must have been the happiest of her life."

Elizabeth looked at her aunt hesitantly.

"Mr. Darcy wrote Papa a week ago—immediately after he proposed to me. We begged Papa to keep the secret for a while. We wished to allow Jane and Mr. Bingley to enjoy their time. We will inform Mama soon."

"I see." Mrs. Gardiner laughed. "Very clever, indeed. So, the invitation to Pemberley might have a greater importance than we thought. This should be a lovely summer."

Their conversation turned lighter when Mrs. Gardiner begged her niece not to forget to invite her to Pemberley for Christmas and to offer her a phaeton to ride around the estate. They were in the middle of a pleasant conversation about the beauties of Pemberley when a servant suddenly announced Mr. Darcy.

With surprise and no little emotion, Elizabeth rose to greet him. However, his countenance and his evident haste were not what she expected, and her smile faded.

"Forgive me for this inappropriate visit," he addressed Mrs. Gardiner while he glanced at Elizabeth. "I am afraid we will not be able to keep our previous engagement for today. Something unexpected has happened."

"Is everyone well? May we be of any help?" Elizabeth inquired, her face pale.

"You are very kind, but no, there is nothing you can do. We are all well, only…" He hesitated a moment, then said in a lower voice. "My cousin Anne unexpectedly arrived in town last night. There seems to be a conflict within the family that needs to be solved."

"Oh…" Elizabeth replied, her pallor growing more visible.

"There is no need for worry; I shall take care of everything as soon as possible."

"Will you… I imagine you will have to postpone your plans for travelling to Netherfield tomorrow," Elizabeth concluded, and his hesitation was apparent.

"I hope it will not be necessary. I am afraid I cannot stay longer. If everything proceeds satisfactorily, I hope you will allow me to call again later."

"You are welcome at any time, sir." Mrs. Gardiner smiled with perfect politeness.

He thanked them and made his farewell with a fond look at Elizabeth. When the door closed behind him, a claw of doubt gripped Elizabeth's chest. She felt things were not as easy as he pretended them to be. She knew she was being ridiculous and childish, but she could barely fight the tears that stung her eyes.

She spoke little during breakfast and even less afterward. Her mind was seized by countless questions and speculations regarding Miss de Bourgh's visit. Was Lady Catherine also in London? Why was Anne staying at Darcy's townhouse? They were relatives, of course, but it would have been a more natural choice for her to stay with Lord Matlock or Lady Selina. Was it possible that Lady Catherine had devised a scheme to force Darcy finally to marry her daughter? Elizabeth was aware of the absurdity of such a thought, but somehow it did not appear impossible.

A couple of hours later, Mr. Bingley called, and his presence brought joy to one Bennet sister and equal disappointment to the other. He was queried, but he seemed oblivious to what had happened at the Darcys' home. Elizabeth had little to do except wait—and hope.

THE EARL'S LIBRARY WAS MUCH too small for such a heated debate; it became increasingly strident and harsh, every thoughtless word spoken in anger. The argument had begun in the drawing room, but the earl was certain that every servant was listening behind the doors, so he moved the battle to the library, where he hoped to handle it better.

"Catherine, you shall not convince me by shouting. We should at least attempt to speak normally if we intend to accomplish anything at all."

"There is nothing to accomplish, Henry. I have little else to say to you. I must go to Darcy, recover my daughter, and make the proper arrangements. She spent the night in his house; we must make the announcement immediately."

"Are you out of your mind, Catherine? You have taken this entirely too far. Even you must comprehend by now that Darcy will never marry Anne."

"Of course he will; why would he not? Besides, there is little he can do now. Anne has spent the night alone in his house!"

"Yes, Aunt," said the colonel, "you mentioned that a moment ago. As father said, it means nothing; Darcy will never marry Anne, and he has no reason and no wish to do so. And I dare say neither has Anne."

"Quiet, Robert! You cannot possibly understand what duty means; I dare say you never will after indulging yourself for so many years in wild, careless activities. I am leaving now; I have no time to waste here. I shall make my opinion known, and I am sure Darcy will agree with me. I must speak to him immediately."

"That is fortunate, as I wish to speak to you too, Aunt."

Darcy's appearance in the doorway startled all of them. His appearance was its usual perfection as was his composure. At his right, holding his arm, was Lady Selina, greeting her aunt with proper respect. Lady Catherine ignored her entirely.

"Darcy, thank the Lord you are here! Where is Anne? I must speak to her this instant; I do not have a moment to lose. Where is she?"

"Anne is at Lady Selina's, and she is resting. She was properly accommodated into a large apartment in the guest wing more than adequate for her comfort."

"What is she doing there? We must fetch her at once. I made arrangements for us to return home immediately. You will accompany us, I presume. During the ride back to Rosings, we will have time to discuss all the necessary details."

"Anne has no desire to return to Rosings for the present. She has told me she wishes to stay in Town until the end of the season."

"Stay in Town? What kind of nonsense is this? Anne cannot stay in Town; her health will not permit it. What has happened to that girl? Has she lost her senses? She runs away like a wild wanton, and now she refuses to return home? I must talk to her this instant! She will not dare disobey her mother!"

"Anne insisted she wished to rest undisturbed. She said she does not want to speak to anyone, at least for the moment."

"Nonsense," Lady Catherine repeated as she walked towards the door.

"Aunt Catherine, I promised Anne I would respect her wishes, and I intend to do so. We shall not disturb her today. Hopefully, before tomorrow we can all judge the situation more properly."

"Darcy, it is not for you to speak for Anne. In order to do so, you first must wed her! And speaking of that, I hope you will carry out your duty as soon as possible; you must realise she is utterly compromised after spending the night in your house. I am sure the rumour has spread around the entire Town by now."

Darcy looked at Lady Catherine, preoccupied and severe. Suddenly it was silent

221

in the library, so silent that each breath could be heard.

"I am not speaking for Anne; she can speak for herself perfectly well. I only intend to respect my cousin's wishes. As for wedding Anne—that matter has long been settled between us. I have no intention of marrying Anne—not now or ever. And about Anne's being compromised—it is too ridiculous to mention."

Lady Catherine's stupefaction was equalled only by her fury; red-faced with her eyes wide in utter shock, she seemed unable to speak. When she finally found her voice, the torrent of her anger was impossible to interrupt.

"You have no respect for your parents' memory or for your duty or your legacy! How can you show so much disdain for your mother's wishes? You and Anne have been meant for each other since you were infants; no other settlement is possible. Anne cannot think properly, but you—I expected much more from you!"

"Aunt Catherine, it pains me to see that you are unwilling to accept the truth, as well as my wish and Anne's." Darcy replied with serenity and perfect politeness, as though Lady Catherine's words had not affected him in the slightest. "I have great hopes that you will shortly change your mind for the benefit of our family"

Darcy's calm attitude seemed to increase Lady Catherine's anger, and she continued her offensive tirade until he interrupted her politely but decidedly.

"I would suggest postponing this discussion for now, Aunt Catherine. I have some business to attend to, but I shall be happy to speak to you again tomorrow."

"You will not dare to leave now, Darcy! You cannot possibly—"

"Catherine, you are indeed out of your mind," Lord Matlock intervened, his temper obviously lost. "It is no wonder that poor Anne ran away and does not wish to return. What has happened to your reason? Can you not see how ridiculous your behaviour is? You will cease offending Darcy this instant if you wish to be welcome in this house. If not, you will force me to ask you to return to Rosings immediately!"

"*I* am out of my mind? What about *Darcy*? Do not believe me oblivious to the reason for his dishonourable behaviour! Do not believe me oblivious to the fact that he is involved in a sordid affair with that Bennet girl—a shameless hussy who had the benefit of my benevolence and repaid me in the most ungrateful manner! How can this be borne? A country nobody interfering in our family? You may have your way with her as much as you like; that is not my concern. But you cannot abandon your duty and—"

"Lady Catherine!" Darcy interrupted her with barely concealed anger. "Offending Miss Elizabeth will only put you in a more pitiable situation and make me forget my manners. Please do not force me to answer you as I would any other person who dared to malign her reputation."

His cold countenance and the sharpness of his voice silenced Lady Catherine for the moment, enough for him to continue in the same manner.

"Besides, the subject of this conversation is not Miss Elizabeth," Darcy continued, attempting a reasonable explanation. "I understand you are upset, Aunt, and I admit that to be my fault. I should have told you clearly long ago that your expectations about marriage to Anne would never be fulfilled and—"

"Of course the subject is Elizabeth Bennet; do not try to fool me as she fooled you! Can you not see that you have been trapped by her arts and allurements? Lady Sinclair was shocked by how easily you allowed yourself to be deceived; she told me as much in her letter! Can you not understand that the Bennet girl would do anything to secure a wealthy husband? Should her father die, she and all her sisters and mother would be thrown out by Mr. Collins; he will inherit everything, you know. Can you not understand her motives? That girl has no respect for decorum and propriety; Mr. Collins gave me a detailed report of her wild behaviour. Do you know he intended to marry her, but after knowing her better, he did not consider her qualified to be a clergyman's wife? That is why he decided to make a marriage offer to the present Mrs. Collins—a much better choice! Do you prefer such a girl to my Anne? I can imagine how she charmed you, but be aware! She will force you to marry her, undoubtedly!"

Darcy's countenance changed dramatically as he listened to his aunt's outrageous speech; his face darkened with rage and showed only cold fury. He stepped towards his aunt, and Selina instantly grabbed his arm tightly.

"Cousin, please," Lady Selina whispered, but Darcy ignored her and replied with cold civility in an unsuccessful attempt to overcome his anger.

"As I said, my decision regarding a marriage with Anne has been of long standing and has nothing to do with any other lady. Besides that, I believe Miss Elizabeth Bennet to be a most extraordinary woman, whose accomplishments make her worthy of admiration. Unlike Mr. Collins, I do consider her perfectly qualified to be my wife. I suppose this opinion places me in opposition to Mr. Collins—a wise, reliable clergyman who has shared all his intimate secrets with you. It is beyond any doubt that you deserve each other. And now you will excuse me; as I said earlier, I have business to attend to. This discussion cannot have a resolution in your favour, so I would rather end it immediately. I shall see you again later." He turned to leave.

"Darcy, where are you going? You cannot leave us with such a lack of consideration. Come back; I have not finished speaking to you!"

"I would suggest you write Mr. Collins and complain about my behaviour, Lady Catherine," Darcy concluded as he closed the door behind him.

"Catherine, not a single word more!" the earl shouted, his face red with fury. "Have you not made a fool of yourself long enough? I doubt there is a single servant who has not laughed at you by now! How dare you speak to Darcy in such a manner? And how dare you offend Miss Elizabeth Bennet, who is dear to our family? Do you hear yourself? Such vulgarity is unacceptable for someone with your education!"

"How dare you speak to me like this? I have always been known for expressing my opinion openly. I shall not be silenced!"

"If it is so, you will have to bear others' expressing their opinions equally openly, and I dare say you will not enjoy the result. For instance—my opinion is that you should return to Rosings immediately. You are not welcome in this house any longer."

"I shall not return! I shall not abandon my daughter! I must speak to her at once! You cannot refuse my staying here. This was our parents' house!"

"I can do whatever I please. And your daughter is not willing to see you. You should contemplate her motives during your journey home."

"Father, it is very late, and Aunt Catherine is tired." Lady Selina tried to bring a trace of calmness to the din. "Perhaps she should rest a couple of hours, and you can speak again later. I am sure things will resolve for the better."

"Selina is right." The colonel supported his sister's reasonable suggestion. "Father, should I ask the maid to prepare Lady Catherine's apartment?"

The earl glanced at his children, breathing deeply a few times to regain some composure. He then turned to his sister, who stood in the middle of the room, an expression of disdain and arrogance on her face, barely favouring them with a glance.

Lady Selina took his arm and patted it gently. "Please, Papa…"

"Very well then, be it as you wish. Catherine, I shall give you one more chance, and you must thank my children for their wisdom. You may stay here for tonight, but you will apologise to Darcy without delay!"

"I shall never apologise to Darcy, and I shall not find rest until he is forced to see reason. The way he spoke of that Bennet girl proves he is out of his senses. And you are no better, Brother. How can you say Elizabeth Bennet is dear to your family?"

"Catherine, go to your room before I change my mind. Spending a night in London on the street is not as enjoyable as it might appear, and you are close to seeing it for yourself."

Lady Selina quickly grabbed her aunt by the arm and took her out of the library before any other reply was expressed.

As the door closed, Lord Matlock turned to his sons. "I must speak to Darcy immediately. Catherine will have no rest until she has her way. I wonder whether he was serious about Miss Bennet. Robert, do you know where Darcy might be?"

The earl paced the room in distress, asking questions without waiting for answers until his sons forced him to sit and have a glass of wine. It was then settled that they would all try to fetch Darcy and meet at Lady Selina's house to discuss the best course to be taken. As they left the library together, the two young men heard their father cursing in a low voice.

"Damn, Eve Sinclair! Just wait until I have a word with her husband."

An hour later, Colonel Fitzwilliam was the first to discover Darcy at his solicitor's office. Following a brief discussion, they rode together to Selina's house. Neither the viscount nor the earl was there, but she greeted them with obvious joy and relief. She invited them into the music room, and they were pleasantly surprised to find Anne de Bourgh, tentatively trying a song on the piano. At their sight, her cheeks coloured, and she rose quickly, curtseying to them.

"You look well, Anne," the colonel said affectionately. "I was afraid this mess would affect your health. How did it cross your mind to drive alone to London? Why did you not send me a note? I would have come and fetched you. On the other hand, I can understand your running; I would run myself to escape Aunt Catherine. She is just insupportable."

"I am sorry I gave you all so much trouble," Anne whispered, lowering her eyes. "I should not have come... Forgive me, I should have known that my coming here would upset Mother and increase her anger. Forgive me for placing you all in a difficult situation. Do not worry; I will return home; that is the best way..."

"Anne, you know too well you are like a sister to us!" said Darcy. "You must not apologise! It is entirely our fault; we should have done more to protect you. You will not go anywhere until we are certain Aunt Catherine is more reasonable. Even better, I think you should consider spending the summer at Pemberley with us."

Anne's eyes became brighter in a moment, and she looked at her cousin, as she was afraid to believe his words. "You want me to come to Pemberley?"

"That is an excellent idea," Selina concurred. "You will stay with us for the moment; it will be a pleasure to have you here. And we will go to Pemberley together; we will be a large party. I am sure you will enjoy yourself very much!"

"Well, I am not certain about that," said the colonel. "Anne does not seem to enjoy herself very much in large parties. Even more, if we try to keep Anne here over the summer, we must take drastic measures. Aunt Catherine surely will hire an army to take her back to Rosings!" The colonel laughed, waiting for his sister and Darcy to join in his amusement. They remained stern while Anne instantly paled.

"Robert, what on earth happens inside your head?" Selina's voice, full of angry reproach, surprised the colonel, who still seemed oblivious to their displeasure.

"What do you mean? I was only joking," he explained, but the moment his gaze rested on Anne, he frowned. Her eyes were tearful and her expression pale; her hands were trembling in her lap, and the colonel suddenly embraced his cousin tightly.

"Anne dearest, I did not mean to upset you! I was only joking; I wanted to make you forget about this ridiculous fight and... Please forgive me," he said as he tenderly caressed her hair. "Darcy is right; it is entirely our fault—his and mine. We come every year to Rosings, and we should have observed that Aunt is too severe with you. Please do not cry; we will take care of you now. I will take care of you! Will you forgive me?"

He was still holding her tightly, her head leaning against his shoulder, and she tried to hide her sobbing as she whispered, "There is nothing to forgive."

A few minutes passed in silence until Darcy intervened. "Anne, we must discuss what you wish to do, and I must be sure of your safety. I planned to go to Netherfield tomorrow; Georgiana has decided to remain in Town. She wished to stay with you, and I encouraged her in this decision. But I can change my plans if necessary. I shall be away for a fortnight."

"There is no need to change your plans," said the colonel. "We shall take care of Anne."

"I shall be fine." Anne forced a tearful smile. "Forgive me for worrying you so. Please do not change your plans for me... I shall be fine. And I thank you... I would love to come to Pemberley if it is no trouble. I have not seen Pemberley in years."

"It will be interesting to see how Aunt Catherine takes this news." The colonel laughed again, his amusement impossible to conceal. "She will go distracted, I dare say. Perhaps I should move here for the time being to protect Anne. Better said, I should move into Anne's room, to be certain Aunt will not hire someone to kidnap her."

"Robert!" Darcy sharply interrupted him, but the colonel dismissed him with a gesture.

"Oh, you are so serious, Darcy. Go to Hertfordshire and take care of your business; we shall be fine here. We shall take care of Anne, and Father—poor fellow —will take care of Lady Catherine. We must calm her as soon as possible; she will become wild again when she receives certain news from Hertfordshire."

He glanced at Darcy then continued to laugh. "Forgive my indiscretion, Cousin, but really you cannot hope that your news is still a secret from anyone in our family."

"Did you propose to Miss Bennet? That is wonderful news," said Anne shyly, and the colonel and Selina burst out in laughter. After a first moment of shock, Darcy had no other choice than to join them.

"It appears not to be much of a secret any longer. I wonder what betrayed us; Elizabeth and I tried to be discreet about the engagement," Darcy inquired seriously, which only increased the others' amusement. Even Anne could not stem her laughter.

That very moment the library door opened, and the earl and viscount entered. They remained motionless in the doorway, staring at the happy group.

"Well, this is unexpected. We walked around town, looking for Darcy, and you seem to have a jovial party here. May I ask what is so amusing?"

"Welcome, Papa," Selina greeted him with a gentle kiss on his cheeks. "We have made plans for the summer; I will tell you immediately. And Darcy informed us of his plan to go to Hertfordshire tomorrow."

"Oh, good. You will finally speak to Mr. Bennet. I think we should put the announcement in the papers as soon as possible.," The earl spoke with perfect calmness, as though it were a matter long discussed and agreed to; the others began to laugh again while Darcy stared at them sheepishly.

Lord Matlock and the viscount watched the laughing group in bewilderment and then concluded that the argument with Lady Catherine had affected the family's sanity.

As he enjoyed a drink at the end of that distressing day, the earl was informed of the plans regarding Anne. He approved but expressed his concern that Catherine would be difficult to convince, and though Anne was of age and could make her own decisions, staying away from her mother was not easy to accomplish. His main goal was to avoid a scandal, which would surely hurt their family's reputation. Lady Catherine could not be expected to behave in a reasonable manner when she was upset.

"Well, we shall see. We must find a way to settle this eventually, although I expect Catherine's reaction on hearing a specific news item from Darcy to be quite violent."

"Mother will be so angry if she finds that… You must be careful, Cousin," Anne said, emotional and tearful. "If mother meets Miss Elizabeth, she will be very harsh with her. If I can do anything to protect you from all this trouble… If I could convince Mama that our marriage was never a possibility—"

"Anne dear, you must not worry about me—or about Miss Elizabeth Bennet. Neither of us is afraid of Aunt Catherine." Darcy smiled.

"Oh, I am aware of that," Anne replied. "I saw her when she was in Kent. I must say I never met anyone so courageous! She was not intimidated in the slightest by Mama. I can easily see her confronting Mother quite forcibly if needed!"

"Quite." Darcy smiled again.

"Well, Anne, you could find someone to marry you just to escape Lady Catherine's obsession. That would be quite a joke." The colonel laughed once more, and again the others did not share his amusement. The colonel was puzzled.

"Robert, would you join me at the club?" Darcy said suddenly. "I have some last-minute business to attend to before I leave tomorrow."

"Gladly. I shall see you all tomorrow as I have some fixed appointments for tonight." He smiled mischievously as he took his farewell. "Anne, you must promise me you will rest and not worry about anything."

"I promise," she whispered with a forced smile.

"I shall see you tomorrow morning before I leave," Darcy added warmly.

"Thank you, Cousin," said Miss de Bourgh as her cousins closed the door behind them.

"Robert, what in the world is wrong with you? Damn it, man, how can you be so insensible? How can you make Anne so uncomfortable?" Darcy asked severely as soon as they entered the carriage.

"Pardon me? Pray tell me, how do I make Anne uncomfortable? What nonsense is this?"

"Why do you keep making fun of her timidity? You did the same when we were in Kent! And how could you joke about your moving into her room? And about someone marrying her just to foil Aunt Catherine? Can you not imagine how painful such jokes are for her—especially coming from you? You believe she has no feelings?"

"Darcy, I do not understand what you are talking about! I am quite fond of Anne; you know that. How could I make fun of her? They were just harmless jests!"

"You may be fond of her, but you have no compassion! You know she takes every word from you seriously. And on that subject: I do not want to sound hypocritical, nor do I pretend to be the master of proper behaviour, but you should be careful when you embrace Anne. She is very sensitive now—even more so than before—and she could easily misunderstand your care."

"Misunderstand? What do you mean? Be careful when I embrace Anne—what silliness is this?" Darcy looked at his cousin, who seemed completely at a loss, and hesitated continuing the conversation. Was he really so oblivious to Anne's feelings—he, of all people, who was so accustomed to ladies' company?

"Darcy, this is a very unfortunate moment to be silent! You must explain to me what is bothering you; it seems I am not smart enough to comprehend your meaning. Apparently, I do not even know how to behave with my cousin—"

"There is no need to be upset; it was not my intention to offend you. But I was certain that, by now, you were aware of Anne's tender feelings for you. For heaven's sake, I guess you and Aunt Catherine are the only ones who missed it."

"Anne has tender feelings for me? You mean—" The colonel appeared so shocked by the revelation that it was Darcy's turn to quell the temptation of laughing at *him*.

Eyes wide, face pale, speechless, and as nervous as a boy, Colonel Fitzwilliam looked nothing like the charming gentleman who was known as the ladies' favourite.

"Anne has tender feelings for me? Are you certain, absolutely certain?"

"Yes, Cousin, I am absolutely certain. I cannot see how this could possibly have happened and what you did to deserve it, but I am certain." Darcy attempted to lighten the tension.

The colonel looked at him sharply. "If we begin a conversation about how deserving each of us might be, it would be difficult to understand how Miss Elizabeth possibly accepted your proposal. So let us not dwell upon the subject any longer. Better, tell me how you can be so certain? About Anne…do you believe she has hopes that…? Did I encourage her in any way? I would hate to know I made her suffer, even if it was most unwittingly."

"Robert, Anne is a reasonable person—and very wise. She surely did not inherit this trait from the Fitzwilliam family." Darcy smiled. "I do not think she had any particular hopes…but we both know how difficult is to command the heart. I only want you to be careful. Forgive me if I offended you."

"No, no—you are right of course," the colonel replied with no little worry. "I am grateful that you pointed out this particular situation to me. I shall be careful…"

For the rest of the ride, Robert said nothing. His preoccupation was impenetrable, and Darcy attempted unsuccessfully to raise his spirits until they reached the club.

ELIZABETH FELT TRAPPED INSIDE THE house while her mind travelled through London in search of Darcy, and her heart startled each time a door opened.

After the happy anticipation of Darcy's visit to Hertfordshire, his brief call and the disturbing news of Miss de Bourgh's arrival brought her countless worries and fears. The sharp-clawed grip did not abandon her chest the entire day while she waited in vain for any scrap of news. It was settled they would depart for

Longbourn the following day after breakfast, and she felt something would intervene to prevent Darcy from accompanying them. Mr. Bingley was in Gracechurch Street almost the entire afternoon, and he received a dinner invitation; his joyful and enthusiastic acceptance sounded almost annoying to Elizabeth, though she knew she should be ashamed of such feelings.

She finally returned to her room to prepare for dinner when a servant entered to announce that her presence was required in the library. Startled, trying to read something on the servant's stern face, and too embarrassed to ask the reason, Elizabeth hurried downstairs. She opened the library door tentatively, and her heart nearly stopped when she saw Darcy by the window, staring outside.

She took a few steps, and he heard her; he turned slowly, and she glanced at his preoccupied countenance, attempting to guess the news he was bringing. Then he smiled.

"I am so happy to see you," he whispered, holding her hands. Their eyes held, and his low voice sent cold shivers through her. They were inches apart, and she found no words to say how happy she was to see him. He leaned forward until his lips touched and lingered a few moments over hers.

"Mrs. Gardiner was very kind and allowed me to speak to you a few minutes. And she congratulated me." His smile increased, and his eyes still held hers.

"Yes, she… I…" Speaking—as well as breathing—was still difficult. "I spoke to my aunt; I hope you do not mind. I have never kept any secrets from her. Besides, I think she guessed the truth long ago."

"I do not mind. I would not wish you to keep any secret from Mrs. Gardiner. Besides, it seems we are poor at keeping secrets; my entire family guessed, too, without my telling them a thing. Including Anne," he laughed, and Elizabeth stared at him.

"Miss de Bourgh? But how could she—?"

"What can I say? It is another proof that we are the least perceptive people in the world when it comes to each other. Everyone guessed our feelings long before we did."

"That should be cause for worry, do you not think?" she replied, her heart lighter.

"Not quite… But I would suggest we always speak our minds openly to avoid any further misunderstanding." His lips gently pressed against hers again.

The kiss began lightly, but her hands wrapped around his waist, and she leaned against him, seeking shelter in his embrace. His arms closed around her.

"Mrs. Gardiner allowed me a few minutes to speak," he said breathlessly. She glanced up at him, her cheeks crimson and her eyes sparkling. He placed another quick kiss on her forehead. "I feel horrible to betray Mrs. Gardiner's trust, but I also feel horrible to be so close to you without kissing you. We must settle a date —*you* must settle a date. Do you think you will be able to decide by tomorrow? I would like to be able to present it to Mr. Bennet when I speak to him. Do you think we should fear any opposition from him?"

Darcy spoke with such unusual haste and nervousness that Elizabeth was not certain whether he were joking or not. His final words puzzled her even more.

"You will speak to Papa tomorrow? So you will come to Hertfordshire with us?"

"Why would I not come? Have the plans changed?"

"No, no...but I was afraid that... What happened to Miss de Bourgh? Is she well?"

His face changed, and he moved her to sit on the couch, holding her hands tightly.

"Anne is as well as can be expected. She is staying at Selina's house, and she seems to be pleased with the present arrangement. But Aunt Catherine arrived in Town, and she is very upset. She wished to take Anne back to Rosings...and..." He stopped and looked at Elizabeth then kissed her hand. She caressed his face, her hand resting on his cheek.

"Forgive me; I am afraid I have exposed you to a most unpleasant situation. My aunt's main purpose seemed to be to force me to marry Anne as soon as possible." Elizabeth looked at him, stern and pale, and he placed another kiss on her hand. "I decidedly refused, and she became very angry. It seems she received a letter informing her about my...interest in you. She is furious with you as she holds you responsible for my rejection. We had a violent disagreement. She has declared she will not rest until she has her way. She is even less reasonable than we knew her to be. I am truly sorry..."

"Please do not apologize; it is not your fault in the slightest. Do you know who might have sent her the letter? And how does Miss de Bourgh bear all this?"

"Lady Sinclair sent the letter. And it is my fault. I am disappointed in myself for not settling this situation long ago. Both you and Anne are now exposed to Lady Catherine's anger because of my cavalier attitude. Oh, you asked about Anne —she is well now. She will stay with Selina for the next few weeks...and Georgiana will keep her company. I invited Anne to join us at Pemberley for the summer. I hope you do not mind."

"I think it is a wonderful idea—Miss Anne's company will be a valuable addition to our party. So Georgiana will not join us? I shall miss her dearly, but I think her presence will be very beneficial for Miss de Bourgh."

"Georgiana will miss you as well, but you will meet again soon. Besides, I confess it is convenient for me; I was a trifle worried at the prospect of her going to Hertfordshire while Wickham is in the area."

"I understand your worry. So—you will come to Hertfordshire with us?" she asked again, her voice hopeful.

He laughed, and his hands cupped her face as he gently kissed her eyes.

"You do not seem to have much trust in my word, Miss Bennet." His lips pressed against hers with tender passion.

"I do trust your words...and we should settle a date. I already have a suggestion," she managed to whisper with a last breath, until she abandoned herself to his kiss. He suddenly started to laugh, his lips still pressed against hers.

"Am I correct in presuming that Lady Catherine's menace has hastened your decision? Her presence in town seems to be of infinite use, which ought to make her happy for she loves to be of use."

"No, not really... I had decided a couple of days ago, but I did not dare to speak earlier. I thought six months, perhaps?" Her cheeks instantly turned crimson, and she blushed even more when he stared at her in surprise. "Do you believe it would be too soon?"

"Surely you are mocking me, Miss Bennet! Six months? You might as well have said six years! You are teasing me, are you not?"

He seemed equally surprised and upset, and his eyes seemed to plead for a positive resolution to the stressful situation. She started to laugh.

"You do not believe it would be too soon, it seems. Then by all means, please do choose a date yourself. I promise I will accept any date that my father would agree with."

He looked at her with perfect seriousness.

"It would only take a few days for a special license. I do not believe I need more than a week to make all the arrangements," he declared, and her eyes opened wide in disbelief.

It was his turn to laugh.

"If I were to think only of my wishes, a week from today would be a perfect time; but I do not wish to raise any speculation about a hasty marriage, so I believe three months would be a perfectly reasonable and properly long engagement. It would give us time to inform your family and to make all the announcements as required."

"It sounds a perfect arrangement, Mr. Darcy." She smiled with delight.

"It will be perfect—almost two months of engagement at Pemberley. It will give you time to became accustomed to the estate and to make any changes you like."

"I am certain I will love being engaged to you at Pemberley, Mr. Darcy," she said teasingly, her smiling eyes moist with emotion.

His gaze became darker, and his voice lowered as he leaned to whisper to her.

"I am certain you will, Miss Bennet."

A determined knock at the door interrupted their interlude. They separated hastily, and Elizabeth was certain her cheeks were burning when she greeted Mrs. Gardiner.

Their hostess glanced briefly at the couple; he was still holding Elizabeth's hand. It was obvious something special had happened between them, and Mrs. Gardiner smiled to herself but said nothing.

She invited Mr. Darcy to join them for dinner, but he declined as he had some business to finish that evening. It was settled that Mr. Darcy with Mr. Bingley would return the next day around noon to fetch Elizabeth and Jane. A few minutes later, Mr. Darcy left, followed through the window by Elizabeth's gaze; the happiness shining from her face was more dazzling than ever.

As busy as he was with preparations for his trip to Hertfordshire, Darcy thought little about the previous day's events. Anne was well settled at Selina's house, and there was no reason to worry about her, so Darcy turned his mind to more pleasant subjects—like the time he would spend with Elizabeth. Therefore, when the door opened and Lord Matlock and the colonel entered, red-faced and furious, Darcy needed some moments to understand his uncle's anger.

"That woman is completely out of her mind. Where on earth can she be? I thought she came to see you! She left the house early this morning; heaven knows where she went. Upon my word, if she does something stupid, I shall never speak to her again!"

"Lady Catherine left without a word," the colonel explained.

Darcy looked up in surprise. "Perhaps she returned to Rosings?"

"That would be reasonable behaviour, which is why I suspect you are wrong," the earl replied. "I was afraid she was here, continuing to argue with you. We also checked with Selina, but she is not there either."

"Uncle, you should not worry so much. Aunt Catherine has servants with her; she is not in danger, wherever she might have chosen to go. There is little she may do, really."

"I surely hope so. Well, I think we should return home; I have wasted my morning in a most stressful manner. We shall call at Gracechurch Street to say goodbye to Miss Elizabeth and Miss Bennet. I trust you will take care of them during the journey, Darcy."

"I would not worry about that," said the colonel, laughing. "So, Darcy, you will return in about two weeks if I remember rightly."

"Yes. I plan to finish all my business in town before summer, and then I shall travel to Pemberley before you to have everything prepared for your arrival."

"Oh, nonsense," the earl said. "Everything is always prepared at Pemberley. Mrs. Reynolds is taking care of the house perfectly. You worry too much. Well, convey my best wishes to Mr. Bennet; I hope to see him again very soon. If not for this mess with Catherine, I would surely join you in Hertfordshire."

"I have great hopes that you and Mr. Bennet will have many opportunities to spend time together in the future." Darcy smiled as he made his farewell to his relatives.

MR. BENNET COULD NOT REMEMBER another time in his life when he felt equally happy and content nor more grateful for the surprises that had permeated his life in recent weeks.

Though he had suspected it since his visit to Town, the confirmation that his eldest daughters were bound through deepest affection to two remarkable gentlemen filled his heart with joy, and it dissolved all the worries that had burdened him for years.

It was not only the knowledge that his family would have a secure future, no matter what happened to him, but the certainty that his daughters would have lives filled with love.

He felt his eyes burning with tears as he recollected all his discussions with Elizabeth since she was an infant—how proud he felt to have such a spirited, bright, witty daughter and how much he feared that she would never find a man to appreciate her qualities and allow her spirit to live free. He always feared that Elizabeth would choose never to marry, as her openly expressed wishes and expectations from a man were unlikely to be fulfilled. Even she used to joke about being a spinster and spending her life caring for Jane's children. But his fears slowly dissipated when he met Darcy in London and easily guessed the gentleman's admiration for his daughter.

Yes, he had never felt equally happy and content before, he thought, as he continued to enjoy the peace and silence of the library.

Mrs. Bennet was visiting her sister Philips in Meryton, together with Lydia and Kitty. Since he received and shared the news of Mr. Bingley's proposal to Jane, Mrs. Bennet had little else to live for except making arrangements for a wedding whose date was not even settled and sharing her good fortune with everyone she knew. Regarding Mr. Darcy's proposal, Mr. Bennet maintained perfect secrecy; if Mrs. Bennet discovered *that* truth, her entire attention would descend on Mr. Darcy—and that would be unfair to both gentlemen. Mr. Bennet laughed to himself at the prospect.

A mild source of disquiet at Longbourn was Lydia and Kitty's behaviour. They were strangers to discipline and restrictions, and for the last two weeks as Mrs. Bennet was occupied with other things, Lydia and Kitty were left completely to themselves. They would come and go as they pleased, walking almost daily to Meryton to meet the officers, purchasing useless articles and then arguing over them for hours. Not a single moment of their time was spent in a beneficial way, and Mr. Bennet was neither oblivious nor indifferent to the consequences that might be suffered by their young minds and weak characters. However, since his wife seemed pleased and content with their younger daughters' behaviour and saw no reason to restrain them, Mr. Bennet could do little that would not create friction within the family—which he did not wish to do.

With the latest fortunate events, Mr. Bennet hoped that his younger daughters would have opportunities to spend time with Jane and Elizabeth away from their mother's lenience, and that their behaviour might change as they grew older.

However, until such time, it was distressing to bear the daily grievances about the regiment's departure from Meryton and Lydia's constant complaints about not following them to Brighton for the summer. He knew it would be foolish to allow Lydia to leave his sight—especially to a camp full of soldiers—but to have her constantly crying of her misfortune in being kept at home was even more difficult to endure.

His musings were abruptly interrupted by a din of voices that shattered the house; he thought he could recognise Hill but the other voice—so strong that he was uncertain whether it was a woman or a man—he had never heard before.

The library door was thrown open and slammed against the wall; Mr. Bennet had no time to rise from his chair before the guest invaded his room.

"You are Mr. Bennet, I presume!"

A puzzled gaze was his only reply while Mr. Bennet kept to his chair with perfect calm. The guest allowed the silence no longer and demanded with severity, "Well? Are you Mr. Bennet or not? I would appreciate an answer; I have no time to lose."

"Forgive me; I was under the impression that you already had decided I was Mr. Bennet, so I never suspected you might require an answer regarding my identity," the gentleman said with amusement after the first puzzling moments. "And speaking of identity, may I inquire to whom I have the pleasure of speaking in *my* library?"

"I am Lady Catherine de Bourgh!"

Mr. Bennet was positively shocked. All amazement, he finally rose from his chair.

"Of course—I should have guessed immediately; forgive my ignorance," Mr. Bennet responded in all honesty. How was it possible that he did not recognise the formidable lady instantly as the noble patroness so warmly described by Mr. Collins? He attempted to form a proper invitation to the house, but she interrupted him.

"You have very small rooms here," she said with a brief glance around. "Even smaller than Mr. Collins told me. This could hardly be called a library."

"Yet, I do call it a library." He did not dare presume what brought the illustrious lady into the neighbourhood, but obviously, it was not a courtesy visit. Lady Catherine was unhinged about something, and Mr. Bennet quickly anticipated an opportunity to amuse himself while solving the mystery.

"Lady Catherine, though your presence honours me, I confess I cannot imagine to what we owe your ladyship's extraordinary visit. May we be of some assistance?"

"Yes, you may. I did not come here for the pleasure of the trip; you can be sure. I have rarely had such a disagreeable journey. Is your daughter at home? I need to speak to her."

Mr. Bennet's puzzlement increased as well as his amusement.

"You need to speak to my daughter? Is there a specific daughter you have in mind, or will any of them do? My eldest are expected from London later today, but my youngest will be home any minute."

"Mr. Bennet, you should not assume me tolerant of your mockery! I did not come here to be the brunt of your jokes. I wish to speak to your daughter Elizabeth immediately!"

"With Lizzy? On what subject, if I may ask?"

"On the subject of her preposterous behaviour and questionable character! And you, as her father, should take appropriate measures to remedy this intolerable situation."

"Lady Catherine, of what situation are you speaking? And I must insist that you explain your harsh words regarding my daughter. I can see you are upset, and I cannot imagine why." At the offensive words about his favourite daughter, Mr. Bennet immediately became serious. There was no room for amusement.

"You can be at no loss, Mr. Bennet, to understand the reason for my journey hither. No matter how indolent you might be in your family, I was told you are perceptive enough to understand the situation."

"Though your ladyship's trust in my perception flatters me, I am afraid your praise is undeserved. I am not at all able to account for the honour of seeing you here."

"Then I shall explain immediately! A report of a most alarming nature reached me two days ago, which involves your daughter Elizabeth. Your daughter, to whom I was exceedingly kind and generous in Kent, has repaid my generosity in the most detestable way. She used all manner of arts and allurements to make my nephew forget his duty and his family. She has addled his wits and is ready to expose him to ridicule."

Suddenly, the relief of revelation washed away all Mr. Bennet's worry.

"When you speak of your nephew, dare I presume you refer to Mr. Darcy?"

"I do refer to Darcy! So you are not as ignorant as you pretend to be!"

"I am ignorant about your ladyship's displeasure, but I do know of Mr. Darcy's admiration for Elizabeth. However, I do not understand in what way she would make him forget his duty and his family."

"The admiration you are speaking of caused Darcy to break his promise to my daughter, Anne! What would a gentleman say to that?"

"Mr. Darcy is engaged to your daughter? I did not know that."

"He is… In fact, their engagement is of a peculiar kind. From their infancy, they have been intended for each other. It was the wish of his mother as well as hers. While they were in their cradles, we planned the union; and now, at the moment when the wishes of both sisters would be accomplished in their marriage, to be prevented by a young woman of inferior birth, of no importance in the world and wholly unallied to the family!"

"Lady Catherine, I am afraid I am lost again. I understand your ladyship wants Mr. Darcy to marry your daughter, and I suspect he is not willing to do so. You pretend he was engaged to your daughter, but I understand it was not he who promised anything to his cousin but you and his mother planning for them. I have difficulty comprehending what my daughter's fault is in this unfortunate situation. If Mr. Darcy admires Elizabeth, he surely cannot be bound either by affection or by honour to his cousin."

"Your daughter's fault is that she attempted to insinuate herself with him, to gain his attention by all manner of schemes, to trap him into a marriage, no doubt very advantageous for her and for your family but disastrous for him and his good name. But that will never happen—I shall never allow it to happen! And you, if you know the best interests of your family, will help me with this. If you are as sensible as I hope—"

"Lady Catherine, though I find this discussion entertaining, I still do not understand what your ladyship proposes to accomplish by coming here today. What would you expect me to do? Should I forbid Mr. Darcy's admiring my daughter?

Should I force him to marry your daughter? Do you believe he will obey if I ask him to do so?"

"You should demand that your daughter stay away from my nephew forever! You should keep her at home and make her understand that, no matter how hard she may try, a union with my nephew will never be possible."

"Now...forgive me for being so bold, but I must ask—why would I do such thing? As far as I can see, there are only two choices here: either Mr. Darcy accepts your notion of his marrying your daughter or he does not. In the first instance, things would be settled to your liking. In the second, even if I keep my daughter at home and never allow her to see Mr. Darcy again, it would not make him return to his cousin. And if he indeed admires Elizabeth and has any serious design on her, why would I intentionally ruin my daughter's chance for happiness? Why would I not welcome the union of such a worthy man with my daughter?"

"Because honour, decorum, prudence, even interest forbid it! If you love your daughter, you should not expose her to ridicule by attempting to attain a goal so far above her! Mr. Darcy and my daughter would be a perfect match in all the ways that matter; anyone can see that. Your daughter is merely a temporary distraction for him; he will never ask for her hand in marriage, and you will be left with only disappointment and shame!"

"Lady Catherine, does Mr. Darcy know of your visit here? Have you spoken to him lately?" Mr. Bennet was suddenly weary of their conversation.

"I did speak to him yesterday! I told him everything I told you!"

"And, considering you came such a long way to repeat everything to me, I imagine he was not receptive to your interference."

"He was not—because he is already addled! That is why I came here with the determined resolution of carrying my purpose! I wished to speak to your daughter directly, but perhaps it is better that I spoke to you instead. Mr. Bennet—you must know I never fail in my plans, and I am always willing to pay the price. Here is what I propose to you: if you agree to help me with this situation, I shall insist that Mr. Collins take care of your family after you are gone. I shall see that he allows your widow and your daughters to remain in this house as long as they wish!"

Mr. Bennet looked at her with great interest and complete seriousness.

"Lady Catherine, your offer is generous indeed. It makes me happy to know that, after I die, your ladyship—who undoubtedly will live much longer than me —will convince my cousin not to throw my family out of their home. On the other hand, were my daughter to marry Mr. Darcy, the problem would be solved in a more desirable manner. So I am afraid my choice is final, and I must refuse you."

"How dare you! You refuse to obey the claim of duty and honour? You and your daughter are determined to ruin my nephew and make him the contempt of the world!"

"Neither duty nor honour would be violated by my daughter marrying Mr. Darcy—quite the contrary. And with regard to the resentment of his family, I had the pleasure of meeting Lord Matlock, and I am certain he would welcome such a union. As for the world in general, I dare say it would have too much sense to join in the scorn."

"And this is your real opinion! This is your final resolve! Very well—I shall now know how to act. Do not imagine, Mr. Bennet, that your ambition will ever be gratified. I hoped to find you reasonable, but depend upon it, I will carry my point."

"I am sorry I must disappoint you even more, but there is little you can do now. It pains me to give you more bad news, but there is something else you must know. I suspect Mr. Darcy did not inform you because he wished to speak formally to me first. Our entire discussion was pointless, because Mr. Darcy asked for Elizabeth's hand in marriage a week ago. He wrote and asked for my consent; I await his arrival at any moment as he accompanies Elizabeth home. You are more than welcome to wait for him if you wish. It would be exhilarating for all of us to debate his engagement to Elizabeth."

Mr. Bennet smiled, but he suppressed his mirth when he saw Lady Catherine turn white and lean slowly against the settee. She seemed unable to breathe, and he hurried to pour her a glass of water when the room was suddenly invaded by Mrs. Bennet, Lydia, Kitty, Mrs. Philips and Lady Lucas. Mrs. Bennet's voice almost made him drop the glass.

"Oh dear Lord, did I hear you correctly? Lizzy is engaged to Mr. Darcy? Oh heavens! Mr. Darcy and Lizzy? Hill, where are you? Lady Catherine, Hill told me you were here, and I was wondering about your visit... Oh dear Lord, you came to tell us about the engagement? Lizzy and Mr. Darcy? Oh, Lord, this cannot be! My dear Lizzy, she is such a smart, spirited girl! So bright, so well read! And such a good dancer! Oh, such a handsome man! Tall and handsome! Oh, dearest Lizzy! Hill, Hill, where are you?"

Mrs. Bennet's cries of happiness continued for a time, and Lady Catherine, suddenly recovered from her shock, strove to find the exit from the house. Her retreating steps attempted to outpace Mrs. Bennet's persistent words of gratitude for bringing them such extraordinary news.

Mr. Bennet asked John to help Lady Catherine to her carriage and then closed the library door with a heavy heart. Why could he not manage to control his anger better? He should have kept the secret as Darcy and Elizabeth requested. How could he betray their confidence? Surely they would be upset with him—and reasonably so. He was upset with himself, but there was little he could do for the present.

Lady Catherine—with tentative steps, unable to interrupt Mrs. Bennet and looking desperately from one woman the other, all of whom were discussing her nephew's engagement—finally entered her carriage, wailing at the coachman to make haste.

As the carriage departed, Mrs. Bennet's voice still rang loud and clear.

Looking out the carriage, Elizabeth thought there could be no day more

237

perfect for travel.

They had left London immediately after breakfast with a tender farewell from Lord Matlock, his sons, Miss Darcy, Lady Selina, Mrs. Gardiner and the children. After spending such a long and eventful time together in London as well as at Matlock Manor, Elizabeth felt as though she were departing from one family to be reunited with another.

They journeyed together in Darcy's carriage, and Elizabeth blushed as she remembered her shameless scheme: Jane was the first to enter the carriage. Elizabeth followed her sister and immediately sat opposite. Consequently, when the gentlemen entered, each had little choice but to sit by his betrothed.

The moment he took his seat, Darcy's glance, smiling and mischievous, acknowledged his approval of the seating arrangements and made her blush.

She had slept little the previous night, imagining the ride home. How many things had happened in such a short time and how much her life had changed in only one month! She had left Longbourn with so many uncertainties, fears and hopes, and now she returned with a heart filled with overwhelming happiness.

She looked briefly at her dear sister, whose felicity glowed on her beautiful face, then turned briefly to the man near her—the source of her own felicity. He was smiling—a smile that was more obvious in his eyes than on his face. Opposite them, Mr. Bingley spoke much and laughed frequently, his joy impossible to conceal.

Mr. Darcy—her future husband—spoke little and laughed even less, but his face, even more handsome when joy was brightening it, gave little doubt of his feelings.

From time to time, he leaned towards Elizabeth, pointing to something out the window that she could admire. In these moments, which were neither few nor rare, his body touched hers, and his lips, whispering into her ear, daringly touched her. His hand, resting on her shoulder, and his fingers, brushing over her nape, seemed to burn her skin.

Such small gestures were unnoticed by Jane and Mr. Bingley—both being preoccupied with each other—but for Elizabeth, it was sweet torture, a storm of fire and ice sending countless shivers throughout her body.

Three times, at Mr. Darcy's suggestion, the carriage stopped at some lovely place, allowing them time to enjoy refreshment and take short walks near the carriage.

Nothing seemed more natural to Elizabeth than to enjoy the beauties with her intended, to walk at his side and to take offered fruits from his hand as they sat together on a blanket. The smallest touch, the most innocent smile or joke, made her blush, and he did not miss her disquiet. He tried to reduce her uneasiness with light jokes and teasing, and she gladly entered his game.

During the last part of their journey, Elizabeth became more comfortable —even managing to bear his thigh tightly pressed to hers—and their conversation unfolded in a light, pleasing manner.

It was late in the afternoon when the carriage stopped in front of Longbourn. Mr. Darcy and Mr. Bingley helped the ladies out, and they were approaching the main entrance together when the door opened and Mr. Bennet appeared.

A moment later, he was unceremoniously shoved aside as Mrs. Bennet ran out the door, decidedly moving in their direction, and did not stop until two steps away from Mr. Darcy, expressing loudly and incoherently her happiness at seeing him at Longbourn again. She then turned briefly to Mr. Bingley, greeting him too with a rushed welcome, and then returned her attention to Mr. Darcy, complimenting him on his carriage—the most exquisite she had ever seen.

Darcy looked at her, completely lost, his arm still held by Elizabeth, and glanced briefly at Mr. Bennet. The gentleman's guilt and embarrassed expression dissipated any remaining doubts: his engagement to Elizabeth was no longer a secret.

After a short hesitation, Darcy lowered his eyes to Elizabeth, who was looking at him with a pale expression, troubled and ashamed. He smiled and replied warmly:

"Mrs. Bennet, I thank you for your warm welcome. Mr. Bingley and I are happy to be at Longbourn again. We have always regretted that we did not have a chance to accept the dinner invitation you so generously extended us last autumn. We hope to have numerous opportunities to benefit from your generosity on this visit."

Lord Matlock, Colonel Fitzwilliam, and the viscount were at their club in London, debating the last days' events. All were worried as they had not discovered Lady Catherine's whereabouts and feared she might do something that would expose them all to ridicule. They were at least content that Anne was safe and healthy in Selina's house, protected from the foolishness of her mother.

Shortly, two gentlemen approached their table and stopped to greet them.

"Lord Sinclair—so glad to see you," said Lord Matlock. "I was hoping to meet with you, as I need to speak about a rather private and important matter."

"I am glad to see you, too, Matlock. Well, well, I wonder what important matter that might be." Lord Sinclair laughed in obvious good humour. "Can we sit at your table? By the way, do you know John Stoddart from *The Times*?"

"Of course; Mr. Stoddart, very pleased to see you again. Please take a seat, gentlemen."

"Lord Matlock—it is an honour, sir. And such a surprise—I just spoke to your sister Lady Catherine earlier today. She came to visit me at my office," said Mr. Stoddart.

"Quite a surprise indeed." Lord Matlock glanced at his sons. "Mr. Stoddart, I hope you will accept a dinner invitation on short notice. I feel we have many things to discuss, many things indeed."

Chapter 19

"There is something of great delicacy about which I wish to speak to you, Sinclair," said Lord Matlock, choosing his words carefully. They were sitting at a table slightly apart from the rest of the group in a large room at their club. The other gentleman looked at him with curiosity, so he continued.

"It regards Eve."

"Eve, my wife? What did she do? You seem quite serious; should I be worried?"

"I am very serious; I am sorry to upset you, but drastic measures are required. Her actions intentionally jeopardised the good name and peace of my family."

"I must demand that you be more specific when you bring such a serious accusation."

"A few days ago, she sent a letter to my sister Catherine with offensive content directed to my nephew Darcy and Miss Elizabeth Bennet—the niece of our late friend Mr. Gardiner. This action brought painful consequences to those whose names were maligned and to others associated with them."

As he spoke, Lord Matlock grew angrier. Lord Sinclair paled.

"How can you be certain it was Eve?"

"My sister Catherine told me. Should I ask her to hand me the letter?"

"No...no—that will not be necessary. Please accept my apologies on behalf of my wife and myself. I cannot imagine what Eve was thinking; sometimes she is just... How can I atone for this unfortunate outcome? What should I do?"

"There is no reason for you to apologise, and no compensation is possible. I depend on you to take the proper measures to avoid similar situations in the future. I was thinking... Your estate is beautiful. I have known Eve since she was an infant, and I am certain that spending a few months there for the summer would benefit her. Solitude can be rewarding at times."

"True... I think that to be wise advice. Again, please accept my apologies..."

"There is nothing further to say on the matter. Let us return to the others."

"Matlock, please do not think me oblivious to what happens around me. I see and hear everything. It is just that...sometimes I am weak. Doing what is proper is not always easy. Eve is a very beautiful woman. I know you never approved my marriage, but there was little I could do. I am not as strong as you."

"I am not as strong as you believe me to be, Sinclair—not at all. As for your marriage—I only gave you my opinion as a friend. It was never for me to approve it or not. But enough of this. I trust you will find the best solution."

"At least I will search for the best solution; I can promise that."

The discussion ended in awkward tension for both gentlemen as they reunited with the group. Lord Sinclair seemed to have lost most of his joyousness, and he was more silent than ever; it was no surprise when he made his farewell rather sooner than later.

The evening ended at Matlock's house with a pleasant dinner and a single guest —Mr. Stoddart. As Lord Matlock guessed and feared, it was revealed that Lady Catherine visited the editor of *The Times* earlier that day, insisting that an announcement be posted in the next edition, announcing the engagement of Mr. Darcy to Miss Anne de Bourgh. With great effort, Lord Matlock managed to maintain a calm appearance as he tried to explain to his guest—without maligning the good name of their family and his sister—that such an announcement was in error.

Mr. Stoddart was quick enough neither to miss the truth behind the earl's words nor to ignore the potential interest in such gossip. But his wisdom assisted him in choosing the side he should take. The interest of the editor was overcome by the gentleman's common sense and his awareness that Lord Matlock was not to be trifled with. Therefore, Mr. Stoddart politely accepted the explanation without further inquiry; he even suggested that Lord Matlock should be certain that such an announcement had not reached other newspapers, too, in order to avoid unpleasant surprises.

After dinner ended and Mr. Stoddart left, the three gentlemen were enjoying a brandy in the library when the door was thrown open. As Lord Matlock feared, the day, which started so badly, turned even worse.

"Did you know Darcy is already engaged to that Bennet girl?" Lady Catherine cried.

"Catherine, where have you been? You disappeared like a lunatic. What were you thinking?" Lord Matlock instantly became as furious as his sister, and no attempt by his sons succeeded in calming him. "I warned you to behave reasonably or you would be forced to return to Rosings. You will leave the house first thing in the morning."

"Did you know Darcy is engaged?" she repeated. "Her father himself informed me of it, and her horrible mother nearly drove me insane with her deranged outburst. That woman is out of her senses, I am telling you! What should we do? What should we do?!"

"CATHERINE! Silence, not a word more! You are not allowed to speak about anyone being insane! You are completely unbalanced! Yes, I do know Darcy is engaged, and I could not be happier. I imagine he will be married as soon as possible, so there is nothing you can do. I shall ask servants to prepare your luggage!"

"You have been to Hertfordshire? To Longbourn?" inquired the viscount.

241

"Oh, and just so you know—Mr. Stoddart had dinner with us today. Do not expect to see your preposterous announcement in the newspaper. What was in your mind to do such a thing? Can you imagine the consequences if the announcement appeared and then Darcy married Miss Bennet? Can you imagine what that would mean for poor Anne—and for our entire family?"

"Stoddart is a betrayer; I shall go to other newspapers instead!"

"You have been to Longbourn?" the viscount repeated while everyone ignored him.

"Go to your rooms until the morning, or I shall be forced to throw you out this very moment. Gibbs, help Lady Catherine to her apartment, and be certain her carriage is ready at daybreak," the earl addressed a stunned servant, lost in the middle of the din, then the earl himself took his sister's arm and directed her out of the library.

The viscount and the colonel looked at each other in frozen disbelief.

"You must be correct; she surely was at Longbourn," the colonel finally replied sternly.

As soon as Mrs. Bennet's nerves allowed her to calm and she felt well enough to inquire after her sister Gardiner's health, Mr. Bennet suggested that Jane tell her mother and younger sisters all the details of their long trip while he discreetly invited Darcy and Elizabeth to follow him into the library.

Immediately, Darcy began a formal address regarding his proposal to Elizabeth, but the elder gentleman interrupted him with a wave of his hand.

"Indeed, sir, as I already told you in my letter, I could not think of anyone better for my Lizzy. I feel grateful and honoured by your request, and I never gave my consent as warmly as I do now. But we shall talk about all this later. What I wanted to tell you before my wife does is that we had a most surprising visitor earlier today."

Darcy's countenance softened and warmed with each of the gentleman's words, but the final statement did not make an impression on him. He turned to Elizabeth with a small smile, certain that she was the one to guess about the visit.

"Can you not guess who the visitor was, Mr. Darcy?"

"Me?" He was completely lost, searching for a sign of mockery.

"You indeed, as the matter concerns you quite a lot. I dare say not everyone in your family approves your engagement with Lizzy, am I correct?" Mr. Bennet was positively amused, but Darcy turned pale and silent, staring at his host with obvious worry.

"Lady Catherine was here?" Darcy's voice sounded lost and incredulous. Mr. Bennet laughed.

"She was, indeed. I must say, Mr. Collins's description did not do her justice. Lizzy dear, it seems she was quite upset with you; she declared you ungrateful that, after she invited you for dinner at Rosings, you somehow deceitfully charmed Mr. Darcy."

Elizabeth blushed and attempted to laugh, but Darcy's distress pained her. She tried to form a reply, but the gentleman spoke first.

"Mr. Bennet, words are insufficient to express my regret for the dreadful situation you endured. I never suspected such a thing might occur; please forgive me, I—"

"Sir, there is really no need for such distress. I had quite an amusing time, and it became even more diverting when Mrs. Bennet returned home unexpectedly. Did I mention that Lady Catherine's loudly expressed indignation allowed Mrs. Bennet to discover the secret of your engagement? Mrs. Bennet and half of Meryton, to be more specific."

"I am truly sorry, sir, truly sorry," Darcy repeated.

"Do not be sorry; nobody ever made Mrs. Bennet so happy. My only concern is about Miss de Bourgh. I understand it was expected that you would marry her? How does she bear your engagement? This is not something to trifle with."

Without even asking permission, Darcy poured himself a glass of brandy then managed to reply coherently.

"Nobody expected me to marry Anne except my Aunt Catherine. Please be assured that I did not break my word, nor did I pain anyone with my engagement. I happened to speak to Anne a few days ago when she arrived in town. She was quite happy about the news, I might say. The matter of a marriage between us was long settled."

"Good. Now, be so kind as to pour me a glass of that brandy, and have a seat. Now would be an excellent time to give me more details about your arrangements."

Elizabeth breathed in relief and glanced at Darcy; his discomfort was still darkening his expression, but he attempted to speak lightly as he informed Mr. Bennet about what they decided. Mr. Bennet interrupted him a few times in obvious good humour, declaring he had expected the news of their engagement since they shared those few short letters. He then asked Darcy whether the invitation to Pemberley was still valid since he already secured Elizabeth's hand and did not need to be polite any longer.

Mr. Bennet's teasing brought little comfort to Darcy's embarrassment; Elizabeth could see that. He rarely smiled, and he seemed to struggle to understand whether Mr. Bennet was joking. Her father's next question, however, took her by complete surprise.

"So, this is your plan… And may I ask why you think a three-months' engagement is necessary? I do not mean to intrude; I am just curious. It is my understanding that no more than a week is needed to apply for a special license."

Elizabeth felt her cheeks burning, and she dared a glance at Darcy; his expression suddenly changed, though he seemed equally uneasy.

"We thought it would be proper not to rush… We believed that it would be better if…" As he spoke, he kept glancing at Elizabeth as if waiting for her intervention. His words seemed weak and his arguments unconvincing.

"To be honest, sir, I thought an engagement of three months would be comfortable for Elizabeth. If it were my choice alone, I would say two weeks would be long enough. However, Elizabeth's comfort and wishes are more important than mine."

"I would imagine as much." Mr. Bennet laughed while Elizabeth turned crimson. A moment later, Mr. Bennet became more serious.

"As I said, I do not mean to intrude but I was thinking—perhaps you should choose a shorter engagement, considering the circumstances. From what I observed earlier, Lady Catherine will not cease interfering until everything is settled and publicly acknowledged. I would say the best way to avoid a scandal is to be done with it."

Darcy's expression darkened again, and he avoided Mr. Bennet's eyes for a moment.

"Mr. Bennet, I could have all the arrangements completed in a week, and nothing would make me happier. But I shall not force Elizabeth to hurry or to decide against her wishes only because of my aunt's behaviour. Despite anything my aunt might do, I will find a way to protect Elizabeth and our families. Please do not worry about that."

Elizabeth gently touched his arm with her hand, and he turned to meet her eyes. She smiled, her cheeks still burning, her eyes sparkling.

"I think we should discuss this…the engagement, I mean. And no, I do not worry about Lady Catherine either."

"Good—excellent," Mr. Bennet said while the couple looked at each other in silence. "Discuss this, and let me know what you decide. And your mother too —she will never forgive you if you do not allow her time for proper arrangements. Now let us return; I am certain Mrs. Bennet is anxious to ask Mr. Darcy what he would prefer for dinner."

"Papa, may I have a few more minutes with Mr. Darcy? We will join you shortly."

"Sir, would you be so kind as to lend me a pen and some paper? I intend to send an express for my uncle. I was thinking that an announcement in the papers —about our engagement—would be necessary," Darcy said.

"Yes it would—yes indeed. Lizzy will show you everything you need."

Mr. Bennet left the library, but no words were spoken for some time. Meaningful, deep looks attempted to share each other's feelings before the silence was broken.

"Elizabeth, I cannot say how sorry I am. I cannot forgive myself for exposing you and your family to my aunt's malicious actions. I never would have believed her capable of such things. You cannot imagine how ashamed I am and—"

"You take too much upon yourself, truly. It is done and cannot be changed. I am certain my parents took the situation much better than you did." She laughed, gently caressing his face. "As for being ashamed—I believe I know your feelings. I love my mother dearly, but her exuberant behaviour has frequently made me uncomfortable."

"Your mother would never behave like Lady Catherine did; of that I am sure."

"Oh, yes she would." Elizabeth laughed heartily. "Only try to tell her you decided to marry someone else after she was convinced she would have you as a son-in-law, and you will see. But that is quite easy to understand; nobody would ever accept easily the loss of such a faultless man—tall and handsome and worth ten thousand a year!"

Her eyes laughed along with her teasing, and his countenance brightened at the sight. He captured the hand that was still caressing his face and placed a long kiss in her palm while his other arm encircled her waist.

"You are generous to forgive me so easily. I shall abuse your generosity by insisting on listening to your father and choosing another wedding day—a much earlier one," he said while he gently pulled her closer.

His lips brushed small, warm kisses on her palm and along her wrists, then further to each finger while his eyes never abandoned hers. She rested her other hand against his chest while she wondered how it was possible to shiver on such a warm day.

"You said I would enjoy being engaged at Pemberley," she whispered, smiling shyly.

"Indeed. But you will enjoy even more being newly wed at Pemberley." He wiped her smile with a warm kiss that took her breath away and left little doubt about his meaning. She moved closer, and her hands curved around his neck as she daringly accepted the passionate demand of his lips.

"I do not believe I can finish preparations in less than two weeks," she managed to whisper, her lips almost touching his. "I will need a new trousseau, new dresses…"

His lips captured hers again with more passion. He allowed her to breathe again, enough to respond.

"Do not bother yourself with new clothes; you will not have time to wear any of them…"

She froze then pulled away, staring at him in shock. "Mr. Darcy!"

His hands were still around her waist, and he looked at her—her eyes sparkling, her cheeks and neck red, her lips wet and crimson—and he was at a loss to understand what offended her. Then suddenly the revelation struck him, and he started to laugh while his arms crushed her against him and he gently kissed her hair.

"What I meant was that I plan for us to leave for Pemberley immediately after the wedding, so there will be no special occasions to require new dresses. And you will have plenty of time to order everything you need after we marry."

She looked at him, incredulous at his explanation, and he laughed again and kissed her hand. She started to laugh, too.

He leaned closer to whisper in her ear. "However, I confess I am exceedingly pleased that your imagination equals the quickness of your mind. And it gives me one more reason to insist we decide on an earlier date."

"Very well, sir. I should have known that you would not have it any other way but your own. We shall marry as soon as you make all the arrangements. Two weeks should do."

The expression of heartfelt delight diffused over his face warmed her heart, and with no trace of shyness, she rose on her toes so her lips could reach and join his. Another kiss brought them closer, with growing passion, until he began to laugh against her lips.

"Though my previous explanation was genuine and honest, now that I come to think of it, I confess your guess was not far from what I had in mind as well."

She looked at him again, struggling to be serious and reproachful, but he demanded her lips once more, and she was not strong enough to fight against it. The shivers travelling wildly along her body almost equalled her imagination.

It was more a spectacle for the servants than a breakfast, as Lady Catherine repeatedly declared she would not leave town without her daughter.

After pointless arguments, Lord Matlock accepted his sister's request to at least speak directly with her daughter. Colonel Fitzwilliam disapproved the arrangement immediately, but the earl argued that a discussion between the two was necessary and fair.

The colonel left the house much earlier than the others, so he had time to reach his Selina's house and warn Anne about the imminent visit.

Half an hour later, Anne was waiting in the drawing room, her countenance calm, her distress betrayed only by her hands entwined in her lap and by frequent glances directed to the colonel. Lady Selina watched them with a smile.

Lady Catherine entered, followed by the earl, and did not favour them with a greeting. She stopped in front of her daughter.

"Anne, I came to fetch you. There is no need to worry about your luggage, I will send after it later. If we leave now, we shall arrive at Rosings by the end of the day."

"Good day, Mother, I am happy to see you again," Anne replied shyly.

"Yes, yes, good day. Now go and prepare yourself; we must go."

"Mother, I am not returning to Rosings. Selina invited me to stay with her."

"I will not hear any of this, Anne. I will never allow you to stay in town; you know your health does not permit it. You will return home with me without delay."

"Selina fetched a doctor to examine me yesterday. I am perfectly well. I thank you for your concern, but you cannot force me to return. I have decided to remain with Selina."

"Obstinate, headstrong girl! I am ashamed of you! Is this your gratitude for everything I have given you? I have dedicated my entire life to taking care of you, and this is how you repay me? I am now convinced that you have not the smallest affection for me, but you owe me respect and obedience!"

"Mother, it pains me that I hurt you, but please do not doubt my affection as I do not doubt yours. I am grateful for your care and concern, but—"

"You believe Selina or anyone else would take care of you as I do? Do you think anyone else cares about your well-being as I do? Foolish child! They will soon tire of you and send you back home—alone! Do you want to expose yourself to such shame?"

"Forgive me for upsetting you, but I shall not return home," Anne repeated weakly.

"I think there is not much to discuss at this point," the colonel interfered. "Anne has decided, and we should not upset her more on this subject." Without allowing any contradiction, he offered Anne his arm and showed her out of the room.

Behind them, Lady Catherine began another argument with the earl but with no success. The viscount closed the door to avoid servants witnessing their debate.

"Catherine, you should leave now, and do not worry about Anne; she will be provided with the best possible care. She will return to Rosings when she is ready."

"This will not end here; I promise you! I shall not allow you to interfere in my family!"

"Catherine, go home. I shall accompany you to your carriage," the earl repeated, and he took her arm decidedly.

Finally, the impressive carriage left; from the library window, Anne, holding tightly to the colonel's arm, watched her mother depart.

THE NEWS THAT ELIZABETH AND Mr. Darcy decided to marry in two weeks' time threw Mrs. Bennet from extraordinary joy into the deepest despair. That her daughter would marry at Longbourn with a special licence and that Mr. Darcy expected his uncle—Lord Matlock—to attend the event with his entire family was almost too much happiness to bear for her sensitive nerves. However, a tragedy almost followed as she was certain she could not possibly finish all the arrangements for such illustrious company in so short a time And the realisation that Elizabeth would not have time to complete her trousseau was another reason to fear that Mr. Darcy might become upset and change his mind.

It was the gentleman himself who assured Mrs. Bennet that he insisted on a short engagement, and he expressed his wishes that, once they were married, Mrs. Bennet would be kind enough to advise Elizabeth on purchasing everything she might need. Mrs. Bennet almost fainted at such compliments.

As promised, Mr. Darcy spent quite a lot of time at Longbourn with Mr. Bennet. They studied all the papers of the estate, searching together for the best way to administer Longbourn in the future.

Elizabeth served them coffee and refreshments and stayed with them for hours, watching her betrothed with equal admiration and pride as he patiently explained to Mr. Bennet any mistakes he observed and how they could be remedied.

At one point, he even asked Elizabeth's opinion, and they began a small debate. Mr. Darcy won, but he admitted Elizabeth's observations were valid and could be useful. Mr. Bennet again declared that, if Elizabeth were a man, Longbourn would have been a perfectly managed estate, and his life would have been so much better. Mr. Darcy laughed and responded that, in such a case, his own life would have been considerably worse.

At that moment, Mr. Darcy became more serious and assured Mr. Bennet that he must worry about nothing from then on. Mr. Bennet replied, with gratitude and emotion, that all his worries vanished the happy day he received news of their engagement.

On the third day after their arrival, as Darcy, Elizabeth and her father were having a light discussion in the library, they were interrupted by Lydia's impetuous entrance.

"Papa, I want to go to Brighton! The regiment will leave soon, and I want to go there. You must allow me! Mama is very unfair to me; she doesn't even listen to me anymore!"

"I want to go, too, Papa," said Kitty behind her.

"Thank you for sharing your wishes with me, girls. Now please be so kind as to pull the door behind you when you leave."

"But, Papa, what do you say?"

"About what, child?"

"About Brighton, of course! I want to go; Mrs. Forster has told me there will be many balls and parties with all the officers. This is my dream, Papa."

"I am sure it is, Lydia. Now go and let me finish my business."

"Oh, this is so unfair," cried Lydia. "So unfair!" She groaned as she left the room.

Mr. Darcy glanced at Elizabeth; she was embarrassed, and he smiled to comfort her then looked at Mr. Bennet. The gentleman seemed perfectly calm, resuming their conversation with obvious amusement. For him, it was a normal disturbance.

Sometime later, they joined the others in the drawing room. Lydia was still upset, and Kitty was not far away. Jane attempted to moderate them while Mr. Bingley stood by the settee and simply admired Jane.

"So, my dear Mr. Bennet, how are things going on? Mr. Darcy, are there hopes of improvement for Longbourn, do you think?" Mrs. Bennet inquired with a broad smile.

"According to Mr. Darcy's expertise, it seems we can estimate great improvements in the future," Mr. Bennet replied with perfect calmness.

"Oh, such a relief indeed! I expected nothing less from Mr. Darcy—no indeed. I can only imagine how much larger your estate is; you must be extraordinarily clever to take care of it. I have always said you must be extraordinarily clever, Mr. Darcy."

"No, you did not," Lydia intervened, and Mrs. Bennet turned white.

"Of course I did, silly child, but you did not hear me because you never hear anything. I was always certain that Mr. Darcy was the only one who might help Mr. Bennet."

"I thank you for your kind words, madam. I did nothing more than to share with Mr. Bennet some aspects I already had to solve in the past. There was not much help needed," the gentleman replied with perfect politeness.

"But you know, I wonder if it is such a good thing to improve Longbourn. It pains me so much to know that after Mr. Bennet passes away the estate will be inherited by Mr. Collins. I cannot even bear to think of that. Perhaps it would be better to allow the estate to fall into ruin."

"Mama!" cried Jane and Elizabeth at the same time.

"Well, my dear, I understand your distress, but let us hope I live long enough to benefit from the improvement of Longbourn. And, if we are both fortunate, perhaps you will be protected from any suffering by simply passing away before me," replied Mr. Bennet.

Mrs. Bennet started to laugh. "Oh, Mr. Bennet, you are such a tease! God has been so good to us by helping our daughters to marry so well. I could not care less about Mr. Collins. If I were never to see him again, I would be perfectly content. I never liked him!"

"Yes, you did, Mama," Lydia said. "Do you remember when Lizzy refused to marry him and you almost forced her to accept his proposal? Oh, it was so much fun! Mr. Collins running after Lizzy and Mama running after him! And now Lizzy marries Mr. Darcy! What a joke!" Lydia ended her tirade with a burst of laugher while everyone else froze.

Elizabeth was crimson, unable to raise her eyes from the floor. Mrs. Bennet was pale, staring at Darcy in the greatest panic; Mr. Bennet himself was speechless and lost.

Darcy looked from one to other, undecided what to do next.

"Bingley, I think we should leave and change for dinner," Darcy eventually said.

"Yes, yes indeed," Mr. Bingley approved with great relief, and only a few minutes later, both gentlemen left the house. The next moment, Mrs. Bennet's voice shattered the walls.

"How could you say such a thing in front of Mr. Darcy? Are you out of your mind, child? What if he gets upset and annuls the engagement? It is miracle enough that he wishes to marry Lizzy. Now you try to scare him away? Stupid, mindless child!"

"You should let me to go to Brighton, and then I will say nothing more! You promised me as much before you found out about Lizzy's engagement. You promised!"

"Brighton? You may go way beyond Brighton. You may go beyond Paris, if you wish; I do not care! If you find someone to pay your expenses, go! I will surely not ask your father for a single farthing for you; you do not deserve it! I do not wish to hear or see you again until after Lizzy is married—that is, if Mr. Darcy ever returns! Upon my word, if he refuses to marry Lizzy, I shall never buy you a single bonnet or dress ever again!"

Mrs. Bennet shut the door behind her and cried after Hill. Lydia left the house, followed by Kitty, and declared she would visit Maria Lucas.

Elizabeth noticed Jane attempting to speak to her, but she grabbed her bonnet, left through the back door, and moved at a quick pace along the garden path. She could not speak to anyone. When she was far enough, she ceased fighting her tears. Her eyes burned, and her chest ached from shame. She had hoped that, once he came to know and accept her family, she would have no reason to be embarrassed again, but she was wrong.

The revelation of Mr. Collins's failed proposal should not have been a reason for distress; she would have told him herself eventually. Or she might have kept it secret; after all, it was a private matter and propriety demanded that it remain private. But the way the entire conversation flowed and her family offended each other once again in front of him—Lydia's wild behaviour and her impertinence were too painful to watch.

She climbed the hill through the grove, wiping her eyes furiously. She wished for nothing but to be alone for a time. She sat on a fallen tree trunk and allowed her eyes to travel down to the valley. She would surely miss those beloved grounds.

Elizabeth startled at the sound of a horse approaching. She was angry that anyone would disturb her peace, and for an instant, her heart hoped it might be Mr. Darcy.

"Miss Bennet, what a lovely surprise to find you here," said a well-known voice.

"Mr. Wickham. A lovely surprise, indeed," she replied sternly.

"You look more beautiful than ever! I understand you had a lovely, long trip. And I also understand there is reason for me to congratulate you!"

"Indeed, you are well informed, sir. I thank you."

"In truth, I never would have expected such an ending. Engaged to Mr. Darcy —that is something I would never imagine. I remember how much you disliked him a few months ago; I only hope he softens his manners somewhat and makes you happy. Although, being the mistress of Pemberley will surely compensate for any faults its master might have."

"I am sure it will. I am even more fortunate that the master of Pemberley has few faults for which to compensate. And how are you, Mr. Wickham?"

"I am as well as can be expected. The regiment will leave Meryton; I am sure you heard. There are a few friends whom I will dearly miss," he said meaningfully, but her expression remained unchanged.

"You will surely find a way to compensate for that loss; I do not doubt."

"So—what did Lord Matlock say about the engagement? Did he approve?"

"Lord Matlock has always been kind and generous. We are happy to have his blessing."

"Well, surely things have changed lately. The Darcys and the Matlocks never would allow anyone so beneath them to enter their family. You must have some special charms, Miss Bennet, to convince them to accept you. I am speaking from personal experience; I was always tolerated but never accepted. They did not even give me what was rightfully mine..."

Elizabeth was angry and tired and not in the slightest as patient as she should be. Mr. Wickham's large smile, insinuating tone, and that particular, cold glint in his eyes were too much to bear at such a time. She stepped closer to him.

"It is quite strange that you say such things, Mr. Wickham. From what I heard, you were always treated as a part of the family. I was told that the late Mr. Darcy held you in high esteem, which you did not quite deserve. I also understand that Lord Matlock never abandoned you, not even when your behaviour was less than honourable. Even more, I was informed that the living you told me about was left to you under special conditions that you did not fulfil. However, you did receive a large sum of money to compensate your loss. And, when you speak about not being

250

allowed into the family, is it possible that you refer to the fact that you tried to compromise Lady Selina and Georgiana and were stopped before you succeeded?"

Each of her words twisted his countenance, and he stared at her open-mouthed. Her voice became cold and accusing while her entire presence demanded respect. When she took a step closer, he staggered back.

"It is true that I liked you from the very beginning of our acquaintance, Mr. Wickham, but you betrayed my trust and my friendship. You misled me with malicious gossip about Mr. Darcy and, even worse, about Georgiana—who you knew very well to be a delightful, sweet creature. You offended the memory of your godfather by hurting his children, and you shamelessly take advantage of Lord Matlock's generous affection. And you dare speak of not being allowed in their families?"

"Miss Bennet, I shall not allow anyone to speak to me in such a manner. And you should be more prudent than to begin an offensive argument in the middle of the woods where nobody can hear you!"

"Is that so, Mr. Wickham? Perhaps you intend to take advantage of our present solitude and harm me in some way? That would be the final dishonourable thing you might do to show your true character!"

He took another step back and glanced sharply at her.

"I have no intention of harming you, Miss Bennet, but I shall not allow you to place the entire fault on me. Your accusations might be true, but everything I told you, you accepted willingly. Perhaps it was dishonourable the way I spoke of Darcy, but what would you say about a young lady, the daughter of a gentleman, who agrees to share gossip with a complete stranger from the first moment of their acquaintance? In what way was your behaviour better than mine? And now suddenly you discover a genuine affection for the same man you hated a few months ago. Could it be that your love suddenly appeared after you saw his properties? Do not attempt to fool me, Miss Bennet; I am not naïve!"

"I do not attempt to fool you, Mr. Wickham, and I shall not deny that your reproaches are deserved. My behaviour was wrong and unfair; my prejudice clouded my judgement while my pride and vanity blinded me to your deceptive amiability. But I shall not repeat my mistake; I shall not discuss with you my love or the changes of my heart. I am quite certain we will not see each other much in the future, so I wish you wisdom and humility and as good a life as possible. Good day, Mr. Wickham!"

"I would not be certain about how often we might meet in the future, and—"

"I said good day, Mr. Wickham. I would appreciate if you would not continue this conversation. I must return home now."

She stepped back to return to the same path, and she was suddenly startled and released a small cry. Only a few steps away stood Thunder, waiting patiently. A short glance was enough to observe Mr. Darcy walking towards them slowly.

He bowed to her properly, his countenance stern, fixed upon her shoulder.

"Mr. Darcy! I was just returning to Longbourn. Such a surprise to see you— I thought you were at Netherfield by now."

"A fortunate coincidence—please allow me to keep you company. Bingley has returned to Longbourn, and I will meet him there."

"Darcy, very pleased to see you. I was just congratulating Miss Bennet on the news of your engagement. Please allow me to do the same."

"Wickham, save your breath. As I told you last year, there are very few circumstances that would compel me to speak to you again. This is not one of them."

He offered Elizabeth his arm, and they walked away together as Wickham called to them, "Darcy, Miss Bennet—I hope to see you both again sometime soon!"

Wickham mounted, and the sound of his horse galloping away gradually diminished along the path. Only then did Elizabeth stop and ask Darcy to rest a moment. She glanced at him briefly.

"I met him a few minutes ago; we argued very harshly and—"

"I know; I heard. Forgive me, I did not mean to skulk, but your voices were loud, and I could not find a convenient moment to interfere."

"You heard?" She blushed than instantly paled.

"Yes. Thank you for defending us. I do not know whether anyone ever told Wickham all those things straight to his face before. I was very proud of you—and a little frightened, I confess. I must be careful in future not to upset you in any way." He laughed, but she felt her eyes burning.

"He was right; I was silly and blind and mindless. I allowed myself to be so easily deceived. I practically invited him to malign your name and Georgiana's…"

"We have already discussed this, Elizabeth. The behaviour of neither of us was faultless since we first met. But all that is ended. Let us not think of the past."

She laid her head against his chest as they stood side by side, and her hands slid around his waist. He held her tightly and lifted her chin so he could see her eyes. She was still tearful, but she laughed at him. He stole a brief kiss; then he suddenly moved and sat on the grass, pulling her to sit by him. A moment later, he lifted her and placed her in his lap. She gasped in surprise but only hesitated briefly before she allowed herself to enjoy his warmth. Her head was now a little higher than his, so she leaned down to his laughing mouth. She expected a kiss, which did not come. Instead, he trapped her in his embrace, almost crushed to his chest, and spoke seriously.

"So, Miss Bennet, I understand that I have something in common with Mr. Collins. I never would have expected that."

She paled, and her heart nearly stopped. "I am very sorry for the uncomfortable situation you have been put in. My sister is always accustomed to have her own way and—"

"I see you attempt to change the subject, so I shall not insist further. I have only one question: between my proposal and Mr. Collins's, which was worse?"

She stared at him incredulously, then suddenly cupped his face with her small hands and said, just an instant before her lips finally met his and she abandoned herself to his tender caresses: "Yours was worse, by far, sir."

They became lost in a passionate kiss, their arms holding each other close. With guilty pleasure and embarrassment, she could feel his strong legs moving beneath her, his hands travelling daringly along her back, his lips abandoning hers to escape along her jaw to her neck and her shoulders then to the edge of her gown... She shivered and sighed, waiting, but the burning touch of his lips ceased.

"We should stop," he suddenly whispered. "We must return to Longbourn; Bingley is expecting me—and your father too, I imagine."

"Yes," she admitted, struggling to breathe, but some time and more kisses were necessary before they finally succeeded in separating.

He gently brushed her hair with his fingers and arranged a few rebellious locks then fixed the edge of her gown, which had almost fallen down. He called Thunder, and a brief glance was enough for her to understand his meaning. They mounted together again, and this time she adjusted her body against his in the saddle almost immediately.

They rode towards the house, and each time the trees happened to shelter them from the main road, their lips sought and found each other, eager and starved to be joined. He carefully looked around each time to be certain they would not be caught. His hands daringly touched and caressed her thighs through the fabric of her gown with slight moves that could not possibly be noticed by anyone passing by but strong enough to make her skin tingle. Most of the time, she looked straight ahead to admire the view, allowing her nape, neck, and shoulder to bear the rushed, tantalising touches of his lips.

"Pray tell me how it happened that you returned. I thought you left to change for dinner."

"I did. But I turned my head towards Longbourn for a moment and saw you walking towards the groves. I could not be certain it was you from such a distance, but it was a lucky guess."

"Very lucky guess, indeed." She laughed.

Finally, Longbourn was in view and their posture—though awkward as they rode together—became perfectly proper. Just before they reached the main garden, he leaned to whisper, "I might reconsider my previous decision to teach you to ride. I find this way of riding much more rewarding."

She laughed again, laying her head back against his chest. When they stopped, he dismounted and helped her down.

At that moment, Mr. Bennet appeared from the back door and stopped in surprise to look at them with curiosity and then reproach, studying their crimson faces, hair in disorder, and embarrassed looks. They glanced at each other and realised they looked far from proper.

"Mr. Darcy! I thought you left long ago, sir."

"I... We..." They both turned red while struggling to speak.

"Well, well... I guess I must congratulate myself on insisting to shorten your engagement."

"Papa, we—"

"Lizzy dear, go and change for dinner before your mother sees you. I shall see you soon," Mr. Bennet said gently, highly amused.

Darcy stepped further and tried to arrange his coat as he struggled to speak coherently.

"Mr. Bennet, it is my fault. I saw Elizabeth going for a walk, and I returned to meet her. I know it was not proper; I am sorry. But please believe me, I shall never do anything to harm Elizabeth nor expose her to a compromising situation. Please be assured that—"

"Do not excuse yourself any more, sir; it is really not necessary. I would warn you to be careful to avoid other awkward moments like this one, but I confess I am pleased to see my daughter so happy. At least I am not concerned she might have married you for your wealth." Mr. Bennet laughed, enjoying the chance to tease his guest.

"Tomorrow I plan to go to London and make all the arrangements for the wedding. In the mean time, I shall not allow any other similar situation to occur; that I promise."

"Oh, do not promise such a thing; you may not be able to keep it. Do not be embarrassed, sir; I do remember what love and passion mean. I have been passionately in love with my wife since we married. Unfortunately, we had little in common except that. I have great hopes that things will be different with you and my Lizzy."

"Thank you, sir," Darcy replied, astonished by such a confession.

"Now go and change, too, before Mrs. Bennet spots you. As fond as she is of you, it would be difficult to explain to her why your clothes have grass stains. You must hurry; dinner will be ready in an hour. I am hungry, and Netherfield is not that close. Oh, and I forgot to mention: Mr. Bingley might keep you company to London tomorrow. He seemed determined to force me to accept a double wedding. My wife is exceedingly upset with that arrangement, but it is very likely Mr. Bingley will eventually win."

THE NEXT DAY, MR. DARCY and Mr. Bingley left for London after a short visit to Longbourn. To Elizabeth's surprise, Mr. Darcy handed her a small package a little larger than a book. He whispered she should open it only after his leaving, which made Mrs. Bennet speculate about the possibility of its being a box of jewels.

It was settled that the gentlemen would stay in Town until the licenses and settlements were ready. Mrs. Bennet was still upset with Mr. Bingley for stealing the opportunity of arranging a second wedding. Even more, she was worried that a double wedding would not satisfy Mr. Darcy's notions of grandeur. She was certain he would not want to share such an important event with anyone else, and nothing Elizabeth said to convince her otherwise had any success in calming her nerves.

As soon as the gentlemen departed, Elizabeth retired to her room and, with eager hands, untied the package; inside, she found four envelopes. She searched them carefully and found a number on each of them. Beside the envelopes, there was a note, with no envelope to protect it. She understood it was the first to be read.

My beloved Elizabeth,

I will be away for four days, and I hope you will miss me as much as I shall miss you.

I cannot believe that less than two weeks have passed since our engagement—two weeks, as long as a lifetime and as short as a heartbeat. I still have so many things I wish to share with you, to tell you, to show you, that I wish to trap the time and chain it to last longer.

I have enclosed four letters, one for each day I will be gone.

Open them one by one and try to understand my chaotic thoughts and my tormented feelings; if anyone can understand, you are surely the one.

In two weeks' time we will be together forever, and perhaps I should wait until then to tell you everything that remains unsaid. But I am certain, beyond any doubt, that we will not have time to discuss the past nor to trouble ourselves with it.

In two weeks' time, there will be only the present and the future—our present and our future.

And our love.

Forever yours, FD

She read the note over again, pressed her lips over it, then read it again. A sharp pain in her chest betrayed her love and the cold sense of loneliness. He would be gone for four days—four days as long as a lifetime.

Slowly, she opened the envelope with number one on it.

Inside, she found four sheets, fully covered with his handwriting. She glanced at the first page, and with surprise and equal pleasure, she saw the letter was a close confession of his thoughts from the first day they met at the Meryton assembly.

Day by day, hour by hour, moment by moment, everything was there. The first letter ended at the moment she left Netherfield after Jane's illness.

His thoughts, his fears, his hopes, his mind, and his heart—everything was there and there was so much more to come!

She read the letter several times, then rushed to her desk, took a pen and paper and started to write.

My beloved soon-to-be-husband,

I always said I wished to marry only for the deepest love, but I never knew what love meant until you captured my soul, my mind, and my body. I never imagined what true love might be until you taught me—and I can only count my heartbeats until the moment we shall belong to each other and step together into our future.

But, as you know, my thoughts were not always so—not at all.

The first moment I saw you entering the Meryton assembly, I said to myself that you were the handsomest man I had ever seen. Half an hour later, I was certain beyond any doubt that you were the handsomest man I had ever met—and the most aloof—and the most proud—and the most unpleasant—a man who considered me not handsome enough to tempt him to dance. Can you imagine, my love, what that means to a 20-year-old young woman? Surely you did not know for some time, but you learned it quite painfully..."

She continued to write, word by word, row by row, page by page, with no restraint, no hesitation, no self-censure. She allowed her thoughts, her memories, and her feelings to flow out on the page. She put her mind and her soul on the page—to meet his.

And when he returned, she would give them to him—one letter for each day —his letters and hers.

THE RIDE TO LONDON PASSED sooner than Darcy expected.

He had spent the entire previous night writing the letters, so fatigue overcame him immediately. That was a very good thing as he already felt—most painfully —Elizabeth's loss. The more time they spent together, the more she opened to him and allowed him as close to her as he wished; and the more he got from her, the more he desired and the more he missed and craved her.

Opposite him in the carriage, Bingley talked, happy and animated, but Darcy could not attend.

He was relieved when they finally reached London. First thing, they went to the solicitor's office to apply for the special license, which would take a few days. Afterwards, each of them left for his own house with the promise of meeting again the next day.

Alone in his carriage, Darcy decided to call briefly at Selina's to inquire after Anne and, if possible, to find Georgiana there, too. His intuition proved correct: in the drawing room were his sister, Anne, Selina and her children, all of them hurrying to welcome him.

He briefly asked about Anne's health and about Lady Catherine, and he was provided with satisfactory answers.

Georgiana and Selina asked countless questions about Elizabeth, as if she had been away for months. He explained the reason for his return to town, and news of the imminent wedding brought a storm of inquiries, suggestions, advice, and laughter. Immediately, Selina began to write Elizabeth and Jane, to ask if they needed her to purchase anything for them. Then she sent a note to the modiste to schedule an appointment.

Darcy looked at them sternly. After all, there was not such a difference between Mrs. Bennet and the ladies of the *ton*.

"And Lord Brightmore? Is he away?" Darcy finally asked a reasonable question.

"He is with Robert and Thomas at the club. They tried to take Father too, but he refused. I do not know what to do with him; I cannot allow him to continue in such a way. He has not wished to speak to us for more than two days."

"Who?" Darcy asked dumbfounded.

"Father, of course. I just told you, Darcy; pay attention."

"Lord Matlock does not speak to you? Why?"

"We do not know; that is precisely the problem."

"What do you mean, Selina?"

"I just told you—since two days ago, the day after you left. He went to his club then called on Mrs. Gardiner then went home, but neither Robert nor Thomas was there, so we do not know what happened. When they returned, Father was alone —with his drink—and from that moment he has refused to speak to any of us."

"Did you fetch a doctor? He might be ill. I shall go to visit him immediately."

"We did, but he would not admit us—or the doctor."

"That is extraordinary!"

"Perhaps my mother's visit affected him," Anne spoke up. "It was such a trying time, and poor Uncle was so kind and protective of me and—"

"I doubt that is the reason, Anne. I shall insist on speaking to him immediately. Have you spoken to Mrs. Gardiner? She might help us. You know how much he respects and admires her. He would not dare refuse to talk to her."

"I went to Madeleine to ask her help, but she is ill. She has not left her bed for more than two days. She is weak and cannot eat, and the doctor said she was feverish too."

Darcy stared at them in utter shock. "Lord Matlock refused to speak to you for two days and Mrs. Gardiner is ill? She has been ill for the same length of time?"

"Yes, quite strange, is it not?" asked Georgiana.

"Very strange," repeated Lady Selina. "I do not know what to do. I send the doctor to Madeleine daily. I go to check the children. I try to make her eat but—"

"Do you remember, William? It was the same with you back in January. Do you remember when you left Town for more than a week without a word? It is almost the same with Uncle. Oh dear, what a strange coincidence. Elizabeth was ill that time, too. Do you remember?"

"I do remember, dearest; I could never forget that week. I do remember quite vividly."

"Perhaps you should talk to Uncle. Maybe you can find a way to speak to him."

"I will, my dear; that is exactly what I will do. But first, Selina, may I have a glass of brandy—a very large one, please?"

Ten minutes and two glasses of brandy later, Darcy was still in the drawing room, staring out the window while his sister and cousins watched him with worried looks.

Then, suddenly, he began to laugh.

Chapter 20

"You will marry in two weeks? You cannot do such a thing!"

"Of course I can, Caroline. We will marry with Darcy and Miss Elizabeth."

Caroline Bingley looked at her brother in astonishment. Charles Bingley poured himself a glass of wine, a broad smile on his face.

"Charles, what do you mean? Darcy marrying Elizabeth Bennet? That cannot be!"

"Caroline, I hate it when you repeat my words! I just told you, and I am quite surprised that you are surprised," he replied with good humour.

"Mr. Darcy is marrying Eliza Bennet? That cannot be, that cannot be…"

"You see? That is precisely what I was saying! I shall send for Louisa, so you can repeat the news to each other before dinner."

Caroline Bingley needed many minutes to recover from such disastrous news. Her mind could barely comprehend such nonsense. Eliza Bennet managed to trap Mr. Darcy in marriage? The same Mr. Darcy who agreed that a union between Charles and Jane Bennet would be a catastrophe now agrees to join that family? It must be a nightmare, and if she were strong enough, she would surely wake from it.

Sometime later, Louisa arrived, and at last, Caroline had the comfort of her sister's sympathy. Caroline was certain that it must be a conspiracy on the part of Lady Selina because she showed her disapproval for those small, wild lads of hers. Eliza Bennet was so sly, pretending she liked children! And now Mr. Darcy would marry her! If Caroline could only find a way to speak to him, she would tell him that she liked children too and was willing to give him as many heirs for Pemberley as he wished!

The Bingleys' evening became worse during dinner. Louisa and Caroline's complaints, their malicious comments towards the Bennets, and their beliefs that Mr. Darcy would soon realize his enormous error all ruined Bingley's appetite, and he hurried to his apartment to finish his meal in peace. He briefly considered how it would be after his marriage: Would Caroline change her behaviour towards the Bennets? Most likely not. How would dear Jane bear to hear her family insulted?

And what about Mrs. Bennet? She surely would consider Netherfield to be her home, too, and would expect proper courtesy.

Would Caroline consider moving to Louisa's? Surely, he could not allow anyone to upset Jane; that would not be fair to her. But could he ask his sister to leave their house? Would that be fair to Caroline? Charles Bingley suddenly realised that his marriage might bring pain along with the joy.

As his carriage rolled towards the earl's house, Darcy considered the best course of action. Though he had laughed in the library as he immediately guessed the reason for the earl's state of mind and spirit, the sharp pain in his chest never released its grip. He remembered—in quite painfully vivid colours—those dreadful days after his disastrous proposal when he was certain happiness would be an unknown word to him.

Surely, things could not be as bad in this case. Even if he were correct in his assumption that his uncle proposed to Mrs. Gardiner and she refused him, the earl's proposal could not possibly equal his own. They had known and respected each other for many years; the earl always valued Mrs. Gardiner's opinions and she seemed to enjoy his company. However, it did not bode well if the earl was in such a poor state and Mrs. Gardiner was unwilling to speak even to Selina.

He finally reached the house and entered; a servant received him reluctantly and, with obvious uneasiness, declared Lord Matlock was not home to anyone. Darcy thanked him then passed decidedly towards the library. The first knock on the door remained unanswered; the second one received a harsh "go away" in reply. He entered.

"I would appreciate a glass of brandy. The ride from Hertfordshire was quite long, and it is hot outside."

"Darcy. I did not expect you so soon. So—did your brandy disappear that you barge into my library to take mine?" The earl only favoured him with a brief glance.

"I have not been home yet; I have to finish some business first. I went to apply for a special licence. Did you know? We decided to marry in two weeks."

"Yes, I imagined you would do that. I am very happy for you."

"And then I went to see Anne and Selina."

"Yes, I imagined that, too. You may go home now; there is no business for you here."

"Oh come, Uncle, will you offer me a glass of brandy or not?"

"You may pour it yourself if you insist; in the meantime, I shall dismiss the idiot doorman; I told him not to allow anyone into the library, but he failed to understand."

"Nonsense; you will do no such thing." Darcy took the first gulp from his full glass and sat in an armchair near the earl. He stared at him in silence.

"Darcy, what is it you want from me? You should go home and mind your own business. I am not ill as I told my children a thousand times; I only need to rest in peace. I might leave town for the summer. I find that London's air does not suit me at all. Country air would do just fine—country air and silence. I do not expect you to understand."

"I understand quite well. There was a time in January when I thought London air did not suit me at all. I believed country air and silence would be better for me. I was wrong."

They were sitting near each other, glasses of brandy in hand, gazing at the wall in front of them. Their conversation was stern and neutral; no emotions were involved.

"The situation cannot be the same," the earl replied after a short hesitation.

"I am aware of that. This situation cannot be as bad as that situation was in January."

"One always believes that one's situation is worse than others'."

"It might be so, but I have reason to suspect I am correct in my statement," Darcy said.

For some time, there was silence; the glasses were filled again. They continued to stare at the wall rather than each other.

"I remember you were all very worried for me, but I gave little import to your concern. I was reckless and self-absorbed. I cared nothing about others' pain. I believed I was correct in my behaviour; not for a moment did I consider I might have done something wrong. But I was—so very wrong!" Darcy spoke calmly, his hand clenching his glass.

The earl finally turned to look at his nephew; he accepted and held the inquiring gaze.

"I have never spoken to anyone about that, and I never shall. Only my affection and respect for you as well as your genuine care for Elizabeth—which I know to be reciprocated—convinces me to make this confession."

He paused and rose, beginning to pace the room.

"I was attracted and charmed almost from the first day I met Elizabeth. I was bewitched in a way that was completely new and frightening for me, and I spent many days and nights convincing myself that such feelings were inappropriate and dangerous. I left Hertfordshire on the pretext of saving Bingley from an unsuitable marriage, but I also did it to remove myself from Elizabeth. I shall not give you more details; it suffices to say that you were right to question the reasons for my interference in Bingley's affairs, but it took a long time to understand that. Then I met her again, and again I was wrong; you noticed almost immediately her dislike for me. I chose to misinterpret her behaviour and convinced myself she was shared my feelings and welcomed them. So, the day after the ball, I went to Gracechurch Street and proposed to her. I diligently exposed to her my feelings along with my doubts and uncertainties. I told her I had to fight against my pride, duty and even common sense to accept a connection to her family, which was so much beneath me. I hurt her in every possible way, and I had no doubt that she would accept my proposal with gratitude. After all, I am Fitzwilliam Darcy, and she is the daughter of a country gentleman with a small estate."

Darcy stopped and looked at his uncle, whose countenance expressed shock and disbelief. He continued, attempting a smile to lighten the tension.

"She rejected me without hesitation. She accused me of being selfish and insensitive to the feelings of others, which we both know to be the truth. She properly humbled me as neither you nor my beloved parents ever did. My parents taught me what was right but never taught me to correct my temper. I was taught good principles but left to follow them in pride and conceit. Elizabeth placed a mirror in front of me and forced me to see myself in it—to see myself in her eyes. She showed me how insufficient were all my pretensions to please a woman worthy of being pleased. Her words were as harsh and as painful as they were true, but for some time I did not allow the truth to touch my mind—that is, until I realised that running away does not bring relief and that happiness does not come from solitude. And then I returned to London."

The tension was so burdening that each of them felt the weight of it. The earl rose, opened two windows, then continued to pace the room, glancing at his favourite nephew from time to time. Then he finally spoke.

"Damn, Nephew, I am amazed that you can be such an idiot at times! It is a wonder how you inherited this trait from me!"

Darcy smiled but said nothing. He stared at his uncle, waiting for him to continue.

"I... It is just that... I have always admired Madeleine Gardiner, but I have never considered... I valued and treasured my friendship with Edward Gardiner, and I would never dare to..."

"Of course," Darcy replied calmly.

"But during the last year I found myself enjoying her company more than anyone else's. And I kept searching for it—for her company, I mean. And...I was certain she accepted my attentions...so...a couple of days ago as you left for Hertfordshire, I proposed."

"It did not go well, I presume."

"No, it did not... In fact, yesterday I would have said it was horrible but now that you have shared your own experience, I must change my assessment. I did not make a fool of myself as you did—at least I hope not; my age should give me some small advantage. Neither of us was either impolite or offensive. But I believe I was too hasty. She was certainly surprised, and she even seemed frightened. She confessed she never thought I might come to her with such a proposal. She declined me decidedly, though she was kind and generous in her refusal, but I felt I pained her. I attempted to take the proposal back and assured her she had no reason to feel uncomfortable—that I would wait for her answer as long as she needed. I expressed my hope that the incident would not affect our friendship, and I assured her of my esteem and affection."

His emotion made the earl's speech difficult, and Darcy thought he never before saw his uncle in such a state. He patiently waited.

"She was extremely disturbed; I could see she was tearful though she tried to conceal her distress. She apologised many times and assured me of her gratitude for my support and friendship, and she asked my forgiveness for upsetting me. It was so painful to watch her barely fighting her tears—without daring to do anything to comfort her. I... I had little else to do except leave, though I wished to stay and talk to her as I used to do when I had a problem and needed advice. I hoped I could return the next day after we both had time to reconcile with our feelings. But...the next day I received a letter from her, saying she was forced to sever our friendship and begging me to allow her the time and distance to come to peace with herself. She asked my forgiveness if something in her behaviour misled me and raised expectations that could not be fulfilled. And she has refused to speak to me—or Selina—since then."

The earl gulped the remaining brandy and filled his glass again. Darcy stood silent.

"So, Nephew—any wise advice for your old and unwise uncle?" He laughed bitterly.

"No indeed, sir. I have no advice, and I dare say none is needed—except not to leave Town for this reason and not to be hasty anymore. And to respect her request. I speak from my own painful experience, not necessarily from wisdom."

"Hmm—you said no advice and yet here are three pieces of advice, all reasonably wise I might say. Do you think...considering what you said to me and how things changed for you and Elizabeth...do you believe there might be a change of mind by Mrs. Gardiner?"

Darcy looked at his always self-confident, daring, mocking, and sometimes-impertinent uncle, now watching him display the uncertainty of a schoolboy.

"As your lordship once said, I am not the most reliable person in matters of the heart. Besides, I was wrong once in estimating a lady's feelings for my friend Bingley, so I would not dare form an opinion. What I can say from my own observation is that Mrs. Gardiner obviously enjoyed your company. But she is a very proper lady, and she would never allow her feelings to be openly displayed, even if those feelings did exist. And more so, I imagine how difficult it must be for her to consider binding herself to another man after she shared a life based on the deepest affection with a most beloved husband who died unexpectedly. I would imagine such a woman would not open her heart easily or allow her feelings to be exposed with haste, but that would only make it more worth the effort to conquer her heart."

The earl stared at his nephew in silence, both their countenances stern and unmovable.

"Damn, Nephew, you might be an idiot sometimes, but you are as wise as Georgiana always said—very wise, indeed. You surely inherited that from your father."

Another glass of brandy and some tentative smiles were shared before they finally left the library. Just before they stepped out, the earl turned to Darcy again.

"Nephew, this conversation never took place. None of these subjects have been discussed."

"What conversation, sir?"

"Indeed—what conversation? Now—you and Georgiana should join me for dinner at Selina's. I dare say she will be pleased to see us."

"So I would imagine, Uncle. I shall see you later tonight."

Darcy exited Matlock's house and hesitated a moment before he gave orders to the coachman. When he arrived in Gracechurch Street, he was still uncertain whether his decision was the correct one, but he dismissed any thought that might advise against it.

The servant introduced him to the drawing room where Mrs. Gardiner and the children were. He was greeted as warmly as he expected, but Mrs. Gardiner's charming smile could not hide the dark circles around her eyes or her pallor. He took the offered seat while the hostess ordered drinks and refreshments and sent the children to their room.

"I am very pleased to see you, sir. I hope everyone at Longbourn is in good health?"

"Indeed they are; thank you. Mrs. Bennet is quite busy with all the wedding preparations. We changed the wedding date; we shall marry in two weeks' time."

"Two weeks? That is extraordinary news. Sir, please allow me to tell how happy I am. I truly believe there cannot be a more perfect couple than you and Elizabeth."

"Thank you, Mrs. Gardiner, your approval means so much to us. I hope Elizabeth is as happy as I am—that is all I want and hope for."

"I have no doubt she is. In fact, nobody who saw you together lately would doubt that."

He laughed nervously. "Yes, those who saw us lately might have no doubts. But anyone who saw us a few months ago would never imagine such a happy ending, I am sure."

Mrs. Gardiner released a delicate chuckle. "True. The beginning of your acquaintance was quite challenging, I might say."

"It is amazing how fate chooses to play with us sometimes. Less than six months ago, I never would have imagined I would be married by summer—and certainly not to Miss Elizabeth Bennet."

He looked at his hostess with great seriousness, and then continued.

"I admired Elizabeth from the very beginning, and my feelings for her began to grow long before I admitted those feelings to myself. I never thought I might attach myself to her, as I was certain she was not suitable to be my wife; I forbade my mind and my heart even to consider her. However, there came a painful moment when I had to face the danger of losing her forever. The despair of never seeing her again forced me to ask myself about my true wishes and to take proper measures. It took me a long time to recognise that my happiness was Elizabeth. I learned in a most painful way that sometimes two people might not like each other in the beginning or might have a wrong first impression about each other or might begin as mere acquaintances—or quite the contrary, be long-time friends—only to discover that fate has different plans for them. And if one fails to recognise one's true feelings and wishes, the distance from happiness to despair is a mere step away."

Darcy's voice remained calm even as he struggled to smile. However, by the time he ended his confession, Mrs. Gardiner's eyes were tearful, and she was biting her lips in a valiant attempt to maintain her countenance. For a time, there was a heavy silence in the room. Mrs. Gardiner's pale face coloured red while her hands trembled in her lap.

Finally, Darcy rose and bowed to her. "Mrs. Gardiner, please forgive me if my words upset you; that was never my intention. You know how greatly Elizabeth admires and loves you, and please have no doubt about my affection and gratitude for you."

"Thank you, sir. And please do not worry; you did not upset me. I shall be fine."

"I am glad to hear that. And I hope you feel better soon; my cousin and my sister were quite worried about you. I hope you know how much they value your friendship."

"Yes, I know… Please convey my apologies to them. I hope we shall meet again soon."

"Perfect. I shall leave you now; I must send a detailed letter to Elizabeth and assure her you will attend our wedding in two weeks. She was most insistent about that."

Mrs. Gardiner forced a gentle smile. "Mr. Darcy, you are a wise man, sir."

"Believe me, I am not; but I thank you nevertheless." He smiled back.

"Sir, I was wondering… Is Lord Matlock well, I hope?"

"Not at the moment, but I am quite sure he soon will be. Good day, Mrs. Gardiner!"

Outside the house, Darcy took a deep breath of fresh air. Only then did he feel the tension and understand how delicate his intervention had been. Fortunately, Mrs. Gardiner was a woman of great intelligence and remarkable wisdom, so she surely took his words properly. And she did not seem upset—sad, troubled maybe, even fearful, but not upset.

Perhaps he was a wise man after all since both the earl and Mrs. Gardiner declared it so.

THERE WAS A DIN DURING meal at Selina's, and everyone spoke more than they actually ate. The Matlock siblings, along with Anne and Georgiana, were utterly surprised to see their father almost his usual self. He did not miss the opportunity to tease Darcy about the disappointment of half the ladies in London at his marriage, a comment that made Anne and Georgiana blush violently.

Darcy inquired about Lady Catherine, but he was told they had no news since she returned to Rosings. The announcements about Darcy's engagement to Elizabeth were already in the newspapers, so it was presumed Lady Catherine was resigned that there was nothing she could do. Anne then asked whether Mr and Mrs. Bennet were upset over Lady Catherine's visit to Longbourn, but Darcy could assure them—with complete honesty—that they had been delighted. By
264

the end of the evening, Anne's distress diminished enough to smile and enjoy the good dinner and the joyful company.

For the next days, Darcy's time in Town was split among his solicitor's office, his club and his uncle's house.

Two days after his visit to Gracechurch Street, Georgiana and Selina each received a note from Mrs. Gardiner, thanking them for their concern. The note also said that, if they happened to be in the neighbourhood, they would be most welcome to visit at anytime—which event occurred that same afternoon. On her return, Georgiana was happy to report to her brother that Mrs. Gardiner seemed if not fully recovered then certainly improving.

Darcy decided to spend the remaining time finishing his business, so nothing would disturb their newlywed time. Keeping his mind occupied was a good idea as, the moment he had nothing else to think of, his thoughts returned to Elizabeth and the pain of being separated from her. He was content, though, that there was such a distance between them, or else he surely would not be able to keep his promise to Mr. Bennet.

After the wedding, they would go directly to Pemberley, he suggested to Elizabeth in a letter, and she happily accepted. He wished to be alone with her so that they could dedicate themselves to each other without any distractions or disturbances.

He had already ordered Mrs. Reynolds to have everything perfectly arranged for Mrs. Darcy's arrival. Mrs. Reynolds replied with two pages of questions about Miss Bennet's favourite colour, her preferences in dishes, her wishes to change the furniture in the apartment, and personal maid of the future Mrs. Darcy. He assured the housekeeper that Mrs. Darcy would not require any changes, at least for the present, and declared he trusted Mrs. Reynolds to find the most suitable maid to serve Mrs. Darcy personally.

He had been in Town for six days and expected the papers to be ready the next day as his solicitor assured him. Two more days would pass until he could return to Netherfield with his family. Even Anne insisted on attending—to everyone's surprise and to Bingley's great delight as he had long wished to have Netherfield filled with dear guests.

The earl had not decided whether he would attend, and Darcy did not insist as he knew Mrs. Gardiner would be there. Since the day he talked to both his uncle and Elizabeth's aunt, Darcy had not brought up the delicate subject again. He did not intend, nor would he ever dare, to interfere further between the earl and Mrs. Gardiner.

A couple of days before, Darcy was forced to bear a stressful and disturbing visit from Miss Bingley. To his utter shock, she arrived alone, asked for Georgiana —who was not at home—and instead of leaving, simply took a seat. She than declared that she could not believe he decided to marry Eliza Bennet and reminded him of his unfavourable comments in November about the Bennet family. Then, suddenly, she changed the subject and confessed to him that she always loved children exceedingly and wished nothing more than to have at least four children when she married. Darcy could do little but listen to her—dumbfounded, clueless, and fearing what she would say next.

She left only when Bingley unexpectedly appeared at the door, questioning the reason for his sister's presence there and offering to escort her back home.

On the evening of the sixth day, Darcy and Georgiana had a late and peaceful dinner alone as they had for the past three days. These were the last days of their solitude, and Darcy tried to spend as much time with her as possible. He already warned her that after the wedding she would have to bear his utter neglect as he intended to spend an entire month at Pemberley alone with Elizabeth. Georgiana laughed and assured him that the joy of having Elizabeth as her sister would be worth being neglected for a while.

They were enjoying the second course when a servant entered to announce a visitor, and the most surprising appearance lifted Darcy from his seat.

"Mr. Bennet! What an extraordinary surprise, sir! Please come in, what—" He was shocked into silence as he saw Elizabeth step shyly from behind her father, her appearance in great disorder, her eyes red and swollen. Georgiana cried in surprise and ran to her, while Darcy quickly took her hands and sat her in a chair.

"Good Lord, what happened? Elizabeth, are you ill?"

Elizabeth did not reply, only her hands held his tightly while she avoided looking either at him or at Georgiana. "Perhaps you and Papa should talk privately," she whispered.

Mr. Bennet, however, replied with reasonable coherence. "She is not ill; do not worry sir. Please forgive us for such an intrusion, but we did not know where to go as we are quite desperately in need of all the help we can find... We... This is quite ridiculous, and I would laugh if I were not so ashamed... My daughter Lydia... She eloped with Wickham. Poor stupid, mindless child. She ran away from home with Wickham."

Darcy looked at Mr. Bennet in disbelief. His common sense wanted to deny the possibility of what he just heard while his mind painfully comprehended the gravity of it. He glanced at his sister, whose pale countenance seemed burdened by sadness, then at Elizabeth, whose eyes were still averted to the floor. He returned his attention to Mr. Bennet without releasing Elizabeth's hands.

"I am grieved, indeed. Grieved, shocked... How did this happen? When? Where?"

"It happened last night, but we discovered it only this morning. It was my fault... Lydia was very upset that we did not allow her to go to Brighton, and she argued with her mother daily. I confess I could hardly bear all their fights; so when she asked me to allow her to spend some time with Maria Lucas, I was quite pleased. She went to Maria three days ago, and the first night everything was fine. Then the second night... When Maria went to wake her for breakfast this morning, the elopement was discovered."

"But are you certain, absolutely certain that she eloped?"

"I am certain, unfortunately. She left a letter for Maria that is very clear. And I suspect Kitty was aware of her plans. She said they would go to Gretna Green to marry, but I somehow doubt it. I left Longbourn immediately, and Lizzy insisted she on coming with me. I confess I did not wish to bring her, but I had no strength to fight with her—so here we are. We stopped at every station, every inn from Meryton to London, asking about them. We have reason to believe they are in London, but from this point on, I am completely lost. I do not know how I could possibly trace them in Town. If you have any information…"

Darcy suddenly released Elizabeth's hand and started pacing the room. Mr. Bennet followed him with a preoccupied gaze, not daring to interrupt him.

Elizabeth's pain and the coldness in her soul froze the tears on her face. Her hands trembled, hanging in their loneliness, while the shame forbade her eyes to rise from the floor. She could hear his steps and feel his anger while she feared what he must be thinking. What would he do in such a horrible situation that could possibly have a favourable solution?

"Mr. Bennet, before we take any other steps, you and Elizabeth must change and eat something. You will need to recover your strength and—"

"Mr. Darcy, that will not be necessary; I would rather go and—"

"Sir, please let us not argue; there is no time. As I said, you must refresh yourselves and eat something; I will not have it any other way. I shall send for Colonel Fitzwilliam; he will be very useful in our quest."

He suddenly resumed his place near Elizabeth and took her hands again. "Mr. Bennet, if it is acceptable to you, I would like for Elizabeth to remain here with Georgiana. I would not wish to leave my sister alone." Mr. Bennet silently nodded, and Darcy continued.

"Dearest, please show Elizabeth a room near yours and help her change and refresh herself. I shall have some food sent to your apartment, as I doubt you will wish to return downstairs. I trust you will take good care of each other while we are gone. I need to be certain of that; I do not wish to worry about your well-being. Will you be fine?"

"I need to inform my aunt," Elizabeth whispered, her gaze still on the floor.

"Mr. Bennet and I will speak to Mrs. Gardiner. I believe it is the best way. Will you be fine?" he repeated, looking at both of them and they nodded in silence.

Darcy called Mrs. Spencer and gave strict orders; when the housekeeper left the room with Elizabeth and Georgiana, Darcy hurried to the library, wrote three notes and rang for Miles.

"Please take this to Colonel Fitzwilliam at once. After that, you will deliver these two notes; the directions are on them. This needs to be done with the utmost urgency."

Miles left without a single word, and only then did Darcy return to Mr. Bennet in the dining room and pour himself a glass of wine.

"Mr. Bennet, you do look tired; I am afraid you are not well. I believe you should rest. I understand your worry, but there is not much you can do for the moment. I will attempt everything possible to discover them; please have no doubt about that."

"Surely you are mocking me, sir. I have done little but rest my entire life, which is why I have come to such a disastrous situation with my youngest daughter lost —perhaps forever—and my other daughters in despair. You must at least allow me to look unwell and tired. What pains me more is that I do not even have the comfort of knowing Lydia felt anything for Wickham. I believe she was so silly that she would have been fooled by any officer who smiled at her. What I cannot understand is why *he* would do such a thing? He could not possibly feel much for her, and he must know Lydia has little dowry, if any; he could not possibly intend to actually marry her. And if he intended only a brief distraction, why take the risk of choosing a girl who, as silly as she might be, is not alone in the world? He must imagine I would look for her, and he would be forever compromised in the militia and lose his only source of income. As much I think on it, I cannot understand his reasoning."

Darcy paced the room for some time, sat on the chair, then rose and paced again.

"It is my fault, Mr. Bennet. First, because I refused to expose Wickham's deceitful nature as I should have done long ago. And second, because I allowed myself to be overwhelmed by everything that has occurred lately and put aside my caution. I should have anticipated this. Since he knew I would marry Elizabeth, he would not hesitate harming your family to accomplish his plans."

"His plans? What plans are you speaking of, sir?"

"To assure himself of an easy living, of course—and to revenge himself on me. The more I think of it, the more I believe he intends to marry Miss Lydia. In that way, he believes he will be part of my family. However, even if that is his plan, I fear things will not be easily solved."

"What you say astonishes me, sir. I believed Wickham to be a worthless sort of man, but I never imagined him capable of planning such a scheme."

"He is capable of anything if it is convenient for him." The hasty appearance of the colonel interrupted their discussion. Colonel Fitzwilliam seemed equally angry and worried, and before Darcy had the chance to give him more details, he began to curse.

"Robert, growing furious is not very useful. We must think rationally; if they are in Town, as Mr. Bennet rightfully suspects, there are few places he could afford to stay. If we are lucky, we shall receive news about their whereabouts shortly."

"I believe we should speak to my father; he might have valuable information about where Wickham might stay in London. You may trust the earl's secrecy, Mr. Bennet."

"Please do whatever you think is necessary, sir. There are many things that worry me considerably more than the secrecy of this situation, even if I did not trust Lord Matlock."

"There is no need to involve the earl for the moment. I would suggest that we talk with Mrs. Gardiner and then have a word with Mrs. Younge."

"Mrs. Younge? I thought she left London last year after Ramsgate," the colonel exclaimed.

"Quite the contrary—she settled in London. She took a large house in Edward Street last year and has since maintained herself by letting lodgings."

"Then he surely must be there; let us go there directly," said the colonel; Mr. Bennet looked at them both with little understanding.

"Forgive me for a moment; I must speak to my sister before we leave. I shall return directly," Darcy said and he almost ran up the stairs.

He nervously knocked at Georgiana's door; he found his sister alone and tearful. She glanced at him, uncertain whether she should dare to approach or not. He gently embraced her, and she started to sob in his arms wordlessly.

"Dearest, why are you crying? Where is Elizabeth?"

"I do not know...forgive me... Elizabeth said she wished to be alone. She is so upset and...I did not know what to say to her. I do not know how to speak to her."

He caressed her hair as he spoke gently. "I am sorry to tell you this at such a delicate moment, but there is something you should know. I told Elizabeth about Ramsgate..."

She stared at him, her eyes wide and tearful. "You told her? When? What will she think of me now? Why did you tell her, Brother? I shall never dare speak to her again."

"My dear, I told Elizabeth in January... Believe me; it was necessary, but you should not let it worry you. She knows you were not to blame. And she thinks highly of you, as you well know. I dare say it is for the best; you may speak openly to each other."

"I do not believe she wishes to speak to me. She is so troubled, so distressed and—"

"I shall talk to her briefly, then I must leave; we have not a moment to lose."

Darcy gently kissed Georgiana's forehead and smiled at his sister as he closed the door behind him. He hesitantly knocked at Elizabeth's door; he heard no reply, so he entered carefully. In the chair, staring at the window, lost in her thoughts, Elizabeth seemed oblivious to everything around her. He called her name, and when no answer came, he sat near her. Her eyes, red and swollen, finally dared to meet his.

"Forgive me," she said. "Forgive me for coming to you with our troubles and disturbing you. I am so sorry for hurting Georgiana; she seems so pained and... I still cannot understand how this happened. It is my fault; I could have prevented it had I but explained to my family some part of what I knew... Wretched, wretched, mistake..."

He took her hands in one of his while the other gently caressed her face.

"I would have been upset if you had not come to me directly. Never again apologise for coming to me with your troubles, my love. As for this stressful situation, I am the only one who should apologise. It is entirely my fault; I never allowed my business with Wickham to be known, not even by my family. That is why he succeeded in deceiving Georgiana and my uncle and now Miss Lydia. But that will all change today; we will find them, and I will be certain proper measures are finally taken."

"Perhaps we are both culpable in some way, but I am afraid little can be done. You know him too well; he will never marry Lydia. He has no interest in her, and he will not take such a burden on his shoulders. She is lost forever and…what shall we do now?" she whispered, looking at him hesitantly, her hands trembling in his.

He seemed scarcely to hear her; then he suddenly started walking up and down the room in earnest meditation, his brow contracted and his air gloomy. Elizabeth gradually observed that her power must be sinking while her eyes followed his movements.

"What shall we do now?" she repeated, her voice weak.

"I have sent people to make inquiries, and I hope to receive news soon. I will leave now with Mr. Bennet and the colonel. Please try to speak to Georgiana; she is upset and worried for you. I just told her that you know about Ramsgate. She is afraid that you might think ill of her… Please go to her and take care of each other…"

"I will take care of her…but William, what shall we do? About our wedding…"

"I am not certain; let us see what comes of this situation, and we will decide later about the wedding. I am afraid I cannot think clearly now; I am only thinking of the best way to solve this. We will speak more tomorrow."

"As you wish," she answered weakly. He embraced her tightly and left in haste.

Elizabeth remained unmoving in the middle of the room, her eyes fixed upon the door closed behind him. The question she feared most—the one that had tortured her since the news of the elopement—remained unanswered. Mr. Darcy seemed not to have an answer himself; he was obviously uncertain of his own decision. She did not doubt his feelings for her or his desire to share his life with her. But would his duty allow him to go further with that decision now that her family situation had changed so dramatically? Yes, perhaps he was right; perhaps it was somehow his fault that Wickham had not been exposed earlier. But in the end, it was Lydia's lack of maturity and decorum that threw her into Wickham's arms at his slightest notice, and the shame and disgrace had fallen entirely on her family. It was true that he had a duty to her, too, now that the announcement of their betrothal was made public. Would the duty to his family and his name overwhelm his duty to her? And if so, would she allow him to marry her only to keep his word? To force him to become Wickham's brother? Every fibre of his body must be appalled at that horrible thought. Could she put him and Georgiana into such a painful situation?

She did not fail to notice that he called her '*my love*' but made no gesture of real tenderness. He did not kiss her nor even touch her as he used to. She covered her face with her handkerchief to hide her tears; her mind, her soul, and her body vividly remembered the happiness that had overwhelmed her those last weeks and now seemed lost forever.

A few minutes later, she wiped her eyes and glanced at her image in the mirror. She promised him she would take care of Georgiana, and she could not disappoint him.

The moment Elizabeth saw Georgiana, her own distress vanished; the girl's pallor and her blue eyes—tearful, lost, surrounded by dark circles—created a disturbing image. Elizabeth gently embraced her young friend then took her hands as they sat together.

"Georgiana, I think we should talk. There are not enough words to tell you how sorry I am for all the pain you must endure because of us. If there were any way to take your distress upon myself, I would not hesitate to do it…"

"Oh no, please do not say that! It is not your fault! I am only upset for my own folly, my own silliness… It is true that I am pained but only because I imagine what your sister must be going through, how ashamed and how troubled she must be… I know that very well," she whispered.

"I feel sorry for her, too. I feel it is my fault that I took no better care of her; she is young and not very wise…"

"Do you think he might have tender feelings for her? Perhaps he is in love with her."

"I doubt that. I saw them together many times, and I never observed any inclination on his part. I am afraid his motives are not as genuine as you wish to believe."

"Yes, I always tend to misjudge his motives…"

"Please do not say that. I know what you are thinking, and you are unfair to yourself."

"No, I am not… I was almost in the same situation as your sister. It was only a fortunate happenstance that William arrived the day before we planned to elope. If not, I would have disgraced my family—my brother—forever. I still cannot believe that William forgave me. I certainly did not deserve it. I am not being unfair to myself at all; I have only begun to know myself. I am nothing but a silly girl who made a fool of herself—very much like poor Miss Lydia. Mr. Wickham never would attempt such a scheme with a woman with sense and good judgement, someone like you or Miss Bennet."

"Georgiana, please look at me," Elizabeth said gently as the girl still refused to meet her eyes. "As I said, you are being unfair to yourself. You might have been correct when you said Jane would never allow herself to be deceived, but you were wrong about me. I did allow myself to be deceived by Mr. Wickham's charming manners; I allowed myself to be flattered by his appearance of goodness, and I trusted him implicitly. I permitted and welcomed his stories about his past dealings with your brother without even considering how improper such confessions were. I believed the malicious words he did not hesitate to throw upon your brother, without questioning his motives or his character. I am quite certain I never would have agreed to elope with him, but other than that, I showed only a bit more maturity than Lydia, and there were likely many other women who fell for Mr.

Wickham's charms. So you should be proud of yourself for having the strength and maturity to report the intended elopement to your brother. That speaks highly of your worthiness and your character."

While Elizabeth spoke, Georgiana's eyes expressed all the tumult of feelings inside her: shame, embarrassment, doubt, disbelief, relief, concern, and, finally, understanding. When Elizabeth finished her confession, burdened with guilt and distress, it was Georgiana's turn to comfort her friend. They continued to speak to each other, sharing blame, guilt and hopes, and none of them noticed when midnight came and went or when dawn shyly appeared at the window.

INSIDE DARCY'S CARRIAGE, THREE MEN found nothing to say to each other, so preoccupied were they in blaming themselves for the unfortunate elopement.

Darcy's thoughts were torn between anger and pain. Elizabeth's despair, his sister's distress, and his departure in haste without being able to comfort them only increased his fury against Wickham and against himself.

They had briefly visited Mrs. Gardiner—who was shocked and frightened to see them at her door—and informed her about the events. She insisted she should go with them as she hoped she would be able to speak reasonably with Lydia if they found her, but the gentlemen refused her decidedly. However, Mr. Bennet promised he would return to her with all the details.

They easily reached Mrs. Younge's place, but speaking to the woman herself proved to be more difficult. First, she denied knowing anything about her old acquaintance and even less that he was there. They first tried a polite approach, and Darcy even offered a substantial compensation for her effort. But the lack of success made the colonel declare he would enter by force and knock on every door until he discovered Wickham, and his increasing anger left no doubt about the veracity of his intentions. Eventually, Mrs. Younge showed them to Wickham's room, but his situation was not what they expected.

It was a small chamber with only a bed, a table, and two chairs. A bottle of brandy, half-empty, betrayed Wickham's occupation; he greeted them incoherently, a large smile on his face. "Mr. Bennet, gentlemen, what an unexpected pleasure."

"Where is Lydia?" Mr. Bennet inquired severely.

"Oh, she is not here. I could not possibly bring her to such a place; it is surely not proper for a young lady like her. I assure you she is very well, resting in a friend's house."

"Very well, put your clothes on, and let us go and fetch Miss Lydia immediately," the colonel demanded.

"I am afraid I cannot do that, sir. I would surely not disturb my friend in the middle of the night. Besides, I dare say it would be better if Miss Lydia is not involved in our discussion; it is not a proper conversation for a lady."

"Then we are done here," said Darcy. "There is nothing to discuss until we see Miss Lydia and speak to her. Send me a note when you think we can disturb your friend." He rose to leave, and the colonel followed him.

"I believe it would be useful to talk now, though," Wickham replied. "There are things that must be settled tonight for the benefit of all."

"There is only one who might benefit from this disgraceful situation, Wickham," said Mr. Bennet bitterly. "All I wish is to see my daughter."

"Mr. Bennet, I assure you Miss Lydia is unharmed. I understand you are upset, sir. I know I would be upset in a similar situation. I deeply apologise for all the distress I caused you; my only excuse might be that one cannot command the desires of one's heart. Falling in love might be dangerous sometimes, and nothing can be done now except to make the best of it. I am well aware there is only one honourable thing to do, and I would gladly do it were my own present state not so desperate. I am afraid I am unable to support myself; I could not possibly afford to take proper care of a wife."

"And now it begins; please do share with us your misfortunes," the colonel said sharply.

"Mr. Wickham, I am afraid you have miscalculated," said Mr. Bennet, "or you have given me too much credit. Whatever desperate situation you might have, I am in no position to be the remedy. Surely you must know I am a man of limited resources."

"I am well aware of that, sir, and it pains me to be forced to burden you further. Yet, I see no alternative. I cannot return to Meryton even if I wished to. There were some delicate problems that forced me to leave the regiment. I…sadly, I have some debts of honour that I was unable to cover, and I cannot possibly return until I am able to solve them. So you see, the small income I had in the militia is now gone, too."

"It is ironic that you have debts of honour, when you seem to have no honour at all," Mr. Bennet responded bitterly. "It makes your present situation even more pitiable, but again there is nothing I can do."

"I understand that; however, if there is a desire for a reasonably discreet solution, I am certain resources could be found in your…extended family."

"What do you want, Wickham?" Darcy inquired coldly. "Spare me your appalling tirade; there are no fools here."

"It is not what I want but what I imperatively need in order to assure a decent living for my future wife. I cannot enter into a marriage unless my debt problems are entirely solved. I cannot expose my wife to the shame of—"

"Enough, Wickham! Your voice sickens me. What else?"

"I wish nothing more than that Mr. Bennet gives Lydia what is her right. However, I will need another living…perhaps another commission somewhere… And of course, a special license will be needed, but unfortunately I cannot afford to apply for one, so…"

Darcy stepped closer, his cold eyes fixed on Wickham's face.

"I need a detailed list of your creditors by tomorrow morning. I will return around noon, and by then I want to meet Miss Lydia, too. I shall speak to her alone before taking any further steps. I hope it does not cross your mind to refuse this; you must know that I will send my men to search for her immediately, and you will be followed closely. You cannot hide from me. Do not trifle with me, Wickham. If I once showed weakness in dealing with you, it is over. Do not try my patience."

"Darcy, I am not—"

"Wickham, I have wasted enough of my time with you. We shall see you again tomorrow at noon. There is only one more thing I wish to make clear: if Miss Lydia is harmed in any way, if she was in any way forced into this situation, there will be no escape for you; you must be aware of this."

"She is unharmed," Wickham said. "And, though it is ungentlemanlike of me to say it, she entered into the situation willingly. I might say the elopement was her idea."

"Of course it was. I am certain a girl of fifteen convinced a man of twenty-five to elope with her. You are a pathetic joke, Wickham," the colonel replied and cursed.

"I will see you tomorrow at noon," Darcy concluded and left the room at a quick pace, followed by the other two gentlemen. Outside the house, he stopped near the carriage and breathed deeply a few times to regain his composure.

"I have never been so ashamed or so angry in my entire life," said Mr. Bennet. "We should not satisfy his demands; I should not give him more than I can afford. It is not fair to take full responsibility, Mr. Darcy. What do you think he will do if you refuse him?"

"I am not certain, but I will not take the risk of finding out. I cannot possibly allow this situation to burden Elizabeth any longer. Besides, I am truly worried about Miss Lydia; we must ensure that he fetches her. I fear she might be in danger."

"What do you mean? He said she is with one of his friends."

"Wickham has no friends whom he might trust except those who truly worry me. We must solve this as soon as possible. In truth, I consider the best solution for Miss Lydia would be to marry him and then become a widow," Darcy said, and both gentlemen looked at him in shock. He smiled bitterly. "I am only speaking in jest."

"Well, the idea is not entirely uninteresting," the colonel said seriously.

"Mr. Darcy, you said Lydia might be in danger. Would it not be too late to wait until morning? Could we not try to find her now? The night is still early and—"

"Mr. Bennet, forgive me for worrying you more than is necessary. There is nothing we can do for now. Please trust me. We should all go home and rest; hopefully we will have everything settled by tomorrow evening."

"Very well. Please leave me in Gracechurch Street, sir. There are many things I need to discuss with my sister Gardiner. I will stay at her house for the night."

A few minutes later, Mr. Bennet entered the Gardiners' house, worried, thoughtful, his shoulders down, and burdened by distress. Darcy looked after him helplessly.

The next stop was Lord Matlock's house, and the two cousins separated, planning to meet again first thing in the morning.

Darcy's carriage departed at a steady pace while the colonel entered the house and did not stop until the library. He hastily poured himself a glass of brandy, emptied it with one gulp and then filled it again.

"Well, you seem to be quite thirsty. An interesting evening, I presume?" The colonel startled and almost dropped the glass as he saw the earl watching him with a smile.

"Father...why are you not sleeping at such a late hour?"

"I might ask you the same question, son," the earl replied, well humoured.

"Forgive me—I shall go to my room. I am not inclined to speak at the moment."

"What happened, son? You seem upset. Is something wrong? I understand Darcy's man was here earlier. What is the matter?"

The colonel glanced at his father then averted his eyes and poured himself another glass of brandy. The earl took the bottle, but the colonel found another one.

"Robert, for heaven's sake, what is wrong?"

"Do you wish to know what is wrong, Father? Do you truly want to know? Your all-time favourite is wrong—as he always has been. It is nothing more than further proof of Wickham's unworthiness and his true character. Now that you know, I imagine you are not interested in the details. Even if I should bother to tell you, you would surely find an excuse for his behaviour. I shall go to bed now; I must meet Darcy and Mr. Bennet early in the morning. You should go too, Father."

"Robert, please, let us talk! What has Mr. Bennet to do with this? Robert!"

"Good night, Lord Matlock."

When Darcy arrived home, it was so late that he was certain Elizabeth and Georgiana were long asleep. He briefly stopped at Elizabeth's door and hesitantly opened it; there was no one inside, and the bed was untouched. He knocked at his sister's door, and her voice invited him in immediately. As he expected, Elizabeth was there too, both of them in nightgowns, talking. He held their worried, inquiring gazes for a moment then allowed a smile to spread on his face.

"Why are you ladies awake at this hour?"

"Oh, Brother, we were so worried that we could not possibly sleep. What news do you have?"

"Come, let us sit," he said gently. "I have as good news as can be expected for the moment. We spoke to Wickham and discussed a few things; we will meet again tomorrow, and hopefully we will settle everything as favourably as possible."

"Oh, did you hear, Elizabeth? Everything will be fine as we hoped," she said with excitement while Elizabeth remained silent and still.

"Now let us go to sleep; we will all meet at breakfast in the morning. Elizabeth, allow me to show you to your room. Good night, my dear," he said as he gently kissed his sister's forehead. Georgiana embraced her brother, then Elizabeth, and looked after them as they left the room together. A smile lit her face as she finally felt she could breathe.

In front of her door, Elizabeth stopped and glanced at him, pleading weakly. "Can we speak for a moment, please? I am begging you... I know you are tired but—"

He leaned and whispered to her ear, his lips touching her skin. "It never crossed my mind to go to sleep without speaking to you. I just need to go and clean myself a little; then I will come to you shortly. Are you hungry? Do you need anything?"

"I need nothing but you," she whispered then blushed violently at the meaning of her own words. He kissed her hands and opened the door for her; she entered, and he held her arm and forced her to stop for another moment, enough for his lips to meet hers briefly.

Inside her room, Elizabeth felt her entire body quivering and wrapped her hands around herself. Unexpectedly, her heart was filled with warm joy, which burst from inside her chest and spread along her body. His gentle touch, his deep voice, the scent of his lips on hers and his promise of coming to her room soon turned her despair into hope and her pain into joy. The sharp claw was still clutching her as she had little optimism about Lydia, but she felt there was hope; *he* was her hope.

She looked around and climbed into bed, covering herself with the sheets. After the fatigue, lack of sleep, and distress that almost defeated her, she allowed herself to be spoiled by the soft fabric and closed her eyes. She did not hear the door open, but she could feel his presence in the room long before she opened her eyes.

Darcy wore nothing but his trousers and a white shirt, unbuttoned at the neck, and his hair—a little wet—curled around his temples. His smile warmed her heart while a trace of coldness made her shiver. She smiled back.

"May I sit near you?" he asked, and she nodded, her cheeks burning.

He leaned back in the bed next to her, both resting against the pillows. His right arm encircled her shoulders, and he gently pulled her to his chest. His fingers found their way into her loose, silky hair while his other hand entwined with hers.

"I missed you so much," he said, and she sighed, brushing her cheek to his chest, only the thin fabric between them. He continued to play with the rebel locks, his fingers briefly touching the bare skin of her neck.

"Pray tell me, how was the meeting? How is Lydia? And my father? Did you speak to my aunt? What did Papa say? And how dared Mr. Wickham face you all?"

"We spoke to Mrs. Gardiner earlier and Mr. Bennet returned to spend the night at her house. I am sure he will give her all the details. Mr. Bennet is as well as can be expected. I hope he will regain his usual spirits when this affair is ended. As for Wickham—we met him as we expected, but Miss Lydia was not there. He said she is in the house of one of his friends. I hope to see her tomorrow."

"Do you think she is well? Could you not see her tonight? What if he has harmed her?"

"I am certain she is well; he has no reason to hurt her. I strongly believe that he wishes to marry her; it was his plan from the beginning."

"Because of you... He wished to marry Lydia because he knows you will marry me."

"Probably," he replied hesitantly.

Suddenly, she raised her head to meet his eyes and spoke with a trembling voice. "What shall we do now? I cannot force you to become Wickham's brother—not for the world. I am appalled only thinking of it; I cannot imagine what you must feel…"

"Elizabeth, what do you mean? Please tell me you do not imply what I think you do…"

"I do not want you to be forced into this marriage; I do not want to expose you to the shame of being related to such a man. I do not want—"

"Elizabeth, is this what you meant earlier, just before I left? When you asked me what we will do next, you wished to know whether I intended to annul our wedding?"

"Yes…I know you would never refuse to comply with your duty, but I wish you to know I would understand if you— Oh, I see you are upset now, are you not?"

"I am still considering whether I should laugh or be truly upset, Elizabeth. And I wonder how well you know me and how well you trust in my love if you could even consider such a possibility. Am I to understand that, if some unfortunate event should befall my family, you would break our engagement?" he said in earnest.

"How can you say such a thing, sir? You know that is not true!"

"How can I know that? And how can I trust your commitment when you doubt mine so easily? Am I so unworthy of your confidence?"

"Please do not be angry with me," she said gently. Her eyes, moist with tears, locked with his, and she stretched to reach his face. Her fingers gently brushed along his jaw then daringly caressed his hair. Her face was close to his.

"I confess I was afraid you might wish to end our engagement; my judgement knew I should trust you, and my mind told me I had nothing to fear, but my heart rarely listens to my mind. I do trust you—I learned to trust you a long time ago—but I still cannot believe that such extraordinary happiness can last. I am afraid that something might happen to break my heart into pieces. And now, you may decide whether you would rather laugh or be upset, sir. I am entirely at your mercy, Mr. Darcy."

She was lying atop him, pressed against his chest, her lips almost touching his, her fingers caressing his face. One of his arms encircled her waist, pressing her closer to him while the other hand gently caressed her nape then travelled down to her spine and back to her shoulders. The thin fabric of her nightgown fell from her shoulder, so nothing separated her skin from his burning fingers. Their eyes still held, searching each other's souls; their lips tantalised each other without really touching. She felt her breasts crushed against his chest while his gentle hands turned more eager, more daring, and more compelling. His movements suddenly stopped, and he cupped her face with both hands.

"So, Miss Bennet, you feared that I might not wish to marry you any longer, but you still allowed me to come to your room and relax in your bed? Am I correct?"

She hesitated a moment, as her mind could not comprehend his words easily, and her lips, suddenly dry, did not wish to speak.

"To be perfectly honest, by the time you came to my room, I already understood that my fears were for naught. Your gaze, your smile, the way you held my hand, the way you whispered into my ear that you would come to my room—all of these made me see the truth. But even if I were not certain of your intentions, I would have allowed you to come to my room; I am ashamed to admit it, but I have no wish to deceive you. I was uncertain whether you intended to marry me or not, but I was never uncertain of your feelings as I was never uncertain of mine—well, at least not in the last month or so…"

"I am glad you trusted me enough to confess that, Miss Bennet. And I shall forgive you for the time being as I blame your distress and your drowsiness for your bad judgment."

"You are very generous, Mr. Darcy…"

As she spoke, her lips twisted into a small, teasing laugh. Their eyes were still locked, her lips—now moist and red as she licked them repeatedly—only an impudent inch away from his while she brushed her body against him, attempting to find a more comfortable position and oblivious to the sensations aroused within him. Her lack of experience was deliciously compensated by her fresh awareness of her own desires and her newly discovered sensuality.

He smiled at her and to himself, his heart melting with love while his body painfully bore his restrained passion. With one arm, he pulled her body closer to his, and with the other gently pressed her head to his, until their mouths almost touched—and then he released his grip and closed his eyes, allowing her the liberty of choosing what to do next. Gently, shyly, her lips brushed over his, tantalizing them; he still did not move. As though demanding their rights, her lips pressed against his with more daring, and he could not help laughing against her mouth as he easily recognized her mirroring his own kisses as she learned from them.

He allowed himself to savour her tentative seduction for a few more moments; then he suddenly rolled her over against the pillows and trapped her with his arms. She was surprised and puzzled, glancing at him in wonder; the thin nightgown had fallen from her shoulders, barely protecting the silky skin of her breasts, which moved heavily with each breath. He leaned towards her, gently removed the locks of hair from her temple then kissed her eyes.

"Did you read my letters?" he asked, his fingers playing with her hair.

"Oh, yes…yes I did…thank you," she answered, lost under his gaze.

"I hope you enjoyed them, though there were things that are not easy to read or to forgive. I did not want to conceal anything from you. I wrote them honestly with my heart and my mind open to you—my soul and my love in four letters."

"I do love them dearly. And I wrote four letters of my own." She smiled, and his eyes lit immediately. "I wrote down all of my thoughts, all of my feelings, day by day and moment by moment since the first day we met—just as you did."

"I want to read them," he said, and his eagerness made her laugh.

"You will—tomorrow. I brought them with me—my soul and my love in four letters."

For some time they looked at each other in perfect silence. Then his left hand slowly caressed her face, and as gentle as a breeze, his fingers traced the line of her neck, slowly brushing over her bare shoulders then down to the edge of her gown. She shivered under his touch, and her breathing became heavier; their eyes continued to hold so each could read the other's tumult of feelings. His hands continued their conquering journey with gentle tenderness, brushing tentatively through the silky fabric over her breasts, lingering a long, sweet moment; she moaned and closed her eyes though she was not certain whether he truly touched her or she merely craved the warmth of his hands.

His caresses glided further, still gentle and patient, down to her belly, along her hips, and over her thighs… Not for an instant did he attempt to remove her nightgown; his fingers only touched her bare skin where it was already revealed to him—on her arms, her shoulders, and her neck. His gaze eventually released hers as his lips slowly followed the burning trace of his fingers; countless kisses covered her face, neck, and shoulders until his lips, warm and moist, reached the edge of her gown. Against her desires and hopes, his kisses travelled back until his yearning mouth found hers, and for a time their passion found release in a game of conquest and surrender, of demand and neglect.

Hardly catching his breath, his hands still caressing her with restless desire, he separated from her a little, watching her beautiful, flustered face, the sparkle in her eyes, and the moist redness of her swollen lips.

"It is time to stop now, or we might not be able to stop soon enough," he whispered.

She daringly held his gaze, her hands encircling his neck. "Do you wish to stop?"

"I wish nothing more than to continue, my love. But I made a promise to your father, and I plan to keep it. Besides, I certainly do not want to remember our first night together connected to the painful distress you had to bear because of Wickham. Let us sleep now, shall we? I will stay with you a little longer if you wish."

"Thank you for your care, my dearest Mr. Darcy. And for your wisdom and for your tenderness and…"

"I believe you should stop, Miss Bennet, or I shall be lead to believe that I truly am a man without fault." He laughed, caressing her hair.

"It pains me to admit it, but I am afraid Miss Bingley might have been right. I shall acknowledge my error to her the first time we meet again," she said, and he laughed again, accusing her of being mean and vicious while she sighed in delight as she found a perfect spot near his heart to rest her head.

"William?"

"Yes, my love?" he replied, surprised that she was not yet asleep.

"I love Lydia, and I would do anything to help her. I wish nothing but the best for her."

"I know… I never doubted that…"

"Then how is possible that she is in such a dreadful situation and I can think of little else except how happy I am to be in your arms? How can that be?"

He kissed her hair and pulled her even closer to him. "I will bring Lydia to speak to you and Mrs. Gardiner tomorrow. Anything you decide—anything she wants and it will be accomplished. That I promise you."

He felt her place a kiss on the spot where his heart was as she whispered, "Thank you."

She soon fell asleep, sighing from time to time, tightly cuddled in his arms. As she moved in her sleep, her nightgown shifted, and for a moment, the splendour of her soft, silky breasts was revealed to him. He pulled the gown back to her shoulders and arranged it carefully while he covered her with the sheets.

He watched her sleeping, rejoicing in the greatest success of his life; soon, they would be bound together in all ways and for all time, and they would have nothing else to worry about. If only the next day would pass as he planned...

Darcy did not sleep at all; his mind was fully preoccupied with the next day's events while trying to command his tortured body to resist the painful, delicious torture of having her so close.

It was finally morning.

Chapter 21

M rs. Gardiner was stunned when the servant announced that Lord Matlock was calling. It was so early that she had barely left her bed, a terrible headache troubling her after the long discussion with Mr. Bennet.

She could not possibly send the earl away, even more so as she suspected something of great importance must have happened. But what could he possibly need to drop in unannounced at that hour? As if guessing her thoughts, the servant explained that the earl had asked to see Mr. Bennet, a fact that immediately made Mrs. Gardiner suspect the reason for his call.

She sent the servant to fetch her brother Bennet while she prepared herself as quickly as possible. Her hands were slightly trembling as she arranged her hair; she could not decide whether she felt composed enough to meet him alone, so she intentionally delayed her appearance in the parlour as long as possible.

When she finally appeared, the earl greeted her then hastily apologised for barging in so unexpectedly. She assured him no apologies were necessary and asked whether something had happened. A short glance was enough to prove to her that the earl was equally uneasy and distressed by their meeting. Before the earl had time to respond, Mr. Bennet entered.

"Lord Matlock—what a surprise!"

"Mr. Bennet—I am very pleased to see you again, sir, though I suspect your sudden arrival in Town does not have a pleasant cause."

"Unfortunately, you are correct, sir, but I am happy to see you again nevertheless."

"Forgive me if I presume too much, but…I had an argument with my son last night, and he briefly mentioned you were in town; dare I presume this has something to do with George Wickham? Forgive my intrusion, but if it is so, I believe I might be of some help."

"I see no reason to conceal the facts from you, your lordship, or to doubt your secrecy; Mr. Wickham… He eloped with my youngest daughter a couple of days ago."

The earl's surprise, as well as his disbelief, was clear. He immediately asked for more details, and Mr. Bennet related to him everything that had happened in the last two days.

"I cannot imagine what might have occurred to make him do such a thing. I have known Wickham for many years, and I know he is sometimes reckless and impulsive, but he is not as bad as he might appear. I am certain I can reason with him."

"Forgive me, but I doubt that very much. Mr. Darcy suspects that Wickham planned this scheme when he knew of Elizabeth's engagement, and after our discussion yesterday, I am convinced he is correct. Wickham almost forced us to accept his demands, and he seemed to know what to ask for and how. We are certain he intentionally hid Lydia, so we could not speak to her until he had the chance to negotiate his requests."

"That is quite extraordinary, sir; I do not doubt your words, and I know Darcy might have reason to suspect the worst, but I still hope there is some kind of misunderstanding."

"Well, you are more than welcome to join us, sir, and see for yourself. I must confess I am deeply ashamed; my family put Mr. Darcy in this horrible situation. Wickham actually forced him to pay all his expenses, to assure him an occupation and to accept him as a future brother. In truth, I would not be surprised if Mr. Darcy should break his engagement and run as far as he can, if only to escape Wickham's plans."

"Please do not think so tragically; I thank you for your trust, sir. I shall leave you now, but we will meet again very soon. Mrs. Gardiner, I apologise again for my intrusion."

Lord Matlock's dark countenance and troubled expression worried them. Despite the earl's confident words, his expression was disturbing. However, there was little they could do for the moment except wait and hope.

DARCY POURED HIMSELF A SECOND cup of coffee while listening to the colonel's complaints. His cousin had arrived earlier, and a short glance was enough for Darcy to see that the colonel also had not slept much the previous night. Troubled and angry, the colonel confessed the argument he had with his father, and Darcy chose to listen in silence.

"So, you think the earl guessed what happened?" Darcy inquired.

"Probably but that is not what bothers me. I know my father to be a man of his word, and I do not doubt his discretion. But his blindness, his partiality to Wickham—"

"That is something we cannot change, and you should not argue with the earl about it. Let us finish our breakfast; I want this situation solved today."

"It will cost you a great deal; I hope you are aware of that."

"I am aware, but what worries me more is to find a solution that avoids further trouble in the future. Wickham will never change. Should we allow that girl to marry him?"

"First we should talk to her and see what she wishes. Do you think your men could find her in time? It would be helpful to have her before we negotiate with him."

"I will send Miles to collect the reports, but I doubt there is much news; if she were found, I would already have been informed."

"If nothing else works out, we can make her a widow at any time. For a hundred pounds, I can have someone take care of Wickham."

"Surely you are joking, Robert!"

The earl's voice startled them both, and they had no time to respond before Lord Matlock closed the door behind him and took a seat at the table. The earl watched them closely; the colonel rose and moved to the window.

"No, I am not joking!" he said coldly.

"Good morning, Uncle, how are you? Would you like to have breakfast with us?"

"I need to speak to you both; I went to visit Mr. Bennet in Gracechurch Street."

"What is it you wish to discuss, Father? Darcy will pay off Wickham—as he always has—and then we will hope that Wickham changes for the better—as we always do—and nothing will change. He will always be the same worthless man; everybody can see that except you. And do not worry, I will not murder your favourite," he said bitterly.

"Robert, why are you so angry with me? I imagine you believe it is my fault, but—"

"Of course it is, Father; it was always your fault! You allowed him to take advantage of you for years—as he did with Darcy—but at least Darcy was never deceived by his shameless hypocrisy. You spent your life finding excuses for Wickham's wild behaviour, even when he asked Darcy for compensation for the living and then shamelessly returned to demand his inheritance, even when he attacked that servant girl, even when he was almost thrown in jail because of his gaming debts. You always refused to see the truth, and the scoundrel is so confident in your blindness that he dared to harm your own family!"

"Robert, let us all calm; there is no use to start this argument now…" Darcy intervened, but the colonel, furiously pacing the room, did not hear him.

"What do you mean, Robert? How did George harm my family?"

"Surely you cannot believe his eloping with that Bennet girl was his first attempt! He always did everything in his power to be admitted into our family! He first tried to seduce Selina, but my sister was too smart for him; then he did the same with Georgiana, and only Darcy's intervention prevented a tragedy. Now, as soon as he discovers Darcy's engagement, he elopes with Elizabeth's sister! Even you must see it was a well-prepared plan! What excuses will you find for your protégée, your lifetime favourite now? What a joke—your favourite! Do you believe us all fools? We have known for many years that he is your son; why the hell did you not acknowledge him from the very beginning and be done with it? You obviously love him more than your other children, so why not do it openly?"

The colonel filled his glass again, emptied it in one gulp then threw it in the fireplace.

The earl, now pale, looked at his son in complete shock, immovable in the middle of the room. He tried to find something to support himself, and with great difficulty, he found a chair. Darcy hurried to help his uncle; the colonel glanced briefly at his father but did not move towards him.

Darcy offered the earl a glass of cold water; he took it with trembling hands, and for some time it seemed that he struggled to breathe. Eventually, he broke the heavy silence.

"You believe George is my son? And you believe I love him more than I love you? My dear boy, you could not possibly be more wrong. There is nothing more important in the world than you three are; I do care deeply for George, but I am surely not his father."

His words fell like intense darkness over the room, and only their breathing was heard. The colonel stared at his father in disbelief, and the earl held his distrustful gaze. Darcy stood near his uncle, lost and troubled, wondering what he should do while a thousand thoughts spun in his tired mind.

The door opened, and Miles entered, handing a note to his master; the next moment he disappeared, closing the door in silence.

"I must leave now," the earl said suddenly, rising from his seat.

"Uncle, let us talk to clear this misunderstanding," Darcy said gently.

"I cannot talk now; I must leave. I have something to do. I must go," the earl repeated and hurried away. Darcy tried to follow him, but the colonel's voice stopped him.

"Darcy, let him leave."

"Robert, you had no right to judge the earl as you did, nor to hurt him so. His care for you has always been beyond reproach, though you know very well that it was not easy for him. I cannot believe you truly doubt his love for you or that you are jealous of his affection for Wickham."

"I do not doubt his love for us, and perhaps you are right; I undeservedly hurt him. And I was a complete idiot to tell him about Selina and Georgiana in such a careless way; forgive me. But I could not hold back my anger. It is best that he left; I cannot possibly talk to him now."

When the hour was reasonable enough for a visit to the solicitor's office, Darcy and Robert Fitzwilliam still had not succeeded in finding a reasonable explanation for the extraordinary argument. The consequences of the colonel's lack of sleep and the early morning brandy had almost vanished—after two cups of coffee and a repeated refreshing of his face with cold water—so he could reasonably see the errors in his conduct of the discussion with his father. Neither he nor Darcy could believe that what they had suspected for a long time—that Wickham was the earl's son—proved to be wrong. However, neither of them had the smallest doubt that the earl told them the truth.

Miles was sent to bring the list of Wickham's debts; a quick calculation showed that the amount was as large as the colonel feared. It was then discussed what kind of living Wickham could be provided, assuming Lydia was determined to marry him.

With news to share, Darcy and Colonel Fitzwilliam went to meet Mr. Bennet. It was already noon, and Darcy considered whether he should see Elizabeth and Georgiana. Besides being slightly worried for them, he had not spoken to Elizabeth at all that day, and he missed her. He also remembered that he promised Elizabeth she would have the chance to speak to Lydia before any final decision was made, and he intended to keep his promise.

They arrived at Mrs. Gardiner's house and asked to see Mr. Bennet. Before the servant had time to make the announcement, a din of voices startled the silence of the house; without hesitation, they headed to the library where they found the most astonishing gathering: Mr. Bennet, Mrs. Gardiner, Lord Matlock and Miss Lydia Bennet in the midst of a most animated and not quite civilised debate.

"Papa, you cannot forbid me to marry Wickham, no matter what you say! I love him dearly, and I wish for nothing but to marry him! I care for nothing but him!"

"Miss Lydia, be reasonable; surely you can see that we want what is best for you."

"Oh, I do not wish to talk to you anymore, Lord Matlock! I will not let myself be deceived again! You tricked me to come with you, and you promised to take me to see George. Just wait until I tell him you lied to me! George said you are his friend and said you will help us, but it looks like you lied to him, too. You are mean and dishonest!"

Mr. Bennet took a step forward and slapped Lydia with such force that her cheeks reddened instantly. She looked at her father in shock; never in her life had she been punished by her father; he never even raised his voice to them. The angry expression on his face made her step back in disbelief.

"One single disrespectful word to Lord Matlock and I will send you away with no hesitation. I will easily find a place across the sea to have you locked up for the next five years—without revealing your location to anyone. You must see I am not joking, girl. I shall not even demand that you apologise to the earl, as not even your excuses are worth hearing. Now—you wish to marry Wickham? Be it as you like. You will write me a note this very moment, asking my permission to marry him. That way, every time you complain about how unhappy you are with no means to support yourselves, I will remind you of this note. You are very young, it is true, and your reckless behaviour is entirely my fault; I shall not deny that. This is why I am willing to take you home and bear the shame of your elopement if only to protect you from a lifetime of suffering. But if you refuse to see reason and reject any advice coming from me, as well as from your aunt and from the man who generously took the trouble of finding you, then you deserve no concern and no care. Write me the note, and marry Wickham."

As Mr. Bennet spoke, his voice turned more cold and severe; his attempt to conceal his anger, disappointment, and self-reproach defeated his strength. He needed to sit; only then did he notice Darcy and the colonel entering the room.

"Lord Matlock, I beg your forgiveness, I do not mean to upset you or Papa, but you cannot convince me to leave Wickham! Papa, I want to marry him; I love him so much, and he makes me so happy! Please, Papa! You cannot send me away or lock me up only because I want to marry the man I love. Lizzy and Jane are marrying two wealthy men, but I am sure they do not love their betrotheds half as much I love my Wickham. Please, Papa," Lydia pleaded in an entirely different voice, which Mr. Bennet easily recognised. It was what she always did when she wished to have her way—first ask, then demand, then beg and cry. And she always succeeded. Mrs. Gardiner took her arm.

"Lydia, let us go upstairs and find you something to change into. We will discuss more of this later. Excuse us, gentlemen," Mrs. Gardiner said with a glance at the earl.

They left the room, and Mr. Bennet covered his face with trembling hands. "She is right; I cannot lock her away to forbid her marrying him. What should I do?"

"She seems determined to have him," the earl said. "She seems even to be in love with him. We can keep her away from him by force if you wish, but...I believe none of us would dare to offer you any advice in such a delicate situation. The decision must belong to you, Mr. Bennet, and we will do what needs to be done to accomplish it."

"She is not sixteen yet," Mr. Bennet said in a pained, low voice. "I never took proper care of her before, so I am lost as to what is best to be done now. I do not know... I would like to speak to Madeleine...and to Elizabeth, too."

"I believe that is best," Darcy intervened. "Since Miss Lydia is here, we have no reason to rush a meeting with Wickham. Elizabeth is with my sister; I have not spoken to either of them today, but I will bring her to speak to you."

"Very well; we must decide what is best, not only for Lydia but for our entire family. I thank you, gentlemen. I cannot begin to tell you how grateful I am for everything you have done. I would have been lost without your help."

"Unfortunately, it seems there is not much we can do either, sir; we will see you again later and do what you have decided" said the earl, while all three of them left the house.

"May I ask where you found the girl?" the colonel asked once they were out on the street.

"There are few places George could afford to leave her. Except for Mrs. Younge, there is another house where he usually stays. The...lady who owns the house is a close friend of his. I had met her before, so she did not hesitate to allow Miss Lydia to come with me."

"So fortunate that you have such a close knowledge of Wickham's favourite friends and haunts," the colonel replied with sharp mockery.

"You helped us solve a very delicate situation, Uncle; we thank you for that." Darcy gave his cousin a reproachful glare.

"Yes, well... Unfortunately, it looks like there is little that can be done; Miss Lydia has made her decision. However, there is something that troubles me, Robert.

Please explain what you meant about George seducing Selina and Georgiana. I know he has been ungrateful and disrespectful to you, Darcy, but I fear there is more—"

"There is much more, Uncle, and I would rather not speak of that, but since Robert already mentioned it—I believe we may trust your secrecy. It is important, however, that this matter remain between us."

"Do not doubt my secrecy, Darcy; perhaps I have not proved myself trustworthy when it comes to George, but you must know I would never betray your confidence."

"Very well then—we shall relate the facts to you as soon as we arrive home. Perhaps it is time to discuss everything openly before something else occurs."

"I could not agree more. That is precisely why there is something else I need to ask you—both of you. While Miss Elizabeth speaks to her father and her aunt, I would like to talk to you two—and Thomas and Selina. I believe it is time to openly discuss George."

"Uncle, this is not something to be done in haste—or in the heat of a difficult moment."

"Father, I have had enough talk of Wickham!"

"Please, Darcy…Robert; let us not argue. I shall be home, waiting for you. Please…"

The younger gentlemen reluctantly agreed to meet later at Matlock's house, and they were ready to depart when the sudden appearance of a Darcy carriage surprised them exceedingly. Nervous and worried, Georgiana and Elizabeth greeted the gentlemen.

Darcy immediately informed them that Miss Lydia was in the house, news received with great relief. He then told them that Mr. Bennet wished to speak to Elizabeth and suggested that Georgiana should return home. His proposal was readily accepted, so Darcy helped Elizabeth into the house then left with his sister.

Lord Matlock and his son returned home together without saying a word to each other during the journey. Once there, the colonel retired to his rooms while the earl wrote a short note to his daughter.

An hour later, inside the Matlock library, the earl, pale and silent after Darcy related to him the unknown details of Wickham's behaviour, glanced with worry at the four young people who waited uneasily.

"Papa, please sit," Selina said gently, inviting her father near her. He forced a smile while he gently kissed his daughter's hand and started his confession without meeting their eyes.

"I never imagined I would have to carry out this discussion with my own children, to bear the shame of your judging me, perhaps even hating me and most likely never forgiving me. I have kept this story in deep secrecy, not to protect my pride but to protect you and to protect me from losing your affection, which is the most important thing in the world to me."

"Papa," Selina said, tearfully, "you shall never lose our affection!"

"My confession is a delicate family matter, but I invited Darcy too—first, because he is as close to me as you are and, second, because my actions affected him directly and painfully. But in order to go further, there are some things that need to be clarified, though you may know some of them. Our family, though one of the oldest in England, was sometimes more successful in preserving its good name and social place than in securing the pecuniary resources required to sustain a luxurious life. My grandfather and my father refused even to consider entering into any kind of business, limiting the fortune of the Matlock family to what God gave us through our several estates. After a few years of unfavourable weather, this proved insufficient for the estates' needs, and it was not long before the family found itself in the shameful position of being forced to either sell some of its properties or bear relative poverty."

He paused a moment, breathing deeply before he continued.

"As you may imagine, as the eldest and the only son in the family, it was expected of me to save the family. Once I finished my studies, I diligently involved myself in seeking a way to improve Matlock's situation. In the meantime, however, my parents found an easier and more immediate means of settling things, arranging for me and for my sisters—Catherine and Anne—the most advantageous marriages our name and social status could buy. You might disapprove of the way I judge my parents, but it is difficult to conceal my feelings. By the time I was twenty, I knew I would marry Harriet, whose dowry was more than fifty thousand pounds. I knew little about her except that her family was an old and respectable one with a remarkable fortune that had improved miraculously during the past ten years. She was a few years older than me, beautiful and accomplished, as I was told."

He stopped again and took a glass of wine while pacing the room. He quickly glanced at his companions then returned his eyes to the window.

"The summer before my wedding, I was in Bath with some friends when I first met Julia, the daughter of an attorney who also owned a shop. I was almost one and twenty; she was almost seventeen. Suffice to say, she was a most charming creature, full of joy, witty and playful; her blonde hair and blue eyes easily stole my heart. But, as I knew I should be married soon, I did everything to enjoy her company in a proper way during long walks and sparkling discussions. I confessed to her that I was engaged, and she said she was aware, even if I were not, that she would not have been a proper choice for a future earl."

The earl paused again as speaking became too difficult; Darcy left his chair and went to pour himself a glass of wine while moving into a farther corner.

"We separated with affection and regret as I had to return home. I promised I would write to her, but she said it was not proper to do so. However, she said she would always be pleased to see me again if I ever happened to be in Bath. Needless to say, I returned to my duty with a heavy heart. For many days and nights, I could think of nothing else but her. Forgive me, my children; I am certain this is hard for you to understand, but I feel I need to explain to you how things turned out as they did…"

"I understand you, Papa," said Selina with gentle tenderness.

"As do I, Uncle," answered Darcy, his voice a low whisper.

"I married in October, and God is my witness that I was determined to do everything in my power to love and honour my wife, but it proved to be more difficult than I feared. Harriet was very reserved; she spoke little, and she rarely enjoyed other people's company, including her parents and me. We received and paid calls only if it was absolutely necessary. We attended the theatre and opera from time to time, but she seemed to take little pleasure in art. I confess that, at first, I imagined she must have been forced into the marriage as I was. I even suspected that her heart was otherwise engaged and she could not easily bind herself to me. I tried to be patient and not to force my presence on her unless it was necessary. But things between us never improved, and the fact that we were living at her father's estate did not help."

His emotions overwhelmed him, and for some time, the earl was unable to speak. As he struggled to regain composure, the viscount stepped up to him.

"Father, there is no need to torment yourself so. We remember our mother quite well, and we remember how difficult those years were. We also remember how kind and affectionate you always were with us."

"You are generous, Thomas, though I do not deserve your kindness. The truth is those years I was gone most of the time, meeting business partners and searching for ways to improve the financial situation of the family as my father and father-in-law never failed to remind me of my duties. I confess to you that I rather preferred being away as your mother seemed to dislike my presence, and I wished to avoid fights and scandal. My only joys were you, my children; the days of your births were the happiest of my life, and all my work was meant to secure your futures, so that you would have the liberty of making your own choices in life. Each time I returned home, I anticipated your running to me, to see your sweet faces welcoming me, to see how much you had grown... Unfortunately, your mother and I always argued about you. She loved you in her own way, and she was protective of you, so she did not allow me to spend much time with you. She accused me of spoiling you too much for your own good; she pretended that I tried to turn you against her, that I allowed you to be disobedient, that I was too preoccupied to give you enough education. You were so small—just two little boys who wished to play. Then, when your mother was carrying Selina, things changed for the worse, as she could not bear my presence at all. My father-in-law sent me on a long business trip outside the country, and I was away for more than two years."

"We believed you left us," the colonel said sternly.

"Forgive me, son. I should have refused to be away from my children for so long, but I was not strong enough to demand my rights. In the meantime, my sisters married advantageously as our parents arranged: Catherine to Sir Lewis de Bourgh —a man of considerable wealth, and Anne to George Darcy—the descendent of an old, respectable, though untitled family. Both my sisters were fortunate to receive what they wished: Catherine—an obedient baronet as a husband, and Anne—a man who loved her deeply and proved to be a close, reliable and helpful friend to me."

A long pause followed, as all of them found a need to satisfy their thirst.

"On one of my business trips, I unexpectedly met Julia again in Brighton. I confess to you that, in all those years, I never forgot her and I attempted to find news of her several times. Her father passed away when she was nineteen, and she married her father's business partner; they left the country together, so I was told. And then, one day, I saw her on the beach. She was there with her two-year-old son—a beautiful boy, remarkably resembling her. I found she had married Mr. Wickham, who had been appointed as my brother's steward. What a strange way destiny had of playing with me..."

"The boy was George," whispered Selina.

"Yes... I stayed in Brighton two weeks, as I could not force myself to leave. We met daily on long walks as we used to do. And all my sorrow for not seeing you children for such a long time was palliated by having little George around—who was the sweetest boy one could imagine. They were in Brighton for the summer without Mr. Wickham, as the salt air seemed favourable to Julia and her son. It does not honour me to confess it, but my relationship with Julia grew deeper than we wished. I knew her husband to be a good, honest man, very loyal to my brother; she always spoke highly of him, but as happened with me, her marriage was made by need rather than affection, and neither of us could fight our mutual feelings.

"Two weeks later, I returned home and stayed there for the summer. My heart was torn between the joy of seeing you—I barely recognised you boys, so grown up, so handsome, and Selina was the most precious gift I could ever imagine—and the pain of seeing how much your mother had changed for the worst. She seemed to separate herself from the world, and every attempt to speak to her turned into a horrible scandal. It was the first time I noticed her bad treatment of her own children, and that I could not accept."

"Yes, we remember it well," the colonel intervened angrily. "I shall never forget her continuous fury, her yelling, her heavy hand when she slapped us or grabbed us by the hair, and all the other punishments when we were not quiet enough or when we were too quiet, when we ate too little or too much, when we were outside or inside. Any reason was good enough to teach us discipline! And where were you, Father? Spending time with George Wickham while your own children were suffering!"

"Robert, you are being unfair!" the viscount intervened severely.

"No, he is not being unfair, though, as I said, the time I spent with George was less than two weeks. You have every reason to judge me, Robert. I shall not attempt to excuse myself nor hope for your forgiveness; I know that you, as a middle child, were the one who suffered the most. Thomas was older and more able to protect himself while Selina was too small to stay without her nanny. But you, my dear boy, were the main object of her anger until that day when, in a furious moment, she pushed you and you fell down the stairs. I cannot tell you what I felt when I saw you tumbling down then lying on the floor, lifeless. If I were not so frightened for you, I do not know what I might have done to her. It took you two weeks to start recovering, and it was not until the end of the summer that we knew you would be well."

"I remember you were with me all that time," the colonel said, his eyes fixed on the floor. "For the first days I could not see, so I used to stretch my hand out to feel you. You never left. I did not forget that; I remember praying that you would never leave me again…"

"After that dreadful accident, my anger turned quite wild against your mother, my father-in-law and even my own parents. I decided that, as soon as Robert was fully recovered, we would move to the Matlock estate. I allowed your mother to join us if she wished under my strict conditions. It is enough to say that I found ample arguments to force my father-in-law to accept my demands. So in September we moved."

"Mama did not come to us at first," said Selina.

"No, she did not. She came later, and she stayed only a couple of weeks because she could not bear my requirements. She was not allowed to do what she pleased, and she was not allowed to spend time alone with any of you. I cared for nothing but your safety. Every two months, she used to come and stay a few days…until she simply stopped coming…"

"Yes, we remember… What about Mrs. Wickham?" asked Selina gently.

"Matlock was an easy distance from Pemberley, and we spent quite a lot of time with the Darcys. My brother was little George's godfather, so he was at Pemberley, playing with you all the time. And my sister Anne, who did not have many friends, seemed to enjoy Julia's company. So we met quite often. But there was no…improper interlude between us while we were at Pemberley—never. It was enough for us to have the opportunity to enjoy each other's presence, to speak to each other, to walk the grounds of Pemberley with you children, to watch you all playing. It is true, however, that for several years, Julia and George spent the summer months in Brighton, and I visited them as often as I could without staying away from you more than a few days…"

"So all those years you and Mrs. Wickham… And neither Mr. Wickham nor Uncle Darcy suspected anything?"

"I could not be certain of Mr. Wickham, but Darcy surely did not know or he would have confronted me. He would not have allowed my betrayal."

"And this is how you became so attached to George?" inquired the viscount.

"Yes…and it was not even difficult; he seemed to possess the sweetest, friendliest nature, and he always knew how to charm people around him, including me and my brother Darcy. Then, when Selina and George were eight, Julia passed away in only one summer. I do not know what happened; my brother Darcy fetched the best doctors for her, but no remedy was found. She was simply gone as gently as she had lived. My heart and my mind were broken, and I was never the same

291

after I lost Julia. When she began to feel ill, she made me promise—again and again—that I would take care of George. I promised her, and I tried to keep my promise every day, but now I understand I failed miserably. She asked me for only one thing, and I was not worthy of her trust. I betrayed her confidence. A year after Julia, my own dear sister left us only a few months after Georgiana was born. George was lost, I was lost, two men attempting to take care of our young children—Georgiana only an infant—and of young George Wickham, who always remained dear to our hearts.

"It did not take long for us to notice that George was thinner and weaker than all three of you boys. He did not excel in anything; he used to complain of pain all the time, and we were afraid he might inherit Julia's illness, so we never forced him to do anything. He was not very easy or quick in learning either, and it soon was obvious that he did not like studying very much. His own father was disappointed in him and often told him so. I even remember Darcy arguing with Mr. Wickham for being too severe with George. Mr. Wickham was worried that his son would never be able to support himself, so my brother promised he would give George a living, to have an easy and honourable way to make a good life close to Pemberley. And George knew and expected that he had nothing to worry about or fight for. I believe this was our most painful mistake. While we gave George the same care and the chance of having as good an education as our children, we never gave him equal responsibilities or duties. He was allowed to believe he deserved everything and owed nothing. Even later, when George grew up and his preference for easy rewards and little effort became obvious, both Darcy and I found reasons to forgive him; I believe that is why, at some point, you children abandoned the hope of seeing me reasonable about him, so you ceased telling me about his wild behaviour."

No reply came from his children, so after a short pause, the earl continued.

"Later, after Mr. Wickham and my brother Darcy passed away, George told me I was all he had left in the whole world and his mother would be grateful to know he had my protection. That moment I knew I would never be able to abandon him. I knew about his past dealings with William regarding the living, and I never doubted that it was a good decision to deny it to George as he would never be a cleric. But I could never refuse him when he asked for my support—especially when he admitted his faults and deeply apologised and promised to change. I knew he would never keep his promise, but was I better if I broke my promise to Julia? George's faults are mine, too."

The last words were barely heard, as it seemed the earl had lost his voice. Selina stepped closer and took her father's arm then put her head on his chest.

"You blame yourself too much and undeservedly so, Papa. You cannot possibly consider yourself guilty of George Wickham's faults just because you gave him too much affection! He had all the chances, all the support, all the care one could hope for. Many others have so much less and accomplish so much more! Also, George is not unique in his failure. There are many others, born from the most illustrious families, who had everything in life and turned out even worse than George. You know, Papa, I have two boys, and I would give my life for them any moment. I love them dearly, and I often spoil them, and I am happy to see you and their father and grandmother doing the same. We try to give them affection and care and good principles and good education, but more than that, we can only pray God to allow them to become worthy, honourable young men. Until then, I will never cease to love them."

"Perhaps it was your fault, Father," said the colonel. "You and Uncle Darcy were guilty of affection and leisure; you gave him everything and demanded nothing. You taught him he could have his way easily, and he did not have to work hard for anything. You encouraged his weakness and never built his character. You might have showed him good principles and generous care but never taught him how to apply them."

The earl's shoulders fell as he listened to his son's harsh words, admitting their justice.

"But I believe Selina is right," the colonel continued. "It is not fair to blame you for the way Wickham grew up; it is enough to look at the three of us and see how different we are. And how different you and Aunt Catherine are... And just look at Mr. Bennet, who also blames himself for failing to be a good father; perhaps he is right, too, but he was the same for all his daughters. Then how did it happen that two of them grew up so admirably while the last one, who had the proper example of her elder sisters, turned out so differently? Could it be only the father's fault?"

The earl faced his younger son and their eyes finally met after avoiding contact for such a long time. A brief trace of relief lit the earl's stern countenance while the colonel forced a smile.

"You are more generous than I deserve, my children. You cannot imagine how much easier my heart is now that you endured this painful confession. And now I must beg for your help once more: what is to be done? How can you change a man who does not want to be changed? Darcy, where are you, son?"

In the far corner of the library in half darkness, Darcy was silent and overwhelmed by his own painful memories. He vividly remembered the years his uncle spoke of—the love and joy of his parents, the frightening behaviour of his aunt Harriet, the gentle smile of Mrs. Wickham, he and George playing together, the sadness of being forced to hurt his father with disappointing reports of George's behaviour then his fights with George over the years. But his most recent memories were equally heartrending.

His uncle's story of a lost love was as powerful as the sharp tightness in his chest. He almost lost Elizabeth without even trying to win her, and the earl gave him a disturbing vision of how things might have turned out had he entered an arranged marriage and, perhaps, met Elizabeth again over the years. The mere thought sickened him, and he suddenly could not breathe, so he hurried to open the window.

"Darcy, are you unwell?"

"I am perfectly well, Uncle; please do not worry for me. I just wish to express my gratitude for allowing me to be part of this distressing revelation. Your trust honours me, sir. Do not worry; we will find a way to deal with Wickham as we always have."

"You will surely not change him, but perhaps it is time to teach Wickham a little about responsibility, Father," said the viscount. "I do not expect that either you or Darcy will refuse to pay for his foolishness once more, but I believe it would be useful to show him he cannot always have his way so easily. Though you never did it when he was a child, perhaps it is time to 'spank' George Wickham and teach him a lesson."

"Wickham should be beaten senseless to finally understand the lesson," whispered the colonel bitterly while his sister looked at him with reproach. "Do not worry; I have learned that I cannot always have what I wish for." He poured himself a glass of brandy.

Selina went to her brother and embraced him tightly, placing a tender kiss on his cheek. The colonel's countenance remained stern even when Selina gave him a second kiss.

The tension in the large room had almost vanished when a servant entered and, with obvious unease, informed them that a Mr. Wickham demanded to see Lord Matlock.

"LET MR. WICKHAM WAIT a little longer, Gibbs. I will ring for you to bring him in soon."

"Papa, I shall leave," said Selina. "I do not wish to see Wickham"

"I shall, too, as I do not believe I can be of any use to you. I never dealt with Wickham in the past, and I will surely not do so now or in the future," added the viscount.

The three gentlemen who remained in the library exchanged quick glances and stepped closer to each other. Then the earl rang for the servant to invite Wickham in.

George Wickham entered quickly and froze near the door as he observed three men instead of the one he expected. He looked around, disconcerted, then smiled.

"Lord Matlock—such a pleasure to see you again, sir. And what a wonderful surprise to meet Darcy and the colonel. In truth, I had prepared myself to receive your visit later."

"I am surprised to see you too, Wickham," said the colonel. "You have not been in this house for quite a long time if I remember correctly. It must be something very important that induced you to come unannounced. You should have sent your card first."

"I appreciate that you never lose your sense of humour, Colonel. Forgive me for intruding, but I must speak with Lord Matlock. I understand his lordship knows where Miss Lydia Bennet is at present. I am truly worried for her."

"Well, George, you have no reason to worry," said the earl. "Miss Lydia is safe and sound at her aunt's house. I suspect she is resting now."

"I am glad to hear it. It is good to know she is well, I was concerned that—"

"Oh stop the nonsense, George. What kind of fool do you believe me to be? You were not concerned for the girl but for losing your advantage in your negotiation with Darcy. You took the girl and hid her from her father to increase his despair, as you knew too well that Darcy would not allow this situation to affect Elizabeth's family! Good plan, boy!"

"I assure you, your lordship, that your suspicions are ill founded. Miss Lydia's well-being is all that matters to me. I did not hide her, but I had reason to believe Mrs. Younge could not offer her a proper accommodation and—"

"And leaving her in a brothel was a better accommodation? Are you out of your mind to believe I will accept your stupid explanations? Do I look like a complete idiot to you?"

"Lord Matlock, please believe me that Miss Lydia Bennet was very well taken care of. She was hosted in a guest room, separated from the rest of the house. Mrs. G is a close friend of mine, and I trusted her to handle Lydia with great care."

"Is that so? What if Darcy and Mr. Bennet denied the payments you demanded? What if Darcy refused to honour your debts? What then would have happened with Miss Lydia?"

"Your lordship is very severe with me and most deservedly so, but I never thought to put Lydia in any danger. I care deeply for Lydia and I do wish to marry her, but I had no pecuniary resources to support a wife, so I have few choices. I might have been reckless and hasty in allowing myself to be overcome by my feelings and eloping, but I hoped that your lordship would heartily understand that one cannot command passion and love."

The earl, stepped closer, anger darkening his features. "Do not dare suggest what I think you are suggesting, or I shall rip you apart! How can you speak of feelings, passion and love? I understand a few years ago that you had strong feelings for Selina—am I wrong? And then for Georgiana? And now suddenly for Miss Lydia Bennet only a week after you discovered that her sisters will marry well. Do you believe me a mindless, old fool?"

Wickham turned pale and stepped back against the wall as if the earl's proximity had propelled him. He blinked repeatedly, struggling to hold the earl's piercing gaze.

"Your godfather would have killed you without remorse if he knew you attempted to use his beloved daughter in such a shameless way; you should not doubt that!"

"I did no harm to Georgiana...nor to Selina..." Wickham mumbled.

"I would imagine not, or else my sons or Darcy would have long since killed you! But to take advantage of Georgiana's sweet temper, to persuade her to elope with you only to force Darcy to repay you—is this not harm?"

"Your lordship cannot blame me so harshly for trying to be part of a family that I have always loved and respected or for trying to secure myself a way of living. You know very well that I have nothing left in the world. My own father did not leave me much, and…and there is no one in my own family to help me… my beloved mother…"

"Silence, George! Do not force me lose the rest of my temper. You had so much more than others, and yet you accomplished nothing at all. Had I seen you struggling to secure a future, attempting to enter into any sort of profession, working hard to study or any such thing, I would have supported you entirely—even more than I have already foolishly done! And I am sure Darcy would not hesitate to give you the living even now if we had any real hope that you would use it properly. Your lack was not in support but in honour. I am happy and relieved that your poor mother did not live to bear such a disappointment. And do not ever use her name again in an attempt to melt my heart, or I shall not be responsible for my actions!"

"I am astonished at what an idiot you are, Wickham," the colonel intervened. "I know that, for many years, you reached your goals by deceiving Uncle Darcy, my cousin, and my father, taking advantage of their affection for you, of their fondness towards the past, or of their sense of honour, adjusting your schemes to convince each of them separately. But I cannot believe you attempt the same strategy when we are all here together and actually hope to be successful again. I say we should find a way to be certain you will never bother us again."

"Wickham, how can we be certain that, if you marry Miss Lydia, have your debts paid, and a commission of some kind assured, you will not return to your old habits?" Darcy inquired sternly. "How can I be sure that you will treat your wife properly and not squander your income in the same reckless manner then return to me for additional funds?"

"I assure you, Darcy, that things will change; I promise you that. I believe it is time to decide upon my future career, and I feel that being a clergyman will suit me quite well, after all. If you could be so generous as to give me the living, I—"

"George, stop your whining; that will never happen. There will be no living for you; I shall not allow it. And I am not certain I will allow you to marry Miss Lydia either."

"In truth, your lordship, forgive my impertinence, but I dare say this marriage does not depend on anyone's will but mine and Lydia's. We both wish it, and we have already bound ourselves to each other by expressing our love and passion—"

"So you imply that you have taken her to your bed, and you believe you can use this to force your will over ours. George, you surely would not dare to compete with my will and my decisions. You must know better than that! Even were Miss Lydia with child, I could offer her a better life without you. And I will spare Darcy from wasting his money on you once more. Yes, I think this would be the best way of solving the situation—you shall go and take care of your debts as well as you can and try to find yourself a way of gaining an income to live since I understand you cannot return to your regiment. Your problems are ours no longer, boy. And do not bother me again until you can show some proof that you have improved your behaviour, which I expect to happen in no less than fifty years."

"But your lordship, how can I do that since I am without support and have fallen into poverty with the threat of being thrown into debtors' prison?"

"To be honest, I do not really care. You will find a way out of this mess; you always do. Perhaps Mrs. G will give you an assignment in her house," the earl added sharply.

"But I spoke to Mr. Bennet yesterday and he said…and Darcy and I already settled the matter… I already sent Darcy a list of my creditors as he required…"

"As I said, I do not really care. I forbid Darcy to take further measures, and I do not wish to allow you marry to Miss Lydia. That is all I will say for the moment. And I see very little chance of changing my decision by tomorrow—very little chance indeed. I would suggest you return to Mrs. Younge and devote your time to considering your choices. I would dare presume that your present situation makes it difficult for you to pay for your room, so here are ten pounds to cover your present expenses."

"I cannot believe that your lordship is so harsh with me; why are you offending me so cruelly. Why do you enjoy humiliating me with so little consideration?"

"For more than twenty years I showed you nothing but care, affection and understanding, and the results were disastrous. It is time to change my approach."

"Lord Matlock, please do not desert me, sir. Please tell me what I can do to convince you I have decided to change, that I want to change—that I shall not betray your trust this time. I understand I cannot continue as I have, and I am determined to do my duty. I wish to marry, to have a family… How can you deny me this joy?"

"George, that was an entertaining discussion, but I will leave you now. I must prepare to go out; have a pleasant day," the earl said with perfect calm as he left the library.

Wickham was immobile and shocked in utter disbelief. He stared at the closed door then his eyes pleaded in panic to the other two gentlemen.

"Darcy, you must help me! Do you wish me to beg you? I will, if that is what you want. I have nowhere to go, and Lydia is waiting for me! I promised her we would marry in a few days! She is Elizabeth's sister. How can you pain her so deeply?"

"I must leave, too," Darcy told his cousin, completely ignoring Wickham. He stepped to the door then turned and faced him.

"Wickham, you must know by now that your insincere begging impresses no one. I shall speak to Elizabeth and Mr. Bennet now. Your fate depends upon them and upon Lord Matlock's will. I would suggest you go home as the earl said and think on what you truly want to do. We might allow you to speak to us later; by that time, I expect you to present yourself with a promise you can keep. You said you wish to marry Miss Lydia. Think diligently on what this signifies, what your responsibilities will be, and whether you will be able to fulfil them. Do not expect that, in doing that, you will find an open door to my house. You will need many years to prove yourself worthy of enjoying our company again. Go home, Wickham; meditate on what you did and what you wish to do and we might send for you later tonight. Have no expectations, only hopes—and pray!"

"Gibbs, please show Mr. Wickham out," said the colonel. The servant escorted Wickham out, having to push him, as he seemed as steadfast as the wall.

Inside the library, the colonel quickly filled three glasses of brandy then took one, offered the second to his cousin and the third to Lord Matlock, who returned a moment later, looking as troubled as when he left.

"I am glad you understood my intentions so easily," the earl said.

"Of course we understood; it was quite obvious—as it is obvious that you are not well!"

"No, I am not well, Robert. In truth, I have not been so unwell in a very long time; since we spoke yesterday, I have spent not a moment without blaming myself and—"

"Father, I am truly sorry for upsetting you so; I know I have been unfair."

"No, Son, please do not apologise; it was my duty as a father to see that my favouring George did not affect you all—and I failed. Your well-deserved outburst opened my eyes; and now I ask again—what should we do with him?"

"Do you believe Wickham will change, Father?"

"Not at all. Unless something truly dramatic occurs to him, George will never change. He will find a way to convince us of his good intentions and promise us again that he will change. But he will not. And to be honest, I could not allow him to fall without lending him a hand. I cannot leave him in debtors' prison. I know I am weak, but at least I admit the truth."

"So you or Darcy will pay his debts, and you will allow him to marry Miss Lydia."

"Cousin, it was a truly joyous moment to see Uncle tormenting Wickham. But, to be honest, Wickham was correct: this marriage does not depend on Uncle's will—or mine."

"And George will easily understand that as soon as he considers the entire situation. He is no fool. I believe he will be more worried about having his debts paid and a living offered to him than about the marriage itself."

"I agree, Uncle. We must speak to Mr. Bennet; hopefully, he and Elizabeth had more success in changing Miss Lydia's mind. In any case, I had already arranged for a special licence to enable a quick marriage. Also, I will see to his debts, and we must consider an adequate commission for him. At this point, I can think of nothing to suit him."

"Darcy, give me the list of George's creditors. George is my responsibility; please allow me to fulfil it without further arguments. As for a living, if the marriage takes place, I believe the best arrangement will be to purchase him a commission in another regiment somewhere in the North. I shall speak to my friend, the general."

"It will be an important sum," Darcy said, handing the earl the list, as he understood he had no other choice. "It will very likely be nearly ten thousand pounds."

"I appreciate your concern, Darcy, but Matlock's pecuniary situation has significantly improved, especially during the years I worked with Edward Gardiner.

298

Besides, I truly depend on your excellent estate management skills to help me recover that sum shortly," the earl said, smiling bitterly.

THE MOMENT THEY ARRIVED IN Gracechurch Street, all three were invited into the library where Mr. Bennet seemed to be even more distressed and angry than he was earlier; he could do nothing to convince Lydia against marrying Wickham. He apologised for the dreadful situation that affected them all so greatly—until the earl interrupted him. Calmly, Lord Matlock informed Mr. Bennet of their decision regarding Wickham since the marriage seemed likely.

As they spoke, Elizabeth entered the library, glancing with worry from one man to another. She greeted the colonel, then the earl—who embraced her affectionately—then moved towards Darcy, who took her hands and tenderly put his arm around her shoulders.

"You seemed troubled," she whispered, holding his gaze.

"I am very well now that I see you again." He smiled, placing a kiss on her hands.

"Perhaps you two wish to speak in private; do not allow us to disturb you," the earl said with obvious mockery. Elizabeth's face turned red.

"Since you mention it—yes I would like to speak to Elizabeth privately with Mr. Bennet's permission. The music room would suffice, I believe," Darcy answered in earnest. The others stared at him, uncertain whether he were serious or not.

"The music room would be fine," said Mr. Bennet, and without hesitation, Darcy took Elizabeth's arm and left the library.

He closed the door of the music room and finally looked at Elizabeth, whose eyes were darkened in concern. He put his arms around her and crushed her against his chest, as though he thought she might escape. She first remained still in his embrace, obviously surprised, then she allowed her hands to glide around his waist and tightened herself to him until there was only one heart beat and one breath sound.

"Will you not tell me what troubles you so?" she whispered when the silence became unbearable. He allowed some distance between them then took her hand, and they sat together on the settee. He just looked at her, his fingers gently caressing her face, then kissed her forehead, cheeks, and temples. When he stopped, he looked at her again.

She cupped his face with her small hands, her eyes sparkling with tears. "You must tell me what pains you so, my love."

He turned his head so that his lips could reach her palm. He then embraced her again, and another long silence followed. She ceased asking, resting her head on his chest and listening carefully to his heart, beating wilder than usual.

"It pains me to think how close I came to never knowing love, happiness and passion. It pains me to realise how different my life would be now. When I left Netherfield in November, I willingly ran away from the most frightening feeling I have ever known—from you—and I was certain my duty demanded it. My heart breaks to know you might have been only a memory."

His face was as pale, lifeless, and troubled as it was that horrible day in January. Her heart ached, and her own pain left her breathless. She cupped his face again, but as he was much taller, his face was still too far from hers, so she daringly struggled to her knees on the couch, so she could hold his eyes. He smiled at this childish gesture and unexpectedly pulled her onto his lap. Then he tightly embraced her once more. "You are my joy, Elizabeth," he whispered.

"And you are my life, William. I have had the same frightening thoughts so many times. Now that I am so close to my happiness, I often worry about how close I came never to know the strength of such feelings. But we should not worry any longer! You must learn some of my philosophy: think only of the past as its remembrance gives you pleasure," she said, caressing his handsome face.

He smiled. "You are very wise, Miss Bennet. I shall diligently learn any philosophy you will teach me. And you are perfectly right—we should not worry any longer."

They spent the next moments in a tender embrace, silently comforting each other. Elizabeth did not dare to inquire further, though she suspected something quite dramatic must have occurred to trouble him so; he seemed unwilling to share more details, and she respected his decision. After some time, he gently placed her back on the couch.

"Speaking of troubling situations—I understand Miss Lydia is determined to marry Wickham."

Elizabeth blushed. "Unfortunately, she is. We could not convince her otherwise. I…my aunt and I suspect that they already…you know…"

"Yes, I suspect that, too. We spoke to Wickham earlier; the earl was exceedingly harsh with him. He finally seems to understand the extent of Wickham's wild behaviour, and he was very upset to be deceived and betrayed for such a long time."

"I feel sorry for the earl's pain, but I am glad he eventually realised the whole truth. But…what shall we do now?"

"We discussed all the details. I must confess that the earl insisted on taking upon himself all Wickham's expenses. I would have gladly borne it, but there was no room to argue with my uncle. He said Wickham is his responsibility."

"Oh dear, what a shame. Because of Lydia's reckless behaviour, the earl must—"

"My love, please believe me that your sister's situation is not the only reason for the earl's involvement. You must not trouble yourself. Wickham will have his debts paid, and he will receive a new commission in the North. They will likely marry in a few days and leave immediately. I wish them to be far away before our wedding. I hope you and your father approve these—"

"Thank you, my love," she whispered.

"Now we must return; I would not force your father to come after us," Darcy said laughing. "And… I cannot hope for you to sleep at our house again."

"No indeed." She laughed, blushing. "I must be here to help my aunt take care of Lydia, Besides, I do not believe my father would approve in any case."

"Sad news, indeed." He sighed, quite serious. "Fortunately, before long I will not need anyone's permission for you to sleep in my house." He stole a kiss from her moist lips.

Their return to the library was received with meaningful smiles and sharp glances. Elizabeth declared she would retire, but before doing so, she placed a gentle kiss on the earl's cheek. He looked at her in surprise as she thanked him with a smile and left.

"We sent for Wickham," the colonel said. "He will be here shortly."

"Excellent; if this marriage must take place, it is better to do it sooner rather than later," said Mr. Bennet. "When everything is settled with Wickham, I shall send a letter to Longbourn. Elizabeth and I will stay in town for the wedding."

"Excellent arrangement. If all goes well, we will have no reason to delay our own wedding," Darcy said only a moment before Wickham was announced.

"Mr. Bennet, Lord Matlock, such an honour to see you again," the newly arrived said.

"Be quiet, George, and listen to me carefully. We wish to know whether you have given your situation proper consideration. Are you decided to marry Miss Lydia Bennet?"

"Indeed I am, sir!"

"Do you remember what we discussed earlier?"

"I do remember every single word, your lordship."

"Very well. You will marry as you wish. Now—here is the list of your debts. I took it from Darcy, and I will pay it. You are now in my complete debt, George. You shall never bother Darcy again under any circumstance. Am I clear enough so far?"

"Very clear, sir. And I thank you deeply for your kindness—"

"Darcy arranged for a special licence; you will be married in a few days. You will receive a commission in a northern regiment and leave immediately after the wedding. I expect you to prove your intention of changing your habits immediately. I shall keep an eye on you every moment, George. Do not disappoint me again. I expect you to comply with your duties and take care of your wife."

"I will, your lordship. I shall not disappoint you. I—"

"Oh, George, I am so happy to see you again," cried Lydia, bursting into the library. "Your uncle made me leave with him; I wished to wait for you, but he said you sent for me! And they tried to convince me not to marry you, and Lizzy was so mean to me. She said I will not be happy with you, but I imagine she is just jealous."

"Lydia!" exclaimed Elizabeth, mortified.

"Oh, it is true, Lizzy; you are jealous. Everybody knows George was your favourite! Oh, I am so happy to see you, my love!" She almost threw herself onto Wickham's neck while the others looked at each other in deep embarrassment.

"These will be very long days—very long indeed," Mr. Bennet said, and nobody attempted to contradict him.

TWO DAYS LATER, LIFE IN Gracechurch Street was neither easy nor comfortable. Lydia's behaviour did not change in the slightest; she remained just as careless, and nothing interested her except her "dear Wickham."

Since the wedding was a certainty, Mr. Wickham dined in Gracechurch Street every evening. Consequently, neither Darcy nor his sister accepted a dinner invitation.

Lord Matlock came the next day at Mrs. Gardiner's special invitation. He found her alone in the drawing room, her expression preoccupied and slightly flushed.

"Lord Matlock, I could not allow another day to pass without thanking you for your unexampled kindness to my poor niece. Ever since Elizabeth told me, I have been most anxious to acknowledge to you how gratefully I feel it."

"Mrs. Gardiner, I am exceedingly sorry that you have been informed about these particulars. To be honest, I asked for Mr. Bennet's confidence, but it seems I forgot to tell Darcy. Please do not speak of gratitude; I did nothing more than what was my duty. I would not want this situation to make you uneasy."

"It does give me uneasiness as it makes Elizabeth uneasy. We cannot but feel sorry that Lydia's behaviour cost you and Mr. Darcy such exorbitant expense—"

"Mrs. Gardiner!" the earl interrupted her, stepping closer and gently taking her hand. She averted her eyes but did not withdraw her hand. "Mrs. Gardiner, this situation is settled. Let us speak of it no more. I thank you for your kind words, though they are unnecessary. Now, is Mr. Bennet home, I hope? Oh, and I almost forgot, Selina said she will call later; she wished to introduce my niece Anne to you."

"I… Yes, my brother Bennet is in the library. I look forward to seeing Selina and Miss de Bourgh," she said, a warm smile on her face.

"Excellent; I want to take him to the club. Darcy and my sons will join us."

"He will be pleased, I am sure. And I was wondering…if you are not otherwise engaged, we would be honoured to have you as our guest for dinner tonight."

"No, I am not otherwise engaged—thank you. I shall see you again later, then."

"Excellent," she said, and the earl laughed, as his words sounded quite strange coming from her.

ELIZABETH DIVIDED HER TIME BEFORE Lydia's wedding between her sister and Georgiana, who was reluctant to come to Gracechurch Street. The second evening, just before dinner, Elizabeth received a note from Lady Selina, informing her that Lady Brightmore was hosting a party in three days' time and insisted that Elizabeth and her father attend.

"Well, if you wish to go, we will go," said Mr. Bennet. "What do you say, Madeleine?"

"Lady Brightmore is a kind lady, and she is fond of Elizabeth. Her parties are pleasant and amusing; I see no reason not to go."

"Oh, I want to go," said Lydia. "Will there be a ball, too?"

"Ball or no ball, you will not be able to come," Mr. Bennet intervened. "You will marry that very day, and as Lord Matlock said, you are expected to leave London immediately."

"Oh, but I am certain we can stay a night longer."

"No, and you will not even have time to stop in Hertfordshire. A married woman must understand that nothing is more important than her husband's duty."

"Oh, that is so unfair! But I am sure we will have enough balls later. I shall invite Kitty to come and visit as soon as we are settled. Oh, but I would so like to go to Lady Brightmore's party! It is so unfair!"

"So unfair, indeed," replied Mr. Bennet sternly.

Without any particular incidents, the day of Lydia's marriage came. Elizabeth, her aunt, and her father were joined by the earl and Darcy, and they went together to the church. The colonel and the viscount excused themselves, declaring they had other engagements. And so, the ceremony went as easily as expected, and Mr. and Mrs. Wickham departed in their carriage—a gift from Darcy—to start a new life, followed by the circumspect and worried faces of their relatives. It was done!

Elizabeth's heart was heavy; she had little hope that her sister would be happy. She held Darcy's arm tightly, her dazed eyes lost to the sky. She felt Darcy's hand press hers as he whispered, "Do not worry; we will not abandon her."

She returned to him a loving, grateful gaze, whispering, "Thank you."

Later that day, after much torment, long discussions and shared concerns, Elizabeth, her father, and her aunt prepared themselves for Lady Brightmore's party.

Darcy and Georgiana came to fetch them, and the group, happily reunited, arrived at Lady Brightmore's residence with the pleasant anticipation of a delightful evening.

As before, the party seemed to number about thirty persons at least. Mr. Bennet was introduced to Lady Brightmore, who welcomed him; she kissed Georgiana, and then her attention moved to Darcy and Elizabeth.

"Oh, my dears, I was so happy to hear of your engagement! The best news since my son married Selina! My dear Elizabeth, you look so beautiful! And Darcy—you are more handsome than ever. I am sure all the ladies will envy Elizabeth. Oh, you are such a beautiful couple! Just look at you! And you will marry in two weeks? Well, just seeing how you look at each other, I understand why you want to marry sooner! And I imagine you will lock yourself in at Pemberley after the wedding!"

"Your ladyship is very kind and amusing, as always," said Darcy with his usual composure while Elizabeth blushed violently. "Yes, we will go to Pemberley."

"Oh, well, I am so happy! Who can believe Darcy would make a love match with a girl from Hertfordshire?" Lady Brightmore laughed. "The heart has strange ways."

"Yes, very strange. Who would believe such a thing, indeed? Mr. Darcy, such a surprise to see you here!" They turned in surprise at the newly arrived guest, and Elizabeth startled, slightly uneasy as Darcy greeted the lady.

"Eve, such a surprise to see you here," Lady Brightmore said, and Lady Sinclair smiled.

"I came with my cousin as I did not receive an invitation myself. I imagine you forgot to invite me, Lady Brightmore."

"I did not forget; I purposely did not invite you as Lord Matlock seemed quite upset with you," Lady Brightmore said bluntly. Lady Sinclair attempted a laugh.

"You are so amusing, Lady Brightmore—and so is Lord Matlock."

"No, I am not. And I really wish you to leave, dear."

"Excuse us," Darcy said as he took Elizabeth's arm and walked to where his cousins were standing, allowing the two ladies to continue their argument. They noticed Lady Sinclair pass undisturbed through the group, ignoring Lady Brightmore's disapproving gaze.

"I hope you will not permit her to ruin your evening," Darcy whispered.

"Fear not—the days when Lady Sinclair succeeds in upsetting me have passed."

"I cannot believe Eve dared to come here," Lady Selina said angrily. "What on earth is to be done to keep her away?"

"Are we to talk about Eve the rest of the evening?" asked the colonel. "For heaven's sake, a whole week we talked about Wickham; now we change to another annoying character. Anne, you must secure me a dance tonight, and so too Miss Bennet."

Anne de Bourgh stared at her cousin, eyes wide in disbelief. "What do you mean dance? This is not a ball, is it?"

"It is not a ball, but surely there will be a chance to dance."

"But I never dance in public," Anne whispered.

"Well, this would be an excellent moment to start," said the colonel.

"Then I must secure a dance, too." Darcy smiled, and Anne turned to him in surprise.

"Well, Cousin Darcy, it is strange that you discover a willingness to dance precisely when it will make me uncomfortable," Anne said seriously while the others could only laugh.

The first part of the evening passed equally pleasantly; at supper, they sat close together, a united family sharing joy and support. After dinner, the gentlemen briefly retired to the library for brandy; as the colonel anticipated, four musicians were preparing to perform, and the ladies happily anticipated the pleasure of dancing. Elizabeth poured herself a cup of tea and moved into a far corner, needing a peaceful moment as her thoughts were still preoccupied with Lydia. She was surprised and puzzled to see Lady Sinclair approach and address her directly.

"Well, well, Miss Bennet—I must say you are the author of the most astonishing surprise of this year. To make Darcy marry you—it is quite extraordinary."

Elizabeth smiled politely and made no reply.

"In truth, one cannot help wondering what sort of accomplishments a woman must possess to convince a man of excellent position and wealth—desired by many eligible young ladies—to marry her. Especially as she does not have anything exceptional—neither beauty, nor fortune or title—except a sister married in haste to hide the shame of an improper elopement. Will you be so kind as to enlighten me, Miss Bennet? I must say I misjudged you completely when we first met. I thought you to be a little country girl of not much consequence. My first impression of you has proven completely wrong."

Elizabeth turned her eyes to Lady Sinclair, holding her impertinent gaze for a moment in a silent battle of wills. Then she allowed a large smile to spread over her face.

"That is true for both of us, Lady Sinclair; my first impression of you was wrong, as well. I thought you to be a lady. It seems we both misjudged the other completely."

Lady Sinclair went white; then her cheeks coloured with anger.

"I was told your chief quality is your insolence, and this has proven to be true. How dare you speak to me in such a manner? Do you have the presumption to believe that, in marrying Darcy, you will become our equal? Do not expect to be noticed by anyone of consequence. You will be censured, slighted, and despised by everyone connected with Darcy. Your alliance will be disgraced and your name will never be mentioned by any of us. You shall never be invited nor visited by any of us, you must be aware of that!"

Elizabeth smiled again, glancing quickly to the other side of the room.

"These are heavy misfortunes,," she replied without attempting to hide her amusement. "But the wife of Mr. Darcy must have such extraordinary sources of happiness necessarily attached to her situation that she, upon the whole, could have no cause to repine. And if no one ever issues an invitation, as you so kindly warn me, I shall be forced to spend more time at home alone with my husband. I dare say that would be to my advantage, would you not agree?"

As Lady Sinclair paled again and seemed to stop breathing, Darcy approached them, a glass in his hand, watching with uneasiness. He met Elizabeth's eyes and noticed their mischievous sparkle. He smiled at her.

"Forgive me, ladies. I hope I am not interrupting anything."

"No, not at all," answered Elizabeth, returning his smile. "Lady Sinclair was curious to know how I succeeded in convincing you to marry me."

"Oh, I see...and did you tell her the truth—that it was I who struggled for months to convince you to marry me?"

"No... *that* I did not tell her," Elizabeth replied as his dark gaze and mischievous smile caused her heart to race.

"Well, it is fortunate that I came just in time to extend to Lady Sinclair all the details she needs. Now, if you will excuse us, I wish to dance with Miss Bennet. In truth, I can hardly stay away from her for more than a few minutes."

Darcy took Elizabeth's arm and held it tightly. She turned her head to meet his eyes and smiled at him. He leaned his head and kissed her hands, then took her to the dance floor while Eve Sinclair, her pale face barely concealing the anger that twisted her usually beautiful features, left the house in haste.

Lady Brightmore, a glass of her finest port in hand, considered that she should host such parties at least once a month as this one proved to be most diverting.

Chapter 22

Mrs. Bennet was certain that her nerves would never survive the distress of such extraordinary events.

After Lydia's unexpected marriage—at the precocious age of fifteen—to the handsome but reckless Mr. Wickham, Mrs. Bennet struggled now to endure the greater happiness of soon having three daughters married. In two days, both Lizzy and Jane would be wedded more advantageously than she had ever imagined.

Until then, however, she had to rise to the expectation of having Lady Selina, Lord Brightmore, Lord Matlock and his youngest son as guests for dinner. So many titled persons gathered together were unheard of both at Longbourn and in Meryton.

Of course, Lady Lucas dared to presume that she could offer advice and support. *What a joke, indeed! Charlotte marries Mr. Collins, and suddenly that makes Lady Lucas qualified to deal with the nobility? Oh, where is Hill?*

In the library, Mr. Bennet returned to his usual habits. He was quite devastated at the thought that he would lose his favourite daughter and seldom have the joy of sensible conversation, but he was content to know that he was losing his eldest daughters to lives full of joy and happiness. Besides, Darcy already told him—repeatedly—that he was most welcome to visit any of their homes whenever he pleased, so he anticipated that he would travel frequently in the future.

Two days earlier, Mrs. Gardiner and her children had arrived; Darcy and Bingley were already at Netherfield, and the Matlocks and Miss Darcy were expected later that day. That evening, they were all invited to dine at Netherfield, and the next evening they would enjoy a great dinner at Longbourn.

To distract him from his emotions, Mr. Bennet opened the letter he received a week before from Mr. Collins. Until that point, he was not particularly curious to discover what his cousin had to say, but now he thought it might be an amusing diversion.

Mr. Bennet started to read, and each passing moment the smile on his face grew. Mr. Collins began with congratulations on the approaching nuptials of the eldest daughters and gave a fair amount of attention to Elizabeth's wedding to Mr. Darcy, a *"young gentleman who is blessed, in a peculiar way, with everything the heart of mortal can most desire—splendid property, noble kindred, and extensive patronage."* Yet in spite of such obvious temptations, Mr. Collins generously warned Elizabeth and Mr. Bennet of *"what evils you may incur by a precipitate marriage to that gentleman, which, of course, you will be inclined to take immediate advantage of. My motive for cautioning you is as follows: we have reason to imagine that his aunt Lady Catherine de Bourgh does not look on the match with a friendly eye; her ladyship expressed very clearly her opinion against this alliance, which she termed so disgraceful a match. I thought it my duty to give the speediest intelligence of this to you and to my cousin, that she and her noble admirer may be aware of what they are about and not run hastily into a marriage that has not been properly sanctioned."* Mr. Collins moreover added, *"I am truly rejoiced that my cousin Lydia's sad business has been so well hushed up, and I am only concerned that their scandalous elopement before the marriage took place should be so generally known and will greatly affect the reputation of your entire family. I hope that you will not encourage the vice by receiving them at Longbourn any time again; you ought certainly to forgive them as a Christian but never to admit them in your sight or allow their names to be mentioned in your hearing; Lady Catherine herself was very specific about this."*

The rest of his letter was only about his dear Charlotte's situation and his expectation of a young olive branch, and Mr. Bennet could hardly contain his laughter, imagining the discussion between Lady Catherine—wildly furious—and Mr. Collins—struggling to direct her anger towards any other person than himself. By then, Mr. Collins surely must know that Elizabeth's marriage to Mr. Darcy would happen, no matter how little Lady Catherine approved it. Surely, her anger had become a deadly storm, and Mr. Collins was a willow in her wind.

Mr. Bennet amused himself a little longer; then he took up pen and paper and wrote with a contentment he had rarely felt.

Dear Sir,

I apologise for my late reply, but we have been busy with the latest preparations for the wedding. As I am certain you know, Elizabeth will be the wife of Mr. Darcy. Console Lady Catherine as well as you can. But, if I were you, I would stand by the nephew. He has more to give.

Yours, &c.

EACH DAY SINCE THEY RETURNED from London, Elizabeth and Darcy took long strolls on the paths around Longbourn. They reserved this time only for each other, a time for sharing and bonding, a time meant to prepare themselves for a lifetime together.

The content of their exchanged letters—their love and souls put on paper—was examined. Every moment spent together brought them closer to a complete understanding of each other, and two days before the wedding, there was nothing in their past together that remained hidden. Even the most painful disclosures —such as the malicious gossip Elizabeth overheard from Lady Sinclair at the ball in January—became easier to bear, and each confession taught them how to better comfort the other, how to dissipate the sadness from the other's face, and how to bring joy into each other's hearts.

"These days have been quite trying for you," Elizabeth said, laughing and holding his arm tightly as they walked towards Oakham Mount. "Last evening, you seemed desperate to escape from Mrs. Philips's attention."

"I hope I was not rude. I confess I simply do not know how to reply when Mrs. Philips speaks openly of my 'exceedingly handsome posture.' I believe she told me at least ten times in the last week how much I was admired when I first came to Hertfordshire and that I would surely be a 'perfect husband.'"

"Well, as Lady Brightmore wisely said, all women envy me for marrying you."

"Hardly… Anyone who knows me can testify that I am far from perfect."

"I know you are not perfect, but I do know you are perfect for me," she replied in earnest.

"I hope that is so, as you will have to bear me quite a lot; there will be a whole month with no better company than mine, so you should enjoy the large party while you can as you will surely miss it."

"I am sure you will be excellent company." She laughed again. "But I confess that I will miss Meryton and those four and twenty families at whom you once laughed. I feel the need of looking at every spot one more time to fix it in my mind."

"That was unkind, Miss Bennet! I remember the discussion clearly, and I did not laugh at the four and twenty families—" He stopped and turned her to him, looking into her eyes, and suddenly changed his tone. "I imagine you will miss your home, but you must know that we shall return any time you wish. And your family will visit us at Pemberley in a month. I do not like to see you sad."

"Yes, I know. I thank you for worrying about me, but I am not sad—not at all." He embraced her, and she laid her head against his chest.

"What would you say to a last, long ride—from Longbourn to Netherfield and back? We can return before the others arrive."

Elizabeth nodded without hesitation, a bright sparkle in her eyes. He called Thunder—who walked calmly behind them—and they both mounted.

This time she was neither frightened nor embarrassed; she cuddled in Darcy's arms, adjusting her body to fit the saddle, her hands holding his tightly. He held her forcibly close to him while he commanded the stallion; Thunder started at a slow pace that gradually increased to a full gallop.

Elizabeth knew the surroundings well; every path, every tree, and every prospect moved past at a dizzying speed. Up on Thunder's back, tightly clenched in

Darcy's arms and the wind blowing gently through her hair, Elizabeth took her farewell of beloved places with tearful eyes, her heart torn by bittersweet feelings.

They rode in silence for some time until they noticed two carriages below in the valley, heading towards Netherfield. The guests had arrived; it was time to return home.

As Thunder slowed his pace and entered a protected grove of trees, Darcy turned her head to face him. She immediately understood his gaze and felt nervous anticipation as he claimed her lips, first gently then more daringly. She allowed his passion to overwhelm her; his demanding mouth and hands firmly caressed every part he could reach—back, neck, shoulders, hips, thighs—with increased possessiveness, and she thought of nothing but the sensations that caused her to tremble. Her mind briefly warned her that someone could see them, but she dismissed it immediately. She cared little for such thoughts since she had surrendered her heart and body to him.

"I have always enjoyed riding, but never as much as in the last weeks," he whispered as he tried to breathe; she laughed.

"I am not quite sure that this can be called *riding*," she said, breathlessly. "And I am certain poor Thunder is not at all fond of having to carry such a heavy burden. He will be delighted once I learn to ride on my own."

"Well, Thunder may have to wait a little longer. I am seriously considering a delay of our riding lessons for the time being," he said as his lips enjoyed the soft skin of her neck. "Things are quite perfect as they are; I do not think there is a need for you to learn to ride anytime soon," he mumbled then claimed her lips once more while his hand tightened its grip on her thigh.

She briefly wondered how far away Longbourn was and whether anyone could see them. One of her hands found support on his thigh, and he moaned; then his fingers brushed down from her neck to the edge of her gown and rested on the spot where her heart was beating wildly. She could feel his tongue tantalising her lips, which parted with a smile, and his teeth gently bit her lower lip. She laughed against his mouth, whispering:

"I believe you are right; I see no reason to learn horseback riding for the present…"

When Thunder neighed forcefully, both laughed as though the horse had responded to their teasing. However, the stallion neighed again and became slightly nervous, so Darcy finally separated from Elizabeth and looked around: a carriage had stopped in the middle of the road in front of them. At the window, Mr. and Mrs. Collins were staring at them, one with laughing eyes, amusement evident on her face, the other speechless and unable to breathe from the severest shock of his life.

After a moment of discomfiture, Darcy was the first to recover. He moved the horse closer, then dismounted and helped Elizabeth down.

"Mrs. Collins, Mr. Collins, what a surprise," Darcy said with perfect solemnity. "I was just teaching Miss Bennet how to ride; she will need this skill once we are at Pemberley."

Barely able to maintain her countenance, Charlotte embraced Elizabeth with great affection. "I am sure Lizzy will be a dedicated student in everything regarding her future position as Mrs. Darcy; she has always been an adept student."

Elizabeth blushed even more as Darcy coughed forcibly to cover his amusement. He had always liked the former Miss Lucas.

"Oh, let me look at you, my dearest Charlotte," Elizabeth said, admiring her friend whose aspect spoke of her happiness at being with child. "You are so beautiful!"

"I am very happy, Lizzy," Charlotte said with her usual calmness as they walked together, arm in arm, followed by the gentlemen. "And I am happy to see you so happy."

Elizabeth blushed again. "Your presence will only add to my happiness. You arrived just in time. Do you know Jane and I will marry the day after tomorrow?"

"Yes, I know. The subject has been discussed at great length at Rosings for the past several days. Lady Catherine disapproves any connection with the event, and Mr. Collins would never do anything to disobey her ladyship's commands. It is only a fortunate coincidence that my mother has not been feeling well, and I wished to see her before my condition prohibits my travelling." Charlotte smiled meaningfully.

"Indeed a fortunate coincidence, my dearest Charlotte…"

Behind the ladies, a different conversation was carried out on the same subject. While Mr. Collins attempted to find a proper way to compliment Mr. Darcy without upsetting Lady Catherine, the former interrupted him decidedly.

"Mr. Collins, I confess I am upset with you, and only consideration for the friendship of Miss Elizabeth and Mrs. Collins prevents my calling you out."

Mr. Collins stared at him wide-eyed, incredulous at such a statement; he repeatedly worked at dispelling the lump in his throat.

"Mr. Darcy, you must believe that I do not know why—"

"You have given Lady Catherine vicious descriptions of Elizabeth that malign her reputation. You described her as a wanton, wild woman, and you declared that you refused to marry her when we both are aware of the truth. You cannot possibly imagine that I would overlook such offences!"

"Mr. Darcy, I assure you, sir, that—"

"Are you attempting to deny it, sir? Do you suggest that Lady Catherine has deceived me? If so, I will go and confront her directly!"

"No, no, I beg you to listen to me… Lady Catherine would never do anything wrong… I am sure it is all a great misunderstanding… I would never—"

"Mr. Collins, be man enough to admit your error; that is the least you can do! Are hypocrisy and lies accepted by the church? For heaven's sake, you soon will be blessed with children, and you must set a good example for them. You must try to be worthy of your wife and your child, Mr. Collins, for I strongly believe at this moment you are not!"

Mr. Collins, his face pale, stepped hesitantly, his shoulders slumped in a submissive posture. Longbourn soon appeared, and the ladies stopped to wait for them, so Darcy finally took pity on his companion.

"You should take care of your family, Mr. Collins; it is surely more important than attempting to please Lady Catherine all the time. I hope I have no reason to be upset with you next time we meet!"

"Sir, I assure you—"

"Good day, Mr. Collins. Mrs. Collins, as always, it is a pleasure to see you." Darcy bowed to Charlotte with warm politeness.

As the Collinses' carriage departed for Meryton, Elizabeth and Darcy entered the Longbourn yard, her laugher mixed with distress while she remembered what occurred.

"I cannot believe that, of all the people in the world, Mr. Collins should happen upon us in such a scandalous situation. I can only imagine what he will tell Lady Catherine!"

"You have no reason to worry, I assure you. I am quite certain that Mr. Collins will have nothing to say to Lady Catherine."

"How can you be so certain? He is such a gossip and—"

"Elizabeth, trust me; you have no reason to worry. But enough of Collins now —we have only a few minutes to spend in silence before we are invaded by my entire family."

"That was rude." She laughed. "I cannot wait to see Georgiana and Lady Selina. Oh—and I hope Lord Matlock comes, too; Papa looks forward to seeing him again."

They entered the house, and Mr. Bennet inspected them curiously, his right eyebrow rising in wonder. "You have been away quite some time," he said sternly.

"You will not believe what happened." she replied, slightly flustered. "We met Charlotte and Mr. Collins; they just this moment arrived from Kent. Is that not a pleasant surprise?"

"Oh, who cares about Mr. and Mrs. Collins," Mrs. Bennet interrupted. "You should go upstairs and prepare for dinner, Lizzy; it will soon be time to leave for Netherfield. And, for heaven's sake, child, why do you keep Mr. Darcy outside so long? Surely, he is not accustomed to staying out in the sun for hours! I hope you will excuse her, Mr. Darcy; she means well, I assure you, but she has this strange habit of walking out. I am not sure where she got it from; no one else in our family does such a thing!"

"I thank you for your concern, ma'am, but please believe me that I find Elizabeth's passion for walking quite enchanting," Darcy said with perfect politeness, bowing to Mrs. Bennet, who blushed with pleasure as she considered how fortunate Elizabeth was to find a man with not only peculiar tastes but also ten thousand a year.

Later that day, the Bennet family reached Netherfield hours before dinner. Introductions were made, and Elizabeth—as well as Mr. Bennet—was pleased to see that Lord Matlock had decided to attend.

Mrs. Bennet was completely charmed by not only Lord Matlock's handsome appearance and amiable manners, but also the colonel's lively presence, Lady Selina's remarkable beauty and kindness, and Miss Darcy's impeccable manners and soft voice. While all the others took their places at the dinner table, Mrs. Bennet silently looked up to the sky and thanked the Lord that Elizabeth did not agree to marry Mr. Collins last November. For the first time, Mrs. Bennet admitted that there was no other girl as smart as Lizzy. It seemed that all her reading was eventually useful. Now if she could only manage to keep her tongue under control and be obedient to Mr. Darcy's wishes. Yes, she would have to speak to Elizabeth the very next day specifically about her duties.

Mr. Bingley considered there had never been such a pleasant, joyful dinner at Netherfield since he had leased it. To host all the people he loved and admired in his house, to have Jane shining at his side, and to make the final arrangements for his wedding—he still could not believe it was truly happening.

Caroline and Louisa were still displeased—Bingley could easily see that—but they would have to accept his decision eventually. He was disconcerted that both of them seemed determined not to return to London after the wedding, and he was distressed to know they would be in the house during his wedding night. He cast a quick glance at Darcy, who seemed to have no worry since he would be leaving for Pemberley in less than two days. Darcy always had the luck.

Darcy watched Elizabeth with heartfelt delight; she was so easy in her manners, and her presence was so bright, her eyes sparkling as she found amusement in everything. She was happy; anyone could see that, and that very thought made him happy. From time to time, she turned to meet his gaze, and each time she blushed. He could sense that his staring made her nervous, and he found that disturbingly pleasant, so he allowed his eyes to caress her face, her neck, her bare shoulders and arms, then down to—

"So, Nephew, may I ask what you are contemplating so seriously?" The earl's voice brought Darcy back from his reverie, and he needed a gulp of wine before he could reply. The earl followed the direction of his gaze and laughed.

"Well, well, it is not difficult to imagine what you are thinking of. She is a remarkable woman; I hope you know how to take care of her."

"I hope that, too." Darcy smiled. "But speaking of remarkable women, I am glad you decided to come. I trust everything is well?"

"Yes, everything is well. Now let us go and relieve Bingley of his brandy; he must pay in some way for the good fortune of marrying Jane Bennet. I say, he hardly deserves that beautiful girl!"

"Uncle, leave poor Bingley alone; you have tormented him enough," Darcy said laughing.

"I say, Nephew, since he depended entirely on your opinion last November when he left Netherfield, Robert and I were wondering whether he asked your advice about the wedding night, too. By the way, Darcy, do you need any such advice?" the earl inquired in a low voice, and Darcy spit his brandy and coughed until his face turned red.

The earl patted his back gently as he whispered with mocking kindness, "Oh, come, son, do not be nervous; all will be well, you will see…"

As Darcy struggled to regain his composure under the inquiring, worried glances of the other guests, Lord Matlock never attempted to conceal his laughter.

Later after dinner, the gentlemen briefly retired to the library while the ladies amused themselves in the drawing room. Shortly, they were reunited, and the gentlemen asked the favour of some music. Elizabeth was not inclined to play and—strangely—Miss Mary did not offer herself, so Bingley asked Mrs. Hurst to indulge them, and she accepted with superior condescension.

While Mrs. Hurst exhibited her talent, Elizabeth felt Darcy behind her, his hand resting on her shoulder. She rose from her seat and stood by him against the wall. He took her arm, and for some time he seemed to pay attention to the pianoforte, but as the others became interested in the performance or in their own little conversations, he silently moved towards the door, pulling Elizabeth with him. Curious, she followed him; he exited the room along the main hall then entered another room and locked the door behind them. Elizabeth looked around, saw the pool table and blushed while her eyes gleamed with mirth.

"I recall an evening in this room last year; it was the first time I saw you without your coat," she said, slightly nervous under his dark gaze. He said nothing but suddenly lifted her to sit on the table then put his arms around her.

"That night was the first time I wondered what you would say if I locked the door and kissed you senseless," he whispered, and her heart raced wildly.

"You wished to kiss me senseless that night?" she wondered in disbelief. "I believed you were displeased that I disturbed your game—"

He kissed her words away, and his lips were neither patient nor gentle; his mouth was starving for hers, and his palm traced a circuit along her legs, thighs, ankles and back again. Her arms encircled his neck, and he moaned in pleasant surprise when he felt her teeth gently biting his lip.

"They will wonder where we are… We should return," she said, her lips as daring and impatient as his.

"Yes…" He took her down from the table as quickly as he lifted her, but he did not break the kiss for a few moments. "We have a billiard room at Pemberley, too," he finally said.

"I am sure you have, but I am happy you brought me here tonight…to kiss me breathless in this very room," she said, her eyes sparkling, her lips moist and red, her face flushed.

"Your father would shoot me if he knew how many times I broke my promise. If I were your father, I would shoot myself for the way I behave," he said as he unlocked the door.

"Do not worry; my mother would protect you." She laughed.

"There is also something serious I would like to discuss with you, Elizabeth."

"What is it? Though I believe this discussion *was* quite serious," she teased him, and he smiled, kissing her hand.

"Would you rather go to London tomorrow and stay there a few days? It will be a very long journey from Longbourn to Pemberley."

"I would rather go to Pemberley directly. I have had enough of London for a while. I do not mind its being a long journey if we are together. I want to go to Pemberley with you," she said passionately, and he tenderly embraced her and placed a gentle kiss on her hair.

"Very well, my love, we will do as you wish. I will make all the arrangements."

When Darcy and Elizabeth joined the others, it seemed nobody had noticed their absence. The ladies—aside from Miss Bingley and Mrs. Hurst who spoke only to each other—were chatting animatedly with frequent interruptions of excitement from Mrs. Bennet while Kitty and Mary intervened in the conversation with unusually shy politeness. Elizabeth moved towards Jane, and Darcy returned to the group of gentlemen. The colonel glanced at him with sharp irony.

"You know you are being quite ridiculous, are you not? We *all* know what you are doing. I never expected you to behave like a schoolboy, Darcy."

"Oh, be quiet, Robert," Lord Brightmore intervened. "He is not being ridiculous at all. The days of courtship are the most beautiful days of a man's life—"

"Until the wedding, of course," the earl said, laughing.

"Well, you have been equally ridiculous and still are." The colonel dismissed him with a gesture. "I shall not argue with you about that."

"Robert, you should not laugh at others; it might happen to you, too." Darcy smiled.

The colonel took a gulp of his brandy. "Not bloody likely."

Very late in the evening, the Bennets left Netherfield with the promise of meeting again the next day at Longbourn. That night was restless for the soon-to-be-married couples. Elizabeth and Jane talked to each other until dawn, sharing not only joy but also the sadness of separation.

Elizabeth insisted that Jane and her husband should have a very long visit to Pemberley. She believed—but did not dare tell Jane—that Mr. Bingley should have been more decided in asking everyone to leave Netherfield after the wedding; the newly wedded surely must have some time for themselves. She felt somehow that she would benefit from the complete solitude of Pemberley with only her husband, while Jane would have to bear the Bingley sisters and their mother at the same time. But Jane seemed utterly happy, so Elizabeth could only be happy for her, too.

Back at Netherfield, the resident gentlemen were still enjoying brandy long after midnight. With a full glass in his hand, Lord Matlock addressed Bingley.

"Well, well, son—somehow you succeeded in trapping that beautiful girl into marriage. You know you do not deserve her, do you not?"

Surprisingly, Bingley, well animated after several glasses, laughed. "I do know that, your lordship. I still cannot believe I will be married in two days."

"You should take good care of her, and do not dare allow your sisters to upset her!"

"I shall not... I shall allow no one ever to upset Jane and—"

"By the way, Bingley, what is this nonsense that your sisters will stay a couple of weeks at Netherfield? Hurst just told me earlier."

Bingley sighed in deep preoccupation. "They said they wished to stay..."

"They said they wished to stay? What do you mean? So no matter what anyone says, you just agree with it? Have you lost your mind, boy?" the earl thundered. "You are the master of the house! People should do what *you* say!"

"I know, sir, but I cannot throw my sisters out—"

"Not out, but off to London, if I may say so, but of course, that is your decision after all. Why on earth do you think Darcy is in such a hurry to leave for Pemberley with only his bride? I am sure that, when you wake up after your wedding night, you will be thrilled to meet Caroline and Louisa, asking you how everything went."

Bingley stared at the earl, blinking repeatedly as though trying to comprehend his words. As revelation began to dawn on him, his face quickly effected several expressions, his gaze moving from the earl to Darcy. He emptied his glass in one gulp and poured another.

"London can be lovely in the summer," he eventually said.

HAPPY FOR ALL HER MATERNAL feelings was the day on which Mrs. Bennet got rid of her two most deserving daughters.

Mrs. Bennet had not slept a single moment the previous night, so excited had her nerves been, on the one hand because of the dinner she hosted—which was declared to be marvellous, especially by Lady Selina, Miss Darcy, and Lord Matlock—and on the other hand because of the weddings the next day. All of Meryton was gathered to see Miss Bennet and Miss Elizabeth marry illustrious and exceedingly handsome gentlemen—as Mrs. Philips wisely pointed out many times.

Elizabeth was surprised at how little nervous she was during the ceremony; she felt nothing but overwhelming happiness. She looked around and saw her father watching her closely, a trace of sadness on his face. She also noticed her mother whispering to Mrs. Philips, Kitty and Mary whispering to Georgiana, Mrs. Gardiner sitting between Lady Selina and Lord Matlock, and Colonel Fitzwilliam and Lord Brightmore smiling mischievously. Jane was bright and charming at her side, and at her other side stood Mr. Darcy—the last man in the world she ever imagined she would marry. Mr. Darcy—her husband, her happiness.

After the wedding breakfast, Elizabeth took her husband's arm with a light heart and complete confidence; he covered her hand with his, and their gazed at each other as their smiles grew together. They walked to the carriage, followed by their families but oblivious to the rest of the world.

Elizabeth rewarded everyone with a bright smile, her eyes as sparkling as stars; Darcy sat near her and put his arm around her as she rested her hand on his thigh. The footman closed the carriage door and took his seat, and the carriage moved slowly, retreating step-by-step from the joyous crowd until nothing could be heard but the horses' steady pacing and the coachman's low voice commanding them.

Darcy turned to his wife and kissed her hand tenderly.

"We are finally going home, Mrs. Darcy."

She sighed and laid her head on his shoulder as her fingers entwined with his. The carriage moved through the landscape of her childhood, leaving it and the familiar grounds behind; she felt him kiss the top of her head, so she removed her bonnet and threw it on the opposite seat. She lifted her eyes to him.

"Do you remember when we returned from the sleigh ride and you were home? You took my bonnet off and unbuttoned my coat."

He smiled mischievously as he kissed her hair again. "Of course, I remember; you were so cold and frozen that I could think of nothing but how better to warm you."

"Oh, you are only teasing me. I am sure you did not think of such a thing that day."

"Believe me, I did." He laughed, and her eyebrows rose in disbelief.

"If I were to believe what you are saying, it seems you had nothing but improper thoughts about me," she said reproachfully, and he laughed louder.

"I might have had a few proper thoughts." He then turned serious and lowered his head to her, his fingers brushing over her face.

"I think I began to desire you and dream about you even before I realised I was in love with you. During your stay at Netherfield, there was not a single hour that I did not imagine how it would feel to embrace you, to kiss you, to touch you…

"I cannot imagine those kinds of thoughts crossed your mind when I was certain you were looking at me only to find a blemish. I never read passion or desire in your eyes."

She paused a moment then admitted with a smile, "It is also true that, at that time, I did not really know what passion and desire look like."

"And you do now?"

"I most certainly do…" she responded, daringly lifting her face to meet his lips. He stole a brief kiss then caressed her face tenderly.

"You must help me to behave properly on this long journey, and that will be a very difficult task."

Before she had time to reply, he captured her lips eagerly while his left hand cupped her face and neck. His tongue tantalised her lips then moved down to her throat; he cast a short glance through the small window to ascertain that the coachman had his back to them, then he gently bit her ear and spoke hoarsely. "I cannot possibly bear to wait until Pemberley…without touching you…but I promise I will be careful not to disturb your appearance…too much…"

His hand touched her bare arms then ran over her ribs and lingered upon her breast. His fingers did not move, only cupped her soft roundness then brushed slowly, tenderly, barely touching the soft fabric. She sighed, and his mouth covered her moan.

"We must behave properly," she said breathlessly after some time. He smiled and nodded then separated from her but did not release her from his embrace. His
316

right arm remained around her shoulders, and she cuddled to his chest, silently admiring the passing landscape.

They stopped every few hours to change horses and refresh themselves. Everything was perfectly arranged for their journey, a good sign that Miles, who had been sent ahead, was managing his duties most diligently. Inside the carriage, their behaviour became less proper several times, as Elizabeth pointed out with equal amusement and embarrassment.

Finally, at the end of a distressing, warm, and lengthy day, they stopped for the night at a small inn in Northamptonshire. It was a nice building—not large but well cared for—with a lovely yard full of flowers and lit by several torches.

The owner and his wife hurried to welcome them; it was obvious that Darcy had been their guest previously, and they seemed pleased to see him again. Darcy introduced Elizabeth to Mr. and Mrs. Johnson, who offered warm congratulations.

"Mr. Darcy, we have prepared the upstairs rooms for you."

"Thank you, Mrs. Johnson. Do you have other guests?"

"No, sir. Miles paid for all the rooms yesterday."

"Excellent. Thank you." Elizabeth watched her husband with equal amusement and anxiety. He certainly knew how to have his way. He had paid for the entire inn, so nobody would disturb them, she thought, feeling her cheeks flush.

The rooms were large and nicely furnished. There was a small office separating the bedroom doors, which were now open.

"There is hot water prepared in your rooms. I will send a maid to help Mrs. Darcy."

"Thank you, Mrs. Johnson. Everything is perfect, as always."

"I will ask for dinner a little later," he whispered to Elizabeth, and she smiled, flustered.

She had no patience to enjoy a long bath, so she prepared herself rather quickly. She glanced at her image in the small mirror and was pleased enough. She then dismissed the maid and hesitantly knocked at his door. He opened and looked at her so intently that she could feel his eyes caressing her. He took her hand, kissed her and invited her to sit at the small table in the middle room.

"This is lovely," she whispered, "but I doubt I will be able to eat much."

"You have to." He smiled. "You must eat well and sleep well; it was a long day, and we have another one and half ahead."

She laughed nervously. "I guess I must obey you, now that we are married."

"True..." He watched her closely then suddenly took her hand and raised her from the seat; he gently embraced her and kissed her temple.

"Are you nervous?"

"No, no...yes...a little..."

He cupped her face, and his gaze deepened into her eyes.

"There is no need to be nervous. This will not be our wedding night..."

"It will not?" She stared at him in disbelief, uncertain of his meaning.

"I would like our first time as man and wife to be in our home if you agree..."

"Oh…" She averted her eyes from him a moment, her cheeks burning. He smiled and stole a hasty kiss, his thumbs caressing her cheeks.

"I do not want anything or anyone to disturb us; I want to have my mind and my heart and my body preoccupied with nothing but you. I want us to love each other as we please in comfort, without hurry, then to sleep if we like then love each other again…"

She could feel his gaze deep inside her, invading her soul, and she shivered at each word. She put her palms over his hands.

"I think it a perfect arrangement…" she said with a trembling voice, attempting a smile.

"No, it is not perfect; a perfect arrangement would have been to marry at Pemberley and take you to our rooms a minute after the wedding, but we must make the best of this. Now let us eat; you must be starved. Then we shall try to get some sleep; we must wake early in the morning since we have a full day of travel. We will see how far we can go tomorrow, and we will decide whether we spend another day on the road."

When they returned to the dinner table, Elizabeth's anxiety had vanished completely, and her appetite seemed to increase with every bite. He poured her a little wine, and after the first gulp, her cheeks turned crimson, and she grew more animated. To the contrary, Darcy's hunger for food diminished as he could think of nothing but the beautiful woman who was now his wife—the one who gazed at him with adoring tenderness, blushed for him, and laughed at him, her long, dark hair falling on her shoulders in heavy, silky curls. He wondered whether he would be able to restrain himself 'til they reached Pemberley. He planned to use the time to allow her to become more at ease with him, more comfortable with his touch, to become aware of her own wishes and determine she desired him as much as he desired her. It was a little scheme he had planned since they decided to journey to Pemberley after the wedding, yet he was uncertain whether he would have the self-restraint to control his passion.

"Should we go to sleep?" she asked timidly, and her voice brought him back from his reverie. She seemed to wait for his indication as to what to do next. He gently took off her robe then lifted her in his arms. She released a small cry of surprise and encircled his neck with soft, warm arms; then a moment later, their lips joined passionately. He put her on the bed, went to blow out the candles, and returned to sit on the bed beside her. She snuggled to his chest, and he put his arm behind her to pull her closer.

"I have long wished to sleep in your arms again," she whispered while her fingers touched the thin fabric of his nightshirt.

"And I have wished to have you in my arms again even longer, my love." He gently nestled her against the pillows, his fingers brushing over her eyes and cheekbone, and lingering on her lips a moment; then suddenly his mouth captured hers with tender passion. The kiss started gently, but soon the tenderness turned into breathtaking desire. As his lips became more demanding, his hands eagerly caressed her throat, her shoulders, her bare arms, then returned to reach the edge of her nightgown. The soft fabric was pulled down from her shoulders and gathered on her breasts; he broke the kiss and withdrew from her a moment, but her hands were tightly clasped around his neck, and she seemed unwilling to allow his departure. He smiled and returned to her lips until their need for air became stronger. He looked at her through the darkness; the moonlight shyly entered through the windows, and her eyes sparkled like stars.

"I want to show you how much I love and desire you…" he said hoarsely.

"Please show me," she whispered, closing her eyes and parting her lips for him.

But his mouth was eager to taste more; his lips slowly traced warm kisses on her chin, then lower, along her jaw, down to her throat, then back to her ear and finally back to her own thirsty mouth. He lowered her nightgown, and countless chills overtook her; she moaned and he stopped, trying to hold her gaze. His stare made her breathing rapid, and her heart beat wildly. His eyes lowered, resting with passionate greed upon her soft roundness. Her breathing increased even more as his fingers—gently and so very slowly—brushed a trace of fire from her neck, down along and around her left breast again and again then cupped it with tender possessiveness, perfectly fitting in his palm. She moaned louder, and her back arched into his hand while his thumb daringly caressed her hard nipple. She released a soft cry, and he silenced her with another kiss; his hand moved to her other breast, starting the sweet, unbearable torture again. Her moans increased together with her breathing, and her body started to move as if of its own will.

"I want to taste you," he whispered, but she could not comprehend his words until she felt his mouth abandon hers and travel down, following the burning trace left by his fingers.

She shivered as her mind told her what would come only a moment before her body felt it. His lips soon reached the place where her heart was beating wildly; her skin, still burned by his fingers, had to bear the torturous touch of his mouth, which kissed, tasted, savoured, and then closed around her nipple. She moaned again, covering her mouth with her hand. He suddenly stopped and lifted his head to look at her, kissing her lips softly. His hand returned to her breasts, unable to abandon their softness.

Then he withdrew a bit, watching her closely; she opened her eyes and held his own, her desire matching his. His hand slowly resumed its journey and stopped a moment on her belly; lifting the nightgown, it moved down slowly and patiently, tantalisingly brushed over her right thigh then slid gently between her legs. A deep moan escaped her dry lips, and she licked them as her legs moved. His eyes still held hers, and she could feel his gaze burning her as much as his hand, which slowly moved against her inner thighs. His eyes seemed to tell her what would happen; she slowly parted her legs, and a smile lit his dark gaze. His caresses increased, becoming more daring, more demanding, and more determined.

His fingers persisted on her thighs for some time then moved up tentatively and remained still, pressing on her most intimate place. She gasped and looked at him in disbelief, holding her breath. He smiled and kissed her again; slowly, his fingers found their way to her bare core with tender caresses. His mouth suddenly captured hers again in a possessive kiss, his tongue conquering her mouth while his fingers moved in torturous, daring strokes, burning her core. Her mind could not understand what was happening while her body melted under the fire he built within her. She felt her mouth abandoned as his lips travelled down her neckline; his mouth tasted her skin and lowered again to her breasts, conquering her skin inch by inch, while his fingers conquered her core until everything vanished around her and there was nothing but his mouth, his fingers and a storm of fire and ice that shattered her senses.

She remained still, struggling to breathe again and to comprehend what had just happened; she needed some time before she dared to open her eyes. Slowly her senses recovered, and she could feel his hand still caressing her thighs, her belly, her hips…

Their eyes met, and a smile was softening his face; she briefly wondered how she looked and what he might think of her. He gently placed a kiss on her lips, then he leaned over her, covering them both with the soft sheet, his lips tantalising her ear.

"William, that was… I never imagined anything like that…"

"It makes me so very happy that my caresses please you. I have dreamed about that for such a long time… I have dreamed about *you* for such a long time, my love…"

She turned to face him, and unexpectedly, she put her hand upon his, which was cupping her breast. "Words cannot possibly describe what you made me feel… Is this how much you love and desire me?" she asked with blushing shyness.

"Not really; I love and desire you much more than that…" He kissed her hair.

"It cannot be much more… I know there is something else, but it cannot be more than what I felt. Such pleasure is unbearable…" Her voice trembled slightly.

"You must trust me, Mrs. Darcy—there is much more than that. Much more indeed," he whispered, and he could feel her tense in his arms. He chuckled and caressed her face.

"Let us sleep now; you must be tired. Good night, my love."

There was a long moment of silence, and he was certain she was asleep. He could not possibly rest, as their little interlude was pure torture for him. He smiled as he remembered her beautiful face aglow and her eyes darkened with passion and pleasure—the passion and pleasure she had experienced for the first time.

"William?" she unexpectedly called his name and he startled. "I wish to show you how much *I* love and desire you. Will you teach me?"

His heart nearly stopped, and he could barely breathe. Her earnest request made his blood boil, and he was instantly so warm that he had to remove the covers. Every part of his skin craved the hidden promise behind her words, and his body cried to him to reply. He glanced at her eyes, tenderly raised to meet his, her face lit by a bright smile. She offered herself to him without knowing what she was offering. He kissed her temple.

"I shall teach you everything, my love...as soon as we are home. Now close your eyes and speak no more because you are in great danger of not sleeping at all this night."

It was already light when Darcy awoke. He had not slept much, and his body ached, but his mind and his heart were light and easy.

Elizabeth was still asleep, her bare body covered. She breathed peacefully, her hair falling over her back as she rested on her side. He slowly removed himself from her, dressed and closed the door quietly as he went downstairs. Mrs. Johnson offered to send a maid to help Mrs. Darcy, but he refused. The servants prepared food and drink for the road; when the carriage was ready, he returned to fetch Elizabeth.

He sat on the bed and stroked her hair; she sighed with delight and smiled but did not wake up. Then he gently pulled down the sheets, and as her skin was revealed to his eyes, his fingers brushed over it; then he pressed his lips to her shoulder and bit her skin gently. She moaned and turned to him, covered with nothing but her hair. When she finally met his smiling eyes, she allowed herself to be caressed by his gaze for a moment then suddenly realised her state. She gasped and grabbed the sheets to cover herself.

His smile grew larger, and he caressed her face—flushed in the daylight—then kissed her hand. "We must leave; the carriage is ready."

THE SECOND DAY OF THEIR journey passed uneventfully. The newlyweds planned only to change horses as necessary and not to stop for the night, as they wished to get home as soon as possible; but Pemberley was still far away.

Consequently, they stopped at an unknown inn that appeared civilised enough and asked for rooms and food. The place was crowded, and as soon as they entered the main room, many pairs of eyes were on them. The owner easily recognised a worthy customer, so he hurried to comply with their demands. It was settled that driver and footman would sleep for several hours in order to be able to continue their journey safely.

Darcy and Elizabeth retired to their room, far from the noisy dining area. Servants brought the luggage, some hot water to refresh themselves, and a tray with food and wine. Darcy inspected the dishes, tasted the wine, then looked around the chamber severely and seemed displeased with it.

"I am sorry; we should have stopped two hours ago at the inn where Miles made the arrangements. I thought we could push on to Pemberley, but I was wrong. I have unwisely placed you in an unpleasant situation only a day after our wedding," he apologised with obvious distress, but she smiled at him.

"William, please do not worry about me; I shall be happy only to sleep in your arms." She caressed his face and pressed her lips to his.

"Are you not hungry? We should eat a little," he said, but their lips were already otherwise engaged. A moment later, overwhelmed by her tenderness, he sat in a chair and pulled her into his lap. The long kiss ushered in many others, their lips separating only to breathe. She felt his arms caressing her legs and lifting her dress, and all she had in mind was the pleasant anticipation of what would happen next. She briefly considered that they should move to the bed and blow out the candles as her dress was already up to her thighs. Instead, she felt his strong, demanding hands placing her astride his lap; she gasped in surprise and attempted to break the kiss, but he would not allow it. His hands encircled her back, caressing her spine, her neck, and her shoulders; then he removed the hairpins to release her heavy tresses while defeating her weak resistance with his eager passion.

After long, tormenting minutes, he finally freed her lips and withdrew his face a bit to look at her. He was smiling while she felt her cheeks burning with embarrassment.

"My beautiful, beloved wife…" He tightened his arms around her, and they remained in the silent comfort of each other's arms for some time. "We should try and rest, my love," he said eventually. "I will go to the other room to allow you to wash and change. Then we must eat a little and try to sleep a few hours."

"Very well…thank you," she said while trying to move as she became increasingly aware of the awkwardness of their present position. He left the chamber, and she finally dared to look around the small, simple room—the chair where she sat in his lap and her own image in the mirror. As other feelings diminished, embarrassment coloured her cheeks while she cleaned and changed herself.

Shortly, he returned, his appearance more proper; he had changed his trousers and shirt, and his slightly wet hair curled more than usual.

"You look beautiful, Mrs. Darcy. Now—shall we eat? These dishes seem quite tasty after all." He proved to be right; the dinner was brief, but the food and wine were much appreciated, more so as both were hungry and thirsty.

Finally, it was time for what sleep could be had; they shared the same bed, gently embraced, her head on his chest, one of his arms tightened around her shoulder, the other entwined with hers. Not a single kiss was shared as he declared she needed to rest. She attempted to tease him a few more times, but he was unmoved in his decision and eventually insisted with perfect seriousness, which only made her chuckle and blush.

"Mrs. Darcy, we absolutely must rest now. You should take advantage of this rest, as I suspect you will not have much sleep tomorrow at Pemberley."

WELL BEFORE DAWN, THEY RESUMED their journey. Despite her assurance that she was rested, Elizabeth soon fell asleep again on Darcy's shoulder. He held her gently and allowed her to rest for a couple of hours.

When the sun was up, she woke and discovered, with happy anticipation, that they had entered Derbyshire. She eagerly inquired about each remarkable place through which they drove, and rather often, she asked how much longer they had to go.

When Darcy told her they would arrive at Pemberley in less than an hour, Elizabeth's anxiety increased significantly and unexpectedly; she watched for the first appearance of Pemberley Woods with great perturbation. The park was large and contained a great variety of ground. They entered it at one of its lowest points, and drove for some time through a beautiful wood, stretching over a wide extent.

Elizabeth eagerly admired every beautiful spot and point of view, her mind and heart overwhelmed by a myriad of emotions. They gradually ascended for half a mile, and then found themselves at the top of a considerable eminence, where the wood ceased, and the eye was instantly caught by Pemberley House, situated on the opposite side of a valley into which the road, with some abruptness, wound.

Elizabeth gasped in wonder and asked to stop the carriage. Darcy smiled as she quickly exited and stood spellbound, her hands pressed over her chest to quiet her emotions as she marvelled at her future home.

It was a large, handsome, stone building, standing well on rising ground and backed by a ridge of high woody hills, and in front, a stream of natural importance was swelled into a greater width but without any artificial appearance; its banks were neither formal nor falsely adorned. It was simply perfect in its natural splendour.

"I have never seen a place more beautiful," she whispered, and he put his hands on her shoulders; she could feel his warmth near her back and leaned against him. "It is just breathtaking. I never would have imagined it to be so wonderful!"

He wrapped his arms around her. "I am glad you approve of it."

"Approve of it? It is as impressive as it is astonishing in its beauty. You know, until now, I did not fully comprehend what it means to be the 'master of Pemberley.'"

"Pray tell me, had you known before what it means to be the 'master of Pemberley,' would you have accepted my first proposal? After all, the beauty of the house should compensate for my faults," he said, laughing.

"No, I would not have! But I surely would not have teased you so when we were in Hertfordshire, and I might have offered to mend your pen as Miss Bingley did." She joined him in his amusement, and he laughed louder.

"Well, my dear Mrs. Darcy, now you will have the chance to rectify your errors. Come, I am in quite a hurry finally to be home, but I promise I will show you every spot of the estate during the next few days. You will come to know it and love it as much as I do."

When the carriage stopped in front of the manor, Elizabeth forgot to breathe. She looked around, her eyes wide, her heart racing. She took Darcy's arm, but her feet seemed unable to obey her will. Darcy kissed her hand and put his arm around her shoulders.

"We are finally home, my love."

"Oh, dear Lord! Mr. Darcy, you arrived early, sir! We did not expect you until dinnertime! I hope you are well. Oh, forgive me, Mrs. Darcy; we are honoured to receive you at Pemberley. Welcome! Oh, I am such a fool; please enter. I am standing in the way; I heartily apologise... Oh Lord, and we are not completely ready; I am so sorry..."

"Mrs. Reynolds!" Darcy's voice was gentle but decided and immediately silenced the anxious housekeeper. "Mrs. Reynolds, there is no need to be nervous or to trouble yourself. We are happy to be home at last. Everything is well, I trust?"

"Yes, everything is well, but I am afraid Miles misled us; he said you would arrive later in the afternoon; and the meal is just—" Darcy started to laugh, and his amusement seemed to disturb the woman even more.

"Mrs. Reynolds, in four and twenty years I have never seen you so distressed! I will show Mrs. Darcy around for a short while; in the meantime, please send Miles to take care of the luggage and prepare us something to eat. We shall need our baths ready as soon as possible. We are very tired and will retire early today."

"Very well, sir. Oh, and the staff are eager to meet Mrs. Darcy; shall I fetch them now in the main hall?"

"I would rather have Mrs. Darcy meet the staff tomorrow. She has not slept well for two nights, and she needs to rest."

"Oh, you are right, of course; forgive me," Mrs. Reynolds said, lowering her eyes.

Elizabeth glanced at Darcy briefly then put her hand over his.

"In fact, if it is acceptable to you, William, I would like to meet the staff now. I am eager to make their acquaintance," she said, looking from Darcy to Mrs. Reynolds. "William always speaks so highly of you, Mrs. Reynolds, and of his entire staff that I would be delighted to see them. Would half an hour be acceptable? I would like to refresh myself a little and to arrange my appearance. I would not make a poor first impression to them," she said in confidence.

Mrs. Reynolds looked at her master, slightly disconcerted but pleasantly surprised, waiting for his indication. He smiled. "Mrs. Darcy is right, of course."

"Oh, that is wonderful! Thank you, Mrs. Darcy. Should I come to help you refresh yourself? Not that you need it—you look beautiful if I may be so bold as to say so!"

"Mrs. Reynolds," Darcy interrupted her again. "We thank you, but we do not need your assistance for now. I shall ask for the maid later."

He took Elizabeth's arm and directed her along the main hall, stifling a laugh. "She is nervous because of you," he whispered. "She wrote me several letters, asking me if you wished to change the furniture and what your favourite dishes are."

"She seemed very kind and quite fond of you. I think we shall get along well."

"I have no doubt of that. I must thank you for being so considerate; I believe it meant a lot to them that you wish to meet the staff today. So, what else do you wish to see?"

"Whatever you wish to show me. I am overwhelmed by so much beauty, and I imagine it would take a long time to see everything."

"Indeed... I would rather have a longer tour of the house tomorrow. For now, we shall go and see your apartments then return to meet the staff, and then I intend not to leave our rooms again until late tomorrow. Is that acceptable to you?"

"Do I have a choice, Mr. Darcy?" She laughed.

"Not really; I plan to lock the doors and throw away the key if necessary."

"Such a demanding husband! I cannot possible contradict you, so I had best obey."

"Very wise, indeed," he concluded and stopped in the middle of the hall to claim her lips.

Finally, he opened the door widely. "These are your rooms, Mrs. Darcy."

She entered tentatively and remained near the door, looking around in silence. He placed his hands on her shoulders and she put her hands over his.

"This is exquisite," she whispered. "Splendid..."

"I am glad you like it. And here are my rooms," he said, opening the adjoining doors. She stepped inside, holding his hand tightly.

"The apartments are perfectly matched," she said in deep admiration. "So beautiful..."

"Yes, they were furnished to belong to the master and mistress of the house. And they must be matched as I expect never to keep the door between them closed," he smiled and attempted to kiss Elizabeth again, but she resisted.

"I had better arrange my hair a little before I meet the staff. I cannot afford to let you kiss me again, or we shall never be downstairs in time," she said teasingly.

She admired the rooms in silence for some time, bewitched by the view from her balcony. The beauty around her overwhelmed her again and her husband's tender caress was not enough to put her at ease. She allowed herself to rest in his arms for a short while, then they returned together to the main hall, where the entire staff was in line, waiting for them.

With no little nervousness, Elizabeth glanced at the staff; she had not imagined so many. One by one, Mrs. Reynolds introduced all thirty-five servants to Mrs. Darcy. They were of many different ages, with different responsibilities but equally nervous and somehow worried at meeting the new mistress.

Elizabeth greeted each of them with a smile; after the first five, she suddenly stopped and confessed that she was nervous and wanted to make a good impression. She also said she hoped they would help her to learn her responsibilities and thanked them for greeting her so warmly. Immediately, everyone's faces lit with relief, and whispers of approval could be heard. The introductions then continued in a calmer and lighter manner. At the end, Mrs. Reynolds introduced to Elizabeth her new maid, Molly—a girl close to her age who seemed unable to breathe in front of her new mistress.

The staff finally returned to their duties, and the Darcys enjoyed a light, hasty meal, to Mrs. Reynolds obvious disapproval; she insisted they should eat more to regain their strength after two days of exhausting travel. Afterwards, they retired to their apartments; Molly came to help Elizabeth while Darcy entered his own rooms.

After the lengthy journey, tired from lack of sleep and heightened emotions, Elizabeth looked forward to a warm bath and abandoned herself to the huge tub, allowing the water to wrap her exhausted body while her mind wondered about what would come next.

However, she had no patience to lie in the hot water for long. She called for Molly to help her prepare for the night. Surprisingly, a few minutes later, Mrs. Reynolds appeared, inquiring whether Mrs. Darcy was pleased and needed anything else. Elizabeth thanked them both warmly and assured them everything was perfect and they could retire for the time being.

"Very well, I trust that Molly prepared everything you need for the night. We shall not disturb you tomorrow unless you specifically ring for us. Good night, Mrs. Darcy."

Finally alone in her chamber, flustered and slightly uneasy, Elizabeth started to laugh, glancing in the mirror then to the closed door of his room. She took off her robe and moved onto the bed, enjoying the soft caress of the silk while she waited for her husband.

DARCY HAD JUST FINISHED HIS bath, and impatiently waited for Miles to shave him, but the man seemed to move slower than ever before. When he was finally ready, he dismissed Miles, asking not to be disturbed again. He then wrapped himself in his robe and knocked at Elizabeth's door, but no answer came. He knocked again then entered carefully and stopped in the doorway, a huge smile on his face.

Elizabeth had fallen asleep on the bed, her hair spread over the pillow in great disorder, her breathing steady and calm. He approached closer, leaned over the bed near her then removed a lock of hair from her face. She sighed at his touch, and a smile twisted her lips.

She slept so peacefully that his heart ached at the idea of disturbing her. For a moment he even considered allowing her to sleep a few hours, but the next moment, his body, painfully aroused by long restrained passion, commanded him otherwise.

He removed his robe and joined her, covering himself with the sheet and pulling her towards him. She moaned sweetly and cuddled to him, unwilling to waken. He briefly touched her lips with his then traced warm, soft, gentle kisses down her throat; his hand cupped her breast through the soft gown. At first she only moaned, enjoying his touch, but did not awaken. His caress grew more intense, and his mouth captured her other breast; she let out a moan and opened her eyes, then she rolled on her back, offering herself to his tender hands.

"I am sorry I woke you, my love… I hope you do not mind…" His hands travelled hastily along her body, caressing her with a tenderness that soon grew into desire.

"I would be upset if you allowed me to sleep," she teased him, but he silenced her with an unexpected kiss that became almost violent in its intensity. He rolled until he was completely upon her, his body crushing hers. He supported himself on his elbows to allow her to breathe, her hands tightly clasped in his hair, her mouth trapped in his kiss; her breasts were still crushed against his chest while his hips pressed against her thighs. She could feel him growing harder as he slowly brushed against her.

"God, I cannot bear this any longer," he moaned against her lips. Her own moans were the only reply, and she reached down, trying to slide her hands between their thighs.

"William, I want to touch you, too," she begged, barely able to speak through his kisses.

"Later, my love—later. It is my turn now. I want to touch, to feel, to taste every part of you," he said, stealing a hasty kiss. Then he suddenly rose on his knees, and to her utter amazement, he grabbed the lower part of her nightgown and ripped it apart in an instant.

She stared at him, eyes wide in disbelief, but instead of being frightened by his violent gesture, she seemed equally embarrassed and amused, her eyes laughing. She stretched her hands to him, and he leaned towards her; she thought she knew what he would do next—but she proved to be wrong. He hastily parted her legs, lying atop her again. His face reached only as high as her breasts, and this time the touch of his fingers, his lips, and his tongue were neither patient nor gentle; he seemed driven by a stronger, more demanding urge. Certain that she could not possibly endure more pleasure, she called his name, and his lips stopped—but only for a moment as his hands and lips ventured lower, tantalising her ribs, her belly, her navel, then lower, brushing over her hips and her thighs. She remembered his touches from two nights before, and her breath quickened in anticipation of the torturous pleasure he would soon give her again.

Her waiting was not in vain; his fingers gently slid between her thighs, caressing her. She moaned and cried his name again, but his caresses ceased and his hands abandoned her warm core and gently pressed her legs apart even more. She breathed deeply, waiting, hoping that somehow he would extinguish the fire inside her. Her mind suddenly splintered into countless pieces when, a moment later, she felt the softness of his lips upon the warmth between her legs. Her moans turned into cries, wondering whether it was real or only her imagination, but all her doubts vanished as his mouth began a maddening exploration. If two nights ago the torturous movements of his fingers taught her what pleasure meant, his mouth now enlightened her to further delights.

"William, please…" she begged, grabbing the sheets with her fists as her hips began to move instinctively. She bit her lips painfully when she felt his tongue exploring her core, tentatively at first then more daringly, tasting her with an intimacy that was difficult to accept, but she craved more. He was gently conquering her inch by inch with an insatiable need until she knew nothing else. A deep moan escaped her as she struggled for air, and she shattered violently under the countless chills that shivered throughout her burning skin.

Slowly, his caresses returned up along her body; his lips returned to taste her breasts then her arms, shoulders and throat; then he stopped to tantalise her ear.

"Are you well, my love?"

"You are a cruel man to tease me so," she whispered, her mouth finally joining his. "You cannot possible imagine what I feel…"

"I do not tease you, my beloved; what you feel cannot be more powerful than my own feelings, and your pleasure is mine, too." He lay atop her again between her parted legs then abandoned her mouth and kissed her closed lashes.

"Open your eyes, my love. I want to see you… I want to watch you become my wife," he said, and she forced her eyes to meet his. She felt his hand gently brushing between her thighs, then his hardness pressing against her core; she moaned, a strong sense of fear and happy anticipation making her heart race. She thought she knew what to expect, and neither her body nor her mind could bear to wait longer—so she opened herself to him.

"You know it will be painful at first," he said, and she nodded, her eyes never leaving his. Slowly, gently, he entered her only a little. She gasped but she held his gaze. He smiled, and his hands grabbed hers, entwining their fingers in a tight grip while a strong, eager, powerful stroke was enough for him to enter her completely. Her body instantly arched and stiffened from the pain—stronger and sharper than she expected and a deep cry escaped her lips.

"Oh, God, my love," he moaned, remaining still, trying to breathe steadily, his eyes caressing her face as their hands remained clasped. "You are completely mine now," he moaned, his lips brushing over hers.

She felt there was not enough air to cool the fire enveloping her. He was completely inside her, filling her with his burning heat, with his powerful passion, and she could feel him pulsing in her. "I can feel you inside me," she whispered.

"Is it very painful?" he asked, and she silently denied it, tying to smile at him. It was painful indeed, as she felt her body split apart, but the happiness of having him inside her, of finally becoming his wife in every sense, made it worthwhile.

He began to move slowly, watching her face intently. He knew it was painful for her, he could see it on her beautiful face, but he could also see that she was welcoming their first joining.

"I love you so much, my beautiful wife," he said, fighting an urge that almost overcame his patience, struggling to control his movements and be gentle for her.

She moaned from the painful pleasure building inside her, and her fingers caressed his handsome face. "I love you, my husband," she replied, her eyes sparkling.

Her body tried to learn the rhythm of their shared love, moving tentatively beneath him but his slow movements soon became thrusts—faster, deeper, stronger —his deep moans burning her skin. He spoke to her but she could not understand his words. Nothing mattered but his love overwhelming her as their rhythms grew wildly fervent; ecstasy, possessiveness, abandon, tenderness, and passion seemed to grow every moment in astonishing repetition. After a seemingly endless time, his moans covering her soft cries, he finally reached his long desired completion; his body shattered in release while warm waves spread inside her trembling body and everything else vanished around them…

Breathless and exhausted in their happiness, tightly embraced, they lay next to each other. A silence surrounded them as peaceful as their complete happiness. He tenderly kissed her hair, and she cuddled in his arms, wrapped in her husband's love.

"You were right," she whispered after a few long minutes. He said nothing, so she continued, puzzled. "Will you not ask me what I mean?"

"Hmm...not really..." he said teasingly, fondling her ear and neck. "Please allow me to try to guess your meaning, Mrs. Darcy. Could you possibly mean that I was right when I told you there is much more than we experienced two days ago at the inn?"

She was speechless for a few moments then looked at him in obvious surprise. "Are you reading my thoughts now, Mr. Darcy? You must be a 'man without fault,' after all," she teased him, finding a better place to rest her head on his chest. He took her hand and tenderly kissed it then placed it upon his heart.

"As I said before, I am not perfect, my dearest wife. I just hope that I am good enough for you."

"Of that, you may have no doubts, my love. We are to be the happiest couple in the world," she sighed only a moment before fatigue finally overcame her.

Late in the night, tightly wrapped in their own happiness, Mr. and Mrs. Darcy finally fell asleep in the comfort of their own home—at Pemberley.

Chapter 23

D arcy woke long before dawn; he breathed the scent of Elizabeth sleeping peacefully in his arms, and he smiled at her enchanting image, remembering her beautiful, glowing face after they loved each other. He could easily recollect every moment of their first joining as husband and wife, each expression on her face while he conquered her body: surprise, wonder, pain, delight, tenderness, passion, desire, completion—each of her feelings was vivid in his mind.

She was so exhausted that she had not moved since she fell asleep; her long hair tickled his neck, and his body seemed painfully aware of her presence. He glanced at her beautiful curves, protected only by the remnants of her nightgown, and the temptation to caress her soon became an urge. He gently removed a lock of hair from her face, and his finger brushed against her lips so slowly that she likely did not feel it. But she did; her sweet sigh proved it. She moved slowly and turned on her side towards him; suddenly her breasts pressed to his chest as her hand slid around his waist and her leg climbed his thigh. He felt his body stiffening and he wondered at his complete lack of self-restraint. In truth, he was not master of himself with Elizabeth. To regain control of his senses, he directed his gaze towards the large windows. Through the heavy curtain, he noticed the shy dawn attempting to appear. He gently laid her against the pillows and rose from the bed. He pulled the curtain away and opened the French window; immediately, the fresh breeze of early summer delightfully invaded the room. He stepped onto the balcony and looked around; the beauties of Pemberley seemed more enchanting than ever before as the sunlight tentatively broke the darkness.

Suddenly, a thought crossed his mind, and he hurried inside, leaning over her and covering her face with small kisses while he whispered, "Elizabeth, wake up, my love!"

A deep moan was her only reply, and her hand stretched to touch him; but her sleep remained as deep as before. He took her hand and kissed it then whispered again. "Come, my love, you must wake up this very moment," he insisted, and her lashes opened wider.

To her utter surprise, she saw him abscond with a few pillows, taking them out to the balcony; then he returned and lifted her into his arms. She gasped, staring at him in wonder, but she had no time to inquire as he placed her on the pillows spread across the balcony. He then sat by her, his back against the wall, and enveloped her with his eyes. Still half asleep, she leaned against him without even asking his intentions. As long as she was in his arms, nothing else mattered.

"Look, my love," he said, pointing in front of them. "This is our first sunrise together!"

All her fatigue vanished as her eyes finally spotted the beauty of the sun rising shyly from behind the hills. She pressed her hands against her chest to settle her heart.

"What splendour..." she whispered, her voice trembling. They rose, and she slowly turned to face him, her eyes sparkling with tears. "Thank you for sharing this with me, my love." Her eyes then returned to admire the beauty before them whilst she rested more closely against him, his hands embracing her waist, entwined with hers.

"After breakfast, I will show you the estate—or at least some parts of it. I thought we could have a thorough tour of the grounds in the evening before dinner."

"That sounds wonderful," she answered, shivering while he gently fondled her ear.

"It will be a long ride, but I am sure you will enjoy it."

"I am sure I will... Will we go on Thunder?" she asked, and he started to laugh, suddenly turning her head so he could meet her lips.

"No, indeed. I really want to show you Pemberley, so we will take a phaeton. I do plan a ride on Thunder, though...in a few days..." he whispered against her ear, and she chuckled, then finally their lips met.

She was still in his arms, wrapped between his strong legs, her back against his chest; only her head was half turned so her lips could fully enjoy his passion. Slowly, his hands became eager and gently caressed her thighs, her hips, and then up along her arms. She attempted to turn to him, so she could return the caresses, but his arms entrapped her, so she abandoned herself to his tender caress, their lips joined in a growing, passionate kiss. Then his hands continued to explore tenderly; his left hand stroked her thighs while his right hand glided inside her nightgown, brushing her breasts with burning fingers. Her moan was strangled within the kiss while his caresses became more urgent.

"William, please stop," she begged, but for a long moment, he ignored her plea as his gentleness became insistent. "Please stop; we cannot... Please..."

Her voice, more strong and clear, stopped his movements immediately. "Forgive me, my love. I did not intend to force your will... I was just... Please forgive me..."

She rolled in his arms, so she could face him then cupped his face with her small hands. He looked at her; she was flustered, her lips red and moist, her eyes bright.

"We cannot do this on the balcony... Someone might see us..."

He finally understood the reason for her plea; his eyes lit in delight and relief, and he turned to kiss her palms. "You are right, of course. Shall we return to our room?"

She nodded, still flushed, and they entered, holding hands. He closed the window and pulled the curtain then hurried to the bed and lay against the pillows, waiting for her to join him. With a mischievous smile, her eyes laughing at him, she placed herself with her back against him, to resume the identical position from the balcony. He laughed hoarsely. "You seemed to guess my wishes, Mrs. Darcy."

He trapped her with his hands, placing countless kisses on her head, neck and shoulders; she chuckled as his lips tickled her ear, but he turned her head to silence her with a kiss. Without releasing her lips from his demanding kiss, he removed her nightgown; the room was half-dark from the heavy curtain, and she wrapped her arms over her breasts.

He gently pulled her back closer to his chest then slowly lifted her arms. His fingers brushed along her bare arms, her skin shivering from his touch, then cupped her breasts. Their soft roundness fitted as perfectly in his palms as he remembered; he stroked them with slow movements, his thumbs tantalising her nipples, which hardened at his touch. He was never more pleased than when hearing her moans of profound delight. He felt her moving slowly against him, painfully arousing his desire.

"I wish so much to be inside you that it hurts me…" he moaned against her ear while his hand possessively caressed her breasts.

"Please do not toy with me…" she begged, and he suddenly rolled her on her back, his weight crushing her. He watched her closely, their faces almost touching. Her hands encircled his waist; his legs parted hers even more while he tenderly kissed her lips. He tried to be gentle as he was certain it was still painful for her. With great delight, he found her warm and moist, and he entered her slowly, smoothly, moaning with exquisite pleasure.

She released a cry, and he stopped, looking at her intently. "Am I hurting you?"

"No…no… Please do not stop…" she begged.

"You are so sweet…and warm…" he moaned, moving slowly with long, deep strokes.

Her moans and his combined, her hips joining his rhythm and their hands caressing each other, their lips tasting. His thrusts increased their pace, stronger, harder and deeper, with equal pleasure and pain until her body shattered violently and she bit his lips, her fingers clinging to his hair. Their lovemaking continued with growing desire and insatiate demand for each other, and they did not find rest until sometime later when the sun was already up and the day had started.

But their embrace lasted even longer; in the comfort of his arms, Elizabeth fell deeply asleep again, and he watched her sleep in perfect silence and stillness. He barely dared to breathe, afraid that he might disturb her. He allowed her to rest until she finally woke on her own, her eyes smiling at him with bright happiness.

"Good morning, my dearest wife; how are you feeling?" He smiled tenderly.

"Good morning, my dearest husband." She smiled back. "How am I feeling? Very happy…and very hungry." She laughed, and he kissed her hair.

332

"Then I must make amends... I shall first take care of your hunger and give proper attention to your happiness later. But for now, I asked for our baths to be prepared, and after breakfast I have a surprise for you."

"What surprise?" Her eyes sparkled even more in delightful anticipation.

His eyebrow rose in disapproval. "Mrs. Darcy, how can it be a surprise if I tell you what it is? But enough of this for now; Molly will be here in a moment to help you."

In their separate rooms, they bathed and reunited a half hour later. They went down arm in arm, happily welcomed by Mrs. Reynolds's contented smile. She asked if they were well and hoped they would enjoy their breakfast; she was rewarded with Darcy's approving smile.

After breakfast, Elizabeth barely had time to gather her bonnet and her spencer before Darcy decidedly escorted her out onto the lawn. The soft warmth of the summer day and the splendour of the surroundings made Elizabeth gasp and sigh. She looked at her husband, her eyes moist with emotion. "So beautiful..." she whispered.

"It is beautiful, indeed. And now you have brought joy and liveliness to Pemberley—the only things that were missing for it to be perfect." Then, in front of the house, spotted by several curious eyes from the windows, the master of Pemberley tenderly kissed his wife's lips then her hand.

A small phaeton with two horses appeared; Darcy helped Elizabeth into it then sat beside her and took the reins. The horses stepped calmly and steadily along the avenue, the gentle summer breeze caressing Elizabeth's face. She closed her eyes to enjoy the scent of freshness, but Darcy soon stopped the phaeton in front of the impressive stables. They climbed down from the phaeton, and Darcy guided Elizabeth to the entrance, where a man of middle age was waiting for them.

"Elizabeth, allow me to introduce to you Mr. Walter Colton, who has been taking care of our stables and horses in the most excellent manner for more than fifteen years."

"I thank you, sir; your words honour me. Mrs. Darcy, we are all happy to have you here."

"I am happy to be here, Mr. Colton," she said, smiling genuinely whilst she glanced around at the remarkable specimens.

"Walter, we are in kind of hurry. Can you show us, please?"

"Certainly, sir. Please follow me; here she is," he said, and he stopped in front of a box. Darcy turned to Elizabeth and spoke gently.

"This is Spirit. If you like her, she will be your horse."

A splendid paint horse, white and black, stepped reluctantly towards them. Elizabeth gasped in surprise, her eyes wide open while she moved closer, entranced.

"What a beauty!" she exclaimed rapturously as she took another step forward. The horseman stretched his hand to the mare, which shyly sniffed it.

Hesitantly, Elizabeth barely touched the mare's neck. Darcy took her hand in his, and with entwined fingers, they petted the horse affectionately.

"William, she is the most beautiful horse I ever saw! Except Thunder, of course…"

Darcy laughed, and Mr. Colton covered a smile with his hand.

"She is more beautiful than Thunder, which is expected as she is a lady," Darcy said.

"If I may intervene, Spirit is truly remarkable. If Mrs. Darcy decides to keep her, I am sure she will have no cause to repine."

"Who could possibly not want her? I only wonder if I will be worthy of her qualities; I am not at all a good rider," she confessed; then her face suddenly coloured as she noticed Darcy's hidden smile. Walter Colton was certain that Mrs. Darcy blushed from modesty, a trait he greatly admired in the new mistress of Pemberley.

"Excellent," Darcy replied. "I am certain you will get along wonderfully with Spirit."

"Should I prepare her?"

"No, thank you, Walter. We shall not ride today—tomorrow perhaps."

Elizabeth remained near the mare, petting her gently, and Darcy needed to call her name twice before she finally left the horse. Eventually, they resumed their places in the phaeton, and Elizabeth, impromptu, leaned towards her husband and started to kiss him. He immediately entered her playfulness, but she withdrew only an instant later.

"Oh, I do not want to be seen by anyone. I just wished to thank you for your kind generosity; I am not certain I deserve all these—"

"My love, I am hardly as generous as you say just because I offered you a horse. Mrs. Darcy needed one; it cannot be otherwise. And speaking of that, I unpardonably forgot to show you the Darcy jewels, which belong to you now."

She held his arm tightly then leaned against his shoulder. "There is no hurry… As you said, I will have plenty of time to see them later. But Spirit—oh, she is beautiful. I already love her and cannot wait to start riding her."

"For someone who does not like horses much, you are quite excited, Mrs. Darcy," he said laughing. "We shall start the riding lessons tomorrow. I am very glad you like Spirit."

The phaeton glided along the path at a steady pace. While the beauty of the land opened to their view, with rapture and deep admiration, Elizabeth became accustomed to her new home, guided by her husband.

Darcy told her that his steward had scheduled an introduction to all their tenants in a week's time during an informal party at Pemberley. He briefly informed her about each family on his estate while she listened with complete enchantment and intense curiosity. At one point, he showed her the road to Lambton—the small town where Mrs. Gardiner grew up—with the promise that they would visit it soon. From time to time, they stepped down so she could touch the grass, the flowers and the trees, and he took every opportunity to claim a kiss or steal a caress. However, while her delight was obvious and her happiness made her face glow, it was not difficult for Darcy to notice that a trace of worry and uneasiness shadowed Elizabeth's eyes. He inquired about the reason for her preoccupation, and she only hesitated a moment before replying, her eyes meeting his.

"Until today, I did not understand what it meant to be the mistress of Pemberley. Everything is so beautiful, yet so overwhelming, that I cannot but wonder—again—whether I will rise to such high expectations."

"My love, are you teasing me? How can you doubt yourself when I trust you so completely? I know Pemberley can seem impressive with all its wealth and grandeur—"

"Oh, but this is not what troubles me, my love. However impressive your fortune might be, that is not what makes me wonder and worry but the responsibilities attached to the master and mistress. You speak with so much passion about your legacy, about all the people who depend on you... I can hardly imagine how difficult it must have been for you to be in charge of everything at such a young age. Lord Matlock praised your skills so many times, but now I understand his meaning. I shall do everything in my power to bear my share of responsibilities, but you know I was not prepared for this. Neither my knowledge nor my experience are at such a high level."

"Perhaps not, but do you truly believe other women are more prepared? Had I married the daughter of an earl, who had lived all her life in luxury, would she have been more prepared for the responsibilities of a large estate? Even more, do you believe she would have even worried about such thing? The fact that you are so preoccupied with your duties is the best proof that you will be the perfect mistress for Pemberley. I have not the slightest doubt or concern. If you want to learn something, I shall be happy to teach you."

"Thank you, my love," she replied, laying her head against his shoulder. "Your trust is what matters most to me. I want to learn everything you want to teach me."

The ride continued for another couple of hours, with more and unexpected beauties revealed to Elizabeth's curious eyes. When they returned to the house, it was already late in the afternoon. Mrs. Reynolds seemed displeased that they had been out so long without "anything to eat or drink properly in such hot weather," and she hurried to inform them that dinner would be ready in no time.

Unlike the previous evening when nerves and fatigue prevented her really enjoying the meal, Elizabeth was now ravenous and eager to taste the rich dishes that were served. Mrs. Reynolds inquired whether Mrs. Darcy was pleased with the courses and had any special requests for the next day. Elizabeth assured her that she had rarely had anything so tasty, and she declared she had nothing more to wish for.

Soon after dinner, Mr. and Mrs. Darcy returned to their rooms, whilst downstairs the reports about the new mistress grew more favourable with every hour.

As they waited for the servants to prepare their baths, Darcy turned to his wife. "Tomorrow morning I will order the largest bath tub that can be found—one to easily accommodate two persons," he whispered, obviously amused by his wife's sudden blush, her incredulous expression and the slight trembling of her hands.

The servants' appearance broke off any further conversation on that subject, but some time later, lying in the hot water, her eyes closed, Elizabeth shivered at the image of Darcy and her together in the bathtub—or perhaps he was only teasing her again.

Elizabeth enjoyed her bath for quite some time; eventually, her eyes still closed, she heard steps, and she imagined it was Molly coming to help her out. Yet, she did not wish to break her thoughts, so she remained still a little longer. When she finally opened her eyes, she gasped in surprise when she saw not the maid but Darcy, kneeling by the tub, dressed only in his robe, an enigmatic smile on his face.

"You scared me," she whispered nervously.

"I am sorry," he replied, though his smile said otherwise. "I dismissed Molly until the morning. Any help you might need, I will provide. I hope you do not mind."

"No...I just did not expect that..." Her shyness grew, and she looked around, attempting to avoid his eyes. His fingers gently caressed her face—wet and crimson—then he leaned to steal a kiss. "Are you ready to come out or should I join you?"

She laughed but replied daringly, "I doubt the tub is large enough for both of us; besides, the water is already cold, so I shall take your first offer for the time being."

"Excellent choice." His tenderness washed away some of her uneasiness, and a smile brightened her eyes. He wrapped her in a large towel then lifted her in his arms and took her not to her bed but to his; the candles were extinguished, and the only light was from the moon and the stars shyly stealing through the curtain. He gently put her down against the pillows, his eyes never leaving hers, and slowly dried her skin, spot by spot.

When he finished, he pulled off the towel and his robe and reclined beside her, covering them both with the sheet. They lay in silence, their bodies feeling and craving each other without actually touching. His fingers caressed her face while his lips tantalised hers before claiming a long-desired kiss. For a time, their lips joined and danced together, passionately yet patiently, with restrained desire. Their bodies, with nothing to keep them apart, tentatively brushed against each other. His hands slowly travelled along, burning her skin, making her shiver, and she could hardly think or do anything but surrender to him. As with a will of their own, her hands shyly stroked his chest then moved lower to his waist. He moaned, and suddenly her mind vividly woke up.

She broke their kiss and withdrew enough to meet his eyes. "I wish to touch you," she whispered, and his eyes darkened; after a brief hesitation, he turned on his back, his breathing deep and slow, then remained still. She smiled and climbed on her side so her lips could reach his and her hand rested on his chest. Her long hair, slightly wet, fell in heavy curls, tickling his skin.

"I love your hair," he moaned. Slowly, watching his face, she gathered her hair on one side and allowed it to fall over his shoulder and chest. His hand glided along her nape, and he tried to pull her head closer to capture her lips, but she resisted.

336

Instead, her lips traced light kisses along his jaw, his neck, then lower until she stopped at the spot where his heart was beating. Her fingers brushed against the curly hair on his chest with shy curiosity while her lips touched, explored, and tasted his skin as he had done to her. As all attention was turned to the novelty of her exploration, her breasts brushed against his chest, and a joint moan escaped their lips. A moment later, she repeated the gesture again and again, the pleasure of his chest hair against her hard breasts growing unbearable. Her hand slid lower to his waist, towards his hips, her fingers stroking his skin.

"Elizabeth…" he begged, and she stopped for a moment, lifting her eyes to him; it was dark, but the moonlight was enough for their eyes to meet.

"What should I do now to please you? Please teach me…" she whispered.

He gently caressed her hair. "I have nothing to teach you, my love. Each of your touches gives me more pleasure than I ever felt before. This is perfect," he said, and she smiled then resumed her caresses, her upper body now completely lying atop his. While her small kisses burned his chest, her hand lowered even more until it finally reached the object of her interest, brushing it tentatively. The sensation was so powerful that his hips shuddered and his hands tightly entwined in her hair while her fingers remained still, barely touching him.

"Oh God, please," he begged her, and she was not certain what she should do next. Her fingers moved slowly along his hardness; with complete shock, she explored every inch of it, amazed at its size, strength, and softness. His deepest moan was the sign she needed to increase her caresses and her other hand moved to the same spot, searching with curiosity; then her fingers entwined and closed around it.

"Please, my love," he begged again, and his hips shuddered and arched towards her hands; her fingers resumed their movement along the hard softness, daringly, strongly, then, without much consideration, her lips pressed upon it. Then, slowly, her lips joined her fingers in caressing him and her tongue curiously tasted him. The sensation, so new, so strange, so unexpected, disconcerted her for a moment, and she wondered whether she should continue. But his hoarse voice, his pleading, his hips moving to the rhythm of her fingers, reminded her of the torturous, exquisite pleasure he had given her so many times—and she thought of nothing but to offer him what he desired. Her fingers and lips together resumed their caresses, and each of her kisses, each of her touches elicited deeper moans from him. She could feel his hardness pulsing in her hand as if it was alive, growing even harder when her lips touched and tasted it, and a strange sensation built and burned inside her as his pleasure became hers.

"Elizabeth, wait… I want to touch you, too," he said but she could not understand his meaning. A moment later, however, she felt his strong hands moving her body, and with the deepest shock, she felt his hands and his mouth caressing her legs, then tantalising her inner thighs and gliding between them. She needed only an instant to understand that he wished for them both to share the same sensation, to bear the same torturous feelings. She resumed her caress, whilst her own body craved and was gratified with his passionate touches, each of them more preoccupied with the other's pleasure, trying to offer more than they received, until everything collapsed around them.

As quick as a heartbeat, she found herself turned again, and his weight crushed her as he entered deeper, stronger, and faster than ever before. She cried but not from pain—as her mind anticipated with some worry—but of unexpected pleasure and of the fulfilled desire of feeling him inside her. She clasped her legs around his waist, and he tried to catch his breath while he conquered her with long, slow, deep thrusts. She bit his shoulder while the rhythm of his hips increased and his passion invaded her stronger and stronger, deeper and deeper until pleasure shattered her violently while his body convulsed upon hers, bursting inside her.

For a long time, neither of them had the strength or the will to move. He only freed her from his weight as she needed to regain her breathing, but their lower bodies remained joined. She could still feel him inside her, not as large or as strong as before but pulsing lively. Their hands continued to caress each other tenderly as they struggled to recover from the storm of sensation that left them completely spent, exhausted in mind and body.

"You are so wonderful, and I love you so much," he whispered while he kissed her forehead. "That was... The pleasure you gave me was the most exquisite sensation I have ever experienced... If I ever dreamt that you would someday touch me in such a way, my dream was a pale shadow of the reality."

She looked at him with a slight uneasiness he did not miss. "I cannot believe what we just did... It was so unexpected, so hard to imagine... Yet, it feels so natural when we are together. I love you so deeply and completely," she replied, caressing his face.

It was almost midnight when they finally fell asleep, tightly embraced in the large bed of the master of Pemberley, ending their day as passionately as it began.

Chapter 24

During their first week of marriage, the master and mistress rarely left the house, partly because of rain during the first days but also because Mrs. Darcy needed time to visit Pemberley's rooms—all of them, one by one, in the company of the master, who had postponed all his other business. A great amount of time was spent in the library, for which Mrs. Darcy seemed to have the same passion and fondness as the master; also, a fact that raised some rumours downstairs, Mrs. Darcy showed an unexpected interest in the billiard room, which was uncommon for a lady. After much speculation, whispered carefully in order not to be heard by the severe Mrs. Reynolds, it was decided among the staff that surely Mrs. Darcy learned to play billiards in order to keep her husband company —yet another proof of her worthiness.

By the second week, however, the newly wedded couple spent a few hours out-doors every day—taking long strolls around the gardens, visiting Lambton or one of the tenant families, and conducting Mrs. Darcy's riding's lessons. The information that the new Mrs. Darcy did not excel in riding was somehow disconcerting to the Pemberley staff, as everyone had been certain that Mr. Darcy's wife should be the most accomplished lady in every respect. However, Mr. Colton reported that Mrs. Darcy's improvement in riding was the fastest and most impressive he had seen in years, which, he admitted, was to Mr. Darcy's merit entirely as the master did not allow anyone but himself to tutor Mrs. Darcy. One aspect puzzled Mr. Colton, though, and he did not dare discuss it with anyone else: From the first days of their arrival, Mr. Darcy and his wife rode together on Thunder, which was only natural since she could not mount her own horse. But why they would continue that habit even after Mrs. Darcy became proficient at riding by herself, Mr. Colton could not understand.

A month after Mr. Darcy wedded Miss Elizabeth Bennet, everybody who saw them together could testify that he could not possibly have made a better choice. The new Mrs. Darcy brought the only things the master of Pemberley lacked: liveliness, joy, and laughter to warm Pemberley. The master himself was seen smiling more than he had in years, and to everyone's shock, he even danced several times at the small party he held for his tenants. Even more, the way Mr. and Mrs. Darcy gazed at each other all the time left no room for doubt regarding the feelings they shared.

A new, shiny day dawned beautifully at Pemberley, and the entire household was in an agitated state. In two days' time, a large party of houseguests was expected, and everything must be more than perfect as Mrs. Reynolds repeated countless times. In truth, Mrs. Reynolds seemed to be the one most concerned about the event—unlike Mrs. Darcy, who assured the staff that she trusted their efficiency implicitly and there was no need for them to do anything different from what they usually did. No matter how much she came to appreciate her new mistress, Mrs. Reynolds could not possibly approve such a leisurely approach; surely, everybody must and would do much more than usual as it was the first large party hosted by her master since he married!

Elizabeth knocked at the study door, and her husband invited her in, a well-known, tender smile on his face. They had spent the morning riding, and afterward, while she went to change her gown, he had an appointment with his steward, which had just ended.

Since they married, they were separated only when he had some fixed appointments, and she usually employed that time discussing with Mrs. Reynolds matters related to the household. The rest of the time, even if he had to take care of business or study a report, she took a chair close to him, reading in silence. He gladly remembered his promise from the first day and did not hesitate to inform her about the most important aspects of his business. He was pleased and eager to answer any of her questions, and he always encouraged her to disagree and argue with him.

He took her hand and closed then locked the door behind him. She smiled and blushed; he always locked the door when they were in a room, which proved a very wise gesture as, most of the time, what started as an innocent, enjoyable activity—reading, playing the piano, or playing billiards—quite often became an intimate interlude.

"Was your meeting successful, I hope?" she inquired.

"Yes, everything is settled. I hope nothing urgent will appear in the next days as I plan to focus my attention on our guests."

"I can hardly wait for their arrival; I have missed them all so dearly."

"Yes, I imagine it must have been difficult for you to have no other company than mine."

She raised her eyebrow in harsh reproach. "Such an unfair statement does not even deserve a reply. I believe you are only craving more compliments to flatter your pride. So fortunate that Miss Bingley will be here in no time," she replied impertinently.

He unceremoniously sat in his chair by the desk and pulled her onto his lap.

"You are quite disrespectful, Mrs. Darcy," he said as he claimed her lips. "I think I shall complain to my mother-in-law about your wild behaviour."

"Forgive me, sir, I was not aware that you were displeased with my behaviour. Had I known before, I surely would endeavour to make amends."

She laughed against his mouth, and he silenced her with another kiss, deeper and more demanding as she encircled her hands around his neck, her mouth as eager as his. He suddenly pulled up her dress and turned her to face him, astride on his lap. She was neither surprised nor reluctant; their kiss grew wilder as well as their caresses. He lowered the dress from her shoulders while she untied his cravat. She could feel his hands gliding between her thighs, and she laughed within the kiss at how expert he had became at removing their clothes in every possible situation. However, her laughter soon became moans of torturous pleasure when he entered her slowly, deep inside. He slowly put her back against the desk to expose her soft, heavy roundness to his hungry mouth, eager to enjoy her sweetness. Their rhythm increased, and they struggled to quiet their moans within the kiss, biting each other's lips. When pleasure vanquished her strength and she could move no longer, he rose from the chair and laid her along the desk, her legs entwined on his back, and he continued to love her there on the wooden desk—where he had spent so many lonely hours—until she took her pleasure again and again. Only then did he allow his own body to feel its long-restrained relief.

Their clothes in great disorder, they rested together on the sofa, breathing heavily. "It has been eight hours since we made love; it is no wonder I missed you so much…"

She smiled at him, flustered. "I cannot believe how little shame we have…to make love on your desk; it is preposterous."

"No, it is not; this is passion, my love. However, I remember how reluctant and embarrassed you were when it happened the first time." He laughed.

"Oh, you should not laugh. I still remember that stormy night—with rain and thunder and lightning. I could not believe that you wished to do such a thing, and I only agreed because you caused me to lose my mind and my good sense. And I am still embarrassed…"

"But you must admit that the embarrassment means little compared to the final reward," he answered, a mischievous smile on his face. He then kissed her hand and her forehead. "My passion for you knows no restraint, and I know sometimes I embarrass you with my insistence, but I hope I never forced my will on you. I would never want you to do anything against your wishes."

"You know very well that I always welcome your attention and that my passion is no more restrained than yours. I love to feel your gazes, your touches, your caresses, your kisses; I love to know your passion overcomes your well-known self-restraint. But that does not eliminate the fact that sometimes I am embarrassed and uneasy with the things we do…and the places we do them. As it happened with the billiard room—you placed a settee there, and I am certain the entire staff guessed your reason for doing so."

He laughed and kissed her hair again. "Forgive me, my love. Should I ask for the settee to be removed? I can do so immediately."

She stared at him and hesitated briefly before replying with complete seriousness. "Well, the damage has already been done, so you might just as well leave it where it is."

"Yes, I thought the same." He laughed, covering her face with small kisses. "Now, Mrs. Darcy, you should try to fix your clothes as I am tempted to embarrass you again."

A sudden, strong knock at the door interrupted their teasing conversation, but Darcy did not hurry to reply. She glanced at him inquiringly with amusement.

"Mr. Darcy!" Miles's voice startled Elizabeth, and she looked at Darcy with worry. Since they married, Miles had never knocked on a locked door, let alone called his master.

"Go away, Miles."

"Mr. Darcy, please sir—you are wanted in the drawing room," Miles repeated, and Darcy finally rose from Elizabeth's side.

"Someone had better have died, or else I will kill Miles," he mumbled as he walked to the door, glancing at the mirror briefly to button his vest. He opened the door only enough to talk to Miles for a few moments then closed the door again and returned to Elizabeth, who was looking at him, half amused and half puzzled; he took her hands gently.

"You should go and change, my love. Lord Matlock is here; he seems to have some urgent news for us."

A FEW MINUTES LATER, ELIZABETH returned to the drawing room in a great hurry. She was pleased at the prospect of seeing the earl again, though she could not restrain her worry regarding the news he had so unexpectedly brought. She expected a happy, joyful reunion, and she stepped to the earl, her hands stretched to greet him.

"Lord Matlock! I am so happy to see you again!"

"Thank you, my dear," he said, kissing her hand politely. "You look more beautiful than ever." His voice trembled slightly.

Darcy put his hands on her shoulders. "Elizabeth, Uncle brings us sad news. Please sit down, my dear." She looked from one to the other, her eyes darkened with distress.

"George was murdered two nights ago. He was shot during a card game," the earl said.

Elizabeth forgot to breathe, her fingers tightly gripping her husband's hands.

"I am on my way to his regiment," the earl continued. "I stopped briefly to inform you; I received news at Matlock Manor from his colonel early this morning and…I thought about sending news to Longbourn or to Mrs. Gardiner, but I know they are already on their way here. Robert and Thomas are in London, too. I must go now; it is late…"

"I will come with you, Uncle," Darcy said decidedly. He turned his eyes to Elizabeth and spoke gently. "My love, I must go. We will bring Wickham home to bury him at Pemberley near his parents. We cannot leave him there among strangers."

"Darcy, you cannot leave your wife alone; there is no need for you to come. I will take care of everything. I should not have sent him away alone; it is only my fault…"

Elizabeth squeezed her husband's hand. "Do you think I should go, too? For Lydia?"

"By no means," he said severely. "I cannot allow you to expose yourself to such a situation. We will take the best care of your sister, I promise. Besides, you must be here to receive our guest, we might not return in time for their arrival. Uncle, I will be ready in no time," he said then hurried to prepare himself, leaving Elizabeth and the earl alone in the drawing room.

"I am so sorry, sir," she said gently. "I know you were very fond of Mr. Wickham, and I can imagine how you must suffer. But you cannot possibly believe it was your fault."

"Yes, I was very fond of him but it was for naught… He died alone in the street, I was told… Somebody shot him, alone in the dark…and it is my fault. Did Darcy not tell you?" At Elizabeth's puzzled expression, he continued. "It seems he did not—I should have known that he would not betray a secret, not even to you. When he returns, please ask him… Tell him I said so… I am so tired, my dear, so very tired… "

Elizabeth looked at the earl, disconcerted; he seemed lost and incoherent. She could not comprehend his words, nor could she miss his pale countenance.

Darcy appeared with a small valise in his hand, his face dark and troubled. He embraced her tenderly, so tightly that she could barely breathe.

"You do understand why I must go… I do not want to leave you alone, but…"

"Of course, I understand. Please take care of Lydia…and his lordship; he is not well. Do not worry about me, my love. Pemberley is my home now; I am not alone here."

"It is your home, indeed, beloved. I shall return in no time…"

Alone in the impressive drawing room, Elizabeth watched her husband leave with Lord Matlock. She clasped her hands to stop their trembling then ran upstairs to the balcony, following them with her gaze until they disappeared behind the hills. Only then did she begin to cry.

DARCY WAS GONE FOR A full day, and Elizabeth had barely slept a few hours. She spent her time moving from one room to another, looking at the portraits in the gallery, trying to play the pianoforte for a few minutes, walking in the back garden among the spectacular rose bushes from which he brought her a fresh flower every day and visiting Spirit at the stables, but nothing could comfort her for his absence. Her happiness, so complete and perfect only a day before, was now crushed by the tragic death of George Wickham.

Mrs. Reynolds offered her warm support and care with the delicacy and discretion of an elder and wise aunt while Molly seemed to suffer together with her mistress.

Elizabeth, tired and confused, could not forget the earl's words and troubled countenance, nor could she stop trying to guess the secret about the connection between the earl and his favourite. Her husband knew it but did not share it with her, which was easy to understand. He could not possibly betray his uncle's trust—not even to her. Now he was allowed to tell her, but to what purpose? Mr. Wickham was gone forever, and nobody could help him. Did they make the wrong decision to purchase him a commission in Newcastle? Would things have been different if he had remained in Meryton?

And what about Lydia, a girl of fifteen who had been through so much distress in such a short time? What tragedy she must have suffered to have her husband dead less than two months after their wedding. Perhaps she should have gone with them to help Lydia. It could not possibly be worse than staying home alone with an ocean of tears.

Mr. Wickham's death affected the entire Pemberley staff as most of them were acquainted with him. It was the general opinion that Mr. Wickham's behaviour had always been reckless and frequently dishonourable—and turned even wilder in the last years. But the memories of a child with a bright smile and blonde hair, running along Pemberley's paths, were still vivid in the minds of the eldest, and they could not remain untouched by his fate, so Mrs. Reynolds said, her eyes tearful.

Though the precise time was still uncertain, Darcy had decided that George Wickham would be buried at Pemberley, so Elizabeth took it as her duty to have all the arrangements made. With the precious help of Mrs. Reynolds and Miles, the parson was invited to discuss the sad event, and everything was settled properly.

It was the most painful coincidence that, during the days when Pemberley was prepared to receive all Mr. Darcy's extended family, George Wickham would leave it forever.

By the second evening of Darcy's departure, Elizabeth's distress overcame all her other feelings as well as her common sense. Sleeping was impossible even to consider and so was eating. She walked around the drawing room, moved to the library, to her rooms, then to the library again, her restless steps breaking the silence of the house. Then finally, she asked for Molly to help her prepare for the night. The next afternoon, her family was expected, and what was happily anticipated was now a reason for worry and deep distress. She could only imagine and fear her mother's reaction at such dreadful news. She must handle such a difficult situation properly, so she must try to rest, at least a little.

The night was dark and warm, the stars shadowed by heavy clouds. A gentle breeze blew through the curtain, disturbing Elizabeth's restless sleep. She turned from one side to another and the sheets tightened around her, her mind twisted by frightening thoughts; light, followed by deafening thunder, awoke Elizabeth while a shiver froze her spine. She looked around disconcerted, and her heart skipped a beat—first of dread then of happiness. Kneeling at the edge of the bed, her husband was watching her protectively, tenderly. She threw herself into his arms, and he gently caressed her hair.

"I am so happy you are back! How are you? Where is Lydia—is she well? And the earl? How are you, my love?"

"Dearest, you should not get too close to me; I am filthy. A maid is already taking care of Lydia; she was offered a room in the guest wing. She must bathe and eat something; Mrs. Reynolds is in charge of everything."

"Oh, I will go to her. And Lord Matlock? And…Mr. Wickham?" she inquired tentatively.

"The coffin was placed in the chapel. We will have the funeral tomorrow morning; it will be dawn soon. Mrs. Reynolds told me you already had everything settled; I thank you. And she told me you have not slept in two nights. You must be exhausted."

"My love, it seems quite unfair to worry about my fatigue…and please do not thank me. Mrs. Reynolds and Miles deserve all the credit. I will go to Lydia now… But, William…where is Lord Matlock?"

He hesitated a moment, his countenance dark. "He is in the chapel. He said he could not leave George alone. I tried to convince him otherwise, but I doubt he even heard me."

She caressed his face with both hands. "My love, you did everything you could. You should bathe and eat something while I take care of Lydia. Then we will go to the chapel…to pray together. We cannot leave Lord Matlock alone."

He put his arms around her and kissed her forehead in approval, and she lingered in his arms a little then reluctantly left. She entered her sister's room, worried about her present state, and a moment later, she was startled by Lydia's loud wails.

"Oh, Lizzy, I am so glad to see you! Did you hear my dear George was killed? I am going to lose my mind; what should I do now? How can I be a widow at fifteen? Oh, you have such a beautiful house—you were so clever to marry Mr. Darcy, though George was your favourite first! Look at this expensive furniture —I never saw anything like that. Poor George always said how beautiful Pemberley is. How could Mr. Darcy have been so cruel, so mean to him? If Mr. Darcy had given him the living, my dear George would not be dead now! What should I do now, Lizzy? I will have to wear black forever!"

Elizabeth turned pale, glancing at the maid and Mrs. Reynolds who were busy preparing Lydia's bath. She gently embraced her sister, trying to excuse her unfair accusations.

"Lydia, you must take a warm bath and eat something then rest a little. Mr. Darcy and I will go to the chapel; Lord Matlock is already there. Do you wish to come with us?"

"Oh, I could not possibly do that, Lizzy. I must sleep—the journey was horrible!

345

I could not rest since I found what happened to my poor George!"

"Mrs. Darcy, I prepared a special tea for Mrs. Wickham; it will help calm her. I think she should not leave her bed for the time being," Mrs. Reynolds said gently.

Elizabeth nodded in approval, her head spinning from ire and distress at her sister's thoughtless words; she struggled to comfort and calm Lydia, who was savouring her tea and food and continued to wail about how her George was harshly treated by Mr. Darcy and Lord Matlock—who forced him to move to Newcastle—then repeated three times that she would be forced to wear black, which was very unbecoming to her complexion, and that she would miss all the balls for the rest of the year.

When dawn broke, Lydia finally fell asleep; Elizabeth and Darcy, hearts and arms entwined, went towards Pemberley's small chapel to join Lord Matlock in prayers and sorrow. The earl glanced briefly at them and forced a sad smile then gently embraced Elizabeth. Neither of them said a word for a long time as there were no proper words for such an occasion. It was George Wickham's last night at Pemberley...

In the morning, the rain stopped briefly then started again just before the funeral.

Unlike his life—where he liked to be the centre of everyone's attention and surrounded by as many people as possible—only a small procession followed George Wickham on his last way. The funeral service was only interrupted from time to time by the sound of the rain, and it ended rather soon.

In the carriage on their way back to the house, Lord Matlock informed them he would return to Matlock Manor, but Elizabeth and Darcy strongly opposed him. They insisted that the earl could not possibly leave since his entire family would arrive at Pemberley later that day. Eventually, he admitted he would stay for another week.

After a hasty and mostly silent breakfast, Lydia returned to her room, accompanied by the maid. Lord Matlock retired to his apartment, and Elizabeth and Darcy finally had some time alone to rest and comfort each other.

"It must have been very difficult," Elizabeth finally whispered.

He hesitated a moment before answering. "It was very difficult...and disappointing. He... After only a month, he had lost all the money he was given...and he already had debts. It appears he attempted to cheat during a card game. Later, when he left, the other player shot him in the back. They were both drunk. The other is already in gaol, but..."

"This is so hard to believe, to understand... Everything you did for him was for naught... "

"From the beginning, we feared this would happen. It saddens me to say that I did not trust his promises for a moment. But my uncle wished and hoped for a change..." He stopped for a moment and looked at Elizabeth, their hands held together, then kissed her temple. "When you wish, I shall tell you a story...my uncle and George's story. I know you have always wondered as we all had... Uncle said I should tell you."

"Please tell me now… I mean, if you wish…and if you are not too tired."

"I am never too tired when you ask something of me." He forced a small smile, briefly kissing her lips. Then, with a low, hesitant voice and heavy heart, Darcy began his narration. Elizabeth listened in complete silence, only the alternate rhythm of her breathing and her beating heart betraying her emotions. When he ended his heart-wrenching story, Elizabeth needed a long time to recollect enough to speak.

"It explains so many things…" she whispered. "Poor Lord Matlock…first impressions and appearances can be so misleading. Considering his easy manners, his tendency to joke all the time, his forwardness and straightness—I never would have imagined all the struggles he had to bear."

"Poor men who do not choose wisely whom to marry…" Darcy replied. "And yes, first impressions can be very misleading," he agreed, kissing her hands. "I love you so much, my darling Elizabeth." She cuddled to his chest and, his arms wrapped around her, they finally fell asleep, embraced in love and comfort, exhausted by fatigue and emotions.

Darcy was the first to wake, carefully rising so as not to disturb Elizabeth. It was already afternoon, and a glance through the window showed him the rain had long stopped, vanquished by a bright sun. He prepared himself and went downstairs to be certain everything was prepared to receive their expected guests. He inquired after Lord Matlock, and was informed that the earl had not yet left his apartment.

At four o'clock in the afternoon, Elizabeth joined him in the library. She seemed rested, and despite a trace of visible pallor, her countenance was bright. She greeted him with a small smile, and he tipped her chin and claimed her lips tenderly.

"I went to see Lydia," she whispered. "She is still asleep; I hope she remains upstairs until we speak to my family. I do not expect my mother will take the news well and—"

A determined knock at the door interrupted them, and a footman brought the news that the carriages had been spotted entering the park. As the servant left, Darcy stole a few more moments to claim another kiss. "Do not worry; the park is quite large," he said while his patience seemed to vanish and the kiss turned more passionate.

Eventually, arm in arm, they exited in front of the main entrance, waiting. Six large carriages stopped in a row, allowing a wave of exuberance and joy to spread. Four small children impatiently ran from one carriage, closely followed by the governess. Four stern gentlemen—Lord Brightmore, the colonel, the viscount and Mr. Bennet stretched their legs after the long journey. Mrs. Gardiner, Lady Selina and Georgiana, followed by a shy Anne de Bourgh, stepped down, smiling with beautiful elegance while Mr. and Mrs. Hurst, together with Miss Bingley, impassively looked at the noisy gathering. Finally, Mr. and Mrs. Bingley, arm in arm and gazing at each other, exited their carriage, and immediately after them, Mrs. Bennet, with Mary and Kitty, made no effort to hide their enthusiastic appreciation.

"Oh, this is absolutely astonishing! Dear Lord, I never imagined that one of my daughters would live in such a house! Surely, there are not many earls who have such splendid houses. My poor nerves cannot bear so much excitement, but upon my word, I would not mind if I died this very minute," Mrs. Bennet exclaimed while her husband expressed his hope that her nerves would resist at least until after dinner as he was very hungry.

Mr. and Mrs. Darcy greeted their guests with much joy and love. Elizabeth embraced and kissed the ladies—except Mrs. Hurst and Miss Bingley, who curtseyed to their hosts with cold politeness—while the gentlemen complimented Elizabeth on her appearance. Mr. Bennet embraced his favourite daughter, kissing her cheeks, and he was rewarded with the warmest embrace, but not longer than a moment as he was pushed by Mrs. Bennet, who claimed the full attention of her "favourite" daughter.

With a great din of voices, the guests finally entered, and this time, the grandeur of the interior silenced Mrs. Bennet. The children were first directed to their rooms, then servants were assigned to help the guests; the first who were directed to their apartments were Miss Bingley and the Hursts, an honour that both ladies noticed and appreciated. Then Miss Kitty and Miss Mary were showed to their rooms as well as Miss Anne de Bourgh. Surprisingly, Darcy invited the rest of the guests into the main drawing room, offered them some refreshments and drinks, and then dismissed the servants.

"Forgive me for delaying you. Unfortunately, I must share news that is equally unpleasant and painful" His grave voice wiped the smiles off their faces.

"I do not know another way of saying this, so I shall be direct: three days ago, Mr. George Wickham tragically died. He was buried here at Pemberley earlier this morning. Mrs. Lydia Wickham is upstairs, resting in her own apartment."

A deep, heavy silence gripped each of the guests, their expressions frozen in stunned disbelief. The tension was unbearable, yet nobody dared to break it with a single word. Eventually, Mrs. Bennet's voice cried her despair while she deplored the loss suffered by her youngest and most beloved daughter. With great difficulty, Elizabeth and Jane managed to speak to her rationally and take her to her rooms, supported on their arms. With a brief glance, Elizabeth noticed her husband's dark expression and, in a corner, Georgiana's white face and tearful eyes as she bit her trembling lips.

One by one, silenced and troubled, the ladies left the drawing room while the gentlemen remained still, staring at each other, unsure what to do next. The colonel filled a glass with brandy and emptied it with one gulp, his gesture instantly mirrored by the others. After a second round of brandy, the colonel and the viscount inquired after their father. They were informed that the earl had not left his rooms since the funeral and had asked to be allowed to rest. A new round of brandy was the start of discussion and speculation about the astonishing event, asking Darcy for all the details.

"We all knew this would happen sooner rather than later," the colonel burst out. "God have mercy on his soul, but he was always mindless and careless, looking for trouble and surrounded by the most worthless people. We are all sad and shocked, certainly, but this could have been easily anticipated and not prevented."

"I know you are correct," Darcy replied. "God knows that more than once I said I would kill him with my bare hands. But now I cannot help but feel sad and somehow guilty. It might be because my life is so happy, so complete in the most beautiful way. I have been so fortunate while he had such bad luck…"

"That is nonsense, Darcy," Lord Brightmore intervened. "Your present happiness is not a matter of luck but of wise choice, hard work and struggle. Wickham's tragedy was also a matter of choice—of different choices."

"I agree," said Mr. Bennet. "We should pray for him; there is nothing else to do…"

Elizabeth's appearance in the doorway turned the gentlemen's full attention towards her. She stepped to her husband, who hurried to take her hand and offer her a chair.

"I only came to inform you that everything has been settled; everyone is resting in their rooms and dinner will be ready in an hour," she said gently then glanced at her husband and whispered, "I will go to Georgiana now; I think she needs me." Darcy only approved silently and then kissed her hand with gratitude. With a small, warm smile, she left the library, followed by the gentlemen's gazes.

"Mrs. Darcy seems to fit perfectly at Pemberley," Lord Brightmore said kindly.

"She does," Darcy replied. "Elizabeth is the most astonishing woman. She has brought so much joy, warmth and liveliness to Pemberley…and she has already become accustomed to all her duties. And Mr. Bennet—I can only say how amazed I am at how quickly Elizabeth learns everything related to business. In truth, I feel blessed and fortunate; there cannot be a better wife nor a better mistress than Elizabeth—as my housekeeper insists." His enthusiasm was boundless as he spoke of his wife. He noticed Mr. Bennet's moist eyes and contented smile, then he suddenly met Bingley and Lord Brightmore's gazes and wisely added, "All three of us have been extraordinarily fortunate in choosing our wives."

"So you have been," a voice said from the doorway, and everyone turned to greet Lord Mattock's unexpected presence. "Darcy, would you care to share that brandy, or do you keep it for yourself?" the earl inquired then turned to Bingley. "How are you, boy? I hope you are making Jane happy; I will ask her—depend upon it."

Bingley, unexpectedly at the centre of attention, almost choked on his drink while Mr. Bennet and the younger gentlemen began to laugh.

Sometime later, everyone retired to prepare for dinner—except Mr. Bennet, who remained a little behind. Darcy offered him another drink, but Mr. Bennet refused.

"Darcy, I only wished to tell you how impressed I am with everything I have seen so far…and to thank you for your care. Our family has much to be grateful to you for."

"Please do not speak of that, sir. I am pleased you approve of Pemberley. I hope you know you may consider it your home and do anything that pleases you. To-morrow I have planned a full tour of the house. Also, we will take a ride around the park; we have horses and phaetons prepared for everyone if the weather permits."

"That sounds an excellent plan. Please reserve me a seat in the phaeton with Lizzy."

"Actually, sir, I think Elizabeth would rather ride."

"Lizzy is riding? On a horse?" Mr. Bennet inquired with disbelief, and Dar-cy laughed.

"Indeed she is; in fact, she is an excellent rider—and a very competitive one."

"That is quite astonishing. I cannot even imagine what other things she has learned since she married," Mr. Bennet said, and Darcy turned towards the window to hide his suddenly red face.

After that exchange, Mr. Bennet went to his room and Darcy in search of his wife. She was not in their rooms, so he knocked on Georgiana's door and found them together, speaking on the settee, holding hands. He embraced his sister, asking how she was.

"I am fine, Brother, thank you. I was telling Elizabeth how happy I am to be home."

"We are happy, too; we missed you dearly."

They spoke for some time then separated to change for dinner and reunited later in the large dining room, more crowded than it had been in many years.

The dinner went as perfectly as expected, and the exquisite courses were as-sociated with—mostly—pleasant conversation. Mrs. Hurst and Miss Bingley expressed their opinion about recent events, and they did not forget to point out that Mr. Wickham had been a favourite of the entire Bennet family, who surely must suffer the loss.

Mrs. Bennet did not hesitate to praise Mr. Wickham's amiable manners and his handsome appearance while Lydia continually repeated what a wonderful rider her husband was and how all the ladies envied her. A few minutes later, however, Mrs. Bennet's attention turned to the furniture and to the grandeur of the chamber, and Kitty impatiently asked if they would host a ball sometime soon, worthy of such a beautiful room. Lydia argued that a ball would be completely inappropriate as her dear husband had just passed away and she would not be allowed to dance. Mrs. Bennet hushed them both and expressed her impatience to tour the estate the next morning, which surely was larger than "Meryton, Longbourn and Neth-erfield together" while she concluded that Netherfield was nothing to Pemberley. Elizabeth froze in embarrassment, Jane turned pale, and only Mr. Bingley hurried to agree with her, declaring he had always taken Pemberley as a model and was tempted to purchase an estate just like it.

After dinner, the gentlemen retired to the library while the ladies were left to themselves. Miss Bingley lost no opportunity to ask Elizabeth how she bore the difference from the world in which she had been brought up and her new life. She also inquired whether Elizabeth kept to her old habit of walking. Though Miss Bingley's malice was impossible to miss, Elizabeth tried to remain perfectly polite.

She cared little about Miss Bingley but was content to see Jane happy. The very short time they spoke together was enough to understand that marriage suited her sister very well.

Mrs. Gardiner was as elegant and beautiful as ever, though a little more restrained. However, a significant improvement was easily observed in Miss Anne de Bourgh's aspect and manners. She seemed livelier, often showed a charming smile, and was less fearful to take part in conversation. She seemed easy with all her cousins, as well as with Mrs. Gardiner, and her behaviour towards Elizabeth was friendlier than ever.

The gentlemen seemed to get along very well together, but the stressful journey and the overwhelming events exhausted the ladies, who expressed their wish to retire soon, and they did so after a short farewell from the gentlemen.

Alone in her room after a day as long as an age, Elizabeth bathed with some haste then fell into a deep sleep for the first time in three days. She finally allowed her mind and her body to rest while, through the opened window, the summer breeze blew gently.

Close to midnight, Darcy entered the apartment, opening the door carefully; Elizabeth was sleeping in her bed her breathing calm and steady. He gently caressed her hair and wrapped the covers around her. Then he briefly washed and changed to his nightshirt then lay near her. Her back was to him, so he spooned her, wrapping her in his arms; she sighed and cuddled closer. He breathed deeply and moaned as her closeness aroused his desire. They had slept like that—her body spooned within his arms—many times, though sleep was not precisely the fair word. He smelled her silky hair and fondled her ear for a moment. She moaned and pressed her back against him. For a short while, as he saw her sleeping peacefully, enjoying the warmth of his closeness, he felt content that she was finally resting after such trying days.

However, his generous concern vanished in a moment when her bottom pressed against his thighs. He nuzzled her ear and her neck as he lowered her nightgown and cupped her breasts, caressing her roundness with impatient desire. She moaned and pushed against him harder. "Are you tired, my love? Should I allow you to sleep?"

"I am very tired, but I miss you more," she whispered, turning her head as she begged a kiss. His lips captured hers while his hands adoringly explored every inch of the body he so dearly missed. Her skin craved his touch; he pulled up the nightgown to her waist and one of his hands slid between her thighs, caressing her, as he well knew she liked most; then he entered her slowly, deeply, throbbing inside her. Their moans joined in a passionate kiss.

"This is so good," she whispered, and he bit her ear, thrusting deeper inside her while his hands travelled from her breasts—tortured by the pleasures of his touch—down between her thighs, tantalising the burning spot between her legs. He never freed her lips from the passionate kiss; his hands became less gentle and more possessive, more conquering, more demanding, giving pleasure and taking pleasure from her while his thrusts grew stronger, deeper, and faster until pleasure overwhelmed their senses.

They fell asleep afterwards, but their passion and yearning for each other awoke them once again during the night. Luckily, the next day none of the guests left their rooms until very late, so nobody could complain that Mr. and Mrs. Darcy neglected their visitors by oversleeping.

Two weeks had passed since the guests arrived at Pemberley, and the subject of Mr. Wickham's tragic end was mentioned less frequently. The newly wedded couples were rarely aware of anything else around them, whilst the other guests found ways to amuse themselves and enjoy the beauties of Pemberley. Mr. Bennet rarely left the library; however, from the window, he had a full view of everyone who wandered outdoors, especially his most beloved daughter; he had never seen his Lizzy more beautiful, glowing in her happiness. She and her husband seemed to complete each other perfectly, and the change—the improvement—was visible on both of them as was their mutual support and passion. Mr. Bennet smiled to himself as he spotted Elizabeth and Darcy escape the crowd whenever possible, riding at a gallop through the fields and returning with grass-stained clothing. He had never imagined his Lizzy riding so well, just as he had never imagined Darcy laughing so much. This match was truly perfect, and he could not have prayed for more.

As a father, he was worried for his youngest daughter, but as he bitterly estimated, Lydia's attachment for her husband—and, consequently, her sorrow at losing him —was not strong enough to really pain her, so two weeks later, she was rarely heard to mention her dear Wickham's name.

The only person who visited Wickham's grave daily was Lord Matlock. Though he struggled to return to his usual self, his countenance was still darkened by sadness, and his spirit never rose to what it had been when Elizabeth first met him.

From time to time, Lord Matlock spent time on the lawn, watching the children playing and talking to Mrs. Gardiner and his daughter. One day, Elizabeth saw her aunt riding with Lord Matlock through the small grove behind the house then other times walking together in the garden.

A few days later, Lord Matlock asked Darcy and Elizabeth for a short meeting. They were surprised when Lady Selina and her brothers joined them; then Lord Matlock finally appeared with Mrs. Gardiner on his arm and Mr. Bennet beside them. They all sat, staring at each other in an awkward silence until Lord Matlock, distressed and agitated, spoke.

"There is something of importance that I wish to share with you, and I prefer you all be here as this news affects each of you…" He paused, all eyes fixed upon him, except Mrs. Gardiner's who seemed determined to look at the fireplace.

"I wish to announce to you all that I am courting Mrs. Gardiner," he said, looking from one to the other, waiting for their response. Elizabeth glanced at her husband, who smiled at her, and then at her aunt, who searched their faces with worried eyes.

"Do you have nothing to say?" the earl inquired when the silence became difficult to bear.

"What is to be said? We await your news," the colonel answered.

"What do you mean?" the earl replied harshly. "*That* is the news."

"The news is that you are courting Mrs. Gardiner? Surely you are joking—forgive me for being disrespectful, Mrs. Gardiner—but, Father, I was certain you had been courting Mrs. Gardiner since last year," the viscount said, politely puzzled.

"I was not!" the earl interrupted him severely, pacing the room. He suddenly stopped, gazing at Mrs. Gardiner, whose face turned from pale to red, then at his children. "It is true I had always admired Mrs. Gardiner, and in the last year, I had the chance of spending more time in her company and... But I did not court her...properly. I just now asked her permission, and I want you to know I will start courting her."

"Oh, that is wonderful," Lady Selina said to break the silence. "My dearest Madeleine, I have long considered you part of my family, so you must know how happy I would be if one day... This is wonderful news, indeed," she concluded, and her brothers agreed.

When they left the library, the colonel grabbed his father's arm tightly while he asked his brother and Darcy to stay a little longer. He closed the door and filled his glass again.

"It is I who have news that might shock you. I thought it would be better to inform you before the ladies. I asked Anne to marry me, and she accepted," he said sternly.

Darcy stared at him in silence while the earl threw his glass into the fireplace.

"Son, why on earth did you do that? Did you learn nothing from what I told you? This cannot bring any good, and it is not fair, neither to Anne nor to you. You might think it is the easiest, most convenient and comfortable way, but—"

"Father, please listen to me! I understand your worry, but there is no need for it. I am not doing it for convenience only. I might not be passionately in love with Anne—not like Darcy is with Elizabeth—but we have spent enjoyable time together in the last two months, and we have come to know each other very well. I...I confess I miss her when I do not see her every day and...I have known many women before, but I never missed anyone. I think we will have a good marriage —better than many others."

While he spoke, he became increasingly animated, and the earl's countenance softened as he listened to his son. He glanced at Darcy and saw the same worry on his nephew's face. Yes, Lord Matlock would want nothing more than to see his sons marry for the deepest love—as Darcy did or even Selina. He wished to protect them from a loveless marriage and a lifetime of regrets. But true love was not easy to find and did not always manifest itself in the same way. And he could not possibly forbid his son from marrying Anne. He could only hope, pray, and give them his blessing, which he did, his heart still heavy. The colonel, nervous as a schoolboy, hurried to speak to Anne and then to his sister while Lord Matlock, somehow dizzy after all the events and the generous glasses of brandy, began to write the startling news to his formidable sister.

A week later—under a special licence and in the presence of his entire family —Colonel Fitzwilliam wedded Anne de Bourgh in Pemberley's small chapel. Lady Catherine did not attend the wedding, but she sent a letter declaring she disapproved such a hasty marriage, decided without the approval of the mother of the bride, and mentioning she was not well enough to bear the long journey. However, during the next month, after the earl and Anne's third letter, Lady Catherine officially invited her daughter and son-in-law to visit Rosings whenever it was convenient for them. But she did not forgive so easily either her brother or her formerly favourite nephew and his new wife.

THE WARM, GREEN SUMMER DAYS turned windy and cold, but the beauty of the grounds did not diminish; they only changed their colours.

Pemberley Manor was more silent than in the summer, but the sound of the piano and joyful laughter could still be heard all day long. At Miss Darcy's special invitation, Mary and Kitty remained at Pemberley after their parents and Lydia returned to Hertfordshire The long stay in such superior company brought a remarkable improvement in both Bennet sisters, making one less voluble and the other more so.

To the newlyweds, the presence of Mary and Kitty was fortunate and beneficial as it helped them feel less guilty for all the time they spent alone together, almost neglecting their beloved Georgiana.

After planning things carefully for several months, Mr. Bingley left Netherfield and, with Darcy's help, purchased a property in the neighbourhood, and Elizabeth and Jane, in addition to other sources of happiness, were within thirty miles of each other.

The first days of December increased the fever of preparations, as the entire party that visited Pemberley in the summer was expected to return for at least six weeks during Christmas time, then to return all together to town for the Season.

Mrs. Gardiner frequently wrote Elizabeth long, detailed letters. In one letter, she informed Elizabeth that, by a strange coincidence, she and Lady Selina happened upon Lady Sinclair at the modiste, and so received the information that Lady Sinclair was expecting a child sometime at the end of January. When she shared this news with Darcy and speculated that the happy event might have occurred during the hunting party at Matlock, Elizabeth was surprised to see Darcy more preoccupied than amused, but she presumed it was because of some other business on his mind.

Mrs. Gardiner sent detailed reports of everything except the progress of her courtship with Lord Matlock and a certain date that everyone expected. Elizabeth, who loved her aunt dearly, did not dare insist on more information about such a delicate subject. She knew how strong the bond was between her aunt and uncle and how difficult it must be for her aunt to decide to start a new life with another man, no matter how exceptional that man might be. She discussed the matter with Darcy more than once, and both agreed that it was the best decision for both not to hurry such an important step as they had difficult, painful pasts to overcome, despite their strong, mutual affection and respect.

One cold night, as Elizabeth was sleeping deeply and peacefully in her husband's arms, covered in warm blankets, she found herself abruptly awakened. She opened her eyes, disconcerted, looking at the fire burning warmly and listening to the wind blowing.

"Lizzy, wake up my love," he said hastily, and she moaned and smiled. She adored hearing him call her Lizzy. She glanced at him, wondering why he hurried to the window and pulled open the curtains.

"Look Lizzy—this is our first snow at Pemberley," he said, and she immediately rose from the warmth of the bed, the cold of the room shivering her skin. She stepped in front of the window, and he immediately wrapped his arms around her, kissing her neck.

"Oh, William, this is so beautiful," she whispered.

"We should return to bed; it is cold," he said caringly, but she begged him to stay a little longer. He could not possibly refuse her, so he hurried to push the settee close to the window, throwing a few pillows and a blanket on it. Then he took her in his arms, and they lay together on the couch, wrapped in each other's arms and covered with the blanket, warming their bodies and hearts as they admired their first Pemberley snowfall.

The next morning, everything was white, and Elizabeth, Georgiana, Kitty and Mary spent a couple of hours before breakfast walking in the garden through the snow while Darcy watched them from the library window.

The snow continued to fall the entire morning then stopped, and the wind demanded its share of time. Later in the evening, however, after dinner, while Elizabeth and Darcy prepared for the night, it started to snow again, steadily, peacefully. On the balcony, Elizabeth forgot to breathe under the spell of such beauty.

"Mrs. Darcy, I will meet you downstairs in a quarter of an hour. Dress yourself warmly; it is freezing outside," her husband said abruptly, putting more wood on the fire.

He was gone before she had time to reply or to attempt to guess what he planned to do. She had long ceased trying to anticipate the meaning of his words or his intentions, but she did not need to know more as she trusted him completely.

A quarter of an hour later, the butler opened the main door and invited her out. In front of the entrance, her husband was waiting beside a huge sleigh pulled by Thunder and another black horse. Her face turned crimson from her own emotion and the chilling breeze as the snowflakes caressed her cheeks and rested in her hair.

He took her arm and directed her into the sleigh; then he settled himself beside her and took the reins. The horses impatiently started to move, and soon the sleigh was flying over the white ground.

Elizabeth closed her eyes as she breathed the cold, fresh air. She nestled to her husband's chest while her heart seemed afraid to beat from overwhelming happiness.

Darcy's arms gently encircled her shoulders while his other hand covered them both with a smooth wool blanket. Her own hand slid around his waist. He secured the reins, and the horses instantly slowed the pace; his free hand gently stroked her face and then lowered to her neck, brushing tenderly along her skin. His lips captured hers in a kiss, at first tender and then more passionate, to which she happily surrendered. One arm travelled along her spine, while the other continued its journey from her neck lower...then tried to find its way inside her coat. She laughed against his mouth and shivered as his fingers tried to unbutton her spencer but were caught between it and her dress. His kiss became more daring, while his fingers became more eager and less skilful in their attempt to reach the softness of her skin.

The snowfall increased, and so did his impatience. Her face was freezing while his lips were burning and her body seemed on fire...

"Mrs. Darcy, tomorrow night, please indulge me and dress yourself less diligently. A single coat over your dress would suffice, I think, and one with very few buttons would be a perfect choice." She laughed, her fingers hurrying to help his in their daunting task.

"But sir, you said I would freeze if I did not dress securely"

"Well, my love, this outside activity in full winter is very new for me, too, so I am learning from experience. However, I think I may safely promise you that you will not freeze. In fact, I dare say you will be quite warm...quite warm indeed," he whispered, and his strong hands placed her astride his lap.

She encircled his neck with her arms, allowing her lips to be captured by his. Covered in blankets—with the horses moving at a slow pace and the snow falling on their hair, their faces and their skin—they subdued the frozen air with the warmth inside them on their first sleigh ride alone together—only them, their love and the winter covering Pemberley in frozen whiteness.

Nine months later, in the middle of August, young William Darcy, a beautiful, healthy boy, claimed his place in the world and in the hearts of his parents.

Epilogue

Five years happily passed after Mr. Fitzwilliam Darcy of Pemberley wedded Miss Elizabeth Bennet.

Mr. and Mrs. Bingley, blessed with two daughters as beautiful as their mother, remained as kind and gentle as they had been when they first met. Their proximity to Pemberley allowed the two families to meet often and spend as much time together as they wished. Under Darcy's wise supervision, Mr. Bingley's estate became as profitable as it was beautiful, adding further to Mr. Bingley's good name.

Mrs. Bennet could hardly bear the happiness of seeing Lydia and Kitty married —three years after her eldest daughters—to two officers about ten years older, handsome enough for the girls to be charmed and wise enough for Mr. Bennet to trust them. Even more fortunately, Mary developed a strong affection for Mr. Thornton, the parson who was offered the living at Kympton village, and she married him when she turned one and twenty.

Miss Georgiana Darcy had come out when she was seventeen, and since then, she had been greatly admired and courted by many eligible, London bachelors. However, she was in no haste to marry quickly as she set her mind and heart to accept nothing less than the love and happiness she witnessed in her brother's marriage.

Two years after the Darcy's wedding, the London *ton* was stunned by the announcement of Lord Matlock's marriage to Mrs. Madeleine Gardiner. Though Mrs. Gardiner's character and elegance were praised by anyone who knew her, her low situation by birth—as well as the fact that her father had owned a small shop in a village—were reason enough to raise gossip and speculation, which ended several months later when other subjects required the interest of the *ton*. Their unexpected marriage was shockingly blessed with a beautiful baby girl born a year later. Together with Mrs. Gardiner's other children, she gave Lord Matlock the joy of a second youth. It was strange, however, that Lord Matlock's *daughter* was a year younger than his *granddaughter*—the daughter of Colonel Fitzwilliam and Anne. And so, as he had long wished and prayed for, Lord Matlock, who always complained of not having enough beauty in his family, was gifted with a daughter and granddaughter to fill his life.

The young master William Darcy was followed by his brother, Robert—two years his junior—and his sister, Elizabeth Anne—born two years after Robert. The children brought blessed joy to their family, each of them taking particular traits from their parents, so they were much alike, yet completely different. However, they all had one thing in common—the unconditional love of their parents.

Five years and three small children did not change or diminish Elizabeth and Darcy's love and passion for each other. Their bond only grew stronger, and their knowledge of each other's heart and mind became so complete that they rarely needed words to express their wishes. For everyone who had the chance to meet them or see them together, it became a truth universally acknowledged that Mr. Fitzwilliam Darcy of Pemberley and his wife—née Miss Elizabeth Bennet—were perfect for each other, and as Mrs. Reynolds told anyone within her hearing, they were indeed the happiest couple in the world.

CPSIA information can be obtained at www.ICGtesting.com
Printed in the USA
LVOW08s2349240714

395883LV00004B/487/P